TOME
OF THE
UNDERGATES

Sam Sykes

GOLLANCZ

LONDON

The right of Sam Sykes to be identified as the author of
this work has been asserted by him in accordance with the
Copyright, Designs and Patents Act 1988.

First published in Great Britain in 2010 by Gollancz
An imprint of the Orion Publishing Group
Orion House, 5 Upper St Martin's Lane, London WC2H 9EA

An Hachette UK Company

A CIP catalogue record for this book is available
from the British Library

ISBN 978 0 575 09028 6 (Cased)
ISBN 978 0 575 09029 3 (Trade Paperback)

1 3 5 7 9 10 8 6 4 2

Typeset by Deltatype Ltd, Birkenhead, Merseyside

Printed in Great Britain by Clays Ltd, St Ives plc

The Orion Publishing Group's policy is to use papers that
are natural, renewable and recyclable products and made
from wood grown in sustainable forests. The logging and
manufacturing processes are expected to conform to the
environmental regulations of the country of origin.

www.orionbooks.co.uk

TOME OF THE UNDERGATES

ACT ONE
Few Respectable Trades

Prologue
NO ROOM FOR HOPE

The Aeons' Gate
Sea of Buradan, two weeks north and east of Toha
Summer, late

Contrary to whatever stories and songs there may be about the subject, there are only a handful of respectable things a man can do after he picks up a sword.

First of all, he can put it down and do something else; this is the option for men who have more appreciable talents. He could use it to defend his homestead, of course, as protecting one's own is nothing but admirable. If he decides he's good at that sort of work, he could enlist with the local army and defend his kin and country against whatever entity is deemed the enemy at that moment. All these are decent and honourable practices for a man who carries a sword.

Then there are the less respectable trades.

There's always mercenary life, the fine art of being paid to put steel in things. Mercenaries, usually, aren't quite as respected as soldiers, since they swear no allegiance to any liege beyond the kind that are round, flat and golden. And yet, it remains only a slightly less respectable use for the blade, as, inevitably, being a mercenary does help someone.

Now, the very bottommost practice for a man who carries a sword, the absolute dregs of the well, the lowliest and meanest

3

trade a man can possibly embrace after he decides not to put away his weapon is that of the adventurer.

There is one similarity between the adventurer and the mercenary: the love of money. Past that fact, everything is unfavourable contrast. Like a mercenary, an adventurer works for money, be it gold, silver or copper. Unlike a mercenary, an adventurer's trade is not limited to killing, though it does require quite a bit of that. Unlike a mercenary, an adventurer's exploits typically aid no one.

When one requires a herd of cattle guarded from rustlers, a young maiden protected, a family tomb watched over or an enemy driven away, all for an honest fee, one calls upon a mercenary.

When one requires a herd of cattle stolen, a young maiden deflowered, a family tomb looted and desecrated or an honest man driven away from his own home, all for a few copper coins and a promise, one calls upon an adventurer.

I make this distinction for the sole purpose that, if someone finds this journal after I've succumbed to whatever hole I fell into or weapon I've run afoul of, they'll know the reason.

This marks the first entry of the Aeons' Gate, the grand adventure of Lenk and his five companions.

If whoever reads this has a high opinion of this writer so far, please cease reading now. The above sentence takes many liberties.

To consider the term 'adventure', one must consider it from the adventurer's point of view. For a boy on his father's knee, a youth listening to an elder or a rapt crowd hearing the songs of poets, adventure is something to lust after, filled with riches, women, heroism and glory. For an adventurer, it's work; dirty, dusty, bloody, spittle-filled, lethal and cheap work.

The Aeons' Gate is a relic, an ancient device long sought after by holy men and women of all faiths. It breaches the barriers between heaven and earth, allowing communication with the

4

Gods themselves, an opportunity to ask why, how and what.

Or so I've heard.

My companions and I have been hired to seek out this Gate.

To address the term 'companions', I say this because it sounds a degree better than a 'band of brigands, zealots, savages and madmen'. And I use that description because it sounds infinitely more interesting than what we really are: cheap labour.

Unbound by the codes of unions and guilds, adventurers are able to perform more duties than common mercenaries. Untroubled by sets of morals and guidelines, adventurers are able to go into places the common mercenary would find repulsive. Unprotected by laws dictating the absolute minimum one must be paid, adventurers do all this for much, much less coin than the common mercenary.

If someone has read this far, he might ask himself what the point of being an adventurer is.

The answer is freedom. An adventurer is free to come and go as he pleases, parting from whoever has hired him when the fancy strikes him. An adventurer is free to stop at whatever exotic locale he has found, to take whatever he has with him, to stay for as long as he wants. An adventurer is free to claim what he finds, be it knowledge, treasure or glory. An adventurer is free to wander, penniless and perpetually starved, until he finally collapses dead on a road.

It also bears mentioning that an adventurer typically does leave his employer's charter if the task assigned proves particularly deranged.

Thus far, my journey has taken my companions and me far from Muraska's harbour, where we took on this commission. We have travelled the western seas for what seems like an eternity, braving the islands, and their various diseases and inhabitants, in search of this Gate. Thus far, I've fought off hostile natives, lugged heavy crates filled with various supplies, mended sails, swabbed decks and spent hours upon hours with one end of mine or the other leaning over the railing of our ship.

My funds have so far accumulated to twenty-six pieces of copper, eleven pieces of silver and half a gold coin. That half came from a sailor who was less lucky than the rest of us and had his meagre savings declared impromptu inheritance for the ship's charter.

That charter is Miron Evenhands, Lord Emissary of the Church of Talanas. Miron's duties are, in addition to regular priestly business, overseeing diplomatic ties with other churches and carrying out religious expeditions, as which this apparently qualifies. He has been allocated funds for the matter, but spends them sparingly, hiring only as many adventurers and mercenaries as he must to form a facade of generosity. The ship he has chartered, a merchantman dubbed the Riptide, we share with various dirty sailors and hairy rats that walk on two legs.

My companions seem content with these arrangements, perhaps because they themselves are just as dirty and smelly. They sleep below deck even as I write this, having been driven up top by foul scents and groping hands. Granted, the arrangements are all that they are content with.

Every day, I deal with their greed and distrust. They demand to know where our payment is, how much money we're getting. They tell me that the others are plotting and scheming against them. Asper tells me that Denaos makes lewd comments to her and the other women who have chartered passage aboard the ship. Denaos tells me that Asper mutters all manner of religious curses at him and tells the women that he is a liar, lech, lush, layabout and lummox; all lies, he tells me. Dreadaeleon tells me the ship rocks too much and it's impossible for him to concentrate on his books. Gariath tells me he can't stand the presence of so many humans and he'll kill every one to the last man.

Kataria ... tells me to relax. 'Time at sea,' she says, smiling all the while, 'amidst the beauty of it all should be relaxing.'

6

It would seem like sound advice if not for the fact that it came from a girl who stinks worse than the crew half the time.

To be an adventurer means to have freedom, the freedom to decide for oneself. That said, if someone has found this journal and wonders why it's no longer in my hands, please keep in mind that it's just as likely that I decided to leap from the crow's nest to the hungry waters below as it is that I died in some heroic manner.

One

HUMAN LITTER

In the span of a breath, colour and sound died on the wind.

The green of the ocean, the flutter of sails, the tang of salt in the air vanished from Lenk's senses. The world faded into darkness, leaving only the tall, leather-skinned man before him and the sword clutched in his hands.

The man loosed a silent howl and leapt forwards. Lenk's sword rose just as his foe's curved blade came crashing down.

They met in a kiss of sparks. Life returned to Lenk's senses in the groan of the grinding blades. He was aware of many things at once: the man's towering size, the sound of curses boiling out of tattooed lips, the odour of sweat and the blood staining the wood under their feet.

The man uttered something through a yellow-toothed smile; Lenk watched every writhing twitch of his mouth, hearing no words behind them. No time to wonder. He saw the man's free hand clutching a smaller, crueller blade, whipping up to seek his ribs.

The steel embrace shattered. Lenk leapt backwards, feeling his boots slide along the red-tinged salt beneath him. His heels struck something fleshy and solid and unmoving; his backpedal halted.

Don't look, he urged himself, *not yet.*

He had eyes for nothing but his foe's larger blade as it came hurtling down upon him. Lenk darted away, watched the cutlass bite into the slick timbers and embed itself. He saw the twitch of the man's eye – the realisation of his mistake and the instant in which futile hope existed.

And then died.

Lenk lunged, sword up and down in a flashing arc. His senses returned with painful slowness; he could hear the echo of the man's shriek, feel the sticky life spatter across his face, taste the tang of copper on his lips. He blinked, and when he opened his eyes, the man knelt before his own severed arm, shifting a wide-eyed stare from the leaking appendage to the young man standing over him.

Not yet.

Lenk's sword flashed again, biting deeply into meat and sliding out again. Only when its tip lowered, steady, to the timbers, only when his opponent collapsed, unmoving, did he allow himself to take in the sight.

The pirate's eyes were quivering pudding: stark white against the leather of his flesh. They looked stolen, wearing an expression that belonged to a smaller, more fearful man. Lenk met his foe's gaze, seeing his own blue stare reflected in the whites until the light behind them sputtered out in the span of a sole, ragged breath.

He drew a lock of silver hair from his eyes, ran his hand down his face, wiping the sweat and substance from his brow. His fingers came back to him trembling and stained.

Lenk drew in a breath.

In that breath, the battle had ended. The roar of the pirates' retreat and the hesitant, hasty battle cries of sailors had faded on the wind. The steel that had flashed under the light of a shameless staring sun now lay on the ground in limp hands. The stench ebbed on the breeze, filled the sails overhead and beckoned the hungry gulls to follow.

The dead remained.

They were everywhere, having ceased to be men. Now they were litter, so many obstacles of drained flesh and broken bones lying motionless on the deck. Pirates lay here and there, amongst the sailors they had taken with them. Some embraced their foes with rigor-stiffening limbs. Most lay on their backs, eyes turned to Gods that had no answers for the questions that had died on their lips.

Disconcerting.

His thought seemed an understatement, perhaps insultingly so, but he had seen many bodies in his life, many not half as peacefully gone. He had drawn back trembling hands many times before, flicked blood from his sword many times before, as he did now. And he was certain that the stale breath he drew would not be the last to be scented with death.

'Astounding congratulations should be proffered for so ruby a sport, good sir!'

Lenk whirled about at the voice, blade up. The pirate standing upon the railing of the *Riptide*, however, seemed less than impressed, if the banana-coloured grin on his face was any indication. He extended a long, tattooed limb and made an elaborate bow.

'It is the sole pleasure of the *Linkmaster*'s crew, myself included, to look forward to offering a suitable retort for,' the pirate paused to gesture to the human litter, 'our less fortunate complements, of suitable fury and adequately accompanying disembowelment.'

'Uh,' Lenk said, blinking, 'what?'

Had he time and wit enough about him to decipher the

tattooed man's expression, he would, he assured himself, have come up with a more suitable retort.

'Do hold that thought, kind sir. I shall return anon to carve it out.'

Like some particularly eloquent hairless ape, the pirate fell to all fours and scampered nimbly across a chain swaying over the gap of quickly shifting sea between the two ships. He was but one of many, Lenk noted, as the remaining tattooed survivors fled back over the railings of their own vessel.

'Cragsmen,' the young man muttered, spitting on the deck at the sight of the inked masses.

Their leviathan ship shared their love of decoration, it seemed. Its title was painted in bold, violent crimson upon a black hull, sharp as a knife: *Linkmaster*. And in equally threatening display were crude scrawlings of ships of various sizes beneath the title, each one with a triumphant red cross drawn through it.

Save one that bore a peculiar resemblance to the *Riptide*'s triple masts.

'Eager little bastards,' he muttered, narrowing his eyes. 'They've already picked out a spot for us.'

He blinked. That realisation carried a heavy weight, one that struck him suddenly. He had thought that the pirates were chance raiders and the *Riptide* nothing more than an unlucky victim. This particular drawing, apparently painted days before, suggested something else.

'Khetashe,' Lenk cursed under his breath, 'they've been waiting for us.'

'Were they?' someone grunted from behind him, a voice that seemed to think it should be feminine but wasn't quite convinced.

He turned about and immediately regretted doing so. A

pair of slender hands in fingerless leather gloves reached down to grip an arrow's shaft jutting from a man's chest. He should have been used to the sound of arrowheads being wrenched out of flesh, he knew, but he couldn't help cringing.

Somehow, one never got all the way used to Kataria.

'Because if this is an ambush,' the pale creature said as she inspected the bloody arrow, 'it's a rather pitiful excuse for one.' She caught his uncomfortable stare and offered an equally unpleasant grin as she tapped her chin with the missile's head. 'But then, humans have never been very good at this sort of thing, have they?'

Her ears were always the first thing he noticed about Kataria: long, pointed spears of pale flesh peeking out from locks of dirty blonde hair, three deep notches running the length of each as they twitched and trembled like beings unto themselves. Those ears, as long as the feathers laced in her hair, were certainly the most prominent markers of her shictish heritage.

The immense, fur-wrapped bow she carried on her back, as well as the short-cut leathers she wore about what only barely constituted a bosom, leaving her muscular midsection exposed, were also indicative of her savage custom.

'You looked as surprised as any to find them aboard,' Lenk replied. With a sudden awareness, he cast a glance about the deck. 'So did Denaos, come to think of it. Where did he go?'

'Well ...' She tapped the missile's fletching against her chin as she inspected the deck. 'I suppose if you just find the trail of urine and follow it, you'll eventually reach him.'

'Whereas one need only follow your stench to find you?' he asked, daring a little smirk.

'Correction,' she replied, unfazed, 'one need only look for the clear winner.' She pushed a stray lock of hair behind the leather band about her brow, glanced at the corpse at Lenk's feet. 'What's that? Your first one today?'

'Second.'

'Well, well, well.' Her smile was as unpleasant as the red-painted arrows she held before her, her canines as prominent and sharp as their glistening heads. 'I win.'

'This isn't a game, you know.'

'You only say that because you're losing.' She replaced the bloodied missiles in the quiver on her back. 'What's it matter to you, anyway? They're dead. We're not. Seems a pretty favourable situation to me.'

'That last one snuck up on me.' He kicked the body. 'Nearly gutted me. I *told* you to watch my back.'

'What? When?'

'First, when we came up here.' He counted off on his fingers. 'Next, when everyone started screaming, "Pirates! Pirates!" And then, when I became distinctly aware of the possibility of someone shoving steel into my kidneys. Any of these sound familiar?'

'Vaguely,' she said, scratching her backside. 'I mean, not the actual words, but I do recall the whining.' She offered a broader smile to cut off his retort. 'You tell me lots of things: "Watch my back, watch his back, put an arrow in *his* back." Watch backs. Shoot humans. I got the idea.'

'I said shoot *Cragsmen*.' Upon seeing her unregistering blink, he sighed and kicked the corpse again. 'These things! The pirates! Don't shoot *our* humans!'

'I haven't,' she replied with a smirk. 'Yet.'

'Are you planning to start?' he asked.

'If I run out of the other kind, maybe.'

Lenk looked out over the railing and sighed.

13

No chance of that happening anytime soon.

The crew of the *Linkmaster* stood at the railings of their vessel, poised over the clanking chain bridges with barely restrained eagerness. And yet, Lenk noted with a narrowing of his eyes, restrained all the same. Their leering, eager faces outnumbered the *Riptide*'s panicked expressions, their cutlasses shone brighter than any staff or club their victims had managed to cobble together.

And yet, all the same, they remained on their ship, content to throw at the *Riptide* nothing more than hungry stares and the occasional declaration of what they planned to do with Kataria, no matter what upper assets she might lack. The phrase 'segregate those weeping dandelions 'twixt a furious hammer' was shouted more than once.

Any other day, he would have taken the time to ponder the meaning behind that. At that moment, another question consumed his thoughts.

'What are they waiting for?'

'Right now?' Kataria growled, flattened ears suggesting she heard quite clearly their intentions and divined their meaning. 'Possibly for me to put an arrow in their gullets.'

'They could easily overrun us,' he muttered. 'Why wouldn't they attack now, while they still have the advantage?'

'Scared?'

'Concerned.'

'About what?'

Largely, he told himself, *that we're going to die and you're going to be the cause.* His thoughts throbbed painfully in the back of his head. *They're waiting for something, I know it, and when they finally decide to attack, all I've got is a lunatic shict to fight them. Where are the others? Where's Dreadaeleon?*

Where's Denaos? Why do I even keep them around? I could do this. I could survive this if they were gone.

If she were ...

He felt her stare upon him as surely as if she'd shot him. From the corner of his own eye, he could see hers staring at him. *No*, he thought, *studying*. Studying with an unnerving steadiness that exceeded even the unpleasantness of her long-vanished smile.

His skin twitched under her gaze, he shifted, turned a shoulder to her.

Stop staring at me.

She canted her head to one side. 'What?'

Any response he might have had degenerated into a sudden cry of surprise, one lost amidst countless others, as the deck shifted violently beneath him, sending him hurtling to one knee. He was rendered deaf by the roar of waves as the *Riptide* rent the sea beneath it with the force of its turn, but even the ocean could not drown out the furious howl from the *Riptide*'s helm.

'More men!' the voice screeched. 'Get more men to the railing! What are you doing, you thrice-fondled sons of six-legged whores from hell? *Get those chains off!*'

Not an eye could help turning to the ship's wheel, and the slim, dark figure behind it. A bald beacon, Captain Argaol's hairless head shone with sweat as his muscles strained to guide his bride of wood and sails away from her pursuer. Eyes white and wide in furious snarl, he turned a scowl onto Lenk.

'What in Zamanthras's name are you blasphemers being paid for?' He thrust a finger towards the railings. '*Get. Them. OFF!*'

Several bodies pushed past Lenk, hatchets in hand as they rushed the chains biting into the *Riptide*'s hull. At this, a lilting voice cut across the gap of the sea, sharp as a blade to Lenk's ears as he pulled himself to his feet.

'I say, kind Captain, that hardly seems the proper way to address the gentlemen in your employ, does it?' The helmsman of the *Linkmaster* taunted with little effort as he guided the black vessel to keep pace with its prey. 'Truly, sirrah, perhaps you could benefit from a tongue more silver than brass?'

'Stuff your metaphors in your eyes and burn them, Cragscum!' Argaol split his roar in twain, hurling the rest of his fury at his crew below. 'Faster! Work faster, you hairless monkeys! Get the chains off!'

'Do we help?' Kataria asked, looking from the chains to Lenk. 'I mean, aren't you a monkey?'

'Monkeys lack a sense of business etiquette,' Lenk replied. 'Argaol isn't the one who pays us.' His eyes drifted down, along with his frown, to the dull iron fingers peeking over the edge of the *Riptide*'s hull. 'Besides, no amount of screaming is going to smash that thing loose.'

Her eyes followed his, and so did her lips, at the sight of the massive metal claw. A 'mother claw', some sailors had shrieked upon seeing it: a massive bridge of links, each the size of a housecat, ending in six massive talons that clung to its victim ship like an overconfident drunkard.

'Were slander but one key upon a ring of victory, good Captain, I dare suggest you'd not be in such delicate circumstance,' the *Linkmaster*'s helmsman called from across the gap. 'Alas, a lack of manners more frequently begets sharp devices embedded in kidneys. If I might be so brash as to suggest surrender as a means of keeping your internal organs free of metallic intrusion?'

The mother claw had since lived up to its title, resisting any attempt to dislodge it. What swords could be cobbled together had been broken upon it. The sailors that might have been able to dislodge it when the Cragsmen attacked were also the first to be cut down or grievously wounded. All attempts to tear away from its embrace had proved useless.

Not that it seems to stop Argaol from trying, Lenk noted.

'You might,' the captain roared to his rival, 'but only if I might suggest shoving said suggestion square up your—'

The vulgarity was lost in the wooden groan of the *Riptide* as Argaol pulled the wheel sharply, sending his ship cutting through salt like a scythe. The mother chain wailed in metal panic, going taut and pulling the *Linkmaster* back alongside its prey. A collective roar of surprise went up from the crew as they were sent sprawling. Lenk's own was a muffled grunt, as Kataria's modest weight was hurled against him.

His breath was struck from him and his senses with it. When they returned to him, he was conscious of many things at once: the sticky deck beneath him, the calls of angry gulls above him and the groan of sailors clambering to their feet.

And her.

His breath seeped into his nostrils slowly, carrying with it a new scent that overwhelmed the stench of decay. He tasted her sweat on his tongue, smelled blood that wept from the few scratches on her torso, and felt the warmth of her slick flesh pressed against him, seeping through his stained tunic and into his skin like a contagion.

He opened his eyes and found hers boring into his. He saw his own slack jaw reflected in their green depths, unable to look away.

'Hardly worthy of praise, Captain,' the *Linkmaster*'s helmsman called out, drawing their attentions. 'Might one suggest even the faintest caress of Lady Reason would e'er do your plight well?'

'So ...' Kataria said, screwing up her face in befuddlement, 'do they all talk like that?'

'Cragsmen are lunatics,' he muttered in reply. 'Their mothers drink ink when they're still in the womb, so every one of them comes out tattooed and out of his skull.'

'What? Really?'

'Khetashe, *I don't know*,' he grunted, shoving her off and clambering to his feet. 'The point is that, in a few moments when they finally decide to board again, they're going to run us over, cut us open and shove our intestines up our noses!' He glanced her over. 'Well, I mean, they'll kill *me*, at least. You, they said they'd like to—'

'Yeah,' she snarled, 'I heard them. But that's only *if* they board.'

'And what makes you think they're not going to?' He flailed in the general direction of the mother chain. 'So long as that thing is there, they can just come over and visit whenever the fancy takes them!'

'So we get rid of it!'

'*How?* Nothing can move it!'

'Gariath could move it.'

'Gariath *could* do a lot of things,' Lenk snarled, scowling across the deck to the companionway that led to the ship's hold. 'He *could* come out here and help us instead of waiting for us all to die, but since he hasn't, he *could* just choke on his own vomit and I'd be perfectly happy.'

'Well, I hope you won't take offence if I'm not willing to sit around and wait with you to die.'

'Good! No waiting required! Just jump up to the front and get it over quickly!'

'Typical human,' she said, sneering and showing a large

canine. 'You're giving up before the bodies are even hung and feeding the trees.'

'*What does that even mean?*' he roared back at her. Before she could retort, he held up a hand and sighed. 'One moment. Let's ... let's just pretend that death is slightly less imminent and think for a moment.'

'Think about what?' she asked, rolling her shoulders. 'The situation seems pretty solved to you, at least. What are we supposed to do?'

Lenk's eyes became blue flurries, darting about the ship. He looked from the chains and their massive mother to the men futilely trying to dislodge them. He looked from the companionway to Argaol shrieking at the helm. He looked from Kataria's hard green stare to the *Riptide*'s rail ...

And to the lifeboat dangling from its riggings.

'What, indeed—'

'Well,' a voice soft and sharp as a knife drawn from leather hissed, 'you know my advice.'

Lenk turned and was immediately greeted by what resembled a bipedal cockroach. The man was crouched over a Cragsman's corpse, studying it through dark eyes that suggested he might actually eat it if left alone. His leathers glistened like a dark carapace, his fingers twitched like feelers as they ran down the body's leg.

Denaos's smile, however, was wholly human, if a little unpleasant.

'And what advice is that?' Kataria asked, sneering at the man. 'Run? Hide? Offer up various orifices in a desperate exchange for mercy?'

'Oh, they won't be patient enough to let you offer, I assure you.' The rogue's smile only grew broader at the insult. 'Curb that savage organ you call a tongue, however, and I might be generous enough to share a notion of escape with you.'

'You've been plotting an escape this whole time the rest of us have been fighting?' Lenk didn't bother to frown; Denaos's lack of shame had rendered him immune to even the sharpest twist of lips. 'Did you have so little faith in us?'

Denaos gave a cursory glance over the deck and shrugged. 'I count exactly five dead Cragsmen, only one more than I had anticipated.'

'We don't get paid by the body,' Lenk replied.

'Perhaps you should negotiate a new contract,' Kataria offered.

'We have a contract?' The rogue's eyes lit up brightly.

'She was being sarcastic,' Lenk said.

Immediately, Denaos's face darkened. 'Sarcasm implies humour,' he growled. 'There's not a damn thing funny about not having money.' He levelled a finger at the shict. 'What *you* were being was facetious, a quality of speech reserved only for the lowest and most cruel of jokes. Regardless,' he turned back to the corpse, 'it was clear you didn't need me.'

'Not need *you* in a fight?' Lenk cracked a grin. 'I'm quickly getting used to the idea.'

'We should just use him as a shield next time,' Kataria said, nodding, 'see if we can't get at least some benefit from him.'

'I hate to agree with her,' Lenk said with a sigh, 'but … well, I mean you make it so *easy*, Denaos. Where were you when the fighting began, anyway?'

'Elsewhere,' the rogue said with a shrug.

'One of us could have been killed,' Lenk replied sharply.

Denaos glanced from Lenk to Kataria, expression un-changing. 'Well, that might have been a mild inconveni-ence or a cause for celebration, depending. As both of you are alive, however, I can only assume that my initial theory was correct. As to where I was—'

'Hiding?' Kataria interrupted. 'Crying? Soiling your-self?'

'Correction.' Denaos's reply was as smooth and easy as the knife that leapt from his belt to his hand. 'I *was* hid-ing and soiling myself, if you want to call it that. At the moment ...' He slid the dagger into the leg-seam of the Cragsman's trousers. 'I'm looting.'

'Uh-huh.' Lenk got the vague sensation that continuing to watch the rogue work would be a mistake, but was unable to turn his head away as Denaos began to cut. 'And ... out of curiosity, what would *you* call what you were doing?'

'I believe the proper term is "reconnaissance".'

'Scouting is what *I* do,' Kataria replied, making a show of her twitching ears.

'Yes, you're very good at sniffing faeces and hunting beasts. What I do is ...' He looked up from his macabre activities, waving his weapon as he searched for the word. 'Of a more philosophical nature.'

'Go on,' Lenk said, ignoring the glare Kataria shot him for indulging the man.

'Given our circumstances, I'd say what I do is more along the lines of planning for the future,' Denaos said, finishing the long cut up the trouser leg.

Heavy masks of shock settled over the young man and shict's faces, neither of them able to muster the energy to cringe as Denaos slid a long arm into the slit and reached up the Cragsman's leg. Quietly, Kataria cleared her throat and leaned over to Lenk.

'Are … are you going to ask him?'

'I would,' he muttered, 'but I really don't think I want to know.'

'Now then, as I was saying,' Denaos continued with all the nonchalance of a man who did not have his arm up another man's trouser leg, 'being reasonable men and insane pointy-eared savages alike, I assume we're thinking the same thing.'

'Somehow,' Lenk said, watching with morbid fascination, 'I sincerely doubt that.'

'That is,' Denaos continued, heedless, 'we're thinking of running, aren't we?'

'*You* are,' Kataria growled. 'And no one's surprised. The *rest* of us already have a plan.'

'Which would be?' Denaos wore a look of deep contemplation. 'Lenk and I have rather limited options: fight and die or run and live.' He looked up and cast a disparaging glance at Kataria's chest. 'Yours are improved only by the chance that they might mistake you for a pointy-eared, pubescent boy instead of a woman.' He shrugged. 'Then again, they might prefer that.'

'You stinking, cowardly *round-ear*,' she snarled, baring her canines at him. 'The plan is to neither run nor die, but to *fight*!' She jabbed her elbow into Lenk's side. 'The leader says so!'

'You do?' Denaos asked, looking genuinely perplexed.

'Well, I … uh …' Lenk frowned, watching the movement of Denaos's hand through the Cragsman's trousers. 'I think you might …' He finally shook his head. 'Look, I don't disapprove of looting, really, but I think I might have a problem with whatever it is you're doing here.'

'Looting, as I said.'

Denaos's hand suddenly stiffened, seizing something as a

wicked smile came over his face. Lenk cringed and turned away as the man's long fingers tensed, twisted and pulled violently. When he looked back, the man was dangling a small leather purse between his fingers.

'The third pocket,' the rogue explained, wiping the purse off on the man's trousers, 'where all reasonable men hide their wealth.'

'Including you?' Lenk asked.

'Assuming I had any wealth to spend,' Denaos replied, 'I would hide it in a spot that would make a looter give long, hard thought as to just how badly he wanted it.' He slipped the pouch into his belt. 'At any rate, this is likely as good as it's going to get for me.'

'For us, you mean,' Lenk said.

'Oh, no, no. For *you*, it's going to get much worse, since you seem rather intent on staying here.'

'We are in the employ of—'

'We are *adventurers* in the employ of Evenhands,' Denaos pointed out. 'And what has he done for us? We've been at sea for a month and all we've got to show for it is dirty clothes, seasickness and the occasional native-borne disease.' He looked at Lenk intently. 'Out at sea, there's no chance to make an honest living. We're as like to be killed as get paid, and Evenhands knows that.'

He shook a trembling finger, as though a great idea boiled on the tip of it.

'Now,' he continued, 'if we run, we can sneak back to Toha and catch a ship back to the mainland. On the continent proper, we can go anywhere, do anything: mercenary work for the legions in Karneria, bodyguarding the fashas in Cier'Djaal. We'll earn *real* coin without all these promises that Evenhands is offering us. Out here, we're just penniless.'

'We'll be just as penniless on the mainland,' Lenk countered. 'We run, the only thing we've earned is a reputation for letting employers, *godly* employers, die.'

'And the dead spend no money,' Denaos replied smoothly. 'Besides, we won't need to take jobs to make money.' He glanced at Kataria, gesturing with his chin. 'We can sell the shict to a brothel.' He coughed. 'Or a zoo of some kind.'

'Try it,' Kataria levelled her growl at both men, 'and what parts of you I *don't* shoot full of holes, I'll hack off and wear as a hat.' She bared her teeth at Denaos. 'And just because *you* plan to die—'

'The plan is *not* to die, haven't you been listening? And before you ask, yes, I'm certain that we *will* die when they return, for two reasons.'

'*If* they return,' Kataria interjected. 'We scared them off before.'

'*When* they return,' Denaos countered. 'Which coincides with the first reason: this was just the probe.'

'The what?'

'Ah, excuse me,' the man said as he rose up. 'I forgot I was talking to a savage. Allow me to explain the finer points of business.'

Lenk spared a moment to think, not for the first time, that it was decidedly unfair that the rogue should stand nearly a head taller than himself. *It's not as though the length of your trousers matters when you piss them routinely*, he thought resentfully.

'Piracy,' the tall man continued, 'like all forms of murder, is a matter of business. It's a haggle, a matter of bidding and buying. What they just sent over,' he paused to nudge the corpse at his feet, 'is their initial bid, an investment. It's

24

the price they paid to see how many more men they'd need to take the ship.'

'That's a lot of philosophy to justify running away,' Lenk said, arching an eyebrow.

'You had a lot of time to think while hiding?' Kataria asked.

'It's really more a matter of instinct,' Denaos replied.

'The instinct of a *rat*,' Kataria hissed, 'is to run, hide and eat their own excrement. There's a reason no one listens to them.'

'Forgive me, I misspoke.' He held up his hands, offering an offensively smarmy smile. 'By "instinct", I meant to say "it's blindingly obvious to anyone *but* a stupid shict". See, if *I* were attacking a ship bearing a half-clad, half-mad barbarian that at least *resembled* a woman wearing breeches tighter than the skin on an overfed hog, I would most certainly want to know how many men I needed to take her with no more holes in her than I could realistically use.'

She opened her mouth, ready to launch a hailstorm of retorts. Her indignation turned into a blink, as though she were confused when nothing would come. Coughing, she looked down.

'So it's not *that* bad an idea,' she muttered. Finding a sudden surge of courage, she looked back up. 'But, I mean, we killed the first ones. We can kill them again.'

'Kill how many?' Denaos replied. 'Three? Six? That leaves roughly three dozen left to kill.' He pointed a finger over the railing. 'And reason number two.'

Lenk saw the object of attention right away; it was impossible not to once the amalgamation of metal and flesh strode to the fore.

'Rashodd,' Lenk muttered.

He had heard the name gasped in fear when the

Linkmaster first arrived. He heard it again now as the captain of the black ship stood before his crew, the echo of his heavy boots audible even across the roaring sea.

Rashodd was a Cragsman, as his colossal arms ringed with twisting tattoos declared proudly. The rest of him was a sheer monolith of metal and leather. His chest, twice as broad as any in his crew, was hidden behind a hammered sheet of iron posing as a breastplate. His face was obscured as he peered through a thin slit in his dull grey helmet, tendrils of an equally grey beard twitching beneath it.

And he, too, waited, Lenk noted. No command to attack arose on a metal-smothered shout. No call for action in a falsely elegant voice drifted over the sea. Not one massive, leathery hand drifted to either of the tremendous, single-bit axes hanging from his waist.

They merely folded along with the Cragsman's titanic arms, crossing over the breastplate and remaining there.

Waiting.

'Their next bid will be coming shortly,' Denaos warned. 'And *he's* going to be the one that delivers it.' He gestured out to the crew. 'They're dead, sure, but they're Argaol's men. We have to think of our own.'

'He's just a human,' Kataria said derisively, 'a monkey.' She glanced at the titanic pirate and frowned. 'A big monkey, but we've killed big ones before. There's no reason to run.'

'Good,' Denaos replied sharply, 'stay here while all sane creatures embrace reason.' He sneered. 'Do try to scream loudly, though. Make it something they'll savour long enough so that the rest of us can get away.'

'The only one leaving will be you, round-ear,' Kataria growled, 'and we'll see how long your delusions of wit can sustain you at sea.'

'Only a shict would think of reason as delusional.'

'Only a human would think of cowardice as rational!'

Words were flung between them like arrows and daggers, each one cutting deeply with neither of the two refusing to admit the blood. Lenk had no eyes for their snarls and rude gestures, no attention for their insults that turned to whispers on his ears.

His stare was seized, bound to the hulking figure of Rashodd. His ears were full, consumed by another voice whispering at the back of his head.

It's possible, that voice said, *that Denaos is wrong. There are almost as many men on our ship as on theirs. We could fight. We wouldn't even have to win a complete victory, just bloody their noses. Teach them that we aren't worth the trouble. It's business, right?*

'What's the big deal over a big monkey, anyway?' Kataria snapped. 'The *moment* he raises that visor, I'll put an arrow in his gullet and we'll be done here! No need to run.' Her laughter was sharp and unpleasant. 'Or do you find his big muscles intimidating, you poor little lamb?'

'I can think of at least one muscle of his that you'll find unpleasant when he comes over,' Denaos replied, a hint of ire creeping into his voice. 'And I wouldn't be at all surprised if *it* was bearded and covered in iron, too. He's seen what you've done to his men. He won't be taking that visor off.'

It's possible, Lenk answered his own thought, *but not likely. Numbers are one thing, but steel is another. They have swords. We have sticks. Well, I mean, I've got a sword ... fat lot of good it will do against that many, though. Running is just logical here. It's not as if Denaos actually had a good idea here, anyway.*

'If you run, you don't get paid,' Kataria said. 'Though,

really, I've always wanted to see if human greed is stronger than human cowardice.'

'We get paid slaves' wages,' Denaos said. 'Silf, we get worse. We get *adventurers'* wages. Stop trying to turn this into a matter of morality. It's purely about the practicality of the situation and, really, when has a *shict* ever been a moral authority?'

When have any *of them ever had a good idea?* Lenk's eyes narrowed irately. *I'm always the one who has to think here. He's a coward, but she's insane. Asper's a milksop, Dreadaeleon's worthless. Gariath is as likely to kill me as help. Running is better here. They'll get me killed if we stay.*

'Well, don't get the impression that I'm trying to stop you,' Kataria snarled. 'The only reason I'd like you to stay is because I'm almost certain you'll get a sword in your guts and then I won't even have to deal with the terrible worry that you might somehow survive out at sea. The *rest* of us can handle things from here.'

'And if I *could* handle it all by myself, I would,' Denaos said. 'Feeling the humanitarian that I am, though, I would consider it a decent thing to try to get as many *humans* off as I possibly could.'

'Decent? You?' Kataria made a sound as though she had just inhaled one of her own arrows through her nose.

'*I* didn't kill *anyone* today.'

'Only because you were busy putting your hands down a dead man's trousers. In what language is that decent?'

They're going to die, Lenk's thoughts grew their wings, flew about his head violently, *but I can live. Flee now and live! The rest will ...*

'And what would you know of language?' Denaos snarled. 'You only learned how to speak ours so you could mock the people you kill, *savage!*'

... waiting, waiting for what? To attack? Why? What else can you do? There's so many of them, few of us. Save them and they kill each other ...

'And you mock your own people by pretending you give a single fart about them, *rat*.'

... to what end? What else can you do?

'Barbarian!'

What else can you do?

'Coward!'

WHAT ELSE?

The thoughts that formed a blizzard in Lenk's mind suddenly froze over, turning to a pure sheet of ice over his brain. He suddenly felt a chill creep down his spine and into his arm, forcing his fingers shut on his sword's hilt. From the ice, a single voice, frigid and uncompromising, spoke.

Kill.

'What?' he whispered aloud.

Kill.

'I ... don't—'

'Don't what?'

He felt a hand on his shoulder, unbearably warm. He whirled about, hand tight on his sword. The shapes before him looked unfamiliar for a moment: shadows of blue lost in the sky. He blinked and something came into view, apparent in a flash of blazing green.

Kataria's eyes, brimming with disquiet.

With every blink, the sunlight became brighter and more oppressive. He squinted at the two people before him, face twisted in a confused frown.

'What?'

'It's up to you, we agreed,' Kataria replied hesitantly. 'You're the leader.'

'Though "why" is a good question,' Denaos muttered.

'Do we fight or run?'

Lenk looked over his shoulder. His eyelid twitched at the sight of the pirates, visibly tensing, sliding swords from their sheaths. Behind the rows of tattooed flesh, a shadow shifted uneasily. Had it always been there, Lenk wondered, standing so still that he hadn't noticed it?

'Fight?' Kataria repeated. 'Or run?'

Lenk nodded. He heard her distinctly now, saw the world free of haze and darkness. Everything became clear.

'I have a plan,' he said firmly.

'I'm all ears,' Denaos said, casting a snide smile to Kataria. 'Sorry, was that offensive?'

'Shut up,' Lenk growled before she could. 'Grab your weapons. Follow me.'

Don't look, Dreadaeleon thought to himself, *but a seagull just evacuated on your shoulder.*

He felt his neck twist slightly.

I SAID, DON'T LOOK! He cringed at his own thoughts. *No, if you look, you'll panic. I mean, why wouldn't you? It's sitting there … all squishy and crawling with disease. And … well, this isn't helping. Just … just brush it off nonchalantly … try to be nonchalant about touching bird faeces … just try …*

It occurred to the boy as odd that the warm present on his shoulder wasn't even the reason he resented the birds overhead at that moment.

Rather, he thought, as he stared up at the winged vermin, they didn't make nearly enough noise. Neither did the ocean, nor the wind, nor the murmurings of the sailors gathered before him, muttering ignorant prayers to gods that didn't exist with the blue-clad woman who swore that they did.

Though, at that moment, he doubted that even gods, false or true, could make enough noise to drown out the awkward silence that hung between him and her.

Wait, he responded to his own thoughts, *you didn't say that last part instead of thinking it, did you? Don't tell her that the gods are just made up! Remember what happened last time. Look at her ... slowly ... nonchalantly ... all right, good, she doesn't appear to have heard you, so you probably didn't say it. Wait, no, she's scowling. Wait, do you still have the bird faeces on you? Get it off! Nonchalant! Nonchalant!*

The problem persisted, however. Even after he brushed the white gunk from his leather coat, Asper's hazel eyes remained fixed in a scowl upon him. He cleared his throat, looked down at the deck.

Mercifully, she directed her hostility at him only for as long as it took to tuck her brown hair back beneath her bandana, then looked back down at the singed arm she was carefully dressing with bandage and salve. The man who possessed said arm remained scowling at him, but Dreadaeleon scarcely noticed.

He probably wants you to apologise, the boy thought. *He deserves it, I suppose. I mean, you* did *set him on fire.* His fingers rubbed together, lingering warmth dancing on their tips. *But what did he expect, getting in the way like that? He's lucky he escaped with only a burned arm. Still, she'd probably like it if you apologised ...*

If she even noticed, he thought with a sigh. Behind the burned man were three others with deep cuts, bruised heads or visibly broken joints. Behind *them* were four more that had already been wrapped, salved, cleaned or stitched.

And they had taken their toll on her, he noticed as her hands went back into the large leather satchel at her side and pulled out another roll of bandages. They trembled,

31

they were calloused, they were clearly used to working.

And, he thought with a sigh, *they are just so strong.* He drew in a resolute breath. *All right, you've got to say something ... not that, though! But something. Remember what Denaos says: women are dangerous beasts. But you're a wizard, a member of the Venarium. You fear no beast. Just ... use tact.*

'Asper,' he all but whispered, his voice catching as she looked up at him again, 'you're ...' He inhaled sharply. 'You're being completely stupid.'

Well done.

'Stupid,' she said, levelling a glare that informed him of both her disagreement and her future plans to bludgeon him.

'As it pertains to the context, yes,' he said, attempting to remain bold under her withering eyes.

'The context of ...' she gestured to her patient, 'setting a man on fire?'

'It's ... it's a highly sensitive context,' he protested, his voice closely resembling that of a kitten being chewed on by a lamb. 'You aren't taking into account the many variables that account for the incident. See, body temperature can fluctuate fairly quickly, requiring a vast amount of concentration for me to channel it into something combustible enough to do appreciable damage to something animate.'

At this, the burned man added his scowl to Asper's. Dreadaeleon cleared his throat.

'As evidenced visibly. With such circumstances as we've just experienced, the risk for a triviality increases.'

'You set ... a man ... on fire ...' Asper said, her voice a long, slow knife digging into him. 'How is that a triviality?'

'Well ... well ...' The boy levelled a skinny finger at the man accusingly. 'He got in my way!'

'I was tryin' to defend the captain!' the man protested.

'You could have gone around me!' Dreadaeleon snapped back. 'My eyes were glowing! My hands were on fire! What affliction of the mind made you think it was a good idea to run in front of me? I was clearly about to do something *very* impressive.'

'Dread,' Asper rebuked the boy sharply before tying the bandage off at the man's arm and laying a hand gently on his shoulder. To the sailor: 'The wound's not serious. Avoid using it for a while. I'll change the dressing tomorrow.' She sighed and looked over the men, both breathing and breathless, beyond her patient. 'If you can, you should tend to your fellows.'

'Blessings, Priestess,' the man replied, rising to his feet and bowing to her.

She returned the gesture and rose as well, smoothing out the wrinkles creasing her blue robes. She excused herself from the remaining patients with a nod and turned away to lean on the railings.

And Dreadaeleon could not help but notice just how hard she leaned. The irate vigour that had lurked behind her eyes vanished entirely, leaving only a very tired woman. Her hands, now suddenly trembling, reached to the gleaming silver hanging from her throat. Fingers caressed the wings of a great bird, the phoenix.

Talanas, Dreadaeleon recalled, the Healer.

'You look tired,' he observed.

'I can see how I might give off that impression,' Asper replied, 'what with having to undo the damage my companions do as well as the pirates' own havoc.'

Somehow, the softness of her voice cut even deeper than its former sharpness. Dreadaeleon frowned and looked down at the deck.

'It *was* an accident—'

'I know.' She looked up and offered him an exhausted smile. 'I can appreciate what you were trying to do.'

You see, old man? That fire would have been colossal! Corpses burning on the deck! Smoke rising into the sky! Of course she'd have been impressed. The ladies love fire.

'Well, it would have been difficult to pull off, of course,' he offered, attempting to sound humble. 'But the benefits would have outweighed the tragedy.'

'Tragedy?' She blinked. 'I thought you were going to try to scare the rest of them off with a show of force.' She peered curiously at him. 'What were you thinking?'

'*The exact same thing*,' he hastily blurted. 'I mean, they're pirates, right? And Cragsmen, on top of that. They probably still believe wizards eat souls and fart thunder.'

She stared at him.

'We, uh, we don't.'

'Hmm.' She glanced over his shoulder with a grimace, towards the shadows of the companionway. 'And what was the purpose of that?'

He followed her gaze and frowned. He wasn't quite sure why she looked at the sight with disgust. To him, it was a masterpiece.

The icicle's shape was perfect: thick enough to drive it into the wood of the ship, sharp enough to pierce the ribcage in which it currently rested comfortably. Even as the Cragsman clung to it, hands frozen to the red-stained ice in death, Dreadaeleon couldn't help but smile. He had expected something far messier, but the force used to hurl it through the air had been just enough.

Of course, she probably won't understand that. He rolled his eyes as he felt hers boring into his. *Women.*

'Prevention,' he replied coolly. 'I saw him heading for the

34

companionway, I thought he might try to harm Miron.'

She nodded approvingly. 'I suppose it was necessary, then, if only to protect the Lord Emissary.'

Well done, old man, well done. The exuberance coursing through him threatened to make him explode. He fought it down to a self-confident smirk. *Talking to girls is just like casting a spell. Just maintain concentration and don't—*

'After all,' he interrupted his train of thought with a laugh, 'if he died, who would pay us?'

... do anything like that, idiot.

She swung her scowl upon him like a battleaxe, all the fury and life restored to her as she clenched her teeth. She ceased to resemble a priestess at that moment, or any kind of woman, and looked instead like some horrific beast ready to rip his innards out and paint the deck with them.

'This is what it's all about, then?' she snarled. 'Pay? Gold? Good Gods, Dread, you *impaled* a man.'

'That hardly seems fair,' he replied meekly. 'Lenk and the others have killed far more than me. Kataria even made a game out of it.'

'And *she's* a shict!' Asper clenched her pendant violently. 'Bad enough that I should have to tolerate *their* blasphemies without you also taking pleasure in killing.'

'I wasn't—'

'Oh, shut up. You were staring at that corpse like you wanted to mount it on a wall. Would you have taken the same pride if you had killed that man instead of just burning him?'

'Well ...' His common sense had fled him, his words came on a torrent of shamelessness. 'I mean, if the spell had gone off as it was supposed to, I suppose I could have appreciated the artistry of it.' He looked up with sudden terror, holding his hands out in front of him. 'But no, no! I

35

wouldn't have taken pride in it! I never take pride in making more work for you!'

'It's not *work* to do Talanas's will, you snivelling heathen!' Her face screwed up in ways that he had thought possible only on gargoyles. 'You sound like … like one of *them*, Dread!'

'Who?'

'Us.'

Lenk met the boy's whirling gaze without blinking, even as Dreadaeleon frowned.

'Oh,' he said, 'you.'

'You sound disappointed.'

'Well, the comparison was rather unfavourable,' the wizard said, shrugging. 'Not that I'm not thrilled you're still alive.'

He still sounded disappointed, but Lenk made no mention of it. His eyes went over the boy's head of stringy black hair, past Asper's concerned glare, through the mass of wounded sailors to the object of his desire.

The smaller escape vessel dangled seductively from its davits, displaying its oars so brazenly, its benches so invitingly. It called to him with firm, wooden logic, told him he would not survive without it. He believed it, he wanted to go to it.

There was the modest problem of the tall priestess before him, though, arms crossed over her chest to form a wall of moral indignation.

'What happened at the railings?' she asked. 'Did you win?'

'In a manner of speaking, yes.'

'In a manner of …' She furrowed her brow. 'It's not a hard question, you know. Did you push the pirates back?'

'Obviously, we were triumphant,' chimed a darker voice

from behind him. Denaos stalked forwards, placing a hand on Lenk's shoulder. 'If we hadn't, you'd like have at least a dozen tattooed hands up your skirt by now.'

'*Robes*,' she corrected sharply. 'I wear *robes*, brigand.'

'How foolish of me. I should have known. After all, only proper ladies wear skirts.' As she searched for a retort, he quickly leaned over and whispered in Lenk's ear. 'She's never going to let us by and she certainly won't come with us.'

Lenk nodded. Ordinarily, that wouldn't have been a problem. He would just as soon leave her to die if she insisted. However, she could certainly call the sailors' attentions to the fact that they were about to make off with the ship's only escape vessel. Not to mention it would be exceedingly bad judgement to leave the healer behind.

'So just shove her in,' he muttered in reply. 'On my signal, you rush her. I'll cut the lines. We'll be off.'

'What are you two talking about?' Asper's eyebrows were so far up they were almost hidden beneath her bandana. 'Are you plotting something?'

'We are *discussing* stratagems, thank you,' Denaos replied smoothly. 'We are, after all, the brains of this band.'

'I thought I was the brains,' Dreadaeleon said.

'*You* are the odd little boy we pay to shoot fire out of his ass,' the rogue said.

'I shoot fire out of my *hands*, thank you. And it requires an *immense* amount of brains.' He pulled back his leather coat, revealing a massive book secured to his waist by a silver chain. 'I memorised this whole thing! Look at it! *It's huge!*'

'He raises a good point,' Denaos whispered to Lenk. 'He might try to stop us.'

'I can handle it,' a third voice added to the conspiracy.

Kataria appeared at Lenk's side, ears twitching. 'He weighs even less than me. I'll just grab him on the way.'

'I thought you didn't like this idea,' Lenk said, raising a brow.

'I don't,' she replied, sparing him a grudging glare. 'It's completely unnecessary. But,' she glanced sidelong at Lenk, 'if you're going to go ...'

The moment stretched uncomfortably long in Lenk's head, her eyes focusing on him as if he were a target. In the span of one blink, she conveyed a hundred different messages to him: requests for him to stay, conveyance of her wish to fight, a solemn assurance that she would follow. At least, he thought she said that. All that echoed in his mind was one voice.

Stop staring at me.

'Yes, good, lovely,' Denaos grunted. 'If we're going to do this, let's do it now.'

'Do what?' Asper asked, going tense as if sensing the sin before it developed.

'Nothing,' Denaos replied, taking a step forwards, 'we're just hoping to accomplish it before—'

'*By the Shining Six,*' the voice cut through the air like a blade, '*who wrought this sin?*'

'Damn it,' Lenk snarled, glancing over his shoulder at the approaching figure.

Despite rumours whispered in the mess, it was a woman, tall as Denaos and at least as muscular. Her body was choked in bronze, her breastplate yielding not a hint of femininity as it was further obscured by a white toga.

Hard eyes stared out from a hard face, set deep in her skull and framed by meticulously short-trimmed black hair. Her right eyelid twitched at the sight of them all huddled together, the row of red-inked letters upon her cheek dancing like some crimson serpent that matched her very visible ire as she swept towards the companions, heedless of the puddles of blood splashing her greaves.

'Quillian Guisarne-Garrelle Yanates,' Asper said pleasantly as she stepped forwards unopposed, she being generally considered the person best suited to speak with people bearing more than two names. 'We are pleased to see you well.'

'*Serrant* Quillian Guisarne-Garrelle Yanates,' the woman corrected. 'Your praise is undeserved, I fear.' She cast a glimpse at the human litter and sneered. 'I should have been here much sooner.'

'Yes, scampering in a bit late today, aren't we, Squiggy?' Denaos levelled his snide smirk at her like a spear. 'The battle was over before you even strapped that fancy armour on.'

'I was guarding the Lord Emissary,' the Serrant replied coldly. 'You might recall it being your duty, as well, if you could but keep your mind from gold and carnage.'

'Carnage?' Kataria laughed unpleasantly. 'It was a slaughter.'

Quillian's eyes sharpened, focusing a narrow glare of bladed hatred upon the shict.

'You would know, savage.' She forced her stare away with no small amount of effort. 'I had hoped to arrive to see at least some modicum of rite was being followed. Instead, I find ...' she forced the word through her teeth as though it were poison, '*adventurers*.' She spared a cursory nod to Asper. 'Excluding those of decent faith.'

'Oh,' the woman blinked, 'well, thank you, but—'

'*She's* with us,' Denaos interjected, stepping up beside the priestess with a scummy grin. 'How's that stick in your craw, Squiggy? One of your beloved, pious temple friends embroiled in our world of sin and sell-swording, eh?' He swept an arm about Asper, drawing her in close and rubbing his stubble-laden cheek against her face. 'Doesn't sit too well, does it? *Does it?* I can smell your disgust from here!'

Lenk caught the movement, subtle as it was, as the rogue gingerly tried to ease his blanching captive towards the escape vessel. Dreadaeleon, too, looked shocked enough that he'd never see Kataria coming to grab him. He readied his sword, eyeing the ropes.

'That would be me,' Asper snarled, driving an ungentle elbow into his ribs and ruining his plans. 'Get *off*.'

'The hallowed dead litter the deck,' the Serrant said, sweeping her scorn across the scene, then focusing it on Lenk. 'Innocent men alongside the impure. All sloppily killed.'

'What?' Dreadaeleon asked, pointing to his impaled victim. '*That* is, by far, the cleanest kill in this whole mess!'

'Incredibly enough,' Lenk added with a sigh, 'killing is a sloppy business.'

'These vagrants should have been routed before *one* of Argaol's men could be driven below,' she snapped. '*You* allowed this to happen.'

'Me?' Lenk said.

'*All* of you.'

'What?' Kataria looked offended as she gestured to Denaos. '*He* didn't even do anything!'

'Yeah,' Lenk said, nodding. 'How do you figure we're at fault?'

'Because of the horrid blasphemies that continually spew from your bile-holes. You *anger* the Gods with your disregard for the sacred rites of combat! Your crude tactics, your consorting with heathens,' her stare levelled at Kataria again, 'as well as inhuman savages.'

Her eyes were decidedly warier when she swept the deck again.

'And where *is* your other monster?'

'Elsewhere,' Lenk replied. 'Look, we have a plan, but it doesn't need you around. Is this really—'

'Respect for the Gods is *very* necessary,' Quillian said sharply. 'Yes. *Really.* Bad enough that you bring your Godless savages here without questioning the divine mandate.'

'Savage arrows took three already.' Kataria's threat was cold and level. 'I've got plenty more, Squiggy.'

'Cease and repent, barbarian,' the woman replied, just as harshly. Her gauntleted hand drifted dangerously close to the longsword at her hip. 'The name of a Serrant is sacred.'

'I'd disagree with that, Squiggy.' Denaos chuckled.

'Me too, Squiggy,' Kataria agreed.

Stay calm, Lenk told himself as he watched the Serrant fume. *This might be better. Neither Asper nor Dread is paying attention. We can still salvage this, we can still—*

Kill.

The thought leapt, again, unbidden to his mind. He blinked, as though he had just taken a wrong turn.

Run, he corrected himself.

Kill, his mind insisted.

And, like a spark that heralds the disastrous fire to come, the sudden concern on his face sparked Quillian's suspicion. Her glance was a whirlwind, carrying that fire and giving it horrific life as it swept from the companions, standing tensed and ready, to the escape vessel.

By the time it settled on Lenk, wide with shock and fury, he could see his plan consumed in that fire, precious ash on the wind.

'She knows,' Lenk whispered harshly to Kataria. 'She *knows*.'

'Who cares?' the shict growled. 'Stick to your plan.'

'What? Shove her in, too?'

'No, shove her *over*. She'll sink like a stone in all that armour.' She paused, ears flattening against her head. 'It was my idea, though, so she counts as my kill.'

'Deserters,' Quillian hissed, 'are the most grievous of sinners.'

Damn it, damn it, damn it, Lenk cursed as he watched her sword begin to slide out of its scabbard. *This complicates things. But we can still—*

Kill.

'I suppose you would know,' Denaos said with a thoughtful eye for the brand under her right eye, 'wouldn't you?'

Her shock was plain on her face, the kind of naked awe that came from the knowledge of a secret revealed. Her lip quivered, her spare hand going to the red ink.

'You—'

'Yes,' he replied smoothly. 'Now, if you wouldn't mind scampering off to scrawl another oath on your forehead or something? We've got stratagems to—'

'You ...' she hissed again, brimming with rage as she hoisted her sword, 'you *dare*!'

There was a flash of steel, a blur of black. In the time it took to blink, the Serrant's sword was out and trembling, its point quivering at Asper's throat. The priestess's eyes were wide and unmoving, barely aware of what had happened as two broad hands clenched her arms tightly.

Denaos peered out from behind her, grinning broadly and whistling sharply at the blade a hair's width from the priestess's throat.

'Dear me.' The rogue clicked his tongue chidingly. 'You

ought to be more careful, oughtn't you? That was nearly another oath right there.'

Quillian's eyes were wide, the bronze covering her knuckles rattling as she quivered horribly. Empty horror stared out from behind her gaze, as though her mind had fled at the very thought of what she had nearly done. It was an expression not entirely unfamiliar to Lenk, but it was usually plastered on the faces of the dying.

'I ... I didn't mean ...' She looked at Asper pleadingly. 'I would never ...'

This is it, Lenk thought, *she's distracted. Denaos has a grip on Asper. Time to—*

Kill.

No, time to run. We have to—

KILL!

WE HAVE TO RUN!

'Now,' he whispered.

'What?' Kataria asked.

'*NOW, GENTLEMEN, NOW!*'

The voice of the Cragsman was accompanied by many others, boiling over the railings of the ship like a stew. The panicked cries of the sailors, mingled with Argaol's shrieks for order, were hurled into the broth, creating a thick, savoury aroma that Lenk well recognised.

Battle.

Damn it.

Chapter Two

BLOOD AND SALT

In the span of a breath, colour and sound exploded.
They came surging over the railings in numbers unfathomable, the twisting wire of their tattoos blending together to create some horrible skeleton of black and blue outside the tide of flesh they arrived on. Their zeal was loud, joyous, the song of impending slaughter joined by the humming of their upraised swords and the clinking harmony of the chains they came clambering across.

'Now, *now!*' Denaos cried, lunging at the rigging and pulling a knife out. 'We can still make it!'

'*What?*' Asper's expression drifted from incredulous to furious. 'You *were* planning on deserting?'

'Oh, come on,' the rogue protested sharply, 'like you weren't expecting this!'

'I knew it,' Quillian snarled. She shoved herself in front of Asper, blade extended. 'Stay behind me, Priestess. The danger is not yet great enough that I cannot deal with a deserter first.'

'*I say, look lively, gentlemen!*'

In the sound of whistling metal, the Serrant was proven violently wrong. The hatchet came whirling over the sailors' heads, a bird of iron and wood that struck the woman squarely in her chest. A human gong unhinged, she went collapsing to the deck, Asper quickly diving to catch her.

'Well, there you are,' Denaos said. 'Providence. Now, let's *go*!'

'No!' Kataria's bow was already in her hand, arrow kissing the string. 'Even if we get that thing off, we won't get far.'

As if to reinforce her point, a flock of hatchets came flying over the railings. The bold and unlucky sailors who had rushed forth to intercept the boarders went down under the sound of crunching bone and splashing liquid. The first of the boarders came sweeping over the railing, yet more of the thirsty weapons in their hands.

'Dread!' Kataria snarled, seizing the boy by the arm and shoving him forwards. 'Do something!'

'Right … right …' He stepped forwards hesitantly. 'I can … do something.' He cleared his throat, then glanced over his shoulder to see if Asper was watching. 'Er … you like fire, don't you?'

'*NOW!*' Kataria shrieked in unison with the wailing weapons.

The boy's eyes snapped wide open, hand up instinctively as he whirled about to face the onslaught of metal wings. His lips twisted, bellowing a phrase that hurt to hear, crimson light sparking behind his eyes.

The air rippled before him, hatchets slowing in their twisting flight, before finally stopping and falling to the deck.

'Well, hell,' Denaos grunted, 'we can just have him do that and we'll be fine!'

'We can't leave!' Asper protested. 'Quillian is hurt.'

'So she can stay behind and be a decoy!' the rogue retorted. 'Am I the *only* one who's thinking here?'

'We don't have time for this,' Kataria growled. Her eyes, along with everyone else's, turned towards Lenk, who was

45

watching the ensuing fight impassively. 'What do we do?'

He did not hear them. He did not feel her hand on his shoulder. Everything seemed to die; the wind ceased to blow, the sky ceased to move, the sea ceased to churn. He felt his eyes closing of their own volition, as though something reached out with icy fingers and placed them on his eyelids.

And that something reached out, whispered on a breathless voice into his ear.

When he opened his eyes again, there were no more enemies. There were no Cragsmen, no pirates, no sailors rushing forth to meet them. All he could see before him were fields of wheat, swaying delicately in the wind he could not feel. All he could hear was the whisper of their insignificance.

All he could feel was the blade in his hand and his boots moving under his feet.

'Lenk! *LENK!*' Kataria shrieked after him as he tore away from them, rushing to the railing.

'Well, fine,' Denaos said, 'see? He volunteered to be the decoy. It's a non-issue.'

The others fell silent; she continued to shout. He still didn't hear her. The timbers quaked under him as several pairs of feet added their rhythm to his charge. Emboldened by his actions, possibly, or spurred on by the wordless call to battle Argaol sent from the helm.

He didn't care.

His eyes were for the pirates that just now set their feet upon the timbers. His ears were for the sound of their last hatchets flying past his ears and over his head as he ducked low. His blade was for the man that just now set a hand upon the railing.

The sword lashed out quickly, catching the boarder by

surprise as the Cragsman looked to see where his projectile had landed. It bit deeply, plunging below the pirate's breastbone and sinking into his flesh.

His breath lasted an eternity, even as his mouth filled with his own life. The pirate looked down to see his own horror reflected in the steel, then looked up and Lenk saw his own eyes reflected in his foe's unblinking gaze as the light guttered out behind them.

Chaff from wheat.

He pulled hard, his blade wedged so deeply in the man that he came tumbling onto the deck. Lenk smashed his boot against the man's throat and pulled again, jerking his sword free in a spattering arc.

His senses were selective, ignoring the sound of sailors colliding into their foes in favour of the sound of feet coming up behind him. He whirled, lashing out with his blade, not caring who it was that had dared to try to ambush him.

Sparks sputtered in a quick and hasty embrace as his sword caught the pirate's cutlass. It was enough to drive the man back with a surprised grunt, enough to give Lenk room to manoeuvre. He sprang backwards, felt something collide with his heel.

He looked.

A sailor; he recognised the face, if not the name. Such a task was difficult though, given that a hatchet had lodged itself in said visage, leaving little more than half a gasping mouth and one very surprised eye. At that, Lenk's own eyes widened and the world returned to him.

Battle.

He could barely remember what had brought him this far: the fields of wheat, the unmoving sky and the silent screaming. What stood before him now was not something

47

to be scythed down carelessly, but a man, towering and swinging his cutlass wildly.

Surprised, but not shocked, Lenk brought his blade up to defend. He felt the blow more solidly this time, shaking down to his bones. Behind his opponent, other tattooed, leering faces erupted over the railings, rushing to meet the defenders. He heard feet shuffling, bodies hitting the deck behind him. He was surrounded.

Imbecile, he thought. *At what point did this seem like a good idea?* His foe swung again, he darted to the side. *Charging headlong? Who does that?* He lunged, sought the pirate's chest and caught his blade instead. *Well, Gariath does, but he's … well, you know.*

An errant kick caught him, sent him staggering backwards. His foe, apparently, had long legs. Long arms, too, Lenk noted; this wouldn't be a fight he could win if it continued to be this dance.

Run away, he thought, *escape through the crowd and you can—*

Kill.

No, no! Stop that! You just have to get away long enough to—

Fight.

NO! If … if you can't escape, just keep him busy. Keep him distracted long enough for Denaos to stab him in the back or Kataria to shoot him in the neck or—

Alone.

'What?' he asked his own thoughts.

He whipped his gaze about the carnage that the deck had become. He could see flesh, faces rising up and down from a sea into which the sailors and Cragsmen had blended seamlessly. But they were only faces filled with fear or covered in tattoos. He could see no sign of a skinny youth, a tall and lanky cockroach, a flashing silver pendant.

Or, he noted ruefully, twitching ears and bright green eyes.

Whatever twinge of despair he might have felt must have made itself apparent on his face, for when he turned his attentions back to his opponent, the Cragsman had discarded his battle-hardened concentration in exchange for an amused grin.

'I say, dear boy,' he said, 'you look to be possessed of a touch of the doubting dung beetle.'

'I'm fine, thanks,' Lenk grunted in reply, hoisting his blade up before him.

'More's the pity, I suppose. Had you, indeed, succumbed to the previous hypothesis of being a man of the utmost practicality and, synonymously, cowardice, I would have invited you to congenially excuse yourself from the antici- pated social of disaster about to be wreaked.'

Lenk blinked. 'I'm sorry, did you just offer me an escape route or invite me to tea?' He made a half-hearted thrust at the man, who easily darted away. 'Either way, you would seem to be in a poor position to guarantee either. You're not the captain.'

'Indeed. Our dearest chum and astute tutor Rashodd has excused himself from this particular bloody fete to better assure you of his honour. All we wish to partake of is the women in your charter, as well as a portion of your cargo, us being pirates and all.' He tilted his head slightly. 'And a particular priest who has decided to associate himself with your uncouth captain.'

Lenk drew back at the mention, suddenly cocking a brow.

'Evenhands?'

'Ah, the delicate ladies of your employ would certainly

be unimpressed at the object of your concern, sir.'

'What do you want with the Lord Emissary?'

The Cragsman offered a smirk coy as he could manage with lips like a shedding centipede. 'A proper gentleman never tells,' the pirate said, advancing upon the young man and grinning as his opponent took a step backwards. 'Unfortunately, in the time it took to deliver that stirring bout of eloquence, my patience, and thusly the offer, did decline. Alas …' He raised his cutlass high. 'Generosity wasted is generosity insulted, as they—'

He was interrupted suddenly by the sound of an out-of-tune lute being plucked, followed by a whistling shriek that ended in a wet, warm punctuation. The pirate jerked suddenly, he and Lenk sharing the same expression of confusion before they both looked down to see the arrow's shaft quivering from between two of the Cragsman's ribs.

'Ah,' he slurred, mouth glutted with red, 'that would do it, wouldn't it?'

Lenk watched him until he stopped twitching, then turned his stare upwards.

He caught sight of Kataria's smile first, her canines broad and prominent over the heads of the combatants as she stood upon the railing. She held up a hand, wiggling four slender fingers before scampering up the rigging, a trio of Cragsmen at her heels.

It was a well-believed idea of less-practical men that removing oneself from the reach of their opponent was low. *Scampering* away from them, however, was simply insulting. Kataria doubtlessly knew that. With dexterity better befitting a murderous squirrel, she turned, drew and loosed a pair of arrows at them, giggling wildly as they fell back, one dead, one wounded and the third apparently ready to find easier prey.

The saying was old and well-worn amongst men, but true enough that the pointy-eared savages had adopted it as their own.

Shicts don't fight fair.

The Cragsmen, too, seemed equally aware of the phrase and voiced their retort in a whirl of thrown hatchets. She twisted, narrowly avoiding the gnawing blades, but found herself caught in the rigging as they glided over her head and bit through the rope. She shrieked, fell, disappeared into the melee.

Go back, was his first thought. *Find her. Save her.* But his legs were frozen, his head pulling towards another direction. *She's a shict. Savage. She doesn't need saving. Keep going, keep going and—*

Kill. The thought came again, more urgent this time. It hurt his head to think it, chilled his skull as though it came on icy breath. *Fight.*

He couldn't help but agree; there would be time enough to worry about Kataria later, likely when she was dead. For the moment, something else caught his attention.

The sound of wheels turning with such force as to be heard over the din of battle reached his ears. A groaning of wood and metal sounded across the gap of the sea. Lenk could see, over the heads of the pirates who remained aboard the *Linkmaster* to hold their boarding chains steady, a monstrosity being pushed towards the railing.

'A siege engine?' he muttered to himself, not being able to imagine what else the wheeled thing might be. 'If they can afford a damn siege engine, why are they raiding *us*?'

No answer was forthcoming from either the four Cragsmen pushing it, nor from the visor-bound gaze of Rashodd. It was not them that Lenk looked at, but rather the wisp of a man standing by the side of the titanic captain.

51

Or at least, Lenk *thought* it was a man. Swaddled in conservative black where the pirates displayed their tattoos brazenly, the creature's clothing was the least curious thing about him. He was heads shorter than the others, looking like a mere shadow next to Rashodd, and his head resembled a bleached bone long scavenged of meat: hairless, pale, perfectly narrow.

Whether he saw Lenk staring at him or not, the young man did not know. But as the insignificant person's lips twisted slightly, the bone showing a sudden marring crack, Lenk couldn't help but feel as though it was intended for him.

To your left.

The thought came with greater clarity, with greater will, as though it was no longer even a part of his own mind, but another voice altogether. Lenk was highly surprised to hear it.

Not quite as surprised as he was to feel the rounded guard of a cutlass smash against his jaw, however.

He staggered backwards, his heel catching a dead pirate's arm as though his foe reached out in death. His senses reeled as his sword fell from his hand, his vision blurred as he felt blood trickle down his nose. He looked up, blinking and shaking his head; the first thing he made out, shortly before the tattoos, was a long, banana-coloured grin.

'It could hardly be said of me that so noble a man of the Crags does not endeavour to make good on his word,' the pirate said. 'But I do beg your pardon, kind sir. You do us no honour by sitting quietly and watching.' He looked down at the man Lenk had tripped over and frowned. 'Nor by the theft of so fine a fellow as this gentleman was to me.'

'I'm … sorry?' Lenk's voice was hoarse and weak, his hands trembling as he reached for his fallen sword.

'Ah, of course, your apology is accepted with the utmost gratitude,' the pirate replied. 'Even if the idea of repairing such egregious breaches of conduct is more than a tad absurd.'

His fingers felt numb, unable to sense the warmth of the hilt, the chill of the steel. He tried to regain his footing, the ringing in his skull and the uncertainty beneath his feet conspiring to keep him down. The Cragsman seemed less than concerned with the young man rising, if his very visible pity was any suggestion.

'I don't suppose it would help if I said I wouldn't do it again?' Lenk asked, trying to talk through his dizziness.

'I'm more than a mite remorseful to inform you that such would hardly be the proper retort.' The pirate shook his head and levelled his blade at the young man's face. 'Regrettably, this is the point in proper protocol where we resolve and absolve alike through the gouging of eyes and spilling of entrails upon the uncaring deck, if you'll excuse the crudeness.'

'Ah.'

Absently, Lenk regretted not having thought of something better for his last words.

That thought was banished as his hands thrust up weakly, catching the pirate's wrist and holding the blade fast a hair's length away from his face. The gesture was futile, both Lenk and his foe knew; his arms trembled, his fingers could not feel the skin and metal they sought to hold back. His breath gave up before he did, becoming short, rasping gasps in his throat.

He clenched his jaw, shut his eyes, felt his arms begin to yield.

No.

That thought lasted for but a moment, while the moment

existed as a drop of moisture on the pirate's blade, dangling for a silent eternity. Lenk felt his breath run cold in his lungs, felt his blood freeze in his veins and time with it.

Fight.

His muscles did not strengthen beneath his skin, rather they denied strength entirely in favour of the frigid fingers that crept through him. In one long, cold breath, he felt the numbness sweep up his arms, into his chest.

Into his mind.

Deny!

The thought grew stronger, louder with every twitch of his hands, every fingerbreadth he gave to the blade. It echoed through his head, down into his chest, into an arm that involuntarily broke from his opponent's grip and sought his fallen blade.

Through shut eyes, he could see the moment dangling off his opponent's sword.

He felt it drop.

'KILL!'

Blue flashed, pitiless and cold, behind his eyelids. Eyes not his own stared back into him. Teeth that were not his clenched. Fingers that were not his gripped a hilt. The thought did not leap to his mind, did not whisper inside him.

It had a voice.

It spoke.

Lenk felt something move, a snap of cold air that sent his hair whipping about his face. He opened his eyes and stared down the long steel blade of a sword he didn't remember swinging, life dripping down it, upon which the Cragsman's shock was violently etched.

He looked up, just as surprised as his opponent, and met the man's eyes. No fear this time, no moment of futile hope and extinguished life. The pirate stared at him with eyes that could reflect nothing, the blow having come too swiftly to grant him even the privilege of a horrified death.

He mouthed, 'No fair.'

And fell to the deck.

The numbness did not flee from Lenk's limbs, but rather seeped into his body, as water disappearing into the earth. He felt suddenly weak, legs soft under a body suddenly unbearably heavy, breath offensively warm and jagged in his throat.

Slowly, he staggered to his feet. Slowly, he felt the sun again, heard the din of battle. But the warmth was faint, the sounds distant. He could feel the chill, he was aware of it as he was of his own shadow. It seeped away, dissipated into blood that began to run warm, leaving only a single thought given a voice behind.

'*More.*'

'What?' he gasped, his own voice suddenly alien to himself.

'*More.*'

'I ... I don't—'

'MORE, YOU IDIOT! THERE'S MORE COMING!'

Argaol's roar came from the helm with desperation. Lenk glanced up to see four sailors locked in combat with a pair of Cragsmen, desperately trying to keep the blade-wielding pirates away from their captain with their staves. The dark man himself looked directly at Lenk, pointing to the railing.

He shrieked, of course, as he usually did when addressing the young man, but Lenk didn't hear him. He didn't need to as he saw two more tattooed men leap from a boarding chain onto the deck. Instead of rushing towards the battle to aid their fellows, they instead cast wary looks about, hungry eyes and bare feet immediately setting off for the companionway.

Evenhands.

'Damn, damn, damn, damn, damn, damn, damn, *damn*.'

A curse for every step as he charged after the boarders. Ironic, he thought absently as he pushed his way through the melee, that moments ago he was ready to leave the Lord Emissary to die. Then again, it was hardly surprising; so long as he had been hit in the face once today, he might as well get paid for it.

Which wasn't likely to happen if his employer was gutted below decks.

'Protect the charter, boys!' Argaol roared to his own crew. 'Protect the Lord Emissary! The Gods demand it and smile on us for it!'

Lenk's pace was quick as he leapt over bodies, side-stepped brawls, darted around stray blades. The battle raged with no clear victor; he passed corpses both familiar and tattooed. But the sailors held, the Cragsmen had not overrun them yet, and the two boarders were not as swift as Lenk was. For a moment, he felt a rush of victory as he drew closer.

For a moment, he thought that maybe the Gods *did* smile upon him.

That belief died with the sudden twist of an ankle and a shriek as he recalled that the Gods loved irony far more than they loved their servants. He hit a patch of red-tinged seawater, his boot slid out from under him and he went sprawling, sword clattering to the deck.

There was barely enough time to spew out a curse before he lunged to his feet, seizing his weapon. Too late;

he saw the two boarders vanish into the shadows of the companionway, laughter anticipating the impending looting ringing in their wake. Once inside, they would easily lose any pursuit in the maze of cargo holds and cabins, chopping up passengers at will, cutting and pillaging in a few breaths. And he was too late to stop it.

Too late, too late, too late, too late, too—

Stop it! Stop, he scolded himself as he forced his boots into a run. *Fight first, fear later.*

Just as the darkness of the companionway loomed up before him like a gaping maw, he was forced to skid to a halt. Something squirmed in the shadows. Someone screamed.

He threw himself to the side just in time to see the body of one of the invaders sail through the air, landing limply on the deck with his neck twisted at an angle at which necks clearly were not meant to twist.

'G-GET AWAY FROM ME!' the remaining pirate squealed from inside. He came shrieking out of the gloom, weapon lost, mouth gibbering. 'MONSTER! THEY'VE GOT A GODS-DAMNED DRAG—'

His scream died in his throat, his feet torn from the deck as a great red arm ending in a set of brutal claws reached out from the darkness to wrap about his neck. The hand tightened, the sound of bones creaking between its massive fingers. Lenk cringed, but only for a moment. He knew the smile that then spread across his face was unwholesome, but he could hardly help himself.

The sight of Gariath brought out all sorts of loathsome emotions in people.

The dragonman emerged from the companionway, holding the writhing pirate aloft with an arm rippling with crimson muscle. He surveyed the battle through black eyes, his captive a mere afterthought.

57

The expression across his long snout was unreadable as he swung his horned head back and forth. The ear-frills at the side of his head twitched in time with the leathery wings folded on his massive back, as if stretching after a long nap.

'I thought you weren't coming up,' Lenk said.

Gariath looked down at the young man, who only came up to the lowest edge of his titanic chest. He sneered, far more unpleasantly than either Lenk or Kataria could ever hope to, baring rows of sharp, ivory teeth.

'It was stifling below,' he grunted. 'I came up for air and find humans dying.' He glanced over the melee. 'I can't say I'm not pleasantly surprised.'

He became aware of the captive pirate thrashing in his hand, pounding at the thick red wrist wrapped in a silver bracer. His scaly eye-ridges furrowed as he turned to the companionway.

His snarl was short and businesslike as he slammed the pirate's face against the wooden doorframe, staining it red. His roar was loud and boastful as he drove it forwards again, bone fragments splintering with the frame. His snort was quick and derisive as he crushed the pirate once more, reducing a formerly grisly visage to featureless red pulp. Already bored with his now-unmoving prey, the dragon-man dropped him to the deck, raising a clawed foot to rest upon his head.

'Who needs to die?' he asked.

'Pirates,' Lenk replied.

Gariath ran his obsidian glare from one end of the ship to the other in long, patient stares.

'Which ones are the pirates?'

'What do you mean, "Which ones are the pirates?"'

'You all look the same to me,' Gariath grunted, folding his arms over his chest. 'Ugly, stupid, smelly.'

'So look for the ugliest, stupidest and smelliest ones and give it your best guess,' Lenk replied. 'Are you going to help or not?'

The dragonman's thick red legs tensed. His weight shifted to the foot resting on the pirate's skull. Lenk winced and turned away at the sound of something cracking, the sight of something grey and sticky oozing out onto the blood-soaked deck. Gariath snorted.

'Maybe.'

Contrary to what her elders had said of the teeming race, Kataria didn't find humans entirely awful. The only thing that truly annoyed her about them was their grossly under-rated ability to adapt. It was a subject of routine discussion amongst those few shicts who grew old enough to stop killing their round-eared foes and start theorising about better ways to kill them.

'They're just monkeys, of course,' it had often been said. *'They spend their whole lives searching for food and, when they don't find it, they just run around in circles, smelling their fingers and eating their own scat.'*

In the year since she had followed a silver-haired man out of the woods, she had been keeping track of her own addenda that she might someday offer by the fire. And, as the possibility of her living that long quickly began to dwindle, she thought, not for the first time, that the elders' description neglected to mention that, when faced with food, humans proved particularly motivated.

And the Cragsmen surrounding her proved to be particularly clever monkeys.

Should've stayed in the rigging, she told herself, *should've climbed back up. Easier target for hatchets, sure, but you could've shot more of them.*

She had hardly expected them to figure out what arrows were, much less corner her against the railing. But they had adapted; they had found her, pursued her, showing the extreme discourtesy of not giving her enough room to shoot them.

And now a trio of them surrounded her, their eyes locked on the gleaming arrowhead that drifted menacingly from body to body.

One shot. One arrow was all that kept them at bay, each one hesitant to rush, to force her to choose him to plant the angry metal seed in. After that, they would be upon her faster than she could pull another one free of her quiver.

Her ears twitched, recalling the threats and declarations they had inflicted upon her from the safety of their ship. Those same threats, that same hunger lurked behind their eyes now, dormant for fear that she would see them in their gazes and extinguish them with an arrow.

The sea roared behind her; the terror of humans was an invitation for her. It would be better that way, she knew, to kill one and then hurl herself into the froth. She would die, certainly, but it was infinitely better than the alternative, better than submitting to the human disease.

A bit late for that, isn't it? she asked herself, resentful. She forced that from her head, though, determined to think.

Options were unsurprisingly limited, however: shoot and die in the sea, shoot and die in the arms of a human ... skip the third party and just shoot herself?

'*Get down, Kat!*'

She heard Asper's voice first, Dreadaeleon's second. The instant she recognised the alien babble emanating from the boy's mouth, she fell to the deck as her assailants looked to the source.

Then screamed.

Fire roared over her head in a wicked plume, the smell of stray strands of her own hair burning filled her nostrils. The stench of burning flesh, however, quickly overpowered it, just as the angry howl of flame overpowered the shrieks of the Cragsmen. She could feel the deck reverberate as feet thundered past her, carrying walking pyres over the railing to plunge into the water below with a hiss.

She got up, patted her head for any stray flames, then looked at the fast-fading plumes of steam rising from the sea.

That works, too.

'Are you all right?' Asper's voice was joined by the sound of bronze on wood as she dragged Quillian to the shict's position. 'One moment. I can check you over as soon as—'

'Oh, yes, sure, be certain to check her over.' Dreadaeleon wore a look of ire as he walked beside her, one hand folded neatly behind him, the other flicking embers from his fingers. 'I mean, it's not like I did something incredible like *conjure fire from my own body heat*.'

'Like *that's* hard,' Kataria growled. She pointed out to sea. 'Those don't count, by the way.'

'Don't ... what?'

'Only kills you do yourself count. Wizard kills aren't real kills.'

'*Real* kills?' Asper looked up, disgusted. 'These are human lives we're taking!'

'*We?*' Kataria asked with a sneer. 'What did you do aside from try to choke me with moral indignation?'

'I ...' The priestess stiffened, looking down with a frown. 'I can fight.'

'Don't waste your breath on a reply, Priestess,' came a mutter from the deck, ire unimpeded by her barely conscious stagger. Quillian rose to her feet on trembling legs, turning a scowl upon the shict. 'One can hardly expect inhumans to understand things like mercy and compassion.'

'What? Your sword is just for show, then?' Kataria asked, smiling.

Quillian did not smile back, did not even offer a reply.

Perhaps it was the clarity that the hatchet blow had robbed her of that caused the Serrant's mask of contempt to crack, or perhaps it was that she simply didn't want to bother keeping it up anymore. But in that moment, the displays of righteous indignation and palls of virtuous disgust fell away from Quillian's face.

Hate remained in abundance.

It was a pure hate that Kataria had seen before, albeit rarely, a hate that flowed like an ancestral disease. Quillian hated Kataria, hated her mother, hated her father, hated everything with pointed ears as she hated nothing else, not even the pirates swarming about the deck.

'Go! *GO!* He'll kill us all!'

Or running, anyway, she thought as a tattooed blur rushed past her.

The moment of tense readiness collectively and quickly faded into befuddlement as the Cragsmen rushed towards the companions and then, without even looking, right past them. Precious steel was forgotten, wounded men were ignored, terror shone through every inked face. Kataria watched, baffled and wondering whether shooting them in the back counted.

More men rushed past, these ones belonging to the

Riptide's crew. She knew the source of the panic before she even turned about, much less before she heard the screaming.

'MONSTER!' one of the Cragsmen howled. 'RUN, GENTS! THE LOUTS BROUGHT A BLOODY DRAGONMAN!'

Blood-soaked, she thought, would be a more accurate descriptor of the towering creature striding casually after them. A small heap of broken bodies, twisted limbs and ripped flesh lay behind him: the brave and foolish few who had decided he might not be quite as tough as he looked.

Gariath looked as unconcerned as someone covered in gashes and blood could be. Almost bored, she thought, as he stepped upon, rather than over, the bodies before him, continuing a slow pursuit after the fleeing pirates.

That expression gave her the courage to shoot him a pair of scowls. Once for his cold, arrogant stride when he clearly had only about one more kill to his name than she did, *if that*. Her deepest scowl, accompanied by a matching frown, was for the fact that he walked alone.

Lenk was nowhere to be seen.

'Stop running, rats,' Gariath growled. 'The *Rhega* were made for better fights than you can offer.'

A body stirred on the deck. A Cragsman, apparently trying to hide amongst his dead fellows, came sprinting off the deck, only to crash back down as a corpse selfishly tripped him.

He did not remain there for long, however.

'No! *NO!*' he shrieked, a pair of clawed hands gripping him by the heels. 'GET AWAY, BEAST!'

'Oh, Talanas.' Asper flashed a sickened look as Gariath pulled the man off the deck. 'Gariath, don't.'

The dragonman didn't seem to notice her, much less

acknowledge her words. Kataria stepped forwards, looking past his terrified victim and into his black eyes.

'Where's Lenk?'

He looked at her as he might an insect, shrugging.

'Dead?' she asked.

'Probably,' he grunted. 'He's human. Small, stupid … not quite as stupid as the rest of you, but still—'

'Put me down,' the Cragsman pleaded, 'please. *PLEASE!*'

'Shut up,' Kataria snarled at him. Her eyebrows rose suddenly. 'Wait a moment.' She knelt before him, looking into eyes that threatened to leap from their sockets. 'Did you kill a silver-haired man?'

'Looks kind of like a silver-haired child,' Dreadaeleon piped up.

'You're one to talk,' Asper replied snidely, 'and he's not *that* short.'

'I … I didn't kill anyone! I swear!' the pirate squealed.

'You're only making this more unpleasant.' Gariath sighed. 'Shut up and see if you can't die without soiling yourself.'

'How come you didn't watch him?' Kataria asked the dragonman.

'If he can't watch himself, he deserves whatever happens to him.' Gariath snorted. 'Hold that thought.'

'NO!' the man screamed as his captor pried his legs apart with no great effort. 'It's … it's all cultural! I was pressed into service! Please! *PLEASE!*'

One by one, groans of impending horror escaped the companions. No one dared to look up, much less protest, as Gariath drew his leg back like a hammer and aimed squarely between the pirate's legs. Kataria stared for as long as she could, until the sight of the dragonman's grin finally made her look down.

There weren't hands big enough to block out the crunching sound that followed.

She looked up just in time to see a flash of red and brown as Gariath tossed the man overboard like fleshy offal. That, she knew, was about as much honour as he would offer creatures smaller than himself. That thought, as well as his massive, suddenly wet foot, kept her tense as she addressed him.

'We have to go back,' she said, 'we have to find Lenk.'

He glanced over his shoulder. 'No.'

'But—'

'If he's alive, he's alive,' he snorted. 'If he's dead ... no great loss.'

He's right, you know, she told herself. *It's one human. There are many of them. You shouldn't want to look back, shouldn't care. It's one human, one more disease.*

She sighed, offering no further resistance as he pushed his way past her, trying to convince herself of the truth of her thoughts as he moved through the companions. No one bothered to stop him. No one she cared about, at least.

'So!' Quillian placed a bronzed hand on her hip, unmoving as Gariath walked forwards. 'The battlefield is further profaned by the presence of abominations? There is hardly any redemption for this—'

'Shut up.'

The dragonman's grunt was as thunderous as the sound of the back of his hand cracking against the Serrant's face. Her armour creaked once as she clattered to the deck and again as he stepped on and over her.

'What ... I ...' Asper gritted her teeth at his winged back. 'I *just* pulled her *off* the ground!'

'Don't encourage him,' Kataria warned. 'Come on. We look for Lenk. Gariath handles the rest.'

'Oh, is that all?' Dreadaeleon pointed over her shoulder. 'There's one part of our problem solved, then.' He coughed. 'By me.' He sniffed. 'Again.'

She turned, fought hard to hide her smile at the sight of the young man rushing across the deck. That task became easier with every breath he drew closer. For with every breath, she saw the blood on his sword, the uncharacteristic fury in his stride …

The angry cold in his narrowed eyes.

'Does this mean we have to help Gariath?' Dreadaeleon asked, sighing.

She ignored him, cried out to the other short human.

'Lenk!'

'Chain,' he grunted as he sped past. '*CHAIN!*'

It occurred to him, vaguely, that the voice snarling those words from his mouth was not entirely his. It occurred to him that she looked at him with those same, studying eyes and he had ignored her. It occurred to him that he was weary, dizzy, surrounded by death and rushing heedlessly into more.

What did not occur to him was that he should stop.

Something was driving him like a horse, spurring him on. Something compelled his feet to move beneath him, to ignore the footsteps following him. Something forced his hand on his sword, his eyes on the mother chain.

Something spoke.

'*Go.*'

The chain grew larger with every step, as did the sight of the crimson hulk in the corner of his eye. Gariath had stopped before the chain, muscles tensed and quivering.

No matter, Lenk thought, he must keep going, he must fight, he must obey the need within him.

In some part of his mind, he knew this to be wrong. He felt the fear that crept upon him, the terror that the voice was some part of the void to which his mind was slowly being lost. Madness; what else could it be? What else could compel him to fight, to rush into impossible odds? What else could override reason and logic with its own frigid thoughts?

'*Stop.*'

He obeyed, not knowing what else he could do.

The reason became apparent quickly enough, reflected in the jagged head of a bloodied axe clenched in meaty, tattooed paws. The Cragsman was massive, apparently of the same stock that had bred the giant Rashodd, with grey hair hanging about a grizzled visage in wild braids.

He stood upon defiant legs, regarding the companions with eyes unwary, challenging them to take the mother chain. Lenk looked past his massive shoulders to the chain itself, swaying precariously as leathery bodies twisted over each link.

'*Reinforcements.*'

'And this one's the vanguard,' Lenk grunted in reply to the thought.

'*Meant for me ...*'

Lenk glanced up at the dragonman as he heard the others come to a halt behind him.

'What?'

'This is it,' Gariath whispered, taking a step forwards. 'This one was made for me.'

'That's stupid,' Kataria said, 'I can put an arrow in him from—'

'*MINE!*'

She recoiled, with everyone else, as he whirled on her, teeth bared and claws outstretched. 'Those other ones were weak, stupid. This one …' He turned back to the massive man, snorting. 'I might die.'

She blinked. 'What?'

'More than a chance of that, dear boy,' the vanguard boomed, hefting his weapon over his shoulder. 'Defiance of man's law is our trade, but expunging an abomination is the work of the Gods, I am assured.'

'Yes.' Gariath's eyes lit like black fires, his hands tightened into fists. '*Yes.*' His wings unfurled behind him, tail lashing angrily. His jaws craned open, a roar tore free from his throat. '*YES!*'

'COME, DEMON!' the Cragsman howled, beating his chest. 'COME AND TASTE THE—'

His speech was cut short as his body stiffened with a sudden spasm. He smacked his lips, furrowed his brow, as though he had just forgotten what he was going to say. When he opened his mouth to finish the challenge, a faint trickle of red appeared at his lips.

'Well … that's …' The light behind his eyes extinguished along with the fire in Gariath's as the pirate collapsed to his knees. 'That's …' He groped uncertainly at his chest, seeking to scratch an itch beneath the skin. 'That's … rather …'

He fell face down. A bright-red flower bloomed from his neck, dripping onto the wood.

Denaos's grin was short-lived as he looked at his companions, wiping clean the long knife in his hands.

'That one was *MINE!*' Gariath exploded in a roar, the deck shaking with the force of his stomp. 'He was put here to fight *ME!*'

68

'He just crawled over the chain, actually,' Dreadaeleon said quietly.

'You gutted him like a fish!' Asper said, grimacing at the corpse. 'You killed him as if he was nothing!'

'Is that … praise?' Denaos shook his head. 'No, no. Of course, you're whining. Isn't that typical? I'm demeaned for not killing anyone and the *moment* I save us all some trouble by indulging in an act of practical butchery, *I'm* suddenly at fault?'

'*I* never asked you to take a life,' Asper protested.

'*You* don't even think that it might be necessary!' Kataria spat back. 'If you had your way, we'd all sit around praying to some weak round-ear god for an answer while they sodomised us with steel!'

'Don't talk to her like that!' Dreadaeleon piped up, trying hard not to wither under her scowl. 'She's right to have conviction, even if it is in imaginary beings on high.' He blinked, eyes going wide. 'Did I say that part aloud or think it?'

A hand cracking against his head made a proper answer.

'Who told you to even scurry out of your hole, rat?' Gariath growled. '*You* were meant to eat filth and drink your own tears. The *Rhega*,' he thumped his chest, 'were made to kill and die.'

'Plenty of time for the latter,' Denaos replied, holding his arms out wide. 'Humanity didn't fight its way to the top of the food chain to be condescended to by lizards.'

Well, that figures, Lenk thought to himself. *The one time he musters the spine to confront someone, it's one of our own.*

'*Useless …*' the voice muttered.

Agreed. He blinked. *No, wait. Don't talk to it.*

'*Fight.*'

Fight back! Resist! It's madness, you know it's madness! You aren't mad! You can—

'*NOW.*'

The voice came with a sudden insistence, a frigid howl that drowned out the sounds of argument, the sounds of clinking chains. The voice left no room for fear or for thought as it gnashed its teeth, fangs sinking into his brain, grinding his skull between them, filling his mind with fury.

'*Command.*'

'S-stop ...' he whimpered.

'*Lead!*'

'Hurts—'

'*KILL!*'

'*STOP!*'

He didn't know how loud he had screamed, but everyone had snapped to attention. He didn't know what expression he wore on his face that caused them to look at him so.

He didn't care.

'Dread,' he snarled, pointing to the chain, 'burn them.'

'Right ...' the boy said, swallowing hard and moving towards the links. 'But I need time to—'

'*NOW!*'

No time even to stutter an agreement, the cold rigidity in Lenk infected Dreadaeleon as well. His fingers knotted together in a gesture that was painful to watch, his lips murmured a language that was painful to hear. Lenk watched him open his eyes, watched the crimson energy flower from behind his eyelids as tiny electric sparks began to dance along his sleeves.

'*Enemies.*'

'Right,' Lenk muttered, spying the hatchet-bearing pirates move to the chain on the *Linkmaster*. 'Kat.'

'Uh-huh,' she replied, already drawing the fletching to her cheek. The arrows sang in ugly harmony, wailing from her string to catch them in the throat and chest. She wasted no time in turning a smug grin upon Gariath. '*I win.*'

'What ...' Asper asked, her voice as hesitant as her trembling hands, 'what should I do?'

'What *can* you do?' Lenk replied coldly, his mind focused on other things.

No cry had arisen from the *Linkmaster*, none of the collective panic that had plagued them upon Gariath's appearance, not so much as a harsh word from Rashodd. The pirates simply took a collective step backwards, their expressions unnervingly serene. Even Rashodd appeared not at all displeased as failure loomed in his iron-clad face.

Why?

They parted like a wave of flesh, opening up a space at the railing. Lenk's eyes widened.

The siege engine.

It rolled to the railing, a mass of iron and wood whose immediate purpose he could not decipher. A ballista? Of course, how else would they have got the chain across? Then why weren't they firing it?

'What are they waiting for?'

No answer was heard over the sound of Dreadaeleon's chant as it rose to an echoing crescendo. The sparks that were birthed on his sleeves grew into full electric snakes, crackling eagerly as they raced down his arms and into his knuckles. He extended his fingers, trembling as though they sought to jump free of their fleshy prisons, and knelt down to press two single fingers against the chain.

'*Yes ...*'

It came too quick for anyone to scream, the lightning leaping from his fingers and onto the chain with electric vigour. Men became insects in a hail of sparks, tattoos lost amidst the blackening of skin. They collapsed, fell into the water and were lost to the tide.

'*Good.*'

'Gariath,' Lenk muttered.

The crimson hulk stared down at him for a moment, eyes narrowed, challenging him to give an order. Whatever the others had seen in Lenk that made them obey, he didn't see it or didn't care.

Inside his head, Lenk's mind clenched, as if agitated that the dragonman would not obey. Whether he finally resisted out of inner discipline or pure fear, Lenk kept such ire from reaching his lips. He did not break his stare from Gariath's black gaze, did not back down.

And when Gariath finally did move to the chain, he did not care why. He looked, instead, to the deck of the pirate ship and their siege engine. He spied the shadow there again, the man with the bone for a head who looked like some displaced spectre amongst the crowd. Again, the man met Lenk's gaze, again the man smiled.

The dragonman hooked his hands into the mother chain's clawed head, gripping it firmly. Snorting, he gave it a great shake, dislodging a corpse caught by the wrist in its links, throwing off the pirates who still tried to set foot on it. Lenk watched with narrowed eyes and empty thoughts.

Gariath grunted, muscles straining, wood cracking as he began to pull.

The shadow of a man held up a hand, waved it.

'*No.*'

Sailors flocked to the railing of the *Riptide*, roaring challenges at their calm foes.

Two Cragsmen rushed to the engine, pulled a rope.

'*No!*'

Gariath's wings unfurled like great sails, the wind filled with a shower of splinters as the chain's head came tearing loose. With a great iron wail for its lost charge, the mother chain collapsed into the sea and its little linked children followed, clinking squeals, while the *Riptide* drank the wind and tore away from its captor.

Men cheered. Denaos and Kataria shared an unpleasant cackle at the victory. Dreadaeleon managed a smile, looking to Asper, who managed a sigh of weary relief. Gariath snorted disdainfully, folding his arms over his chest.

It was too soon for Lenk to rejoice, not while his ears were fixed to a sound.

The siege engine came to life without boulders or spears or arrows. It shifted upon its wooden wheels, an iron monstrosity of spikes and blades, swinging back and forth. It sang.

A church bell, he suspected, by the look and sound, but forged from a mould more misshapen than was intended for any godly instrument. Its chorus was no echoing monotone droning, but something of many voices that sang out in horrid, discordant harmony.

A shriek banged against a moan, raucous laughter scraped against agonised weeping, a wistful sigh ground against a violent roar. The bell spoke. The bell sang. And it did not fade from Lenk's ears, even as the *Linkmaster* shrank in his eyes.

'That was it?'

Lenk turned to see scorn in Gariath's eyes, the dragonman looking down at him with scaly lips pulled into a snarl. The young man regarded him coldly, forcing the horrid song from his thoughts long enough to meet him with an equally contemptuous look.

'You got to kill someone, didn't you?'

73

'I barely bled,' Gariath replied.

'That's … a problem, is it?'

Gariath regarded him carefully for a moment before snorting. He turned, forcing Lenk to duck the sweeping tail that lashed out spitefully behind him, and began to stalk along the deck.

'Don't call me again,' he grunted, 'unless there's real blood to be spilled.'

'One wonders,' Asper said snidely as he passed, 'just how much blood needs to be spilled before it qualifies as "real".'

Gariath did not reply, did not even seem to notice her or the bodies he crushed under his feet. That only seemed to cause her face to contort further, teeth grinding behind her lips. Her voice still brimming with ire, she turned to Lenk.

'I'm going to help the men remove the bodies, someone has to—' She hesitated, flinching, and seemed to exhale her anger in one long, weary sigh, offering the young man something of a smile. 'At least it's over and we're safe.'

'Yes, isn't that interesting?' Denaos commented as he walked away. 'Violence solves yet another problem.'

'That doesn't mean I have to like it.'

'You don't, of course,' he replied, 'but what would you have done differently?'

She looked down, rubbing her arm. 'Nothing, I suppose.'

'Then let us content ourselves with the present, bloody and body-strewn as it may be.'

'Don't act like you're some great warrior,' Kataria snarled at his back. 'You were more than willing to run away when it was still an option.'

'I was,' he said without turning around. 'And if we had

74

done as I suggested, there'd be much less dead and we'd *all* be happy.' He offered a limp-wristed wave as he headed for the companionway. 'Let us consider this the next time we all decide that I'm not worth listening to.'

Asper muttered something under her breath, fingering her pendant as she walked towards the sailors who were already pulling up bodies, sighing over their companions and tossing their fallen adversaries over the railing. Dreadaeleon made a move to follow, but staggered, leaning on the railing.

'I can ...' He paused to take a deep breath, a thin sheen of sweat on his brow. 'I can help. I'm ... just a little winded, is all. Strain and all that. Just ... just give me a moment.'

'Take all the time you need,' she said coldly. 'There will be a lot of prayers to be said. I wouldn't want you to subject yourself to that kind of ordeal.'

He made an awkward attempt to follow her after an even more awkward attempt to retort. Instead, he was left furrow-browed and sneering as he stalked the opposite way, leaning heavily on the railing.

'As though it's my fault I'm surrounded by the ignorant masses.' He stopped, glowering at Lenk. '*You* swing a big piece of metal and make a mess on the deck and *you* get a smile.' He poked himself hard in his sunken chest. '*I* electrocute *three* men as humanely as possible and *I'm* the heathen?'

'Well,' Lenk replied, admiring his own blade, 'you must admit ... it *is* pretty large.'

The boy's face turned as red as his eyes had just been as he staggered past the young man and disappeared into some corner of the ship, muttering under his breath.

Lenk paid it no mind as he walked to the railing and the angry chew-mark where the chain had been dislodged.

The *Linkmaster* continued to dominate the horizon, even as it became a black beetle on the water. Even as its prey continued to outrun it, he could see no hurry aboard, no frenzy of movement as orders were barked for the ship to give chase. It faded into the distance, until he could see nothing of the men aboard it, hear nothing of their voices.

But he continued to hear, continued to see. The bell's song lingered, echoing inside his head just as loudly as if it were next to him. Just as if they were before him, he could see the black-clad man's bone-white lips, twisted into a wide and knowing smile.

And, lingering behind them all like gently falling snow, the sound of a thought given a voice, muttering …

'Are you aware that we won?'

He whirled about with a start to see Kataria smiling, leaning on her bow. Her eyes were soft now, two emeralds gleaming lazily under heavy lids.

'If you want to cheer,' she said, 'I won't think any less of you than I already do.'

'If there's anyone who should be cheering and demeaning themselves, it's you,' he replied, glancing at the clean-up taking place along the deck. 'Lots of dead humans … must be a good day for you.'

'Only a few over a dozen,' she said with a shrug. 'Barely a dent in their numbers. Nothing worth celebrating.'

'You're aware that I'm human, right? Because, really, I'm not sure how I'm supposed to take that remark.'

'Well, it's not as if any of the humans I *like* died.' She followed his gaze as a drowsy-looking Quillian appeared to assist Asper. 'In fact, several humans I don't like survived.' She sniffed the air, scratched herself. 'Still, good day.'

Supposedly.

He suspected he should agree; a day that ended with someone else dead instead of himself usually qualified as 'good' for an adventurer. He suspected that his next thought should have disturbed him quite a bit more than it did.

This time, dead bodies just aren't enough.

Had this been a chance raid, some simple act of piracy like he had originally suspected, of course he could take pride in the fact that he could still stab people and thus was still employable. But this hadn't been a chance raid, there were too many factors screaming that this was something worse.

The calm demeanour of a famously bloodthirsty and deranged breed of murderers, a man who had no business being in the company of such towering and fierce creatures, a bell that sang instead of a ballista that shot.

A chill crept up his spine.

'*Staring . . .*'

He could feel it immediately, almost heard her eyes turn hard behind him as they bore into him, digging under flesh, searching, studying. He gritted his teeth, tried not to twitch under her gaze. But something inside him lacked willpower. He felt something shift under his skin.

'*Make her stop.*'

'You're worried.'

When he turned, her smile was gone. He saw her, then, without the heat of battle to cloud his mind. She was weary: sweat slicked her skin and seeped into the cuts on her muscular physique, her hair clung in dirty clumps and the feathers she wore whipped about her wildly. She was the very vision of savagery, the image conjured up when people spat the name '*shict*'.

And she was staring at him with eyes full of concern.

'You're thinking.' Her ears twitched, as if hearing his very thoughts.

His breath caught in his throat at that idea. 'We won,' he gasped, 'they lost.'

She nodded intently.

'But they didn't curse. They didn't scream. Wouldn't you have?'

'If we had lost and I wasn't dead, probably.'

'They were calm.' He turned a glower over the sea. 'They shouldn't have been.'

A hand was laid on his shoulder. He felt her through the leather of her glove and the cloth of his tunic, felt her heartbeat just as he knew she could hear his. Just as he knew he should pull away, just as he knew that she didn't touch humans if she wasn't pulling arrows out of them.

Just as he knew he could not.

Everything went silent inside him. The wailing drone ceased, the smile vanished from his mind. He could feel himself grow warm again, feel the blood pump through him, coursing under her touch.

She turned him to face her, he did not resist. Her eyes were not soft, but not hard. He had no idea what lurked behind her green orbs as she stared into him, just as he had no idea what to do.

'It's over,' she said with a certainty he hadn't heard from her before. She smiled. 'Stop thinking.'

He watched her lay her bow upon her shoulders, looping her arms up and over it. Her hair drifted in the breeze and carried the scent of her sweat into his nostrils as she walked away. It filled his breath, now deep and regular again as he repeated calming words to himself.

'It's over.' He rubbed his eyes, laid his sword against the railing and leaned backwards. 'It's over.'

He heard the voice. It was soft, fading even as it spoke, but he heard it. He heard it speak a single word, ask a single question.

'*Over?*'

And then, he heard it laugh.

Three

PRESIDING OVER RUIN

By the time Lenk clambered up the stairs leading to the helm, the cheering had died down. A few fellows enthused at not being killed had dared to clap him on the back once Kataria had left his side, finding boldness in the absence of his maligned companion. Their enthusiasm was slain as surely as their fellows, however, when they cast a glance upon the deck and surveyed the work that had to be done.

There were dead to tend.

Lenk spared a glancing frown for the men below. Some were veterans, having seen the deaths of comrades before, though likely none so gruesome. Most were young men who'd only seen elders pass away in their sleep. He hesitated at the top of the helm, his gaze lingering upon a young man dragging one of the dead from the deck.

A part of him wanted to turn back around, put a hand on the young man's shoulder and move him below where Asper tended to the wounded, mortally or otherwise. The sailor was possibly the same age as Lenk. Hands on shoulders should be wrinkled, he thought, weathered with age and experience, broad from embracing children and wives. Young hands, calloused hands, were not meant to be placed on shoulders.

Old hands grip people. Young hands grip swords.

His grandfather had told him that once. His grandfather's hands had been young to the day he died. He blinked, drew in a deep breath. Something in his mind stirred: the roar of fire, shadows dancing against sheets of orange, people falling beneath flashes of silver, smiles that twisted into screams. His grandfather ...

No. He commanded himself to force the images from his mind. *Not today. Not now.*

He turned his back on the deck. There were plenty of men with weathered, wrinkled hands on the ship. His still gripped a sword.

At the ship's impressive wheel stood Captain Argaol, looking decidedly less fazed than he should have with dead men on his deck. His dark features were stern, eyes fixed straight ahead, not even looking at the young man. His only movement was to reach down and smooth the sash of commendation medals he had earned from his various charters.

His mate, Sebast, a man who had spent so much time in the sun that he had both the appearance and smell of jerked beef, dutifully moved aside as Lenk stepped onto the quarterdeck. He sniffed, dipped a mop into a wooden bucket and proceeded to wipe away the blood that had been spilled on the ship's timbers as casually as if he were wiping away the lunch that Lenk had spilled some days earlier.

Lenk gave him a cursory nod before stepping up to the captain's side.

'Well, we did it.' His voice sounded alien to his own ears.

'Did what?' The captain's voice seemed much deeper than it should have, given his size. The man stood only a little taller than Lenk, his height perhaps diminished due to the lack of hair upon his head.

81

'Drove off the pirates.'

'And?'

'I thought you'd like to know.'

'I can see the whole Gods-cursed ship from up here, boy. You think I didn't see that?' He glanced at the young man with a sneer. 'What? You wanted some credit for breaking the chain? Smart move there – wish you'd thought of it early enough to spare my men.'

'It was a fight,' Lenk replied coldly. 'People die.'

'How fortunate we have you to be so casually nonchalant about it. I've been in this business awhile, boy. I know what happens.'

'Then you'll also know to choose your insults carefully. Many more of your men would have died if not for us.' The young man gestured to the deck. 'Or did you not see how many pirates we killed?'

'Oh, I saw,' the captain replied, seething. 'I also saw you making eyes at the escape vessel while you were down there.' He levelled an accusing finger. 'You'd have run like the heathens you are and left the rest of us to die if you could have.' He grunted and glowered at his first mate. 'What'd I tell you about taking adventurers aboard?'

'Bad idea,' Sebast replied without looking up. 'Bad philosophically, bad practically. Still, they *did* undoubtedly save about as many as they killed, Captain. Perhaps a little gratitude wouldn't be inappropriate?'

'I'm grateful enough that the heathen scum didn't decide to slaughter us to try and curry favour with the Cragscum, aye,' the captain agreed.

The adventurer reputation for opportune betrayal was not unknown to Lenk, but he still took slight offence at Argaol's accusation. It wasn't as though he had *seriously* considered turning on the crew.

Not until now, anyway.

'So, you'll forgive me if I'm not at the pinnacle of appreciativeness' Argaol continued, scowling at the young man. 'And you'll forgive me for saying that if you ever so much as think of fleeing and leaving my men without escape again, I'll chop you up and serve you in the mess.'

'Hope you've got a bigger sword,' Lenk muttered under his breath.

'What was that?'

'I said if you're so concerned for your crew, perhaps you should be down there moving corpses and grieving.' Lenk cast a sneer of his own back at the captain. 'I promise I won't look if you start crying.'

'Ah, we've got a merry jester here, in addition to a filthy adventurer. I bet a man of such diverse talents would like a lovely strawberry tart.' He snapped two thin fingers. 'Sebast, fetch the fanciful adventurer a tart!'

'As you like, Captain.' The mate set aside his mop and began to trundle down the steps.

'Get back here, you nit,' Argaol snarled. 'I was being sarcastic.'

'Facetious,' Lenk corrected.

'What?' He sighed, slumping at the wheel slightly. 'You got word for me, boy? Or did you come up here to demonstrate your impeccable wit?'

'A little over a dozen of the Cragsmen dead, fewer of our own.'

'*My* own,' Argaol snapped back fiercely. 'The *Riptide* sails under Argaol, the men serve under Argaol, not some runty adventurer.'

The mate leaned upon his mop, peering thoughtfully at the young man. 'Where is it you said you came from, Mister Lenk?'

'Steadbrook,' the young man replied, 'in Muraska.'

'Steadbrook, is it? That can hardly be right. I've travelled up, down, through and around Muraska and I've never heard of any such town.'

Lenk opened his mouth. His voice caught in his throat as he blinked. 'It's gone,' he whispered, choked, 'burned.'

'Such a shame.' Whatever sincerity the first mate might have hoped to convey was lost as he returned to his mopping. 'It would have been interesting to visit a place that produces such short men with grey hair.'

Before Lenk could respond, Argaol interjected with a rough cough. 'What of the Lord Emissary?'

'Evenhands is—'

'Kindly refer to our charter by his proper name,' the captain interrupted sharply. 'This ship is free of all blasphemy, no matter how minor. I won't have a …' He stared hard at Lenk. 'What's your faith, boy?'

'None of your business,' Lenk responded hotly.

'Khetashite,' Sebast muttered. 'All adventurers follow the Outcast, I hear.'

'The proper title is the Wanderer.'

'Khetashe gets a proper title when he's a proper God and not some patron of misfits.' Argaol coughed. 'At any rate, what of the *Lord Emissary*?'

'*Evenhands* is safe. No pirate managed to get through us.'

'Aye, thanks to that monster of yours, no doubt.' Argaol laughed, his humour tinged with an edge of hysteria. 'Your boys are good at killing, Mister Lenk, no doubt about that. A shame you couldn't find a more decent skill to devote your life to.'

Lenk's only response was an acknowledging hum. There was no real sense in getting angry at slights towards his profession. He had heard them all, up to and including slights against his God, Khetashe. There was, after all, little sense in getting irate about insults to a God who watched over people who killed things for money.

'Speaking of faith, your men are all Zamanthrans, I hear.'

'All men of the *Riptide* pay homage to the Sea Mother, ayc.'

'Should we not stop to give them their proper burial, then?'

'Not with Rashodd's boys on our backsides, no.' Argaol shook his head. 'We'll attend to the rites when we're free and clear.' He turned to his mate and gestured with his chin. 'Mister Sebast, inform the men to trim up the sails. They won't be catching us anytime soon.'

As the sunburned man nodded and scampered off, Lenk stalked to the edge of the railing. The *Linkmaster* wasn't fully out of sight, but far enough away to resemble a glistening black beetle on the horizon.

'Are you sure it's wise to trim the sails?' he asked. 'They might catch up.'

'Not so long as Zamanthras loves us,' Argaol grunted. 'And I don't need the wind ripping my sails while it's on our side. We'll be out of their sight before the Sea Mother even realises I'm carrying a shipload of heathens.'

'Of course, Captain,' Sebast interjected as he clambered back up the stairs, 'you *are* also carrying the Lord Emissary of the Church of Talanas and one of the Healer's holy maidens.' He rubbed his chin thoughtfully. 'Perhaps the two cancel each other out?'

'And *that's* why you're first mate, Mister Sebast.' The captain sighed. He jerked his chin towards the railing. 'Have a glimpse, then. Tell me how far they are behind us and see if you can't assuage the adventurer's fears.'

The man came up beside Lenk and peered out over the rail. 'A good ways, I should say, Captain.' Sebast hummed thoughtfully.

'How the hell far away is a "good ways", Mister Sebast? Can you see their faces?'

'Nay, sir. I wouldn't wager they can see me, neither. They look a mite busy loading up that huge crossbow.'

'Crossbow?' Lenk's eyes widened at the calm expressions of the captain and mate. 'So they *do* have a ballista.'

'How do you think they launched that chain in the first place, boy?' Argaol snorted, then spat. 'Back in the day, a pirate would be as concerned with the condition of a ship he meant to take as her captain would be. Nowadays, they don't even bother. Who cares for the condition of a ship if you're just going to scuttle it, aye?'

'A tragic example of the decline of ethics, Captain,' Sebast agreed.

'Should we be worried?' Lenk asked, though their expressions seemed to answer that already.

'As I said, not so long as we've got the wind on our side,' Argaol replied. 'And the Sea Mother is apparently overlooking your various blasphemies today and giving us Her blessing.' He glanced over his shoulder. 'Tell me, Mister Sebast, have we lost Rashodd yet?'

'Correct me if I'm wrong, Captain, but assuming we *are* losing him, he should be getting smaller, shouldn't he?'

'What are you trying to say, Sebast?'

'He's right.' Lenk pointed out to sea as the black blot that was the *Linkmaster* gained shape and definition. Dozens of figures swarmed over its deck. 'They're catching up.'

'Whoresons must—' Argaol paused, staring at the wheel as though it were suddenly something alien. It remained unmoving, even as his thin, dark fingers gave it a swift jerk. The helm made no response. Nor did it move even as he gritted his teeth, set his feet and pushed with his shoulder.

'Gods-cursed piece of ...' The captain's words faded into an angry snarl as he pushed. 'Move, you stupid thing!' A growl became a roar. '*MOVE!*'

The wheel obeyed.

It spun with such ferocity and suddenness as to hurl the captain to the deck, whipping around in opposition to his will. Everyone's eyes went wide, staring at the possessed device with horror as it continued to spin, whirling one way, then the other. The roar of the sea became a low, dejected sigh. The ship rocked, its headway dying to a crawl.

'Something's wrong,' Argaol gasped, 'something ... something's wrong with the rudder.'

Lenk peered over the railing, glancing down at the ship's stern. His breath caught in his throat, denying him any curses he might have uttered. Beneath the pristine blue, stark against the white froth of the ship's wake, was blackness, an inky, shapeless void that clung to the *Riptide*'s rear like a sore.

'What the hell are those?' Sebast muttered.

It took Lenk a moment to realise the first mate wasn't referring to the lightless stain at the rudder. He then saw the flashes of pale skin in the water, gliding towards the *Riptide* like fleshy darts.

'Are those ... men?'

Lenk blinked; they were indeed men. Bereft of hair, bereft of clothing save for what appeared to be black loincloths wrapped about narrow waists, a small company of men swam towards the ship with unnerving speed. In bursts of white froth, they leapt from the sea, arms folded, legs pressed tightly together, in a flash of bone-white and black, before diving below the waves to re-emerge moments later.

'Oh, no, no, no.' The captain's growl had degenerated into a sharp whimper as he pointed out to sea. 'No, no, not now, *not now*!'

The *Linkmaster* had closed with such swiftness as to make it seem like a shadow upon the waves cast by the *Riptide*, a trailing darkness that quickly shifted, gaining on its prey. Lenk could see faces, tattoos, nicked blades clearly. More than that, he could see their chain, its massive links attached to a great spear ending in a claw, once more loaded in the massive ballista.

'This is what they were waiting for—' Lenk muttered.

'*This* is all *your* fault!'

He whirled at the accusation, facing a wide-eyed, clenched-teeth Argaol.

'*My* fault?'

'You and your wretched blasphemies! Your wretched God and your wretched profession! You've brought the damned wrath of the Gods on my ship!'

'Why, you simpering piece of—'

'*BOARDERS! WE'RE UNDER ATTACK!*' The call rang out from the deck.

'*AGAIN!*' someone added.

Argaol's mask of scorn was quickly replaced with shock. 'Well?' he demanded harshly.

'Well, what?' Lenk responded, equally vicious.

'Get down there!'

'You just called me wretched. Why should I do anything you say?'

'Because you're on the Lord Emissary's coin, the Lord

Emissary's on *my* ship and *my* ship is about to be simultaneously boarded by Rashodd's boys and …' his face screwed up as he searched for the words, 'some manner of *fish-men.*'

'They look more like frogs from up here, Captain,' Sebast offered.

'That had occurred to me,' Lenk replied, stroking his hairless chin and hoping that was as effective as caressing a beard. 'And rest assured, I'll get right on it … after you pay.'

Shock, anger and incredulity gave way to a moment of sheer, unexpected consternation on the captain's face.

'*Pay?*'

'Blasphemers live by coin.'

'Are you actually trying to extort me while our lives hang in the balance?'

'I can't think of a better time for extortion, can you?'

It was a purely bitter demand, Lenk knew, as much motivated by pettiness as pragmatism. Still, he couldn't deny that it was purely satisfying to watch the captain reach into his pocket and produce a well-worn pouch, hurling it at Lenk as though it was a weapon.

'Of all the vile creatures you consort with, Mister Lenk,' he forced through his teeth, 'you are by far the most disgusting.'

Lenk weighed the pouch in his hand, hearing the jingle of coins within. Nodding, he tucked it into his own belt.

'That's why I'm the leader.'

In a perfect world, Lenk would have faced well-trained ranks of soldier-sailors armed with steel and discipline scrawled on their faces as he arrived on the main deck. In a less-than-perfect but still optimistic scenario, he would have found shaken but stalwart men, armed with whatever they had to hand.

Perfection and optimism, however, were two words he had no use for.

He shoved his way through herds of visibly panicked sailors, shrieking and screaming as they tripped over bodies and fought over the swords their foes had left behind. He didn't spare a glance for them as he heard the senior members of the crew barking orders, trying to salvage a defence from the mob.

Let them deal with their squealing, milksopping idiots, he advised himself, *you've got your own psychotic, cowardly idiots to deal with.*

The sight of said idiots, for whom hope of perfection or optimism had long ago died a slow and miserable death, was modestly heartening. After all, he reasoned, if they hadn't already looted the bodies and fled he could likely hope for them to put up a fight long enough to abandon him in the middle of it.

Gariath stood at the centre of the deck, Dreadaeleon little more than a dwarf beside his towering form. Kataria and Denaos were at arms, arrow drawn and dagger at the ready. Quillian stood distanced from them, a crossbow strapped on her back to complement her sword; why she lingered, Lenk could only guess. Perhaps she wished to be present to deliver a smug lecture as they lay dying shortly before being impaled herself.

If Khetashe loved him, he thought, he'd be dead first.

'Where's Asper?' he asked, noting the absence of the priestess.

'Tending to the wounded below before tending to the soon-to-be dead above,' Denaos replied. 'As well as saying whatever prayers she says before engaging in acts of futility.'

'You're not showing her the proper respect,' Dreadaeleon snapped, lifting his chin.

'Warriors get respect. Humans get their faces caved in,' Gariath rumbled as he turned a black scowl upon the rogue. '*You* will get a pair of soiled pants the moment someone turns their back so you can run.'

'If you happen to turn your back on me, monster,' Denaos forced through clenched teeth as he flipped his dagger about in his hand, 'it won't be running I do.'

'*So rarely*,' Lenk interjected with as much ire as he could force into his voice, 'do I find an opportunity where I'm actually pleased you people are around. Would you mind terribly waiting until this uncomfortable feeling has passed to kill each other?' He pointed over the railing to the fast-approaching black ship. 'In a few breaths, we'll be swarming with pirates and Gods know what else is swimming up to the ship. If you've any intention of surviving long enough to maim each other, you'll listen to me.'

Indignant scowls, resentful stares and frustrated glowers met him. Not quite the attention he was hoping to command, but good enough.

'They'll be upon us shortly,' he continued, 'they outnumber us, outarm us—'

'"Outarm" isn't a word,' Dreadaeleon interrupted.

'Shut up,' Lenk spat before proceeding, 'and are likely slightly irate at our having killed some of them. It's not an impossible fight, but we'll have to bleed them, make them pay for every step.'

At the angry call of a gull from above, his eyes drifted towards the top of the central mast. The *Riptide*'s flag, with its insignia of a roiling wave encircling a golden coin, flapped with brazen majesty despite the blood spilled beneath it. His eyes settled on the flag for only a moment, however, before he found the tiny crow's nest perched beneath the banner.

'Kataria, Squiggy,' he said, glancing at the crossbow resting on the latter's back, 'you're both archers.'

'Sniper,' the Serrant corrected sharply.

'What's the difference?' Kataria quirked a brow.

'It is purpose and duty, not mere coin and savage lust, that drive my arrows.' Quillian puffed up proudly. 'I've twice the skill, twice the authority,' she paused, casting a disparaging glance at the shict's muscular, naked midriff, 'and about half a tunic more.'

'Whatever,' Lenk interjected before Kataria could do more than scowl and open her mouth. 'I need you both to climb up there and—'

'*I* serve a higher calling than you, heathen,' the Serrant interrupted with a sneering growl. 'Do you suppose I am one of your raving lunatics to command like a hound?'

'I *suppose* you'd be interested in preserving the life of your employer, as well as that of the priestess below,' Lenk retorted sharply. 'Listen to me and you can avoid earning yourself another red oath, *Serrant*.'

At that, the woman narrowed her eyes and shifted a stray lock of black hair from her rigid face. She didn't make any other move and Lenk supposed that was as close to assent as she would come.

'Right,' he grunted. 'If we put you up in the crow's nest, you can shoot down whoever comes across.'

'A shict can shoot down anything with round ears and two legs,' Kataria said, casting a sidelong smirk at Quillian. 'Squiggy here throws arrows away like flowers at a wedding. Perhaps she'd better stay down here and see if she can't absorb some steel.'

'Why, you barbaric, mule-eared little—' Quillian began to snarl before Lenk's hand went up.

'*Stop.*' He pointed a finger up to the rigging. '*Go.*'

With cold glares exchanged, the two females grudgingly skulked off towards the rigging together. Lenk watched as they nimbly scaled the ropes, if only to make certain they didn't shove each other off, before turning to the others.

'Dread,' he glanced at the boy leaning against the mast, massaging his temples, 'you've got the most important job.'

'Naturally,' the wizard muttered. 'Somehow, having the talent to hurl fire from one's palms always predisposes one to being given the "important" jobs.'

'Yes, you're incredibly sarcastic,' Lenk sighed, 'and if we had more time I'd eagerly indulge your staggering intellect. However,' he gestured over the side towards the ever-growing *Linkmaster*, 'the whole impending disembowelment aspect is a factor.'

'Fine.' The boy rose dramatically, coat sweeping about his feet, book banging against his hip. 'What do you need?'

'A fire. Nothing much, just make something go ablaze on their ship to keep a few of them busy.'

'That's it?'

'Well, Khetashe, don't let me stop you from making their captain eject his intestines out through his ears if you've got that trick up your sleeve.'

'I'm not sure …' Dread scratched his chin. 'I've done so much already. I can only cast so many spells in a day. If I don't rest, I get headaches.'

'A *headache* is slightly better than a sword in your bowels.'

'Point.' Dreadaeleon stalked to the railing. He slid his

legs apart slightly, knotted his fingers together and drew in a deep breath. 'It'll take concentration. Whatever happens, make certain that I'm not disturbed or something could happen.'

'Such as?'

'Where massive fires are concerned, is further explanation really necessary?'

'Point.'

'Here they come,' Gariath said with a bit more eagerness in his voice than seemed acceptable.

The black-timbered ship slid up beside them like a particularly long shadow laden with flesh and steel. The deck swarmed with pirates, their boarding chains and hooks ready in hand, their faces splitting with bloodthirsty grins. The ballista stood drawn and taut, the metal claw of its mother chain glistening menacingly in the sunlight.

No sign of the bell, Lenk noticed, or the black-shrouded man. Or were they simply standing behind the titanic amalgamation of tattoos and iron at the helm? Rashodd was ready to lead this second charge, if the hands that caressed the axes at his hips were any indication.

Young man's hands, Lenk noted.

'Dread,' he grunted, elbowing the boy.

'As I said,' he hissed in reply, '*no distractions.*'

Dreadaeleon's fingers knitted, his mouth muttered as he looked over the *Linkmaster*, seeking a flammable target.

Lenk turned to check the *Riptide*'s preparations. Heartened by their seniors' orders, the sailors had formed themselves into a working defensive line. Their wooden weapons were as shoddy as ever, but they had done the job before. The only difference between this and the previous attack was that this time the men were prepared to face the *Linkmaster*'s crew.

That, Lenk thought, *and the fact that there are about three times as many pirates as there were before … all a degree more psychotic than the last lot.*

His own company was as organised as it was going to be. He hefted his sword, raising it as the ranks of grinning, tattooed faces grew larger with the pirates' approach. Any hope of outrunning the fight was dashed; now, Lenk knew, it was down to skin and teeth.

'The captain sends his best to you, lads,' came a gruff, guttural voice from behind. Lenk recognised the sailor by his bandaged, burned arm if not by name as he came clambering up. 'We'll do our part. The boys are ready to ravage. I hope yours can say the same.' Exchanging a grim nod with Lenk, he swept a glance over the other adventurers. He grinned as he spied Dreadaeleon. 'Look at this brave lad, here. Can't be more than me own boy's age. Good on 'im, even if he did set me on fire before.' He raised a hand over the wizard's shoulder, and Lenk's eyes went wide. 'No hard feelings, eh—'

'*STOP!*'

By the time the word had escaped Lenk's lips, the sailor's hand had come down and clapped the boy on the shoulder. In one slow, painful blink of the eye, Dreadaeleon's stare shot wide open, eyes burning with crimson energy. Lenk barely had time to turn away before his companion instinctively whirled around, bellowed a single, incomprehensible word and extended a palm.

The world erupted into flame, and as the flashing orange faded, screams arose. The sailor's hands went to his head, trying to bat away the mane of lapping fire that had enveloped his hair. The line of sailors parted as he tore through their ranks, his shrieking following him as he hurtled towards the railing.

'*I TOLD YOU!*' Dreadaeleon barked, suddenly aware of what had happened. '*NO* distractions! I told you *NOT* to let anything break my concentration or *THINGS* could happen!'

'Well, I didn't know that *THINGS* involved setting people's heads on *FIRE*, you crazy bastard!' Lenk roared back.

'What in Talanas's name is going on?' Asper appeared on the scene in a flutter of blue robes and a flash of hazel eyes. 'What happened?'

'Isn't it obvious, you shrew?' Denaos barked at the priestess. 'We're under attack!'

'Get back below!' Lenk ordered.

'I should stay,' she contested. 'I ... I should fight!'

'The next time we're attacked by pirates who are deathly afraid of sermons, I'll call you,' he roared. 'Until then, *GET BACK BELOW, USELESS!*'

'No,' the rogue countered, 'stay up here and see if your God loves us.'

Before she could form a retort, her eyes were drawn to the railing. A cluster of sailors had formed, straining to keep their immolated companion from hurling himself overboard while more men poured water on his blazing head. Suddenly, her gaze flitted past Denaos and Lenk, towards the scrawny boy trying to hide behind them.

'Dread! Good Gods, was it not enough to nearly incinerate him the *last* time?' she snarled and turned towards the men at the railing. 'Douse him and bring him below! I'll tend to him!'

Lenk watched her go with a solemn stare. Her medicine, he reasoned, would do little good in the heat of battle. And she was in no mood to linger near Dreadaeleon.

'I knew this was a bad idea.' The wizard shook his head.

'I knew it, I knew it. My master always said I'd face this someday.' He began to skulk off, trembling. 'Oh, Venarie help me, I'm so bad at this—'

'Where the hell are you going?' Lenk howled. 'What about setting something on fire?'

'I already *DID* that!' Dreadaeleon shrieked. 'Venarie help me ... Venarie help me ... why did I listen to idiots?'

'No, no, *no*!' He rushed to seize the boy by his collar, pulling him back to the railing. 'Take a deep breath, mutter something, inhale the smell of your own fart, do whatever it is you do to get your concentration back.' He pointed to the black ship. 'Just do one more little poof.'

'Wizards don't *poof*.'

'Well, you'll *be* one if you don't burn that ship down! Just fire it up! Any part of it! We can still outrun it and let it burn.'

'Right ... right ...' The wizard inhaled sharply, moving to knit his fingers together again. 'I just need to ... to set it on fire.' He licked his lips. 'Then I'll be the hero.'

'Yes.'

'No,' a rumbling voice disagreed.

Before Lenk could cry out, before he even saw the flash of crimson, Gariath's tail had lashed out to smash against the boy's jaw. Dreadaeleon collapsed with a shriek, unmoving. Lenk stared up at the dragonman, eyes wide.

'What was *that* for?'

'Magic is weak. It didn't work. It's a sign.'

'A sign of *what*? That you're a complete lunatic?' He began to glance desperately about the deck, searching for something, anything that might help. 'All right, this isn't lost. Someone just go up and tell Kataria to—'

'No.'

His breath erupted out of him, driven by a hard crimson

fist in his belly. He fell to his knees, gasping. His eyes felt like they wanted to fall out of his skull and roll over the ship's side as he looked up at Gariath, gasping.

'What?' he coughed. '*Why?*'

'This battle was meant to happen. I was meant to fight it.'

'We'll ... *die*.'

'If we're lucky.'

'This is ... insane! I had a ... a strategy!'

Gariath looked down at him coldly. 'I can cave your face in. I make the strategies now.'

'Damn ... damn ...' Lenk cursed at his back as he stalked away He felt the shadow of Denaos behind him and snarled, 'What now? *What the hell do we do now?*'

'Well, you know my advice,' Denaos offered.

'No, what do you—'

He looked up and saw the empty space behind him.

'Right.'

His ears twitched, hearing the sailors behind him take a collective step backwards as the *Linkmaster* loomed up before them, drawing level with the *Riptide*. As the first hooks were thrown, the first war cries bellowed, Lenk's focus was on Rashodd. The great iron hulk's helmet angled down upon him, over the bone-white arms that grasped the railing to pull up slender, hairless bodies.

'Gentlemen,' the hulking pirate boomed, 'good day.'

Four

THE LORD EMISSARY

'*Useless?*'

The rip of bandages being yanked from their roll echoed in the confines of the ship's mess, just as Asper's snarl did, sticking in the timbers like knives. The man struggled, but she didn't pay him any mind. She kept pulling the bandages tight about his charred face, growling.

'Sermons, indeed.' She tied the bandage off with a jerk. 'The stupid little savages could all use one, coupled with a few swift blows to the head.' Her hands trembled as she pulled another roll from her bag. 'Swift blows to the head with a dull, rusty piece of iron ...' She ripped the cloth free, wrapping another layer about the man's face. 'With *spikes*. A few to the groin wouldn't hurt, either ... well, it wouldn't hurt Kat, anyway.'

'No disrespect, Priestess,' her patient meekly said, 'but the bandages, they're—'

'Soaked in charbalm,' she finished, wrapping them around his head. 'I apparently have to keep a lot on hand when I'm dealing with heathens who can't even control their oh-so-impressive *fire*. You know he gets the shakes after he casts that fire? Loses bladder control, sometimes, too. He's probably pissing himself right now.'

Don't piss yourself, don't piss yourself, don't piss yourself.

The boy should have been more worried about passing out, he knew. His body felt drained; the heat that coursed through him was all but spent; he'd already reduced two men to slow, smouldering pyres. His hands felt dull and senseless, the electricity that ran through them having been expended on dislodging a chain.

And still they kept coming. The sailors put up an admirable defence, even in the face of the new, pale-skinned invaders. But they couldn't hold out for ever. Neither could he, and he knew it. Nothing was left of him but spit.

He narrowed his eyes as he spotted two of the pale creatures rushing towards the companionway.

He inhaled sharply, chanted a brief, breathless verse and blew. The ice raced from his lips across the deck between the two and formed a patch of frost in the doorway. His foot came down, hard, frigid spikes rising up to cage the passage off. The creatures turned black scowls upon his red-glowing eyes.

'No one,' he said through dry lips, 'gets in.'

'I cured that,' Asper said to the charred man, 'with a tea I learned after *four years of study*. I can cure the shakes, heal their little cuts and scratches and make sure they don't all die of dysentery. That's what I do. I'm the priestess of the feather-arsed *HEALER*, for His sake!' She coughed. 'Forgive the blasphemy.'

'Of course, Priestess, but—'

'But do they appreciate it? Of course not!' She snarled and jerked the bandage tight. 'The stupid little barbarians think that killing is the only thing in life. There're other things in life ... like *life*. And who tends to that?'

Her patient said something, she wasn't sure what.

'*Exactly!* I'm the Gods-damned shepherd! *I* keep them

alive! They should be following *me*! The only person on this whole stupid ship with more godly authority is—'

'Pray, does there exist some turmoil amongst the good people in my employ?'

She froze, breathless, and turned.

The Lord Emissary spoke with no fury, no sadness, no genuine curiosity at the sight before him. He raised his voice no higher than he would were he consoling a wailing infant. His conviction was that of a mewling kitten.

Yet his voice carried throughout the mess, quelling hostilities and fear with a single, echoing question. Eyes formerly enraged and terrified went wide with a mixture of awe and admiration as a white shadow entered the mess on footsteps no louder than a whisper.

'Lord Emissary.' Asper turned to face him, her voice quavering slightly.

From under a white cowl, a long, gentle face surveyed the scene. A smile creased well-weathered features, eyes glistening brightly in the dim light as Miron Evenhands shook his head, chuckling lightly. One hand was tucked into the cloth sash about his narrow waist while the other stroked a silver pendant carved in the shape of a bird, half-hidden by the white folds of his robe.

'And what evil plagues my humble companions?' he asked gently.

'N-nothing,' she said, suddenly remembering to bow.

'Instances of "nothing" rarely beget so strong a scent of anger in the air.'

'It … it was simply a … disagreement of sorts.' She cleared her throat. 'With … with myself.'

'Good for the soul and mind, always.' The incline of Miron's head was slow and benevolent. 'I find it better to voice concerns before violence comes into play, even if it is with oneself. Many wars and conflicts could be avoided that way.' He turned to Asper pointedly. 'Could they not?'

Her eyes went wide as a child's caught with a finger in a pie – or perhaps a child caught with a finger in burned flesh.

'Absolutely, Lord Emissary.'

Miron's smile flashed for only an instant before there was the sound of something crashing above. He glanced up, showing as much concern as he could muster.

'We are … attacked?'

'My com—' She stopped herself, then sighed. 'Those other people are handling it, Lord Emissary. Please, do not fret.'

'For them? No,' Miron said, shaking his head. 'They have their own Gods to watch over them and weapons to defend themselves.' He looked with concern at her. 'For you, though—'

'Lord Emissary,' she said softly, 'would you permit me the severe embarrassment of knowing how much you overheard?'

'Oh, for the sake of discussion, let us say all of it.'

His voice was carried on a smile, gentle as the hand he laid on her shoulder. She started at first, having not even heard his approach, but relaxed immediately. It was impossible to remain tense in his presence, impossible to feel ill at ease when the lingering scent of incense that perpetually cloaked him filled her nostrils. She found herself returning the smile, her frustrations sliding from her shoulders as his hand did.

'Goodness,' the priest remarked, padding towards the bandaged man. 'What happened here?'

Her shoulders slumped with renewed burden. 'Adventure happened,' she grunted, momentarily unaware of the fact that such a tone was inappropriate in the presence of such a man. 'That is, Lord Emissary, he was wounded ...' she paused, balancing the next word on her tongue, 'by Dreadaeleon. Inadvertently. *Supposedly* inadvertently.'

'A hazard with wizards, I'm informed. Still, this may have done more good than ill.'

'Forgive me, Lord Emissary, but I find it difficult to see the good in a man being torched.'

'There is yet joy in simply staying alive, Priestess.' He looked down at the man's bandages and frowned. 'Or there would be, had you left him a hole through which to breathe.'

She began to stutter an apology, but found no words before Miron gently parted the bandages about the man's charred lips.

'There we are.' He placed a hand on the man's shoulder. 'After your capable treatment, sir, I must insist that you retire to whatever quarters you're permitted. Kindly don't scratch at your wrappings, either; the charbalm will need time to settle into the skin.'

On muttered thanks and hasty feet, the man scurried into the depths of the ship's hold, sparing a grunt of acknowledgement for Asper as he left. Though she knew it to be a sin, she couldn't help but resent such a gesture.

He would have thanked me proper if I had killed for him, she thought irritably, *if only out of fear that I might have killed him. He'd be at my feet and mewling for my mercy if I were a warrior.*

'Tea?'

She turned with a start. Miron sat delicately upon one of the mess benches, pouring brown liquid from a clay pot into a cup: tea that had been left cold when the Cragsmen arrived.

Unperturbed by the temperature, the priest sipped at it delicately, smacking his lips as though it were the finest wine. It was only after she noted his eyes upon her, expectant, that she coughed out a hasty response.

'N-no, thank you, Lord Emissary.' She was suddenly aware of how meek her voice sounded compared to his and drew herself up. 'I mean to say, is this really the proper time for tea? We *are* under attack.'

So much blood.

The air was thick with it. It clotted his nostrils, travelled down his throat and lingered in his chest like perfume. Much of it was his. He smiled at that. But there was another stench, greater even than the rank aroma of carnage.

Fear.

It was in the tremble of their hands, the hesitation of their step, the eyes of the man who struggled in his claws. Gariath met his terror with a black-eyed scowl. He drew back his head and brought his horns forwards, felt bone crunch under his skull, heard breath in his ear-frills.

Still alive.

He drew back his head again, brought forth his teeth. He felt the life burst between them, heard the shrieks of the man and his companion. He clenched, gripped, tore. The man fell from his grasp, collapsing with an angry ruby splotch where his throat had been. He turned towards the remaining pirates, glowering at them.

'Fight harder,' he snarled. 'Harder ... or you'll never kill me.'

They did not flee. Good. He smiled, watched their fear as they caught glimpses of tattooed flesh between his teeth.

'Come on, then,' he whispered, 'show me my ancestors.'

*

'That being the situation, it would seem wiser for us to stay down here, wouldn't it?' Miron offered her that same smile, the slightest twitch of his lips that sent his face blooming with pleasant shadows born from his wrinkles. 'And, when confined to a particular spot, would it not seem wise to spend the time properly with prayer, contemplation and a bit of tea?'

'I suppose.'

'After all,' he spoke between sips, 'it's well and good to know one's role in the play the Gods have set down for us, no? Fighting is for warriors.'

She frowned at that and it did not go unnoticed. The wrinkles disappeared from his face, ironed out by an intent frown.

'What troubles you?'

If fighting is all there is, what good are those who can't fight? Her first instinct was to spit such a question at him and she scolded herself for it. It was a temporary ire, melting away as she glanced up to take in the full sight of Miron Evenhands. *Of course, it's easy for him to make such statements.*

The Lord Emissary seemed out of place in the wake of catastrophe, with his robes the colour of dawning clouds and the silver sigil of Talanas emblazoned upon his breast. She had to fight the urge to polish her own pendant, so drab it seemed in comparison to his symbol's beaming brightness.

The Healer Himself even seemed to favour this servant above all others, as the cloud shifted outside the mess window, bathing the priest in sunlight and adding an intangible golden cloak to his ensemble.

Evenhands cleared his throat and she looked up, eyes wide with embarrassment. One smile from him was all it took to bring a nervous smirk to her face.

'Perhaps you feel guilty being down here,' he mused, settling back, 'attending to an old man while your companions bleed above?'

'It is no shame to attend the Lord Emissary,' she said, pausing for a moment before stuttering out an addendum, 'not that you're so infirm as to require attending to … not that you're infirm at all, in fact.' She coughed. 'And it's not merely my associates – not companions, you know – who bleed and die above. I'm a servant of the Healer, I seek to mend the flesh and aid the ailing of all mankind, just not—'

'Breathe,' he suggested.

She nodded, inhaling swiftly and holding the breath for a moment.

'At times, I feel a bit wrong,' she began anew, 'sitting beyond the actual fighting and awaiting the chance to bind wounds and kiss scratches while everyone else does battle.'

'I see.' He hummed thoughtfully. 'And did I not just hear you rend asunder your companions verbally for taking lives themselves?'

'It's not like they were here to hear it,' she muttered, looking down. 'The truth is …' She sucked in air through her teeth, sitting down upon the bench opposite his. 'I'm not sure what good I'm doing here, Lord Emissary.'

He made no response beyond a sudden glint in his eyes and a tightening of his lips.

'I left my temple two years ago,' she began.

'On pilgrimage,' he said, nodding.

She returned the gesture, mentally scolding herself for not realising he would know such a thing. All servants of the Healer left the comfort of their monasteries on pilgrimage after ten years of worship and contemplation. This, they knew, was their opportunity to fulfil their oaths.

She had been given ample wounds to bind and flesh to mend, many grieving widows to console and plague-stricken children to help bury, and had offered many last rites to the dying. Since joining her companions, the opportunity for such services had doubled, at the very least.

'But there are always more of them,' she whispered to herself.

'Hm?'

She looked up. 'Forgive me, it's just ...' She grimaced. 'I have a hard time seeing my purpose, Lord Emissary. My associates, they—'

'Your companions, you mean, surely.'

'Forgiveness, Lord Emissary, but they're something akin to co-employees.' She sneered. 'I share little in common with them.'

'And that's precisely what troubles you.'

'Something ... something like that, yes.' She cleared her throat, regaining her composure. 'I've aided many and I've no regrets about the God I serve or what he asks of me ... I just wish I could do more.'

He hummed, taking another sip of his drink.

'We've done much fighting in our time, my comp— *them* and myself. Sometimes, we've not done the proper work of the Healer, but I've seen many fouler creatures, some humans, too, cut down by them.'

And it had started as such a good day ...

Lenk hadn't planned on much: a breakfast of hard tack and beans, a bit of time above deck, possibly vomiting overboard before dinner. Nothing was supposed to happen.

'*Unfair.*'

The voice rang, steel on ice. His head hurt.

'*Cheaters. Called to it.*'

'To what?' he growled through the pain.

'*Coming.*'

'What is?'

He felt the shadow over him, heard iron-shod boots ringing on the wood. He whirled and stared up into the thin slit of an iron helmet ringed with wild grey hair that was a stark contrast to the two young, tattooed hands folded across an ironbound chest.

'Oh, hell,' he whispered, 'you sneaky son of a—'

'Manners,' Rashodd said.

An enormous young hand came hurtling into his face.

It was a bitter phrase to utter, but it came freely enough. She had learned many years ago that not everyone deserved the Healer's mercy. There was cruelty in the world that walked on two legs and masqueraded behind pretences of humanity. She had seen many deserved deaths, knew of many that were probably occurring above her at that moment.

While she sat below, she thought dejectedly, waiting quietly as others bled and delivered those richly deserved deaths.

'I heal wounds,' she said, more to herself than the priest, 'tend to the ill and send them off, walking and smiling. Then they return to me, cold and breathless in corpse-carts. I heal them and, if they don't go off to kill someone themselves, they're killed by someone who doesn't give a damn for what I do.'

She hesitated, her fists clenching at her sides.

'Lenk, Kataria, Dreadaeleon, Gariath,' she said, grimacing, 'even Denaos … they kill a wicked man and that's that. One less wicked man to hurt those who Talanas shines upon, one less pirate, bandit, brigand, monstrosity or heathen.'

'And yet there is no end to either the wounded or the wicked,' Miron noted.

Asper had no reply for that.

'Tell me, have you ever taken a life?' The priest's voice was stern, not so much thoughtful as confrontational.

Asper froze. A scream echoed through her as the ship groaned around her. Her breath caught in her throat. She rubbed her left arm as though it were sore.

'No.'

'Were I a lesser man, I might accuse those who were envious of the ability to take life so indiscriminately of being rather stupid.' He took a long, slow sip. 'Given my station, however, I'll merely imply it.'

She blinked. He smiled.

'That was a joke.'

'Oh, well ... yes, it was rather funny.' Her smile trembled for a moment before collapsing into a frown. 'But, Lord Emissary, is it not natural to wish I could help?'

His features seemed to melt with the force of his sigh. He set the clay cup aside, folded his hands and stared out through the mess's broad window.

'I have often wondered if I wasn't born too soon for this world,' he mused, 'that perhaps the will and wisdom of Talanas cannot truly be appreciated where so much blood must be spilled. After all, what good, really, can the followers of the Healer be when we simply mend the arm that swings the sword? What do we accomplish by healing the leg that crushes the innocent underfoot?'

The question hung in the air, smothering all other sound beneath it.

'Perhaps,' his voice was so soft as to barely be heard

above the rush of the sea outside, 'if we knew the answers, we'd stop doing what we do.'

He continued to stare out at the roiling seas, the glimmer of sunlight against the ship's white wake. She followed his gaze, though not far enough; his eyes were dark and distant, spying some answer in the endless blue horizon that she could not hope to grasp. She cleared her throat.

'Lord Emissary?'

'Regardless,' he said, turning towards her as though he had been speaking to her all the while, 'I suggest you spare yourself the worry of who kills who and work the will of the Healer as best you can.' He plucked up his teacup once more. 'Do your oaths remain burning in your mind?'

'"To serve Talanas through serving man."' She recited with rehearsed confidence. '"To mend the bones, to bind the flesh, to cure the sick, to ease the dying. To serve Talanas and mankind."'

'Then take heart in your oaths where your companions take heart in coin. We all serve mankind in different ways, whether we love life or steel.'

It was impossible not to share his confidence; it radiated from him like a divine light. He was very much the servant of the Healer, a white spectre, stark and pure against the grime and grimness surrounding him, unsullied, untainted even as taint pervaded.

And yet, for all his purity, she knew he was her employer and her superior, not her companion, no matter how deeply she might have wished him to be. She looked wistfully to the companionway, remembering those she had left on the deck.

'Perhaps it wouldn't harm any to go up and see what strength I could lend them.' She turned back to the Lord Emissary. 'Will you be—'

Her voice died in her throat, eyes going wide, hands frigid as her right clenched her left in instinctive fear.

'Lord Emissary,' she gasped, 'behind you.'

He spared her a curious tilt of his long face before turning to follow her gaze. Though he did not start, nor freeze as she did at the sight, the arch of a single white brow indicated he had seen it. *How could he not?*

It dangled in front of the window, pale flesh pressed against the glass as it hung from long, malnourished arms. To all appearances, it seemed a man: hairless, naked but for the dagger-laden belt hanging from its slender waist and the loincloth wrapped about its hips. Across its pale chest was a smeared, crimson sigil, indistinguishable through the smoky pane of glass.

Asper had to force herself not to scream as it pressed its face against the window. Its eyes were stark black where they should have been white, tiny silver pinpricks where pupils should have been. One hand reached down, tapped against the glass as a mouth filled with blackness opened and uttered an unmistakable word.

'*Priest.*'

Miron rose from his seat. 'That's irritating.'

'Lord Emissary,' she whispered, perhaps for fear that the thing might hear her. 'What is it?'

'An invader,' he replied, as though that were enough, 'a frogman, specifically.'

'Frog ... *man*?'

He hummed a confirmation. 'If you would kindly inform your companions that their attention is required down here, I would be most grateful.'

Before she could even think to do such a thing, she felt the floor shift beneath her feet as the ship rocked violently. A din rose from above, a shrieking howl mingled with what sounded like polite conversation. A discernible roar answered the call, a chest-borne thunder tinged with unpleasant laughter.

Something had happened on the deck, and whatever had happened had also met Gariath. Another noise reached her through the ship's timbers.

From the cabins beyond the mess in the ship's hold, she heard it: the sound of an iron porthole cover clanging to the deck, two water-laden feet squishing upon the wood, a croaking command in a tongue not human, nor shictish, nor any that she had ever heard.

Something had just crept into the ship.

Something crept closer.

Her hand quivered as it reached for her staff. *Lenk's hands wouldn't quiver*, she thought. Her breath was short, her knees quaking as she trudged towards the cabin's door. *Kataria's knees wouldn't knock.* Her voice was timid, dying on her lips as she tried to speak. *Gariath wouldn't squeak.*

Lenk, Kataria and Gariath were somewhere else, though. She was here, standing between the noise and the Lord Emissary. When her hands wrapped about the solid oak staff, she knew that at that moment, the warriors would have to leave the fighting to her.

'Lord Emissary,' she whispered, stepping towards the hold, 'forgive me for my transgressions.'

'Go as you must.'

She cringed; it would have been easier to justify staying behind if he had been angry with her. Instead, she took her staff in her hands and crept into the gloom of the *Riptide*'s timbered bowels.

Miron turned from the portal towards the foggy glass of the window. The frogman was gone, slid off to join its kin on the deck. No matter; a black void spread beneath the water's surface, a mobile ink stain that slid lazily after the ship as it cut through the waters.

'She sent you, did she?' he muttered to the blackness. Absently, a hand went down to his chest, tracing the phoenix sigil upon his breast. 'Come if you will, then. You shall not have it.'

He turned, striding from the mess towards the shadows of the hold, intent on reaching his cabin. In his mind, a shape burned: a square of perfectly black leather, parchment bound in red leather, tightly sealed and hidden from the outside world.

'They shall not have it,' he whispered.

There was a sound from the shadows, a masculine cry of surprise met by a voice dripping with malice. Someone screamed, someone ran, someone fell.

The man tumbled out of the shadows, the broad, unblinking whites of his eyes indiscernible against the swathes of bandages covering his face. He croaked out something through blackened lips, staring up at Miron as Miron stared down at him, impassively.

A webbed foot appeared from the darkness. A pale, lanky body emerged. Two dark, beady eyes set in a round, hairless head regarded him carefully. Through long, needle-like teeth, it hissed.

'*Priest.*' It raised its bloody dagger. '*Tome.*'

The thing peered through the jagged, splintering gash in the ship's hull that used to be a porthole. Only shadows met its black eyes as it searched through the gloom for another pale shape, another thing similar to this one. Quietly, it slid two slender arms through the hole, a hairless head following as it pulled a moist torso through the rent in the timbers.

The hole was no bigger than its head. Absently, the thing recalled that it should not have been able to squeeze through it.

It set its feet upon the timbers, salt pooling around its tender, webbed toes. Slowly, it bent down to observe a similar puddle upon the floor where similar feet had stood just moments ago. And yet now there was no sign of those feet, nor the legs they belonged to, nor any sign of that one at all.

'It is a stupid one,' the thing hissed. It recalled, vaguely, a time when its voice did not sound so throaty, a time when a sac did not bulge beneath its chin with every breath. '"These ones stay together," these ones were told, "stay together". That one must not have run off. That one must stay with this one.'

This one remembered, for a fleeting moment, that it had once had a name.

That memory belonged to another one. This one knelt down, observing the traces of moisture clinging to the wood. That one had taken two steps forwards, it noted from the twin puddles before it. It tilted its head to the side; that one had stopped there ... but not stopped. It had ceased to step and begun to slide. That struck this one as odd, given that these ones had been allowed to walk like men.

That one's two moist prints became a thick, wet trail instead of footprints, a trail leading from the salt to the shadows of the ship's hold. As this one followed its progress intently, watching it shift from clear salty water to smelly, coppery red, it spied something in the darkness: a tangle of pale limbs amidst crates.

That one was dead, it recognised; it remembered death.

It rose and felt something against its back. It remembered

the scent of humanity. It thought to whirl around, bring knife against flesh, but then it remembered something else.

It remembered metal.

'Shh,' the tall other one behind it whispered, sliding a glove over its mouth while digging the knife deeper into its side. 'No point.' The other one twisted the knife. 'Just sleep.'

Then it slumped to the floor.

Denaos grimaced as he bent down, retrieving the dagger wedged in the infiltrator's kidneys. The last one hadn't made half so much noise, he thought grimly as he wiped the bloodied weapons clean on the thing's ebon leather loincloth. Replacing them in the sheaths at his waist, he seized the pale fish-man by the legs and dragged him behind a stack of crates where his companion lay motionless in a pool of sticky red.

With a grunt, the rogue heaved the fresh corpse atop the stale one.

They were skilled infiltrators, he admired silently; he would never have thought even a child could squeeze through the ship's portholes, much less a grown man. Had he not chosen this particular section of cargo to guard, he would never have found them.

His laugh was not joyful. 'Ha ... guarding the cargo.'

Yes, he told himself, *that's what you were doing. While all the men were dying to the pirates and the women were being violated in every orifice imaginable,* you *were guarding cargo, you miserable coward. If anyone asks why you weren't fighting like any proper man, you can just claim you were concerned for the safety of the spices.*

He caught his reflection in the puddle of water at his feet, noting the frown that had unconsciously scarred itself onto his face. In the quiver of the water, he saw the future: chastisement from his companions, curses from the sailors he had abandoned ...

And Asper. His loathing slowly twisted to ire in his head. *I'll have to endure yet another sermon from that self-righteous, preachy shrew.* He paused, regarding his reflection contemplatively. *Of course, that's not likely to happen, given that they're probably all dead, her included ... if you're that lucky.*

Something caught his eye. Upon the intruder's offensively white biceps lay a smear of the deepest crimson. Denaos arched a brow; he didn't remember cutting either of the creatures on their arms.

He knelt to study the puny, pale limb. It was a tattoo, that much he recognised instantly: a pair of skeletal jaws belonging to some horrid fish encircled by a twisted halo of tentacles. And, he noted with a cringe, it had been scrawled none too neatly, as though with a blade instead of a needle.

As morbid curiosity compelled him to look closer, he found that their tattoos were the least unpleasant of their features.

They lacked any sort of body hair, not the slightest wisp to prevent their black leathers from clinging to them like secondary skins. Their eyes, locked wide in death, lacked any discernible pupil or iris, orbs of obsidian set in greying whites. A glimpse of bone caught his eye; against an instinct that begged him not to, he removed a dagger and peeled back the creature's lip with the tip.

Rows of needle-like, serrated teeth flashed stark white against black gums.

'Sweet Silf,' he muttered, recoiling.

A panicked cry echoed through the halls of the hold, drawing his attention up. He rose to his feet and sprang to the door in one fluid movement. As he reached for the lock, he paused, glancing over his shoulder at the dead frogmen behind. His hand faltered as he pondered the possibility of facing one of these creatures and their sharp teeth from the front.

Slowly, he lowered his hand from the door.

Someone shrieked again and his ears pricked up. A woman.

The door flew open.

Perhaps, he speculated, some sassy young thing slinking down the hall had run afoul of one of the creatures and now cowered in a corner as the intruder menaced her. It was an unspoken rule that distressed damsels were obliged to yield a gratuity that frequently involved tongues.

Surely, he reasoned, *that's worth delivering another quick knife to the kidneys ... of course, she's probably dead, you know.* He cursed himself as he rounded a corner. *Stop that thinking. If you go ruining your fantasies with reality, what's the point of—*

A shriek ripped through his thoughts. Not a woman, he realised, or at least no woman he would want to slip his tongue into. The scream was a long, dirty howl: a rusty blade being drawn from a sheath, a filthy, festering, vocal wound.

And, he noted, it was emerging through a nearby door.

His feet acted before his mind could, instinctively sliding into soft, cat-like strides as he pressed himself to the cabin wall. The dagger that leapt to his hand spoke of heroism, trying to drown out the voice of reason in his head.

You can see the logic in this, can't you? he told himself. *It's not like anyone's really expecting you to come dashing up to save them.*

The door creaked open slightly, no hand behind it. He continued forwards.

In fact, I doubt anyone will even have harsh words for you. It's been about a year you've all been together, right? Maybe less ... a few months, perhaps; regardless, the point is that no one is really all that surprised when you run away.

He edged closer to the door. The sound of breathing, heavy and laboured, could be heard.

And this won't solve anything. Nothing changes, even if she isn't dead. His mind threw doubt at him as a delinquent throws stones. *You won't be any braver for it. You won't be a hero. You'll still be the same cowardly thug, the same disgusting wretch who gutted—*

Enough. He drew in a breath, weak against the panting emerging from behind the door.

But it was not the kind of panting he had expected, not the laboured, glutted gasps of a creature freshly satiated or a fiend with blood on his hands. It was not soft, but hardly ragged. The breathing turned to heaving, someone fighting back vomit, choked on saliva. There was a short, staggered gasp, followed by a weak and pitiful sound.

Sobbing.

Without pausing to reflect on the irony of being emboldened by such a thing, Denaos took an incautious step into the shadowy cabin. Amidst the crates and barrels was a dark shape, curled up against the cargo like a motherless cub, desperately trying to hide. It shuddered with each breath, shivering down a slender back. Brown hair hung messily about its shoulders.

No pale monstrosities here, he confirmed to himself, *none that you don't know, anyway.*

'Odd that I should find you here,' he said as he strode

into the room, 'cringing in a corner when you should be protecting the Lord Emissary.'

Hypocrite.

'I protected the Lord Emissary ...' Asper said, more to herself than to him. Silver glinted in the shadows; he could see her stroking her phoenix pendant with a fervent need. 'They came aboard ... things ... frogs ... men, I don't know.'

'Where?' His dagger was instantly raised, his back already finding the wall.

She raised her left arm and pointed towards the edge of the room. The sleeve of her robe was destroyed completely, hanging in tatters around her shoulder, baring a pale limb. Following her finger, he spied it: the invader lay dead against the wall, limbs lazily at its sides, as though it were taking a nap.

'Lovely work,' he muttered, noting her staff lying near the corpse. 'What? Did you bash its head in?' She did not reply, provoking a cocked eyebrow. 'Are you crying?'

'No,' she said, though the quiver of her voice betrayed her. 'It ... it was a rough fight. I'm ... you know, I'm coming down.'

'Coming down?' He slinked towards her. 'What are you—'

'I'm *fine*!' She whirled on him angrily, teeth bared like a snarling beast as she pulled herself to her feet. 'It was a fight. He's dead now. I didn't need *you* to come looking for me.'

Tears quivered in her eyes as glistening liquid pooled beneath her nose. She stood sternly, back erect, head held high, though her legs trembled slightly. Unusual, he thought, given that the priestess hoarded her tears as though they were gold. Even surrounded by death, she rarely mourned or grieved in the view of others, considering her companions too blasphemous to take in that sight.

And yet, here she stood before him, almost as tall as he, though appearing so much smaller, so much meeker.

'There are …' She turned her head away, as if sensing his scrutinising judgement. 'There are more of those things around.'

'There *were*, yes,' Denaos replied. 'I took care of them.'

'Took care of them how?'

'How do you think?' he asked, sheathing his dagger. 'I found the other two and did it quietly.'

'Two?' She turned to him with concern in her eyes. 'There were four others besides this one'

'You're mistaken, I only saw two.'

'No.' She shook her head. 'I caught a glimpse of them from the porthole as they swam by. There were five in all.'

'Five, huh,' Denaos said, scratching his chin. 'I suppose I can take care of the other two.'

'Assuming they aren't looking,' she grumbled, retrieving her staff. 'Let's go.'

'Are you certain?' he asked, his tone slightly insulting as he looked her up and down. 'It's not like you should feel a need to fight.' He glanced at the pale corpse against the wall. 'After all, you took care of this one well enough.'

He blinked as the thing shifted beneath his eyes. It did not stir, it did not rise. Its movement was so subtle it might have been missed by anyone else. Yet, as he took a step forwards, the body responded to his foot striking the floor. It quivered, sending tiny ripples through the flesh as though it were water.

Flesh, he knew, did not do that.

'Leave the dead where they lie.' Whatever authority

Asper hoped to carry slipped through the sudden crack in her voice. She drew in a sharp breath, quickly composing herself. 'The thing's almost naked; it doesn't have anything you can take.'

His attentions were fixed solely on the thing lying at his feet. The rogue leaned forwards intently, studying it. Its own body had begun to pool beneath it. He let out a breath as he leaned closer and the tiny gust of air sent the thing's skin rippling once more.

'*Leave it,*' Asper said.

Curiosity, however morbid, drove his finger even as common sense begged him to stay his hand. He prodded the thing's hairless, round head and found no resistance. His finger sank into the skin as though it were a thick pudding and when he pulled it back, a perfect oval fingerprint was left in its skull.

No bones.

'Sweet Silf.' His breath came short as he turned to regard Asper. 'What did you *do* to him?'

She opened her mouth to reply, eyes wide, lips quivering. A scream emerged, though not her own, and echoed off the timbers. Immediately, whatever fear had been smeared across her face was replaced with stern resolution as she glowered at him.

'Leave the dead,' she hissed one last time before seizing her staff in both hands and tearing out of the room into the corridor.

Ordinarily, he might have pressed further questions, despite her uncharacteristically harsh tone. Ordinarily, he might have left whatever had screamed to her, given that she could clearly handle it. It was simple greedy caution that urged him to his feet and at her back, the instinct inherent in all adventurers to protect their source of pay.

The scream had, after all, come from the direction of Miron's room.

He doesn't know, Asper told herself as they hurried down the corridor, *he doesn't know, he doesn't know. He won't ask questions. He's not smart enough. He won't tell. He doesn't know.*

His long legs easily overtook her. She sensed his eyes upon her, angled her head down.

The litany of reassurances she forced upon herself proved futile. Her mind remained clenched with possibility. What if he didn't need to ask questions? He had seen the corpse, seen what it was. He saw her sobbing. He was a coward, a brigand, but not a moron. He could be replaying it in his mind, as she did now, seeing the creature leaping from the dark, seeing her hand rise up instinctively, hearing the frog-thing scream …

He heard the scream.

Stop it, stop it, STOP IT! He doesn't know … don't … don't think about it now. Think about the Lord Emissary. Think about the other scream. Think about—

Her thoughts and her fervent rush came to a sudden halt as she collided with Denaos's broad back. Immediately, fear was replaced by anger as she shoved her way past him, ready to unleash a verbal hellstorm upon him. But his eyes were not for her. He stared out into the corridor, mouth open, eyes unblinking.

She followed his gaze, looking down the hall, and found herself sharing his expression, eyes going wide with horror.

'L-Lord Emissary,' she gasped breathlessly.

A pale corpse lay at Evenhands' feet, motionless in a pool of rapidly leaking blood. Miron's sunken shoulders rose and fell with staggered breaths, his hands trembled at his sides. The blues and whites of his robes were tainted black with his attacker's blood. The elderly gentleness of his face was gone, replaced by wrinkles twisted with undiluted fury.

'Evenhands,' Denaos said, moving forwards tentatively. 'Are you all right?'

The priest's head jerked up with such sudden anger as to force the rogue back a step. His eyes were narrowed to black slits, his lips curled in a toothy snarl. Then, with unnatural swiftness, his face untwisted to reveal a bright-eyed gaze punctuated by a broad, gentle smile.

'I am well. Thank you for your concern,' he replied in a trembling breath. 'Forgive the scene. One of these …' he looked down at the pale man disdainfully, 'brutes attacked me as I went to see what was happening on deck.'

'We're still under attack, Lord Emissary,' Asper said, stepping forwards. 'It would be safer if you remained in your quarters.'

'Yes, of course,' he replied with a shaking nod. 'But … be careful out there, my friends. These are no mere pirates.'

'What do you mean, Lord Emissary?' Asper asked, tilting her head at the priest.

As Miron opened his mouth to reply, he was cut off by a sudden response from Denaos.

'It's the tattoos,' the rogue said, eyeing the priest, 'isn't it?'

'Indeed.' Miron's reply was grim. 'They are adornments of an order who serve a power far crueller than any pirate. Their appearance here is … unexpected.'

'A power?' Asper asked, frowning. 'They're … priests?'

'Of a sort.'

'Then why do they side with the pirates, Lord Emissary?'

123

'There is no time to explain,' Miron replied urgently. 'Your friends require your aid above.' He raised his hands in a sign of benediction. 'Go forth, and Talanas be with you in your—'

A door slammed further down the corridor. Miron whirled about, Denaos and Asper looking over his shoulders to spy the fifth intruder darting away from the direction of the priest's quarters. He paused to regard the trio warily for a moment, clutching a square silk pouch tightly to his chest.

'Drop that, you filth!' Miron roared with a fury not befitting his fragile frame.

The creature's reply was a mouth opened to reveal twin rows of pointed, serrated teeth in a feral hiss. Without another moment's hesitation, he stuffed his prize into a burlap sack and tore down the hallway.

'Stop him!' Miron bellowed, charging after the fleeing infiltrator. '*STOP HIM!* He must not have that book!'

'What's so important about it?' Denaos called after him.

The priest did not respond, rushing headlong into the shadows of the hold. Denaos opened his mouth to repeat the question, but the breath was knocked from him as Asper shoved her way past, hurrying after the priest. With a sigh, Denaos shook his head and sprinted after them both.

Pirates, boneless beasts, books worth dying for, he thought grimly, *all in one day. Whatever distressed young ladies* are *rescued from this mess had better be* disgustingly *grateful.*

124

Five

COUNTING *KOU'RU*

Screaming from above, an arrow caught a tardy pirate crawling across the chain. It struck deep into his neck, forcing a blood-choked gurgle from the man as he lost his grip on the bridge of links and went tumbling headfirst into the churning waters below.

'Eight,' Kataria remarked, nocking another arrow.

Her bowstring sang a melancholy dirge for the next pirate struck, the shict grinning as he fell to join his companion in the liquid tomb.

'Nine,' she added, drawing another missile.

'Stop it,' Quillian growled in response, levelling her crossbow towards the deck. 'You're shattering my concentration.'

'You have to concentrate to lose?' Kataria asked coolly as she loosed her arrow. 'How sad. Ten.'

'I have to concentrate to make sure I don't kill *the wrong people*,' Quillian snapped back. She squeezed the trigger on her weapon and sent a bolt flying down to meet one of the deck-bound invaders below.

'So you kill a few of your own along with the pirates.' Kataria laughed. 'It's not like anyone was expecting you to do your job flawlessly.' She winked an emerald eye. 'You're only human.' Her bow hummed and someone screamed from below. 'Eleven.'

'You stupid savage,' Quillian muttered, loading her crossbow.

'You're just upset that you're losing.' She launched another arrow. 'To look, one would think you've never counted *Kou'ru* before.' Before the Serrant could reply, she smirked. 'You see, *Kou'ru* is—'

'What your breed calls humans, I know,' Quillian growled. 'I take no pride in killing my own kind, much less making games of it.'

'Well, no wonder you're so bad at this.'

The Serrant held her tongue, opting instead to focus her aim. It was difficult to ignore the shict; her idle babble was a paling annoyance compared to the grating accuracy of her scorekeeping. That only tightened her resolve, however. She vowed that no simple-minded savage would outshoot a trained Serrant.

'No way in hell,' she hissed to herself.

'Would it help if I shot blind?'

Quillian turned, incredulous. 'What?'

Kataria's grin was broad as she tugged her headband down over her eyes. Her ears quivered, one rotating to the left, the other to the right, like hounds with the scent of prey.

'I can't be blamed for this, you know. Shicts invented archery. We're even named after the sound of arrows hitting flesh.' She let her missile fly and smiled. '*Shict.*'

'Really,' Quillian muttered, 'and here was I thinking you were named after what comes out of my—'

'Your envy certainly smells like that.' Kataria lifted her headband and frowned out. 'Twelve … wait, no, that was just a glancing shot.' The fall in her voice lasted only a moment before she jumped up and down, giggling madly. 'Wait again! Someone got him in the neck with a sword! He's dead! That counts, that counts!'

'Will you *shut up*?'

'Well, you can hardly expect me to help you when you keep shoving that foul attitude at me. Too bad; I could have improved your score to being at least halfway respectable for a human.'

'Help?' Quillian laughed blackly. 'I've seen your kind's "help" first-hand, savage. I know what you've done to my people.'

'If we're talking about crimes and kinds,' Kataria replied nonchalantly, 'we may as well discuss this strange little rabble of vermin called humanity.' She loosed an arrow. 'Thirteen.' She reached for another. 'At any rate, all the shict tribes put together only add up to a fraction of your teeming race. We're smarter than you, quicker than you, craftier than you, and yet all you need to do to beat us out,' she uttered the last words contemptuously, 'is breed.'

'And how many people, innocent people, will never get the chance because of what your kind has done? Your *tribes* slaughter without remorse, discrimination or respect for the rites of combat!'

'We can't afford to discriminate between strains of disease.' Kataria's voice and weapon were one cold, cruel amalgamation, hissing callously in unison as she loosed her arrow. 'Shicts don't fight fair. Fourteen.'

'And your companions, are they strains of the same *disease*?'

Kataria fought hard to keep her body from stiffening, to keep her ears from flattening against her head. The Serrant could not hit a target with arrows. The shict resolved that she could not allow her to see her hit a target with words, either. She could not let the Serrant see her offence at the suggestion. Better to keep the ears upright, proud ears.

Shict ears.

A roar turned her attention to the deck and she glowered. Smoke curled into the sky from smouldering bodies. Men swarmed about the red-skinned brute at their centre, trying to hack at him, trying to take courage in their numbers even as Gariath continued to rip, to pull, to claw and to bludgeon.

Stupid reptile, she thought resentfully, *taking all my kills*. She glowered at the rapidly thinning crowd of foes. *I could kill them all if they'd just stop moving around so much, scampering little monkeys*. Her eyes drifted to the *Linkmaster*, keeping pace with the *Riptide* so easily, its helmsman shouting encouragement as he guided the ship with expert ease.

And his big, fat, ripe head …

'That's it,' she whispered.

She loosed an unpleasant guffaw, which only increased as Squiggy cast her a curious cringe.

'This is how I'll help you,' she said. 'We put a stop to these little pirates moving about and we'll pluck them off one by one.' She glanced to the black ship. 'Of course, we could also just end this game by putting their ship behind us.'

'What?' One of Quillian's eyebrows arched in response to an inner twinge of dread and she whirled about to follow the shict's gaze. 'What do you mean?'

'They can't do much if they can't catch us, can they? And they can't catch us if they can't chase us.' Kataria drew her arrow, aiming it across the gap of sea and the salt-slick deck of the *Linkmaster*, towards its helm. 'Thusly, all we need to do is keep them from chasing us.'

Quillian's eyes went wide as the shict's plan dawned on her. The glistening tip of her arrow was aimed directly at the filthy man at the *Linkmaster*'s wheel, blissfully unaware of her aim as he hurled abuse at Argaol.

'Like so,' Kataria finished.

'Wait, you idiot!'

Quillian's hand snatched an arm already hanging at the shict's side, having loosed the arrow long before the Serrant could even reach for it. With painful slowness, Quillian stared as the arrow hummed with an almost casual speed towards the pirates' helmsman. No heads looked up, far too embroiled in their current battle to foresee the impending disaster.

Quillian's breath caught in her throat as the arrow caught in the helmsman's. He jerked slightly, then stiffened with a curious look on his face, as though unaware of what had just happened.

'There,' Kataria said, shrugging the Serrant's hand off. 'What's so bad about that?'

The slain helmsman answered.

He slumped across the wheel, his body dragging it into a full spin. The chain connecting the two ships went slack as the *Linkmaster* veered suddenly, driven by the corpse's weight. The screams of pirates tumbling off their now-unstable bridge were punctuated by splashes of water. Cries of alarm rose up from the deck as fingers pointed towards the black-timbered titan now careening towards the *Riptide*. The pale-skinned creatures clinging to the hull in mid-climb croaked a collective chorus of terror.

Then, all sounds died in a great wooden scream.

The two huge ships collided, bows splintering. The *Linkmaster*'s momentum sent the *Riptide* spinning as their hulls ground together. Particularly unlucky pirates and pale frogmen were reduced from hostile invaders to smears in the span of two breaths.

The fighting on the deck ground to a halt as the ships did, the sudden shifting sending all combatants sprawling to kiss the salt. Eventually, the spiralling, the screaming and the splintering stopped, leaving two floating behemoths bobbing with unfitting calmness.

Kataria took the opportunity to stagger to her feet, gripping the edge of the crow's nest. She glanced down at the carnage: dizzy men struggling to rise and find their weapons, uttering prayers to various human Gods, flattened chunks of red and pink tumbling into the waters as the hulls eased apart. In the funerary wake of sound, a stray wind caressed her hair, sending her feathers fluttering.

A smile creased her face, breaking into a peal of laughter that was long, loud and unwholesome.

'How many do you think that was worth, Squiggy?' She cast a glance behind her, spying nothing. 'Squiggy?'

When she discovered the bronze-clad fingers clutching at the nest's edge, she had to fight to keep her laughter from overpowering her. She couldn't say at that moment why the sight of Quillian dangling by one stubborn hand was so amusing to her. Perhaps it was her expression, the mixture of fear and outrage at having been hurled from the nest by the force of the collision. Perhaps it was simply the rush of having scored so many *Kou'ru* with one shot, the woman's humiliation being merely the punctuation of a squeal-filled giddy sentence.

Or perhaps it was the opportunity dangling before her.

'Help me up.' Quillian's voice had not even the slightest hint of request.

Kataria's own hand lingered on the rail, her gaze contemplative. There was no real reason to watch the Serrant fall, she realised, but was hard pressed to think of a reason to haul her bronze-clad bulk back up.

And yet, something stayed her hand, a mere finger's length from the Serrant's own reaching gauntlet. Here was a human with genuine hate reinforced with swords, crossbows and blind zeal. Here was a human who saw notched ears as a target.

She had seen such hate before, but only in the eyes of those not content to revile her people and wallow in deluded myth about the tribes. This hate, the undiluted foulness behind Quillian's eyes, was reserved for those who had seen shicts. *Seen*, she thought, *and killed.*

Her suspicions were confirmed, at least as much as she needed them to be, in the grit of the woman's teeth and narrowing of her eyes. She could not disguise her loathing, even as she dangled above the already blood-soaked deck. Even for the sake of her life, Kataria realised, this human couldn't commit the fraud of repentance.

'If you're going to kill me,' the Serrant hissed, 'then cease drawing it out.'

Kataria made no reply besides a careful, contemplative blink. Here was a human who had killed her people. Here was a human who had committed the one sin all shicts were sworn to avenge. Here was a human who could be one less slayer of her tribeskin, a human the world wouldn't miss.

They can always make more, she thought.

'Do it,' the Serrant hissed.

Kataria's hand moved in response, wrapping around the Serrant's wrist.

'Don't be such a whiner,' the shict grunted, straining with the effort of hauling up the bronze-clad woman. 'Just because,' she paused to breathe, 'I took my time,' she gasped, 'Riffid Alive, but you're heavy.'

Suddenly she paused, as the woman's chest rose just above the basket's edge.

'Wait a moment, how many did you say that last one was worth?'

'What?' Hate vanished in a moment of puzzlement in Quillian's eyes.

'When the ships collided,' Kataria repeated, 'how many was that worth? How many did I kill?'

'I don't know,' the Serrant snarled, 'I was a bit busy *nearly falling to my death*.'

'Just take a guess.'

'I don't know ...' She drew in a breath through her teeth. 'You killed ... perhaps eight heathens.'

'*EIGHT?*'

Quillian's shriek was short and brief as the shict released her. She came to a sudden, jerking halt, her bronze fingers digging deeper into the wood to suspend herself. A staggering gasp that sounded as though the woman's stomach was on the verge of spilling out of her mouth went unheeded by Kataria.

'That had to be fifteen,' Kataria protested sharply, '*at least* twelve.'

'You're delusional,' Quillian growled in response. 'Eight is being generous. You didn't do more than shoot one man and send a few others into the sea.'

'In *a chunky jam* I sent them! Give me a better number!'

'Lying is a sin in the eyes of all Gods.'

'Then you'd better cut it out before I send you to meet them.'

Until that moment, it hadn't truly occurred to Kataria that she was prepared to send the woman to her death for refusing to concede a few extra *Kou'ru* when she hadn't been willing to condemn her for supposedly killing her own tribesmen. It bothered her little; whether by righteous vengeance or petty numbers, still one less human.

If, Kataria told herself, *she continues to act in such a human manner*.

'Do you concede?'

'Not a chance,' Quillian snapped back.

'Lovely.' The shict put on a self-satisfied smirk. 'Bid your smelly Gods good day on behalf of Riffid for me.'

She turned about, folding her arms over her chest. She could resume shooting in a moment, when this particular distraction was over. Absently, she scratched her flank as she waited for the sound of bronze grinding against wood, gulls crying above the inevitable shriek, a pompous melon exploding in a barrel.

Either that or a plea for mercy. They'd be equally satisfying.

'Shict,' Quillian gasped.

So soon? Kataria resolved not to turn just yet; that would be too easy.

'Shict!'

She can hold on for a few more moments ... or not.

'Damn it, you long-eared vagrant! Something's happening below!'

Kataria's ears twitched. The Serrant's concerns were confirmed in a cry of pain from a familiar voice. She whirled about, leaning over the dangling woman to peer at what was occurring below.

What had begun as a melee had degenerated into a matter of swaths: swaths fleeing before Gariath as he tore through the ranks of the pirates, swaths collapsing before Dreadaeleon's fiery hands as his arcane chant went unchallenged.

'That hardly counts as a "happening",' the shict sneered. 'I've already killed as many as they have.'

'Not that, you imbecile!' Quillian pointed a bronze finger across the deck.

Kataria's eyes widened immediately, ears pricking up

in alarm at the sight. The greatest swath of all lay at the *Riptide*'s helm, the sailors who had been guarding it now cast to the timbers like scythed wheat. The figure of Rashodd was immense amidst the carnage, wading unhurriedly up the steps towards the sole figure, short and wiry, standing in his way.

'Lenk,' she whispered.

Her arrow was up and nestled in the bowstring in an instant, aimed squarely for Rashodd's massive back. The pirate, however, seemed less than interested in standing still and suddenly twisted, drawing up beside Lenk, uncomfortably close. Even as wiry as he was, as skilled as she was, and as massive as the Cragsman was, her fingers quivered.

No, she resolved at that moment. She would not add Lenk to her score. Besides, she reasoned, a shot from such a distance into a man of Rashodd's girth had no guarantee to kill. To waste arrows on a single *Kou'ru*, no matter how big, simply wasn't acceptable.

Her arrow was back in her quiver, bow in hand, leg over the crow's nest's railing as she prepared to climb down the rigging. Only a sudden shriek gave her pause.

'Hey! *HEY!*'

'Oh, right.' She glanced over the quaking bronze digits and stared down at Quillian. 'I almost forgot.' She smiled. 'Now, we're agreeing that the collision caused at least twelve in my favour, yes?'

'Yes, sure, whatever!' The Serrant nodded fervently. 'Just—'

'Mind yourself, I have to count.' The shict made a show of wiggling her digits. 'Fourteen from arrows alone plus, if we're frugal, another twelve makes ...' She smiled morbidly down at Squiggy, tapping her nose with a finger. 'An even twenty-seven. Lucky number!'

The total dawned on Quillian the moment Kataria leapt from the nest and deftly seized the rigging. Squeals of fury followed her down, but she ignored them. There were more pressing concerns.

A flash of sparks at the helm drew her attention; Lenk was hard pressed against Rashodd's twin axes, his sword nothing more than a weak stinger in the hands of a tiny wasp. Kataria gritted her teeth, splayed her legs against the ropes of the rigging and slid down, ignoring the burn of the hemp that bit through her gloves. She had no time for pain.

The game was not yet over.

Six

THE HERALD

Lenk felt a hammer explode against his belly.

The wind left him, the earth left him as he flew up into the air, sailing blissfully across currents carried by fast-fading screams in the distance. *This*, he thought, *must be what it is to ascend to the heavens.*

The Gods proved not so kind.

He struck the timbers with a crash, sliding like a limp, breathless fish. He collided with the base of the ship's wheel with the meagrest of bumps, giving him the opportunity to lament that the blow hadn't killed him.

'Khetashe,' he gasped breathlessly, 'that didn't work.'

'You thought it would?' Argaol was quick to kneel beside the young man, helping him to a sitting position. 'Rashodd's twice your size if you stand up straight, boy!'

'I thought,' he paused to breathe, 'I could … strike quickly. Use size to my advantage … gnats and frogs, right?'

'What?'

'Something my grandfather told me.' Lenk rubbed his stomach, grimacing; the indentations of Rashodd's knuckles were all too fresh in his skin. 'The frogs are big, slow and lumbering … the gnats are small and quick, they can escape.'

'No gnat ever managed to beat down a frog, runt.'

'Well, I know that *now*. When he told it to me, it sounded like good advice.'

Any further conversation went silent against the sound of distant thunder, the sound of heavy boots. The timbers shook beneath them, the ship trembling with Rashodd's stride. They glanced up as the pirate cleared the last step to the helm.

Rashodd stalked towards them with almost insulting casualness, heedless of the dead beneath his boots, the red flecking his beard, the glistening of his axes. His gaze was unreadable behind his helmet, his voice a metallic ringing.

'It is with no undue fondness that I recall a time when this was a respectable business. It is with nostalgia that I remember when two captains could do business without bloodshed and drinks were always proffered to guests.' He sighed. 'Where is my drink, Argaol? Where is the courtesy extended to a man of my particular prestige? I would give you all the mercy I could spare had you merely displayed a bit of the propriety I am inarguably due.'

Using his sword as a makeshift crutch, Lenk staggered to his feet, steadying himself with the ship's wheel.

Rashodd inclined his head respectfully. 'You seem to be the most decent lad amongst this merry band of rabble we've had the pleasure to treat with.' He hefted one of his axes over a broad shoulder. 'I can't say I don't admire your – if you'll pardon the comparison – cockroach-like tenacity. I've scarce known a man to display such resilience in the face of common sense.' He lofted a great, grey brow. 'Mercenary?'

'Adventurer.'

'That would explain it, wouldn't it? I've no inherent disrespect for the profession, mind you, though it's always seemed to me that an adventurer is naught more than a pirate who couldn't bring himself to admit he's scum.'

'We're all entitled to our opinions.'

'Regardless, I feel compelled to ask you,' he shifted his glance to Argaol, 'both of you … why put up such a fight? While I wouldn't list it as a fault in polite company, are you blind, good man? Can you not see the merry company we keep?' He gestured over his shoulder to the pale invaders, sliding up to reinforce their pirate allies. 'Be frank with me – how many mere pirates do you know that command such beasts?'

'I've met more than a few beasts in my time,' Lenk grunted, standing as straight as he could. 'I'm not impressed.'

'A pity.' Rashodd shook his head sadly and turned to Argaol. 'Then I appeal to your reason, good Captain. Is it too late to call for a cessation that we might converse as proper gents? Must it always come to violence?'

'It came to violence ages ago,' Argaol snarled, 'when you started slaughtering my men.'

'The merry boys of the *Linkmaster* are nothing if not famed for their bravado.'

'What you're famed for is rape, murder and slavery.'

'You do me no honour with flattery, kind sir. Nor have I the patience to continue such an argument. Simply give us what we wish and we can spare you any more tidying-up.'

Argaol regarded the man hesitantly. 'And what, pray, is it you wish?'

'I had come intent on taking away some cargo, but I think it a bit rude,' the Cragsman cleared his throat, 'given that you'll be requiring most of your merchandise to hire on crew to replace the men you've so unfortunately lost.'

'Your hacking them to pieces *was* a bit unfortunate.'

'Details. At any rate, we'll simply search your cabins and take two of your gentle lady passengers.' He held up a pair of fingers. 'One of our choosing, one of yours.'

Argaol hummed; the sound was faint and distant in Lenk's ears, slurred by the thunder pounding through his head. Even through blurring vision, however, he could see the captain's gaze drifting upwards to the crow's nest. Kataria and Quillian had both vanished from the mast; perhaps for the better, Lenk thought.

The captain's thoughts were just as audible. He could see Argaol questioning himself, posing any number of logical scenarios in the tilt of his head. *Why not*, Lenk asked himself, *why not abandon a savage for the sake of the crew? Please the pirates and please the Gods by ridding himself of a heathen adventurer.*

Lenk clutched the hilt of his sword, unsure as to who he should turn it on once enough feeling returned to his arm to heft it.

'As well as the priest below.'

Argaol's neck went rigid. 'Absolutely not! Murder is one thing, Rashodd, but I'll not let you blaspheme this ship.'

'Had I any manner of hat not made of iron, I would doff it in reverence of your godliness, kind sir.' The Cragsman paused to pantomime this. 'But I must attempt to skewer you with logic for a moment: consider the fate of your men. Resist us and the priest comes along with us, cooperate and the priest comes along with us. The only difference that remains is how big a charnel heap you're left with.'

'Zamanthras guides this ship,' Argaol countered hotly, displaying the Goddess's symbol hanging around his neck. 'I will not risk the generosity She's shown me by acquiescing to your logic, no matter how skewering.' He reached for the cutlass at his hip. 'You offer me a quick death by your own hand or a slow one by the Gods' disfavour. I will accept *neither*.'

'We aren't giving up any woman or man, either,' Lenk attempted to say without vomiting as the breath returned to him fiercely. 'Heathen or faithful, adventurer or otherwise.' He hefted his sword and turned an icy glare upon the captain. 'No one dies here without taking someone else with him.'

Rashodd was impassive as Lenk charged towards him, the tiny gnat levelling his tiny silver stinger against the massive, iron-clad frog. The pirate twirled an axe casually in one hand, testing its weight as he might a butchering knife in the face of a particularly choice piece of meat. As he lowered his visored stare upon Lenk's head, he undoubtedly figured that his weapon would split a melon just as well.

The axe swung, bit only a few stray strands of silver as Lenk ducked low and thrust his blade upwards with a triumphant cackle, aiming for the small gap in his foe's armour. Such mirth was drowned in the clamour of steel, however, as Rashodd's second axe came up with an unfair deftness, grinding against the young man's sword.

Undaunted, Lenk pressed the attack. The pirate might have had leverage and strength, but the young man had two hands firmly on the sword's hilt and its tip poised tantalisingly close to the Cragsman's intestines. *Just a little farther*, he thought, *a good push and it's all over*. He saw his grin widen in the blade's reflection, brimming with malicious hope.

It was then that he remembered that Rashodd had two hands.

The flat of the second axe came crashing down and slammed against his ribs. His sword clattered to the ground, hands contorting as muscles locked against the blow.

Paralysed, he was barely able to let out a pained squawk, let alone squirm away from Rashodd's massive hand.

'Kindly use your reason, gentlemen.' The ire boiling in Rashodd's voice was reflected in the fingers tightening around the young man's neck as he hefted Lenk from the deck. 'Perhaps it has been your woe to have dealt with considerably less couth men than myself, but I can most benevolently assure you that my terms would be considered most generous by anyone slightly less deranged.'

'There can be no negotiation where blasphemy is involved,' Argaol snarled in reply.

'Ah, my dear Captain, there can be no victory where Rashodd is involved.' He gestured out over the deck. 'Amongst his allies are counted men who ply the waters like frogs and fight like devils. Look upon them, Captain, embrace the wisdom of our terms and we can begin the long and arduous process of restraining ourselves from the mutilation of fruits, stones and other synonyms for manhood,' he brought his axe up, let the blade graze Lenk's trousers, 'starting with this ardent young lad.'

Being strangled by a giant hand and with an axe brushing his genitalia, Lenk began to see the wisdom in surrender. He hoped between what meagre breaths he could muster that Argaol, too, had enough sympathy for his situation, if not his profession.

While he couldn't twist his neck to see Argaol's reaction, the captain's derisive laughter assured the young man that godliness was, in his eyes, well above concern for an adventurer's dangling bits.

'And what then, Rashodd? Do we see how many more sacks are slashed before you get your men under control?' He chuckled blackly. 'Besides, if you want to negotiate, I suggest you find a more valuable hostage.'

'Truly, good Captain, it is rare that I find myself in a position where callousness overwhelms me.' The Cragsman shook his head. 'I trust the honour isn't lost on you.' He looked Lenk over appraisingly like a particularly gristly piece of beef. 'This upstanding young gent has spilled much blood for your well-being and you would cast him off so crudely?'

'There are always more adventurers. They're like cockroaches, as you say.'

The surprise in Rashodd's voice was genuine. 'It is with no great glee that I admit I hadn't expected this of you.' He twirled the axe in his hands, raising it a little. 'And it is with even less glee that I make this example.'

'You ought to listen to the captain,' someone hissed from behind.

Rashodd turned laboriously with two heavy feet, not nearly deft enough to avoid the arrow that shrieked from the steps and angrily bit at his wrist as it grazed his flesh. His grunt was more of surprise than of pain as he dropped Lenk to the deck, his scowl more of annoyance than anger as he turned to the woman already nocking another arrow.

'Cockroaches are everywhere.' Kataria smiled behind her bow, flashing broad canines. 'Back away from him,' she gestured to Lenk with her chin, 'that one belongs to me.'

'Shicts, is it?' Rashodd's thick lips twisted into a grin that was undoubtedly supposed to be coy. 'My good Captain, you can hardly retain your claims to godliness while consorting with heathen savages.' He raised his hands, taking a step away from Lenk. 'By all means, keep the dear lad if you think it will do you any good.'

Her arrow followed him as he took another two steps backwards. It wasn't until a moment passed that Argaol

142

glanced from the shict to the fallen young man and coughed.

'Shouldn't you … help him?'

Kataria blinked suddenly, glanced down at her companion and sighed.

'Yeah … I guess.'

Rashodd seemed less than worried, even though Kataria kept her bow aimed at him while she came to Lenk's side. The pirate, rather, let out a great sigh, as though a potential arrow through the eyeball was all one tremendous inconvenience. He plucked up his stray axe and twirled it.

'And how do we solve this, then?' He shook his head. 'Kill me, my men will fight harder and, while they weren't particularly restrained boys to begin with, they'll have much less restraint if I'm not here to control them.'

'Every last heathen aboard this blessed vessel will be cleansed by steel, scum.' Quillian's approach was heralded by the hiss of a sword leaping from its scabbard. Though she levelled her blade at the pirate, her scowl was for Kataria. '*Every. Last. One.*'

'She looks mad,' Lenk noted through a strained gulp.

'She always looks mad,' Kataria replied.

'In the interim,' the Serrant said, turning her attention back to Rashodd, 'it is only logical that we begin with the biggest.'

Lenk held his breath as the woman took a menacing step. Rashodd was right, he knew – the Cragsmen wouldn't even notice that their captain had been killed until well after every last man was dead. Such an occurrence, however, rested on the idea that a sword would be enough to stop him.

An idea, he thought grimly, that seemed more ludicrous with every step the Cragsman took to meet the Serrant.

She growled and Lenk winced, though the sound of steel carving flesh never came. Rather, there was the sound of bronze clattering to the floor as a great, clawed hand reached up, seized Quillian by the head and shoved her aside.

Despite having no breath to chuckle, Lenk felt rather satisfied seeing Rashodd leap backwards at the sight clambering up the stairs. If the Cragsman strode with insulting casualness, Gariath stalked with infuriated ease. The leathery skin of his face was twisted angrily, bared teeth as red as every other part of his body. Cuts and gashes crisscrossed his body like so much decoration, which seemed to be all the credit he gave his wounds.

'It's over.'

Gariath seemed to say this with more irritation than satisfaction, though it was difficult for Lenk to distinguish his companion's irritation from his other emotions; all of them involved some manner of rage.

'They barely even fought.'

Red pooled at his feet. Red, Lenk noted grimly, not his own.

'This one didn't even raise his sword.'

Gariath tossed the limp body at the Cragsman's feet. The man was barely recognisable as one of the *Linkmaster*'s crew, so badly broken and crushed was he. Limbs were bent in ways they weren't meant to bend, extra joints had been added, and haemorrhages bloomed in ugly purple blossoms beneath the man's skin.

Lenk quietly wished Rashodd hadn't angled himself to prevent the young man from seeing his face.

The colossal captain gasped at his underling. 'What in the name of All On High did you do to him?'

'I killed him. Isn't that obvious?' The dragonman took

a step forwards and Rashodd backpedalled with uncharacteristic haste, axes raised. 'The rest of them will follow.' Gariath levelled a claw at the captain. 'Unless you kill me.'

A glance at the deck confirmed Gariath's declaration. The battle, it seemed, had taken a definite turn with the dragonman's presence. Many of the pirates lay dead, the remaining ones herded by the now superior numbers of the *Riptide*'s men. Only the pale invaders held strong, pressed into a small mass at one side of the ship, heedless of the Cragsmen's pleas for help.

Those meagre few who hadn't already thrown down their arms collapsed as smouldering husks in the shadow of Dreadaeleon, the boy breathing heavily, hurling gouts of fire from his hands as he strode along the deck like an underfed titan.

'It's an insult,' Gariath growled, tearing all eyes back upon himself. 'I wanted a fight. I wanted *warriors* and you send me babies.' He kicked the corpse harshly. 'Babies.' The foot came up and down with a crack of wood and a spatter of thick, grey porridge. '*BABIES*.'

Rashodd cringed at that. Lenk thought it would have been a satisfying sight had he not also been forced to look away.

'So boldly did you utter condemnation of imagined blasphemies, Argaol,' the Cragsman's voice betrayed not a hint of fear, 'yet now you consort with murderous monsters and do not quiver at your own righteous hypocrisy?'

'Stop talking to them,' Gariath growled, clenching his hands into fists. 'I had to fight through a lot of ugly, weak, smelly humans to get to you. Now, stand still and *fight* so one of us can die and we might be able to get something done today.'

'I care not what atrocities linger before, throughout or herein, reptile.' Rashodd's axes kissed in a challenging clang. 'Nor do I yearn to know what allegiances they hold to. If you seek to die, I'll make your funeral impromptu and decidedly lacking in attendance.'

Not one of the dragonman's smiles had ever been pleasant, Lenk noted as he watched his companion's lips curl backwards, but this particular grin crossed a threshold the young man had not yet seen. Something flashed in the hulking brute's eye, notable only in that it was no glimpse of bloodlust, nor promise of a memorable dismembering. What glimmered behind Gariath's obsidian orbs was anxiousness, eagerness, anticipation better fitting a young man about to bed his first woman.

After that particular metaphor, Lenk did not dare contemplate what his companion was thinking.

'Show me, then,' Gariath's challenge was punctuated by the ringing of his silver bracers clashing together, 'what humans can do.'

'Requested and granted.'

No sooner had the pirate's massive foot hit the deck than a piercing wail cut through the air.

'*Stop him!*' All eyes below and above turned towards the shadows of the companionway as something emerged, pursued by a voice brimming with righteous indignation. '*Stop him, you fools! Retrieve the book!*'

With unnerving speed, something came springing out of the shadows. So white as to be blinding in the sun, the slender, pale creature leapt out onto the deck. It hesitated, surveying the carnage surrounding it with animal awareness, baring black gums and needle teeth in a defiant hiss. The combatants, pirates and sailors alike, ceased their fighting at the sudden appearance of the creature and the booming voice that followed it.

'*I said stop him!*'

At the sound, the creature went bounding through the crowds. Sweeping from the shadows like a white spectre, Miron Evenhands came bursting out, frost flakes on his shoulders. He flung a hand out after the creature in such a dramatic gesture that the figures of Denaos and Asper behind him were hardly noticeable.

'*He has the book! Bring it back to me!*'

'SHEPHERD!' the creature wailed to no visible presence as he rushed past the crowd. 'Summon the Shepherd! This one has the tome!'

'What the hell are you doing?' The roar came from Rashodd. In the angry turn of a heel, the dragonman was forgotten as the captain stormed down the stairs after the fleeing creature. 'We don't need any books, you dim-witted hairless otter!'

'Get back here!' Gariath howled in response, charging after the Cragsman.

Lenk and Argaol shared a blink as a new breed of chaos began to unfurl below. The pale creature nimbly darted between those determined to stop him and rushed to the cluster of his own kind at the ship's railing. All the while, Miron bellowed orders as Rashodd pursued the creature and Gariath pursued Rashodd.

'Well?' Argaol asked, turning to the young man suddenly.

'What?'

'Shouldn't you do something?'

The young man sighed heavily and tapped the toe of his boot on the wood.

'Yeah,' he muttered, 'fine.'

Lenk leapt from the stairs, though he knew not why. His breath was still ragged, his grip weak on his sword, his legs trembling. He charged into a throng of flesh, wood and steel with Rashodd's blow still echoing in his body and he knew not why he did. Yet even as he felt himself stagger, he continued to charge after the pale thief, into the battle, into the sprays of red.

He knew not why.

Voices were at his back: commands from Miron, cries of mingled encouragement and warning from Asper and Denaos, all fading behind him. Arrows flew past his ears to put down particularly bold invaders rushing forth to aid their companion. Rashodd was before him, then at his side as he nimbly darted past the hulking pirate. He caught the flash of an axe out of the corner of his eye, moving to hack his legs out from under him.

There was a roar, a flash of red as something horned, clawed and winged caught the Cragsman from behind.

That threat fled from Lenk's mind with the sound of two heavy bodies hitting the deck. As sounds and screams faded around him, as the world slipped into darkness, leaving only the slender-limbed creature and the burlap satchel it clutched, he knew what sent him in pursuit. He knew, and it spoke to him in a harsh, frigid voice.

'*They cannot flee,*' the voice said, an edge of joy to it, '*they cannot run. Strike. Kill.*'

The command lent him strength, pushed cold blood through his legs, drove him to leap. The pale creature was quick, but Lenk was more so. In the breath between his leap and his descent, the last trace of the world slipped away, bathing everything in darkness. He saw the invader turn, spurred by an unheard shout from his compatriots;

148

Lenk saw the reflection of his steel in the creature's dark eyes.

Then, in a glittering arc, the world returned.

The thief collapsed unceremoniously. Something square and black tumbled out of its satchel, bouncing once upon the deck, then sliding gently to rest in a particularly moist, sticky spot. Even as life leaked out of him, the invader gasped and reached out a trembling, webbed hand for the object.

'Tome ...' he gasped, 'Shepherd ... take—'

Lenk twisted his sword and the creature went rigid, laying its quivering head down in a red pool as though it were a pillow. His blade still glistening, Lenk raised his weapon warily, warning off the small press of pale creatures that took a collective menacing step forwards. They retreated from the weapon, he noted, but with hardly the fear or haste he had hoped. Their eyes were still appraising, their bone daggers still clenched tightly.

'Lenk!' He didn't have to turn around to recognise Miron's booming voice. 'The book! Return it to me!'

A book.

He wasn't exactly sure what he thought the thing should be. It was a broad, black square, only a little bigger than his journal. High quality leather of crimson and ebon bound its pristine white pages; it certainly looked like a book.

And yet, as it slid out of its silk pouch with the rocking of the ship, it somehow didn't seem to be a book.

It was unadorned. No title, no author, no symbol of any faith or people. The pale creatures lurched backwards, regarding it carefully, warily, anxiously. Yet even their reaction went unnoticed beside a fact that hit Lenk as he felt the warmth of the sun on his back.

It doesn't glisten.

Leather of such high quality should shimmer. It should reflect the sunlight in its onyx face. Yet this leather did not glisten, nor shine, nor even flicker in the sunlight.

'Quickly, you fool!' Miron roared. 'Take the book!'

With a swift glance over his shoulder, the young man nodded and moved forwards. Quickly, he reached down to scoop up the item.

'*NO!* Not with your hands!'

He thought it slightly odd that Miron's voice should seem distant, so distant as to render whatever he had just shouted silent. Truly, all the sounds fell silent as Lenk plucked up the book. No seawater, nor blood, though both flooded the deck in excess, clung to the leather cover. He thought that odd for only a moment before he felt a twinge in his palm.

Did ... did it just move?

The book quivered at his thoughts and, in the blink of an eye, responded.

The black cover flipped open, baring the pages to his eyes and, spurred by some unseen, unfelt breeze, began to turn. They went slowly at first, blinding him with hymns, invocations, prayers to things he had never heard of, pleas for things he would never have thought to ask for. An eternity seemed to pass as the words scarred themselves onto his eyes.

He was scarcely aware of the fact that he wasn't breathing any more.

The leaves continued to turn, to flip. Words vanished, blending into images, symbols, pictures that were discernible at first: people in torment, things with horns, claws, feathery wings. Then those too vanished and blended into nothing more than black lines scrawled in shapes that reached out and clawed at him, trying to pull his eyes from his skull with inky fingers.

Someone behind him screamed, told him to put the book down, but he could not will his hand to do so. Even as they made less and less sense, flipping viciously through his mind, the lines began to take a shape. He blinked, and with each passing moment, they continued to form a shape. It was horrible, yet he could not turn his head away, could not shut his eyes. He was forced to stare.

The book looked back at him.

The book smiled.

'*NO!*'

The book snapped shut. His fingers tensed involuntarily around it as the frigid howl reverberated through his head, coating his skull with a vocal rime. He dropped it then, watching it splash in a pink puddle. The liquid did not pool beneath it.

'*Something,*' the voice uttered, '*is coming.*'

Before Lenk could think, a howl filled the air. His eyes rose at the noise, spying the pale creatures as they clustered together at the railing. Standing above them, perched on the ship's edge and clinging to the railing, the tallest of the invaders pressed a conch shell to its lips. Its chest expanded with breath, then shrank as a wailing exhale cut the air.

Voices rose from behind him, excited warnings to the sky. Lenk saw it: the clouds moved suddenly, twisting and shifting. They grew larger, shimmering with a dozen facets as they descended in great drifts.

The sky, it seemed, was falling.

They descended in ominous unity, a flock of frenzied feathers and bulbous blue orbs, to land upon the masts and rigging and railings of the *Riptide*. Lenk watched them, spellbound by their harmony as they settled. Plump bodies covered with feathers, sagging, fleshy faces dominated by two great blue eyes.

How many? He could not find an answer; they seemed to be endless, lines of ruffling, cooing birds. *Seagulls?* No, he told himself, seagulls didn't sit and stare with unblinking eyes. Seagulls didn't gather in such numbers.

Seagulls didn't have long, needle-like teeth in place of beaks.

What, he asked himself, *are they?*

'Harbingers.' Miron's sneering disgust answered his thoughts. 'The book, Lenk! Seize the book! Keep it away from those monstrosities!'

'What are you gentlemen doing?' Rashodd bellowed from the deck, still wrestling with Gariath. 'Your master requires aid!'

'These ones no longer require that one,' the creature with the conch said, levelling a finger at the Cragsman. 'These ones have found the tome they seek.'

'What tome?' All semblance of composure vanished from the captain. 'I ordered you to take no tome!'

'No, that one did not,' the frogman replied, glowering at the captain. 'Yet that one is not this one's master.'

'What in all hell are you—'

Before Rashodd could find the words for his fury, the timbers quaked with sudden, violent force. Another series of gasps coursed through the crowd, hands tightening around weapons as eyes went wide with bewilderment.

Something had just struck the ship.

Distantly, where wood met froth, the hull groaned ominously. The deck shook once more, shifting to one side, sending sailors and defenders alike struggling to keep their footing. An eternity seemed to pass between sounds of wood splintering, punctuated by further wooden whines as something from below crawled up the hull.

The pale creatures whirled, suddenly heedless of the others behind them, the prize they had lost upon the ground. As a single unit of pasty skin and scrawny legs, they collapsed to their knees, pressing their foreheads to the salt of the deck.

All save one.

'Speak not in the Shepherd's presence,' the conch-blower uttered, its eyes on Lenk. 'Dare no movement, dare no impure thought. Be content in salvation.' Its finger trembled as he pointed. 'For that one has seen much purity.'

The ship listed further. Men stepped backwards, caught between the struggle to get away from the railing and to stay on their shifting feet.

And then, all were still; no sound, no movement. Only the groan of wood and the death of wind.

Screams were frozen in throats, hands quaking about weapons, unblinking eyes forced to the edge of the ship. From over the side, an immense, webbed appendage dotted with curling claws and wrapped in skin the colour of shadow reached up to cling to the railing. The wood splintered with the force of the grip, threatening to be crushed as the arm, emaciated and clad in painfully stretched flesh, tensed.

'Sweet Khetashe,' Lenk whispered breathlessly.

With one great effort, the clawed limb pulled the rest of the creature up from the hull and turned the sailors' anxious terror to panic as a great monstrosity landed upon the deck with enough force to crack wood beneath two massive webbed feet.

It stood more than ten feet tall, dwarfing any creature present with its emaciated, ebon-skinned splendour.

Attached to a torso of flesh drawn cruelly tight over a long ribcage were two arms and legs, both longer than spears, jointed in four places and ending in great, webbed claws.

All its thin, underfed horror was nothing compared to the monument atop its long neck. Massive, almost the size of its painfully visible ribcage, resembling the head of a rotted fish, the thing regarded the crew through vast, unblinking eyes: frigid white pools dominated by great blots of darkness. Its wide, toothy maw stretched its entire face to the point of agony, its lower jaw hanging slack. More than one man present retched, cringed or added a distinct yellow tinge to the grisly paint upon the deck as the creature's mouth swung open to speak.

'Where does the salvation lie?' Its voice was lilting, gurgling, the sounds of drowning men. 'Where can it be?

'There, Shepherd.'

Lenk saw their fingers, pale little digits pointed to the deck right at his feet. He glanced down at the tome for only a moment as it lay in a dry space with nothing but wet about it. His attention was then torn upwards once more as he felt the timbers quake beneath his feet.

The thing walked towards him in a loping, unhurried gait. He could see every webbed claw settle into the wood as it set a foot down, see the water cling to its black soles as it raised a foot up.

Was it aware of the fear it inspired? Lenk wondered. Was it aware that there had been so much blood spilled and so many bodies falling just moments ago? Was anyone else still aware? He could feel their frozen presence behind him, feel the ripple of air as they quivered, feel the breath of whimpered prayers.

Were they aware of him, he wondered, or did they merely see a tiny silver shadow before a looming tower of gloom?

'The tome!' Miron's shout was fading, softened by the terrified silence. 'Get the tome!'

By the time Lenk realised there was a world beyond the creature looming before him, the tome was ensconced in webbed claws, examined by empty eyes. It did not blink, did not so much as scowl; whatever it saw in Lenk, Lenk could not see in it.

'Is it tempting? Is it envious?' The abomination's voice was incapable of softness, boiling up in its flabby throat like vocal bile. 'Curious ... and envious, both. The temptation is great to look within and muse on the salvation that lies beneath man-wrought covers.'

'Temptation is strong.' The rotund, feathered creatures chanted in horrifying unison. 'Flesh is weak. Shelter in salvation. Salvation in the Shepherd.'

The black monstrosity leaned down, looking Lenk squarely in the eyes.

'And yet ... is it more faithful to keep eyes chaste, minds pure?'

'Chastity leads to the endless blue,' the chorus above chanted. 'Blessed is the pure mind.'

Its arm extended, reached out to touch the deck as the thing remained unbent and Lenk remained unmoving. It reached over him and he heard its joints pop into place with greasy ease. The warning cries that had been at his back were quiet; all was quiet save for the shifting of the creature as it plucked the book's silk covering from the water.

'It is,' it continued, drawing its great arm back, 'for there is nothing without faith, no hope without chastity.' Like a great, bony crane, the thing dipped its hand, replacing the book into the silk pouch. 'And such great beauty must be kept only for eyes as beautiful.'

Lenk hadn't even noticed the pale creature scurrying up beside the abomination, now accepting the tome with eager hands.

'Is it not so?' The creature did not wait for answer from itself, Lenk or its aide. Without another movement, it gurgled to the pale invader beside it. 'Go.'

'Fools!' Miron cried, though no one seemed to hear him. No one noticed the frogmen retreating, ambling from their prostrate circle and over the railing of the ship, to land in the salt with muted splashes.

No one could see anything beyond the stake of darkness that had impaled the heart of the deck.

'There is no escape from envy,' the creature gurgled, staring down at Lenk, 'however base a sensation it may feel. But to tolerate it … feel it and let it live, that is inexcusable in the eyes of Mother.'

'*Move.*'

He wished he could; the voice was so distant, drowned in the echo of the abomination's gurgle. Between them, the frost and the shadow, he was smothered, frozen, unaware of the glistening black claw reaching down as though it intended to pluck a flower.

'*MOVE!*'

'Understand,' the thing gurgled, 'this is simply how it must be.'

'How it must end,' the chorus agreed with bobbing heads.

When the blackness of the thing's hand had completely engulfed his sight, he felt it. A roar tore the sky apart, ripping through the air as it ripped through Lenk. The creature's hand wavered for a moment, the field of black broken by a sudden flash of angry red, the smothering echo of its voice shattered by thunder.

Gariath struck the creature with all the force of a battering ram, leathery wings flapping to propel his horned head into its ribcage. The abomination staggered, but did not fall. It gurgled, but did not scream. Gashes formed in its chest as it took a great step backwards ... but it did not bleed.

It doesn't bleed.

He was reminded, however, that he did, as the dragonman's knuckles cracked against his cheek. Whatever else had lingered inside him was banished in a fit of bloody-nosed rage as he turned a scowl upon his companion.

'What was that for?'

'Just checking,' the dragonman grunted back.

Lenk blinked as a glob of red-tinged phlegm dripped down his face.

'*For what?*'

'Huh.' Gariath shrugged. 'I didn't think I'd have to follow that up with a reason.' He held up a scarred hand to prevent protest. 'If it makes you feel better, say I was checking if you were too busy soiling yourself to fight.'

'I wasn't—'

'Then what were you doing?'

Lenk opened his mouth to reply, but no words came out. He was muted, blinded, deafened all at once as the images flashed through his head again, the words echoing in his ears: the portraits in the book's pages, the smile across the parchment, '*salvation*', '*MOVE!*' He found himself dizzy suddenly, but dared not sway, lest he find Gariath performing another check-up.

'Never mind,' Lenk grunted. 'Whatever it was, it doesn't warrant you punching your leader in the face.'

'Leaders lead, they don't stand around and wait to die.' Gariath snorted at that, raising a claw to one black eye. 'Cry later. Kill now.'

Whatever fear and frustration had been boiling within left him in one great resigned sigh. He glanced over at Gariath; even in the face of such a horror as the black-skinned foe, even against such walking foulness, he was still tensed for the fight, his wounds and cuts threatening to reopen over the bulge of his muscle. His posture, the eager twitch of wings, the flicking of moistened claws, told Lenk that the dragonman had already prepared to throw himself into a gaping, saw-toothed mouth of death. The sole question that lingered between their gazes was who was going to follow him into the afterlife.

Lenk raised his sword unconsciously. He saw his reflection in his companion's teeth; they both knew the answer.

Thunder burst from Gariath's mouth and crashed beneath his feet as he threw himself on all fours, charging towards the towering creature, wings unfurled, tail whipping behind him. Lenk struggled to keep up, following closely in the dragonman's splintered wake.

The creature regarded them with a curious tilt of its head, as though not entirely sure what was charging towards it. Before it could react, Gariath closed the distance in a sudden spring, leaping up to drive his horns against the monstrosity's ribcage. With an impact that shook the ship in the water, the creature staggered backwards as the dragonman sprang away, landing on all fours as he braced his body.

Lenk was quick to follow, charging up and over Gariath's back as though he were a winged ramp. With a grunt, he went flying off his companion's shoulders, his blade flashing in the air. He swung in a wide, murderous arc, intent on bringing his weapon anywhere he could against the thing's emaciated figure.

Rage turned to confusion in an instant as Lenk felt his

158

blade connect with something, though his feet did not return to the ground. He glanced up with mouth agape at the sight of his blade caught neatly between webbed digits. Slowly, he looked to the creature, who regarded him with the same, unblinking expression as it held him aloft with one long black limb.

'Well … uh …' Lenk began.

Before he could even think to let go of the weapon, the loose flesh about the creature's neck quivered as it gurgled unpleasantly. In a blur of silver and black, the thing's arm rose up and snapped downwards, hammering Lenk against the deck.

The air was robbed from him, sight failed him as he was pulled up from the deck by his sword, his hands wrapped about the hilt in a barely conscious death-grip. His senses failing, he barely felt the sudden lightness of his body as the creature's arm snapped forwards once more, sending him sailing through the air.

In an instant, sound and sight returned to him. Screams and frightened gasps filled his ears as he saw the deck rising up to catch him in his plummet. Bones trembled in flesh with the impact of his fall.

'Gods alive,' his voice was a breathless whisper, 'what made me think that would work?'

'And so it becomes clear.'

The voice was a scar on his brain, rubbed with clawed digits, the drowned gurgle painful even to hear. Through blurring vision, Lenk stared up, pulling himself to his feet just in time to see the ebon hand reaching down for him.

'What God can hear such a voice so far below?' the creature asked.

'They are deaf to your fears,' the chorus muttered.

Lenk fell limp in the creature's grasp as it raised him up

with all the effort it would use to lift a dead fish. He stared into its empty whites, saw the lack of any emotion boiling behind the great black pupils. There was no hatred there, no malice, not even a sinister moment of joy. Nor did the creature's stare reflect any predatory instinct or mindless sense of duty.

Within the thing's eyes, there was simply nothing.

'In the sky where your pitiless Gods dwell, none can hear you.'

A roar tore through the air. Out of the corner of his eye, Lenk spied Gariath rushing forwards, pools of blood quivering on the deck with the force of his four-legged charge. What momentary relief he might have felt was dashed with the sudden snap of a long, black arm.

Gariath was plucked from the deck like a tumbling kitten, a claw wrapping about his throat. It raised him for but an instant, holding him aloft as he thrashed, clawing and kicking at the creature, before bringing him down harshly. Wood splintered beneath the impact, forming a shallow grave of timber and seawater for Gariath to vanish into as the abomination's foot came pressing down upon him.

'But down here,' it gurgled, 'only Mother will hear you.'

The creature's mouth went wide, flesh creaking with the effort of its jaws as it bared rows of jagged teeth glistening with saliva.

'Let your end be a blessing to you.'

'*Fight back.*'

It struck Lenk as odd that he should feel guilty for disappointing the voice, odd that he should feel so guilty for clubbing an impotent fist against the creature's emaciated limb. After all, there were surely worse things than failing a hallucination.

'*Fight!*'

Too little strength, too close to the jaws, he realised. He could do nothing but stare, his scream choked in his throat, as the creature's eyes rolled back into its head, the gaping oblivion of its mouth looming before him.

'DROP HIM!'

The scream was distant in Lenk's ears, as were the cries that followed: shrieks of horror, open-mouthed pleas for someone not to be heroic.

Someone, a man whose name Lenk had never known, burst from the press of flesh like a two-legged horse, a long fishing pike clenched in his skinny hands. His roar was more for his own sake than the monstrosity's, trying to convince himself of his own bravery through sheer volume.

'With me, boys,' he howled, 'we need no heathen adventurers to save us!'

Lenk fell from the monster's grip, suddenly seized by hands about his shoulders as soon as he hit the ground. He glanced up, noting the glint of green eyes and gold hair through his still-swimming vision. A smile tried futilely to worm itself onto his face.

'Kataria,' he groaned.

'Shut up,' she snarled back as she pulled him into the relative safety of the crowd.

His throat aching, he had little choice but to obey. He looked back towards the creature and saw the sailor standing before it, unflinching, unmoving, as he drove the pike through the wisp of flesh that served as the creature's belly. There was the sound of flesh tearing, sinew splitting as the metal head came bursting through the creature's back.

Gariath seized the momentary distraction, reaching up to grab the creature's ankle. With a snarl, he threw the massive webbed foot up and leapt from his half-finished coffin. Splinters jutted from his flesh, weeping gouts pooling at his feet. If he was in agony, he did not show it.

The creature did not fall, but swayed. It did not shriek, but hummed contemplatively. It did not look at the man with scorn, but with nothingness, a strange sort of curiosity that was something between annoyance and sheer befuddlement.

'A mistake.' it uttered. 'Your rage at your uncaring Gods drives you to strike at your saviour. Do you repent?'

The man staggered backwards, lips mouthing a wordless prayer.

'Then let salvation be done,' the creature said.

What composure it had lost was regained in an instant as it rose tall and erect to glance at the pike's shaft jutting from its belly. With no sound but that of its own flesh being mangled, the creature wrapped a claw about the handle and tore it free, sending meaty black blobs plopping to the deck.

'And thus is my part written. I am here to make wide your error, your false hope.'

There was a sucking sound, as of a foot being pulled from mud, and the creature's gaping wound began to quiver. Slowly, the flesh groaned, reaching out with frayed edges to seal itself in a grotesque slurp of sinew.

'What the …' The sailor was breathless, taking another step backwards. 'What … what in the name of Zamanthras *are* you?'

Like a black, rubbery tentacle, the creature's arm shot out to seize the sailor about his head, claws sinking into his cranium as it held the sailor aloft. The man shrieked, kicking about madly, clawing at the creature's webbed hand, writhing in its unquivering grip.

'I am,' it gurgled ominously, 'mercy.'

The sailor's screams died as the beast's claws twitched. With agonising slowness, cloudy, viscous ooze dripped from trembling fingers. The crowd took up their fellow's screams as the slime continued to pour from the creature's hand, coating his head and face to his shoulders. Like a rabbit caught in a trap, the kicking of the sailor's legs slowly died, his thrashing silencing.

In moments, a hunk of breathless meat dangled from the creature's grip, like a condemned prisoner from the gallows, wearing a mask of viscous sludge. The echo of his corpse hitting the deck carried for an eternity.

'A better place, a better dream, free of your uncaring Gods. This is Ulbeccctonth's gift to you.' Its voice was a whisper, could almost have sounded tender if not for the boiling bile in its throat. 'Sleep now ... and dream of blue.'

Even the murmur of the waves had fallen silent, the sea losing its frothy voice as it bore witness to the horrors occurring upon its surface. All present on the ship shared its sentiment, every man breathless, every woman speechless, not so much as a gull to break the choking quiescence. None present dared even a frightened sob, none heard a single sound.

None save Lenk. His eyes were locked on the man's corpse, this sailor he had never met, whose name he had never known, whose death would never be explained to his widow's satisfaction. His eyes were fixed, his ears were full.

'*Needless. Wasteful. Would still be alive if you had killed.*'

'He's dead,' Lenk uttered.

'*Because of you.*'

'Shut up, Lenk,' Kataria urged, squeezing his shoulder. 'It's going to hear—'

Her voice died as two empty eyes rose up. It had heard.

'Curious,' the creature gurgled, as if suddenly aware of the presence of the crew and adventurers, 'what strange vermin swim upon the seas.'

The answer it was offered was subtle, barely more than a whisper. In the wake of sound, however, it began to carry, it began to swell like the waves that had fallen impotent. For the first time in the horrific eternity that began when the creature had risen, eyes managed to blink as they tore themselves away to spy out the source of the new sound that filled their ears.

They parted before Miron like human waves, allowing the priest to stride between them with noiseless steps. The wind rose in his wake, causing his robes to whip about him, as if to silence his quickly growing voice. He spoke louder in response, his chant a series of prayers wrought from words too pure for any present to understand. He raised his hand to the monstrosity, his faith challenging nature and shadow with the gesture.

'No.' The creature's voice was breathless, like a mewling kitten. Its eyes grew wider as it stared at Miron as its victims had stared at it. 'Cease your pitiless wails! Silence your mourning, vermin! I have no ears for it!'

Miron was not silent.

The chorus of feathered creatures was the first to scream. They erupted in a cacophony of noise and flapping feathers, leaping, tumbling, tearing from their perches upon railings and rigging. The sky was painted white, men falling to the deck as great white curtains of ripping, frenzied feathers fell over the ship.

Miron was heedless.

Every breath the priest took seemed to cause him to grow. His presence grew brighter, the whites of his robes suddenly blinding, the fall of his feet causing the deck to quake. His chant became thunder, every word a bolt of lightning, every syllable a crackle of purpose. None dared to stop him, to pull him back as he drew closer to the monstrosity. They fell away, as terrified of him as they had been of the creature.

The creature's jaws tore open as it let out a terrible, unearthly howl that carried the sounds of a thousand drowned voices. Miron did not relent, his chant rising in volume to match the monster's scream as he continued to advance towards the abomination. The creature's claws clutched its skull as it backpedalled on trembling legs, shrieking in agony as it shook its head about angrily. The priest continued forth, his chant a bellowing chorus of alien phrases, his face a mask of wrath as he drew closer, his symbol raised like a shield, his voice a weapon.

Driven to the wind, the chorus disappeared from the ship, becoming clouds as they swiftly disappeared into the blue upon shrieks of terror and agony.

The foul beast itself let out one last, agonised howl and turned, breaking into an ungainly sprint as it loped towards the railing. With one immense leap, it sailed over the edge of the ship and fell into the waters below with a colossal splash.

The waves settled and Miron's chant slowly died as he lowered his hand, his twisted face returning to normal. He took a deep breath and let out a great exhalation, his body shrinking considerably as he released all his air in one great gasp. None dared speak in his presence as he stared out over the waves, his eyes locked upon the unseen creature as it fled beneath the waters.

Men dropped their weapons and their jaws, their eyes agog and their murmurs breathless. Dreadaeleon wore a look of amazement, while Gariath's face was carved into an expression of suspicious concern. Kataria pulled her silver-haired companion to his feet, staring out over the railing with wide eyes. Denaos looked towards Asper for an explanation, but she had none to offer, her eyes locked upon Miron in awed disbelief. From the crow's nest, Quillian gazed out at the waters, hardly believing that the beast was truly gone, believing even less easily the way it had departed.

Sole amongst them, Lenk took a step forwards, his footsteps echoing across the waves. Miron remained unmoving, unchallenging of his employee's approach, unspeaking as Lenk cleared his throat behind him.

'It's gone now, is it?' Lenk whispered. 'The danger's passed?'

'Danger?' Miron cast a smile out from beneath his cowl. 'I suspect you'll soon learn the reason that word was invented.'

Seven

LAST RITES

'On three, right?' Sebast grunted.

Lenk nodded.

'Right, then ... one ... two ...'

They lifted the last of the bodies. The two men had no breath to spare for heaving or grunting as they upended the dead pirate over the railing, sending him tumbling into the eager waters. Lenk grimaced, observing with macabre fascination as the headless man plunged stiffly into the brackish depths.

The sea resembled a floating graveyard, corpses of pirates bobbing at the surface like fleshy lures, their lifeless faces staring up at the darkening skies before they slowly sank in a hiss of froth. Lenk watched the dark, slender shapes of fish gliding between the descending corpses, nibbling, tasting before casually sliding over to the next body. Bigger, blacker fish would join the feast, he had been told, once they caught the scent of blood. By morning, not a scrap of flesh would be left to remember the dead.

A strange thing, the sea, Lenk mused grimly. Hours ago, the men bobbing in the water had been ferocious foes and savage opponents. Now, as they sank in a cloud of swirling dark, they were simply sustenance for creatures that knew or cared nothing for them or their exploits. In the end, for all their bravery, all their savagery, they were nothing but food.

'That's the last of them.' The ship's first mate sighed, dusting off his hands and noting unhappily that such a gesture did nothing to remove the bloodstains. 'Rashodd has been taken below, along with our own boys.'

Lenk nodded. Rashodd had been the only one left alive. What remained of his crew had been swiftly executed and tossed overboard, leaving nothing behind but their captured black ship, a lingering stench and a bloody tarp. Sebast looked to it as his men began to roll it up.

'Once we get some mops up here,' he said, 'you'll never be able to tell we all nearly died on this ship.' His laughter was stale and bereft of any humour. 'Ah, I suspect after I say that a few hundred more times, I'll start believing it, aye?' Quietly, the sailor shoved his hands into his pockets and began to stalk towards the companionway. 'Decent of you to help dispose of the dead, Mister Lenk. I've got letters to write.'

'Letters?'

'To wives … widows, anyway. Orphans, too. Unpleasant business. I wouldn't ask you to help with those.'

Lenk remained silent; it would be an odd thing for the man to ask of him, but he wasn't about to offer his aid, in any case. Sebast took the hint and stalked off across the deck. It was only when he was a thin, stoop-shouldered outline against the shadows of the companionway that a question occurred to Lenk.

'What was his name?'

'Whose?' Sebast called over his shoulder.

'The young man who died today.' Realising his mistake, he corrected himself. 'The one killed by … by that thing.'

Sebast hesitated, staring at the wood beneath him.

'Moscoff, I think … some young breed out of Cier'Djaal. Signed on to make some silver when we last set out from that port.' He suddenly glanced up, staring out over the evening sky. 'I think his name was Moscoff, anyway. It might have been Mossud … or Suddamoff … Huh, you know, I can't even remember any more.' He smiled at a joke only he understood. 'I can't even remember his face … isn't that funny?'

Lenk did not laugh. Sebast did not, either; even his faint corpse of a smile disappeared as he turned and trudged down the steps into the ship's hold.

It only occurred to Lenk after the first mate had departed that his declaration that their work was done had been incorrect. There were still many corpses upon the *Riptide*'s deck, save that these still moved and drew some mockery of breath.

The *Riptide*'s crew traipsed across the deck without purpose, half-heartedly pushing mops over stains that would never disappear, picking up discarded weapons.

Privately, Lenk yearned to see them crack a joke, curse at each other, even brush up against him with a hearty greeting and a full blast of their armpits' perfume in his face. Instead, they muttered amongst themselves, they stared up at the darkened skies above and made unintelligible remarks about the weather. They did not look at each other.

There was no blaming them, he knew. Their hearts were heavy with the deaths of their comrades, their minds trembling with the strain of comprehending what they had seen. He could hardly wrap his own mind about the events as he stared at the splintered dents in the deck.

The creature should not have been. It should have stayed in drunken ramblings and ghost stories, like any other horror of the deep. But he had seen it. He had seen its dead eyes, heard its drowned voice, felt its leathery flesh. Absently, he reached for a sword that was not present as he recalled the battle; he recalled the creature, unharmed by the blows dealt to him by Gariath, himself and Moscoff.

'Or was it Mossud?'

At once, the sailors paused in their menial duties to look towards Lenk. He saw their own lips soundlessly repeat the name before they turned back to their chores.

The moments after the creature had fled returned to him in a flood of visions. Asper had run to tend to the fallen sailor, kneeling beside his still body, looking over his slime-covered visage. He remembered her grim expression as she looked up, shaking her head.

'*He's dead*,' she had said. '*Drowned.*'

Lenk found his knees suddenly weak, his hand groping for the railing to steady himself. *Drowned on dry land*, he thought, *that doesn't happen.*

Where did such a creature come from? What sort of vengeful God had spawned such a fiend that shrugged off steel and drowned men without water? What sort of gracious God would permit such a creature to exist in the world?

Gods, he had found, were seldom of use besides creative swearing and occasional miracles that never actually occurred. He leaned on the railing and cast his gaze out over the sea like a net, trawling for an answer, some excuse for the horrors he had seen. He knew he would not find one.

Kataria watched from the upper deck, a deep frown on her face as she observed Lenk.

His melancholy unnerved her more than it should, as the battle had unnerved him more than it should have. Bloodshed, she knew, had been a big enough part of both of their lives that pausing and thinking about it afterwards was no longer instinct. That he now stood unmoving, barely breathing, eyes distant, caused her to do the same.

She noted the icy glow in his furrow-browed gaze. His thoughts lingered on the dead, no doubt. He did not mourn; Lenk never mourned. The young sailor's death was not a tragedy in his mind, she knew, but a conundrum, a foul question with no decent answer.

Below deck, she knew others *were* in mourning, asking themselves the same questions in teary curses. Their presence was the reason she stood away from them, atop the upper deck, far removed from the humans.

Her belly muttered hungrily.

That was reason enough to be away from them.

None of them would even be able to comprehend hunger at such a time, all choked on emotion and tears they dared not share, just as she was unable to comprehend their grief. No matter how often she attempted to place herself in their position, to understand the people they had lost, the same thought returned to her.

Dozens of humans had died, of course, but only dozens of humans. The world had thousands to spare. Even those who survived the day would likely last only a few more years after. What made these few so special? What if they had been shicts?

She shook her head; they hadn't been shicts, of course. If they were, she would likely feel otherwise. The fact that they were human, weak, close-minded, prone to death, prevented her from feeling anything else.

Once again, her gaze drifted to Lenk, also human.

The young sailor and Lenk: both human, their differences too trivial to note. Why was it, then, that one made her think of food, while she could not tear her gaze away from the other?

'Are we so fascinating?'

Kataria turned at the voice, regarding her new company quietly. A tall, black-haired woman stood at the railing beside her, polishing a bright red apple on the chest of her toga. Quillian had discarded her armour, her flesh no more yielding than the bronze she had worn. All the skin exposed was as white as the garment she wore, save for one patch of crimson at her flank.

Oaths, Kataria noted. In bright red script, the Serrant wore her profession, the condemnation that kept her from the very priesthood she protected. Her sins, her crimes were scrawled from her armpit to her waist in angry, mocking tattoos.

Kataria averted her eyes; given the nature of the brand, she thought it would likely be considered rude to stare. Such a thing wouldn't normally concern her, but she simply had nothing left in her to fight with.

If Quillian had noticed her stare, she didn't reveal it. Instead, she took a bite of her fruit and, chewing noisily, produced another, offered it to the shict.

Kataria lofted a brow. 'You think enough of me now to offer food?'

'No.' The Serrant didn't bother to swallow before answering. 'But I thought to spare these brave men the indignity of hearing your belly rumble.' She followed the shict's stare to the young man below. 'You two are lovers?'

Kataria's ears flattened against her head and her scowl raked the woman. 'Are you stupid?'

The Serrant shrugged. 'It would have been the first I've heard of such a thing. Given your mutual lack of morality, however, it wouldn't surprise me. I know of no adventurer who looks at her boss that way.'

'Lenk isn't my "boss".'

'I thought briefly about using the term "commander",

but I thought you'd be too unaccustomed to proper terms to recognise it.'

'He's my friend.'

'So you say.'

Quillian's chewing filled the air as she stared out, dispassionate.

'You don't have anyone you worry about?' Kataria asked.

'I forsook the privilege of worry when I earned this.' She ran a hand down her tattooed flank. 'Those who fight alongside a Serrant can take care of themselves. From the way your "friend and leader" fought today, I'd say he can more than take care of himself, too. Even if he was an idiot when he charged that ... thing.'

'He's not an idiot,' Kataria snarled. 'He was trying to protect everyone, you included.'

'The only one I need protecting from,' she narrowed her eyes upon the shict, 'is the one right before me.'

Kataria resisted the urge to retort. There was no need for it now.

'I'm not calling him anything more than a good killer,' Quillian continued with a sneer. 'He and that dragonman charged a creature that, by all rights, shouldn't exist.'

'Lenk is different from other humans. He doesn't think like *you*.'

'While I'm thrilled to see a shict stoop so low as to think so highly of a human, I feel compelled to ask ... how *does* he think?'

Kataria shook her head; she didn't know the answer herself. She knew the man well enough to know his patterns, as she knew those of a wolf or a stag. She knew his likes, dislikes, that he wrote in a journal, that he slept little, that he bathed only in the morning, that he made water only when at least two hundred paces from anyone else. What made him think the way he did, however, was a mystery.

All she knew was what he had told her: something had happened in his youth, his parents were no longer alive. She absently wondered what he was like before.

'So much the better,' Quillian grunted at the shict's silence. 'I'd rather not know how you degenerates think.' She swallowed another piece of fruit. 'Argaol, I hear, has taken Rashodd alive … to use the bounty to cover his losses.'

'And the other pirates?'

'Disposed of, not that you care.'

'The world will make more humans.'

Quillian stared hard at her for a moment before snorting and turning about.

'One moment,' Kataria called to her back. 'That phrase can't be enough to make you irate. Tell me,' she tilted her head curiously, 'why is it you hate me, my people, so much?'

The Serrant paused, her back suddenly stiffening to the degree that Kataria could see every vertebra in her spine fusing together in contained fury. Then, with a great breath, her back relaxed and the woman seemed smaller, diminished. She ran a hand down her muscular flank.

'For the same reason I wear this crimson shame,' she replied stiffly. 'I was there ten years ago.'

'Where?'

'I was at Whitetrees,' she muttered, '*K'tsche Kando*, as you call it.'

Kataria froze twice, once for the name and again for the woman's utterance of the shictish tongue. *Red Snow*. She offered no scorn for the woman any more; she could find none within herself. Her hate was no longer misunderstood, no longer unacceptable. Quillian had stood with the humans at *K'tsche Kando*.

She had good reason to hate.

'Given that, and my inability to do it myself, I dearly wish you had died today.' She set the remaining apple upon the railing. 'Your due, should you get hungry later. Expect nothing else from me.'

She was gone before Kataria even looked at the fruit. She glanced at it for a moment before a smirk crossed her face. Plucking up the fruit, she sprang over the railing and glided nimbly across the timbers. As she neared Lenk, she rubbed the apple against her breeches and gave it a quick toss.

Her giggle was matched by his snarl as the fruit caromed off his skull and went flying into the water below. He whirled, a blue scowl locked upon her, as he rubbed his head.

'You're supposed to catch it,' she offered, smiling sweetly.

'I'm not in the mood,' Lenk muttered angrily.

'To catch fruit? No wonder you got hit in the head.'

'I'm not in the mood for your ... *shictiness*.'

'You never are.'

'And yet,' he sighed, 'here you are.'

'Call me concerned,' she said, smiling. She cocked her head, regarding him for a moment. 'What are you thinking about?'

'The creature,' he replied bluntly, scratching his chin.

'What else?' She rolled her eyes. 'Worrying about things you can't help makes your hair fall out, you know.'

'*Someone* has to worry about it,' Lenk snapped, glaring at her. 'Someone has to find out what it was and what can kill it.'

'And that's your responsibility, is it?'

'I've got a sword.'

'You can put it down.'

'I can also get my head chopped off. What's your point?'

'Do you really need to think about this now? The thing is gone.'

'For the moment.'

His hand slid up unconsciously, reaching for a sword that wasn't there. He had left it below after cleaning it, he recalled. His shoulder reacted to the pressure of his fingers, a sharp pain lancing from his neck to his flank. Asper had plucked the splinters from his flesh, though the wounds still ached beneath their makeshift bandages and salve. Still, such a pain felt minuscule against the sensation that clung to his throat like a collar.

He could still feel the creature's claws, its digits like moist leather wrapped about his neck, tightening as it lifted him from the deck. At the thought, his legs even felt weaker, as though the thing still reached out from wherever it had retreated, seeking to finish what it had begun.

'You're hurt?'

He blinked; Kataria's question sounded odd to him, considering that she had seen him be smashed against the timbers, hoisted up and nearly strangled in a webbed claw. In fact, it sounded rather insulting. His hand clenched involuntarily into a fist. Her jaw loomed before him, suddenly so tempting.

He snorted. 'Yeah.'

His shoulder suddenly seared with a lance of pain as she laid a hand upon it. With a snarl, he dislodged her, whirling about as though she'd just attacked him. She matched the murder in his eyes with a roll of her own, placing both hands upon his shoulders and easing him down against the railing.

'What are you doing?' He strained to hide the pained quaver in his voice.

'Hold still; I'm going to check you over.'

'Asper already did.'

'Clearly she didn't do a good enough job, did she?' She slid back the fabric of his tunic, examining the linen bandage wrapped about his shoulder. 'Not surprising. Human medicine is roughly where shictish medicine would be if we were just crawling out of the muck.' She snickered at that. 'Of course, it's *humans* that crawled out of the muck, not shicts, and that must have been centuries ago, so I'm not even sure what her excuse is.'

'It's fine. She gave me some salve and—'

'Bandages. She thinks she can solve everything with bandages and salve.' Peeling back the white linen, she scratched her chin thoughtfully. 'A bit of fire would close these wounds, I bet.'

Had Lenk actually heard her suggestion, he might have objected. As it was, her voice was distant to him, second to the suddenly pervasive presence of her scent.

His nostrils flared soundlessly, drinking in her aroma as she leaned over him. His first thought was that she smelled rather unlike what he suspected a woman should smell like. There was no cleanness to her, no softness. Her perfume was thick and hard, an ever-present scent of wood, mud and leather under an ingrained layer of sweat and dried blood. As he swirled her stink in his nose, he became aware that he should find the aroma quite foul; it certainly smelled particularly disgusting on his other companions.

So why, he wondered, was he so entranced with smelling her?

'That can't be normal—'

'What?'

'What? Nothing.' He blinked. 'What?'

'Fire.'

'What about it?'

'You could seal your wounds with fire,' she repeated, 'assuming you didn't break down in tears halfway through.'

'Uh-huh …'

Her voice had faded again, ears suddenly less important than nose, nose suddenly far, *far* less important than eyes. The scent of sweat, that key ounce of her muscular perfume, became suddenly more pronounced as he spied a bead of the silver liquid forming just beneath the lobe of a long, notched ear.

She continued to prattle on about fire, shictish superiority and any number of topics related to the two. He could only nod, form half-decipherable grunts as he stared at the small trickle of sweat. It slid down her body like a snake, leaving a path of tiny droplets upon her pale flesh in its wake. It trickled down, trailing along her jawline to caress her neck, slithering over a perfectly pronounced collarbone, roiling over the subtle slope of her modest chest to disappear down her leather half-tunic.

Lenk was no longer even aware of her speaking, no longer aware of the dryness of his unblinking eyes or his slightly open mouth.

After a leather-smothered eternity, the bead reappeared just beneath the hem of her garment, settling at the base of her sternum like a glistening star of hope. It quivered there in whimsical contemplation before sliding down the centre-line of her abdomen. It glided over the shadowed contours of her belly's muscle, across each subtle curve as it journeyed ever downwards, his eyes following, unblinking.

Lenk was forced to swallow hard as it finally reached her navel, dangling off the upper lip like some silvery stalactite, quivering with each shallow breath, each tug of her taut stomach, each breath he unconsciously sent its way, growing heavier. It glistened there, stark against the shadow of the oval-shaped depression before something happened. One of them breathed too hard, flinched too noticeably, and the bead quivered once.

Then fell.

It struck his lap with the quietest of splashes, leaving a dark stain upon the dirt of his trousers. Only when its silver ceased to sparkle did he finally blink, did he finally realise what he had just been staring at for so long.

He stiffened, starting up with an incomprehensible grunt. His head struck something and Kataria echoed his noise, recoiling and rubbing her chin. Eyes bewildered, like a startled beast, she regarded him irately.

'What?' she asked.

'What?' he echoed in a shrill, dry crack.

She blinked. 'I . . . didn't say anything.' Tilting her head, her expression changed to one of concern. 'Did I hit a nerve or something?'

'Yeah.' He shifted uncomfortably in his seat. 'A nerve or something.'

She nodded silently, but offered no response. *At least*, he thought, *no decent response*. She spoke no more, did not so much as twitch as she reclined onto her haunches and stared. He cleared his throat, making a point of looking down at the deck, hoping she would lose interest in him and find something else to do.

He had been hoping that for the year he had known her.

Kataria, however, had never found anything else to do

besides follow him. She had never met anyone else in all their travels worth sparing a second glance for. She had never stopped staring.

He cleared his throat again, more loudly. It was all he could do; if he chased her away, she would stare from afar. If he asked what she found so interesting, she would not answer. If he struck her when his temper got the better of his patience, she would strike back, harder. Then keep staring.

She would always stare. He would always feel her eyes.

'Something's on your mind.'

Kataria's voice sounded off. Distant, but painfully close, hissed directly into his ear through a wall of glass. He gritted his teeth, shook his head, before turning to regard her. She was still staring, eyes flashing with an expression he couldn't understand at that moment.

'What is it?' she asked.

You, he wanted to say, *I'm thinking of you. I'm thinking of your stink and how bad you smell and how I can't stop smelling you. I'm thinking of how you keep staring at me and how I never say anything about it and I don't know why. I'm thinking of you staring at me and why someone's screaming at me inside my head and how someone's screaming inside my head and why it seems odd that I'm not worried about that.*

He wanted to say that.

'Today,' was all he said instead.

She nodded, rising up from her knees. She extended a hand and he took it, hauled himself to his feet with her help.

'It's something to worry about, isn't it?'

Really? Worried? Why would we be worried? A man drowns on dry land at the hands of something that shouldn't exist and we should be worried? *You're a reeking genius.*

'Uh-huh,' he nodded.

'You almost died.'

It occurred to him that he should be more offended by the casual observation of her tone.

'It happens.' It occurred to him that this was not a normal answer for anyone else.

She continued to stare at him. This time, he did not look away, absorbed instead by the reflection in her eyes. Behind him, the sun was setting over the bobbing husk of the *Linkmaster*, painting the sky a muted purple, the colour of a bruise. Above him, the stars were beginning to peer, content to emerge after gulls had been chased away. Before him, the world existed only in her eyes, all the silver, purples and reds drowned in the endless emerald of her stare.

'You're staring,' she noted, the faintest of smiles tugging at the corners of her lips.

'I am.' He straightened up, painfully aware that he was barely any taller than she was. He cleared his throat, puffing his chest out. 'What are you going to do about it?'

'I don't need to do anything about it,' she replied smugly. 'Stare as much as you want. I know I'm something of a marvel to behold to beady little human eyes.'

'My eyes aren't beady.' He resisted the urge to narrow said orbs in irritation.

'They *are* beady. Your hair is stringy, and you're short and wiry.'

'Well, *you* smell.'

'Is that so?' She reached out and gave him a playful shove. 'And what do I smell like?'

'Like Gar—' He hesitated, a better insult coming to mind. He returned the shove with a smug smirk of his own. 'Like Denaos.'

Her own stare grew a little beadier at that. Snarling, she shoved him once more.

'Recant.'

'No.' He shoved her back. '*You* recant.'

'Who's going to make me? Some runt with the hair of an old man?'

'Make *you*? I couldn't make you *bathe*, much less recant.' He leaned forwards, making certain he could see the edge of his sneer in her eyes. 'Besides, what do the words of a savage matter to anyone?'

'They apparently mean enough to force a walking disease to put up some pitiful display of false bravado.' Her sneer matched his to a precise, hideous crinkling of the lip. 'If they don't matter to you, why don't you back away?'

'I don't show my back to savages.'

'Shicts don't squirm at stoop-spined swallows struggling to strut.'

'I don't …' He blinked. 'Wait … what?'

She smiled and shrugged. 'So my father taught me.'

He smiled at that. Beneath him, his foot twitched, brushing against hers, and he became aware of how close they stood. He felt the heat of her breath, felt her ears twitch at every beat of his heart, as though she heard past all the grime caking him, all the flesh surrounding him, heard him function at his core.

'Back away,' he whispered, heedless of the lack of breath in his voice.

Her foot did not move. The wind moaned between them, singing a dirge for the dead that went unappreciated. As if in spite, the tiny breeze cut across them and sent their locks of silver and gold whipping across their faces. Between them, though, the air remained unchanging. He could feel the subtle twist of heat as her chest rose with each breath, the cool shift as another bead of sweat formed upon the pale skin of her neck to begin a snaking path down her belly.

'*You* back away,' she muttered, her voice barely audible over the wind's murmur.

The stars were out, unafraid. The sky was the deepest of bruises now. The clouds had long since slunk into black sails on far distant horizons. Behind Lenk, the sky met the sea and the world moved beneath them.

'Last chance,' he whispered.

Before Lenk, the world was eclipsed in two green suns above a pair of thin, parted lips.

'Make me,' she smiled.

There was a heartbeat shared between them.

'*Stop.*'

His eyes snapped open wide. His neck became cold just as it had begun to shift forwards.

'*Staring at us.*'

He didn't hear the voice; he felt it, crawling across his brain on icicle fingers.

'*She's staring at us.*'

'What's wrong?'

Kataria's ears went upright, sensing something. Could she hear it, he wondered, as it echoed inside his skull?

'Stop,' he repeated.

'*Make her stop.*'

'Stop,' his voice became a whine.

'Stop what?'

'*Make her stop!*'

'Stop!'

'Stop *what?*'

'*MAKE HER STOP!*'

'*STOP STARING AT US!*'

183

The sailors glanced up from their routine, eyes suddenly quite wide as his scream carried across the corpses bobbing on the waves. They stared for only a moment before cringing as he turned around, clutching his head, before returning to their duties and taking a collective step away from his vicinity.

Kataria, however, did not look away.

'What's wrong?' she asked.

'Nothing's wrong. I'm perfectly fine.' The statement sounded less absurd in his head, but his brain was choked by frigid fingers, an echo reverberating off his skull. 'Perfectly fine. Would you stop staring at me?'

She did not.

'You're not fine,' she stated, her eyes boring past his hair and skin as if to peer at whatever rang in his head. 'You just broke down screaming at me for no reason.'

'There's always a reason for me to be screaming,' he growled. 'Especially at you.'

'What's that supposed to mean?' Her gaze narrowed; no longer a probe but rather a weapon to stab him with.

'What do you mean, "What's that supposed to mean?" Isn't it obvious? I was nearly killed today!'

And now I'm hearing voices in my head, he wanted to add, but did not.

'You're nearly killed almost every other day! So are all of us! We're adventurers!'

Insanity isn't common amongst adventurers.

'We're not supposed to nearly be killed by hideous *things* that can't be harmed by steel and drown men on dry land! Moscoff—'

'Mossud.'

'Whatever his name was, he rammed the damn … that … *thing* through with a spear and it didn't even flinch! Gariath

and I threw everything we had at it and it didn't budge! I
…' He stalled, then forced the words out through gritted
teeth. 'I looked into its eyes and I didn't see anything.'

'And that's why you went mad a moment ago?'

I went mad because I'm likely losing my mind.

'And you feel that's inappropriate?' he asked with a
sneer.

'Slightly.' She sighed, her shoulders sinking. 'You meet
one thing you can't kill and this is how you react? Is it so
hard to accept that some things exist that you simply can't
change? I would have thought you were used to it, being
a—'

'Human.' He rolled his eyes. 'Of course. How could I
not be used to such things, being a weak-willed, beady-
eyed human?'

'I wasn't going to say that.'

'But you were thinking it.'

Her eyes were hard and cruel. 'I'm always thinking it.'

'Well, if you think so little of us, why don't you leave
and go frolic in the forest with the other savages?'

'Because I choose not to,' she spat back. Folding her
arms over her chest, she turned her nose upwards. 'Who's
going to make me do otherwise?'

'Me,' Lenk grunted, hefting a hand clenched into a fist,
'and *him*.'

She glanced from his eyes to his fist and back to his
face. They mirrored each other at that moment, jaws set
in stone, eyes narrowed to thin, angry slits, hands that
had once been close to holding each other now rigid with
anger.

'I dare you,' she hissed.

*

Asper tied the bandage off at Mossud's arm. A frown ate her face in a single gulp as she looked over the tightly wrapped corpse upon the table. Skinny as he was, with his arms folded across his chest, legs clenched tightly together, the pure white bandages swaddling him made him look like some manner of cocooned vermin.

She hated bandaging; it was such an undignified way to be preserved. Though, she admitted to herself, it was slightly better than being stuffed in a cask of rum. At least this way, when they were stuffed in salt, they wouldn't shrivel up. He would be preserved until the *Riptide* reached Toha and he could be turned over to proper morguepriests.

Still, that fact hadn't made it any easier when she had wrapped the other men up.

She felt sick as she looked over the bandaged corpses laid out upon the tables of the mess hall. The dusty, stifling air of the hold and the mournful creaking of the ship's hull made it feel like a tomb.

She could still recall laughing with sailors and passengers over breakfast that morning …

Tending to the dead was her least favourite duty as a priestess of Talanas. She was bound to do it, as a servant of the Healer, in addition to performing funerary rites and consoling the grieving. When she had trained in the temple, though, she had tended to the latter while less-squeamish clergy had handled the former.

The crew of the *Riptide* would be dead themselves before they let her console them, however. And Miron, the only other man of faith on board, had vanished shortly after he had driven off the beast.

She sighed to herself and made a sign of benediction over the sailor's corpse; if it had to be done, she thought, it was better that she did it than letting him go unguided into the afterlife.

Quietly, she walked down the hall and noted a red stain appearing at the throat of another bound corpse, tainting the pure white. A frown consumed her; that poor man might have lived if Gariath was able to tell the difference between humans a bit better. She reminded herself to rebind him when she could acquire more bandages from Argaol.

The sound of quill scraping parchment broke the ominous silence. She turned to one of the tables, where Dreadaeleon sat, busily scribbling away. She grimaced at the casualness with which he sat next to the bandaged corpse, as though he were sitting next to an exceptionally quiet scholar in a library.

'Have you finished?' she asked, forcing the thought from her mind.

'Almost,' he replied, hurriedly scribbling the last piece of information. 'Do you know what his faith was?'

'He was a Zamanthran, I believe,' Asper said. 'Sailors, seamen, fishermen … they all are, usually.'

'All right,' he said. He finished with a decisive stab of the quill and held the parchment up to read aloud. '"Roghar 'Rogrog' Allensdon, born Muraskan, served aboard the *Riptide* merchant under Captain S. Argaol, devout follower of Zamanthras."' He frowned a little. '"Slain in combat defending his ship. Sixteen years of age."'

With a sigh, he rolled the parchment up and tied it with coarse thread. He reached over the bandaged corpse and tucked the deathscroll firmly in its crossed hands. His sigh was echoed by Asper as they glanced at the pile of scrolls on the bench next to him. With solemn shakes of the head, they plucked them up and walked about the tables, delivering the deathscrolls to their silent owners.

She hesitated as the last one was deposited in stiff, swaddled arms. Dreadaeleon's listless shuffling echoed in the mess.

'Dread.' The shuffling stopped. 'Thank you for helping me.'

'It's not an issue.' He took another step before pausing again. 'I suppose I was duty-bound, being one of the few literate aboard.'

She smiled at that. 'I just … hope you don't begrudge me anything after what I said to you earlier.'

'I said things just as bad,' he replied. 'We all do. It's not that big a deal.'

She felt him look towards her with familiar eyes: big, dark and glistening like a puppy's. It would have felt reassuring to see him look at her that way, she reasoned, in any other situation. Amongst the library of bandages and scrolls, however, she resisted the urge to return the gesture and waited until she heard the shuffling of his feet once more.

'So, what was it?' he asked suddenly.

'Pardon?'

'The creature,' he said, 'that thing. Was it some unholy demon sent from hell? Or an agent of a wrathful god? What?'

'What makes you think I know?' She scowled at him. 'Is there nothing in any of your books that explains it?'

'I have only one book,' he replied, patting the heavy leather-bound object hanging from his waist, 'and it's filled with other things.' He tucked a scroll into the arms of another corpse. 'Nobody knows what that thing was.' He looked up at her suddenly. 'But the Lord Emissary seems to have a better idea than anyone else.'

'What are you insinuating?' she asked, her eyes narrowing

as she drew herself up. 'Lord Miron would never consort with such abominations.'

'Of course not,' Dreadaeleon said, shaking his head. 'I'm just curious as to what that creature was.' He sighed quizzically. 'It's certainly not something I've ever seen in any bestiary.'

'You're as likely to have an answer as I am,' Asper replied with a shrug. 'I've never heard of anything that can drown a man on dry land, have you?'

'There are spells that can do such things. But if it had been using magic, I would have known.' He paused and thought for a moment. 'I wish that ooze hadn't dried off Moscoff—'

'Mossud.'

'I wish it hadn't dried off his face so easily. I could have studied it.'

The priestess chuckled dryly and he turned to her, raising an eyebrow.

'What's so funny?'

'I shouldn't be laughing, I know. But … you're the only man I know who would face something so horrible and wish he could have been closer to it.' She stifled further inappropriate laughter. 'Denaos has sent no word yet?'

'No,' the wizard replied, shaking his head. 'The captain and he have been down there for hours.' He shrugged. 'Who knows what they're doing to Rashodd?'

'I'm not certain I want to know,' Asper replied, frowning. She cast a glance to the companionway leading to the hold below and shuddered.

'And what do you intend to do about *him*?' Dreadaeleon asked, pointing to the far side of the mess hall.

Asper cringed; she had purposely avoided glancing at that particular section. Swallowing her anxiety, she turned

189

and glanced at the cold, limp corpse of the frogman lying on the table under a sheet, eyes wide open and glazed over as they stared up at the ceiling. She hadn't even ventured near enough to close his eyes, she realised, cursing herself for such disrespect. Still, it was difficult for her even to glance at the corpse. Without the rush of combat, the man's appearance unnerved her greatly.

Anxiety was not a word that Dreadaeleon recognised, however, and she gasped as she saw the wizard take a seat next to the corpse and poke it curiously.

'Dread!' she cried out, hurrying over. She skidded to a halt about halfway, cringing, but forced herself to come alongside the boy. 'Foe or not, have some respect for the dead!'

'Look at this,' the wizard said, ignoring her. He held up the corpse's limp arm and she cringed again. He held the arm a little closer to the light and pointed to the skin. 'His skin is still wet and he's been down here for hours and ... my, my, what's this?'

He didn't have to point it out to her, for Asper saw it as clearly as he did. The boy gently pulled the man's fingers apart, stretching the flaps of skin between the digits.

'Webbed hands,' he said, examining the digits. He dropped the hand and spun in his seat, lifting up the man's leg. 'Look here ... he has them between his toes as well.'

'Fascinating,' Asper replied. 'Do you really have to do this now?'

'And if he has webbed appendages ...' Dreadaeleon trailed off as he inched closer to the frogman's head.

Asper reeled back, cringing as he lifted the corpse's head and pulled back his ear. She nearly retched when she saw the thin red slits hidden behind the earlobe.

'Interesting,' Dreadaeleon remarked, sharing none of her disgust. 'He has ... gills.'

'So ... he really *is* a frogman?'

'It'd be more accurate to call him a fishman, I think.'

'Uh-huh,' Asper replied, intentionally avoiding looking at the mutated man. 'It's ... good that the captain didn't order him tossed overboard. Otherwise you might never have found this out.'

'Why does Argaol want him, anyway?' Dreadaeleon asked, examining the webbed toes again. 'Weren't the others tossed overboard after they were executed?'

'I suppose he believes the frogmen have some connection to the creatu—'

Asper stopped short, staring in abject horror as Dreadaeleon dropped the man's leg and began to pull the sheet covering him down. Able to stand no more, she stamped her foot and reached for his hands.

'Even if he *is* a loathsome creature, I won't let you desecrate him like—'

'Do you have any tattoos under your shirt?' he interrupted.

'What?' Asper asked, pulling back with a shocked expression on her face.

'You know, like on your belly or chest?'

'I most certainly do *not!*'

'Really?' Dreadaeleon asked. With one swift jerk, he pulled the sheet from the corpse. Asper reeled back at the sight as Dreadaeleon leaned forwards to get a closer look. 'Our friend here has an interesting one ...'

Emblazoned on the man's chest in ink the colour of fresh blood was a symbol of a pair of skeletal shark jaws, gaping wide and lined with hundreds of sharp teeth. The other frogmen had worn the symbol on their biceps, she recalled. Did they all have them on their chests, too?

'What ... do you think they mean?' At his curious glance, she cleared her throat and continued. 'In your opinion, that is?'

'I'm at a loss. Symbols are really more the dominion of priests, aren't they?'

'Well, maybe I—' She hesitated, suddenly aware of the edge in his voice.

Or rather, she noted, *the lack of an edge. He's doing it again, trying to appear nonchalant and enquiring while secretly smugging it up in his own head.* She felt a familiar ire creep behind her eyes, her hand clench involuntarily. *Not this time, runt.*

'What do you mean by that?' she finished tersely.

'I ... didn't mean anything by it.'

'You leapt straight to linking those symbols to some manner of priesthood. Religious orders are hardly the only organisations to use sigils, you know. What about thieves? Assassins? Merchants? Argaol himself carries his own sigil.'

'Not tattooed on his flesh.' He held up his hands before she could retort. 'Listen, I've neither the time nor inclination for a debate right this moment. I'm simply posing theories regarding a mystery that no one else seems to be thinking about besides you and me.'

Her jaw unclenched so slowly and forcefully that it might have made the sound of groaning metal. She inhaled sharply, holding her breath as her thoughts began to melt into a fine, guilty stew in her head. She had overreacted, of course she knew that now; not everything he posited was a challenge to her faith, nor was he intentionally trying to be snide.

The fact that he was unintentionally quite skilled at it,

she chose to ignore. For now, she forced her irritation down and her smile up, offering an unspoken truce.

'Though, you have to admit,' he scratched his chin, perhaps hoping a beard would magically grow to make the gesture more dramatic, 'it is a little odd.'

'What is?' She felt her jaw set again.

'That the only one who seems to know anything isn't answering any questions *and* is also a priest.'

It unclenched in a creaking snarl. 'Why, you smarmy little—'

Before she could finish expressing her righteous indignation, before he could offer any stammering excuses, a noise filtered through the timbers of the mess. Growing closer with each breath, the sound of cursing, bodies hitting the wood, heavy-handed slaps and more than a little squealing filled the air.

Both pairs of eyes turned towards the companionway as a tangle of flesh, gold and silver came tumbling out of the shadows. They tussled for a moment, all frothing saliva, bared teeth, reddened skin and sheens of sweat, before settling into a mess of limbs. Gloved hands gripped arms, ankles, tufts of hair. Feet were planted in bellies, shins, dangerously close to groins. Their teeth were glistening, their recent use testified by the red marks on each other's skin.

It was a horror to behold, Asper thought, but she had long since spent all her lectures on companionship and scolds for infighting. At this particular tangle, she could only blink once and sigh.

'What's the matter?'

'Ask this savage,' Lenk growled. 'She bit me.'

'This round-ear bit me first!' Kataria snapped back.

'At least *I* don't have teeth like a dog's!' Lenk spat.

'And that's only his most recent crime,' Kataria continued, 'before which came insanity, excessive cursing and
oversensitivity!'

'Lies!' he all but roared. With a shove, he pulled free
from her, clambering to his feet as she did. 'It hardly concerns anyone else, anyway. This is between me and her.'

'Have you no respect for the dead?' Asper protested,
taking a wary step to intervene. 'These men, who fought
and died alongside you, are resting here and *you* have to
bring another squabble into their midst for no reason?'

'There's plenty of reason,' Lenk snarled. 'These *men* are
dead because of us.'

'Why? Because you weren't able to kill the thing that
killed them?' Kataria turned her nose up haughtily. 'Accept
your weakness and move on. There was nothing you could
have done.'

'I could have grabbed the book!'

'You could have had your head smashed in and lost the
book anyway. Then we'd be short a book *and* you.'

'And what do you care about that? What is it you always
say?' He pulled his ears upwards in mockery of hers, his
voice becoming a shrill imitation. '"The world can make
more humans." I'd have thought one more of us dying
would make you happy.'

'In hindsight, it would have, since I wouldn't have to
suffer your voice *now*!' Her ears flattened against the side
of her head in a menacing gesture. 'And don't even think
to try to imitate me, even if you've got the height for it.'

It occurred to Asper at that moment, regarding them so
curiously, that this was no ordinary fight. They had squab-
bled before, as had all in their company, but never with
such fervour. There was something animalistic between
them, a frothing, snarling fury they had not deigned to

194

show each other, or anyone else, before now. For that reason, she thought it wise to keep her distance.

Dreadaeleon, however, had never understood the difference between intellect and wisdom.

'You're disturbing everyone here, you know,' he said, reaching out to place a hand on Lenk's shoulder. 'If you'd just—'

'Back *AWAY*.'

Lenk seized the boy's frail hand roughly, nearly crushing it with his fury-fuelled grip. He shoved Dreadaeleon off effortlessly, propelling his scrawny mass across the floor as though he were a stick wrapped in a dirty coat. And like a dirty coat, he twisted, stumbling across the floor, making a brief cry of surprise that was silenced the moment he came to a sudden halt.

Face-first against Asper's robe-swaddled bosom.

He staggered back as though he had been punched in twelve places at the same time, sweat suddenly forming on his face in streaming sheets, hands held up as though he was facing some murderous wild beast. Given the red-faced, gaping-mouthed, narrow-eyed incredulous expression on the priestess's face, he wagered it would be a reasonable reaction.

'I-I'm truly sorry,' he stammered, 'but you must acknowledge that this was hardly my fault, you see—'

Her slap cut through the air deftly, stinging him across the cheek and sending a spray of anxious sweat into the air. He recoiled, touching the redder mark upon an already reddened face and regarded her with a shocked expression.

'What'd you do that for? I was just telling you it was an accident!'

'Accident or no, a lady is always entitled to deliver a slap for purposes of preserving her dignity.' She flicked beads of moisture off her fingers. 'Rules of etiquette.'

His finger was up and levelled at her in a single breath, an incomprehensible word shouted in another. A small spark of electricity danced down his arm and leapt from the tip, striking the priestess squarely in the chest. She trembled, letting out a shriek as it spread and ran the length of her body sending her hair on its ends and bathing her in the aroma of undercooked pork.

'What was *that* for?' she hissed through chattering teeth.

'Spite,' he replied, flicking sparks off his fingers.

'How utterly typical,' she growled, sweeping a scornful gaze across her companions. 'You people *feed* off each other. When one of you acts like a vagrant, you all do.'

'Us *people*?' Lenk sneered. 'You remember you're with us, don't you?'

'Yeah,' Kataria grunted, 'at least we involved you in the fighting. I don't see Miron out here even talking to you, much less getting ready to jab your eyeballs out.'

'Why, you pointy-eared little—'

The fight died suddenly as the lanterns swayed at a sudden impact. The companions froze, taking a collective hard swallow as they noted a large shadow looming out from the companionway leading to the ship's hold. All looked up to see Gariath standing in the entry, surveying them through eyes glittering with excitement.

'What's going on here?' he asked as softly as he could, hardly enough to prevent them from taking a collective step backwards.

'Nothing's going on,' Lenk said, forcing a weak smile onto his face.

'It doesn't look like nothing to me,' the dragonman

growled, taking a step forwards. 'It looks like you're all trying to kill each other.'

He paused, flashing his teeth in a morbid smile.

'Without me.'

Eight

ENTICEMENT

'What you don't seem to understand is that this is mere courtesy.' Argaol's voice, intended to be a growl, resigned to being a sigh, came out as something of a phlegmless cough. 'Your cooperation here is the difference between a nice comfortable cell in Toha and joining your men in the deep.'

Rashodd looked up from the chair, weary as he had been when the interrogation had begun, but even less impressed with the dark-skinned captain. With his helmet removed, he was all scars and smirks above his long, grey beard. He raised a hand accompanied by the clink of manacles, covering a long, reeking yawn in a gesture one-part manners and two-parts insult. Making a point of smacking his lips, he looked the captain evenly in the eye, as tall sitting as Argaol was standing.

'I can appreciate your desire for information, dear sir,' he spoke curtly, 'as much as I can appreciate your lack of tact and patience. Even so, I must insist that you accept the fact that I simply don't know anything.' His lips curled in an attempt to be coy. 'I should beg your leave to sleep on it, perhaps with a visit from one of your more feminine passengers. It's always been something of a dream of mine to learn what it's like to sleep with a shict.'

Denaos had to stifle an admiring chuckle at that. He'd

often wondered the same thing, hoping to compare it to his beddings with more civilised ladies. *Never did try to talk Kat into it, though*, he admitted to himself, *likely because she'd gnaw my gents off*. Content with that thought, he leaned against the far wall of the captain's cabin-turned-interrogation room, taking comfort in the shadows.

It was all very dramatic, he had to admit: the fineries pushed aside or covered up, a single oil lamp hanging directly over the chair that the Cragsman was seated in. However, it was still Argaol's chair, still far too comfortable for any prisoner to confess in. He had considered bringing this to the captain's attention. Still, he reasoned, it would seem presumptuous to accuse the fellow of not knowing a business he clearly did not know.

With that, he simply plucked a dagger from his belt and began to trim the various stains out from under his nails.

'Regardless, good sir,' Rashodd said, 'don't feign interest in my well-being. I know you full-well plan to recoup your losses with the bounty my head will deliver.'

'However meagre it might be,' Argaol said with a sneer. 'Your ship is damaged, Rashodd. We found scarcely any-thing of value aboard. Even the companion boat had been taken.' He allowed himself a smirk. 'It seems your men jumped ship, long before we could board. Small faith in your cause, had they?'

Not bad, Denaos noted. A cheap shot at a man's esteem wasn't always the best way to get someone to talk, but it might work in this case. Rashodd seemed like the kind of man who wouldn't take kindly to being called small.

'Sensible of them,' the Cragsman conceded with a nod. 'At the very least, they've saved me the hardship of paying for their funerary expenses.' He turned a scrutinising eye upon Argaol. 'You're still a man in good standing with the guilds, yes? You *do* plan to extend that particular courtesy to the families of your slain men, don't you, Captain? I'd offer to chip in, but as you said, not much aboard the *Linkmaster* worth taking, is there?'

The tall man bit back a wince at that. *The captain will be groping his stones tonight, doubtless.*

'I will be, in fact,' Argaol snarled, leaning in close to the prisoner. 'I'll pay for the funerals of those good men who were slain,' he thrust a finger at the Cragsman as though it were a weapon, 'by *your* monsters. Have you no shame, Rashodd? Summoning those ... those *things* to fight for you? Denying my men even the dignity of a death by their own race?'

Weak. Denaos shook his head. Rashodd's response confirmed his judgement.

'In all fairness, sir, *you* threw *your* monster,' he caught a glimpse of Denaos in the doorway and coughed, 'pardon, *monsters* at *my* men first. My ... associates simply had associates of their own. I can hardly be held responsible for their actions.'

'And you still won't tell me anything about them, even while they leave you here to die!'

Rashodd shrugged. 'Friendships are a fickle and mischievous garden, requiring constant tending, with their own share of weeds.'

'I ...' Argaol flinched, his face screwing up. 'What?'

'I'd hardly expect you to understand, kind Captain. After all, most of your precious flowers are dead and trampled into the earth after today, aren't they?'

It was over. Without fanfare or gloating, the verbal spar had ended. Argaol's expression, wide-eyed, slack-jawed, hurt, lasted for only a moment before he turned around to hide the clench of his teeth upon his bottom lip. Rashodd watched him stalk away without contempt or smugness. All he could spare for Argaol was a yawn.

Denaos's own stare lingered upon the pirate for a moment before he felt Argaol's presence next to him. The captain leaned an arm against the wall, regarding the rogue with a tight-lipped, hard-eyed glower.

'Well?' he grunted.

'What?'

'Were you planning on doing anything besides lurking there?'

The tall man rubbed the edge of his blade against his chin contemplatively. 'Well, I was planning on paying a visit later to that one spice merchant you've got chartered here. You know the one, right? Slim little dark-haired thing from Cier'Djaal. She called me a swine before, but I wager she'll change her tune once she realises what I—'

'Yeah, you're adorable.'

'That's a word you'd use to describe something in pigtails and frills. I'm really more of a man possessed of immense gravitas.' He offered the captain a broad smile fit for eating stool. Seeing no reaction, he sighed. 'What is it you expect me to do, anyway?'

'Get him to do what I've been trying to make him do all night,' Argaol growled. 'My boys are up there, terrified that some horror is going to return and do to them what it did to Mossud.'

'Moscoff,' Denaos corrected.

'*Mossud*. I hired the damn boy.' He sighed, rubbing his eyes. 'What this Cragsfilth knows may be what I need to keep my boys safe, and he's not talking.'

'So throw him in the brig. Give him a few days without food or water and he'll tell you.'

'This is a merchantman, you twit. We don't have a brig.

In a few days, we could all be stacked in neat little heaps, ready to be eaten by whatever that thing was.'

'Well, have you tried asking Gariath to help you? He's not bad at this sort of thing.'

'Your monster isn't paying me any mind.'

'Ah, ah.' Denaos winced. 'Keep your voice down. For a fellow with no ears, that reptile hears exceptionally well.'

'*Enough.*' Argaol's voice became as hard as his eyes. He took a menacing step forwards. 'I myself saw you gut two people like pigs on deck today, and we found more of your work down in the hold.'

The rogue shifted, appearing almost uncomfortable if not for the understated smile playing across his lips. It was impossible for Argaol not to notice the aversion of his eyes, however.

'I managed to kill ... what, four? Compared to Kataria, Lenk and Gariath, that's hardly—'

'And your fellow adventurers all say you're the man to talk to about things like this.' Argaol adjusted his stare to meet the rogue's eyes. 'They say you've crawled out of more dark places than they've even heard of. Were they mistaken?'

Denaos's grin faded, his face going blank. With the quietest of sounds, he slid his dagger back into its sheath. Eyes unblinking, he stared at the hilt.

'They said that, did they?' he whispered, voice barely louder than a kitten's.

Argaol's nod was hesitant, but firm. The rogue's voice rang hollow in his ears, bereft of all previous bravado, bereft of any potential scorn. In his voice, as in his eyes and face, there was nothing.

'I suppose they must be right, then.'

'Good,' the captain replied. 'Be sure to get everything

you can out of him. Question him more than once if you need to. Pirates lie. We need to know about that thing and every—'

'Leave.'

'What?'

'Leave me, please. I don't want an audience.' He stared blankly at the shorter man, neck craning stiffly. 'And don't check up on me. This won't take long.'

'What are you going to do?' Argaol asked. Feeling the quaver echo through his throat, he coughed, straightening up in a show of authority. 'It's my ship, my cabin, I have a right to know.'

'Go.' Denaos slid past the captain, striding towards Rashodd. He did not look back over his shoulder.

Rashodd glanced up with a start at the sound of a chair sliding. He blinked blearily, trying to take into account the shape sitting before him. He regarded the tall man curiously for a moment, studying the absence of any expression upon his face, the dark eyes free of any malice or cruelty. A silence hung between them, the Cragsman angling his face to scrutinise this newcomer.

'And what's this?' he mused aloud. 'Perchance, some more stimulating conversation?' He leaned forwards, expressing a smile he undoubtedly hoped would be instigative. 'And, pray, what cabin boy union did the good captain drag you out of?'

Denaos said nothing, his face blank, lips thin and tight.

'Somewhere up north, aye? I say *aye*?' Rashodd forced the word through his teeth, thick with a feigned accent. 'Around Saine?' He settled back into his seat, a satisfied smirk on his face. 'Large men come from Saine, tall men. The Crags are right off the coast. We were once part of the kingdoms. I couldn't truly expect a man of your particular breeding to know such a thing, though.'

Denaos's only response was a delicate shift of his hand as he gingerly took the pirate's manacled appendage in his own and held it daintily in his palm, surveying it as though he were reading a screed of hairy pink poetry.

'Ah.' Rashodd's eyes went wide with feigned surprise. 'Mute, I see. Poor chap.' He glanced over the tall man's head towards the dusky Argaol as the captain shifted closer to the door. 'And simple, I suppose, by the way he fondles me. Tell me, then, Captain, is this the enticement you've sent me? I'd rather prefer the shict, if she's still about.'

Rashodd watched the captain bite back a retort, resigning himself to a purse of lips as the door of his cabin creaked open. Quietly, the man slipped out, the door closing behind him with an agonising groan. Argaol's departure, the lack of fuss and bravado, drew a brief cock of Rashodd's brow, his eyes so intent on the last dusky fingers vanishing behind the door that he scarcely noticed the glimmer of steel at the tall man's hip.

The door squeaked shut and, with a click of its hinges, there was the sound of a raspy murmur, the odour of copper-baked meat and a delicate plop upon the wooden floor.

Rashodd had time to blink three times, noting first the bloodied dagger in the man's hand, second the twitching pink nub upon the floor, and third the red blossom that used to be his thumb. By the time he opened his mouth to scream, a leather hand was clasped over his dry lips, a pair of empty dark eyes staring dully into his own over the top of black fingers.

'Shh,' Denaos whispered. 'No sound.' He set the whetted weapon aside delicately, as though it were a flower, and reached down to scoop up the thumb. He held it before the captain. 'This is mine now. It will remind me of our time together tonight.'

Slowly, he turned it over in his fingers, eyes glancing at every pore, every ridge, every glistening follicle of hair and every clean, quivering rent.

'We're going to talk,' he continued, holding the finger just a hair's width from his lips, 'quietly. You're going to tell me what happened today. Argaol asked nicely. He'd like to know.'

Rashodd dislodged his leather gag with a jerk of his head. He clenched his teeth together as he clenched his bleeding stump. Though tears began to well inside his eyes, he forced them to go harder, firmer, determined to show nothing.

'And what is it to you, wretch?' he snarled through his beard. 'Hm? What makes you think I know anything more than what I said? I don't know anything about that creature.'

'Liar.'

His voice was as brief and terse as the flick of his weapon. The dagger was in his hand and freshly glistening just as another fleshy digit went tumbling to the floor. It came swiftly, so suddenly that Rashodd hadn't even noticed it until the man was scooping it up. He opened his lips to spew a torrent of agony-tinged curses, but found the hand at his lips again, moisture dripping from his nose onto the leathery fingers.

'I said no noise,' Denaos hissed through his teeth, 'it upsets me.' Quietly, he set the digit beside the other. 'You're lying to me, Rashodd. I don't like it.' He shook his head. 'And I don't like what you did today, either. You threatened my livelihood, my career.' He blinked, and, as an afterthought, added, 'My associates.'

'Zamanthras damn you for the heathen you are.' What Rashodd intended to be a fearsome snarl came out as a trembling whimper. 'You'll attack an ignorant, unarmed man for money alone. Mercenary scum.'

'Adventurer,' the tall man corrected.

'Coward is what you are, attacking any man in shackles, preying on those with their backs turned and the helpless. How many people have you gutted before my lads today, hm? How many more unarmed and ignorant did you cut down?'

Denaos did not blink. 'Many.'

'And now you seek to add Rashodd to your tally?' He lurched forwards, something rising up in his gullet, but he bit it back. Clutching his bleeding stumps, alternating between each, he rose up as much as he could in his chair. 'All for naught, heathen.'

'Tell me what you know,' Denaos whispered calmly, rolling one of the fleshy digits between his fingers, 'and I'll give one back.'

'I know only that the frogmen sought to make a deal with us,' he replied, voice quavering. 'They put their services at my disposal, in exchange for attacking a single ship.'

'This ship.'

'This ship. I don't know why.'

'Liar.'

'It's the truth!' Rashodd lunged backwards, pulling his mutilated hands away as the rogue's dagger twitched. 'They offered no reason beyond the need to attack this ship!' He stamped his feet on the floor. '*This* ship! They told me nothing else! I was bound to honour our agreement!'

'They were after a tome,' Denaos replied evenly. 'A book.

I heard them say it. You saw them take it.' He looked up, staring hard. 'You asked for Evenhands, you asked for the priest.' His face twitched. 'Lies upset me.'

'*They* wanted the priest! *THEY*, the frogmen! Not my lads!' He felt the first scrapes of metal against the veins on the back of his hands. 'I thought they simply wanted to ransom him, in which case it'd be in our best interests to keep him safe, wouldn't it?' If he could have seen himself in the rogue's steel, he would have noted the hysterical smile, the wide eyes, the need to appease that he had often observed in his own victims. '*Wouldn't it?*'

'What of the creature?'

'I ... I was as shocked to see it as anyone! You must believe me!'

'The frogmen summoned it.'

'I didn't know! They never told me! They told me nothing but to attack this ship!' He gasped, his voice slurring with coppery saliva filling his mouth. His hands were cold as more of his life wept out from the stumps between them. 'That's the truth! I'm naught but a pawn in whatever game they were planning. I consorted with no spawn of hell. Rashodd is no blasphemer.'

Denaos's head swayed slightly, regarding the man. He did not blink, his lips did not move and he gave no indication that he was hearing anything the pirate said. Slowly, he leaned forwards and squinted, as though regarding Rashodd from miles away. Then his eyes widened suddenly, a flicker of indiscernible emotion, fear, shame, perhaps.

'You're lying again. Argaol said you would.'

'I am no—'

'Hush.'

The blow came more slowly this time; no quick, surgical strike, but an angry, heavy hack. The blade bit halfway through Rashodd's remaining thumb, inciting a scream that went unheard behind Denaos's hand. He whimpered, squealed as the digit hung lazily from the joint before the rogue reached down, seized it between his own thumb and forefinger, and twisted.

Rashodd felt his entire insides jerk with the pain, the shock shifting organs about within him. Bile rose behind his teeth, tasting of metallic acid. He muttered something desperately behind his gag and Denaos pressed his hand harder, narrowed his eyes in response.

'Swallow it.'

He did so, with a choked protest, and lurched as the vile stuff slid back down his gullet. Denaos took his hand away and regarded the pirate carefully, offering no question, no threat beyond a hollow stare. There was no malice dwelling there, no accusation or anger as he had enjoyed with Argaol.

It was the sheer lack of anything in the man's face that prompted Rashodd to pray.

'Zamanthras help me,' the pirate whimpered, 'believe me, I had nothing to do with the creature. Why would I defend those traitors this long?'

'Zamanthras does not exist here.' Denaos shook his head. 'Tonight, the only people in this cabin are you,' he pointed with the man's severed thumb, 'me,' he pressed it against his chest, 'and Silf.'

'S-Silf?'

'"Salvation in secrets,"' the rogue recited, '"forgiveness in whispers, absolution in quiescence."' He paused. 'Silf.'

'The Shadow.' Rashodd uttered the name without reverence or fear for the God. Such things were reserved for the man before him. Quietly, he tucked his hands into his armpits, shivering. 'A deity ... a God for thieves ... and ...' he paused to swallow, 'murderers.'

'Murderers,' Denaos repeated, hollow. A smile, a wistful tug of the lips, creased his face for but a moment. 'Isn't that what we all are?'

'It's one thing to kill in battle, sir, it's another entirely to—'

'It is.' The rogue nodded quietly, setting his dagger aside. 'Perhaps that's how Silf found His flock. Murderers require absolution, don't they?' His hand went inside his vest and came out with another knife, shorter, thicker, sawtoothed. 'Or was He born to serve that need?'

'You can't be serious.' Rashodd gasped at the blade. 'I've told you everything!'

'You might be lying.' Denaos shook his head. 'Silf has seven daughters. This is the second. We'll meet more of them if you don't speak.'

'They ... they wanted the priest for no good deed, I knew.' Rashodd spoke with such squeaking swiftness it would have shamed him under other circumstances. 'They spoke of mothers, queens and names of a Goddess no good Zamanthran has ever heard!' His lips quivered. 'Ulbecetonth ... I am loath to repeat her name, even now. Ulbecetonth is who they worship, who they stole the book for! That's all I know, I swear!'

Denaos paused, the dagger rigid in his hand. It appeared almost disappointed at being stayed, its sawtoothed grin pulling into a curving frown. Quietly, the tall man looked down, observing his reflection in the metal.

Rashodd allowed himself a brief moment of breath, free of saliva or bile. He was suddenly so cold, feeling as though all his warmth was dripping out of him, caking the insides of his arms. He needed something, a shirt, a blanket, anything to stem the loss of warmth coming out of him. Slowly, as his tormentor was absorbed in his own weapon, his eyes drifted towards the captain's wardrobe in the far corner. There must be something there, he reasoned, something that would make him warm again, something to wrap about his hands.

'You say this is all you know.'

There was a change in the rogue's voice, a subtle inflection indicating thoughtfulness. It was a little thing, Rashodd knew, but enough of an alteration to send his head bobbing violently in a nod.

'But you said, moments ago, that you knew nothing.' His eyes lit up suddenly, wide and horrified. 'You were lying.'

Rashodd was up in an instant, manacles rattling. He saw the dagger, but his eyes were focused on the wardrobe. He had to reach it, he knew, had to find something to stem the blood-loss, had to find something to save what remained of his warmth before this murderer took all of it.

There was a flash of black and Rashodd was upon the floor. The oil lamp swayed violently overhead, jostled. With every swing, it bathed the tall man in shadow, then in light, then in shadow. Every breath, the man was closer without moving. Every blink, the man's dagger was bigger, brighter, smiling.

The lamp swayed backwards. There was shadow. The man was on top of him, straddling him.

'No noise,' he whispered.

The lamp swayed forwards. There was light. The man's eyes were broad, wide and brimming with tears. The dagger was in his hand, firelight dancing from tooth to tooth.

'Don't you scream.'

*

After an endlessness of hearing waves rumble in the distance, the door finally opened with a whisper. Denaos's
appearance was just as quiet and swift, sliding out of the
cabin and easing the door back into place with practised
hands.

And there he stood, oblivious to Argaol's stare, oblivious to anything beyond the knob in his grip and the wood
before his eyes. The ship lulled, coaxed by the yawn of a
passing wave.

'How did it go?' Argaol spoke suddenly, his voice strange
and alien to his own ears after so much silence.

'Fine.'

'Fine?'

Denaos whirled about with unnerving speed. A smile
played across his lips, his eyes were heavy-lidded and
sleepy. Argaol cocked a brow; the man appeared more akin
to someone who'd been ratting about in a private liquor
cabinet than someone doing a job.

'Rather well, in fact,' he replied, licking his lips.

'Ah.' Argaol nodded, not bothering to hide his suspicion.
'What did you find out?'

'Not a blessed lot.'

'Were you thorough?'

'Decidedly.' Denaos raised his hands in a shrug. 'I've
a few names, a few theories, but precious little else, I'm
afraid. Whatever else you want to know will come from
someone other than Rashodd.'

'Evenhands,' the captain muttered. He'd been hoping
the Lord Emissary's name wouldn't come up.

'There doesn't seem to be anyone else aboard who might
know about such a thing, does there?' Denaos stalked past
him, offering a ginger pat on the shoulder. 'If you're intent
on finding him, perhaps you can also ferret out a bottle

of wine for me. Or rum, if you've got it. Bring out the expensive stuff, in any case, I feel like celebrating.'

Argaol lingered by the door as the tall man swaggered down the hall, disappearing around a corner, undoubtedly heading for the mess to join his fellows. Even after he had gone, however, the awkwardness of his presence lingered.

Quietly, Argaol glanced towards the door to his cabin, reaching for the knob.

'Don't.'

He looked up with a start. Denaos was at the end of the hall, regarding the captain carefully.

'Not yet, Captain,' he warned quietly. 'Look in there later, if you wish, but don't do anything now.'

'What ...' Argaol caught his breath. 'What did you do in there?'

Denaos did not blink. 'Not much.'

Lenk stared at his companion through one eye, the other tucked under a slab of raw meat. Denaos stared back, resisting the urge to look over the young man's shoulder at the disaster in the ship's mess.

The rogue saw smashed buckets in the periphery of his vision, dishes shattered, mops broken and even the occasional bandaged appendage reaching out as if begging to be spared from the raging carnage. Denaos did his best to ignore that.

The sight of Gariath was decidedly more difficult to ignore.

In one great hand he clutched Kataria by the heel, the shict snarling, raking claws at the dragonman's thigh and twitching her ears menacingly. Beneath his foot, Asper grunted and strained to dislodge herself while Dreadaeleon slapped impotently at the long tail wrapped about his neck, cursing breathlessly. Whatever fight had occurred was obviously over and done with, the clear victor simply enjoying his triumph at his foes' humiliation.

'So, Rashodd doesn't know anything?' Lenk brought the rogue's attention back to him.

'No, he doesn't.' Denaos frowned at the scene. 'Did … something fun happen while I was gone?'

'It's not important,' Lenk replied. 'Are you sure he wasn't lying?'

'Quite sure.' Denaos looked at the glistening meat on his companion's face, then grimaced at the sight of so many nearby corpses. 'Where exactly did you get the meat?'

'I found it.'

'It's … fresh meat,' Denaos said, grimacing. Any flesh from an animal might have been fresh when they set out from Muraska's harbour a month ago, but now … 'And … you just put that meat … that fresh meat … that you found on the floor … on your face?'

'I got hit in the eye. It's not like I'm going to eat it.' The young man scratched his chin, wincing as his fingers grazed a cut. 'That can't be the whole story. We should ask Argaol if he knows anything.'

'Don't be stupid.' Kataria's voice was quickly followed by Kataria's elbow as she pushed herself in front of Lenk. Gariath seemed unconcerned with her escape. 'Argaol doesn't know his head from his foot. You need to talk to—'

'Miron.' Dreadaeleon staggered to join the assembly, coughing. 'Obviously.'

'No!' Asper emerged last, followed by Gariath. 'I'll not have you go after the Lord Emissary with accusations and blasphemies.'

'He's the only one who would know anything,' Kataria

snapped back. 'Are you such a moron that you'd trust him just because he wears a robe fancier than yours?'

'I'm not a moron,' Asper countered hotly, 'and *he's* not the kind of man who needs to be pestered by savages. We need to calm down and—'

'Kill him.' Gariath glanced at the incredulous expressions cast his way and shrugged. 'As if no one else was thinking it. Let's just hunt him down and get it over with.'

'None of that will be necessary.'

The crowd around the entryway parted at the sound of the voice, all figures clearing the way, all eyes settling on the tall, white-garbed figure standing therein. Their eyes flashed with a legion of emotions: defensive reverence, suspicious glares, barely restrained murderous intent. And yet, behind each unblinking stare a confused caution pervaded, forcing them to back away and allow him entry into the mess.

The usual gentle mirth Miron had always worn had vanished from his face, replaced by a baleful frown. He seemed to have grown from the quiet, unassuming priest to a towering, white-clad spectre as he stared out over the companions, his gaze settling on them one by one.

'You … have questions.'

'Brilliant.' Denaos chuckled. 'Did you learn all that by overhearing us or did you ask Talanas for guidance on the subject?'

'Shut up,' Asper snarled, scowling at the rogue.

'Mirth is a fine coping mechanism,' the priest said, offering the faintest trace of a smile that quickly vanished back into his frown. 'But the answers I have for you are nothing to jest about.'

'The questions we have for you don't amuse us in the slightest, either,' Lenk hissed.

'Though I had hoped to reveal more to you when we arrived at Toha, in peace, all questions will be answered.' The priest held a hand up for silence. 'But before all that, I must … ready myself.' He cast a glance towards Lenk. 'I advise you to, as well. What I have to tell you is not easily comprehended.'

'Lord Evenhands,' Asper spoke with reverence, 'you need not explain yourself to us. We know that you have no collaboration with that thing.'

'Thank you, child,' Miron said with a shake of his head, 'but you must hear me.' He cast a glance about the room. 'All of you must hear me.'

'Enough.' Lenk was the first to take a challenging step forwards. 'I'm sure to you, all this cryptic musing is quite dramatic, but I've had enough of it. Before anyone pre-pares *anything*, you will tell us: how did you drive the thing away?'

'If it will calm you, then I will tell you,' Miron said with a reluctant sigh.

He reached under his robe and produced a symbol. Beside the brilliant silver of his pendant depicting Talanas's phoenix, it seemed dull and ominous, little more than a crudely carved chunk of iron. As the companions peered closer, however, they saw a shape within the metal: a heavy, grey gauntlet clenching thirteen obsidian arrows within its cold digits.

'This is a symbol of my station. That is, of the station that is *not* that of the Lord Emissary of the Muraskan Church of Talanas.'

'What?' Kataria asked, screwing up her face in confusion. 'Didn't Lenk just ask you not to speak in riddles?'

'You mean you're *not* the Lord Emissary?' Asper asked

breathlessly, as though she had just been punched in the belly.

'I am,' Miron replied calmly, oblivious to the shock coursing through the room. 'But I have a station and duties above that of being Lord Emissary. To you, I am Miron Evenhands: Lord Emissary of the Muraskan Church of Talanas.'

He held the symbol aloft, letting its cold iron drink in the lantern light as all eyes stared up, some aghast, some shocked and some select few full of more suspicion than ever.

'To Talanas, I am Miron Evenhands: Agent of the House of the Vanquishing Trinity.'

Nine

DEATHSCROLLS

'To begin with,' Miron said, settling in a chair at the head of the long table, 'allow me to thank you for your patience.' He poured a cup of steaming brown liquid from an ornately decorated teapot. 'I would hope that the brief time I have spent in preparation has given you opportunity to reflect on the events you witnessed.'

'Reflection isn't the word for it,' Lenk snapped with unhidden hostility as he pulled up his own chair at the table. 'What we *witnessed* was ...' He looked to his companions as, one by one, they took their seats. 'Well, what would you call it?'

'Horrifying,' Kataria replied.

'Disgusting,' Asper agreed.

'Ominous,' Dreadaeleon uttered.

'Odd.' Denaos coughed. 'From what I saw.'

'Terrifying,' Argaol said as he took his seat at the other end.

A moment of expectant silence descended upon the table. Eyes looked up to Gariath, who spurned a seat in favour of crouching in a nearby corner, cramped as it might have been. He met their stares and snorted.

'Yeah,' Lenk said, nodding.

'Undoubtedly, you have questions,' Miron replied.

'Understandably, Lord Emissary,' Argaol offered, 'my

crew is terrified. They wonder what the hell it was we saw.'

'And what if it comes back?' Lenk added, narrowing a scowl upon the priest. 'And how, exactly, did *you* get rid of it?'

'To begin,' Miron said slowly, finishing a sip of his tea, 'the Abysmyth will not return. It knows my presence, it has heard the words of Talanas. It will not be back as long as I remain on this ship.' His features melted into a frown. 'Beyond that, it already has what it wants.'

'What did you call it?' Kataria asked, grimacing. '*The* Abysmyth?'

'Perhaps it would have been more correct to say *an* Abysmyth,' Miron replied with a nod, 'for there are undoubtedly more where that one came from.' He held up a hand before any questions could be asked. 'I do not know their number, nor who leads them, but I know what they crave and who they serve.'

'That's not the explanation I was hoping for,' Lenk muttered.

'The explanation you seek is a lengthy one,' the priest said.

Slowly, he slid a hand within the folds of his robe. The symbol he had produced before, the gauntlet clenching thirteen black arrows, announced its arrival with a sound far heavier than an object its size should have made as he set it upon the table.

'It begins and ends with this,' he gestured to the pendant, 'the symbol of the House of the Vanquishing Trinity.' He rose up in his seat, clearing his throat as he did so. 'Eras untold ago—'

'Wait!' Denaos held up a hand suddenly. 'If you're going

to begin with that particular phrase, would now be a good time to take a piss?'

'Shut up,' Asper growled, jabbing the rogue in his ribs.

'It's a valid question,' Denaos protested, swatting her arm away. 'I know enough about the clergy to be aware that they're prone to long, dramatic speeches and, frankly, I'm not sure my bladder is up to the challenge.'

'Then invest in some new pants later,' Lenk spat. He turned back to the priest. 'Go on.'

'As you like,' Miron said with a gracious nod to the young man. 'It may shock some of you to know that once, this land was purer than its current incarnation. Ages ago, before any peoples thought to scribe their histories, the Gods were closer to us than we would ever realise.

'Though no text grants us the privilege to know whether they actually set heavenly foot upon mortal soil, our prayers were heard and answered with great frequency. Though heaven and earth were divided by sky and storm, the Gods bade their servants descend from on high and turn sympathetic ears to the plights of mortals below.

'Not quite deific themselves, but leagues beyond mortal, these servants were charged with providing the link between God and man. They heard the woes and prayers of the people and returned them to their heavenly masters. In those ages, the earliest days of creation, miseries were minimal and prosperity of that magnitude would never be known again.'

The priest paused to sip his tea. Eyes held to his gaze by invisible chains went wider. Lenk cleared his throat impatiently, folding his arms over his chest.

'But—' he said.

'Of course,' Miron replied, 'there is always a "but". Being not quite Gods, their servants were not quite perfect. They were the combination of divine power and mortal feeling, and as such, they were susceptible to envy, desire, hatred,' he paused, staring into the steaming cup, 'corruption.

'They saw their duties as beneath them, observing praises heaped upon the names of Gods while they served as mere messengers and errand runners. Within their heavenly bodies, their contempt festered, twisted, grew. The day came when they finally cast off the yoke of duty and rebelled against heaven.

'Unable to touch their godly masters, though, they turned their contempt on the mortal creations below. They scarred the land beneath them and wrought misery and suffering upon the mortal races. Slaves, chattel, sustenance: such were mortals to these servants of the divine. They carved vast empires of death and decay, their own bodies twisting to reflect their hatreds. In the wake of their carnage, they left creations, beasts as vicious and decrepit as themselves.

'The Abysmyth you saw today was one such creation, a twisted mockery of the ability privileged only to the Gods. The Abysmyth is but the servant of another servant.' He let out a breathless whisper. 'And those first servants were the Aeons.'

'Aeons,' Asper whispered breathlessly, her eyes brimming with a realisation she could not bring herself to voice.

'The very same whose gate we seek,' Miron said with a nod.

'You son of a whore,' Lenk growled. 'You've had us seeking a gate that will let more of *those* things out?'

'Please, allow me to finish—'

'Why?' Gariath rumbled from the corner. He approached the table, the furniture trembling with each thunderous step. 'I smelled that thing. I know that it is nothing good.

And *you're* looking for the gate to let whatever created it *out*.' He levelled a clawed finger at Miron. 'We'd be better off crushing his head right now.' He turned to Lenk and snorted. 'Say the word and I'll paint the wood with his face.'

'How *dare* you!' Asper roared, pushing her chair back as she leapt to her feet. 'Even to utter such a threat is—'

'And I'll use *your* scalp to paint it!' Gariath's roar silenced hers as he unfurled his wings. 'Stupid humans,' he growled. 'Only you would defend a man who seeks such a—'

'There is no evidence that he seeks such a creature,' Dreadaeleon protested, rising up to stand beside Asper. 'He's simply informing us of past events and, were you not so allergic to knowledge, you would know that—'

'That what?' Denaos interjected. 'That he's the one who brought it onto the ship in the first place? Don't be stupid. If that *thing* serves other things called Aeons, then it only stands to reason that—'

'To hear *you* calling for an end to stupidity is nearly hysterical.' Kataria forced a laugh to emphasise the point. 'I say "nearly" because it's far more annoying than funny. Now, why don't you just shut up and let him finish and we'll—'

The sound of wood cracking interrupted her as Gariath brought his fists down hard upon the table.

'I will *not* sit here and let another creature like that come and do what it did again!'

'So that's it?' Asper snapped. 'You're just upset that you couldn't kill that thing?'

'Anything that Gariath can't kill is reason enough to worry,' Lenk countered hotly. 'Need I add that neither he *nor* I *nor* a spear to its gut was enough to kill it? So why don't you just—'

'*STOP!*'

A voice not his own burst from a mouth that seemed to stretch too widely. The howl was heard throughout the ship and the waters beyond. The fish swarming the floating dead departed, all thoughts of food forgotten at the sound. Men fell to the deck in fear and even the moon seemed to grow a little dimmer.

Below, Miron regained his composure with a deep inhalation, as all eyes widened and all mouths shut.

'I shall hear no accusations,' he said calmly. 'Not until I have said my piece.' He took a sip of tea, looking over the edge of his cup. 'Any further objections?'

No one dared offer any.

'Delightful.' He smiled. 'As I said, by the time the Aeons had wrought the height of their woe upon mortalkind, they could no longer be called servants of the Gods. As such, a new name was crafted for them.

'Demons,' he said quietly. Slowly, he swept his gaze about the table, challenging anyone to enquire.

Lenk answered it.

'I find myself wondering whether you're madder than I thought you were, Evenhands,' he said coldly. 'Demons … do not exist.'

'There's no evidence for it,' Dreadaeleon agreed.

'Mossud might beg to differ,' Argaol muttered.

'There's no reason for it,' the wizard countered. 'Demons are, theoretically, creatures of distilled evil.'

'And?' the captain pressed.

'And evil as we know it,' the boy replied with condescending smugness, 'or rather, as we like to *think* we know it, doesn't exist. There is instinct, there is law, there is religion. These define action and the intent behind them cannot be classified by subjective definitions. And, above all, things cannot be *made* out of evil.'

'Moral objections aside,' Asper said, casting the boy a sideways glare, 'even the high priests deny the existence of demons, Lord Evenhands.'

'As well they should,' Miron said, nodding. 'It has been ages since anyone has even thought the name, much less seen one. They are too horrible to contemplate and too long forgotten to mention. I assure you, though, they do exist and you have seen one.'

'I believe it.'

Eyes turned towards Kataria with a mixture of horror and suspicion.

'We have legends about them,' she continued. 'Some of the oldest of my tribe claim that their greater ancestors were still alive when demons roamed the world.'

'So you *knew* about this?' Lenk asked accusingly. 'Why the hell didn't you say anything?'

'Oh, come on, imbecile,' she snapped back, 'what were the odds that it would come up?'

'In the interests of preventing further delays,' Miron said, clearing his throat, 'may I continue?'

'Sorry,' Lenk muttered.

'He certainly is,' Kataria added snidely.

'The suffering at the hands of the demons did not go unnoticed by the Gods and did not go unchallenged by mortals,' Miron continued. 'The heavenly ones spoke to the fiercest and most determined men and women, the ones free of demonic oppression, and granted unto them boons of divine power.

'These Gods were the deities of righteousness: Talanas, the Healer, Galataur, the Sovereign, and Darior, the Judge.'

'Who?' Denaos asked.

'Dariorism. An older faith, not much practised any more,' Asper answered.

'Indeed,' Miron said, nodding. 'Some faiths lost much in those times. They vested within these mortals their powers and, with that, the House of the Vanquishing Trinity, an organisation devoted to destroying the demons, was born.

'The fighting began with great bloodshed, but for every demon that fell, more champions rose up, inspired by their rescuers. Many were lost, peoples became extinct in the span of a breath, but ultimately, mortals prevailed. The demons were pushed back and cast into hell, cursed to live in shadow for all eternity.

'The House's life after this was disgracefully short,' Miron continued. 'With no common oppressor, the suffering was forgotten by all peoples. Grudges were born, rivalries surfaced and wars between races tore the unity apart. The House was disbanded.'

'Disbanded?' Kataria said, raising an eyebrow. 'Then why do you—'

'Key positions remain,' Miron said, 'men and women with duties so grave that they must endure the generations. Mine is such a position, mine is such a duty. I remain charged to guard the artefacts born of the suffering, lest they fall into … less worthy hands.'

Lenk's eyes were the first to go alight with the realisation. 'The book,' he uttered, the words heavy on his tongue. 'The book the frogmen stole.'

'It has a name,' the priest replied. 'The Tome of the Undergates, penned by the most heinous of demons and their mortal subjects in the last days of the wars. They were not fools; they foresaw their banishment. Knowing this, they wrought within the pages the rituals and rites necessary to bring them back to the mortal world.'

Miron shrank with the force of his sigh, all authority and cryptic presence lost as he slumped in his seat.

'In my arrogance, I had hoped to use the tome to enable the Aeons' Gate. I believed that the rituals used to establish contact with hell could be used to commune with heaven.'

'How does anything involving the word "Undergates" lend itself to beneficient purposes?' Denaos muttered.

'I have no idea how the Abysmyth and its vile mistress found the book,' Miron continued, 'but it cannot remain in their hands.'

'Again with this "mistress",' Lenk murmured. 'What are you not telling us?'

'You've a right to know,' Miron said. 'Her name is known only to a few, but to them, she is Ulbecetonth, the Kraken Queen, Mother Deep. Once a noble servant of Zamanthras, the Mother, she was corrupted into a creature of wickedness and gluttony. It was she who birthed the Abysmyth, spoke to it, sent it out.' He stared hard at Lenk. 'It is she who seeks to return.'

A deathly silence fell over the assembled as minds struggled to comprehend what had been heaped upon them.

Demons. The word echoed in the quiescence, a lingering cancer in the minds of the companions. Legends of such creatures permeated each of them, instilled by elders seeking to tame them, reinforced by drunkards muttering nonsensical stories. Until that moment, they had seemed nothing more substantial than that.

And yet ...

'All right.' Lenk shattered the silence. 'You aren't telling us this for historical enlightenment.'

'Apologies, but *you* were the one demanding answers,'

Miron replied, smiling with a gentle smugness. 'However, you are correct. I would not tell you this for no reason.'

He took a long sip of his tea and set the cup down. The clink of the porcelain was deafening.

'You will go after the Abysmyth. You will retrieve the tome.'

The silence that fell over them brimmed with tension this time, as every jaw went slack and every eye went as wide as they could possibly go without leaping from their sockets. Questions formed on lips, demands for further explanation, pleas for elaboration, accusations.

None were voiced before Denaos spoke.

'You, priest,' he said, 'are out of your Gods-damned mind.'

'Mind your—' Asper began to scold.

'Don't you tell me to mind *anything* of mine,' Denaos snapped back. 'Did you not just hear what he said?'

'I heard.' Asper nodded. 'And I believe he's right to ask this of us.'

'So it's the whole clergy that's insane?' Denaos's laughter trembled with hysteria.

'I agree,' Kataria piped up.

'Thank you.'

'No, I agree with Asper.'

'Ah, so it's the clergy and the shicts, is it?' Denaos rubbed his eyes and shook his head, as though trying to emerge from some demented dream. 'Am I the only sane one here?'

'Demons are a threat to everything that breathes,' Kataria added with a hiss. She drew herself up proudly, her eyes going hard as steel. 'And it is the duty of a greater race to see them dead.' She glanced sideways at her companions. 'Humans can come along, too.'

'Well, thank Silf the womenfolk are so eager to run off and die.' He glanced at Dreadaeleon, elbowing the boy. 'And what about you?'

'Hm?' The wizard glanced up with a start, roused from some deep reverie. 'Oh. Yes, we might as well go.'

'Oh, *come on*.'

'Knowledge is the dominion of the wizards,' the boy replied sternly. 'There's much we could learn from something that is supposedly distilled "evil", if we ever get hold of a corpse.'

'It's not *their* corpse you'll be holding.' Denaos glanced over his shoulder at Gariath. 'What about you?'

The dragonman merely snorted in reply.

'Possibly the sanest thing spoken yet,' Denaos said with a frustrated sigh.

He cast his eyes to the end of the table, where Lenk propped himself on his elbows, staring into nothingness. Such an expression did not go unrecognised.

'I'm begging you now,' Denaos urged hotly, 'as the only other person here who is a man of reason and not a fanatic, pointy-eared, demented or scaly, *don't* tell me you're considering this.'

Lenk spared the briefest of moments for Denaos, taking in his hopeful expression, before turning back to Miron.

'How do we even know where this ... Abysmyth is?'

The edge of Miron's small smile sheared off the last layer of ease from the room.

'We are about to find out.' The priest looked to the dark-skinned man at the end of the table. 'Captain, kindly bring it in.'

Argaol's face was the colour of a fading bruise when he looked up, a gloomy blend of pale fear and nauseous green.

He looked from the door to the priest, seemingly uncertain which made him more nervous.

'What …' he stammered. 'Now?'

'Now,' Miron replied, nodding.

'Is it really …' The captain hesitated with a cringe before inhaling sharply. 'Fine.' He slipped from the chair to the door, leaning out into the corridor. 'Sebast! Bring it in!'

The first mate came rushing in like a man pursued, his hands trembling with the weight of the large cylinder in his grasp. A black cloth, scrawled with chalk sigils of Talanas, Zamanthras and other less familiar faiths, was draped about it. He set it down upon the table as though it were a carcass, muttering rapid, indecipherable prayers as he wiped his hands violently on his breeches.

'So …' Denaos hummed as he watched the first mate disappear out of the cabin. 'This won't be pleasant, will it?'

'Where these creatures are concerned, there is no such word.'

Miron reached out and slipped the cloth off with a whisper, followed by a chorus of retching and vomiting barely restrained as all assembled laid eyes upon the contents of the brass cage before them. And, with wide unblinking orbs, what lay within laid eyes upon them.

Lenk wasn't sure if he recognised the creature as one of the white-feathered chorus from a day earlier, nor was he sure he wanted to. The creature, a strange and curious thing with the body of a portly seagull, was horrific enough from a distance. As it waddled in a slow circle about the cage, sweeping its bulging eyes around the assembly, more than a few gazes were averted.

And yet, it seemed there was no avoiding its stare. The bulbous orbs peered over the hooked nose of an old woman's face, spotted wrinkles peeled back around its gaping mouth. The teeth within its maw, long yellow needles, chattered wordless curses as it swayed ominously within the cage.

'What ... is it?' The question came from Asper on a bulge of swallowed bile.

'A parasite,' Miron answered, regarding the creature without emotion. 'It heralds the approach of the Abysmyth, gluts itself on the suffering and sinew left behind.' He leaned closer to the cage, sneering. 'Their proper name ... is "Omen".'

'Omen ...' Lenk repeated, apparently the only other one amongst them not so stricken with revulsion as to be rendered speechless.

'So named for their precursorship of all things foul. They are the harbingers and the criers of Ulbecetonth, the cherubs that fly about her crown.' He settled back, steepling his fingers. 'To see them darkening the sky in such brazen numbers is disturbing.'

'Yeah,' Lenk muttered, glaring at the priest. 'That was only *slightly* obvious, thank you.'

The only agreement came from the Omen itself as it chattered its teeth, the yellow needles clicking upon each other as it peered at the companions. Only Dreadaeleon leaned forwards to peer back, observing its lipless mouth with disgust.

'It's ... as if it's trying to speak,' he whispered. There was a flash of movement behind the creature's teeth, a glimmer of saliva that heralded the boy's blanch. 'It's got inner lips.'

'It's got what?' Lenk asked, sharing the wizard's expression.

'Its lips are behind its teeth.' Dreadaeleon tapped the cage curiously. 'Like a gopher ... but why?'

In answer, the creature lunged at his finger, gnashing its teeth with such speed that only the startled shriek that sent him falling out of his chair spared his digit. The Omen hissed, ruffling its feathers as if in challenge as it settled onto its pudgy white haunches.

'Part-gopher, part-bird, part-woman ...' Lenk tapped his chin thoughtfully and glared up at Miron. 'This changes nothing, you realise.'

'It proves the existence of demons, at least,' Asper offered meekly.

'No, the giant fish-*demon* proved the existence of demons,' Lenk spat back. 'What was the point of bringing this out? Shock?'

'Information,' Miron replied coolly. 'An Omen is not a complex creature, living only to eat and cause misery. Neither takes a great amount of intellect, and thus, an Omen is incapable of lying.'

'So ask it a question,' Lenk said, 'and see what it says.'

'It doesn't offer information without incentive,' Miron said.

'You mean ... torture?' Denaos asked, grimacing.

'Not the kind you would be versed in.' Miron affixed a piercing gaze upon the rogue, observing him casually shift his eyes away. 'After all, how does one torture that which feeds on suffering?'

'Rip its wings off and roast half of it until the other half talks!' Argaol slammed his fist upon the table, drawing the creature's attention. 'So long as it gets me further away from that foulness that infected my ship, who cares?' He leaned forwards, snarling. 'Speak, bird, where did you come from?'

The creature replied by tilting its withered head as if

studying him. His facade of fearlessness twitched, threatened to break.

'Speak!'

The Omen's mouth craned open slowly, exposing a tiny void beyond the yellow teeth. A low, gurgling noise emitted from within before a voice, masculine and terrified, boiled out of its throat.

'*Captain,*' it uttered without moving its mouth, '*Captain, where are you? You're ... you're supposed to protect us! Where are you? Why aren't you here? CAPTAIN!*'

Argaol fell back into his chair as if struck. His face was as white as his eyes as he stared, not at the parasite, but at the empty space before him. His jaw hung from his face, his voice oozing out of his mouth like spittle.

'That's ... Anjus. He is ... he *was* the master of wares. What's—'

'*Zamanthras preserve me,*' the Omen continued, its voice now another man's, '*Zamanthras preserve me, Zamanthras preserve me. I'm not going to make it. Mother wash away my sins. I ... I don't want to die. I don't want to die! Please, just let me live long enough to see my wife again, please ... PLEASE!*'

'Nor does the Omen truly speak,' Miron said, sighing. 'It can only mimic what it has heard. But it does so—'

'*IT HURTS!*' the parasite's imitation voice wailed. '*IT HURTS SO MUCH!*'

'Accurately.'

'Make it stop.' Argaol's demand brimmed with tears. 'Make it shut up!'

'Your suffering will be brief, Captain,' the priest said. 'If that is all we require, then let it be so.' He turned to Asper and offered a weak smile. 'Would you kindly do me the favour of reciting, Priestess?'

'Reciting ... what?' the priestess asked, blanching.

'*The Talanic Verses*. Parable four-and-thirty, if you would be so kind.'

'"The Healer Addresses the Masses"? But … whatever for?'

'Allow me to ask the questions, please.' He gestured towards the creature. 'Simply recite.'

'Er … ah, very well.' Asper cleared her throat, drawing the creature's attention. Averting her gaze, she began to speak. '"And it was upon the sixth noon, the sixth dismemberment of the Healer, that he rose again, whole and unscarred. He looked over the people, who raised torch and sickle against him and demanded he be slain again."'

The creature emitted a low hum, like a pigeon being strangled. Its feathers ruffled, teeth chattering a little more violently. Yellow feet plopping beneath it, it marched in place, as if preparing to charge.

'Do not stop,' Miron commanded, staring at the thing. 'Speak, vermin. Where did your master go?'

'"And he said to them, *Do you fear miracles? Have you lost such confidence in the Gods?*"' Asper continued, breathing heavily. '"*Then look upon me with fear, for in fear you will find the need for answers. And it is answers I give you.*"'

The Omen shrieked suddenly, hurling itself against the cage. The brass rattled upon the wood, causing all to draw back, save Miron. The beast hissed, gnawing on the bars of its cage with yellowed teeth and blackened gums, straining to break free, to silence the prayers.

'"*Your suffering is not unknown to me,* He said. *And your dead are with me now, in a place of unending sun and peace. Weep not for them. I shall weep for you. For I say to you, life is sacred.*"'

The creature battered itself against the bars, blood leaking from its head, white feathers stained red as it shrieked and made guttural whines. It gyrated, twisted, writhed upon the floor of its cage. Miron held up a hand to Asper, leaned close to the cage and whispered.

'Where?'

'*North*,' it gasped, through its inner lips, '*north*.'

Miron nodded solemnly, then drew in a sharp breath and finished the prayer. '*Hii lat Udun.*'

'*And so is death*,' Asper translated, eyes going wide. 'That's … Old Talanic. *Old*, Old Talanic. It's never been used outside of hymnal verses—'

'And not since humanity developed one sole language out of many,' Miron said.

The creature twisted once, then lay still, its life escaping on a gurgling, choked sigh. The assembled could do nothing but stare as Miron slowly took up the cloth and draped it over the cage once more.

'A demon's true weakness is memory,' he muttered. 'It recalls the chants that led the House into battle, it fears them.' He lifted the cage off the table and set it aside. 'But more importantly, we have our answer. We know where they are heading.'

'You can't be serious,' Denaos whispered.

'Can I be anything but?'

'You bring out a flying gopher-demon, do a few tricks and expect us to go chasing after the Abysmyth?' The rogue made a flailing gesture. 'All that convinces *me* of is that we shouldn't be chasing demons! Lenk *and* Gariath couldn't even scratch that thing! You're sending us against something that can't be hurt!'

'It can't be harmed by mortal creations, no,' Miron replied quickly, 'but there are weapons that even demons fear. Fire, you see, is their bane. The smallest heat source burns them unmercifully, and they cannot bear the presence of smoke.'

'Dreadaeleon is a wizard,' Asper said thoughtfully. 'He can make fire.'

'Well, thank goodness he did that when it was here earlier,' Denaos sneered.

'If I had known that *then*, maybe I'd—' Dreadaeleon began.

'Quiet,' Lenk snapped.

'Regardless,' the priest continued with a sigh, 'you are hired to me as adventurers. You are free to leave my company at any moment and free to make your own decisions.' He held his hands up in resignation. 'Man's fate is his own to weave.'

Glances were exchanged, myriad emotions captured in every eye. Terror, excitement, purpose, anger, anxiety, all reflected in stares that slowly, one by one, turned to the silver-haired young man scratching his chin absently.

Despite everything said between them, despite their harsh words for each other, they looked to him for their answer, their uniting purpose. Whatever had been said in the name of duty and fury, every word and oath could be revoked in the blink of an eye.

All rested on what would emerge from his mouth.

'We'll do it.'

Kataria and Asper beamed with simultaneous smiles of pride as Dreadaeleon's brow arched and Denaos's head fell into his hands with a dramatic moan. Gariath's fierce visage remained unchanged, save for a snort and a nod to Lenk. Argaol, meanwhile, stared at the young man with the same curiosity with which he would regard a fire-breathing tortoise.

'For one thousand pieces of gold.'

Suddenly, smiles disappeared, brows went flat and the rogue's head snapped up like a cat catching the scent of dead fish.

'How dare you, Lenk?' Asper was quick to hurl her voice brimming with scorn. 'To ask any money for such a duty is a sin in itself, but to ask for such an exorbitant sum is—'

'Done.'

'Lord Emissary!' Her wrath turned to shock as she whirled upon Miron. 'The Church doesn't have that kind of wealth to flaunt on a quest with no guarantee of success.'

'As well I know, child.' Miron sighed. He looked to Lenk without judgement. 'The money will come from my personal funds and will be paid in full upon return of the book.'

'I can agree to that,' Lenk replied, 'assuming you pay for supplies we'll need.'

'Done.'

'We have a deal, then.'

Miron's only reply was an ominous hum as he rose from his chair like an ivory tower.

'I suggest you retire shortly. The Abysmyth has a lead on you and you'll be leaving at dawn if you're to catch it.' He glanced at Argaol across the table. 'Captain, if you would kindly assist me in consulting the sea charts?'

'Aye ... aye,' Argaol muttered, rising on shaking legs. He wore an expression of disbelief, unwilling to comprehend what he had just heard, what he had just been a part of.

Quietly, on knocking knees, he followed the priest out of the cabin, pausing only long enough to look at Lenk and shake his head.

No sooner had the door slid shut before all eyes turned to the young man as he reclined in his seat, folding his hands behind his head as though he were at a picnic and not at negotiations regarding beings from hell.

'So, then,' Denaos began angrily, 'will you give reason as to why you just signed all our deathscrolls?'

'I gave you one thousand,' he said smugly.

Asper shot him a vicious glare. 'Perhaps then you'll give a reason why you just extorted from my church like a street hawker?'

'No.'

'So why should we follow you on this expedition at all?' the rogue demanded.

'You probably shouldn't,' Lenk replied with a shrug. 'I never asked any of you to follow me wherever I went and I won't ask you now.' He glanced to Asper. 'If you object to what I just did, I'm sure Argaol will let you stay aboard until you reach Toha.'

Slowly, he leaned forwards, sweeping them with his piercing gaze.

'I don't know how far along I've figured this out,' he said, 'but I want to kill this thing. I don't know how, or why, but I will.' He turned to Asper. 'And if I'm being sent to kill something that, up until this point, was simply legend, I deserve a bit of compensation.' He leaned back again. 'So, the way I figure, you can leave this table right now for whatever reason you may have. If I go alone, then I go alone. When I come back with the book, I'll never have to work a day in my life again.' He grinned broadly. 'Man's fate is his own to weave.'

Once more, the glances were exchanged. The silence lasted but a moment.

'I'll go,' Kataria said. 'Demons and cleansing aside,' she smirked slyly, 'I happen to need a new set of leathers.'

'I will, as well,' Dreadaeleon piped up, the faintest hint

of excitement in his voice. 'There's a lot to be learned here and I intend to be the one to find out what's going on. The Venarium will need to know.'

'Freak,' Denaos muttered.

'I'll go.' Asper spoke with some reluctance. 'But only because it's the right thing to do. I forego my share right now.'

'And since everyone is intent on killing themselves,' Denaos sighed, 'I should come along to pick up the bodies.' He immediately shot up a single finger. '*If* I get Asper's share.'

'Why, you disgusting—' the priestess snarled.

'*You* gave it up,' the rogue interrupted.

'And what about you, Gariath?' Lenk spoke before Asper could start.

Eyes turned to the dragonman, knowing that, of all the companions, his answer couldn't be predicted. He had stayed with them this long, Lenk reasoned, but it would hardly be surprising if he decided the time to leave was now.

'I go,' Gariath grunted. 'Nothing, demon or otherwise, fights a *Rhega* and lives.' He snorted. 'No stupid, weak human will die if I'm there, either.'

'So that's that, then,' Lenk said, rising from his chair. 'Sleep on it. If you change your mind by morning, stay behind. I'll use your share to buy myself new friends.'

'Don't count on me ducking out,' Kataria was quick to snap, springing up. 'I'll put that gold to good use.' She shot her silver-haired companion a glance and winked. 'I wouldn't want you to go spending my share on shoes that'll make you look taller.'

'Stop being stupid,' Lenk grunted. 'If we're done here,

I'm going to sleep. I don't know when one rises to go demon-killing, but I'll wager it's early.'

'Sleep well while you can,' Denaos muttered morbidly as he rose. 'When the Abysmyth eats our heads, you'll hear the screaming in your dreams.'

'By then I'll be able to buy earmuffs.'

ACT TWO
Shores of White and Black

Interlogue

FLEETING NIGHT

The Departure
The Sea of Buradan
Summer, late

I don't remember much about my father, save for the fact that he was a humble man. He made an honest living which, by his definition, was one that involved hacking dirt and killing nothing bigger than a pig as a wedding gift. He lived well, I think, and I try to think of him whenever I have the time, in the moments when I remember the scent of dirt and feel a deep-seated hunger for pork.

I don't recall what he sounded like.

In the dawning hours, however, before the sun has risen, I think of my grandfather. In truth, I think of him quite often: whenever I'm about to be killed, whenever I'm about to make a mistake, whenever I'm ready to do something stupid. I hear his voice, even if it is distant. It's his voice I hear as I clutch his sword, my sword.

Today, I can't hear him. I can't hear anyone. No one's talking.

There's been precious little sleep aboard the Riptide. The crew remains fearful, preferring to go without sleep as they patrol, ever-vigilant for the return of anything that might crawl out of the water. Miron has been locked up with Argaol, discussing

241

whatever it is men discuss when they're about to send people off to die. I should note that they've been avoiding Argaol's cabin, preferring to do their discussing in the ship's hold. I don't know the reason, but I'm finding it difficult to trust the decision behind anything Miron does.

More than that, I'm finding it difficult to trust myself.

The Aeons' Gate, the relic we've been hired to seek out, is named for demons. Not just demons, but arch-demons, demons supreme. Demons with actual titles: 'Kraken Queens' and 'Mother Deeps'. Demon aristocracy, though I'm certain there's a fouler term for their social class. These are the things I've been hired to chase down, these are the things I've been told will be the salvation of mankind, the bridge between heaven and earth.

Despite all the lies ... well, hold it, there's only been one lie, really, but it was rather prominent. At any rate, despite that, I've still agreed to go off in search of the thing in exchange for one thousand pieces of gold.

It's a respectable sum, to be certain, but there remains a tart taste around the knowledge that one's soul, dignity and livelihood come at a price. For a while, I actually began to believe Asper when she told me that the human soul was beyond the weight of metal. I suppose I showed her.

There's time to turn back, to reject Miron's offer, to stay on board the ship and jump off at Toha and find the next priest, pirate or person who requires a sword arm and a lack of questions. For the life of me, however, I simply can't go down there and tell him I quit. I suspect it's because, as I've turned the possibilities over in my head, I continually fail to come up with a reason to turn back.

Dismemberment, death, decapitation, decay and drowning, on dry land or otherwise, are certainly deterrents. On the other hand ... one thousand coins, split evenly amongst five people, still exceed the number most people will ever see in their lifetime.

Certainly sufficient to find more respectable work, perhaps opening a smithy or an apothecary, or investing in slaves in the cities where the fleshtrade is permitted. This is presuming that everyone comes back alive, a staggeringly unlikely estimate by even generous accounts; if someone dies, the shares increase.

I suspect this line of reasoning should strike me as considerably more horrifying than it does.

And yet, it's not just about money, even though I know it ought to be. I suggest that whoever is reading this should season the next few lines with a bit of salt.

I want to find the demon. I want to find it and kill it. I want to find it and kill it and I don't know why.

It's far more likely that the thing will find and kill me first, I know, but all the same, there's something inside me that makes me want to track down the beast and put my sword through it. I never got the chance to strike it directly, as something roiling around in my head reminds me often, and I have to know what will happen when I do. Between blinks, I know this is ridiculous logic: the thing took a spear through its belly and survived, likely my sword won't do anything more than tickle it. And yet … when I close my eyes, it all makes sense.

When I close my eyes, I hear a voice that is not my grandfather's.

I suspect if I were to hear an actual voice, one of reason or even one threatening a stiff blow to the side of my head, I might be able to get these ideas out into the open and, upon hearing my own madness, be able to reject them. My companions haven't been forthcoming, however, indicating that they're either fine with the idea of chasing after demons or simply don't want to talk to me.

It's difficult to tell which.

Denaos slipped away shortly after our little meeting had concluded, citing the need for last indulgences while slinking off towards the cabin of one of the female passengers. Dreadaeleon, rife with 'magic headaches' or some manner of wizardly affliction decent people were never meant to know of, found some dark corner to sip tea in and pore over his book.

Asper, as far as I know, has been in various states of penance, meditation and prayer, tended to by Quillian. The Serrant clings to our priestess like a bloated tick; I suppose this isn't unusual, given the symbiotic or parasitic relationship between their respective callings. All the same, I'm more than a little inclined, at times, to believe the rumours whispered about the Serrant, to give more than just a passing chuckle to the jokes Denaos makes about her.

Gariath, surprisingly, did deign to talk to me beyond grunted derisions of my race. He proved less than helpful in convincing me of the folly of chasing after demons, apparently sharing the sentiments of what may or may not be a symptom of insanity in my head. 'If you're scared, go sleep on a bed of urine,' he suggested. 'Very warm, I hear.'

In truth, I had hoped to speak to Kataria. She was … not forthcoming.

I don't suppose I can blame her, really. Only an hour or two after the Abysmyth was driven off, I managed to not only convince her that I was utterly mad, but savagely attack her and then persuade her to follow me on a chase after the damned thing. If this were any other situation, I'm sure I'd marvel at my ability to turn such a circumstance to advantage.

More than that, I needed to talk to her. I needed to tell her I wasn't mad, so that she would confirm that. If I tell myself I'm not mad, it's not reliable, since it could be the madness talking. But if she tells me I'm not mad, then it's clear that I'm not because she's just a savage shict, not mad, even if the race itself is more than a bit mad.

And beyond even that, I needed to tell her something. I don't know what it was, though. Whenever I close my eyes to think of it, I keep hearing the logic, the voice, the need to go after the demon and kill it. All I can think of to say to her is something about how sweaty she is.

In fact, I did try to tell her. Her response was a shrug, a roll onto her side and a profoundly decisive breaking of wind in my general direction. As one might imagine, negotiations were promptly concluded afterwards.

The sun is beginning to rise now. It strikes me that I should attempt to get at least an hour's sleep. It strikes me as odd that I'm yearning for conversation. My grandfather used to tell me that the moments before an honest killing were tense, silent, no one able to talk, eat or sleep. Maybe I want to alleviate that tension by talking to someone, anyone. Maybe I want them to tell me I'm doing the right thing by going off to chase demons. Maybe I just want to hear something other than the waves.

Maybe I want to stop hearing voices when I close my eyes.

The crew is emerging on deck. Time is short. I'll write later, presuming survival.

Hope is not advised.

Ten

PITILESS DAWN

Silver slivers of the dawn crept through the blinds like spectres, casting ghostly hues on the sheets. Denaos glanced upwards at the shuttered window with disinterest, awaiting the late-dawning sun. Nights without sleep were as common to him as a waking day was.

He had no right to place his feet down on the wood, to rub his eyes and stifle a yawn behind clenched teeth. That sort of thing was reserved for people who had done hard work and slept well, the gestures largely the last appreciation between a man and his bed before he readily faced the dawn like a soldier gallantly marching to battle. Still, he admitted to himself, acting as though he had slept well and was heading to brighter days was one of his lesser lies, hardly worth losing sleeplessness over.

Something rustled in the sheets next to him and he glanced sideways at the nude woman. The sheets hugged her slender body as she blissfully dozed, oblivious to the presence of him or the rising dawn.

She looked peaceful in her slumber. She had met him with suspicion when he had pretended to stumble, lost, through her door late last evening, coming close to casting him out with the coaxing of a bottle of inexpensive wine cracked against his skull. Now, all traces of scorn were vanished from her stately, well-nourished features, instead bearing the expression of something akin to a sated lioness.

Yes, he smiled to himself, *that's a rather good metaphor. I like that one.*

Negotiating his way into her bed hadn't been difficult; it never was. It hadn't taken much but a few false tears shed for his fallen comrades whose names he couldn't remember out of shock to convince her to pour him a glass of the red. The best lies usually began with tears, he knew, and from there it was only a stiff, resolute inhale to convince her of a wound past his brave, stoic shell that was in need of carnal healing.

He eyed the empty bottle on her bureau, regarding the label: Jaharlan Crimson. A lesser wine from a race who regarded lesser wines with all the reverence they did lesser Gods. *To think*, he scolded himself, *if I had recited a bit of poetry, she'd probably have given me some of the expensive stuff.*

That, at least, might have afforded him the opportunity to pass out, to sleep, perchance to slumber right through the call to leave, and a decent excuse not to follow his companions into death. The expensive stuff, at least, might have given him the opportunity for a dreamless, blissful emptiness behind his eyelids.

Lesser wine was his milk. He took it with bread and stew and it had long since failed to do anything but fill his belly and his bladder. Lesser wine never allowed him to sleep.

He rubbed his eyes again, hoping to lower his hands and find an inviting pillow beneath him. He was still awake, eyes still open. He attempted to convince himself that his insomnia was due to the events that had occurred yesterday.

After all, who could sleep after agreeing to chase a beast that drowned men on dry land? Certainly not Denaos, the average man, the voice of reason amidst the savage, monstrous, insane, zealous and blasphemous. Denaos needed time to digest such horrors, time in bed with pleasurable company and expensive stuff. It could hardly be Denaos's fault that he couldn't sleep.

Denaos told himself this. Denaos did not believe it.

The slivers of light brightened, seeping through the shutters to bathe the woman in muted light. He saw her, then, without the haze of wine or the fleeting euphoria of protrusions in orifices. She was a sculpture, her skin flawless, her hair so dark as to swallow the light as it crept over her.

He blinked. For the briefest of moments the woman was not the merchant who had scorned him previously. For the briefest of moments she was someone else, someone he had once known. He saw her waking as if she were a stranger, rolling over to bat large, dark eyes at him, a smile of contentment upon her face.

'*Good morning, tall man,*' he imagined her saying.

He blinked. In the span of his eyelid shutting and opening, he saw her once more, now still and lifeless upon crimson-stained sheets, eyes closed so peacefully one might never have noticed the gaping hole in her throat …

Stop it, he told himself, *STOP IT!*

Denaos shut his eyes tightly and breathed deeply. The image lingered in his mind like a tumour, growing ever more vivid with each breath he took. Silently, he held his breath, making not a word or sound until he felt his lungs were ready to burst.

When he opened his eyes, she lay there: whole, unsullied, breathing softly.

He slid out of her bed and crept to the crumpled black heap that was his clothes, and felt a chill come over his naked legs. *It would be so easy*, he thought, *to stay here, to let them go and die on their own. It would be easy to lie here beside her …*

He looked at her once more, resisting the urge to blink.

Even as his eyes strained to keep open, he could see her hand on the space he had recently lain upon. She had all her fingers. Without blinking, he saw the red stumps on large, hairy hands. Without blinking, he saw the missing digits rolling about on the floor beside a pair of quivering, glistening globs in a pool of brackish bile. Without blinking, he saw a bearded face, lips cracked and gaping, pleas forced through vomit.

He still dared not close his eyes, nor did he dare return to her bed. It was the scent of linen that was his allergy, spurring images to his mind he never wished to see, those images bringing forth other images. He should be lucky to only recall last night's other accomplishment in such fleeting visions. He should be lucky to escape the nightmare of sheets before he was tempted to sleep.

Quietly, cannily, he slid into his trousers. She would be furious when she awoke, he knew, to find him absent. By then, he would be gone, possibly drowned, possibly with his head bitten off by some horrible monstrosity.

The door shut quietly. The woman turned in her bed, grasping at a space on her mattress that bore no depression or muss of sheets, no evidence that anyone had ever been there.

The sun was the dominion of Talanas.

This, Asper knew, was certain. It was the Healer's greatest gift to mankind, the gate through which He had entered and left the waking, mortal world. Talanas frowned upon

249

no human, cursed no follower of another God; He was the Giver, dispensing His purification freely and without judgement. So, too, was the sun an indiscriminate and generous benefactor of humanity.

More than that, however, the sun was His Eye. Mankind could never truly be separated from Talanas for He observed them always through that great, golden sphere. Through it, He saw all in need, heard every prayer. Only under the cloak of night was He ever hard of hearing. Asper frowned at that; if Talanas had heard her last night, He certainly was not revealing any answers today.

She leaned hard on the railing of the helm, staring out over the sea. The curtains of mist over the sea were parting as dawn crept upon the horizon. She had always welcomed the sun, yearned for the warmth it brought, sought the reconnection with the Healer. When she had studied at the temple, it was a ritual in and of itself to see the sun rise and shine through the stained-glass windows.

Here, far away from the comfort of stone walls, out upon the open sea, the dawn was not quite so dramatic. Instead of arriving in a soundless thunderclap, it staggered up with a silent yawn. Instead of blooming with a glorious burst, it opened its golden eye lazily. Instead of acting as a herald for a new day, a cleansing, it seemed slow, sluggish … bored.

Perhaps that was why she had no prayers for Talanas today.

It had been her routine since she had left the temple to thank the Healer for delivering her through the night once the sun rose again. Following that, she begged safety for her family, her clergy, her temple. Prayers for her companions typically ranked last, pleas for Talanas's watchful gaze requested for Lenk, Dreadaeleon, Kataria and Gariath, always in that order. Whether or not she chose to offer a prayer for Denaos largely depended on her mood.

Today, she was in no mood to ask for any such benevolence. Her lips were still, silent. She could not pray this morning, not when the dawn still failed to cleanse her memories of yesterday's violence.

Images flew on shrieking wings through her mind, scenes of the fury that had raged inside the ship's bowels. Even as she tried to burn the sights out of her eyes by staring directly at the sun, she still saw them. The dawn was in no hurry to assist her.

She saw them, the moments replaying themselves over and over in her mind: the frogman lurching towards her, the white flash of its dagger and needle-like teeth. Her staff was out of reach, useless against the wall; she could not remember how it had left her hand. As desperately as she might wish, she could not help but remember her left hand, reaching out, muscles spasming wildly, tears brimming in her eyes as it reached past the knife and took the pale creature by the throat . . .

NO! She clenched her eyes shut. *Stop it, stop it, stop it. Stop thinking about it! Focus on the dawn! Focus on the sun!*

That proved difficult, as the sun had risen only a hair's width. Dawn had failed to purge her mind. The long, sleepless night had offered her no respite. The new sleeve she had stitched onto her robe failed to offer any comfort.

And so, as she looked down from the dawn to the silver pendant of the phoenix in her hand, she had no prayers. She had but one word.

'Why?'

The holy symbol did not answer. Its eyes, tiny carved gouges, were fixed upwards, staring towards the dawn as though that were enough. She bit her lower lip, not bothering to follow its metal gaze.

'It happened again,' she whispered. 'Why did it happen again? Why does it keep happening?'

The pendant did not answer. The sun rose another eyelash, light caught the silver. A glare was cast over its eyes, the usually stern and uncompromising stare of nobility suddenly turning heavy-lidded and disinterested.

'Why don't you ever answer me?'

'Priestess?'

Asper realised she had demanded that last answer more loudly than she had intended. Swallowing hard, she resisted the urge to whirl about at the voice. Instead, she forced her back to stiffen to a more upright posture, resolute against the dawn. It would not serve, she knew, to look startled under the Eye of Talanas.

'Quillian Guisarne-Garrelle Yanates.' She turned about, forcing a smile upon her face. 'Apologies – *Serrant* Quillian Guisarne-Garrelle Yanates, good morning.'

'To you as well.' The woman's eyes had a peculiar way of remaining still and hard while the rest of her head moved in a respectful nod. 'Quillian is fine.' She cleared her throat suddenly. 'Whichever title pleases you, however, is the one that is proper, Priestess.'

The Serrant attempted a smile; it was not easy for her. It did not flow smoothly over her face, but had to be carved hastily. The twist of her lips revealed strain, teeth set so tight in her jaw as to creak like aged iron. She looked more prepared for a hanging than a conversation.

'The title that would please me most,' Asper replied, her own voice a bit halted by the woman's obvious tension, 'is the one where we have only one name to refer to each other by.'

252

'So noted, Priestess, but I must request you reconsider such a statement. It would be improper to call you anything less than your station.'

Asper blinked at that; she had never considered her name to be beneath her calling before.

'Oaths dictate a certain protocol.'

'Mm.' Asper turned back to face the sun; it had risen a finger's width. 'What can I do for you, Serrant?'

'I was hoping to fulfil my oaths and make certain of your well-being. I know you will … likely be leaving soon.'

It wasn't until Quillian had spoken those words that it dawned on Asper. She would be leaving soon.

All at once, the noise on the decks below began to rise. Sailors were emerging from their sleepless night in the holds below, the sound of ropes sliding on wood, sails unfurling and orders being barked were beginning to mingle with the lazy sizzle of the sun. Asper narrowed her eyes at that; whatever answers she hoped to find, she wouldn't even be able to hear in a few moments.

'Your companions will likely expect you,' the Serrant suggested.

'They can wait.'

The answer came quickly and without thought. Truly, she hoped it would be enough to express her desire to be alone with the silent, uncaring sun, to have the silence to hear its answers.

Even that hope, however, was extinguished.

'A wise decision, if I may say.' Quillian's footsteps were loud and clanking against the wood as she drew closer. 'Frankly, if you think my criticism not too bold, I don't know why you continue to indulge those heathens, Priestess.'

Asper merely let out a hum. She had often been presented

with that query by those who considered themselves worthy of voicing it. She mulled it over herself, frequently. More often than not, she preferred not to think too hard about it; accepting the excuse that she enjoyed the opportunities provided by their company was preferable to the inevitable headaches that ensued further thought.

'Granted, I may not be in a position to question, given that I follow Galataur.' The Serrant hesitated momentarily. 'But ... Talanas only requires you to serve *mankind*, does He not?'

'Ideally, all Gods—' Asper paused, correcting herself. 'All *human* Gods at least gently encourage the improvement of mankind. I seem to do that rather well.'

'Still,' she could almost hear the cracking of Quillian's teeth, 'I wonder if you are perhaps too indulgent of other faiths. Is it not a sin to acknowledge the Gods of savages?'

'Technically, Kataria and all shicts only have one God. Goddess, actually. Gariath, as far as I know, believes in something else altogether.'

'Which is precisely my point: you *are* aware that some of your companions are—'

'Not human?' She rolled her eyes. 'Yes, I had noticed that.'

'May I ask why—'

'I suppose their parents hadn't the foresight to have been human.'

'Your sarcasm is noted.' The lack of ire in the Serrant's voice was oddly unnerving to the priestess. 'It was my intent to ask why you cling to them.'

Likely because they're at least occasionally willing to leave me alone.

She bit back that thought.

'In theory,' she began with a sigh, 'staying in their

company grants me many opportunities to do the Healer's work.' She cast an appeasing smile over her shoulder. 'You might have noticed the abundance of wounds that materialise in my companions' presence.'

Her nervous laughter was met with stony silence. Quillian offered no indication that she understood the jest, much less appreciated it. She lingered in the corner of Asper's eyes for another moment before the priestess turned away.

Perhaps, she thought, if she stood perfectly still, Quillian would simply stand there and say nothing; it would be the same as being alone, just with a strange, silent, bronze-clad woman staring at her.

'You don't seem convinced.'

Asper opened her mouth to retort before she realised the unpleasant truth of Quillian's words: namely, the fact that she was correct.

She closed her eyes at that moment, trying to summon up images of laughter shared, stories exchanged, a reason why she called them 'companions'. All that flashed behind her lids, however, were the images: bodies cut down, blood shed. The frogman lying motionless in the corner, quivering like a blob of jelly …

Stop it!

Her mind disobeyed the command.

Where, she wondered, was the Healer's work? Where were the mended bones and healed flesh? Where had she consoled the grieving? Where were the funerals? Had there been anything beyond swaddled corpses, deathscrolls and steel?

If I stay with them, is there anything beyond that at all?

'Forgive my audacity.' Quillian's voice shifted low at the

priestess's silence. 'I should not have second-guessed your motives.'

'I've been with them for a year now.'

The Serrant's armour shifted noisily as she straightened up. Without looking, Asper could feel Quillian's eyes upon her: expectant, attentive. She realised she had never commanded such expressions amongst her companions.

'I've done a lot of good in that time, you know,' she said softly. 'I don't regret it. It seemed a grand idea, then, to embark on my pilgrimage in the company of adventurers. Where else would one find so much healing to be done?'

'In my humble experience,' there was an edge of venom to Quillian's words, 'there is rarely a good idea that involves shicts and heathens.'

'They're good people.' The counter came neither as swiftly nor as sternly as she expected. 'They're just ...' *Violent? Brutish? Half-mad?* No word summed them up properly. 'Misguided.'

'Does it then fall to you to guide them?'

Once more, the Serrant's words struck her silent. Her mouth did not so much as open as the question echoed in her mind. What hope did she have of mending their ways? It had been a year now, a bloody, fierce year. They had turned their steel and ferocity towards the good of the Church, that much was true, but they still did so uncharitably, demanding exorbitant amounts of wealth ...

What good did she do by remaining with them?

When she turned around, Quillian was close to her, much closer than she had ever seen the woman. Her features became clearer: there was softness between her hard lines, a quiver in her eyes, as though they struggled desperately to remember how women were supposed to look.

The realisation came swiftly upon her. Before that

moment, she had never seen the Serrant in such a position: no sword at her hip, no oaths or battle cries on her tongue, no sounds of battle in the background. It was not Knight-Serrant Quillian that stood before her, it was simply Quillian, woman.

'There is good to be done,' Asper whispered, 'here and now.'

Quillian's hand twitched, the bronze knuckles rattling against her gauntlet. It rose up to her torso and froze there, quivering as though it wanted to go higher.

Then something flashed across her face, so swift that Asper might not have caught it had she not been so close. Quillian's eyes widened for a moment, then shut tightly. When they opened again, they were soft, quivering, the beginnings of a tear forming in the corner of one eye. She bit her lower lip so hard that Asper feared blood might gush out at any moment.

'Forgive me, Priestess,' she said, her voice suddenly stern and brimming with duty once more, 'I must see to the needs of the Lord Emissary.'

The Serrant departed with a haste Asper had never seen before: a loud, clunky, stumbling gait down the stairs of the helm. She even apologised after bumping into one of the sailors before vanishing into the companionway. And yet, even though the woman was gone, the tension remained thick and oppressive around the priestess.

The questions still lingered in the air, echoing in her head. Behind her, the sun had risen halfway out of the ocean, still unanswering.

'*Someone* has a little infatuation, hm?'

Asper blinked and suddenly noticed him: a tall, black stain against the pristine ocean. Tucked in the corner of the helm, Denaos stood, hands at his groin, an arcing flight of golden, foul-smelling angels singing over the railing.

'How long have you been there?' she asked, raising a brow.

'Quite some time,' he replied swiftly. 'And it appears I'll be here for some time more.' The golden shaft suddenly died in the blink of an eye. 'You'd be surprised how little attention a man urinating requires in delicate situations.'

'Given that said attention would require looking at said man, I'm really not.' She formed a glare. 'How much did you over—'

'Wait!' His voice was shrill and hurried. 'Turn around.'

'What?'

'Turn around! Don't look at me!' He offered a bashful smile. 'I can't go if you look.'

'You can't be—'

'*Do it.*'

The order came with such firmness that she found herself hard pressed to do anything but obey. Shortly after returning her gaze to the familiar sight of the sluggish sun, the sound of water singing acrid yellow tunes filled her ears, accompanied by a sigh so filled with relief it bordered on perverse.

'Oh, sweet Silf, that's better,' he moaned. 'This is what I get for drinking the cheap stuff.'

'I thought men outgrew that.'

'Oh, no one ever outgrows their soil habits.'

'Their what?'

'Soil habits,' he repeated. 'Pot practices, golden means, tinkle techniques if you like. Everyone has their own that they discover at birth and they can never get rid of them.' The sound of water stopped; there was a grunt before it resumed. 'For example, did you know that Dreadaeleon, before checking to make certain no one is looking, removes his breeches entirely, no matter which business he has to do?'

She thought she ought to protest that revelation, if only for propriety's sake. However, she found herself silent; she had seen the wizard do that before. A new, slightly more unnerving image flashed behind her eyes.

'Gariath doesn't even take the time to prepare. He just lifts his leg and goes wherever he pleases.' He snorted. 'Must be why he wears a kilt, eh?'

'So, you've seen everyone …' she coughed, 'make water?'

'Everyone except Kataria,' he replied. 'It's true what they say about the shicts. They always go in a secret place.' The sound of water rose suddenly as he tilted upwards. 'Disgusting.'

'Huh.' She chose not to comment on that. 'So, you've even seen—'

'Oh, absolutely.' Without waiting for further prodding, he continued with an obscene vigour, 'I've seen you plenty of times. Now, you're what I've heard called the "chamber-pot philosopher", granted said title through the long contemplations while squatting.'

Her ears went aflame, face going a deeper shade of crimson than had ever been seen amidst roses. She found her mouth open, without a retort, even though it seemed that she ought to have a particularly scathing one. Still, she whirled about to face him, only to be met with a shriek of protest.

'*Don't look!*' he screeched. '*Turn around, turn around, turn around!*'

She did so with only a mild stammer of outrage, more for her own benefit than for his. Undoubtedly, seeing her coloured so would give him *some* bizarre form of pleasure she preferred not to think about.

A breeze, harsh against her cheek, swept over the ship. Asper stood still, facing the lazy, half-risen sun and listening to the vile symphony of water that showed no signs of fading, slowing or otherwise sparing her the unpleasantness.

'So, do you think you'll do it?' His voice was surprisingly soft, nearly drowned by his functions.

'Do … what?'

'Leave.' He grunted slightly, as if forcing himself to concentrate. 'It's fairly obvious by this point that you've considered it.'

'You overheard.'

'"Overhearing" implies a certain degree of innocent accident. I was genuinely and intentionally spying, I assure you.'

'Unsurprising.'

'Few people are anything but, I find. As for myself, there aren't many surprises left.' His sigh was slow and contemplative. 'Maybe that's why I linger around you degenerates.'

'For surprises,' she repeated, sneering to herself. 'I find that hard to believe.'

'So you should. You know me well enough to know that you don't know me nearly well enough to accept that answer.' He cleared his throat. 'Still, everyone needs a purpose for what they do, don't they?'

Another breeze swept over the deck. The tinge of salt was heavy, the song of distant gulls growing louder. The sun was rising stronger now, with more fervour, as though it, too, had heard the rogue and taken the man's advice. That gave her a bitter pause as she bit her lower lip.

'I've been wondering about my purpose.' She surprised herself with the weakness of her own voice; somehow, she thought she would admit it with more conviction.

'That's funny.' He hummed. 'I've always envied the clergy for their conviction. I thought the reason you took oaths was to give yourself purpose.'

'Oaths are a guide, a reminder of our ... of my faith and my duty.'

'A reminder.' He tasted the words. 'That seems acceptable, considering what Quillian's say on her flank.' He added quickly, 'I know you'd like to turn around and raise an eyebrow at that, but I must encourage you to resist. I'm ... sort of in the middle of something.'

'*Still?*' She sighed, but kept her back turned, regardless. 'You ... can read Quillian's oaths?'

'Bits. Dreadaeleon might know more. Suffice it to say, I can pick out parts that are quite interesting to me when she deigns to doff that armour of hers.' Leather creaked as he adjusted himself. 'Hers would seem to suggest a reminder of duty.'

She paused, her lips pursing thoughtfully, then asked, 'Does duty necessarily equate to purpose?'

'That's a decent question,' he admitted. 'I became an adventurer to avoid most accepted forms of duty. I like to *think* I manage to serve that purpose.'

'Don't lie to me,' she snapped. 'You became an adventurer because you were a fugitive.'

'True, but that's not saying much, is it? Prison sentences are a form of duty.'

'For you, perhaps.' Her sigh was long, tired and laden with thought. 'I need more. I need ... to know that I'm doing the right and proper thing.'

'You'll never figure that out,' he answered decisively. 'There's no way to know what the right and proper thing is, you see. Ask a Karnerian, a Sainite, a shict and a dragonman the same question, they'll all tell you something different.'

'I suppose,' she grunted. 'Then again, I suppose I shouldn't be consulting a felon about matters of spirituality and moral rightness.'

'Moral *righteousness*, perhaps not, but I find myself in a unique position to analyse most matters of faith due to my general offensiveness to all Gods, religions and servicemen and -women thereof.'

'Fine, then.' Her patience was a pot of water, boiling as the sun insultingly decided to rise with a hot and yellow unpleasantness. 'What *is* the right thing, if you're such a genius? What are we doing here? What are we *about* to do?'

The question was only half-posed to the rogue; she stared and addressed no small part of it to the sun. It was fully risen now, Talanas's great, golden Eye broad and fully awake, ready to accept her struggle. Yet still no answer came and, as the water rippled beneath it and cast its shifting hues upon the sky, even the great fiery disc itself seemed to blink.

'We're about to go on an adventure.'

His voice was soft, the words spoken with no particular zeal, yet it echoed in her mind. She turned and found herself jumping with a start as she looked into his dark eyes. He stood before her, perfectly still and unmoving, barely a finger's length of space between them. He did not blink.

'And ... what does that mean?' she asked.

'It means that whatever happens is incidental.'

'What do you—'

'We kill a demon, we get a book, we get rich.' He held up his hands in a shrug. 'By that same token, we use that money for whatever good we think it'll do, we prevent that book from being used in anything wicked and whatever demons die as a result will *not* result in more people dying like Moscoff.'

The image of the boy was another wound in her mind: his still corpse, drowned on dry land, the death that should not have been.

'And, as it is an adventure ...' His hands slid down past his waist, tightening his belt and adjusting his breeches. 'Whether you choose to come or stay, and should you find your purpose – or not – as a result, is also incidental.'

With that, he turned towards the stairs of the helm. At the top, he cast a glance over his shoulder. A smile creased his lips, so swiftly and suddenly as to cause her to start.

'Something to think about the next time you squat.'

With silent footsteps, he was gone.

She strained to hear his boots upon the wood, strained to hear over the sounds of sailors rising on the deck and gulls upon the wind. She strained to hear, as though hoping he would mutter some last bit of advice, some solid stone of wisdom that would crush her with the weight of decision.

Such a sound never came. She glanced up; the sun was not providing anything else today. It had risen lazily and now stood stolidly, firmly resigned to another day of golden silence.

On the decks below, life returned to the *Riptide*.

Eleven

BERTH

Kataria leaned over the railing, balancing on the heels of her hands as she stared at the restless sea below. It churned listlessly against the ship's flank, sending up spray that attached to her flesh like swarms of frothy ticks. The small escape vessel looked so insignificant now, in the light of their new intentions. She could hardly recall it being such a salvation when they tried to run the day before.

It had been a temptation then, a betrayal that had beckoned them with promises of redemption from the chaos raging on deck. Today, it threatened her, flashing a smarmy smile of timber as it promised to deliver the companions into the eager, drooling mouth of carnage.

Or perhaps I'm giving it too much credit, she thought. *It's just a boat, after all.*

At the far end of the ship, sailors busied themselves with a pulley, lowering crates and various sundries into the boat. She watched with a frown, noting her bow amidst the mess: unstrung, a bit of its perfectly polished wood peeking out from the fur she had delicately wrapped it in. Her left eyelid twitched as a pair of careless hairy hands plucked it rudely from the spot where she had so carefully placed it and tossed it against the vessel's edge as though it were a common branch.

They did that on purpose, she thought scornfully.

Human hands were without conscience or the ability to lie; what a human desired to say with his mouth, but was prevented from doing by his mind, he did with his hands. Their hands were maliciously clumsy. The whole round-eared race held a grudge over the shictish superiority with a bow.

We can hardly be blamed for that, she told herself. *We did, after all, invent archery. They stole it from* us.

Envy was an instinct for humans, as natural to them as rolling in foulness was to a dog ... a human-trained dog.

'You're going to fall if you keep leaning like that.'

The voice was thundering, even in so casual a mutter. Gariath regarded her impassively, as he might an insect. He snorted, as though waiting to see if she would actually tumble headlong over the railing.

She offered him half a smile and half a sneer, pulling herself backwards.

'Shicts don't fall,' she declared smugly.

'Shicts don't do anything right.' He stalked to her side, making certain to shove her aside with a wing as he looked over the rail. He cast a contemptuous frown at the bobbing vessel. 'What is that?'

'They call it a companion ship; it's used for foraging on islands. Supposedly, it can be manned by two men.' She winked. 'Considering we've three men, two women and one dragonman, we should have an advantage.'

He merely grunted at that, unaware of her resentful scowl. *Lenk would have at least groaned.*

'Five humans are two and a half times as worthless as two humans,' he muttered.

'*Four* humans,' she replied, twitching her ears.

'Pointy-eared humans are still humans.' He didn't even bother to dignify her threatening bare of teeth with a glance. Instead, he merely kept a disdainful eye upon the craft. 'This is a stupid idea.'

'I thought you wanted to chase the demon.' She knew that speaking so coyly to a creature whose arm was the size of her waist was not, by any race's standards, a good idea. Still, she was hungry for a reaction; Lenk would have insulted her back by now. 'Scared?'

He turned to face her, not with any great need to rip her face off, and regarded her through cold, dark eyes. She tensed, ready to leap aside at the first sign of an angry fist. Instead, he merely grunted, ignoring her flicking tongue as she shot it at him. Her sigh was exaggerated and bored, not that he likely heard it.

'Fear is something for lesser races,' he rumbled. 'It's the only gift their weak Gods gave them, since they sought to deny them intelligence.' He thumped a fist against his chest. 'The spirits gave no gifts to the *Rhega*. I'll hunt the demon down.' He narrowed his eyes. 'It was meant for me.'

'Meant,' she paused, cocking a brow, 'for you?'

'I don't expect you to understand.'

'You'd expect a human to understand any better?' It was with some form of pride that she noted the crew, standing as far away as possible from both shict and dragonman.

'I wouldn't expect anyone but a *Rhega* to understand.'

'Yeah, well, there aren't any *Rhega* around.'

For the first time, she hadn't intended any offence. Yet, for all her previous prodding and attempts to incite him into a reaction, her innocuous observation caused him to whirl about and turn an angry gaze upon her.

Obviously.

His step shook the ship as he thundered forwards. The teeth he bared at her, she noted, were far bigger and far

266

sharper than hers. She resisted the urge to back away, even as his hands tightened into fists. Retreat, more often than not, tended to be viewed as even more of an insult by the dragonman.

'*You* don't have the right to utter that word.' He prodded a claw into her chest, drawing blood and sending her staggering backwards. 'The *Rhega* tongue was not meant for *your* ugly lips.'

'Then what am I supposed to call you?' Her attempt to draw herself up seemed rather pitiful when she noted that the top of her head only came up to the middle of his chest, five times as broad as hers. 'Dragonman? That *human* word?'

'There are many human words.' He made a dismissive gesture. 'All of them are equally worthless. *Rhega* words are worth more.'

'Fine.'

He ignored her challenging scowl as she rubbed at the red spot beneath her collarbone. They both looked towards the sea, observing the bobbing craft.

'So,' she broke the silence tersely, 'what is it you think you're meant to do with this demon?'

'Kill it.'

'Well, naturally.'

'A *Rhega*'s kills have more meaning.'

'Of course they do. It doesn't bother you that you couldn't harm it before?'

'Hit something hard enough, it falls down. That's how the world works.'

'You hit it fairly hard before.'

'Then I'll have to hit it harder.'

She nodded; it seemed to make sense.

'Riffid willing, we'll do that.'

'You should save the names of your weak Gods,' he snorted. 'The more you utter them, the less likely they'll be inclined to send you their worthless aid. Besides,' he folded his arms over his chest, '*we* won't be doing anything. *I* will kill the demon and if your Gods aren't useless, they'll kill you quickly and get you out of the way.'

'Riffid is the *true* Goddess,' she hissed, 'the *only* Goddess.'

'If your Gods intended to cure you of your stupidity, they would not have made you that way in the first place.'

She sighed at that, though she knew it was futile. Gariath's response was hardly unexpected. To credit his objectivity, she grudgingly admitted, he had equal disdain for any God, shict, human or otherwise. His interest in theological discussion tended to begin with snorts and end in bloodshed. It would be wiser to leave now, she reasoned, before he decided to end this conversation.

And yet, she lingered.

'So,' she muttered, 'what's got you in such a sunny mood today?'

His nostrils flared. 'There's a scent on the air ... one I haven't sensed in a long time.'

His face flinched. It was such a small twitch, made smaller in the wake of the rehearsed growl that followed, that he doubtlessly hoped no one would notice. But nothing escaped a shict's attention. In the briefest of moments, concealed behind the subtlest of quivers lurked the mildest ruminations of a frown.

His eyes shifted suddenly. They did not soften, as she might have expected, but rather seemed to twitch in time with his face, as though desperately remembering how to.

'It doesn't stay.' His voice was distant, unaware of her presence beside him. 'It goes ... it returns ... then goes again. It never stays. When it does, it is … overwhelmed, drowned out by other stinks.'

One eye rolled in its socket, so slowly she could hear the muscles creak behind it as he narrowed it upon her.

'That, too, would be remedied if you weren't here.'

Even Kataria was surprised by herself when she leapt forwards. She drew herself up, tightening, tensing and baring teeth in an attempt to look imposing: an effort she clearly took more seriously than he.

'Don't you go threatening *me*, reptile,' she spat. 'You seem to forget that *I'm* not a human. Don't act like I have no idea what you're talking about and *don't* forget that no one else even has a hope of understanding what you're going through.' She jabbed a finger against his chest, narrowly hiding a wince behind her mask of ire. '*I'm* the closest thing you've got to one of your own.'

A silence hung between them, an eternity of inaction. The world seemed to fall silent around them. Gariath regarded her indifferently, his shadow choking her slender frame. He took a step forwards, closing the distance between them to a finger's width.

Like a great mountain sighing, he leaned down, muscles groaning behind leathery skin. His nostrils flared as he brought his face closer to hers, sending the feathers in her hair whipping about her cheeks. There was thunder in her ears, her instincts screaming to be heard over the pounding of her heart and the tension of her muscles, screaming for her to run.

The cacophony was such that she barely even heard him when he whispered, 'Is this the part where I'm supposed to cry?'

The thunder stopped with her heart; her face screwed up.

'Wh-what?'

'After this delightful little chat about racial harmony and standing tall against the human menace, are we supposed to be charming little friends? Am I supposed to break down in your puny arms and reveal, through tears, some profound insight about the inherent folly of hatred as you revel in your ability to bridge the gap between peoples? Afterwards, will we go prancing through some meadow so you can show me the simple beauty of a spiderweb or a pile of deer dung or whatever it is your worthless, stupid race thinks is important?'

'I …' His words had struck her squarely in the belly, leaving her breathless. 'I don't—'

'Then *don't*.' He growled. 'Twitch your little ears, if you want. Talk about *your* Gods as if they're any different from *their* Gods, if it's important to you, but *never* make the mistake of thinking you and I are anything alike.' His eyes narrowed to angry obsidian slits. 'In the end, you *all* look the same to me. Small, weak …' His tongue flicked out between his teeth, grazing the tip of her nose. '*Vermin.*'

He punctuated his words with a blast of hot air from his nostrils. In an instant, he rose up before her, seemingly even taller, broader and redder against the clear blue sky. She felt herself take a hesitant step backwards as he turned about slowly.

Whatever retort she might have had buzzing inside her mind was swatted aside like so many gnats as his tail came lashing up in a flash of crimson. It slapped her smartly across the cheek, sending her sprawling to the deck. Even the sound of her body hitting the wood was an insignificant whisper against the thunder of his footsteps.

'You've been squealing those same threats for ages now!' she shrieked after him, rubbing the red mark across her cheek. 'If we're all so beneath you, why not kill us all now?' Her words were little bee-stings against his leathery back. 'Why do you linger around us if you don't like us?'

He paused and she sprang to her haunches, ready to move should he decide to give her more than just a kiss of his tail. Instead, the dragonman merely shuddered with a great breath and spoke without turning around.

'If you're desperate to prove yourself as more than human,' he rumbled, 'prove it to someone lesser than yourself.'

The sea of humanity parted before him as he strode across the deck, sailors practically climbing over each other to get out of his way. The hulking dragonman seemed unperturbed by it, growing taller with each frightened gaze cast his way as he lumbered towards the far side of the ship.

It was with grudging envy that she watched him, for as Kataria stood at the other end of the deck, she was all too aware of the great wall of round-ears that separated her from the only other non-human aboard. Her ears twitched, picking up concerns she couldn't understand, humour she couldn't comprehend, whispers she wasn't privy to.

In Gariath's wake, the humans had re-formed into a great mass of their own race, leaving her sitting beside the railing, alone.

Stupid, stinking lizard. Her thoughts immediately turned to scorn. *Acts like he's so much better than everyone else. As if being large enough to strangle anyone who disagrees with you is reason enough to act as though you're beyond reproach.*

She bit her lower lip; that actually *did* make sense.

Regardless, she countered herself, *he has no reason to treat me like that. He has no reason to look down on me like I'm some filthy ... human!*

Her anger shifted from the dragonman to the sailors bustling about the deck, each one occasionally glancing over his shoulder to see how close she was to them and make room accordingly.

Cowards.

Cowardice was the way of their race. Her father had said as much and now she knew it to be true. She recalled the aftermath of yesterday's carnage. The crew of the *Riptide*, *her* humans had prevailed over the other, filthier humans with *her* help. While they screamed, she laughed. While they fumbled, she shot true. While they had soiled themselves, it was *she* who had pulled Lenk, one of *her* humans, away from danger.

She had deserved their respect from the very beginning as both a warrior and a shict. Now, her very presence demanded it.

And yet, they continued to prove their cowardice. She heard them even now, making envious, lewd remarks about her musculature. They skulked, casting shifty, wary glances her way. They hurried with the loading, undoubtedly eager to see her leave to chase some demon and die out at sea.

None of them had enough bravery to come forth and insult her to face.

'Hey, moron.'

Her lips were curled in a snarl and her teeth bared as she whirled about. The blue eyes that met her fury were impassive and rolling in their sockets.

'Yeah, you're ferocious,' Lenk said, half-yawning. 'I'll be sure to soil myself later.' He extended a tin cup to her, a thick veil of steam rising from its lip. 'Here.'

'What is it?' She took it and gave it a sniff, examining

the thick, brown liquid sloshing about inside it curiously. 'It smells awful.'

'It's coffee,' he replied. 'Tohanan brownbean, specifically; expensive stuff.'

'Coffee,' she murmured. She took a sip and blanched. 'It tastes awful, too.'

'That's how you know it's expensive.'

'I guess that makes sense to a human.'

'Not particularly,' he said, shrugging. 'It never made sense to me, at least.' Taking a sip of his own brew, he forced a smile without much effort to convince behind it. 'I suppose that makes me inhuman, then?'

Kataria should have smiled back, she knew, but her only responses were pursed lips and a heavy-lidded stare.

Inhuman.

The word hung in the air between them and she heard it every time she blinked. In the spaces where she should have seen darkness behind her eyes, she saw him instead. She saw him writhing, clutching his head, snarling at her in a voice that was not his own. In the moments between her breath and the beating of her own heart, she heard him as he shrieked at her.

STOP STARING AT US!

'Stop,' he said.

'What?' She blinked; the images were gone.

'Stop looking at me that way,' he muttered, taking a harsh sip, 'it bothers me.'

'Ah.' She turned her gaze down to the brown brew in her hand and blinked. 'Why are we drinking the expensive stuff, anyway?'

'Argaol's charity,' he replied. 'The good captain apparently wants us to depart in good spirits.'

'Charity?' She cocked a brow; that seemed an unlikely word to describe the man.

'He said to think of it as a last meal for the soon-to-be-corpses.'

'Ah.' She took a sip. 'Thoughtful.'

'Mm.'

The stillness of the morning was broken suddenly by the sound of something shrieking across the sea. The two glanced up and regarded the looming black spectacle approaching the *Riptide*.

The *Linkmaster* was alive in the waters, or at least alive in the same way a carcass crawling with flies was alive. Men scurried across its decks, pink dots against black timbers, variously swabbing, stitching and otherwise mending. From its railings dangled crude rope swings, men ensconced and busy at the hull. At the prow, one such man worked at the bright red lettering of the ship's title, smothering its identity under a shell of black paint.

Kataria noted with some pride the wound where the ship's hull had been shattered by the *Riptide*'s prow. It had been her precise shooting, shictish shooting, that had given the great wooden beast such a blow. Now, men dangled around the great mess of timbers, prying from its splinters what appeared to be thick, reeking chunks of quickly browning beef.

Kataria's grin was small, restrained and wholly unpleasant.

'Disgusting.' Lenk grimaced as what might once have been a thigh was tugged free of the wood and plopped into the waters below, the latest course of a feast tended to by a noisy pack of gulls. 'And to think, that's our freedom.'

'It is?'

'According to Argaol.' Lenk nodded. 'He even renamed it *Black Salvation* for the occasion.'

'I'm not sure I follow.'

'Well, if that demon we questioned is to be believed, the Abysmyth headed for the islands to the north. The waters there are too shallow for a large ship like the *Riptide* to navigate, so we're taking the companion craft,' he gestured over the ship's starboard side, 'out there.

'Now, you might have noticed that thing is far too small to take us *back* to Toha, where civilisation and our pay await when and if we retrieve the tome and assuming at least one of us is still alive to deliver it.'

She nodded; the thought had occurred to her.

'So, Argaol's apparent plan is to let Sebast take the *Black Salvation* out after us.' He took a hard swig, finishing the rest of his coffee. 'In a few days, the ship should be ready for sailing. Presumably, it should take another day or two for Sebast to catch up with us.'

'I see.' Her ears twitched. 'So, that gives us how much time to find the tome?'

'About six days before we meet up with Sebast.'

'So, going by what we know of the Abysmyth, you figure that gives us, what, one day to find where it went, another day to get the tome, two more days to reach wherever it is we're supposed to reach and one more day to find Sebast.' She blinked. 'What do we do with the other day?'

Lenk's nostrils quivered as he inhaled deeply. 'Presumably?'

'By all means,' she answered.

'Bury the dead.'

A stale wind swept across the deck. The feathers in Kataria's hair wafted across her face as she stared down into her cup and swirled the liquid thoughtfully.

'Good coffee.'

'Mm.'

In the brightness of the morning, Kataria couldn't help but notice a sudden change in Lenk. He was not a large man, standing only about as tall as herself, far shorter than most of his kind. Yet, today, as the sun gnawed at his back with hungry golden rays, he seemed smaller than he had been the night before … diminished, somehow.

It was no mere physical change, nothing that sleeplessness alone could account for. He had changed so subtly that no one but she might notice. He stood slightly less straight, his back a little more crooked. His silver hair that had once gleamed bright and flowed in the breeze like liquid metal now hung limp and grey at his shoulders, still even as the wind tried to goad it into movement. For all that, though, his eyes had lost none of their lustre. They were still blue, still hard.

Still cold.

'Lenk,' she whispered.

He turned on her swiftly, a beast sensing danger, and her breath caught in her throat as he levelled his gaze at her. His eyes glimmered with an intellect not his own, flashing with a hard and stony presence for but a moment. When she blinked, his stare was softer, but no less wary.

'Last night …' she continued, unintimidated.

'You couldn't sleep, either,' he finished, nodding. 'Frankly, if I broke wind as much as you do, I'd have a difficult time breathing, much less dozing off.'

'That's not what I was going to say.'

He sighed, and diminished further, something leaving him with the force of his breath.

'I know.' His voice was weaker now, closer to a whimper

than an answer. 'I know what you want. I know it every time you stare at me.'

'I don't mean to.'

'Yes, you do. That's simply how you ask for things. You stare.' When he looked back up at her, his eyes quivered at the corners, stars sparkling against red-veined whites. 'But it's far too early for that sort of thing just now, wouldn't you agree?'

'For what sort of thing?' She strained, with no small effort, to conceal the indignation in her voice. '*Talking?*'

'About what *you* want to talk about, yes,' he replied sharply. 'So, kindly indulge me when I ask you to simply keep your peace today.'

'Keep my ...' Her face twisted into an expression of incredulousness. 'For how long?'

'Hopefully,' he turned from her and began to trudge away, 'until one of us is dead so that it no longer matters.'

She watched him go for a moment, venom boiling on the tip of her tongue. Moments before he stepped out of earshot, she struck, like a spitting asp, and hissed at him.

'And will it be you who kills me?'

He stiffened and, in a sharp, shallow breath, he was restored. No longer diminished, he turned on her, standing as tall as he could, wiry muscles tensed and eyes bright with anger. She forced herself not to recoil as he stepped towards her, boots heavy upon the deck.

'What was that?' He had no growl or snarl to his voice, no passion or anger.

'You heard me,' she responded swiftly. 'By walking away from me, you're putting my life in danger.'

'Stop this.'

'Are you just going to pretend that last night didn't happen?' She took a challenging step forwards. 'Are you going to hope it was a bad dream? That it won't happen again?' She shook her head. 'I'm sure you can live with that, but *I* can't.'

'*Stop.*'

'I *remember* what you did last night.' She continued unabated, despite the rigidity of his body, the narrowing of his eyes. 'I remember you screaming at yourself, screaming at *me*. Now we've got a chance to find out what's going on inside that thick head of yours and you don't even want to spare a moment to talk about it for *my* sake, let alone yours.'

'Kat—'

'Lenk.' She took a step closer, peering intently at him. Her hand trembling, she reached out to lay it upon his shoulder. 'What happened to you?'

The answer she received was unspoken. Beneath her hand, beneath the fabric of his tunic, she felt something stir in his bones. Even as the sun hissed, steadily climbing, she felt a sudden chill coursing through her fingers.

'That's enough.' His own hand was up in a flash, batting hers off his shoulder. 'If I *don't* want to talk about something, you're in no position to question me. Over the past few days, I've been stabbed, slashed, punched, pummelled and smashed by various people and things *without* the luxury of pay or anything more than a bowl of beans and the complaining of the people I somehow manage always to find myself surrounded by.'

She blinked and he was face to face with her, his breath frigid against her lips. Her own lungs seemed to deflate under his gaze, her eyes refusing to look away from his. She wanted to blink, she craved any reason to close her eyes, praying that when she opened them again, his eyes would be dotted by black pupils.

But she could not blink. As he stared at her, she was forced to stare back into two orbs of pristine, pupilless blue.

'Listen to me when I say,' he whispered harshly, 'that I have *earned* the right to walk away from you.'

And with a turn that cut the wind, he was off, stalking across the deck. She stared at him; though he was no longer diminished, no longer so small against the day, he did not appear whole, either. He walked with his back straight, but his hair still hung limply upon shoulders that were heavy with some unseen burden.

Though she had spoken to Lenk moments ago, she was unsure who now walked away from her.

A mass of people were congealing at the railing. She spotted her own companions amongst them, huddled about the dark shape of Captain Argaol. Quietly, she began to move towards them, rubbing her arms as she went to nurse circulation back into her skin.

It hadn't been so cold a moment ago.

'Damn,' Denaos grunted, looking up accusingly at the sky. 'What happened?'

'What do you mean?' Asper asked.

'It was warm,' Denaos muttered, stamping his feet. 'Now it's colder than a whale fart.'

'Do ... do whales fart?' She cocked a brow.

'Everything farts; it's what makes us human.'

'But whales aren't—'

'That's why *their* farts are *cold*,' he snapped. The tall man glanced up as Kataria elbowed her way into the huddle, his eyes darting from her bare arms to her bare midsection. 'Not that I've any particular grievance with it, but are you sure you wouldn't like a cloak or something?'

'I don't need anything,' she muttered, not looking at him. Her stare was distant, though the corner of her gaze occasionally flickered to the silver-haired man standing beside her. 'It's not that cold.'

'*Not that cold?*' Denaos shivered at the very words. 'It feels like I've just sat on an icicle and twisted.'

'She said she's not cold,' Lenk spat, glowering at him. 'Shut up.'

While a number of scathing retorts leapt easily to mind, ones he was certain would leave the young man fumbling for his stones, Denaos opted to clamp his lips together. Something between his and the shict's stare confirmed the wisdom in that.

'You'll be sweating out of your pants in an hour, anyway,' Argaol replied, glancing up at the sun. 'The sea changes weather quickly. While those soft and dry porkflanks in the cities won't be up to face their warm morning for another two hours, we men of Zamanthras have to be up before dawn so we can face Her when She's cold and angry.'

'And this has never struck you as blatantly stupid?' Dreadaeleon offered the man a smirk.

'I'm in no mood for a smug-off, boy,' the dark man snapped. 'The Lord Emissary has requested I point you in the direction of your demon and that's just grand by me. The sooner you learn where you're going, the sooner you can be off my ship and out of my life. So, unless there are any objections,' his eyes darted between the assembled, 'we can proceed.'

'This is probably unnecessary,' Kataria muttered with a sneer, 'since Gariath can apparently just *sniff* his way to victory.'

'Victory smells like a pair of ripped-off ears,' the dragon-man said in reply, dismembering the argument before it

280

could begin, 'just in case anyone was wondering.'

'All right, if there aren't any *other* objections,' Argaol sighed, 'we can get underway.' He swept about, pointing towards the distant horizon. 'Now, if you strain your eyes a bit, you can see your destination on the edge of the world there.'

Lenk squinted, peering out over the railing and shaking his head.

'I can't see anything.' He made a gesture. 'Kat, get up here and tell me what you see.'

'No need for that,' she replied. 'I see a speck of white in the distance and, in the fore, a silvery piece of—'

'*Anyway*,' Argaol interrupted, 'she's correct. The island you're looking for has the renown of being the whitest. See, it's the furthest from Toha, the Heart of Buradan, where the Sea Mother plummeted from the heavens to submerge Herself in the deep. As one sails from Toha, where the sands are so blue as to render the shores useless, one finds the sands getting progressively whiter until you reach Ktamgi.'

'Ktamgi?'

'Aye, Ktamgi.' He nodded. 'The uttermost reach of Toha and her Blue Navy.'

'What do you mean by that?' Lenk asked.

'He means it's a former Tohanan colony, as far as an island can be from Toha and still be considered theirs,' Denaos replied before the captain could. 'Though he's a bit mistaken; smugglers have been using the Reaching Isles for decades now.'

'Check with whatever vile sources you have, you thug,' Argaol snapped back. 'The Reaches have been cleared of pirates for the past five years.'

'My mistake.' Denaos coughed. 'I just figured, what with

the fact that we were *attacked* by pirates yesterday, they might still be active. You yourself said that some of the *Linkmaster*'s crew escaped on their companion boats.'

'First of all, it's the *Black Salvation* now. The *Linkmaster* was a pirate vessel and I command no such thing.' He held up a finger. 'Further, however many of Rashodd's boys escaped are likely headed for safer waters than Ktamgi's.'

'You're implying that Ktamgi's waters are not safe.' Lenk glowered.

'Well, pardon the abruptness, but I figured since you're eager to go chasing after gigantic black demons that rip heads off, safety wasn't that big a concern for you.'

'No one's ever actually seen an Abysmyth rip anyone's head off,' Dreadaeleon pointed out.

'*Be that as it may*,' Argaol replied, 'the threat of pirates, sharks or whatever man-eating parrots or similar creations may be out there are the *least* of your worries, I can assure you. As it stands, according to the Lord Emissary and our …' he paused to clear his throat, '*other* source, Ktamgi is the most likely island the demon has fled to with the Lord Emissary's tome. As stated, you'll have about six days to get your business done before Sebast catches up with you.'

'And Sebast will pick us up at Ktamgi?' Asper asked.

'Well, not as such, no.' Argaol shook his head. 'The waters around Ktamgi are shallower than most. He'll be meeting you on an island another day north, on an outpost called Teji.'

'Of course.' Lenk rolled his eyes. 'Why convenience us when you can make a profit?'

'If you prefer not to meet up with us, you can try making it to Port Destiny in the companion craft.'

'All the same,' Dreadaeleon tapped his chin thoughtfully,

'aren't there a number of islands closer and more suitable to serve as a meeting site?'

'Well, if you check the charts, you'll—' He glanced at the boy, searching the shadows of his coat. 'Where are the charts I gave you?'

'Likely down in the hold below. I memorised them last night.'

'You memorised sixty sea charts in the span of a few hours.'

'Wizard.' The boy tapped his temple. 'If I can figure out how to turn a man into a puddle of liquid entrails, I can assuredly memorise a few crude drawings of an ocean.' He smirked again. 'Though I did enjoy the pictures of compasses and sea monsters on the charts. Your handiwork, Captain?'

'Sebast's.' Argaol sighed. 'Look, the Lord Emissary insists on you having the charts and I'm not one to deny him. I've been all over the sea and—'

'You have,' Dreadaeleon interrupted, 'and that's why *you're* overseeing thirty-odd unwashed, hairy men in various states of greasiness and undress and *I'm* about to—'

'Get your head eaten by a demon,' Argaol finished.

Dreadaeleon's grin vanished. 'Quite.'

'At any rate, Teji is the only island that possesses a desirable combination of attributes,' Argaol continued. 'In addition to being relatively close to Ktamgi and friendly to merchants, it's also as close as one can possibly get to the more northern islands before entering Akaneed territory.' He grimaced. 'I'll *not* send even you into those waters during breeding season.'

Lenk almost hesitated to ask; no creature that he knew of was ever particularly desirable company during any kind of breeding season. Kataria, however, asked for him.

283

'What … is an Akaneed?'

'Well, it's like a giant, angry—' He paused, smacking his lips. 'You know, I shouldn't even encourage you. *If* you stick to the plan and head for Ktamgi, then Teji, you won't even encounter one, so there's no sense in telling you what one looks like.' He coughed, lowering his voice. 'Not like you could do much against one, anyway.'

'What?'

'Nothing,' he replied. 'Any questions?'

'What did you just say a moment ago?'

'Any *other* questions?'

'It occurs to me, Captain,' Dreadaeleon mused, 'that there are a dozen or so Reaching Isles, most of them likely possessing these white sands you speak of. If we get lost, how are we to know we've arrived on the right one?'

'Decent point.' Argaol cast a sideways glance at Kataria. 'Ktamgi is the furthest Reach, so you'll be looking for sands that are just a shade less white than her.' He cleared his throat before she could respond. 'Anything else?'

'There yet remains,' a voice spoke, slow and methodical, 'one point of business.'

All other sounds were penitent before the voice of Miron Evenhands: gulls going silent, men pausing to swiftly look up before bowing their heads, and the great waves dying to a quiet, respectful murmur as the priest emerged from the companionway.

The wind, however, did not abate. As he strode towards the companions, his sleeves and cowl billowed behind him, white wings, stark and pure against the dawning gloom. His eyes glimmered like fading stars, his smile as easy and familiar as the sun.

It struck Lenk as only a brief, fleeting moth of a thought,

but the Lord Emissary looked as though he hadn't even been present for the carnage the previous day.

'I would hope you aren't planning to send my humble agents out before I can offer the proper benedictions, Captain,' Miron said, reaching them. He appeared to be even taller today, threatening to challenge Gariath's own impressive height.

'I'm not one for lying to priests, Lord Emissary,' Argaol replied, 'so I'll not *tell* you I was hoping to be rid of them as soon as possible, no.'

Miron ignored that, instead surveying the assembled with his unflinching gaze.

'I hope the significance of this excursion has been impressed upon you all,' he spoke softly, 'not merely for the consequences that are to come from the Abysmyth's holding of the tome, but also for those brave souls who have assembled here to pursue the beast.

'Whether they worship Talanas,' he glanced to Asper, 'Silf,' to Denaos, 'the flow of magic itself,' to Dreadaeleon, 'Gods I've no wish to disrespect by uttering their names improperly,' to Kataria, 'forces beyond our own comprehension,' to a smugly smiling Gariath, 'or ...'

He hesitated, blinking for the first time at Lenk. The young man blinked back, coughing.

'Khetashe,' he said. 'The Wanderer.'

'Oh.' Miron bit his lower lip. 'Really?' He waved a hand, dismissing further conversation. 'Regardless, a most momentous journey is about to be undertaken. For never before have so many gathered under a common cause since the House was first founded. And I hope—'

The Lord Emissary's voice died for Lenk, fading into such pious rhetoric as could only be spoken by someone *not* about to be off to be killed. He was jerked aside by a dark hand, pulled away from the circle towards the railing and turned to face Argaol, the captain's face grim.

'Listen,' he muttered, 'you know I'm no blasphemer.'

'Uh … yeah?'

'As well you know I'm none too fond of you.'

'Oh … yes.'

'But I'd be no man of Zamanthras if I sent you off without encouraging you to a wiser course of action.' He pointed down to the bobbing companion craft below. 'I'm going to have the boys plant the sea charts in your cargo. There are a few islands safer than Ktamgi that you can land on out there.'

'But Ktamgi is where—'

'Don't think I'm an idiot, boy, I know damn well what lies on Ktamgi.' He sighed, resting a hand on the young man's shoulder. 'That's entirely my point. There's nothing to say you can't just find a decent place to squat and wait out the six days before heading for Teji. Avoid the demon entirely, forget the tome and preserve your life.'

'That's a bit sentimental for a man who's wished me dead before.' Lenk quirked a brow.

'And if you manage to die of your own idiocy, the world won't miss one or six adventurers,' Argaol replied. 'But …' He paused, clenching his teeth. 'I didn't sleep last night. I kept seeing Mossud in my mind, over and over, I kept seeing what became of him.' His eyes were red-rimmed, heavy. 'I wouldn't wish that on anyone, much less one who has, I'll admit, helped me in the past. We *might* have been sunk if not for you and your boys yesterday.'

Lenk was at odds with himself; his first instinct was to shove the captain's hand away, to launch some smarmy retort and walk away strengthened by the power of the last word. His second instinct was to nod, thank the captain for his advice and discreetly pursue that course of action later.

He settled for the third and least satisfying instinct.

'I don't have a lot of options here, Captain,' he said softly, so as not to be heard by his companions nearby. 'I don't *have* any shipping business, any farm, any shop or anything even resembling a decent life to go to if I don't get paid from this.'

'No amount of gold can be worth dying like Mossud did.'

'It's not the gold,' Lenk spoke with a swiftness that surprised himself, 'not just the gold, anyway. It's also … the demon. I have … I have to go and find it. I have to kill it.'

'You're skirting dangerous thoughts there, boy.' The captain grimaced. 'You can just tell me without soiling yourself that you're going to chase after this demon for the *fun of it*?'

Lenk opened his mouth to reply, but nothing even remotely less insane came to mind. Instead, he sighed, rolled his shoulders and offered a half-smile to the captain. Argaol, in response, stared for a brief, horrified moment.

'I'll only say it once more because I suspect you'll change your mind when the truth of your situation sinks in, boy,' he hissed. 'When you see white, you turn the other way … *quickly*.'

Not sparing another moment for a conversation that was clearly already quite deranged, Argaol spun on his heel and stalked off towards his sailors.

'What was that about?'

The young man did not start at the voice; he had felt her eyes on him since Argaol had dragged him off.

'Well-wishing,' he replied without turning.

'Don't insult me any further,' Kataria growled.

'You're right, I'm sorry.' Lenk sighed, his head drooping. 'Argaol just had a few last words to spare me.' He glanced up; Kataria was already at his side, staring out at the horizon. He followed her gaze. 'Can you really see Ktamgi?'

'Slightly.' Her pupils dilated swiftly, encompassing her eyes for a moment as she sought out the island. 'It's distant, though. It'll take a few days to get there in this wind.'

'We've got our own wind.'

'Mm.'

They stood for a moment. Lenk couldn't help but notice as the breeze kicked up, sending the shict's feathers playing about her face, caressing her skin with the locks of gold that whipped in the breeze. He clenched his teeth, making the same expression he did when he had once pulled an arrow out of his thigh.

'Kat, let me—'

'I'd rather not,' she replied.

With that, she was gone, returned to her spot between Asper and Gariath. Lenk stared at her for a moment before forcing himself to turn away. His eyes could spare nothing for her now, he knew, not so much as a blink. He leaned out over the railing, squinting.

Odd, he thought, that Ktamgi, no more than a distant black dot, should be capable of looming.

Twelve

WAKE

The companion craft tore through the waves like an overeager child. Its canvas sails bubbled and giggled with the air fed into them, it slipped over wave and surf with a grace both enthusiastic and distinguished.

Lenk would remember to savour the imagery later.

For the moment, his world was one of wood. Fingers aching, he clung to the vessel's railing, knees wobbling in nauseous rhythm with his churning stomach. His lunch rose up in protest for the sixteenth time, narrowly fought back by a tightening throat, as they cut over another wave. Near-faint, he was spared a violent uprising of jerked beef and fruit as a fist of froth struck him squarely in the face.

'Fourth time that's happened.'

Wet strands of silver obscuring his vision, Lenk scowled towards the prow. Kataria leaned on the edge, perfectly balanced, an obnoxious smile beaming in time with the oppressive sun.

'Choke on it,' Lenk snarled in reply.

'You wouldn't get wet so often if you didn't put your face over the side,' she chided. 'Though, frankly, the concept of water being wet may be too much for me to expect you to grasp.'

'If you'd like to clean up my mess after I spill it on the floor, be my guest.' He cast a sneer at her, chiefly to hide his nauseous grimace. 'Perhaps you could take a moment to roll around in it first.'

'I didn't even know you got seasick.' The shict gave no indication she had even heard the insult as she tilted her head. 'Where was this love of lurching when we were on the *Riptide*?'

'Buried below deck,' Lenk replied sharply. 'Since I lack that privacy here, I have the distinct pleasure of hearing *you* while I—'

His sarcasm caught in his throat, overtaken by a stampede of half-digested meat. In one vile swoop, he tilted overboard.

'If you're feeling a bit fragile, I could ask Dreadaeleon to slow down,' Kataria offered, none too gently.

'I doubt he'll listen.'

Their eyes slid towards the stern, narrowing upon the scrawny, coat-clad figure seated upon the sole bench. Legs folded, hands knitted in a gesture that looked painful to even consider attempting, Dreadaeleon's eyes were shut tightly, lips quivering in a series of incomprehensible murmurs.

Above his head, the air shimmered and waxed, the sails billowing with every rapid twitch of his mouth. Behind him, the combined strength of Denaos and Gariath fought to control the rudder against the fury of the artificial wind. The rogue looked not at all pleased with the task; perhaps due to the proximity of the dragonman, perhaps due to the boy's coat-tails whipping him about the face.

'Fortunate that the companion vessel is small enough for him to move, isn't it?' Kataria spared a smile for the wizard. 'I'd wager even the Abysmyth can't swim so fast.'

'Yeah … fortunate,' Lenk grumbled, narrowly avoiding a rogue wave. 'We'll be food for it that much quicker.' His cheeks bulged momentarily. 'And here I am, courteously marinating in my own juices.'

'If it bothers you that much, wake him up.'

'You don't know much about wizards, do you?' Lenk cast a baleful glare at the youth. 'He's focusing at the moment. If he's disturbed, something could go wrong.'

'Such as?'

'I woke him up one time while he was trying to keep a fire lit without wood.' A sour frown creased Lenk's face. 'He got startled and I walked away with no hair anywhere, save on my head.'

Kataria blinked for a moment before her eyes widened.

'You mean even—'

'*Yes.*'

'Sounds painful.'

'It was,' he replied. 'Anyway, if you feel like being blasted by whatever he's messing with, go right ahead. Maybe then I can be sick in peace.'

Kataria chose to hold her tongue as his head bowed back beneath the railing. An expression that lingered uncertainly between lamentful and resentful played upon her face as she stared at him. There was a quiet comfort in his lurching, she thought, not without a modicum of distaste for the idea. She could see him now, vulnerable, as she had not seen him for ages. She could stare at him now without agitating him.

Without him screaming at me.

His head snapped up suddenly, his gaze fixing on her with a cold intensity. She resisted the urge to jump, even as he narrowed his eyes at her, as though he had heard her thoughts. In an instant, whatever malice lurked behind his glare dissipated, replaced by something hovering between meekness and resentment.

'So,' he whispered softly, 'this will sound rather odd to hear.'

She quirked a brow.

'And, rest assured, it's not that easy to say, but …' His eyes flitted to the side, indicating a lock of silver that had been coated in a thick brown substance. 'Would you mind terribly?'

The other brow went up, eyes widening as she realised his request.

'Mind?' she asked. 'Yes, of course I mind, and more than a little of it is quite terrible.'

He blinked at her. 'But can you do it anyway?'

'Yeah.' She sighed, doffing her gloves. 'Just don't get any on me.'

With a roll of her eyes, she slid behind him just as his head went back over the railing. Gingerly, she knitted her fingers into his hair and pulled it back gently, holding it out of his face as he sent a wave of brown cascading from his maw.

It occurred to her, with no small amount of grimacing, that she shouldn't be looking so intently, much less smiling so broadly, at the sight of his liquid corkscrews. His sickness was a comfort to her, however; perhaps it was simply morbid amusement at his suffering, perhaps it was simply pleasant to feel needed once more. Either way, she could not turn away nor banish the smile from her face as he let out a gurgling sound, choking on pleas for mercy to his own innards.

She resolved to be disgusted with herself later.

'This is nice, isn't it?'

'Nice,' he repeated, gasping. His head tilted upwards slightly. 'I'm vomiting up my intended last meal so that I'll be nice and lean before something out there in the wide, blue sea of death decides to devour me.' He shuddered. 'Yes, this is very nice.'

'What I mean is,' she continued, 'this is like how things used to be.'

'That's odd, I don't remember this part.'

'Just shut up and listen for a moment.' Her ears twitched for emphasis. 'What do you hear?'

'I really don't think—'

'Wind and water,' she speared his sentence with a smile, 'nothing more.' From behind her, a shrill voice rose to an alien crescendo. 'Well, wind, water and Dread, anyway.' She leaned closer, skewering him a little further on her grin. 'But that's all there is. There's no screaming, no dying. It's just the sound of the world. Do you even remember when we were last able to hear this?'

He raised his head from the sea, casting a glimpse over his shoulder. Despite the sopping strings of hair clinging to his face and the brown streak creeping from the corner of his mouth, some hint of a smile shone through, like the merest sliver of sunlight through a boarded-up window. With a sigh, the first sigh, she noted, not to brim with resentment, he turned away.

'I'm not sure I'd put it in those words,' he said, 'but I do remember a time less red ... and brown.' He made a choking sound as he bit back a meaty uprising. 'I suppose if we could have such things all the time, though, they wouldn't mean anything.'

'Not necessarily.'

'Hm?'

'Well, given the circumstances, you think we might ...' She let the thought dangle off her tongue, hanging ominously in the air over his head.

'Run away?'

293

'Yeah.'

'The thought had occurred to me.' His second sigh bore not even a hint of contentment. 'What of you? You seemed eager enough to go chasing the Abysmyth last night.'

'Well, I wasn't about to be shown up by *you*,' she retorted, less hotly than she thought she ought to. 'But I've had time to think on it.'

'And now you want to run?'

'Not really,' she spoke evenly. 'I'm merely putting it forth as a possibility. It doesn't matter much to me.'

'Doesn't matter,' Lenk repeated. She could hear his brow furrowing. 'How does it not matter? Have you *not* figured out that we're all going to die?'

'Well, if you're so certain about our fate, it would seem a bit pointless to worry about it. But that isn't what I've been thinking about.'

'Go on, then.'

'It just occurs to me,' her voice grew hesitant, as though she were attempting to soothe an irate beast rather than pose a question, 'I don't know why you're out here.'

Lenk's response was a wet gurgle as he nearly toppled overboard with the fury of his heaving. The sea giggled a mocking, salt-laden tune as it reached up to slap him with a frothy palm. He pulled back a scowl dripping with resentment.

'I ask myself that same question,' he muttered, 'every Gods-damned day.'

'That's not what I mean.' She spoke more harshly. 'Why are *we* out here? Why did *you* decide to go after the demon if death is so certain?'

'I believe we covered this last night,' he replied, 'with one thousand golden responses.'

'Don't you dare pretend to think that I'm an idiot by

pretending *you're* an idiot, Lenk.' All traces of sensitivity had given way to ire, anger spurred by his evasion. 'All the gold in the world won't do you any good if you're dead. There's another reason you're out here, one you're not telling me.'

He drew in a deep breath suddenly and, as though he had inhaled the sun, the air seemed to go cold around her. Before her, he went stiff and rigid, his fingers threatening to dig deep furrows in the railings, so white did they become. His voice was low and soft, though not at all gentle, as he hissed through his teeth.

'Then why would I tell you now?'

Kataria found herself shivering at his response. For an instant, something else spoke from his mouth, another voice that lurked between his words. An echo of an echo resonated in her ears, lingering in the air around his lips and sucking the warmth from the sky with each reverberation.

'Lenk, that's not—'

No, no, NO! Her instincts thundered in her brain, drowning out all other sounds. *Don't you apologise to him, don't you try to make peace. If he wants to be difficult, let him be difficult.*

And yet, the voice that seeped out of her mouth was not that of her instinct.

'Lenk,' she whispered, 'does it have to be this way?'

'What way?'

Let him be difficult … and let him remember what it means to be difficult.

Whether it was instinct or simple, vengeful pride that forced her to tighten her grip on his hair, she could not say. Whether it was instinct or the last layer before a shell of quiet resentment gave way to a boiling core of anger that caused her arms to tense, she could not say.

'This way.'

If it was anything other than a perverse pleasure that caused her to slam his head down against the railing, bringing a smile at the cracking sound that followed, she did not care.

'Khetashe!' he screamed, fingering the red blossom under his nose. 'What was that for?'

When his fist lashed out to catch her jaw, he found nothing but air. A quick glance over his shoulder saw her crawling across the vessel's meagre deck. Had he energy for anything besides heaving, he might have scrambled for his sword and pursued. As it stood, he merely vomited again.

Asper glanced up as Kataria sprang forwards over the shifting deck. Her eyes went wide at the chorus of curses from Lenk's lips and she turned a befuddled stare to her companion as she sat down beside her.

'What was that all about?'

'Nothing to worry about yet,' Kataria replied swiftly. With unnerving speed, she forced a smile onto her lips. 'All's well here?'

'I suppose,' the priestess replied. She noticed the bright red spot upon the railing and frowned. 'Should I—'

'No, you shouldn't,' Kataria snapped. 'He's fine. How are you?'

'Decent enough,' Asper replied with a weak shrug. She furrowed her brow at the shict. 'Why do you care, anyway?'

'I can't care about my companions?' She gave Asper a playful slug on the arm, her grin growing broader as the priestess let out a pained squeak. 'What's the matter with you, anyway? You haven't spoken for hours.'

'I'm fine.' Asper's voice was as distant as her gaze, her eyes staring out over the endless blue. 'I'm just … distracted.'

'By?'

'Well … nothing.' The priestess shook herself angrily, as if incensed by her own lie. 'Nothing that I can help, anyway. It's just … I *hear* something. My ears are ringing, I have a headache,' she fingered the phoenix medallion in her palm, 'but I don't know why.'

'Seasickness, perhaps.' Kataria sneered in Lenk's direction as the young man let out a saliva-laden groan. 'It could be worse.'

'It's not that.' Asper shook her head. 'It … well, it sounds strange to say, but it feels … like something's calling to me.' Seeing her companion's baffled expression, she continued hastily. 'It-it's not a sound, not a normal one, anyway. It's not like the ringing of bells or the crying of children. It's … an ache, a dull pain that I hear.'

'You hear …' Kataria's face screwed up, 'pain?'

'Something like that.'

'Well.' The shict clicked her tongue thoughtfully. 'If there were something out there that you could hear, I think chances are that I would hear it first.' Her ears twitched. 'And if it were something I couldn't hear, I think Dreadaeleon would sense it.' She glanced back at the entranced boy and frowned. 'Then again—'

'I know.' Asper sighed. 'It's just nerves, I suppose.' Her hand tightened around the pendant, squeezing it as she might a lover's hand. 'I don't think I can be blamed for it, knowing what we're going after.'

'The Abysmyth can be hurt.' Kataria spoke as much for her own assurance as for Asper's; the quaver in her voice, however, seemed to convince neither of them. 'We've seen it, right?'

'We saw the Lord Emissary chase it away with prayers.'

'Well, I suppose we're in luck, since you seem to do a lot of that.'

'It's not the same and you know it.' Asper glowered at her companion. 'Further, we *also* saw it take a harpoon through the belly and ...' Her face twisted slightly. 'Mossud, bless him—'

'I remember.'

Kataria paused to force a frown upon her face. It felt awkward, like pulling a muscle, to strain such false sympathy through her teeth. Yet it was infinitely preferable to trying to explain her thoughts on the matter. Mossud's death had been something appalling, the shict readily admitted to herself, but he was still just one human amongst many.

The fact that the world would make more did not seem as consoling as it once had.

'Even if there is something out there, you don't need to worry.' Kataria shifted her face into a smile, hoping the priestess wouldn't notice the pain with which she did it. 'Leave matters of death and dying to the warriors.'

Asper frowned. As though her brain were wrought out of lead, her head bowed to stare dejectedly into the dull silver of her pendant, fingers caressing its metal wings.

'Yeah ... the warriors.'

Kataria fought back a sigh; humans never seemed satisfied by anything. They exuded fear, yet despised being reassured against it. They blatantly craved admiration, yet had no desire to earn it. *They're all nothing but a bunch of slack-jawed hypocrites*, she thought resentfully, *cowards*.

Quietly, the urge to sigh twisted within her, becoming an urge to do to Asper what she had done to Lenk.

Before she could so much as tense her fingers, however,

she suddenly noticed the waters calming. Curious, she leaned out over the railing, watching the waves slow until they finally came to a bobbing stop. She glanced up; the sails hung impotent against the tiny mast.

'Well,' she snorted, 'maybe Dread can ease your apprehension, since he seems to be done with whatever he was doing.'

'Are we close to land?' Asper cast a glance about the waters. 'I don't see anything here.' Her eyes shifted towards the rear of the boat. 'Dread, are you—'

All eyes, in addition to the priestess's, had turned towards the vessel's bench. Dreadaeleon stood upright upon it, stiff as a board and eyes wide with an expression that could only be described as baffled shock. A few moments of silence passed before Denaos cleared his throat.

'Did you get tired or something?'

The boy did not respond. Rolling his eyes, the rogue rose to his feet and reached out to place a hand on his shoulder.

'Listen, we're on a bit of a schedule, as you might recall. If I'm going to die, I'd like it to be before lu—'

In the blink of an eye, Dreadaeleon's hands flung out, palms wide and aimed at the sail. His voice was an incomprehensible thunder, a furious phrase that erupted from his lips. The air shimmered for a moment before it rippled and quaked, as though threatening to burst apart like an overstuffed pillow.

The vessel responded immediately, rocking at the sudden burst of wizardly force and flying forwards like a javelin. Its prow rose so far out of the water as to threaten to capsize; bodies were forced to cling to wood to avoid being hurled from the deck, their protests inaudible over the boy's chanting.

'Sweet Silf,' Denaos howled, 'what is he *doing*?'

'Turn the rudder!' Lenk shouted from the prow. 'Try to stop it!'

Hands, both human and dragonman, went to the steering rudder, arms quivering with effort as they grunted, growled and spat curses at the stubborn mechanism. It would not budge, except at the beck of whatever force Dreadaeleon imbued in it, jerking it wildly back and forth.

'Stop *him*, then!' Kataria shrieked above the sorcerous gale.

Gariath responded with a roar that nearly silenced the wind, pulling himself up the deck by his claws, the gleam in his black eyes suggesting that however he intended to stop the wizard, he also intended it to be permanent. As he came closer, his claws reached out to grasp at the boy's fluttering coat-tails.

Dreadaeleon's voice grew louder and, like a wooden slave, the vessel obeyed, lunging out of the water violently. Gariath tumbled backwards, his massive red bulk slamming into Denaos and nearly crushing the tall man against the ship's gunwale.

'Fine,' the dragonman snarled, making ready to pull himself up again, 'he can't work his magic if his head is ripped off.'

'No!'

He narrowed his fury at Lenk. 'Why *not*?'

'He's focusing on … something,' Lenk hollered. 'If you disrupt him now, this whole ship may be blown apart!'

'How is this any better?' Denaos countered.

'He's not acting of his own will,' Asper shouted in retort.

'How do you know that?' the rogue howled. 'His magic may have driven him insane! It's not unheard of! We need to put him down!'

'Calm down,' Lenk shouted back. 'I don't think he's going to bring us to harm.'

'How can you be so sure?' Kataria cried loudly as the gale intensified.

'I can't, really.'

'Oh … well.'

He managed to pull himself up enough to see a rapidly approaching bank of sand in the far distance. As the waves lapped around the island, revealing jagged rocks jutting from the shore, he winced and braced himself as the island grew closer with each blinking eye.

Lenk stared upon the wreckage with dismay.

The companion boat lay on its side upon the beach, several yards up a shore marred by a deep skid-mark. Its red ribs jutted from the jagged hole gaping in its flank, as if it had been harpooned. Its shredded sail hung from a splintering mast like flesh flayed from bone. His frown grew so long it hurt his face as he waited for the carrion flies to begin swarming over it.

'At least no one was hurt too badly,' piped up a cheerful voice from beside him.

He glared at the grinning shict and then at the bandage wrapped tightly around his arm. He flexed it a little, wincing as the cut beneath it seared his skin.

'Well.' She coughed. '*I* wasn't hurt too badly.'

'Lucky for us,' he grumbled.

He cast a glance over Kataria, who bore no physical injuries aside from a few scuffs and sand stains on her pale skin. When the vessel had hit the shore, she had been tossed into a nearby shrubbery. He had had the misfortune of nearly impaling his arm on a jutting timber rib.

Disdainfully, he twitched his forearm again and saw a bit of red seep through the white bandages.

He glanced at the long skid in the sand where he had landed after being hurled from the vessel. He winced and made a silent prayer of thanks to whatever deity had prevented him from striking any of the bone-white jagged stones jutting from the sands like teeth. The tips of the same stones, their white hues mottled with coral the colour of vomit, emerged from the surface of the blue, foamy seas beyond.

A sea of trees, rising from a blanket of shrubbery, roots and vines, stood behind them; the only landmark breaking a nearly perfectly endless sheet of white sand and rock. At a glance, it seemed lush, Lenk thought, but he knew well that forests could be just as unforgiving and desolate as deserts. The corpse of the vessel, sprawled out on the sand like a beached whale, wood drying under the sun like bones bleaching, seemed a charming example.

'It could be worse,' Kataria offered, snapping him from his gloomy reverie.

It certainly could, Lenk thought.

He glanced over his shoulder to where Gariath squatted. The dragonman had taken the worst of the crash, having been tossed from the prow violently, skidding across the sands until his violent journey ended abruptly at a nearby palm tree. Cuts from the beach rocks and thorny shrubs covered his red skin and splinters from the tree jutted from his back.

Regardless of his injuries, the hardy dragonman had refused all aid.

'Human medicine,' he had growled, 'is for skinned knees and constipation.'

Instead, he had skulked over to the shade of the same tree he had caromed off and sat quietly.

Dragonmen, particularly red ones, Lenk had been told, were resilient creatures and had an innate ability to heal themselves through sheer force of will. If there was a will stronger than Gariath's, Lenk had never seen it, for the dragonman's wounds were no longer bleeding.

He would have thanked his companion for declining aid if it was out of generosity. There weren't a great many supplies to go around for the purposes of treating injuries.

His arm had required a good deal of Asper's bandages and Denaos's scrapes had required a good amount of salve. Most of the priestess's aid, however, had gone to the one who had caused the wreck in the first place. Lenk's eyes narrowed to thin, angry slits as he cast a glare further down the beach.

Dreadaeleon sat propped up against a rock, Asper squatting by his side, working to tighten the bandage around his head that covered the gash at his temple. *A lot of bandages*, Lenk noted with a wince, *too many to hold in such a small brain.*

Even now, the wizard clutched his head as he lay against the rock, pampered like a baby. Lenk's teeth ground together so hard, sparks almost shot from his mouth. He felt his hands clench into fists, heedless of the strain it put on his wounded arm. Kataria noticed his ire rising and laid a hand on his shoulder.

'Now, calm down,' she said soothingly. 'He already told you—'

'He told me nothing,' Lenk snarled. 'If we're going to be stuck on some Gods-forsaken island and starve to death because of him, I want to know *why*.'

Not waiting for a reply from his companion, the young

man stormed over to the boy's resting place with such fury in his stride as to burn the sands beneath him. He paused nearby and folded his arms over his chest, focusing his icy scowl upon the wizard. Asper said nothing and continued working on her patient's splint, though her hands trembled more than a little under Lenk's frigid stare.

'Well?' Lenk snarled after several moments' silence.

'Well what?' Dreadaeleon replied, not opening his eyes.

'Well, how's your little scrape, you poor little lamb?' Lenk said, his sarcasm burning. 'What the hell were you thinking?'

'Well, I don't know,' the wizard replied, equally vitriolic. 'I suppose I thought: "*I bet Lenk would find it hysterical if I decided to crash the boat.*"' He snorted. 'I already told you, I don't know what happened.'

'How?' the young man spat back. 'How do you not know what you were doing?'

'The intricacies of my mind are of such staggering complexity that they might very well cause yours to explode, leak out of your ears and puddle at your feet.' He tilted his nose up. 'Suffice it to say, I knew exactly what I was doing, I just wasn't sure why.'

'Oh, well, thank Khetashe for *that* distinction!'

'Lenk,' Kataria said, creeping up to his side. 'You know Dread wouldn't do it on purpose.'

'Well, I'd like to know whose purpose he *did* do it on,' the young man growled, casting a sideways glare at the shict.

Despite the protests of his conscience, his rage cared neither for compassion nor logic. It took all his willpower not to flay the boy alive and use his skin to patch the vessel's wound.

'I'm not sure what happened,' Dreadaeleon said, finally opening his eyes and looking at Lenk. 'I was focusing on moving the ship, as you asked, when I suddenly ... heard something.'

'Heard something?' Lenk asked, screwing up his face in confusion. 'When you focus, you can't hear bloody murder two inches from your ear.' His sniffed, glaring at Kataria. 'I know from experience.'

'Baby,' Kataria grunted.

'It wasn't in my ears,' Dreadaeleon said softly, 'it was ... in my head.'

'So you were just going mad?'

'No, Lenk,' Asper said, looking up. 'I ... I heard it too.'

'Really?' Lenk asked, more in sarcasm than genuine curiosity. 'So tell me, why didn't you go insane?'

'She's not sensitive to magic,' Dreadaeleon said, 'I am.'

'If she's not sensitive, then how did she hear it at all?'

'I don't know,' Dreadaeleon said, shaking his head. 'It's possible that—'

He cut himself off and fell back against the rock, his face screwed up in pain as he clutched his skull.

'What now?' Lenk asked, an inkling of concern seeping through his anger.

'Magic headache,' Dreadaeleon replied with a halting, pain-filled voice.

'What?'

'Wizard's headache,' Asper said, a hand going to Dreadaeleon's shoulder. 'Magic takes a toll on the body.'

'If I use magic too much,' Dreadaeleon replied, breathing hard, 'or cast too many spells at once, I get a headache.' He glared up at Lenk through strained eyes. 'I've told you this before.'

Before Lenk could form a reply, he was suddenly aware

of a tall figure standing between him and Kataria. He glanced up, startled as he saw Denaos's concerned face staring down at the wizard.

'And just where have you been this whole time?' the young man asked.

'Asper asked me to get some water for Dread,' the rogue replied, holding up a bulging waterskin.

'We have water on the boat,' Lenk said, casting a glance over his shoulder. 'Most of the cargo was secured, it shouldn't be damaged.'

'True,' Denaos replied with a nod, 'but I thought I might as well take a look around, since we may be here a while.'

'It won't take *that* long to fix the ship,' Lenk replied. 'With any luck, we'll be back out on the sea in a day or two.' His eyes steeled. 'Every day we're on land, the Abysmyth's lead increases. Every day we hesitate, another—'

'We're on it.'

'What?'

'We're here.' He stomped the earth. 'This is Ktamgi.'

'How do you know?'

The rogue reached down to pluck a single grain of sand from the beach. He eyed it for a moment before holding it next to Kataria's midsection.

'Just a shade whiter, as Argaol said.' He pulled back his hand before Kataria could slap it. 'Check the sea charts and you'll see I'm right.' He blinked at Lenk suddenly, cough-ing. 'Sorry for ruining whatever speech you had, though. I'm sure it was astonishingly inspirational.'

'When did *you* learn to read sea charts?' Asper shot a suspicious glare at the rogue.

'Around the time I learned how to avoid angry debt col-lectors by signing on as a deckhand and fleeing the city,' he replied with a wink, 'but that's another story.' He tossed

306

the waterskin to Dreadaeleon, the wizard making only half an attempt to catch it as it bounced off his face to land in his lap. 'Drink up, little man.'

'I see ...' Lenk said, furrowing his brow in brief thought. 'Well, if it is as you say, we'll take a look around, then.'

'Are you sure you wouldn't like to take another moment to berate me for finding the island?' Dreadaeleon asked with a wry smirk. 'Or did you perhaps have some praise for me?'

'What I've got for you is a length of steel and few compunctions about where I jam it,' Lenk snarled. 'Now shut up before I plug the ship's hole with your fat head.'

'Still,' Asper said, 'is it wise to move out now?' She glanced at Dreadaeleon. 'Everyone's more than a little roughed up.'

'We're not too bad,' Lenk said, glancing at his arm. 'We're only looking for traces of the Abysmyth and the tome.' He glanced around his companions. 'If you find it, don't try to fight it on your own.' He cast a concerned glare at Gariath. 'Come and get the rest of us.'

The dragonman merely snorted in reply.

'How are we even going to hurt it?' Denaos asked.

'We'll worry about that later,' Lenk said. 'For now, we just need to find out whether it's still here and still has the tome.' He looked disparagingly at the copse of trees and scratched his chin. 'We might as well spread out to find whatever resources we can.'

'That makes sense.' Asper dusted her hands off, rose to her feet. 'The more food and water we find here, the less we have to use from the ship.'

'Not to mention that spreading out will make it easier for the Abysmyth to hunt us down and eat our heads,' Denaos added with a nod. 'As per usual, your genius cannot be praised with mere—'

'Yeah, we're all going to die, I get it,' Lenk interrupted, waving the rogue away. 'Anyway, foraging shouldn't be a problem. Gariath alone can probably sniff—'

He glanced up at the sound of sand crunching beneath massive feet in time to spy Gariath's wings twitching as the dragonman turned his back to the companions. Without so much as a word, he began to stalk off down the beach, snout occasionally thrust into the air with quivering nostrils.

'There, see?' Lenk smiled smugly. 'That's what you call community-minded. He's already got the scent of some food.'

'You can all starve,' Gariath replied calmly without looking back. 'I'm following something else.'

'What?'

'Die.'

'Ah.' Lenk frowned. 'He's in a mood.' He cast a sidelong glance at Dreadaeleon, gesturing towards the dragonman with his chin. 'You'd better go with him.'

'What?' The boy looked incredulous. 'Why me? I can barely walk.'

'"Barely" still translates to "capable",' Lenk responded sharply. 'It'll be better if we've got two hounds on the Abysmyth's trail.'

'I'm not sure I follow.'

'You can sense magic, can't you?'

'All wizards can.'

'And there you have it,' Lenk replied. 'While I don't know if the demon is actually magical in nature, it probably leaves some kind of reek behind that either you or Gariath can follow.'

'That logic doesn't entirely hold up.' Dreadaeleon rose

to his feet shakily. 'Wouldn't one of us have sensed it before it attacked the *Riptide*?'

'Maybe things work differently when it's out of water.' Lenk placed a hand on Dreadaeleon's shoulder. 'The other reason I'm sending you is to keep an eye on him. If you *do* find the demon, try your best to keep him away from it until we can all assemble. We don't want anyone to fight this thing alone.'

The wizard had no sarcasm in reply. Instead, placing an expression of resolution upon his face, he nodded stiffly to the young man, his tiny chest swelling as Lenk offered him an encouraging smile.

'Beyond that,' Lenk clapped him on the shoulder, 'he looks like he's going to kill someone, and since you crashed the ship, it might as well be you.'

'That does make sense.' Denaos nodded.

'What?' Dreadaeleon's eyes flared. 'You can't be—'

'I am.' With another clap on the shoulder, Lenk sent the boy staggering across the sands in pursuit of the dragonman. 'Off you go now.' He had barely a moment to make certain Dreadaeleon was still on his feet ten paces later before he spied Kataria moving away in the opposite direction. 'Where are you off to?'

'Hunting,' she replied, holding up her bow and patting the quiver of arrows upon her back. 'Gariath is going that way, I'll go this way.'

'Fine.' He nodded. 'I'll come with you.'

'You don't have to,' she muttered in such a way as to indicate that it was not at all a simple suggestion.

'But I should,' he said, less firmly than he might have, 'if only for protection.' He raised a brow. 'Is that disagreeable to you?'

'Slightly,' she hissed. 'But if you can keep up, I can't tell you where to walk.'

And with that, she was gone, vanished into the palm trees like a shadow. A dramatic sigh brought Lenk's attention to the rogue leaning on the remains of the vessel, staring wistfully into the jungle.

'Tell me,' he muttered, 'why is it that you always get to go with Kataria while I'm left behind?' A puzzled expression flashed across his face. 'And what am I supposed to do here, anyway? Not that I'm complaining, but I seem to have been left out of this plot of yours.'

'The boat needs mending.' Lenk gestured to the wreckage. 'You and Asper can tend to it and see if the Abysmyth comes your way.'

'Oh, good,' Denaos said, sighing once again. 'We get to sit here and do busywork while we wait for the demon to come and eat us.'

'More like appetisers than busyworkers, I'd say.'

Lenk didn't linger to hear whatever the tall man might have offered in retort. Pausing only for a moment to pluck his sword from the ruined vessel, he slung it over his shoulder and tore off in pursuit of the shict.

With a resigned grunt, Denaos pulled himself up to perch upon the hunk of wood, frowning at the gaping hole between his legs. Definitely some work to be done here, no doubt, and it was work he hardly felt like doing. There'd be wood to find, wood to shape and wood to attach to the ship's wound.

'So, you know how to take care of this, right?' Asper asked, tilting her head at him.

'It's not too hard,' he replied. 'I did a bit of work under a carpenter back in Redgate.' He scratched his chin. 'His name was Rudder, more body hair than flesh. Nice fellow, but a bit handsy when he tossed back a few. So long as you can—'

A sudden movement caught his attention and he glanced over to see Asper busily at work, altering her garments. After a little bit of tearing, she tied a flap of her skirt to each of her legs, securing the fabric with leather strips to form a pair of makeshift leggings. His interest was piqued and he leaned forwards as she rolled up the sleeves of her tunic to her shoulders, exposing firm arms. The faintest hint of a grin appeared on his face as she grabbed the hem of her tunic and rolled it up, tying it off below her chest and baring a slender midsection.

Suddenly aware of his gaze, she looked up with a suspicious glance.

'What?'

'Nothing,' he said, shaking his head. 'But that's quite a bit of skin to show if you're just mending sails.'

'You can knit,' she said, scowling at him as she moved over to the boat and pulled herself inside. After rummaging around in a few crates, she produced a shiny, well-worn hatchet. Leaping from the vessel, she hiked it over her shoulder and glanced at him. 'There's wood to be cut. If *you're* scared of demons and want to sit here and cry, though ...'

He bit his lower lip contemplatively as he watched her go. Truthfully, he had to admit it *was* a difficult decision: linger here, out in the open where he couldn't be surprised by anything on two or more legs, or follow a hatchet-wielding, half-clad woman into the forest where he might very well accidentally strangle himself with a vine if insects – or demons – didn't eat him alive first.

The decision seemed easy, he thought, until he caught one last glimpse of her before she vanished. It was funny, he thought, but he had never noticed the particular delicacy with which her hips swayed.

Thirteen

AN EARNEST HUNT

Forests, Lenk decided, were places where man was not meant to tread.

It seemed a logical enough theory; humanity built their cities out on the open, where they could see threats coming. In the canopy-choked gloom, everything seemed to be a threat.

What had begun as a tiny copse of trees had blossomed into a lush jungle, deep and green as the sea. And, like the sea, the forest, too, was alive. Hidden amidst eclipsing boughs and grasping leaves, sounds emerged in disjointed harmony. Birds sang shrilly, determined to drown out the thrum of insect wings with their agonising choruses. For all the noises, he couldn't see a single living thing. Not so much as a flicker of movement in the shadows.

Sunlight filtered through the green, twisting net of the forest's canopy, shadowing every tree that crowded Lenk in an attempt to keep him out of their domain. He glanced about warily; in the darkness, the verdant trunks, slim and black, resembled nothing so much as his quarry.

The Abysmyth comes from the sea, right? He asked and answered himself. *Right. It'll stay near water, then.* He paused. *But what if it needed to go into the forest for some reason? What if it had to eat ... demons eat, right?* He considered that for a moment. *Right. They eat heads, probably. They seem like the kind of thing that would eat a person's head.*

If it *had* retreated into the forest, it could stand right in front of him and not be seen. Even worse, it could easily ambush anything that wandered by it; after all, how could anyone tell the difference between it and a tree in the gloom?

Simple, he thought, *a tree won't eat your head.*

That thought brought him no comfort. Instead the same thought occurred to him each time he forced his eyes closed in a blink: he didn't belong here. That thought, in turn, opened his eyes in a scowl at the pale figure shifting effortlessly through the foliage in front of him.

How does she make it look so easy?

'You're moving rather quickly,' he said, if only to break the ambience.

'I'm sorry,' she replied acidly, 'would you like to stop and paint a picture of the scenery?'

Lenk let that particular barb sink into his flesh, not bothering to pull it out or launch one of his own. He sucked in a sharp breath through his teeth; perhaps, he thought, he should wait before attempting to mend things with the shict. She didn't seem to be in the mood for reconciliation at the moment.

No, no, he scolded himself, *if you don't do it now, she'll just get angrier and do worse than bloody your nose.* His eyes drifted down to the hunting knife strapped to her leg. A grimace creased his face.

'What I mean,' he replied, 'is you usually take longer to find a trail.'

'In most cases,' she nodded, 'but this particular quarry has a few exceptional qualities.'

'Such as?'

'For one, there's still a great deal of noise in the forest. Prey, like birds and bugs, always go silent when a predator is about.'

'You said a *few* qualities.'

'Well, there is something more.'

'What?'

'It's a ten-foot-tall fish that walks on two legs and reeks of death, you moron,' she snapped. 'If it's anywhere on this island, it'll be disgustingly hard to miss.'

He chose to leave that one in his flesh, as well. It would be easy, he knew, to sling something equally venomous at her. In fact, as he noted a particularly thick branch just next to her head, he realised it would be even easier to repay her for her earlier violence.

All you have to do is reach out, and ...

He shook his head to dispel that thought. While he knew there to be very few problems smashing someone's head into a tree *couldn't* solve, this was not one of them. Tact, however little use an adventurer usually found for it, was called for in such a situation.

'That's all there is to it, then?' he asked, hoping she didn't note the civil strain in his voice.

'In this particular case, yes.' She ducked under a low-hanging branch. 'Let me ask you something.'

His entire body tensed; questions from the shict, lately, had served chiefly as preludes to violence.

'Have you thought at all about how you're going to fight this thing if you find it?'

'Would it distress you to hear that I don't know?'

'No more than usual.'

'Well, I've been giving it *some* thought,' Lenk replied. 'The Abysmyth can't be hurt by mortal weapons, and that's about all we've got. But it *can* be hurt by fire. Dread can do something about that and, if we've got time, we can get torches.'

'It'll be hard to make a fire when it's eating our heads.'

'You think it eats heads?'

'Sure.' She shrugged. 'It seems like the kind of thing that eats heads.'

He smiled.

'Dreadaeleon has his headache, however.' She grunted as she pressed her lithe body between a heavy stone and a tree trunk. 'I've never seen him use magic in such a state, but I wager it won't be pretty.'

'You mean the spectacle of him straining himself beyond his limits?' Lenk struggled to follow her through the squeeze but found his waist caught firmly in fingers of stone and wood.

'I was thinking more about the greasy splatter that the Abysmyth will make of him.' The shict took his hands in hers and, with a strained grunt, pulled him free. 'This is all assuming quite a bit, though.'

'Right.' He paused to dust himself off. 'We have to find the stupid thing first. Khetashe willing, we'll spot it before it spots us.'

'And then?'

'Then we run away and hide until we can get fire.'

'Not the bravest strategy.'

'Bravery and effectiveness are rivers that run in different directions.'

He caught her staring at his shirt and followed her gaze. Even after he had brushed himself off, the forest proved less than willing to let him go: all manner of burrs, thorns and leaves clung to his garments. He glanced back up and she met his gaze, smugness leaking out of her every pore.

'Perhaps you'd like to take a moment to rest,' she said,

leaning against a tree and folding her arms across her chest.

Reeking, pointy-eared know-it-all.

Despite having led the way through the underbrush, Kataria was completely free of scratches; nothing more than a slight smear of sand marred her flesh. He focused on it unconsciously, observing the sole discoloration to her pale skin, shrinking and growing with each unhurried breath she took.

Arrogant little …

A breeze muttered through the canopy, parting the branches to allow a shaft of light through the greenery. As though the Gods had a flair for the dramatic, the beam settled lazily on Kataria, turning her shoulders gold, setting her hair alight, making the sandy smudge glisten.

Thinks she's so …

The sunlight clung to her, he realised, upon a skin of perspiration. Even as the dirt painted her body bronze, the sweat caught the sun and bathed her skin in shimmering silver. In the moments between the fluttering of the leaves, she looked like something that had sprung from the forge of the Gods, brightly polished metals, rough edges and brilliant, glimmering emeralds.

'What are you looking at?'

He stiffened up at that, going rigid as though he had just been rudely awakened. The reaction did not go unnoticed as Kataria tilted her head to the side, eyeing him as she might a beast, her body tense and ready to flee … or attack.

Not the ideal response.

Now's your chance, he told himself, *you've got to talk to her and you're alone together. Start with a compliment! Tell her about that forge of the Gods thing, she'll like that!*

'You look like—'

Wait, WAIT! He bit his tongue as her face screwed up in confusion. *She's a shict; she doesn't believe in the Gods, just Riffid. Does Riffid use a forge?*

'I look like what?'

Damn it, damn it, damn it. He clenched his teeth. *To the pit with this, just say something.*

'Hey.'

Genius. He sighed inside his head. *Throw away your sword and take up a pen, you Gods-damned poet-general.*

'What?' Kataria's long ears quivered, as though she heard his thoughts.

If she can *hear your thoughts,* he scolded himself, *you might as well just say whatever's on your mind.*

'I want to talk.'

All right, not bad. Straightforwardness is key.

'We don't talk during a hunt,' she replied, 'ancient shic-tish tradition.'

'What?' He blinked at her, puzzled. 'You talk to me all the time when you're tracking.'

'Huh.' She shrugged. 'I guess I just want you to shut up this time, then.'

Easy, he told himself, drawing in a sharp breath of air, *she wants to fight you. Don't fall for it.*

'I want to talk,' he repeated, 'now.'

'Why?'

Because, he rehearsed in his mind, *you're the only person I can trust not to get me killed or murder me in my sleep. It likely sounds stranger to hear than to say, but you're the only person I can sleep easily around and I'd very much like to keep things that way.*

He cleared his throat and spoke.

'Why not?'

Damn it.

'You don't want to do this now,' she replied.

'I do.'

'Then *I* don't want to do this now.'

'Then how are we going to—'

'We're not, that's the point.'

Her stare was different as she slid off the tree, something flashing behind her eyes as she regarded him. He had seen everything in those green depths: her morbid humour, her cold anger, even her undisguised hatred when she met the right person. Up until that moment, though, he had never seen pity.

Up until that moment, he had never had to turn away from her.

'Listen,' she said, 'it's not that I don't trust you any more, but you're just ...' She cringed, perhaps fearing what his reaction might be should she continue. 'You're skulking, secretive, snarling. That *was* charming, in moderation, don't misunderstand me. But now ...' Her body shuddered with her sigh. 'You're not even Lenk any more.'

'*I'm* not Lenk?' He threw a sneer at her as though it were an axe. 'Answer *me* this, then, how is it *you* get to decide who Lenk is?'

'I don't,' she retorted sharply. 'I knew who I *thought* Lenk was, though. Apparently, now Lenk is some deranged lunatic who talks to himself and refers to himself in the third person.'

'Lenk is most certainly *not*—'

He caught himself, bit his lower lip as she caught his sneer, twisted it into a haughty smirk and smashed him over the head with it.

'Point taken,' he muttered. 'Being perfectly fair, though,

you're not Lenk. *You*,' he thrust a finger at her, 'have no idea what's going on in my head.'

'Not for lack of trying, certainly,' she spat back. 'Is it so shocking that someone *might* be interested in your weak, insignificant life?'

'Oh, of course, a reminder of my humanity.' He rolled his eyes and threw up his arms in one grand gesture. 'You held on to that for as long as you could, didn't you?'

'A reminder?' Her laughter was long, loud and unpleasant. 'How could you not be reminded of your race? You're reminded every time you wake up and think: "*Hooray! One more day of being a walking disease!*"'

'Only *I* would think of death so sweetly,' he snarled, 'because the cold hand of Gevrauch is infinitely preferable to sharing my existence with an arrogant, smarmy, pointy-eared shict,' he hesitated, as if holding back some vile torrent, before her hiss forced him to loose it, 'who *farts in her sleep*! There, I said it!'

'*I eat a lot of meat*,' she spat back in an unabated hail of fury, 'and perhaps if you did, too, you wouldn't be the runt that you are!'

'*This* particular runt can easily choke the life out of you, *savage*.'

'You haven't been successful yet, *round-ear*!'

'Then maybe I just need a little more time to—'

'*No*.'

The voice began as a mutter, a quiet whisper in the back of his mind. It echoed, singing through his skull, reverberating through his head. His temples throbbed, as though the voice left angry dents each time it rebounded against his skull. Kataria shifted before him, going from sharp and angry to hazy and indistinct. The earth under his feet felt softer, yielding as though it feared to stand against him.

The voice, however, remained tangible in its clarity.

'*No more time,*' it uttered, '*no more talk.*'

'More time to what, you fart-sniffer?' Kataria was hopping from foot to foot, fingers twitching, though before Lenk's eyes she resembled nothing so much as a shifting blob. 'Not so brave now?'

'I …' he began to utter, but his throat tightened, choking him.

'You what?'

'*Nothing to say,*' the voice murmured, '*no more time.*'

'What,' he whispered, 'is it time for?'

'What the hell does that mean?' If she looked at him oddly, he did not see. Her eyes faded into the indistinct blob that she had become. 'Lenk … are you—'

'*Time,*' the voice uttered, '*to kill.*'

'I'm not—'

'*Kill,*' it repeated.

'Not what?'

'*Kill.*'

'I can't—' he whimpered.

'*No choice.*'

'Shut up,' he tried to snarl, but his voice was weak and small. 'Shut up!'

'*Kill.*'

'Lenk …' Kataria's voice began to fade.

'*KILL!*'

'*SHUT UP!*'

When he had fallen, he could not remember, nor did he know precisely when he had closed his eyes and clamped his hands over his ears, lying twitching upon the earth like a crushed cockroach. When he opened his eyes once more, the world was restored: the ground was solid beneath him, his head no longer ached and he stared up into a pair of eyes, hard and sharp as emeralds.

'It happened again, didn't it?' she asked, kneeling over him. 'What happened on the *Riptide* … happened again.'

His neck felt stiff when he nodded.

'Don't you see, Lenk?' Her whisper was delicate, soothing. 'This isn't going to stop. I can't help you if you don't tell me what's happening to you.'

'I can't.' His whisper was more fragile, a vocal glass pane cracking at the edges. 'I … don't even know myself.'

'You can't even try?' She reached out and placed a hand on his shoulder; he saw her wince at the contact. 'For your sake, Lenk? For mine?'

'I … don't …'

His voice trailed off into nothingness, punctuated by the harsh narrowing of her eyes. She rose, not swiftly as she usually did, but with all the creaking exhaustion of an elder, far too tired of life. She stared down at him with pity flashing in her eyes once more; he had nowhere to turn to.

'Then don't,' she replied sternly. 'Lie here … and don't.'

He felt he should urge himself to get up as he heard her boots crunch upon the earth. He felt he should scream at himself to follow her as he heard her slip through the foliage with barely a rustle. He felt he should rise, run screaming after her, tell her everything he needed to until his tongue dried up and fell out of his head.

For all that, he lay on the earth and did not move. For all the commands he knew he should give himself, he could hear but one voice.

'Weak.'

His head seared for a moment, then grew cold with a dull ache that gripped his brain in icy fingers. His mind grew colder with every echo, the chill creeping into the back of his eyes, down his throat, into his nose until the sun ceased to have warmth. Breathing became a chore, movement an impossibility, death … an appealing consideration.

He closed his eyes, allowing the world to fade away into echoes as the sound, too, faded into nothingness. There was nothing to the world any more, no life, no pain, no sound.

No sound.

He opened his eyes as the realisation came upon him: there was no birdsong, no buzzing of insects.

The prey had stopped making noise.

Cold was banished in a sudden sear of panic. He scrambled to his feet, reaching for his sword, sweeping his gaze about the jungle. Any one of the trees could be the demon, watching him with stark white eyes, talons twitching and ready to smother his head in ooze before eating it.

The only things he saw, however, were shadows and leaves. The only thing he heard was the pounding of his own heart.

'Help.'

The silence was shattered by a faint, quivering voice. It was little more than a whisper, barely audible over the hush of the wind, but it filled Lenk's ears and refused to leave.

'Help me.'

He could hear it more clearly now, recognising it. He had heard more than enough dying men to know what one sounded like. For all the clarity of the voice, he could spy no man to go with it, however. Slowly, he eased his gaze across the trees once more and found nothing in the thick gloom.

'Please,' the man whimpered, 'don't kill me. Don't kill me.'

There was silence for but a moment.

'*DON'T KILL ME!*'

His eyes followed his ears, sweeping up into the canopy, narrowing upon the white smear in the darkness, improbably pristine. From above, a pair of bleary grey eyes atop a bulbous, beak-like nose stared back, unblinking and brimming with fat, salty tears.

I should run, he thought, *the Abysmyth is likely right behind this thing.*

'*No.*' The voice's reply was slow and grating. '*It dies.*'

'It dies,' Lenk echoed.

The Omen's teeth chattered quietly, yellow spikes rattling off each other. Lenk's ear twitched at the sound of wet meat being slivered. Narrowing his eyes, he spied the single, severed finger ensconced between the creature's teeth, shredded further into glistening meat with every chatter of its jaws.

'There are others here.' Lenk's voice sounded distant and faint in his own ears, as though he spoke through fog to someone shrouded and invisible. 'Should we help them?'

'*Irrelevant,*' the voice replied. '*Men can die. Demons* must *die.*'

'Right.'

The Omen shuffled across the branch, tilting its wrinkled head in an attempt to comprehend. Lenk remained tense, not deceived by the facade of animal innocence. As if sensing this, it tightened its broad mouth into a needle-toothed smile, the severed digit vanishing down its throat with a crunching sound.

It ruffled its feathers once, stretched its head up like a cock preparing to crow and opened its mouth.

'Gods help me!' A man's voice, whetted with terror,

echoed through its gaping mouth. 'Someone! *Anyone! HELP ME!*'

The mimicked plea reverberated through his flesh. His arm tensed, sliding his sword out of its sheath. Like a dog eager to play, the Omen ruffled its feathers, turned about and hopped into the dense foliage of the canopy.

'It wants help,' Lenk muttered, watching the white blob vanish into the green.

'Then we shall help it.'

His legs were numb under his body, moving effortlessly against the earth, sword suddenly so very light in a hand he could no longer feel. He thought he ought to be worried about that, as he suspected he should be worried about following a demonic parasite into the depths of the foliage. He had no ears for those concerns, however.

The ringing cry of the dying man hung from every branch he crept under.

Kataria's ears twitched. The world was quiet on Ktamgi.

Insects buzzed in the distance; she heard their wings slap their chitinous bodies. Birds muttered warbling curses; she heard their tongues undulate in their beaks. The sound of water raking sand and clouds drifting lazily in blue skies was far away.

She smiled. How much clearer, she thought, everything was without humans.

She had become used to their sounds, their noises, their whining and their cursing. She had become infected by the human disease, only realising it the moment a breath of air, free of the stench of sweat and blood, filled her lungs. Her ears were upright against her head, a faint sound filled her mind. Her eyes were wide, her smile was broad.

It was time to hunt in earnest.

325

She had barely taken ten paces before she saw the tracks. It might have been a coincidence that the trail only revealed itself after she had left Lenk behind, but she chose to take it as a blessing. Crouching low, her eyes widened as she realised that she both recognised the indentations in the moist earth and that she had spoken too soon.

Humans.

The notion that humans, humans that were not hers, were on Ktamgi did nothing to improve her mood. However, it did not come as a complete surprise to her, either. Argaol, after all, had said that a few of the *Linkmaster*'s crew had escaped. The island *had* also been an outpost for pirates.

Why wouldn't they come here?

The tracks asked her questions, her feet answered. The tracks told a story, her eyes listened. This was the true purpose of the shictish hunt: to learn, to listen, to ask and to answer. Intent on the earth, her eyes glided over the tracks, eager for a new story.

It had begun dramatically, she recognised by the chaos of the prints, though with no great care to establish the characters. The tracks were sloppy and slurred, their dialogue messy and hurried. She rolled her eyes; it was as though these particular humans had no appreciation for the fact that someone might want to hunt them like animals.

Insulting.

Regardless, she followed them further down the trail. They were men, evidenced by the particular depth of the prints, and not graceful men at that. They had been hurried, they had run, but for what purpose?

Perhaps they were chasing down prey? she thought, but quickly dismissed that idea. There was no evidence of another character in this story, no tracks of anything that might be construed as edible. But if not hunger, then what?

There was little else to motivate such speed. Gold, jewels, meat or violence were the typical spurs of flight, but all seemed to be in short supply on Ktamgi. She paused, scratching her flank contemplatively.

There's always fear, she suggested to herself.

She sighed at that; such a predictable twist. Regardless, it forced the story on and compelled her to follow the trail.

The plot only grew more blatantly unimaginative from there, the signs almost disturbingly clear. Here, a boot had become tangled in a root, abandoned by its wearer, who took two more steps before the trail suddenly ended.

That caused her to pause. She glanced up and down the trail but found no more details of this particular character. He had fled only a little further and then, suddenly, disappeared, his feet gone from the earth as though he had sprouted wings. Against her better judgment, she glanced upwards; the canopy remained thick and whole.

Curious, she went further. The cast had been whittled to two, their paths crossing each other recklessly. A pungent aroma filled her nostrils, drawing her eye towards a small depression against the base of a rock.

She grimaced; a vile brew of yellow and brown pooled where one of the characters had fallen onto his buttocks and not taken a step further. *A rather crude ending*, she thought, *but acceptable*.

One set of tracks remained, stretching long and straight through the earth. This one had been spirited, she thought, running for another twenty-three paces before he collapsed beside a tree. Right next to the disturbed dirt where he had fallen, a glisten of ruby, stark against the tree's brown, caught her eye. Her face twisted as she examined the old plant: its bark had been stripped bare in eight deep furrows.

Red flecks glittered like tiny jewels, fragments of dirty fingernails like unrefined ore embedded in the wood.

Spirited, indeed.

Kataria rose, knuckled the small of her back and glanced around. This was hardly the ending she had expected. Three humans run into the forest, leave sloppy trails and then vanish? Where was the tension? Where was the drama?

Her eyes widened with a sudden realisation.

Where was the villain?

She stared down the trail, searching every depression, every track, every broken branch. She found nothing. Whatever had run these men down had left no sign of itself, its prints lost amidst the chaos of the chase, if there had been any prints at all. Her brow furrowed concernedly; there was no sign of the characters either. All that remained of the *Linkmaster*'s crew equated to a few specks of blood and fingernail, an old boot and a puddle of piss and excrement.

Not a proper ending.

The wind shifted, leaves rustled and she felt a sudden warmth on her back. Whirling about, she couldn't help a twinge of pity at the sight of the sun shining through an opening in the foliage. The last man hadn't been ten paces away from reaching open ground.

Then again, she realised, *whatever finally got them likely wouldn't be put off by sunshine and white sand.*

It occurred to her that she ought to return to Lenk and have him listen to the story, as well. He was likely still in the same spot she had left him in, she thought with no small amount of resentment. In fact, if he hadn't moved, whatever unnamed character had ended the three men would likely stumble upon him sooner or later.

Then again ... Her ears twitched thoughtfully. *Is there any need to, really? If these deaths were recent, you would have heard them, wouldn't you? A man who pisses himself doesn't go silently. Whatever killed them is likely far and away, right?*

Right.

She took a step forwards.

And what if it does come across him? He's a big human ... fully grown, or so he says. He can take care of himself. And if he doesn't, what's it matter? He's just one more human, soon to be one less human. For the better, right?

Right. Let's go, then.

Her foot hesitated, having not apparently heard the mental debate. She looked down at the ground and sighed.

Damn it.

Of course she had to go back for him. He had been helpless, curled up on the ground like a mewling infant. *An infant with a giant sword*, she thought, *but regardless.* Her pride could not be his end; pride was a human flaw. While he might be human, he was one of her humans.

She rolled her shoulders, adjusting her bow, and began to trudge back across the trail. She had taken only half a step before an epilogue revealed itself.

A sudden aroma, growing stronger with the change in the wind, filled her nose. She glanced over her shoulder, peering towards the beach, and saw the smoke. Like ghosts, wisps of grey casually rolled across the breeze, drifting further down the shore.

In another twitch of her nostrils, the smoke became heavy with stench, thick with the aroma of overcooked meat. Choked screams carried on its long, grey tendrils. Her ears quivered, nostrils flared as she reached for her bow.

She forgot Lenk, helpless and mewling, and turned

towards the beach. He would wait, she knew, and be there when she returned.

For the moment, Kataria had to see how the story ended.

Fourteen

THE PREACHER

'Where is it going?'

    'The slave returns to its master, the parasite to its host.'

'Are you sure?'

'You cannot sense it?'

'I can hear.'

'Then follow.'

There was no choice in the matter. Lenk's feet moved regardless of his approval, legs swinging up and down methodically, heedless of roots and undergrowth. He was aware of the numbness, but did nothing to fight it. He was aware of the fact that he was talking to a voice in his head, but did not cease to speak.

It had spoken with much less ferocity, much less coldness in its words. It no longer felt like a verbal vice, crushing his skull in icy fingers. Now, it felt like instinct, like common sense.

Now, it felt right.

'Help me,' another voice called, 'please, Zamanthras, *help me!*'

That particular shrieking still grated on him.

He glanced up; the Omen seemed in no great hurry, pulling its plump body from branch to branch on spindly legs. It occasionally stopped to glance down at him, as if

331

making certain he still followed. When he stumbled over a root, it paused and waited for him to catch up.

'It wants us to follow it,' Lenk muttered. 'It's leading us to a trap.'

'*It leads us to an inevitability,*' the voice replied. '*Its master knows of us now, it wants us to find it.*'

'So it can kill us.'

'*So it can find out if it can kill us.*'

'Can it?'

No answer.

The Omen took another hop forwards and vanished into the jungle's gloom, the sound of feathers in its wake. Lenk followed, pressing through a thicket of branches. The leaves clung to him, as though struggling to hold him back. He paid them no mind, brushing them away and emerging from the greenery.

The sun felt strange upon his skin, hostile and unwelcoming. He could spare only a moment's thought for it before glancing down at the wide mouth and bulbous eyes that stared up at him.

'Sea Mother,' it echoed from its gaping mouth, 'benevolent matron and blessed watcher, forgive me my sins and wash me clean.'

A Zamanthran prayer, he recognised, desperate and brimming with fear. The idea of saving whoever the Omen mimicked was nothing more than an afterthought now and Lenk was no longer moved by it. The parasite sensed this, chattering its teeth at him and ruffling its feathers.

'No more,' he said, 'show me.'

The Omen bobbed its miniature head, twisted it about so that it stared at Lenk upside down, then hopped a few steps and took flight. Lenk followed its low, lazy hover across the beach. The forest had not completely abandoned the sand, it seemed, and trees, however sparse, still stretched out their green grasp.

Lush, he thought, but not lush enough to detract from the bodies.

They were Cragsmen, or had been before the Omens had begun their feast. Now the plump demons cloaked them like feathery funeral shrouds, prodding with their long noses, tearing digits off and shredding tattooed flesh in yellow, needle-like teeth. In ravenous flocks, they devoured, slurping skin into their inner-lips and crunching bones in their wide jaws, leaving nothing behind.

Nothing but the faces.

The two men looked to be in repose. Their eyes were closed, mouths shut with only the faintest of smiles tugging at their lips. Perfectly untouched, their faces were pristine and almost pleasant against the mutilated murals of red and pink their bodies had become.

In fact, were it not for the faint glisten of mucus draped upon their visages, they looked as though they were simply napping in the afternoon sun, ready to awaken at any moment, shrieking at what had ravaged their bodies. Lenk could see the shimmer of the ooze, see where it had plugged up their noses, their ears, sealed their lips. These men would never wake again.

The Omens glanced up as he took a step forwards, regarded him for a moment through their unblinking eyes, then rose as one from the corpses. On silent wings, they glided down to the beach to the sole remaining tree, settling within its boughs to stare at him, a dozen eyes bulging through the leaves like great white fruits.

It was only when Lenk drew closer that he noticed the trunk of the tree. It was not slender and smooth, as the others were, but rough and misshapen on one side, as though it suffered some festering tumour.

As he approached it, he felt the noise die in one thunderous hush. There were no more birds singing, no leaves rustling, and even the sound of waves roiling went quiet. Lenk stared at the tree trunk for what felt like an eternity. It was only when it shifted that he realised.

The tree was staring back at him.

The Abysmyth made no movement, at first, nor gave any indication that it even knew he was there aside from the two great, white, vacant eyes glistening in the shadows. Its head lolled slightly, exposing rows of teeth, as something rumbled up through its chest and out through its gaping jaws.

'Good afternoon,' it said.

'Good afternoon,' the Omens mimicked in distant chorus, 'good afternoon, good afternoon, good afternoon.'

'Good afternoon,' Lenk replied without knowing why.

Perhaps it was simply wise to show proper manners to something capable of ripping one's head off, he thought. The creature did not appear to register the politeness, however, and continued to roll its head upon its emaciated shoulders.

'Mother Deep gave us, Her children, many gifts,' it said, far more gently than its wicked mouth should allow, 'and we, Her children, received no greater gift than that of memory.'

There was something unnerving within the Abysmyth's voice, Lenk thought, something that reverberated through its emaciated body and glistened in its eyes as it turned its gaze out to sea. Perhaps the shadows obscured any murderous intent, but the young man could see no malice within the creature. It sat, leaned against the tree and stared out over the waves, at peace.

Like the damn thing's on a holiday, he thought.

'These are the voices I remember,' the Abysmyth continued. 'I remember the wind going silent, the sand losing its hiss and the water closing its million mouths, all respectful, all so that we, her children, may hear the sound of Mother Deep.'

Its head jerked towards him and Lenk's sword went up, levelled at the beast. The creature merely stared at him, giving no indication it had even seen the blade, as it tilted its head, fixing great empty eyes upon the young man.

'Listen,' it said, 'and you, too, shall hear Her.'

'Listen.' The winged parasites bobbed their heads all at once, their voices ebbing like the tide. 'Listen, listen, listen.'

Lenk's ears trembled; he heard nothing but the beating of his own heart and the rush of blood through his veins. Even that, however, fell silent before another voice.

'*Do not deign to indulge the abomination,*' it uttered within his mind. '*To so much as hear the faintest note of Her song is to invite damnation.*'

That, he thought, would have been a much more imposing reply than what he did say.

'I,' he paused, 'don't hear anything.'

The Abysmyth's lolling head rose to regard Lenk curiously. The young man cringed; the thing unnerved him further with every moment. If it had attacked him then and there, he could have mustered the will to fight it. If it had threatened him, he could have threatened back.

Against this display of nonchalance, this utter, depraved serenity, however, Lenk had no defence.

It quietly creaked, resting its head back against the trunk

of the tree, and cast an almost meditative stare across the ocean. Then, with the sound of skin stretching over bone, it snapped its great eyes upon him once more.

'Good afternoon,' it gurgled.

'You … already said that.'

It certainly did not seem wise to offer a colossal man-fish-thing cheekiness of any sort, but the Abysmyth hardly seemed to notice that Lenk had even spoken.

'*Time has no meaning to it,*' the voice replied, '*for it has no use for time. It exists without reason, without purpose, and time is the reason for all that mortals do.*'

'I know you,' it finally said. 'It was upon the blight you call ship that I discovered you. I kept you pure, I kept you chaste.'

'*It babbles,*' the voice within muttered, '*it is depraved, driven mad by its wounds.*'

'What wounds?' Lenk asked.

'*You cannot see them?*'

He squinted, peering into the shadows. Immediately his eyes widened at the gleam of emerald amongst the gloom. Great gashes rent the creature's chest, wounds rimed with a sickly green ichor. Each movement of the demon, each laboured breath and swivel of head, made the sound of leather shredding as the green substance pulsed like a living thing, quietly gnawing on the demon's flesh.

'What happened to you?' It occurred to him that he should be gloating over the creature's wounds, not curious.

'There was a battle,' the creature replied, 'longfaces … many of them, but weak. They could not hear Mother Deep. We could. We knew. We fought. We won.'

'We won,' the Omens echoed above, bobbing their heads in unison, 'we won, we won, we won.'

'We ...' Lenk regarded the demon warily. 'By that, do you mean you and ...' he made a gesture to the winged parasites in the trees, 'those things? Or,' he could barely force the question from his lips, 'are there more of you?'

'More, yes,' the creature replied. 'Our suffering is profound, but a duty we take gladly. Mother Deep requires us to suffer for your sakes and silence the voices.'

Suddenly, its eyes went wide. It rose in a flash of shadows, its shriek causing the Omens to go rustling through the leaves, chattering in alarm. Lenk sprang backwards, his sword up and ready to carve a new set of decorations in the creature's hide. The Abysmyth, however, made no move towards him, not so much as looking at the young man.

It swayed, precarious, before crashing back against the base of the tree, staring up at the sky with eyes full of revelation. Lenk had seen such expressions before, he noted grimly, in Asper's own stare.

'That is it!' It gurgled excitedly. 'It is all so clear. The wind may die, the sea may fall silent, but mortals ... mortals are never quiet. That is why you cannot hear Her, that is why She cannot reach you.'

It turned its eyes towards Lenk and the revelation was gone. Its stare was dead again, empty and hollow as its voice.

'Do not fret, wayward child,' it uttered, 'I am Her will, Her vigilance.' Slowly, its webbed claw slid down to its side; there was a muted moan. 'I can silence the voices.'

'Silence them,' the Omens whispered, 'silence them, silence them, silence them.'

When the Abysmyth's hand rose again, Lenk saw the Cragsman.

He had looked mighty back upon the *Riptide*, ferocity brimming in every inch of his tattooed flesh. Now, dangling upside down in the Abysmyth's talons, he was nothing more than a chunk of bait, wriggling, albeit barely, upon a great hook. The claw marks that rent his flesh glistened ruby red in the shadows, the whites of his eyes stark as the yellow of his teeth as he quivered a plea.

'Help me,' the pirate squealed, 'please!' His gaze darted alternately between the demon and the young man. 'I didn't do anything! I don't deserve this!'

'Ah, you can hear that.' The Abysmyth's voice drowned the man's screams under a multi-toned tide. 'What purpose does it serve to make so much noise? Who can hear with such a tone-deaf chorus? It is a distraction.'

The thing's other hand rose up like a great, black branch.

'The cure is nigh.'

'Cure it!' the Omens shrieked excitedly. 'Cure! Cure! Cure!'

It happened with such quick action that Lenk had no time to turn away. In the span of an unblinking eye's quiver, the demon took the Cragsman's arm in its own great hand and, with barely more than a wet popping noise, wrenched it off.

'*HELP ME!*' the man wailed. '*ZAMANTHRAS! DAEON! GODS HELP ME!*' Tears ran in rivulets down his forehead, mingling with fat, red globs that plopped upon the sand. '*PLEASE!*'

'And for what purpose, my son?' The Abysmyth shook its great head. 'Why do you make so much noise, calling to Gods who know not your name nor your suffering? Where is your mercy from heaven? Where is the end to suffering?'

It flicked its taloned hands, sending the appendage flying to land amidst the sands. The Omens let out a collective chatter of approval, bobbing their heads, their bulbous eyes never looking away from Lenk.

'Where is it?' they asked. 'Where is the end? Where are the Gods? Where is the mercy?'

'Sea Mother,' the man began babbling a prayer, 'benevolent matron, bountiful provider, blessed watcher. Wash my sins away on the sand, deliver me to my—'

'*NO!*'

The Abysmyth's howl echoed across the sea, across the sky. The Omens recoiled, fluttering off their branches to hover ponderously for a moment before settling back down. The demon's black hand trembled as it pointed a claw at the pirate.

'No blasphemies,' it uttered, 'no distractions.' It shook its great head. 'There is but one Mother here, one who may provide you with the mercy you seek.' Its hand lurched forwards, seizing the pirate's other arm. 'Can you not see the truth I seek to give you? Can you not see what woe you wreak upon the world?'

'Can you not?' the Omens muttered. 'Can you not see?'

'The way becomes clear,' the demon nodded, 'with suffering to guide your path.'

Lenk grimaced at the sound of ripping, turned away at the sound of meat sliding along the sand, closed his ears to the sound of the man's shrieking. It was too much.

'*Don't bother,*' the voice replied, effortlessly heard over the pirate's agony, '*he made his path, chose his destiny. He deserves not our aid.*'

'He doesn't deserve this,' Lenk all but whimpered.

'*His sins will be washed clean in the demon's blood. Now, patience.*'

'Can you hear it now?' The Abysmyth pulled the man

up, bringing him to eye level. 'Can you hear Her wondrous song? How it calls to you … how I envy you to hear it for the first time. Let Her hear your joy in the whisper of your tears.'

'Let Her.' The Omens giggled. 'She hears all, She delights in your discovery and Her song shall guide you.'

'Do you hear it?' The Abysmyth shook the man slightly. 'Do you?'

There was nothing left to drain from him, however, no more agony upon his face, no more pain to leak from his stumps. He merely dangled there, mouth agape, eyes barely open. Only the glimmer behind them told Lenk that he was still alive, only the shine of what once had been hope, snuffed out. The Cragsman's lips quivered, mouthing soundless words to him.

Kill me, he pleaded silently, *please*.

'So,' Gariath muttered, 'what was it?'

Dreadaeleon glanced up at the dragonman, licking his lips as he finished slurping a liquid from a tin cup.

'What was what?'

'What called you?'

'Ah.' The boy's eyes lit up. 'It was actually quite interesting. I'm surprised you're curious.'

'I'm not.'

'Then why did you ask?'

'Because,' the dragonman replied, 'if it calls to you again, I plan to kill you before you can do something stupid. To that end, I'd like to know what to listen for so I can act before you do.'

'Pragmatic.' The boy inclined his head. 'The truth is, I'm not entirely sure. It was something of a song without words, music without notes.' He paused, straining to think.

'Flatulence without smell? No, no, it was purely auditory.' His nostrils quivered. 'It occurs to me, though, I'd think you could smell whatever it was long before I heard it.'

'Your thinking tends to be brief and often fleeting,' Gariath grunted. 'I can't smell anything with you drinking that bile.' He pointed to the tin cup clenched in the boy's hands as Dreadaeleon squeezed his waterskin over it. 'What is it, anyway? It smells like bat dung.'

'It is.' Dreadaeleon took a brief sip. 'Some of it, anyway, mixed with the diluted sap of several trees, primarily willow, a few pinches of a powder you're better off not knowing the name of and a drop of liquor, usually a form of brandy or whiskey, for kick.'

'Why drink it?'

'It eases my headaches.'

'Uh-huh.' Gariath scowled at the boy. 'And the bat dung?'

Dreadaeleon smacked his lips thoughtfully. 'Flavour.'

Gariath's eyes glowered, muscles quivering with restrained fury. For a moment, a thought occurred to him, as it often had throughout his company with the humans, that this might be the sign he was waiting for. This might be the one act that indicated that these meagre, scrawny creatures had finally done something so deranged that they needed to be put down like the crazed animals they were.

'What?' Dreadaeleon asked, unaware of how close he was to having his head smashed in.

Not today, Gariath thought, easing his arm rigidly against his side. *If you get his blood on you, you won't be able to follow the scent. Later, maybe, but not now.* Bearing that thought as a burden, he snorted and turned about, continuing to stalk down the beach.

'Where are we going, anyway?'

'There has never been a "we",' Gariath growled. 'There is "I", who stands, and "you", who gets in the way.'

'Right.' Dreadaeleon nodded. '"We."'

'"We" would imply that I and you are on the same standing.' He turned about, making a spectacle of his toothy grimace. '*We* are not.'

'In that case, where are *you* going?'

Just tell him, the dragonman told himself. *If he finds out it's a long way to go, maybe he'll collapse from the thought of so much effort. Maybe then the tide will come in and drown him.* He grinned at that. *Then his stink won't be a nuisance and Lenk won't have anything to complain about.*

'I'm following a scent,' he finally told the boy.

'Food?' Dreadaeleon asked.

'No.'

'Water?'

'No.'

'Other dragonmen?'

Gariath stopped in his tracks, his back stiffening. Slowly, with a look of violation flashing in his black eyes, he turned to regard Dreadaeleon.

'You're using magic on me,' he snarled, 'trying to read my thoughts.'

'Telepathy,' Dreadaeleon corrected. 'And I'm not, no. I couldn't with my headache, at least.' He beamed a self-satisfied smile that begged all on its own to be cracked open like a nut. 'I simply used inference.'

'Inference.'

'The act of—'

'I know what it means.'

'Ah.' The boy nodded. 'Of course. I simply meant that, given the way you seem to be sniffing at the air, there's only a few things you could possibly be seeking. Common beasts, with their advanced senses of smell, usually only seek food, water or mates.'

'Clever,' Gariath grunted. 'Very clever.'

'I thought so.'

'Aside from one fact.' He held up a single clawed finger. 'This particular finger is one of five, which belong to one hand of two, which is the exact same number of feet I have, all of which I've used to split the skulls of, rip the arms off, smash the ribs of and commit other unpleasantries upon,' he jabbed the boy, sending him back a step, 'humans much smaller than you who called me much kinder things than a common beast.'

Dreadaeleon's eyes went wide with a certain kind of fear that Gariath had seen often in him. With predictable frequency the boy, for he was nothing more than a boy, constantly realised he was not the man he pretended to be. Such a reaction was usually caused by his conversations with the tall, brown-haired human woman or with the taller, red-skinned dragonman. Such reactions, too, frequently had visceral effects.

'I ... I didn't ... I mean, I don't want to—'

Stammering.

'It wasn't my intention—' Dreadaeleon shifted his gaze from the dragonman.

Looking at the ground like a whelp.

'You must believe me—' The boy's knees began to knock.

'I do,' Gariath interrupted.

Though he hated to admit it to himself, there was a certain gruesome pride that came with making a human soil himself, but such reactions were reserved for times when he wasn't on the hunt. Human urine was filthy, yellow and filled with the stinks of liquor. He couldn't imagine a bat-dung drink smelling any better coming out.

The boy's sigh, so heavy with relief, did not serve to strengthen Gariath's faith in the human bladder. Rolling his eyes along with his shoulders, he turned about and began to stalk further down the beach.

'Well, can I help?'

'There's a lot of things you can help,' Gariath growled in reply, 'such as your belief that I want to hear you any more.'

'I meant can I help you find whatever it is you're looking for?' Dreadaeleon scurried to keep up with the dragon-man's great strides. 'I'm not bad with scrying.'

'With what?'

'Scrying. Divination.' He beamed so proudly that Gariath could feel the boy's smile searing his back. 'You know, the Art of Seeking. Amongst the wizards of the Venarium, it's not considered worthy of much more beyond a few weeks of study, but it has its uses.'

Gariath paused, his ear-frills twitching slightly.

'Magic,' he uttered, 'can find lost things?'

'Most lost things, yes.'

When the dragonman turned to face Dreadaeleon, the boy no longer saw Gariath as he remembered him. In the span of a single turn, the red-skinned brute's face had shifted dramatically. Wrinkles, once seemingly perpetually carved into his face by an equally perpetual rage, had smoothed out. His lips had descended from their high-set snarl to hide his teeth.

Before, Dreadaeleon had never seen anything within his companion's eyes, so narrow and black had they been. Now they were wide, so wide as to glisten with something

344

other than restrained – or unrestrained – fury, and they stared at him from a finger's length away.

'How does it work?' Gariath growled.

'Um, well …' The boy struggled for words in the face of this new, slightly less reptilian face. 'It's a relatively simple art, which, as I suggested, is what places it so low upon the Hierarchy of Magic.' He began to count off his skinny fingers. 'The first of which being the Five Noble Schools: fire, ice, electricity, force and—'

'Tell me how it works.'

Gariath did not demand, not with any great anger, at least. His tone was so gentle and soft that Dreadaeleon blinked, taken aback.

'I just need a focus,' he replied as confidently as he could, 'something that belonged to the *Rhega*.'

Gariath's face twitched. 'Something that belonged to the *Rhega*.'

'Right.' Dreadaeleon nodded, daring a smile. 'So long as I have something to focus on, something that bears the *Rhega*'s signature, it should lead us to more *Rhega*.'

'As simple as that?'

'Just so.'

Dreadaeleon barely had any time to close his eyes before the fist came crashing into his face. His teeth rattled in his skull, chattering against each other like a set of crude ivory chimes. His coat-tails fluttered behind him like dirty brown wings as he sailed through the air before striking the sand, gouging a shallow trench with the force of his skid before finally coming to an undignified halt.

He heard the thunder of Gariath's footsteps before he felt the thick claws wrap around his throat, hoisting him aloft. His head swam, ringing with the twin cacophonies of his magic headache and the force of Gariath's blow. Through eyes rolling in their sockets, he could barely make out the great red and white blob before him.

'There are *no more Rhega*,' Gariath snarled. '*Your* breed saw to that.' His roar was laced with hot, angry breath that would have choked Dreadaeleon had he been able to breathe. 'And now you want to piss on their memory with your weakling, filthy *magic*! *SIMPLE?*'

The boy's shriek was caught in an explosion of sand as Gariath hurled him to the earth. With the pain echoing through his body in bells of agony, the vicious kick the dragonman planted in his side seemed nothing more than a particularly bloody comma in his furious sentence.

'There are no more *Rhega*,' Gariath repeated, 'just so.'

The dragonman might well have been a ghost, so faint were his footsteps, so hazy his outline in the wizard's eyes. Dreadaeleon tried to speak, tried to choke out a query as to what he had done to deserve such a thrashing, an apology of some sort, or perhaps just a plea for help as he felt something growing smaller within him, deflating as air escaped him without returning.

He had no more mind for questions or pleas, however. The dragonman's shape faded in the distance as he stalked away, his footsteps now silent, as was everything else. The world became numb, all sounds fading before the ringing in his ears.

All but one.

It was faint at first, a slow and gentle lilting of the wind, a voice carried on a stiff breeze that he could not feel. Slowly, it grew louder, searing his ears as it began to drown out the ringing in his head.

So familiar, he was barely able to think, caught between the symphony and chaos murmuring through his brain. *I've heard it before, I know.*

It grew closer and stronger, something between a hum and a purr, escalating to include a faint whistling and breathless gasp. Soon, it began to tinkle, as though it were a gem of sounds being cut into tiny, euphoric crystals.

A song without words, he thought, *so pretty … so pretty …*

His body was numb now. It no longer hurt to blink; the fact that he could not breathe no longer worried him. He lost himself in the song, agony forgotten as he listened to the delicate voice.

Ah, I remember now. He nodded weakly to himself. *From the boat … it's calling to me again.*

And he let himself be called, slipping away into darkness. His vision went blank, eyes closing so that nothing else in the world would matter, not even the shadow creeping over him and the cold, pale hand reaching for him as he lay motionless in the sand.

Fifteen

YOU, TOO, SHALL HEAR

'She is speaking so clearly now.'

Had he any nerve left to be shaken, Lenk certainly would have lost his at the near-orgasmic bliss with which the Abysmyth sighed. His courage, however, was long devoured, vanished under the flocks of Omens who gnawed incessantly at the body parts strewn across the ground. They shredded with their teeth, slurped long strings of greasy meat into their inner lips, all the while chattering their graces over the bounteous meal they had been served.

'We hear Her,' they chanted between chews, 'and so are we blessed. We hear Her.'

The Abysmyth, in response, shook its colossal head.

'But there yet remains no virtue in hearing Her name echoed by the choir.' Slowly, it fixed two great empty eyes upon Lenk. 'And you? Do you hear Her, my son? Have your ears been freed?'

'*Don't answer,*' the voice inside his head uttered, '*it wants an answer.*'

'Why?' he barely managed to gasp to his unseen companion.

'*It is an abomination, and like all abominations, it knows it is nothing. It is a preacher, and like all false preachers, it craves validation. It does not belong in this world. It needs a reason to exist.*'

'And we,' Lenk muttered, 'are that reason?'

'*No,*' the voice replied, '*we are the reason it dies today.*'

'You keep saying that, but how? How do we kill it?'

'*As we kill everything else.*'

Lenk's eyes drifted to the armless man dangling from the Abysmyth's claws, his eyelids flickering, straining to stay open through the pain long enough to mouth his silent plea to Lenk: *Kill me, kill me, kill me.* His wordless chant was like that of the Omens: repetitive, droning, painful to hear, or to imagine hearing.

'Can we—'

'*He is lost,*' the voice interrupted callously, '*he is of no use to us, either.*'

'But we can't just—' Lenk attempted to lift a leg to move forwards.

'*We shall.*' He felt it go numb under him.

'I don't—' He tried to tighten his grip on his sword.

'*We do.*' The weapon felt like a lead weight, useless at his side.

'My son,' the Abysmyth gurgled with an almost sympathetic inclination, 'do not fear what your eyes behold today.' It held up a single, webbed digit and shook it back and forth. 'For the eyes are what weaken you. Through ears, you shall find your salvation.'

'No ...'

The word came too softly from Lenk's lips, his own voice paralysed with fear as he watched the demon's arm crane up to its dangling captive. It pinched one of the Cragsman's meaty legs with two massive fingers, rubbing it between the digits thoughtfully.

'And so do I grant two gifts today,' it continued, keeping a giant black pupil fixed on Lenk. 'To you, the deaf, I grant the gift of hearing.' With a thick, squishing sound, the eye rotated back to the pirate. 'And to you, the misled, I offer you this gift—'

'No.'

Lenk spoke louder this time, but without conviction, his voice little more than a tiny pebble hurled from a limp wrist. Such a projectile merely bounced off the Abysmyth's leathery hide, unheeded, unheard.

'For no God you claim to know has ever bestowed upon you this quality of wisdom.' Against the sound of the leg being wrenched free from its socket, the sound of paper ripping, meat splattering, the Cragsman's shriek was but a whimper. 'Where are they now, my son? Do they hear you, even as you scream? Even as you beg?'

It shook its head with some grim mockery of despair. It rolled its fingers, twirling the severed limb like a daisy petal before tossing it aside, adding to the Omens' sun-ripened buffet.

'They don't hear you. I hear your suffering, my son, as does Mother Deep.' Its eyes brightened. 'Ulbecetonth hears. Ulbecetonth grants you this mercy ...'

With a gentleness not befitting its great size, the creature's hand took the man's head in its palm. It bobbed up and down, weighing the organ as though it were a piece of overripe fruit, pregnant with juices. Then, in the span of a belaboured groan, the creature's talons tightened over the man's skull as its jaws parted and uttered a final pair of words.

'Through me.'

Lenk found not the voice even to squeak at the sight. The creature's arm jerked, stiffened, sank claws into flesh and dripped thick, viscous ooze from its palm. The slime, like a living thing, swept up with an agonising slowness, seizing the man's face with grey-green tendrils, seeping into nose, mouth, ears, eyes until all was nothing more than a glob of moist, glistening mucus.

'Rest, now.'

The Abysmyth laid the Cragsman out before it with an almost reverent delicacy, staring down at the body with eyes that yearned to express pity through their emotion-less voids. The ooze, as if in reaction to the demon, pulsed once like a thick, slimy heart before sliding off the man's face, uninterested, to pool beneath his head.

It was the expression on the man's face that finally drove Lenk to collapse. He fell to his knees, not with a scream, but a slack jaw and quivering eyes that could not look away from the Cragsman. Dismembered, tortured, drowned, the corpse wore no fear upon his face, no anger nor any mask that the young man had seen upon the face of death.

Upon the undisturbed sand, beneath the shade of a tree swaying with the quiet song of a breeze, the Cragsman stared up at the endless blue sky with closed eyes, a slight smile tugging at his lips.

'This is the sound I remember,' the Abysmyth gurgled happily, remorseless, 'the sound of mercy.' It ran its mas-sive hand over the man's face, a sign of benediction from black talons. 'And to you, my son, She grants the gift of tranquil oblivion, through us, Her children.'

'Endless is Mother Deep's mercy,' the Omens chattered in agreement.

'Mercy?'

Lenk's own voice sounded blasphemous in the stillness, echoing against the empty sky. Slowly, he drew himself up from the sand, body rigid and shivering, cloaked by a cold the sun would not turn its eye to.

Such a sound did not go unnoticed. The Omens paused in the midst of their feast, glancing up with bits of pink and black stuck in their teeth, bulbous eyes quivering. The Abysmyth's great head rose, fixing two white eyes out towards the sand.

Two blue orbs stared back.

'Mercy is a purpose.' Lenk could hear the words coming from his mouth, but could not hear them in his head. 'You have no purpose,' the last word was forced from his lips like a spear, '*abomination*.'

He took a step forwards and the Omens scattered, white sheets in the wind as they flew up to the safety of the tree. Behind the net of leaves, their spherical eyes peered out, watching, unblinking, horrified.

The Abysmyth had no such reservations.

'What would a mortal know of purpose?' It rose up, matching Lenk's step with a thunderous crash of its webbed foot. 'A fleeting light in a cold, dark place, quivering and then snuffed for ever, your purpose is only to receive Her infinite mercy.' It stepped out of the shadow, a blight upon the sky and sand. 'Your purpose is to *hear* Her.'

'*Our* purpose,' Lenk felt the urge to pause at that word, but his mouth muttered regardless, 'begins with *you*.' His sword was up and levelled at the beast. 'Where is the tome?'

'Tome? *TOME?*' The Abysmyth howled, scratching at the side of its head as if pained by the very word. 'The book is not for you to see, my son! Its knowledge corrupts, condemns! I won't let you fall to such a fate after all I have suffered for you.' It stomped again, petulant. '*I won't!*'

Only when it stepped into the sunlight, a great stain on the world, did the extent of its suffering become clear. Its wounds pulsated with its rage, the sickly green ichor gnawing at its flesh, carving deeper furrows into its skin and baring masses of bleached white bones and innards that resembled beating patches of dark moss.

'You see,' it all but cackled as it saw Lenk's eyes widen, 'this is the price we paid, we, Her children, for *you*.' It shook its head. 'The longfaces, those purple-skinned *deviants*, would not listen to us, to *HER!* They would not listen! We tried to make them, and what was wrought?' It gestured to its mangled chest. '*Scorn! Impurities!* They cast a disease upon us Shepherds and now *you* say the flock is already brimming with sickness? I will not accept it!'

The creature's roar echoed in Lenk's ears, the same word repeating itself in his head: *We, we, we.* There were more of them, more Abysmyths, more cursed creatures with sharp teeth and glistening ooze.

He felt he should have been terrified by such words. He felt he should run, seek the others and flee the island. Such thoughts were small candlelights in his head, choked out and extinguished by the voice that quieted the demon's howl with its echoing presence.

'You don't belong here,' it spoke through him, 'you were cast out, sent to hell.'

The creature grinned. It did not merely appear to grin, nor did Lenk imagine it grinning. Such an expression seemed painful, the edges of its face cracking, the corners of its lipless mouth splitting with the effort. Still, the demon grinned and spoke.

'We're coming back.'

And then the grin vanished. Lenk stared into a vast, black face dominated by expressionless eyes. The creature tilted its head to the right, as though regarding him for the first time.

'Good afternoon,' it uttered.

It tilted its head to the left.

'I ...' it sounded almost contemplative, 'want you to die now.'

'Riffid Alive,' Kataria whispered breathlessly.

There were very few occasions outside of violent situations where it was acceptable to speak the shictish Goddess's name. Everyday prayers and curses were for weaker deities of weaker races; the shicts were born with all the instinct they would ever need. However, if the Foe of all *Kou'ru* could have witnessed the carnage on the beach through Kataria's eyes, she highly doubted the Goddess would begrudge her.

What had, undoubtedly, begun as a pristine stretch of white sand, completely indiscernible from any other chunk of beach, was now smothered under twisting sheets of grey and white. She stepped upon what had once been the beach, covering her nose as a heavy sulphurous odour sought to choke the life out of her.

The sound beneath her feet was thick and crunching, not unlike walking on pine cones. The sun's warmth paled against the fierce heat that choked the beach. She glanced down; the earth smouldered, red embers burning stubbornly through the blanket of smoke that roiled over sands scorched black. She glanced up; what thin trees remained standing had been charred into dark, lanky arms reaching up towards a sky no longer visible from the ground. Upon their fingers burned bright fires, beacons in the smoke that drew her further down the coast.

They illuminated the earth, however faintly, and the story continued in the charred sand as Kataria spied the first tracks.

There had been a battle, she recognised, and not a clean one. Footprints were muddled: bare feet with webbed toes crossed over heavy, booted indentations in a brawl that sprawled the length of the shore. Here, someone fell hard upon the earth and left a pool of thick, boiling red behind. There, some strange green ichor pulsated hungrily in the sand like a disease. And all across the sand were the vast, webbed prints of something large that had stalked through the melee in long strides.

Abysmyth.

Lenk had told her to regroup with the others if she found any sign of the creature, but, she reasoned, he often told her many things she didn't care to hear. For the moment, she forgot him, forcing down concern and instinct, and leaned closer to the ground, following the story further.

The demon had appeared somewhere in the midst of the brawl, after the earth had been scorched. It had wrought terror upon the field; everywhere its foot had landed, the depressions of fallen bodies lay nearby. *Interesting twist*, she thought, *but unsatisfying.*

If the Abysmyth *had* indeed killed and injured as many as the tracks suggested, where were all the corpses? Where were the drowned victims? Occasionally, shallow trenches had been carved where the bodies had hit the earth, indicating that they had either crawled or been carried away.

Whoever the Abysmyth had struck down had apparently escaped with their dead and wounded. She frowned, uneasy. That only accounted for one side of the battle; where were the frogmen that had rushed into battle beside the demon? For that matter, where was the demon? She paused by the base of a flame-scarred tree, scratching her chin thoughtfully. The wind moaned, peeling back a blanket of smoke.

It was then that she saw the needle-like teeth leering towards her.

She whirled, bow up and arrow drawn, levelling her weapon at the gaping maw that loomed out of the grey. Her hand quivered once, then stayed; the mouth did not move. Instead, the mouth glimmered a shimmering, crystal-line blue.

The smoke retreated further, exposing the face that held the teeth, the large black eyes that dominated the face. From behind a skin of ice, the frogman howled soundlessly at her, immobile and unblinking within its azure prison. His spear was held above his head, icicles hanging from the weapon's tip, the frogman's muscles frozen and unquivering under a sheen of frost.

'Well,' she grunted, 'I'll be damned.'

Somehow, the human curse seemed more appropriate for what occurred next.

In a great sigh, the smoke peeled back. A forest of frozen flesh was laid bare before her eyes. They stood in a charge that had no end, mouths open to utter a battle cry that had no sound beyond the cracking of ice in the distance. Dozens of the pale invaders, turned into an expanse of endless blue, rushed towards some unseen foe that they had never reached. Many of them hadn't even set two feet upon the ground before the ice claimed them.

And now they levelled their hatred, their black stares, upon her.

Kataria, however, had no more attention for them. Her concern was reserved for the emaciated beast that had stridden into battle with them. The Abysmyth's tracks were not apparent in the frost-kissed earth nor the smouldering black sand. However, one set of footprints did catch her attention.

He, or she, for the tracks were made by slender feet set lightly upon the ground, had stood before the frogmen. The frost radiated from that position in a great arcing wave, staining the ground with ice. From there, this new character had turned about, unhurried, by the looks of its shallow, well-defined footsteps, and traipsed down the shore.

Where it had stopped, carnage was born. Fire savaged the land, sending bodies to the ground as burned husks, barely discernible from the scorched earth. Trees were split down the middle, as though by a great blade.

It didn't take the shict long to deduce the presence of magic. Even through the acrid stench of brimstone, the stink of wizardry was thick in the air, a foul amalgamation of sulphur and something metallic, with a somewhat lemon-scented after-aroma.

That answered a few questions right away – for what earthly fire could smoulder for so long? What mortal ice could remain frigid even under the sun's unrelenting warmth?

More questions arose than were answered, however; Dreadaeleon was the only creature she knew capable of the practice of magic, and he was far too frail to wreak such devastation. Besides, he had taken off with Gariath, across to the other side of the island ... hadn't he?

The Venarium, she knew from listening to the boy, were the sole practitioners and custodians of magic. They were, she had learned, a secretive and largely boring lot, more content to study and make rules than actually use their powers for anything interesting.

This character, this set of prints, however, was anything but tedious. She followed the trail, noting each shattered tree, each heap of burned corpses, each patch of ice. So intent on the tracks was she that she hardly noticed the Abysmyth when it appeared through the gloom.

She did not start at the sight of the creature. Rather, she was struck dumb by it and its sudden appearance.

It was dark, far darker than she remembered it, wisps of

smoke pouring from its gaping maw, an enormous wound in its chest and craters that had once been eyes. An icicle the size of the *Riptide*'s bow skewered it through its ribcage, holding it aloft like some demonic kebab, its webbed feet barely grazing the ground as they swayed in the wind.

Despite the oppressive heat, Kataria felt her blood run cold.

The Abysmyth had been a definition up until this moment. Despite being a creature of hell, it had existed according to rules: it killed and it could not be killed. The ending of the trail's story had changed everything. Something had fought the frogmen and Abysmyth, something that left no bodies, only smears of pulsing green ichor.

And amongst it all, someone, a man or woman who strode between infernos and blizzards as casually as one skips through a meadow, had given her a plot that she no longer wanted to read.

Suddenly, finding Lenk seemed like a rather good idea.

Her ears twitched and, for a fleeting moment, she was almost relieved to hear a sound other than the crackling of ice and fire. Such a moment was short-lived; the sounds of steel singing through the air slipped muffled through scars in the smoke, accompanied by faint mutters of voices she had never heard before.

They were vaguely familiar. There was grunting, snarling, the sound of something heavy being swung through the air. Yet there was something odd about the voices: they all spoke at once, echoing and reverberating off of each other to become incomprehensible. Like wisps of smoke, they trickled through to her, brief scents of sulphur and brimstone without the stink of something truly burning.

And then, all at once, they were silent.

She waited, ears twitching, hoping to hear more; she

ought likely to have fled, she knew, but was tempted into stillness by the sounds. She had to find the end of the story that had begun back in the jungle.

Moments passed, a tense eternity of quiescence. In the distance, a seared branch crumbled at its joint and collapsed upon the sand with a faint crash. Her breath was loud, she knew, so loud she might as well have been speaking.

'Ah,' she barely whispered, 'hello?'

She received her answer half a blink later.

Lenk came hurtling through the air like a wiry javelin, cutting through the smog and leaving a trail of clear air behind him. He hit the earth, shifting from missile to plough as he dug a deep trench in the charred sand, a cloud of ash in his wake. There was an alarmed cry, a faint crash as he struck the tree.

Then, silence once more.

She rushed to him, not bothering to call his name, not bothering to shriek out in alarm at whatever had hurled him such a distance. She made no noise, save for the earth crunching beneath her feet and the words hissed between her teeth.

'Don't be dead, don't be dead,' she chanted to herself like a mantra, 'Riffid Alive, don't be dead.'

He might as well have been, lying in a half-made grave with the seared tree to mark it. Motionless, eyes closed, sword held loosely in hands, he looked almost at peace in his trench. So deep was the rent in the earth that she had to leap in to reach his body.

'Don't be dead, don't be dead.'

Two fingers went to his throat; nothing. A long, notched ear went to his chest; soundless.

'Don't be dead, don't be dead.'

She leaned closer to his face; his breath was cold and

icy. Her eyes remained open, watering as the smoke stung them.

'Don't—'

His eyes opened with such suddenness that she recoiled. He rose from the ground like a living corpse draped in an ashen cloak. His sword was in his hand, naked and silver. His eyes pierced the gloom like candles burning blue. His stare shifted over her, merely acknowledging her presence, before he soundlessly pulled himself out of the hole.

'Lenk,' she all but cried after him, 'are you—'

'Not sure,' he replied. His voice was like the sound of the embers beneath his boots. 'Fight now.'

'What fight?'

That, too, was answered as soon as she emerged from the grave.

Sixteen

MOTHER, WHY?

'They won't listen! They can't hear You!'

Kataria's ears twitched. A dozen voices, all choked and speaking at once, tone shifting wildly between each word.

'I've tried! How I've tried! How I've *suffered*!'

Footsteps, embers crunching under massive, webbed feet.

'But for what, Mother? They refuse enlightenment, deny You!'

The crack of ice.

'Have I done nothing to show You my devotion? Is all my suffering in vain?'

Silence. The sound of smoke rising from the earth.

'*NO!*'

The endless grey trembled and scattered, exposing the Abysmyth as a towering tree in the centre of the forest of frozen frogmen. The beast was alight in the gloom, eyes flashing wide and empty, talons wet with ooze, pulsing green ichor pumping in time with each staggered breath it took.

'There's ...' Kataria paused to stare at the creature with ever-widening eyes, 'more of them?'

'More?' Lenk swept the smoke for a sign. 'Where?'

'Behind us,' Kataria replied. 'Dead. Something happened

here.' She glanced from the demon's wounds to a glob of the throbbing green substance on the earth. *Not blood*, she noted, not bothering to wonder what else it might be. 'Probably whatever happened to this one as well.'

'One or one thousand,' the young man muttered, raising his sword. 'We will clean the land of their blight.'

'You think we can?'

'*You* cannot,' he replied sharply, '*we* can.'

'We?' She glanced at him, terrified. 'Who's—'

She never finished the sentence, her breath robbed from her the moment her eyes met his. Perhaps it was the cover of smoke, the angle at which she saw him or stress from the horrors of the battlefield that twisted her vision. She prayed it was, for she saw his stare burning brightly through the smoke.

Pupilless.

She tightened her jaw, turned away, resolved not to look again.

'Then what do we do?'

'Stay,' he commanded coldly. 'We kill.'

'You can't kill that thing.'

'He cannot,' Lenk replied, '*we* can.'

'Damn it,' she muttered breathlessly, 'of all the times for you to go *completely* insane, why did you have to choose the moment when *I* might die, too?'

If the young man had a reply for that, it was lost in the scurry of boots on burned earth. He was up, a flash of silver and blue, carving a path through the endless smoke towards his towering foe. The creature, for its part, seemed unimpressed.

Then, suddenly, it erupted.

'The Shepherd is ever tireless! Ever vigilant!' It roared and the frozen frogmen quaked against the ice. 'It is through his mercy that deliverance is possible! It is through the Shepherd that Her mercy is ever known!'

Lenk lunged, and a great black arm shot out, seizing him about the waist.

Whatever madness or courage had shot him into the beast's grasp vanished once he was drawn close enough to look into the thing's eyes. It gurgled angrily, its blank gaze straining to express the fury its voice could only hint at in disjointed harmony.

That seemed to infuriate it.

'Do not fear, my son,' it murmured, 'for even as you strike at me, I am ever bound to forgive you.'

It craned its arm up, raising him high into the sky, as if to present him to heaven for inspection. Its talons pierced Lenk's flesh, he felt his tunic shredding, five warm pin-pricks painted his body red. He felt a scream burst from his lungs, but heard no reply.

'It is your nature to fear the unknown,' it continued, a deep, resonant bass leaking through its many voices, 'but the Shepherd knows no nature of his own. His life is duty, and his duty is life.'

A ray of sunshine split the smoke, shining down on Lenk.

'Through Her, I grant you this,' it gurgled, tightening its grip, 'my mercy and my duty. I ...'

It tilted its head, hesitant. Its eyes flickered once more as a twisted shriek tore itself from the creature's maw.

'I *HATE YOU!*'

The arm snapped down. Lenk hit the ice, shattered it, and descended below. He ploughed his grave with his body, shards digging into his back and flying up into the air. Even after he had stopped, he felt as though he were still falling, as though something else had torn itself from his body and vanished into the earth.

Through fluttering eyes, he saw the cold powder descending upon him, settling like a blanket, urging him to sleep. Even the sun still shone upon him. It felt warm; somehow, he knew he should have felt colder than he did.

'What,' he whispered, 'what do we do now?'

No one answered him.

'Can we survive?'

No one spoke to him.

'I … think I'm going to die.'

No one reassured him.

The sun vanished behind a blot of ink. His eyes snapped open once, wide enough to see the outline of a webbed foot the size of his head rise above his face. He blinked, and it was still there. Then he felt his eyes shut themselves and it no longer existed.

The world was dark.

'From Mother Deep to child,' it all but whispered, 'from child to mortal. This is your mercy. Sleep now,' its foot tensed, 'and dream of blue.'

The demon's body convulsed suddenly. A sparrow with a silver beak sang through the air, burying itself in the Abysmyth's ribcage. It hesitated, flinching as one flinches at bee-stings. It heard the sound of feet scampering on ice, the sound of something humming a solemn tune, the sound of air parting before metal.

Another arrow struck it, embedded itself in the creature's neck.

It lowered its foot to the ground, swinging its head about to survey the ice. Nothing but still, solitary bodies and frozen faces met its gaze, mirroring the anger it yearned to express.

'How many times must we go through this?' it gurgled. 'How many times must I be scorned before I show you the unreasonableness of your blasphemies?'

Upon hearing no answer beyond the crack of ice, it hurled its head back and screamed.

'HOW MANY?'

Kataria was hard pressed to choke back her scream as the creature's fury raked at her ears. Something tinged its multitude of voices, a gurgling, shrieking squeal that sought to reach inside her head and sink audible talons into her brain. Pain, perhaps, or merely annoyance at having a pair of arrows lodged in its body.

That seemed to aggravate it.

She nocked another arrow and peered around the legs of a frozen frogman who scowled down upon her. The Abysmyth loomed like a tower with a poor foundation, swaying in the impotent breeze that tried to chase the smoke from the beach.

Up to that moment, she hadn't even thought of trying to kill it.

Her plan had simply been to distract it long enough to dig Lenk out of his hole and drag him off to safety. However, as she stared at the creature, temptation manifested in the beast's gaping wounds.

This did not seem like the demon she remembered. This was not the unholy terror that had held a shipful of men in terrified awe, not the creature that had pulled an entire harpoon out of its belly, unfazed. This demon, if it could still be called that, seemed weaker, wounded.

Mortal.

It whirled suddenly, swinging a colossal arm. Glass shattered and a thousand shards of what had once been a man, or something close to it, flew across the beach. Kataria, again, had to bite back horror as a fragment of what had been a face bounced twice across the ice, then skidded to a halt at her feet to stare at her with one eye frozen in hate.

Then again ...

'Forgive the fury, child.'

Kataria froze instinctively; had the thing spotted her?

She dared a glimpse. The Abysmyth stalked towards her, sweeping its eyes across the blue stillness; the look of a predator with the scent of blood.

With all the casualness of a boy with a stick, it brought its arm down to crush another frogman. It pulled back a webbed fist, dark red splinters embedded in black skin.

'You fear for my well-being, perhaps,' it gurgled, 'and that is good. But your fear is in vain. No wolf's teeth can harm the Shepherd. Purple longfaces, they tried. They came out of nowhere with their iron,' it scratched at a green wound, 'their venom. But they could not stop us.'

Longfaces, venom, the words flashed through her mind. The tracks became clear, the other characters revealed. Absently, the shict wished that the creatures that had tormented this demon had decided to linger.

'There is nothing to fear.' The Abysmyth spoke with a poor facade of reassurance. 'There are simply questions, questions that you must answer for yourself.'

Its head jerked away at the sound of ice cracking and Kataria seized her chance. Her feet were quiet as she slid out from behind the frogman, her pale flesh indiscernible from the gloom – she hoped – as she slipped behind another.

'Who will remember you when you die, mortal?' It continued to stalk towards her prior position. 'Will your Gods take you to their elusive heaven,' it levelled its gaze upon a frogman, 'when nothing is left to bury?'

366

Its roar split the smoke as it charged, smashing frogmen underfoot, sending chunks of ice and sinew flying. With one great sweep of its hand, it crushed the frogman that had hidden Kataria. The creature's eyes seemed to go wider, were that even possible, at the sight of empty blue earth, and it collapsed to its knees.

'Why,' its voices were long, loud and keening, 'are You making this *so hard on me?*'

Whether or not the demon was actually capable of sobbing was a matter Kataria would settle later, for at that moment, she saw her opportunity.

As it hunched over, the gaping wound in the Abysmyth's back split a little further open, the green ichor lining it pulsing slightly. Within the wound, through blackened ribs, she saw it: barely visible in the darkness, but round and swollen like an overripe melon.

The heart.

She drew back her bowstring, took aim. She could feel her pupils dilating as the creature's heart pounded, growing larger in her vision with each pump of tainted blood until it was as large as a black boulder. The fletching of her arrow tickled at her lips, which twisted into a grin.

'One,' the whisper of her voice and her bowstring were united.

The missile shrieked, cutting through the smoke and finding its target with a moist, squishing sound. Kataria bit her tongue to keep from giggling madly at her victory.

Her heart went from pounding to still in the time it took the creature to rise, turn and level two empty eyes upon her. She could see the arrowhead jutting from its ribcage, just as she could see it take an unfettered lurch forwards.

'Blessed is Mother Deep,' it gurgled, 'the path is revealed.'

Why she didn't move when it came charging towards her, she knew not. Why she remained standing, slack-jawed, as it reached a hand out for her, she didn't know. Perhaps, she thought through the fog of awe, she was simply terrified. More likely, she was struck into immobility by the vision of the creature's heart, pounding bloodlessly with an arrow stuck through it.

She took two awkward steps backwards before its arm swept out soundlessly, hand closing about her throat and hoisting her high into the air. It did not tremble as her senses returned to her and she hammered at its hand with leather-bound fists, kicking at its ribcage as it drew her closer.

It merely regarded her, tightened its grip and gurgled, 'Sleep.'

Commanded, the ooze began to slide from the creature's palm. Kataria felt it choke her immediately, tightening about her throat as it crept like slugs up her jawline. Instinct demanded that she scream, but survival demanded that she clench her teeth tightly together, denying the ooze a door into her.

The image of Mossud was wrought in her eyes as she stared down at the glistening mucus. In its cloudy reflection, she could see herself in his stead: mouth agape, eyes unblinking with a skin of the viscous slime over her face, still and breathless on the earth like a fish torn from water.

If the Abysmyth saw her fear, it showed nothing in its empty eyes.

'I can hear your thoughts,' it uttered. 'You think the Shepherd mad for slaughtering the flock and calling it mercy.' It tightened its grip; Kataria felt something creak inside her throat. 'Your ears are deafened by so much inane screeching that you call the voice of your God.'

The ooze crept up her jawline, thick, viscous tendrils tugging at the corners of her mouth.

'The truth is not always happy,' it continued, 'but always necessary, and this truth is insistent upon you.' Its fingers twitched, the ooze crawled further upwards. 'This is mercy, for you will be spared the tragedies that are to come.'

Her nostrils quivered, pumping air desperately as the ooze covered her pursed lips and sought the next nearest orifice. She hammered at the Abysmyth's arm, her fists bouncing off its skeletal limb.

'This world will drown,' it spoke, heedless of her strife, 'but only your weak Gods believe in tragedy without purpose. Mother Deep's wisdom is as vast and sprawling as the sea. She shall see this blighted earth reborn into the endless blue it was intended to be. The Shepherd's sole lament is that this sheep will not see such a paradise.'

Instinct and the desperation to wrench free from the beast's grip slowly quieted within her as the ooze slid up her face. Her body seemed to betray her, mouth beginning to loosen, heart slowing, lungs shrinking and wracking her with pain. And as her organs began to surrender, so, too, could she feel her mind fester with a similar disease.

It won't be so bad, she thought, *quick, not much pain, and then it's over. There are worse ways to die ... aren't there?* With none coming to mind, she felt her heart beginning to sink, turning to lead in her chest. *Whatever happens to me won't be half as bad as ...*

Kataria's eyes burst wide open as the ooze crept into the corners of her vision.

Lenk.

She could not surrender, she knew, could not leave Lenk buried in his grave, waiting for the Abysmyth to visit far worse torments upon him. She could not go peacefully into death knowing that he still lay helpless nearby.

With renewed fervour, she hammered at the creature, but even that fury died a swift, ugly death as soon as she had summoned it. Her lungs drew in less and less breath as the slime crept up into her nose, the screams caught inside her threatened to cause her throat to explode. What could she do against the demon? It could not be harmed by mortal weaponry; she had put an arrow through its heart and it hadn't so much as flinched. No, she realised, there was nothing left to be done.

Nothing left, except to apologise.

Lenk, she thought, craning her neck to survey his hole, *I'm—*

Her gaze lingered upon the empty grave for a moment before a new thought struck her.

Where?

The question was answered in an instant as he came, silent as a shadow, silver as the sword he held high, cutting through the smoke. Fast, far too fast for the demon to notice, far too fast for her to flinch, the blade came down in a rainbow of steel.

She felt herself falling, felt fingers loosening around her throat, felt herself collapsed to the ground. She blinked, heedless of the ooze crawling into her eyes, and surveyed the black limb lying limp on the ground beside her, severed neatly at its thin biceps.

If the demon were capable of blinking, it would have, too, as it glanced down at the stump of its arm. It wiggled the remains of the appendage momentarily, shifted its vacant stare about: first to its arm upon the ground, then to the man standing before him, blade bloodless. It tilted its head to the side.

Then, the demon screamed.

The wail was so violent as to pierce even the wall of slime filling her ears, so terrifying as to make her forget the rest of the sludge as she strained to cover her ears. She had heard it laugh, pray, preach and chuckle before. She had heard such things and remained silent.

Only now, when she heard it in pain, did she feel the need to scream.

Lenk, however, was unmoved. His sword lashed out immediately, carving a deep gouge in the creature's wispy torso. Black skin was rent like paper, globs of thick ebon spilling from the wound to plop in quivering jellies upon the earth. The creature shrieked at the wound again, its voice arcing into a high-pitched wail as it grabbed at the cut, straining to keep further parts of itself from slipping out.

'Stop!' it wailed. 'Stop! Stop! You're not supposed to do that!'

Lenk did not stop.

He lunged at the creature as it retreated backwards, thrusting his weapon into its leg so that the tip burst out of the other side in a fan of black. The creature collapsed to its knees and its shriek terrified the gloom, chasing the smoke further from the beach. Its hand quivered, darting between wounds, seeking to contain the thick liquids pouring from it at an alarming rate.

'Not fair!' it screamed. 'Not fair! Get away from me! *GO AWAY!*'

Lenk did not go away.

His stride was soundless, his blade held loosely at his side as he advanced casually upon the creature. The victory was already decided, but rather than end it quickly, Lenk chose to take his time, walking so slowly as to suggest he wasn't even aware that Kataria was nearby, covered with slime, still and breathless upon the ground.

'Mother!' the Abysmyth howled. 'Mother! Help me! *HELP ME!*'

Lenk did not hear.

The demon made a lunge at him, feeble and sloppy, hurling its arm out to claw empty air as he stepped backwards. When the thing landed hard on its hand, he was quick to act, sidewinding about it like a serpent. His boots scraped against leathery flesh as he leapt and raced up the creature's back, seizing it by its great black crest. His sword flashed, a steel fang sinking into the creature's collarbone.

It was in that moment that Kataria realised the Abysmyth was making a sound she had never heard it make, never even thought it was capable of making before that moment: the demon was sobbing.

'It hurts! *It hurts!*' the thing cried out as Lenk wrenched the blade deeper, its mouth gaping wide. '*MOMMY! MOMMY! IT HURTS! MAKE IT STOP!*' It batted at the weapon, digits suddenly becoming pudgy and helpless. '*MOMMY, I DON'T LIKE IT! MAKE IT STOP!*'

Lenk listened.

His foot came up and came down in one quick movement, heel upon the sword's crossguard and burying it to the hilt. The silver blade burst out through the creature's ribcage, sunlight through stormclouds, and shone defiantly.

The demon stopped its wailing. Lenk sprang off its back.

Its breathing was heavy now, laboured and ragged, shining rivers pouring out of it with every gasp. Even as it swayed upon its knees, its eyes could not express the despair it clearly felt as it stared blankly at the weapon. The sword looked back up at it through metal eyes, cruel and remorseless, denying the pity the Abysmyth so desperately wanted.

The wind moaned in the distance. Smoke parted above. A beam of light descended warily to the blackened earth and illuminated the silver spike as the demon reached up and fingered its tip.

'So loud,' it whispered, 'the sky is ... so loud.' Waterfalls of black bile leaked out from between its serrated teeth, stained the ground. 'It hurts ...' Quietly, it looked up to the sky. 'Mother ... how come it hurts?'

Kataria watched it collapse, the sword hilt proud in the sunlight, and a thought struck her.

That should not have happened ...

It was when she blinked and felt her eyes squish that another thought rose.

I can't breathe.

As though it had seemed a foreign concept until that moment, she began to rake at her face, pulling mucus off in great sheets. The slime seemed to resent this, trying to seep further inside her each time she clawed. Her lungs were ready to burst, heart ready to explode, mind ready to turn to stone and drag her head to the ground.

And still she raked.

Boots crunched. She felt a shadow descend upon her.

'Lenk,' she gurgled, choked, 'help.'

He stood above her, unmoving, shadowed by the blend of smoke and sunlight.

'Lenk,' she said again, voice straining to get out through the ooze.

He twitched, knelt down beside her.

She opened her mouth to plead again, but found herself breathless. Blood froze in her veins, breath forgotten as her jaw went slack. She gasped; the ooze found its door into her body and flooded in. Her next breath was the last she took before she felt herself slip away, but even through the darkness of her eyes, she could still see him.

Lenk, skin as grey as a drowned corpse, eyes blue and burning, bereft of pupils.

Seventeen

BURY YOUR FRIENDS DEEP

'Is it working?'

Asper could feel Lenk's eyes with such intensity they threatened to crack her skull. His stare darted between the priestess, sweating and pumping knotted hands over her patient's chest, and the shict, who lay breathless upon the ground.

Asper kept her actual thoughts to herself; it just seemed in poor taste to tell him his concern over his dying companion was slightly irritating.

'I don't know yet.' She pressed a pair of fingers against Kataria's throat. 'This sort of thing works on drowning victims, but only if we get to them quickly.' No pulse; she kept her head low to conceal her frown. 'Really, I just have no idea if it works on drowning by demons.'

'Well, try—'

'Oh, is *that* what I'm supposed to be doing?' she snarled over her shoulder at him. 'I'm not putting hands on her chest for your enjoyment, you know. Back away, moron!'

He nodded weakly, backing away. Such readiness to obey distressed her. It was exceedingly unlike the young man to so willingly bow out of such a situation. Then again, she considered, it was exceedingly unlike him to express any interest in death. Yet he seemed to be dying with the shict,

375

moping about her soon-to-be-corpse like a dog around its dying master.

Asper forbore to tell him this.

She was sorely tempted to tell him to stop staring at her, though. His eyes bored into the back of her skull, drilling into two well-worn spots in her head where other, weary stares had rested. Gazes from mothers with fevered children, fathers with raped daughters had left the first scratches upon her scalp. Soldiers with wounded comrades and sons with ailing elders had bored even deeper.

Lenk's stare, however, went well beyond her skin. He peered past hair, flesh, blood and bone into the deepest recesses of her mind. He saw her, she felt, and all the workings of her brain.

He knew she couldn't save this one.

NO! she shrieked at herself inside her own head. *Don't think like that. You can do this. These hands have healed before, countless people. These hands …*

Her gaze was drawn to her left hand, resting limply upon the shict's abdomen. It twitched suddenly, temptingly. *You could end it all, you know*, her thoughts drifted, *just a bit of pressure, like you did to the frogman. Then, poof! All over! She won't have to suffer any more …*

'No, no, no, *NO!*'

She ignored the concerned stares cast her way, ignored her hand, ignored everything but the placid expression upon Kataria's face and the stillness of her heart.

'I can do this,' she muttered, beginning chest compressions anew, 'I can do this, I can do this.' She found solace in the repetition, so much that she barely noticed the tear forming at the corner of her eye. 'Please, Talanas, let me do this …'

*

Lenk stared at Asper's back, watching the sweat stain grow longer down her robe.

It was a hard battle to resist the urge to rush up beside the priestess, to see if he could help, if he could do something. He was used to fixing things: fixing the fights between his companions, fixing the agreements between him and his employers, fixing to jam hard bits of steel into soft flesh.

That's how it should be.

He should have been able to fix this.

The sound of metal gently scraping against skin was loud, unbearable. He cast a resentful, sidelong scowl at his companion. Denaos, however, paid no heed to the young man, gingerly working at his fingernails with a tiny blade. Eventually, it seemed Lenk's stare became a tad more unbearable and Denaos glanced back at him.

'Sweet Silf, *fine*,' he hissed, 'I'll do yours, if you're so damn envious.'

'Kataria,' Lenk replied sharply, 'is *dying*.'

'To be more precise, Kataria may already be dead.'

Lenk blinked at him. Somewhere in the distance, a gull cried.

'What?' Denaos hardly looked at him as he plucked up a waterskin from the ground and took a drink.

'This doesn't bother you?' Lenk all but shrieked at the tall man, snatching the skin away. 'You can't even keep yourself from drinking *her* water?'

'It's *our* water, you milksop. She'll have her drink if and when she wakes up. Have at least an *ounce* of faith in Asper, would you?' Denaos glanced over to the priestess. 'She's doing her best. She'll do what's right.'

'Really?' Lenk permitted a squeal of relief to tinge his voice. 'You've seen this sort of thing before?'

'Once, aye.' He nodded appraisingly as Asper pressed

her lips against Kataria's once more. 'But the spectacle cost me a pouch of silver.' He became aware of Lenk's angry stare after another moment. 'What?'

'What is wrong with you?' The young man forced an angry snarl between clenched teeth. 'I almost suspect Gariath would be more sympathetic in this than you are.'

'He's further up the beach,' Denaos gestured, 'far more curious about dead demons than he is about Kataria.' He cast a smug smile at Lenk. 'Besides, it's not like he'd do anything more than I am save urinate on her corpse.' He coughed. 'Out of respect, of course.'

'Then maybe you should go and linger with him,' Lenk snorted. 'If we're lucky, I'll only have to come back to see one of you still alive.'

'Unsurprising as it might be, I find the near-dead to be rather more pleasant company than that lizard.'

'Then do me,' Lenk paused, 'and *her* the respect of showing proper manners and worrying a little.' He grunted. 'Or by seeing how many daggers you can fit in your mouth. Whichever.'

'Worry?' Denaos made a scoffing sound. 'Would that I could.'

The wind between them died. Lenk turned a scowl upon the rogue.

'What do you mean by that?'

'Frankly, I'd rather not say.'

'Then you shouldn't have said it in the first place,' Lenk snarled. '*What do you mean by that?*'

The rogue's shoulders sank as his head went low to hide the rolling of his eyes.

'Really, you don't want me to continue. If I do, you'll get all upset and pouty, then violent. You'll do something you'll later regret, then come crawling back like a worm to tell me I was right and, honestly, I'm not sure if I can stand such a sight.'

'Whatever I do, I'm guaranteed to regret it less if you don't have the testicular-borne valor to finish your thought.'

Denaos half-sighed, half-growled.

'Fine. Allow me to slide a shiv of reality into your kidneys.' He shrugged. 'If she dies, it'll be a tragedy, to be certain. She was a fine shot with that bow of hers and a finer sight for eyes used to far too much ugly, I'll tell you. But it's not like we're losing anyone ...' He paused, tilting his head, wincing as though struck. 'I mean ... in the end, she's not one of us. She's just a shict. No shortage of them.'

Lenk blinked once. When his eyelids rose, it was not through his own stare that he saw his hands reach out and seize the tall man by his collar. It was not his arms that trembled with barely restrained fury. It was not his voice that uttered a frigid threat to the rogue.

'The only regret here,' he whispered, 'is that my sword is stuck in a corpse that isn't yours.'

This is it.

The thought rang through Asper's head solemnly, like a dirge bell.

It had to happen eventually.

Her breath was short, sporadic.

You did your best ...

Kataria's face was almost part of the scenery, so unchanged was it. As much as Asper searched, as much as she prayed for a twitch of lips or flutter of eyelids, she found nothing. The shict seemed more in a deep dream than a breathless coma, more at peace than in pain.

That might be a sign, her thoughts flooded her head like a deluge, *that's Talanas's mercy to you. What do you know about this, anyway? You can tie up scratches and kiss scraped knees, but you can't heal a damn thing without bandages.*

She pressed her fingers against Kataria's throat; no pulse … still.

It's not so bad. You can't save them all. Remember the last one? She was in so much pain, but you managed to take that away. Her left hand twitched involuntarily. *You can do the same for your friend, can't you?*

'Shut up,' she snarled, '*shut up!*'

She forced her mind dark, silenced the voices in the rhythm of chest compressions and the futile monotony of breathing. There was solace in monotony, she knew, comfort in not seeing ahead. She forced her gaze away from the future, focused on the now, the lifeless shict and the quiet muttering.

'I can do this,' she whispered, 'I can do this,' she told herself as she had for so long, 'please, I can do this …'

She drew in her forty-third breath and leaned closer to the shict's lips. She hesitated, hearing a sound so faint as to be a shade more silent than a whisper: a choked, gurgling whisper.

'Please,' she whispered again.

The lifeless muscles in Kataria's body twitched. Asper forced herself to continue, biting back hope.

'*Please.*'

The gurgle came again, a little louder. Kataria's body jerked, a little livelier.

'Kat …' She was terrified to raise her voice. 'Please …'

A smile wormed its way onto Asper's face. The shict's pale lips parted, only slightly, and drew in the most meagre, pathetic of breaths.

'Yes,' her giggle was restrained hysteria, 'yes, yes, *yes*!'

Her eyes widened with a sudden dread as she saw something bubble in the shadows of her companion's mouth.

'Oh, no! No, no, *WAIT!*'

As though possessed, the shict's body shuddered violently, her mouth stretching so wide as to make her jaw creak threateningly. A torrent of translucent bile came flooding out of her, arcing like a geyser as her lungs were brutally evacuated.

Groaning, Kataria rolled onto her side and expelled the last traces of the muck with a hack. Body trembling, she had barely the strength to fall upon her back. The sun seemed bright and harsh above her, her breath foreign and stagnant on her lips.

Through fluttering eyes, she became aware of a shadow falling over her. She tensed, her voice forgotten, a scream bursting from her lips as only a faint, ooze-tinged squeal.

Two wicked blue moons stared down upon her. Her heart raced, head glutted with fragmented imagery: grey flesh, silver hair, two blue eyes burning like cold pyres, pupilless.

She opened her mouth to scream again, but caught herself. Or rather, a pair of strong hands caught her by her arms, pulling her closer. She writhed in the grip, unwilling to stare into the eyes that shifted before her. As dizziness and half-blindness faded, she beheld a gaze that was dominated by two big, hound-like pupils.

'Calm down,' Lenk whimpered, 'just calm down. You're fine.'

'Fine,' she repeated as she took in his face, his pink skin and blinking eyes. 'I'm fine.' She paused to cough, forcing a weak smile on her face. 'I mean, as far as nearly dying goes.'

'Fine.' He nodded. 'Just don't strain yourself. Take breaths as they come.' He raised her to a sitting position as he eased a waterskin into her hands. 'Drink. You're sure you're well?'

'A damn sight better than *some* of us,' someone snarled from behind.

Asper's scowl burned two holes in the mask of viscous sludge covering her face. Her lips quivered from behind the vomit, as though she sought to scream but thought better of it. Fuming so fiercely as to make the bile steam, she resigned herself to grumbling indignantly and mopping the substance with her sleeve.

'Oh, you messy little sow.' Denaos giggled as he joined his companions. 'Gone and eaten your pudding like a fat little baby, have you?'

Artfully dodging the glob of vomit she hurled at him, he approached Lenk and Kataria with all the candour of someone who had *not* just recently dismissed a looming death as an unfortunate inconvenience.

'And how are we today?' he asked with a broad smile. 'I was slightly worried we'd have to cut your body into six pieces so that you wouldn't come back.' He added a knowing nod. 'That's what happens when shicts die, you know. They'll come crawling right out of the grave to rip your eyes out and eat them.'

'One would hope she'd have the sense to rip out your tongue first.' Lenk hurled his voice like a spear at the rogue, though Denaos seemed to dodge that just as gracefully as he had the vomit. 'Maybe she'd like to hear what you—'

'Well, that's all fine, fine and dandy.' Denaos interrupted the young man with a timely spear of his own. 'Good to know we all emerged from another near-death experience with only one of us nearly dying. A fine score, if I may say so.'

Lenk opened his mouth to retort, but a hacking cough from Kataria shredded that before it reached his lips. Settling for an icy stare at Denaos's nonchalant expression, he raised the waterskin to her lips, pulling his hand back as she swatted at it.

'I'm not an invalid, round-ear,' she growled, shaking his arm off from around her. After a few frenzied gulps, she wiped her mouth. 'What happened, anyway?'

'We were hoping you might tell us,' Asper piped up. 'Denaos and I came at the sound of screaming.'

'Late,' Lenk muttered.

'*Cautiously* late,' Denaos shot back.

'*At any rate*,' Asper continued, 'we found you unconscious and the whole beach scorched halfway to heaven.'

'Hell,' Denaos corrected.

'What about Lenk?' Kataria asked.

'What *about* Lenk?'

'He was here. He saw what happened.'

'I don't recall.' The young man offered a helpless shrug. 'We were hit pretty hard.'

Kataria's breath caught; she levelled a hard gaze at him. 'We ...'

'Yeah,' he nodded, 'you and me.'

'The demon bashed him good,' Asper added. 'He was just coming out of it when we arrived.'

He wasn't out, Kataria thought.

The visions bloomed in her mind: the onyx sheen of the Abysmyth's black blood, the surgical silver of Lenk's sword. They flooded through her with grotesque vividness, matched only by the horrifying sounds that replayed in her mind.

'*MOMMY! MOMMY! IT HURTS!*' She recalled the demon's wailing voice. '*MAKE IT STOP! MAKE IT STOP!*'

Lenk had said nothing.

Someone else had.

'*Stay*,' it had uttered through his mouth, '*we kill.*'

Whoever had spoken had leaned over her, stood with flesh grey as stone and eyes blue as winter.

Someone not Lenk …

'Whichever of you did whatever,' Denaos added with a grimace, '*someone* seems to have hit the demon back … rather hard.'

'The demon.' Kataria's head snapped up. 'What happened to it?'

The Omen hopped across the sand, sweeping bulbous eyes over the chaos. Despite the smoke seeping into the two gourd-like organs, the thing did not so much as blink. It recalled, vaguely, in what served as its mind, that there had been more of it just a moment ago.

Then there was noise, noise that hurt its ears. It didn't care for that noise, so it stayed away. Now, there were none of it left. It turned about, faced the sea and tilted its head. There was one of it there moments ago, it believed. It chattered its teeth, calling to the other.

All that answered it was the sound of wind and a great, black shadow quickly falling over it.

'Disgusting,' Gariath muttered, wiping thick, black fluid off the sole of his foot.

It wasn't so much the texture of the thing's blood, reminiscent of a large beetle's, that irritated him as it was the smell. He cast a dark scowl over the beach: sand still pumping acrid smoke into the air, fighting the stinging salty reek

384

for dominance, as the stinking panoply of electricity, blood and fear congealed into a fine, vile perfume.

With a growl, he gave the Omen's corpse a kick, sending it spiralling through the air like a feathery, blood-dripping ball to plop at the top of a heap of similar misshapen amalgamations. Gathering them in one spot did nothing for the odour.

With a sigh, Gariath thrust his snout into the air once more, testing it. Nothing but the stink of carnage and fire reached his nostrils. He found his fists tightening of their own volition, his skin threatening to burst under his claws. Every whiff of the air only brought him more of the same stinks, denying him any other scents.

So close, he snarled internally, *I was so close. I was right on top of it ... then THIS!*

The beach's odour had struck him like a wave, drowning all other aromas. It was only because of its sheer overwhelming stench that he had come to it and found two worthless humans agonising over two other worthless humans.

At that moment, he had excused himself to hunt down the remaining Omens that had been hopping aimlessly around the sands. He needed something to vent his rage upon and crushing the tiny parasites seemed only slightly more appropriate than crushing his companions; besides, one of them was already dead.

The Omens, of course, had provided no sport whatsoever. They merely stood there, idle, waiting to die. They didn't even make a sound when he stepped on them, save for one final chatter of teeth.

'Barely worth killing,' he muttered.

'Well, thanks for doing it, anyway,' someone spoke up.

He found his mood further soured with the appearance

of his companions trudging up the beach, the pointy-eared one barely standing. He snorted contemptuously at her.

'Don't look so weary,' he growled, 'it's not as though being killed is some vast ordeal.' He spat on the ground. 'If it was so hard, not everyone would do it.'

'Well, thanks for that,' she replied, blinking at the large pile of lifeless Omens. 'So ... been busy?'

'Hardly,' he grunted. 'Whatever was here before you did all the work.'

'Before?' Asper cocked a brow. 'I didn't see anyone else.'

'Well, you didn't think those two imbeciles could have done all this, did you?' He swept a hand out over the beach, levelling a finger at the frogmen, still frozen even as the sun scattered the last of the smoke. 'There were others here. You *could* smell them, if you were me.' He snorted. 'But you're not.'

'A shame I live with every waking moment,' Denaos muttered. 'Who else was here, then?'

'Longfaces,' Lenk replied curtly. 'The Abysmyth said as much before it died.'

'It did,' Kataria agreed. 'I found tracks to support it, too.'

'You can tell how long someone's face is by their tracks?'

'I can *tell* how many people were fighting, idiot,' she snarled back. 'Not that I needed tracks to tell me there was a fight around here.'

'Regardless,' Lenk continued, 'whoever these people were and however long their faces are, they didn't leave anything behind to let us know what they're up to.'

'What they're up to?' Asper sounded incredulous as she gestured to a nearby tree, split apart by whatever magic had rent it. 'How could anyone that does *this* be up to anything we want to be a part of?'

'Leave it to a zealot to leap to conclusions,' Denaos countered snidely. 'What our dear floor-kisser is missing is the fact that these longfaces not only did this, but they also did *that*.'

He didn't even have to gesture to draw everyone's attention to the hanging Abysmyth.

A particularly fierce gust of wind kicked up, causing the creature's lanky legs to rattle against each other, flecks of charred skin peeling off. The icicle spike that kept it impaled in the air showed no signs of thawing in the sun, shining ominously as its scorched captive continued to stare up at the sky through empty eye sockets.

'How is this even a matter for debate?' Denaos held his hands out helplessly. 'We want Abysmyths dead. Longfaces kill Abysmyths. We should, obviously, find them and kiss whichever part of their anatomy will make *them* die instead of *us*.'

'Afraid of a little death, are we?' Gariath mused grimly.

'Yes, I am afraid of death,' the rogue responded curtly, 'that's a brilliant observation.' He turned to Lenk. 'Listen, you, of all people, must see the wisdom in this. These aren't pirates we're fighting. Whatever help we can get, we need.'

'I didn't think you would want to share the reward,' the young man replied.

'I'm wagering our yet-unseen friends don't do this for mere gold.'

'*Mere* gold now?' Asper feigned shock. 'Have you found a higher calling, Denaos?' She held up a hand to ward off his retort, turning to Lenk instead. 'It's not necessarily a *bad* idea to seek out aid, but whoever did this to the beach clearly didn't have any notion of restraint. Given the circumstances, it'd seem a mite smarter to make sure they won't incinerate us before we throw ourselves upon their mercy.'

'The point is moot for the moment,' Lenk shot at both of them at once. 'The longfaces aren't here. We are.' He cast a glance towards Gariath. 'You've been poking around up here for a while. Found out anything?'

'About what?' the dragonman asked.

'Well, for starters,' the young man pointed behind them, 'how about that?'

The corpse of the second Abysmyth, face-down in a pool of its own black humours, was not exactly difficult to miss. If it were even possible, the thing seemed far fouler in death than it had in life, with its emaciated limbs twisted about its hacked and hewn body, arrow shafts jutting from its black skin, one stump of an arm reaching for the shore as though it still sought to crawl to the safety of the sea.

It was not what was leaking out of the demon that caused Kataria's breath to go short, but rather what was jammed into it.

Jutting from the creature's back, the cross of its hilt shining triumphantly in the sunlight, Lenk's sword glittered with a menace it had never showed her. Whereas before it was merely one weapon amongst many, now the blade seemed alive, smiling morbidly in its steel, remembering well what it had done to the beast.

When the others started stalking towards it, she found herself hard pressed to follow.

'So,' Lenk began, placing his hands on his hips and staring at the corpse, 'what have you found out?'

The dragonman merely rolled his shoulders. 'It's dead.'

'Well, hell.' Denaos sighed dramatically. 'Are the rest of us even needed here? It sounds like the lizard's become so good at this necropsy business as to render Asper obsolete.' He sneered. 'Though, frankly, it's tricky to decide which one's nicer to look at.'

'Keep squeaking, rat,' Gariath snarled in reply, 'and we'll have *two* corpses to admire.'

From seemingly nowhere, he produced something long and black and waved it menacingly at the rogue. It was only after a moment and a sudden wave of nausea that the other companions recognised the Abysmyth's severed arm.

'And one of them will have *this*,' he paused to pluck a stray Omen corpse up from the ground, 'and *this* crammed into it.' He smiled unpleasantly. 'Your choice as to what gets stuffed into which end.'

'It's far too late in the day for this.' Lenk sighed. 'You can kill each other once I don't have need of either of you.'

'Kill,' the dragonman snorted contemptuously, '*each other*?'

'Fine.' The young man rolled his eyes. 'You can kill Denaos once I don't need him any more.'

'I rather take offence at that,' the rogue snapped.

'That was likely why I said it.' Lenk waved the tall man's concerns away and returned to the corpse. 'Now, we know it's dead. We just need to know what killed it.'

'Oh, come on,' Kataria said hotly, 'isn't it obvious?'

Myriad glances cast her way as though she were a madwoman indicated that it was not. With a snarl, she swept up to the corpse and all but seized Lenk's sword and throttled it, so fervently did she gesture.

'The damn thing has a *sword in its back*! That's quite typically fatal, you know.'

'True,' Denaos replied, 'but if you can point out anything

typical about a giant fish-man-demon-thing, I'd love to hear it.'

'They can't be harmed by mortal weapons.' Asper nodded. 'We've seen it. Whatever killed the Abysmyth, it wasn't Lenk.'

'But I saw—' Kataria's protest was slain in her mouth at the sight of Lenk's stare, hard and flashing, levelled at her like a weapon itself. Instead, she looked away and muttered, 'I saw it die.'

'You didn't see Lenk kill it, though.' Denaos pushed his way past her and knelt beside the body. As he extended a hand, stopping just short of its leathery hide, he glanced over his shoulder concernedly. 'We're sure this thing is dead, right?'

'Sure.' Gariath scratched at his chin with the demon's dismembered claws. 'If it isn't, though, the worst that can happen is we lose you.'

'Acceptable losses,' Asper agreed.

'Oh, you two are just a pair of merry little jesters,' he hissed. Without sparing another moment for them, he began to trace his fingers down the creature's hide, no small amount of disgust visible on his face. 'As I was saying, Lenk didn't kill it. Poison did.'

'That can't be right,' Lenk muttered, coming up beside the rogue. 'I didn't see any poison on it.'

'What the hell did you think this stuff was?'

The rogue ran a finger down the edge of one of the creature's wounds, pinching off a few flakes of green ichor, now dried and dusty. He rubbed it between his fingers, brought it to his nose and blanched.

'Granted, it's long past its bottle life, but this is potent stuff.' He brushed his hands off. 'Someone was carving our dear friend up with an envenomed weapon long before you ever hacked at it.' He flicked one of the more prominent tears in the creature's flesh. 'Have a glimpse. These wounds are fresh, even though the venom is old. You remember what happened when Mossud harpooned the thing, right?'

'It healed instantly.' Lenk nodded as he rubbed his shoulder in memory of the thrashing the creature had given him. 'The damn thing didn't even flinch.'

'From *your* attacks, maybe,' Gariath snorted.

'So why haven't these lacerations healed?' Denaos winked knowingly. 'The wounds were trying to close, but the poison kept them from doing so. Rather potent stuff, actually. I haven't seen anything this vigorous before.'

'These wounds, though, are tremendous.' In emphasis, Lenk reached out and flicked an arrow shaft that Kataria had sent into the thing's heart through a tear the size of two fists side by side. 'I've seen some big swords in my time, but nothing so big as to make such a mess.'

'The wounds didn't start that way.' Asper elbowed herself into the huddle, pointing to some of the larger rips. 'See, the edges of the skin are frayed. The poison ate at the flesh, probably continued to do so up until the thing was dead.' She raised her eyebrows in appreciation. 'Not unlike a parasite.'

'I remember.' Lenk nodded. 'The green stuff was pulsating.' He looked over his shoulder to Kataria. 'You saw, didn't you?'

'Yeah.' She nodded weakly. 'Like it was breathing.'

'So,' Denaos bit his lower lip, 'these longfaces are in possession of a ... *living poison*?'

'And you wanted to kiss their rumps,' Asper shot at him smugly. 'Dip your lips in iron, you smelly little sycophant.'

'Well, if you're such a genius,' he snapped, 'maybe you can tell us what did,' he paused to gesture over the scorched beach, '*this*?'

'Isn't it clear?' She paused, held up a hand in apology. 'Pardon me. Isn't it clear to everyone who isn't a colossal moron?' She nearly decapitated him with the sharpness of her smirk. 'Think. What else do you know that can turn sand black and make ice that doesn't melt in the sun?'

'Magic,' the rogue replied, 'but—'

'Precisely,' she interrupted, 'and who do we know who knows something about magic?'

'Dreadaeleon,' he answered, 'however—'

'See? Even *you* can solve these tricky little issues with the miracle of thinking.' She rose, dusting her hands off with an air of self-satisfaction so thick as to choke even the smoke. She set hands on hips and glanced about the beach. 'Now, if Dread would just come up and tell us a little bit about … uh …'

It occurred to her, at that moment, that they had mentioned the subject of magic and had been able to go three breaths without a familiarly shrill voice chiming in with some incessant trivia. She was not alone in her realisation, as Lenk nearly collapsed under the weight of his sigh.

'Right, then,' he muttered, 'who lost the wizard?'

'He was with the lizard last I saw,' Denaos replied. 'Maybe he stopped to sniff a tree or something.'

'Where is he, then?' Asper immediately turned a scowl upon the dragonman. 'What'd you do with him?'

'What makes you think I did something to him?' Gariath replied, raising an eyeridge. 'Isn't it possible that he got lost on his own?'

'Well …' Her face screwed up momentarily. 'I suppose that's possible. I'm sorry.' She sighed and offered him an apologetic smile. 'So, where was he when you last saw him?'

'Writhing on the ground and not breathing.'

'Oh.' She blinked. 'Wait, what?'

'I resent you *assuming* that I beat the stupid out of him until he was lying in a pool of it.' He folded his arms over his chest. 'But, as it stands, I did.'

Asper's jaw dropped. Whether it was from the shock of the dragonman's actions or the sheer casualness with which he reported them, all she could do was turn to Lenk with a look that demanded he do something.

The young man, however, merely blinked; he suspected he ought to do something about it, if he had been at all surprised that such a thing had happened. Instead, he sighed, rubbed the bridge of his nose and cast a glance around his companions.

'Well, you know the routine,' he said. 'Fan out, find him or his body and so forth and so on.'

'Searching for someone we're supposed to care about who was possibly *murdered* by someone else we're supposed to care about is *not* supposed to be *routine*,' Asper shrieked, stomping her foot.

'And yet ...' Lenk let that thought dangle as he reached out to retrieve his sword. 'Anyway, split up.' He cast a fleeting glance over his shoulder. 'Kat, you're with me.'

'What?' She did not mean for her voice to sound as shocked as it did. 'Why?'

'What do you mean, "why"?' Lenk shot her a confused look. 'That's how we always do it.'

'Selfish,' Denaos muttered under his breath.

'Well, yeah, but ...' Her eyes darted about the beach like a cornered beast's. 'It's just that—'

'If you don't want to go with me, fine,' Lenk snapped

back, possibly more harshly than he intended. 'Go with Gariath or whoever else you feel you'd prefer to claw, stab or insult you in the back.' He seized the handle of his sword and gave a sharp jerk. 'All I'm doing is trying to keep people from getting killed.'

No sooner had the steel left the Abysmyth's corpse than the sky split apart with the force of a scream.

Lenk staggered backwards, falling to his rear and scrambling like a drunken crab as the beast, as though possessed, spasmed back into waking life.

Eyes as vacant as they had been in life were turned to the sky as the fish-like head threw itself backwards, jaws agape and streaming rivers of black bile from the corners of its mouth. Heralded by a spray of glistening ebon, it loosed a howl unlike any sound it had made while alive. The noise stretched for an eternity, forcing the companions to choose between gripping weapons and shielding their ears as the shriek echoed off every charred leaf and ashen grain.

Bile streaming from its mouth turned to black blood streaming from every gaping wound in the creature's flesh. Liquid poured with such intensity as to make the creature's entire body seem like a great half-melted candle. As the thing continued to scream, it became clear that it was not just bile that wept from its body.

There was a grunt of surprise from Gariath and all eyes turned to see the severed arm begin to jerk and spasm with a life of its own. The dragonman growled once, then hurled the appendage at the corpse, as though such an act would stop it.

Instead, both member and dismembered began to react as one. Black flesh turned to wax, wax turned to ooze, ooze turned to blood. The creature's flesh began to peel from it, exposing greying bones and settling in a puddle around the thing's knees. The scream intensified with every inch of skin sloughing off and the flesh only crept more quickly with every moment the Abysmyth shrieked.

Only when the last traces of the creature's face dripped off, leaving a fish-like skull gaping at the sun, did the creature finally fall silent.

Leaving no time to curse or pray to various Gods, the pool of black sludge that had been the Abysmyth began to move. It twitched once, rippled like tainted water, then began to creep across the shore like an ink stain, moving slowly towards the sea. A gust of wind kissed the beach; the grey skeleton fell forwards and clattered into a pile of bones.

The tension lasted for as long as it took for the screaming echoes to silence themselves. It was only when everything was silent, save for the waves taking the molten flesh back into the water, that Lenk spoke.

'Spread out,' he whispered, 'find Dread. Kat, you're with me.'

Eighteen

TO KILL AGAIN

Gariath searched the air with his nose, greeted by the same scents he had encountered before: salt and trees. The stink of paper and ink that followed the human boy wherever he went were lost on the wind and in the dirt, and while he did detect traces of dried animal excrement, they weren't the odours of the particular excrement the wizard was fond of drinking.

For a time uncountable, Gariath had to pause and wonder why he was even searching.

It was but one more wonder to add to a running, endless list he had been keeping ever since deciding to follow the humans. Chief amongst them, now, was why they insisted on fanning out to search for the little runt. Surely they must have known that he, a *Rhega*, would find the boy first.

Why even bother attempting to find him without Gariath? Even searching solitarily as he was, there was no chance they would so much as catch a whiff of the boy's farts before he did. They were too slow, too stupid, their noses too small and underdeveloped.

'Stupid little ...' His curses degenerated into wordless mumbles.

Of all the creatures that walked on two legs, he offered grudging, unspoken admiration only to Lenk. Despite the shame of having no family and the humiliation of being shorter than most humans, the young man was bold, disciplined and the only one worthy of something just a shade lower than genuine praise amongst the otherwise useless race.

It was unfortunate that Lenk had chosen to go with the long-eared human. Strong and swift, with a healthy contempt for her round-eared fellows, she might have deserved something a shade lower than what he attributed Lenk, had she not the brain of a squirrel.

The two tall humans were naturally inept at all things: fighting fairly, fighting intelligently and, of course, finding anything. The brown-haired woman was too proud in her false Gods to smell the earth. The rat would run away, leaving a yellow trail, at the first whiff of danger.

And, of course, the human boy had found danger. He was born with a dark cloud over his head, a curse of spirit and body, born of a shamed family and supported by a far more shameful life. The scrawny human was estranged from his father and mother, a wicked omen of itself, and far too feeble to overcome such hardship through the proper channel of bloodshed.

After all, how could one kill to honour one's family if one's family was not worth killing over? Most humans suffered from such a fate.

Fortunately for them, their wretched Gods loved them just enough to allow them the privilege of walking in a *Rhega*'s tracks. The chosen of the spirits, born of red rock shaped by furious rivers, the *Rhega* were the only creation of the world ever to have turned out right. This, he reminded himself, was why he allowed them to walk behind him. They needed him, as sheep needed rams. How else would they survive?

They'd find a way, he thought with a sigh. Luck and

397

stupidity, both desirable traits to them, were things they had in ample supply.

He sighed again, stuck his nose into the air and inhaled deeply. No stink of human.

And yet, this time, he did not lower his snout.

Instead, he sniffed at the air once again, felt his heart begin to pound, ear-frills fan out attentively. The aroma filled his nostrils with memory and he summoned visions and sounds through the scent: clawed footprints in the earth, wings beating on the air, rain on heavy leather, uncooked meat on grass.

Rivers and rocks.

The boy was forgotten, humans disappeared from his concerns as he fell to all fours and rushed along the ground, following the scent as it wound over roots, under branches, around rocks and through bushes. He followed it as it twisted and turned one hundred times in as many breaths, each time growing fainter.

No, no, no, he whimpered inside his head.

The footprints in the earth became his own as he re-traced them.

Not now!

The sound of wings beating on the air became the whisper of waves.

I've almost found you …

The scent of rain was suddenly tinged with salt.

Please, don't go yet!

Rivers and rocks became sand and surf.

He was on the beach suddenly, the forest behind him and the scent gone, a snake stretched too thin around the tree trunks. He rose, turned and thrust his nose into the air. Nothing filled his nostrils. He inhaled until the inside of his snout was raw and quivering and the stink of salt water made him want to vomit.

And salt water was all he received.

The sensation of weakness was foreign to Gariath. He had not felt weak in such a long time, not when blades kissed his flesh and cudgels bounced off his bones; yet he could remember the feeling well. He had felt it once before, so keenly, when he held two bodies not his enemies' in his arms, stared into their eyes as rain draped their faces in shrouds of fresh water.

He had collapsed then, too, as he did now.

He had wept, then, too.

Drops of salt clouded his senses, but not so much that he could not perceive the new stink entering his nostrils. He did not stop to consider what it might be, whether it was something he ought or ought not to kill. His sadness twisted to fury as he drank deeply the aroma and began to anticipate when it would soon turn to the coppery odour of blood.

Fuelled by anger, he tore down the beach on all fours. When he sighted his prey, he stopped only to consider how she might die.

She, for it reeked of womanhood, was pale, beyond even the ghostly sheen of the pointy-eared human. She was so pale as to appear insubstantial, as sunlight shimmering on the sea. Hair the colour of a healthy tree's crown cascaded down her back, its endless verdancy broken only by the large, blue fin cresting her head.

The Abysmyths have such a fin, he thought resentfully.

She was a mess of angles, frail and delicate and wrapped in a wispy sheet of silk that did barely anything to hide the glistening blues and whites of her skin. Through a nose little more than a bony outcropping she exhaled a fine mist. At her neck, what appeared to be feathery gills fluttered.

As vile as she was to behold, the sight of the young boy with stringy black locks in her hands was far more disgusting.

The wizard lay with his head in her lap, a look of contentment creasing his face, as though he were a recently suckled infant. And, as though soothing an infant, the female creature ran webbed fingers through his hair. Through lips a pale blue, she hummed a tune unearthly, one that carried over waves as it carried through the boy, sending both into comatose calmness.

What might temper the sea, however, could not cool the blood of a *Rhega*. She sought to sing him deaf; his ear-frills twitched. She sought to sing his eyes shut; they widened. She sought to carry his bloodlust from his shoulders; he vowed to set it upon hers with two clawed fists.

The fate of the boy was irrelevant; whether she cradled his ensorcelled breathing body or his ensorcelled corpse, she would find herself in a far deeper sleep than she had put him into.

Gariath's wings unfurled like red sails. His hands clenched into fists so tight as to bloody his palms. His terrifying roar seized her weak song and tore it apart in the air. Upon all fours once more, he charged, levelling his horned head at her frail, angular mouth.

It would feel good to kill again.

Lenk staggered as he stumbled over a tree root, kicking up damp soil and leaves. With a sigh, he glanced down at the earth; whatever modest trail had been present was now nothing more than a smattering of dirt and tubers. *If there ever was a trail there at all*, he thought to himself, discouraged. How Kataria routinely made it look so easy, he would never know.

Which begged another question …

'Why aren't you in front?' he asked over his shoulder.

The shict started at his voice, as she had started at every sneeze, cough and curse to pass his lips for the past half-hour. She quickly composed herself, taking a gratuitous step backwards, placing her even further away from him.

'It's good practice,' she replied quickly. 'You need to learn this sort of stuff to survive.'

'Not so long as I've got you around.'

'Well, maybe I won't always be around,' she snapped back. 'Ever think of that, dimwit?'

'Is there something you want to tell me?' The question came with a sigh, knowing full well that whatever she wished to tell him, he wished not to hear. 'You've been skittish ever since we left the corpse.'

'Imagine that,' she sneered, 'near-death experiences leave me a bit jumpy.'

'Sure, jumpy.' He glanced down to the bow drawn in her hands. 'Are near-death experiences something you'd like to share? Because you've had that damn thing drawn and pointed at me for the past half-hour.'

'Don't you blame *me* for being cautious.'

'Cautious is one thing,' he replied. 'You're just being psychotic now. And while I've never begrudged you that before, I have to ask,' he tilted his head at her, frowning concernedly, 'what's wrong?'

Her reaction did nothing to reassure him.

She shifted nervously for a moment, hopping from foot to foot as she glanced about the forest clearing as though noting all possible escape routes. She did not lower her bow, nor relax her grip on its string. She had all the anxiety of a nervous beast while at the same time regarding him as though he were some manner of bloodthirsty predator.

He knew he ought not begrudge her such a mannerism; she had only barely survived the Abysmyth's touch. Surely, he reasoned, fear and panic were reasonable reactions. But towards him? Towards the man who had saved her? Towards the man who thought of her as not just a shict?

He found his hands tensing of their own volition and quickly fought to relax them. Something within him, however, fought just as hard to keep them in fists. Something within him spoke.

'Ignore her,' it uttered. '*If she wishes to scorn us, then let her rot here while we do our work. There will be more Abysmyths. We know this.*'

He clenched his teeth, straining to ignore the voice. His thoughts were glass, however, and the voice was a vocal rock. He felt them shatter and when the voice spoke again, it was a thousand echoing shards.

'*LEAVE.*'

'*KAT!*' he shrieked.

She looked at him, ears twitching as though she could hear what brewed within him. With a grunt, he forced a new face, a frown of concern and narrowed eyes. *Don't upset her*, he told himself, *don't let her hear it* …

'Listen,' his voice sounded strained to his ears, 'you can tell me. I'm not the enemy here.'

She cocked her head uncertainly at that. Once more, something shattered within him. His heart contracted under her wary stare and he felt his face twist to match the pain in his chest.

'Kataria,' he whispered, 'don't you trust me?'

'Usually,' she replied.

Her face nearly melted with the force of her sigh as her shoulders slumped, lowering her weapon. Such an expression brought him no relief; she seemed less remorseful and more weary, as though the thought of talking to him was a surrender.

'Do you remember the Abysmyth?' she asked.

'Uh,' he blinked, 'it's rather a hard thing to forget.'

He felt his heart go numb at the sight of her stare, dire and sharp as an arrowhead.

'Fine,' he continued, 'no, I don't remember it. I can barely remember anything past meeting the damn thing on the beach.'

'You ... *met* it?'

'And had a conversation with it.' He nodded. 'It's rather a polite demon, if you catch it between dismemberings.'

'You said you barely remembered anything.' She seemed unimpressed with his humour. 'What *do* you remember?'

Voices. Or rather a voice, in my head. Icy and angry. Told me to pick up my sword and kill the demon. Told me a hundred times. Told me to kill, to slaughter, to rip it apart. And I did. And I know I shouldn't have been able to, but I was. I killed the damn thing and I don't know why. And when I did, it laughed. The voice laughed and I wanted to laugh, too. I wanted to laugh like a madman and dance in the thing's blood.

That's what I remember.

He told her none of this. Instead, he looked up, and replied in one word.

'You.'

It was not exactly the entire truth, but though it was no lie, Kataria's frown seemed to suggest that she did not quite believe it. He fought back a sigh and instead took a step forwards, feeling at least some relief when she did not tense up, retreat or bolt outright. Instead, she regarded him carefully with a hint of that same probing curiosity he hadn't come to miss before she looked at him like he was a lunatic.

'I saw you,' he continued, unhindered, 'I saw you shoot the Abysmyth. I saw the Abysmyth pick you up and I saw you go still and cold as a fish. Then, I saw you drop.'

'And you know why I dropped?' she asked.

He blinked, shook his head.

'Because of *you*,' she replied, 'because *you* cut the demon's arm off, because *you* killed it.'

'I didn't kill it.'

'I'm fairly sure you did.'

'We settled this already,' he replied, 'the poison killed it. The longfaces killed it.'

'It didn't stop moving until you put your sword in it.'

'The poison took its time, then.'

'Why are you denying this?' She seemed as if she wanted to snarl, to spit the words. Instead, she could only shake her head at him. 'I saw you, too. I saw *you* kill the demon. I saw *you* save *me*.' Her frown twisted and Lenk could see that her heart sank as well. 'Why are you denying *that*?'

Because, he thought, fingering the hilt of his sword, *the Abysmyth can't be hurt by mortal weapons.*

He longed to say such a thing to her, if only so that she might know why he couldn't say it. Instead, he could do little more than roll his shoulders, shake his head and sigh. She returned the expression and, without any fear, walked past him to take the lead.

Her shoulder brushed against his; she felt cold.

'So,' he spoke up, desperate to ease the tension, 'do you see anything that I might have missed?'

'Nah.' She crouched to the earth, glancing over the jungle soil. 'Something came through here, but I can't tell who or what. Nothing's clear.'

The leaves shook in the trees. Birds fled in a sudden burst as a thunderous roar split the forest apart. Kataria rose to her feet, following Lenk's gaze out and away, towards the distant shore.

'That is, though.'

Gariath could tolerate wounds of all kinds: piercings, cuts, gashes, bruises and assorted scrapes were things he could remember, things he could touch, things he could respond to. For those few injuries that drew no blood and beat no flesh, he had no patience.

'Stand still!'

He lashed a claw at the female and, again, she stepped away from him. This routine was becoming quite tiresome. The creature's relentless darting hardly irritated him as much as the serene expression she wore, unflinching, beyond offering him a congenial smile.

'There's no smiling,' he snarled, 'in *battle*!'

His roar drove his fist as he rammed it forwards, preparing to pulp her placid expression. Her sole defence was an upraised hand, a demure smile and a gentle hum.

Music filled his head, smothering him like a tide. His howling seemed so quiet, so meek, his muscles like jelly. When he opened his mouth to curse, he felt his jaw drop and hang numbly. Summoning what remained of his fury, he lunged forwards, arms flopping out before him like flippers.

And then they were lead weights, pulling him to the ground with a crash.

He roared, or tried to roar, both at himself and at her. He tried to rise, to crush her jaw, rip out her tongue, smash her face in so that she might only sputter out a tune with notes of broken teeth. His body, however, would not answer him. His eyelids became heavy like his arms.

A sweet, soothing darkness enveloped him.

The female tilted her head at him, gills flickering curiously, her gaze lingering only for a moment before she glanced up at the sound of shrieking.

The arrow bit angrily through the air where her head had just been, spitefully taking a few strands of green hair as it sped past her and sank into the sands beyond. The female blinked through eyelids that closed like twin doors and regarded the two pale shapes at the distant end of the beach.

'What the hell was that?' Lenk cried, punching Kataria in the arm. 'Shictish archery, my left tes—'

'She moved,' the shict spat back, 'she *moved*, damn it!' Shoving him away, she drew another missile and narrowed her eyes at the wispy creature. 'I'll get her this time.'

Like a silk-swaddled bellows, the female's chest inflated, mouth opening so wide as to threaten to dislocate her jaw. The arrow was lowered in momentary curiosity. Shict and man stared dumbly as the female took one step forwards, turned her mouth upon them and screamed.

The noise was shrill, getting shriller; annoying, Lenk thought through his fingers, but little more than that.

Kataria seemed to disagree.

Collapsing next to her bow, the shict writhed upon the ground, shrieking as she clawed at notched ears that withered like roses. Her legs kicked as she proceeded to bash her head against the sand, straining to pound the noise out of her head.

That left two companions down, Lenk thought, more than enough reason to stick a sword into something.

His weapon was up as he charged towards the female. Her alien features did not cause him to falter; he had killed things much more ferocious than her. He aimed at a spot between her breasts, undoubtedly where her heart was. If it wasn't there, he reasoned, he'd just keep stabbing until he found something.

It was going to be messy. He found himself smiling at that.

It was only when he drew close enough to see her eyes that he hesitated. She cocked an eyebrow, or rather an eyeridge, at him, smiling. He returned the gesture with a confused expression.

Who, he wondered, *smiles at someone charging at them with a sword? It's like the stupid thing doesn't even know I'm about to kill it.*

Even as he continued to advance, his sword held high, still she did not seem to recognise his intent. She cocked her head, regarding him curiously. Good; better that she focus on him than look behind her. Better she lock eyes with him than be tempted to follow his gaze over her shoulder.

If she did, she might have seen Denaos looming up behind her, a long knife clenched in one hand.

The rogue's scowl was as cold as his hand was quick. He slipped a gloved hand around and clasped it over her mouth, bringing his dagger up beneath her chin as she tried momentarily to struggle against his long fingers.

'Shh,' he whispered as he might to an infant, 'no sounds, no singing.' The tip of his blade scraped the bottom of her chin. 'Don't you scream.'

'*STOP!*'

Had the command come from anyone else, Denaos would have cut out her jugular and autographed it before anyone could object. However, the shrill, excited voice forced his blade to a trembling halt a hair's width from turning the female into a cut of choice meat.

He glowered over the woman's head at the boy standing

on trembling legs before him. His face was grave, breath ragged; hardly the sort of visage that should expect to have its commands obeyed, Denaos thought resentfully.

'She needs our help,' Dreadaeleon gasped, even speaking an ordeal.

The rogue glanced from Gariath, unconscious, to Kataria, squirming like a worm on the ground, back to Dreadaeleon.

'What, seriously?'

'Let her speak,' the wizard said, nodding furiously, 'and she'll explain.'

'Don't do it, Denaos,' Lenk ordered, 'she just struck Gariath dead.'

'The lizard's still breathing,' Denaos noted. 'I'd be hard pressed *not* to release her had she actually killed him.' He tugged her closer, bringing his knife a little further up. 'As it stands—'

'*STOP!*' Dreadaeleon shrieked again. 'She hasn't hurt them. Kataria and Gariath will both be fine!'

'Here's a funny fact,' the rogue spat. 'Even if you say something a heap of times, it doesn't actually make it come true.' He levelled a murderous scowl upon his captive. 'We should kill her before she has a chance to do to us what she did to *them*.'

'She won't!' the wizard protested.

'Well, of course she won't if I stick her now.'

'I mean she won't at all,' the boy added hotly, 'not if you let her go. Otherwise, she might—'

'*Not* if I jam a six-finger piece of steel in her face,' the rogue interrupted. 'Sweet Silf, man, try to keep up.'

Dreadaeleon made a motion to protest further, but instead turned two big, brown, puppy-like eyes to Lenk, pleading.

'Lenk, she means us no harm. You've got to believe me.'

'Oh, that's fair,' Denaos sneered, 'go to Lenk for aid.' He turned to the young man. 'The boy might have been bewitched by her. Who says his words are his own?'

'*I* say that you *might* be an imbecile but it's far more likely that you're a bloodthirsty moron! She was only defending herself!'

'She attacked us first!'

'Gariath attacked *her* first!' The boy gritted his teeth. 'Gariath *always* attacks first!' He looked to Lenk once more, eyes going so wide they might roll out of his head. 'Lenk, *please* ...'

The young man remained unmoving, silent for a long moment. He glanced from the unconscious dragonman to the curled-up shict, to the creature with green hair who looked remarkably calm for a woman-fish-thing that had a knife to her throat. He only spoke when the stand-off was joined by a red-faced Asper rushing up to meet them.

'Asper,' he gestured with his chin, 'have a look at Kat and Gariath. See if they're well.'

'What?' she asked, breathless. 'Who's well? What's happening?' She glanced over at the strange captive. 'Who's she?'

'We're a little busy here, Asper.'

The priestess seemed to want to argue, but had no breath for it. With a muttered curse and a wave of her hand, she stalked towards her prone companions.

'Release her, Denaos,' Lenk commanded. 'Keep your knife ready, though. Gut her if she moves funny.'

'She's going to move funny eventually,' the rogue grunted. 'It'd be easier to gut her now.'

'Just do as I say.'

With a grudging snarl, Denaos took a cautious step away, releasing the woman. Both he and Lenk kept their weapons at the ready as the young man approached the creature with a grim look in his eyes.

'If you've injured anyone here,' he uttered, 'I'll take your head before he has a chance to gut you.' He flashed a threatening gaze at Dreadaeleon. 'And if *you* try to stop me, Denaos will take *yours*.'

He let that threat hang in the air as all parties exchanged wary glances. All save the female, who merely smiled as she opened her mouth and spoke in a lyrical, reverberating tune.

'If all death threats have been finished, I should like to solicit your aid.'

Nineteen

LOUD AND NEEDY

While all men can lie through their mouths, and a select few have a talent for lying through their eyes, no man can disguise intent evident in his buttocks.

Lenk's grandfather had said that, or so the young man thought, and while it seemed almost insulting that he would ever find cause to recall such a morsel of wisdom, there was no denying that it was applicable.

Buttocks were firmly entrenched, steeped in tiny sand pits carved of hatred and suspicion. Only Lenk's glare, perpetually flitting between his companions, kept them seated.

It had taken no small effort to get them there in the first place. After discerning that Kataria and Gariath were well enough, it took the strength of all mortal creatures and the possibility of an impending execution to bring their buttocks to the earth in a circle.

Ensconced between them, like a wiry silver battle line, Lenk kept his sword naked in his lap, eyes darting between his companions and the pale creature across from him.

She was a sight that demanded attention. Her features were human enough, in principle: a face filled with discernible angles, five fingers and toes, though webbed, and a long river of hair, though bright green. Her feathery gills, vaguely blue skin and the crest that occasionally rose upon the crown of her head, however, left the young man's buttocks clenched with caution.

Yet whenever she spoke, they became uncomfortably loose.

'I am once again asking for forgiveness.' Her voice was audible liquid, slithering on ripples into his head and reverberating throughout. 'Had I known you meant no harm, I would not have used my voice.'

Lenk frowned at that; before now, he hadn't thought of a voice as a weapon. Before now, he wouldn't have believed it could be used as one.

'WHAT'D SHE SAY?'

He cringed at the sound of Kataria as she leaned over and yelled at him.

'SHE APOLOGISED,' he shouted back.

'YEAH, SHE BETTER!' the shict roared.

'Apologies, again,' the female said meekly, 'the deafness should subside before too long.'

'WHAT'D SHE SAY?'

'It's already been too long,' Lenk muttered, waving down his companion. 'For the moment, your apology is accepted.' At a snort from Gariath, he added, 'By everyone who matters, anyway.'

'I suspect we might feel a degree more comfortable if we knew your name,' Asper offered congenially.

'As well as knowing whatever the hell you *are*,' Denaos added, cocking his head at the female. 'I mean, how are you even *speaking* right now?'

'She has a mouth,' Dreadaeleon muttered, rolling his eyes.

'I mean speaking our language,' the rogue retorted. 'How does some kind of fish-woman-thing learn to speak the human tongue?'

'Don't be crude,' Asper chastised, turning to the woman sympathetically. 'You're more woman than fish, aren't you?'

'I ...' The female appeared to be straining to express befuddlement. 'I am neither fish nor human, though I have spoken extensively with both in my time.'

'So you only *talk* to fish.' Denaos sighed. 'This is going to be another of those conversations I'd rather not hear, I can tell.'

'Then feel free to leave,' Dreadaeleon snapped. 'We can accomplish much more without you here.'

'We could accomplish much more without all of you jabbering like apes.' Lenk fixed a glower upon the female. 'All right, then ... we know how you can speak our language, now tell us what you are.'

'She's a siren, obviously,' the boy interrupted.

'A what?'

'Impossible,' Denaos said with a sneer. 'Sirens are a myth.'

'Yesterday, so were demons,' Dreadaeleon pointed out.

'Demons are a force of pure destruction that want nothing more than to rip us open and eat our innards. It's easy enough to believe such things could exist.' The rogue shook his head. 'Sirens are a legend to explain away navigational errors. Fish-women that lure men to their doom with deadly songs and promises of raucous, violent coitus? Unlikely.'

'Listening to you,' Asper sneered, 'you'd think everything unexplained desired raucous, violent coitus.'

'I have yet to be proven wrong.' The rogue's eyebrow raised appreciatively at the siren. 'Or have I?'

'The young lorekeeper refers to the name that humans are comfortable with calling my kind,' the mysterious female replied fluidly. 'I have never thought of myself as anything requiring a name, however. I am a child of the deep, born of the Sea Mother and charged to warden her waters and protect her children.'

'Fine job you're doing of that,' Gariath growled, 'what with the giant demons prowling about.' He reared up, rising to his feet; buttocks were tensed immediately, but remained in their seats. 'Why are we even having this conversation? If you weren't all so stupid, you'd see what she is.' He levelled a claw accusingly at the crest atop her head and snarled, '*She's* one of *them.*'

Lenk supposed the resemblance to the Abysmyth ought to have occurred to him earlier, as did most of his companions. Tensions rose immediately, daggers were drawn, claws were bared, and even Kataria seemed to figure out the dragonman's accusation accurately enough to nock an arrow. Asper glanced to Lenk, wide-eyed and baffled, but even she seemed to stiffen at the declaration.

Before he could make a move to join or restrain his companions, however, Dreadaeleon acted first.

'She ... is ... *not!*'

With barely more than a flicker of his fingers, he was on his feet, propelled by a burst of unseen energy beneath him. And, apparently envisioning himself as a particularly underdeveloped gallant, stepped to intervene between the woman and the dragonman. Quite unlike the vision his stand conjured up, however, the finger he levelled at Gariath, crackling with blue electricity, delivered a much more decisive message.

'And don't think I won't fry you where you stand if you take one more step forwards.'

'The only thing I *don't* think is that there'll be enough of your treacherous little corpse left to paint the beach with after I'm done with you,' Gariath snorted, apparently unimpressed.

'You tried to kill me just *today*,' the boy warned, his finger glowing an angry azure. 'That didn't pan out so well, did it?'

'If I had tried to kill you, you'd be dead.'

'Gentlemen.' Asper sighed, exasperated. 'Can we not do this in front of the siren?' Met with only a snarl and the crackle of lightning brewing, she turned an incredulous gaze to Lenk. 'Aren't you going to do something?'

That sounded like a good idea; however much Gariath would like to believe differently, Dreadaeleon's magic was more than capable of reducing things far larger than a dragonman to puddles.

Lenk's attention, however, was less on the boy's finger and more on the rest of him: on the way he stood so confident and poised, on the way his eyes were clear enough to reflect the blue sparks dancing across his hand.

'You're using magic again,' he said, more for his own benefit than the wizard's.

'At least *someone* noticed,' Dreadaeleon growled.

'You could barely walk after the crash.' Lenk leaned forwards, intent on his companion. 'What happened?'

At the question, the boy seemed to forget his impending evisceration. He lowered his finger, magic extinguished, and beamed a smile at the young man. With all the propriety of an actor, he stepped aside and gestured to the siren, who merely blinked and smiled.

'She did it,' he said, 'with her song.'

Lenk felt his heart quicken a beat. 'You can heal,' he whispered, 'with your song?'

'It is within my power to soothe.' She nodded.

His mind quickened to match his heart, a flood of

thoughts streaming in. The siren could heal … no, not heal, soothe. She could soothe Dreadaeleon's headache, an affliction that no known medicine could cure. She could soothe the mind.

And perhaps, he thought, the voices within it.

'Sit down.' He waved a hand at Gariath.

'What?' The dragonman growled. 'Why?'

'I want to hear what she has to say,' he replied. 'Not that I'm promising anything, but if Dreadaeleon believes in her, we should give her a chance.'

'The little runt came within an inch of betraying us,' Gariath snorted, 'and the last thing *she* said made the shict deaf.'

Lenk tensed himself at the mention of Kataria, not for any anticipation that she might yell again, but for the fact that he suddenly felt her gaze upon him. Glancing from the corner of his eye, for he did not meet her stare directly, he imagined she could be looking at him for any number of reasons: explanation, impatience …

Or perhaps his suspicions were right and, deaf as she was, those giant ears could still hear his thoughts.

'If I held attempted murder against everyone in this group,' he said calmly, looking away from the shict and towards the dragonman, 'then we'd never get anything done. He's entitled to at least *one* attempt on your life for all the times you've actively attempted on his.'

The dragonman's glower shifted about the circle, from the siren to the young man to the boy, then once more around the others assembled. Finally, he settled a scowl upon Lenk.

'You couldn't stop me, you know,' he grunted.

'Probably not.' Lenk shrugged.

'Good. So long as we all understand that.' He snorted,

took a step backwards, settled upon his haunches and scowled at the siren. 'Talk.'

The female blinked. 'In regards to …'

'Start with your name?' Asper offered. 'I believe that's where we left off before we decided to act like raving psychotics.'

'I … I do not have a name, I am afraid,' she replied meekly. 'I have never had a use for one.'

'Everyone needs a name,' Dreadaeleon quickly retorted. 'What else would we call you?'

'Screechy.' Denaos nodded. 'Screechy MacEarbleed.'

'Don't be stupid,' Asper chastised. 'She needs something elegant … like from a play.'

'Lashenka!' Dreadaeleon piped up, enthused. 'You remember the tragedy, don't you? *Lament for a King*. She looks like the young heiress, Lashenka.'

'Sounds too close to Lenk.' The priestess tapped her chin. 'Were there any other players in it? I never saw it on stage. For that matter, was it any good?'

'It was … decent. Nothing too thrilling, but worth the silver spent.'

'*Silver?* When did theatre become worth that kind of money?'

'Well, this particular one had the Merry Murderers, the troupe from Jaharla, and—'

'*Enough.*' Gariath was on his feet again, stomping upon the ground angrily. He snorted, levelling a claw at the siren. 'Your name is Greenhair. Get on with it.'

'Greenhair?' Asper scratched her head. 'It has a certain charm to it, but I'm not sure that—'

'Tell me,' Gariath almost whispered, 'can you finish that thought with your tongue torn out and shoved in your ear?'

'I don't—'

'Do you want to find out?' With a decisive snort, he glowered at the siren. 'Her name is Greenhair. Get on with it.'

'It's a fine name.' Lenk nodded. 'Just so we're all on even footing, though, our names are—'

'There is no need.' The siren held up a hand while casting a smile at Dreadaeleon. 'I have been informed, Silverhair, of much of who you are and what you do in the Sea Mother's domain.' Her smile broadened. 'And I expect it is by Her hand that I meet you now.'

'Rather high praise,' Lenk muttered. 'But you said you needed our help.'

'And I thank you for it.'

'Save your thanks,' he replied. 'I didn't say we'd give any.'

A smile played across her features. Lenk felt his hand unconsciously resting on his sword; something in the creature's gaze was unsettling. Absently, his thoughts drifted back to the Abysmyth. This thing expressed as much emotion in a twist of pale blue lips as that thing could not in a cacophony of shrieks.

'Your … callings are not unknown to me.' She did not so much as flinch at his bluntness. 'You are … adventurers, yes? And adventurers seek compensation for their trials. Such is the way of the sea. What is given must be earned, what is earned is not easily lost.'

'If that's a lot of fancy talk for gold, then I'm interested.' Denaos eyed the wispy silk she wore. 'I dare suggest I'd be more than tempted to help you if you planned on showing me wherever you hid it, though.'

'I have no riches for you, Longleg.' She shook her hair.

'What I offer, however, is something more precious than gold. Something you have lost.'

Lenk leaned forwards again. He could sense the word resting on her tongue as a hedonist sensed a tongue resting on something else.

'I am informed,' she said, so slowly as to drive him wild, 'that you seek a tome.'

Buttocks tightened collectively.

Not a single face remained unchanged at the word. Expressions went alight with various stages of greed, hope and anticipation. Even Kataria's eyes seemed to widen, if only at the simultaneous reaction amongst her companions. Lenk himself could not imagine what his own face must have looked like, but fought to twist it into stony caution nonetheless. The last time someone had mentioned a tome to him, it had led to him and Kataria nearly being slaughtered.

He had since come to treat the word warily.

'What do you know of it?'

'What I have been told by the lorekeeper and what I am able to conclude on my own,' the siren replied. 'The tome was lost. You, specifically, wish to find it. I am at once filled with joy and sorrow for you.'

Lenk felt his face twitch; good news never began with those words.

'You don't know where it is?' he asked.

'I know where it is,' she replied. 'I have seen much, heard much from the fish before they fled at the presence of the demons.' As if reading his thoughts through his eyes, she nodded grimly. 'The two you discovered on the blackened sands were but the sneezes and coughs of a sickness with many, many symptoms.'

He almost loathed to ask. 'How many?'

'Many,' she said simply. 'They have risen from the depths of the ocean that the Sea Mother has forgotten. They have tainted the waters, as they do all things, and blackened the sea such that no living thing remains between here and their temple.'

Her voice changed suddenly. What had begun as liquid song that slipped through his ears soundless became heavy and bloated, a salt-pregnant wave that seemed to steal the air from the sky as she spoke.

'The fish shall be the first to flee, being closest to their taint. The birds shall be chased from the sky. The clever beasts shall hide where they can. The brave will die. As will all things that walk upon land. Mortals drown. Sky drowns. Earth drowns. There shall be an unholy wave born of no benevolent tide. Nothing shall remain … save endless blue.'

Endless blue.

That phrase had passed through fouler lips before. Lenk tightened his grip on his sword, holding it firmly in his hand, but still in his lap. There would be time to dwell on cryptic musings later.

'Swim to the point, then,' he growled. 'What does any of this have to do with the tome?'

'Consider it a warning,' she replied, unhurried, 'passed through all children of the Sea Mother of what shall come to pass if that foul thing of red and black remains in the possession of the demons. It is a reminder of all that the Kraken Queen craves, all that her children seek to return her for.'

'And the actual location of the tome?'

'It is … not here.'

'Well.' He slapped his knees with an air of finality. 'Thanks for that, I suppose.'

'Not here,' she continued, undeterred, 'but close. You are but an hour away from it, in fact.'

'Now that *is* helpful.' Denaos, who had previously been lying on his back and scratching himself, rose to his feet and stretched. 'Let's get it and put this whole fish and prophecy business behind us, aye? Screechy here knows where it is.'

'I do.' The siren nodded. 'And I know what guards it.'

Denaos paused mid-stretch, sighed and sat back down.

'Of course you do.'

Lenk was less rattled. It was rather apparent that the siren would not be telling them this purely for the sake of their aversion to being choked by ooze.

'What do you want from us, then?' he asked.

She stared at him without expression, spoke without hatred or fury.

'I want you to kill, Silverhair.'

That figures.

'Kill … what?'

'I take no great pleasure in asking you, but the plague must be cleansed. The Sea Mother's dominion must be restored.'

'So you want us to kill more Abysmyths.'

'Curb as many symptoms as you can, yes, silence the coughing and the wheezing where necessary. But for a plague of this nature to be cured, the tumour must be cut out.'

Her lips pursed tightly, eyes narrowed as her utterance reverberated through them like a dull ache.

'You must kill the Deepshriek.'

A moment of silence passed before Lenk sighed.

'You're going to make me ask, aren't you?'

'They …' The siren paused, looked at the ground. 'It …

was once like myself. A child of the deep, a servant of the Sea Mother … but no longer. Long ago, when the skies were painted red and She still befouled the mortal seas, the Kraken Queen sang to the Deepshriek and the Deepshriek listened. Now … it is her prophet, the one who shall return its mistress and mother to the waking world.' She looked back up at Lenk with a swiftness fuelled by desperation. 'Unless you take the tome back to whatever foul hand it came from.'

Lenk hesitated at that, leaning back and sighing. Frankly, he thought, he could have done with just being told the location of the tome *without* hearing the inane claptrap of a deranged sea beast. As it was, the temptation of a thousand gold pieces was slowly beginning to lose its lustre.

He suddenly became aware of Kataria sitting next to him, a blank expression on the shict's face. Leaning over, he yelled.

'SHE SAID THE TOME IS—'

'*I HEARD WHAT SHE SAID!*' the shict snapped back violently. 'The deafness wore off ages ago, you stupid monkey.'

'Oh.' He smiled meekly. 'Well, great.'

'Yeah—'

'This … is rather a lot to take in,' Asper said breathlessly, as though just recovering from some unpleasant coitus. 'Demons upon demons, tomes and diseases … it's hard to decide what to do next.'

'If you're an idiot, I suppose,' Denaos replied. 'Obviously, we run.'

'It's obvious to everyone without a spine, I suppose.'

'I can guarantee you if we decide to go this route, the only spine you'll be seeing is your own as some Abysmyth … Deepshriek … or whatever rips it out and force-feeds it to you.' He cast a glance about the circle. 'Listen, I hate to reinforce your beliefs in my cowardice as much as I hate to be forced to be the voice of reason again, but let's consider a few things.

'First of all,' he held up a finger, 'we can't harm the Abysmyths and it's a decent bet we won't be able to harm something with an even weirder-sounding name. Secondly,' he gestured over his shoulder towards the carnage at the other end of the beach, 'someone else seems to have tried to "cleanse" them without much luck.'

'You speak of the longfaces,' Greenhair replied.

'Seems they get around, too.' Denaos rolled his eyes.

'I witnessed them … from afar. I saw the fire and ice they wrought upon the land.' She leaned back, as though reminiscing fondly. 'They were tall, powerful, skin the colour of a bruise and eyes the colour of milk. There were many, females all but for one male, the one who slew the Abysmyth with a spear of ice.'

'I take it these longfaces didn't take the tome.'

'No. By that time, the servants of the Deepshriek had taken it into their temple.'

Lenk paused, stared hard at her. 'What temple?'

She regarded him unflinchingly. 'I will show you.'

'Well, that's …' Denaos could not find the words to describe the sight looming before him. 'That's … uh …'

'Impressive,' Lenk muttered.

'Ominous.' Dreadaeleon nodded.

'Vile.' Asper blanched.

'Yeah,' the rogue said, 'something like that.'

Like the hand of some drowning stone giant, scraping futilely at the sky as he took his final breath, the granite tower rose to claw at the orange clouds above. A plague of algae scarred its great hide, holes riddling its weathered skin like rocky wounds.

Brackish waves licked against the tower's base, rising and falling to expose the sturdy reef it had been wrought upon. Each time the waves recoiled from the stones, a jagged chorus of rusted spears, blades and spikes embedded in the rocks glistened unpleasantly with the fading sun.

Stomachs writhed collectively as the companions stared upon the impressive mass of impaled corpses in varying stages of decay held fast by the red spikes. Amongst the panoply, a few protrusions impaled incautious sea creatures; many more bore arms with fingers, legs with toes, bodies swaddled by clothing.

Lenk still had trouble believing they hadn't seen it before. Even ensconced on the far side of the island from where they had crashed, the thing was imposing enough to command attention from miles around.

'This is their temple,' Greenhair explained with a shudder. 'They conduct their rites and sermons within.' She narrowed her eyes upon the tower. 'Mortals once lived here, long ago. In those days, they called it "Irontide".'

'And they aren't here any more?' Asper pointedly turned her head away as the waves recoiled once more. 'Who … or what drove them away? The demons?'

'Other men.' Denaos spoke before the siren could. 'Irontide has a rather colourful repute amongst certain circles.'

'Circles that begin and end in activities I've doubtless no pleasure in hearing about,' the priestess muttered. 'But do go on.'

'Fair enough.' The rogue shrugged. 'As you probably know, the main export of the Toha Nations is rum, that being the only place in the world the drink's made. As a result, Toha was quick to extort as much tax gold as they could from other nations desiring the drink. Seeing a profit to be made, pirates were quick to sell illicit barrels of the stuff for far cheaper.

'Towers of this design,' he gestured for emphasis, 'were originally storehouses and protection against the Toha Navy.' He pointed to the stone-scarred reaches of the tower's battlements. 'You can see there what the Navy's catapults thought of *that*.'

'I see.' Asper swallowed hard. 'And … the spikes?'

'First, they were for protection. Then they were used to make examples.'

'Disgusting.' She grimaced. 'What a vile trick that so many lives should be wasted over a drink that has no purpose but to turn good people into sleazy harlots and swillers.'

'That's not entirely fair,' he replied brusquely. 'The same, after all, could be said of any faith.'

'You're actually comparing a house and faith of the Gods to smuggling?'

'They seem fairly alike to me. Crime and religion are the only two things that people are willing to both die for and kill over.'

'Regardless of who lived here for whatever reason,' Lenk interjected, taking a step forwards, 'it appears to have new residents.'

It was plain to see what he spoke of.

Plain and gruesome against the setting sun, a flock of feathers and bulbous eyes formed a white and writhing crown atop the giant. They milled about in great numbers, offering glimpses of hooked noses and yellow teeth that chattered endlessly.

'Omens,' he muttered.

'Ah yes,' Greenhair said coldly, 'the choir.'

Before Lenk could make any agreement, something caught his eye. At the centre of the huddled mass of parasites, a particularly large white tumour pulsated and writhed. He squinted; though it was larger than anything with feathers had a right to be, he could discern no features. He glanced over his shoulder, beckoned to Kataria.

'Have a look.'

She nodded, stalking up beside him, and stared long at the tower. The assembled, in turn, stared long at her, expectant as a grimace crossed her face.

'What is it?' Lenk dared to ask.

'I really have no idea.' Her grimace became a frown as she squinted, trying to find the words. 'It's ... big ... like one of the Omens, except ... bigger. I don't know ... it's got hands and a face, but ... it's upside-down, all angular.' She scratched her head. 'Well ... hell.'

'As good a descriptor as any,' the young man muttered. 'How many Omens?'

'At least twenty, though they all move around so much it's hard to tell.'

'Scavengers.' Greenhair's voice was rife with loathing. 'They feed on the dead and grow glutted on suffering. What you have seen, Notch-ear, is their ... enlightened form.'

'Form?' Asper's eyes went wide. 'Omens ... change?'

'As they feed, yes. They are heralds, after all, and as they change, so too does the Kraken Queen grow in strength.' She frowned. 'To see one here, so soon, is ... troubling.'

'They don't seem to have seen us,' Kataria noted.

'Nor will they, should we keep our distance,' Greenhair replied. 'In their smallest form, they are unthinking,

426

oblivious. The greater one is present to ensure that they attack only what they are meant to attack.'

'A watchdog.' Lenk nodded. 'With a pack of flesh-eating seagulls. Makes sense, given the circumstances.'

'Not to mention a bunch of filthy, corpse-laden spikes,' Kataria grunted, 'and, if Omens *are* heralds, there're enough of them to suggest quite a few Abysmyths inside.'

'And that's where the tome was taken.' Lenk bit his lower lip, sighed. 'Lovely.'

'Lovely, indeed.' Denaos clapped his hands together. 'Rusted spikes to skewer us, Omens to eat us afterwards, Abysmyths waiting to tear us apart barring more fortunate fates.' He giggled, not a little hysterical. 'If we're *really* fortunate, a shark will eat us before we ever set foot on it.' His giggle became a cackle. 'No, if Silf *truly* loves us, he'll send a lightning bolt to strike us down before we even try.'

At that, he flung out his arms and looked to the sky expectantly. All he received, however, was a stagger forwards as Gariath shoved his way to the front.

'A death from a weak God for a weak rat,' he growled, 'the best you could hope for.'

'Let's not get carried away,' Kataria interrupted. 'No one, as yet, has said anything about going in.'

'Of *course* we're going in there,' Denaos snapped. 'It's completely brainless, bereft of any logical reason and totally suicidal. Why *wouldn't* we go in there?'

'It *does* look fairly impenetrable.' Asper frowned once for the fortress and twice for the fact that she agreed with the rogue. 'It's too far to swim without being made into meat for the Omens and I doubt we could get our little boat over there even once we've repaired it.' She squinted. 'I can't even see a way in.'

'There is but one,' Greenhair said. 'On the other side,

amidst the rocks, there is a concealed opening. Seals slumbered by it before the Deepshriek desecrated this place.'

'Regardless,' Lenk muttered, 'there's no way to reach it alive. If we aren't dashed against the spikes by a wave, the Omens will gnaw us to pieces.'

'Not necessarily.' Dreadaeleon scratched his chin. 'I mean, watchdogs aren't the brightest things in the world. Toss a piece of meat out and you can sneak by one, easily.' He glanced to Denaos. 'I suspect you'd probably know more about that than I would, though.'

'You want to distract them?' The rogue scoffed. 'You plan to strip naked, smear yourself with faeces and do the jolly Omen mating dance?' He paused, tapped his cheek thoughtfully. 'That *might* work.'

'Hm … I'm not sure,' the boy replied, oblivious. 'I might be able to do something about it, though. They're scavengers, right? Gluttons?' At a nod from Greenhair, he glanced out to sea. 'So, if they *are* anything like watchdogs, they're probably attracted to blood. In that case, all we need to do is turn the water from blue to red.'

'Oh, is *that* all?' Denaos sneered.

'It's not too difficult. In fact, with a glamer, it should be rather easy … in theory.'

'Nothing with magic is ever easy, in theory or in practice,' Denaos replied. 'And what in Silf's name is a … *glamer*, anyway?'

'Glamer,' Dreadaeleon said, 'from the word "glimmer". It's just a small spectromancy spell, one of the lesser schools. It works on the theory of bending light to produce an image.' He held up a finger. 'To wit.'

His hand danced in front of his face for a moment, a brief murmur expulsed from his lips. His skin shimmered, blinked, then distorted and when he turned back to the companions, he had full lips, long eyelashes and delicate angles. He batted his eyes and gave a demure giggle.

'Just like that,' his voice was a sharp contrast to his new face, 'except on a larger, more distant scale.'

'That's ... actually not a bad idea.' Lenk nodded appreciatively. After an unbearably long moment, he coughed. 'So, uh, are you going to stay that way or ...'

'Oh, right.' The boy waved a hand and returned his face to his own with another, equally feminine giggle. 'Well, I would just lose my own face if it weren't laced on.'

'Right ... anyway, never say or do anything you did in the last few breaths ever again.'

'We don't need magic,' Gariath growled suddenly. 'We don't need cowards, either.' He thumped a fist against his chest. 'We go in. We kill them as they come. We get the stupid book.'

'It's all so easy.' Asper rolled her eyes. 'If we conveniently go insane and forget the fact there are Gods know how many frogmen and Abysmyths in there. Factoring in the Deepshriek, I'd *love* to believe that we could make it in, I really would, but I doubt it.' The waves receded, exposing the decaying buffet of flesh. 'I *severely* doubt it.'

'But it is *not* impossible,' Greenhair protested. 'I have heard the lorekeeper. He has told me much of what you have faced and fought before! He has told me the bravery of adventurers.'

'He lied,' Denaos spat. 'Practicality dictates adventure, not bravery. Besides,' he sniffed, '*you're* not the one to risk your head getting eaten.'

'Don't disrespect her,' Dreadaeleon snapped. 'She can help us.'

'With what? Singing lessons? Unless she can hold you

down while I pound sense into your pudgy head, she's useless to us.'

'My head isn't pudgy.' The boy's eyes flashed. 'But my brain … is *HUGE!*'

'Big enough to come up with a better idea?'

Lenk glanced at the rogue. 'Can *you*?'

'As a matter of fact, I can.' Denaos puffed up, ready to explode with self-satisfaction. 'As much as I'd love to recommend running away, I *do* like getting paid. Obviously, though, charging into a tower that is both ready to collapse *and* brimming with demons isn't a good idea in any language.' He shrugged. 'So, why not just wait?'

'Wait.'

'Wait.' He nodded. 'They'll come out, eventually, to do what demons do. Or we lure them out. Either way, we ambush them, take the book and *then* run away.'

'That's … not completely bad,' Asper conceded. 'They can't stay in there for ever, can they? If they plan to do something with the tome, they'll likely bring it out eventually.'

'I suppose that passes for genius amongst humans,' Kataria sneered. '*Leave* the book in the hands of demons and *wait* to see what they do with it? You stupid monkey.'

'And how do you plan to saunter your mighty shicty self in?' Asper snapped back. 'Are you going to swim in and hope they think your huge ears jutting from the waters are just a white fish with two fins?'

'Miron,' she poked the priestess hard, '*your* almighty lord and master, said himself that we can't leave the tome in their hands.' Her ears twitched threateningly. 'And, frankly, your ear-envy is just sickening.'

'*EAR*-envy?'

'Miron isn't the one risking everything.' Denaos stepped up beside the priestess.

'And you would risk *anything*?' Gariath's laugh was a derisive rumble as he loomed over the man. 'Your eyes and breeches both go moist at the first sign of trouble. The *Rhega* spit in the eyes of death and demons.'

'Oh, it's not *my* death I'm afraid of,' the rogue hissed, 'I'm utterly terrified of the idea that you and I will *both* die and I'll have to share my heaven with some scaly, smelly reptile.'

'There is no heaven for rats,' Gariath snarled, shoving the rogue. 'They get tossed on the trash heap and rot in a hole.'

'*ENOUGH!*' Kataria's cry temporarily skewered the argument. As an uneasy silence descended, she glanced towards Lenk, staring absently across the sea. 'And what do you say? You're the one who usually chooses between bad ideas.'

'Oh, is that what I do?'

He had no more words, only eyes, and they were fixated upon the fortress. The sun was dying at the horizon, descending into a blue grave, and the impending darkness seeped into his thoughts.

One Abysmyth, he reasoned, was invincible. It was a vicious brute capable of ripping people apart and drowning them on dry land, sometimes inflicting both on the same person. The fact that there was more than one had seemed a nightmare too horrifying to contemplate earlier that day.

The fact that there were more than *two*, discounting how many multitudes of frogmen and Omens accompanied them, was too horrifying not to contemplate.

In light of *that* fact, all plans seemed equally insane, save the unspoken idea of just turning around and leaving.

And yet, he thought, *not even Denaos has suggested leaving . . .*

Further, he had entered a contract; not just an adventurer's agreement, but a contract, penned and sealed with promises. He had sold his word to Miron Evenhands, for one thousand pieces of gold.

A man's word, no matter how expensive it might be, is the only thing of any real worth a man can give.

His grandfather had told him that, he was certain.

Don't forget, though, that honour and common sense are mutually exclusive.

His grandfather had also said that.

'Lenk?'

He felt Kataria prodding him, breaking his reverie.

'I . . .' he inhaled dramatically and his companions held their breath with him, 'am hungry.' He sighed and so did they. 'And tired.'

With that, he turned from the fortress and began to trudge away. They watched him for a few moments before Denaos spoke up.

'What? That's it?'

'Night is falling,' he replied. 'If I'm going to my death, it can wait until I've had dinner.'

ACT THREE
The Mouth, the Prophet, the Voice

Interlogue

DON'T ASK

The Aeons' Gate
Ktamgi, a few days north and east (?) of Toha
Summer, getting later

So, why be an adventurer?

Why forsake the security of a mercenary guild, the comfort of a family or the patriotism of a soldier to serve at the whims of unscrupulous characters and perform deeds that fall somewhere in the triangle of madness, villainy and self-loathing?

To be honest, I hadn't actually asked myself that for awhile. Don't misunderstand; I asked myself all the time when I first began doing this sort of thing, three years ago. I don't recall ever finding an answer ...

Eventually, one begins to accept one's lot in life, adventurers included, so I suppose I'd say the chief reason people stay with this, let's be honest, rather abhorrent career decision is out of sheer laziness. But that doesn't really offer an answer to the chief question, does it?

Why do *it in the first place?*

Freedom, perhaps, could be one reason: the need to be without the beck and call of sergeants, kings or even customers. An adventurer is as close as you can get to that sort of thing without declaring yourself outright a highwayman or rapist. Hardly any profit in the latter, anyway.

Greed is certainly another factor, for though adventurers don't get hired often, we do typically end up with whatever gold we acquire along the way from robberies, plundering or looting ... which might be why we don't get hired very often.

That aside, I think the real reason is the first one: laziness.

Wait, let me rephrase.

Comfort.

There's precious little of it to be found in an adventurer's life, it's certain ... and maybe that's why we pick up a sword or a bow or a knife and decide to do it. It makes sense, doesn't it? We all want comfort, in one way or another.

Asper wants the comfort of being able to provide comfort to others in the name of Talanas; being an adventurer gives her plenty of opportunity.

Dreadaeleon wants the comfort of knowing he did everything he could to make himself and his art stronger; again, plenty of opportunity.

Gariath wants the comfort of knowing he did everything he could to reduce the population of every non-dragonman species; I suspect there's a greater reason, but I haven't had any inclination to endure the head-stompings that asking would entail.

Denaos wants gold, I suppose, but why our gold is anyone's guess. He could get gold anywhere else. Maybe he just wants the comfort of knowing he's close to people as scummy as himself.

Kataria ... is a mystery.

She has everything people who adventure typically don't have: family, identity, security, homeland. Granted, I know only as much about shicts as I'd heard in stories and what I've learned from Kataria, but such things, and she's bragged as much, are abundant in shictish society. If she had stayed with them, she'd undoubtedly lead a happy life hunting deer, raising little shictlets and perhaps killing a human or two.

As for me ... maybe by staying near her I can remember what having those things is like ...

... The family and identity part. Not the killing humans part. Though I suspect I've done enough of that to warrant at least a nod from the shicts.

To that end, I briefly considered asking her to stay behind today.

If I die, there's nothing much that will be sorry for my loss. A dead child is a tragedy. A dead man is a funeral. A dead soldier is a loss. A dead adventurer is a lump in the ground and possibly a round of drinks from his former employer. If Gariath or Denaos die, there'll just be one less murderer running loose. If Asper or Dread die, they'll have done so for a cause and, thusly, not in vain.

But if Kat dies ... people will mourn.

I would have liked to tell her to stay ... but, alas, I am an adventurer and it's true what Denaos said: practicality, not bravery, is what drives us.

And having her as a part of my plan is very practical.

The following sentence will undoubtedly prove to be the point of identification in this particular saga where I ceased to be merely foolhardy and became totally mad:

I've decided to go into Irontide, after the tome.

Thus far, I've determined the best means of procuring said book will be through stealth. And, with that in mind, it should come as no surprise that I've decided to divide us up for that purpose. It should come as no further surprise that Gariath won't be coming along.

Nor will Asper or Dreadaeleon – they are too squeamish and too curious, respectively, to be of any use. Denaos, however, is both a thug and possessed of a particular aversion to what lies inside. He'll be perfect.

Kataria is a stalker and a hunter. I need keen senses in there,

437

too; if Gariath's nose can't come, I'll gladly settle for Kat's ears. Her bow will be a welcome asset, as well.

With that in mind, the rest of the plan falls pretty easily into place. Dread's glamer, we're hoping, can apparently draw out the Omens ... and the big one, too. If that doesn't work, we'll find a way to lure them away long enough for us three, who I've deemed 'Team Imminent Evisceration', to swim across and find our way in.

The remainder will stay behind to watch out for anything, to fix the boat ... and to carry what's left of us back to Miron should we fail. Now, I don't mean our remains, since if we do fail, there's most certainly not going to be enough left of us to sprinkle on gruel, much less bury.

But Greenhair, for all her shrieking, made clear something that had plagued me for a while.

These aren't pirates we're fighting. They're demons. Their goals aren't loot and murder, but resurrection. They, themselves something that should not be, are trying to summon something that definitely should not be. And they're succeeding, if a bigger Omen is anything to go by.

If we do fail, I trust Asper, at least, to make it back to Port Destiny to tell Miron exactly what's going on.

Dawn is approaching. After a less than satisfying meal of jerky and fruit, my intestines are in working order and my rear is tightly clenched. If I do die today, I most certainly will not be going out soiled.

I'll write more if I make it out.

Hope is ill-advised.

Twenty

THE PLEASANT LIES

The dawn was shy, too polite to come and chase the stars away, contenting itself to slowly creep into the twilit conversation one wisp at a time. The seas caught between night and day in shiftless masses of molten gold and silver. The night had yet to fade, the dawn had yet to break; the world was mired in an indecision of purple and yellow.

Absently, Lenk wished for more than just a meagre piece of charcoal to sketch the scene.

His desire was for naught; there hadn't been any quills in the companion vessel's cargo. He'd likely miss the flaky black stuff when the time came to build a fire, but for now, all it was good for was writing and sketching.

A breeze cut across the sea, heavy with the cold salt of the pre-dawn mist. It slithered across his body like a frigid serpent, and went unheeded. He rarely felt the cold any more. Rain and winter, sun and spring, all felt the same to him: a faint tingle, a passing shiver, and then nothing.

He paused, staring blankly at the journal in his lap.

He couldn't feel cold any more ...

'You're up early.'

He was torn from further thought by the sound of her voice. Kataria stood behind him, clad in doeskin breeches and shortened green tunic, staring at him with some

439

concern, ears twitching and naked toes wriggling in the sand.

'Yeah,' he said, returning to his sketch.

Her footsteps were loud and crunching against the moist sand; that wasn't good. When she didn't bother to hide the sound of her feet, it usually meant she wasn't going to hide any other sounds she might make.

'You didn't eat much last night.' She took a seat beside him.

'We need to ration.' He didn't look up. 'Gariath eats enough for two men, Denaos eats more to spite Gariath.' He allowed the corner of his eye to drift over her slender, pale form. 'You didn't eat much either, and you're up as early as I am.'

'My people don't eat or sleep as much as humans.' She didn't even bother to hide her smirk. 'We don't need to.'

'Mm.' Even his grunt was half-hearted, long past hearing or caring about the numerous self-proclaimed advantages of shicts.

'I didn't know you drew.' She peered over his shoulder and blanched.

'Mm.'

'You're terrible at it.'

'Mm.'

'You don't seem to understand how this works. I say something to you, you say something back, we fight, maybe someone bleeds. That's how we communicate.'

'Too early,' he replied. 'I'll stab you in the eye a little later and we'll call it a day.'

'I won't be in the mood later.' She leaned over his lap, making him stiffen. 'What do you draw, anyway?'

'Those islands to the north.' He simultaneously gestured to three faint specks of greenery as he shoved her away. 'I hadn't noticed them until today.' He tapped the charcoal to his chin. 'It's possible that one of them is Teji. Seems worthwhile to sketch it, don't you think?'

'You don't want to know what I think. What else do you draw?'

Before he could answer, her hands darted out like two pale ferrets. Before he could protest, they snatched the journal out of his lap. Cackling unpleasantly, she tumbled away from him, evading flailing fists. With a deft leap, she rolled to her feet and began to thumb through the pages, strolling away with an insulting casualness.

'Hm, yes.' She scratched an imaginary beard, eyes darting over the pages. 'Seas … gates … demons … hope.' She smacked her lips. 'A little morbid, you think? It needs a bit of editing. Skip all this gibberish about humans and stick to the parts about shicts.'

'It's for reading, not wiping.'

His hands closed murderously about empty air as she sprang away. Backpedalling without the slightest hint of caution, she continued to peruse.

'Just as well, I'm not so much the literary sort.'

'More of the illiterate sort, are you?'

'If you could be half as clever in your writing, you might actually have some value. Let's see if your drawings are half as terrible.'

'What? Wait a moment!'

'A moment to you is an eternity to me.' She nimbly evaded his hands as she noted the various sketches scrawled in charcoal. 'Not bad, I suppose. If you ever lose your will to fight, you can hack out a living with a piece of charcoal and a dream, can't you?'

She was prepared to slam the book shut and hurl it at

him as he took a menacing step forwards when a frayed edge of parchment caught her eye.

'What's this, then? Something worth reading amongst such drivel?'

No sooner had the page turned than her feet froze in the sand. Her eyes went wide at the sight before her: an image that looked almost wrong in the midst of Lenk's writings. With an elegance she had not seen in his other drawings of demons, landscapes and other combinations of equally boring and horrifying subjects, the page seemed less a sketch and more a memory, revisited frequently in the strokes of charcoal and ink.

It was slender, a wispy figure traced in smooth lines upon the parchment, hair long and unbound, fluttering like wings behind a naked, rigid back. Everything about the figure was hard, fighting against the softness of the lines and winning effortlessly. Even its eyes, brighter than black ink should allow, were fierce and strong.

It wasn't until she noted the pair of long, notched ears that she heard his feet thunder on the shore.

He lunged, wrapped arms about her middle and pulled her to the earth in a spray of sand. She was breathless as he straddled her waist; whether from the drawing, the blow or the physical contact, she did not know. He loomed over her in a burst of blue, two eyes bright and dominated by vast, dark pupils. She found no memories of what that stare had once lacked, only a desire not to look away, a desire to meet his gaze.

And to smile.

Such a feeling lasted for but a moment before she spied the journal held high above him like a weapon of leather and paper. With a snarl, he brought it down and smashed it against the side of her face.

'*OW!*' She shoved him off and scowled as he skulked away. 'How is *that*, to any race, a reasonable reaction?'

'Based on the fact that a man's journal is his sole refuge from the vile and uncouth elements of the world he chooses to name as his companions,' the young man replied snootily. 'And, as a violator of that refuge, I invoked my Gods-given right to bash your narrow head with that refuge.'

'Disregarding the obvious fact that your logic is completely deranged,' she pulled herself to her feet, 'why so secretive about it, anyway? It's not like I haven't seen anything you put in there.'

His stride slowed at that, suddenly afflicted by some degenerative disease that forced him to walk, then trudge, then stop with a painful finality, rigid as a corpse in an upright coffin.

'These are my thoughts.' His whisper cut through the air like a knife.

'Well,' she gritted her teeth, feeling his voice rake against her flesh, 'I mean, they're fine and all, but—'

'But what? You've seen them before, have you?'

'No, but—'

'Heard them, then?'

'Not exactly.'

'*Exactly.*' He whirled on her, hurling his scowl like a spear and skewering her upon the sands. 'You don't *see* my thoughts. You don't *hear* my thoughts. You don't know *anything* beyond what your self-important shicty self believes you do.' His mouth went tight as he tucked the journal under his arm and stalked away. 'Let's not ruin that special relationship we share.'

He had barely taken two steps before he felt her reply impale him and hold him fast.

'I know you don't dream.'

Lenk forced himself not to turn around; he would not give her the satisfaction of seeing his eyes widen, would not let her hear his heart skip a beat. The sound of the waves was suddenly uncomfortably quiet, the creeping of the mist far too slow for his liking.

'Not like other humans, at least,' she continued softly. 'Yours are fevered and wild. You snarl and whimper in your sleep.'

'And what tells you this?' he replied, just as soft. 'Whatever mental illness passes for shictish intuition?'

'You cry out in the night from time to time.' Her voice was emotionless, denying him any anger and any opportunity to end this conversation. 'Not loudly, not lately, but you do. I've seen it.'

His breath caught in his throat. Suddenly, her hand was on his arm, the naked flesh of her fingers pressing against this rapidly tensing bicep. Though desiring not to, though he shrieked at himself not to, he turned and stared into her twin emeralds.

In the year he had known her, he had become accustomed to so much of her: her savagery, her ears, her profoundly morbid laughter. Even her near-total disregard for human life was something he had learned to accept about her. Her stare, however, was something he knew at that moment he would never feel comfortable under.

She never condemned him, never judged him; never did an emotion flicker in the endless green. Her face was blank, mouth small as eyes were wide. He felt vulnerable under her gaze, beyond naked, as though she stared through flesh, bone, sinew, past what some people might call a soul and into something else entirely.

And for all that he strained to deny her, he could not help but stare back.

'What do you dream about?'

'Dawn is rising. The others will be getting up soon.' That he seemed unable to pull himself from her was a fleeting thought. 'Go and bother one of them.'

'Do you dream of your family?' Her grip tightened on his arm. 'Do you see them when you close your eyes?' She clenched his hand in hers. 'Lenk ... is it them you hear?'

'Shut *UP*!'

He ripped himself from her with a shocking ease, meeting her stare with a scowl. Where her eyes were a vast, passionless green, he felt his brim with a scornful blue. He suddenly felt very cold.

'I don't need your interrogations.' His voice leaked between his teeth in a frigid cloud. 'I don't need your sympathy. I don't need to talk about this and I'm not going to.'

At once, her gaze lost its distance and lack of expression. It flitted like that of a beast, darting between fear and resolve, squirming between trembling and firmness. In response, his grew harder, going deep and narrow like a dagger's cut. His jaw clenched, his hands trembled at his sides.

'I *need* you to stop *staring at me*.'

The journal fell to the sand. The sound of it crashing upon the earth echoed through the dawn.

When he turned, all of nature fell silent behind him. The morning took on a thick and oppressive sentience, the mist twisting to angry fingers that sought to impose themselves between the two companions to make room for another presence.

Someone else seemed to step between them, carving a stand with icy feet and turning a hostile, eyeless scowl upon the shict.

And she did not yield.

She had felt it before, seen it walking behind Lenk as an envious shadow, seeking to push others away as it sought to pull itself forwards. She had seen it pull itself into him, overcome him, become him.

She did not fear it, not any more, not for herself.

'Sorry …'

His body shrank with his sigh. She grunted in reply.

'You remember seeing me fall,' she said. 'Do you remember what happened next … with the Abysmyth?'

'I don't.'

'You do. I do.' She took a tentative step forwards. 'I was alive … awake long enough to see it. You fought well, better than I'd ever seen you.'

'Thanks.'

'It wasn't you fighting, though.' Her voice was hesitant, even as her stare was steady. 'It wasn't you who knelt over me. It was someone else.' She forced herself to stare out over the sea. 'Someone with eyes that had no pupils.'

Lenk offered no reply. The beach was reluctant to speak for him, its waves quiet and breezes humble. She rubbed her arms, feeling rather cold at that moment, caught between the silence of the sea and him.

Between them both stood someone else.

She took a step to the side, quietly, as if to get away from the presence. Immediately, she felt a bit warmer, but not because of any removal from an imaginary presence. It wasn't until she felt much warmer that she glanced out of the corner of her eye to see Lenk standing in her footprints, staring out over the ocean, silent.

And they were content to say nothing.

'I can barely remember it.'

He shattered the silence with a murmur.

'I don't remember how they died, only that they were dead.' His eyes were blank and empty. 'I remember shadows, fire ... swords. There was no one left afterwards.' His eyes turned downwards. 'I woke up in a barn, a burned-out thing. I had hidden, I don't remember why I didn't fight. I don't remember whose barn it was, I don't remember what house it was closest to. I don't remember anything about my mother, my father, my grandfather but their faces ...'

She heard his eyes shut tight.

'Sometimes ... not even that.'

He turned away, made a move as if to leave and let the cold presence take his place. Her hand shot out, seizing his and pulling him back.

'I don't want to talk about this,' he whispered.

She squeezed his hand, turned him to face her and smiled.

'Then don't.'

A breeze sang across the sea, heavy with waking warmth. As if possessed of a sense of humour all its own, it pulled their long hair up into the sky, strands of silver and gold batting playfully at each other.

The stars disappeared completely. The sun found its courage in the murmurs of the forest and the shore's crude symphony. Day rose.

'Time to go soon, huh?' She glanced out at the orange horizon. 'I should probably prepare myself.'

'I haven't even told you my plan,' he replied. 'You might not even be involved.'

'Of course I'm involved,' she said with a smile. 'I'm the smart one.'

She patted a pouch at her belt before darting off down the beach, long hair trailing behind her. Lenk watched her go and found a smile creeping of its own accord onto his

447

face. She was pleasant company indeed, he thought, and her imminent death would indeed be a tragedy.

In moments, the sounds of her fleeting feet were replaced by a decidedly lazier step. Lenk glanced over his shoulder to spy Denaos approaching, scratching himself in all manner of places that hardly needed bringing attention to. Hair a mess, vest hanging open around his torso, he casually slurped at a tin cup brimming with coffee.

'Good morning.' He paused to take a long sip, glancing at Kataria's diminishing form. 'My goodness, driven her away at last, have you? Did I miss something fun?'

'Solitude and tranquility,' Lenk grumbled.

'Both hard to come by.' He nodded. 'I'd be rightly irate, were I you.'

'What are you doing up, anyway?' The young man tilted his head at the rogue. 'You don't usually stir before midday unless you have to piss or you're on fire.'

'First of all, that only happened once. And I couldn't sleep. Everyone was keeping me up.'

'Everyone, huh?'

'Everyone,' he grunted. 'Gariath snores like the beast he is and Asper snores like the beast she ought to resemble. Dreadaeleon and his green-haired harlot were the worst, though.'

'What, he wanted a lullaby?'

'Apparently so.' The rogue shrugged. 'He says her songs help him focus his Venarie or clear his mind or empty his bowels or some equally stupid wizardly garbage, I don't know. At any rate, the little trollop of the sea apparently doesn't *need* to sleep, so she just hums all the Gods-damned time.' He quirked a brow. 'What were you two doing, anyway?'

'Not sleeping, same as yourself,' Lenk replied.

'Unfortunate.' He shook his head and sipped. 'I'm not sure what the procedure for marching into a demon's nest is, but I'm certain it requires at least eight hours of rest. You can't scream for mercy if you're yawning, after all.'

'I'm going to miss these little chats.'

'Well, I'll burn a candle for you later, if I happen to remember in between offering thanks to Silf that it wasn't me who got his head eaten.'

'Oh?' Someone giggled. 'You think your God loves you enough to spare you that?'

Both men glanced up, expecting to see Kataria, though neither seemed to recognise the creature stalking towards them. It was her height, same slender build, same pointed, notched ears, but it wore an entirely different skin.

Jagged bands of glistening black warpaint alternated down her body and arms, giving her a dark, animalistic appearance. Her broad canines were white against the two solid bands of black that covered her eyes and mouth. Her ears, also painstakingly painted, twitched excitedly.

'Impressive, isn't it?'

'Not precisely the word I'd use to describe you.' Lenk looked her up and down. 'And yet … I feel compelled to ask – why?'

'Why not?' She rolled her black shoulders. 'I'm about to go to war, aren't I?'

'We've done that before,' Lenk replied, 'and I've never seen you like … this … What the hell are you supposed to be, anyway?'

'A shict about to receive the favour of her Goddess,' she said proudly. 'When the land is smeared with bodies, Riffid will look down and see my colours,' she thumped her chest, 'and know that it was Kataria of the sixth tribe who killed them.'

'I see.' Lenk didn't bother to hide his cringe. 'So ... you expect to make a lot of kills today?'

'You really are stupid, aren't you?' She grinned and tapped a particularly large stripe on her belly. 'This is camouflage, you moron. We're going into some place likely rather dark and, if you hadn't noticed, I'm paler than a corpse.'

'Convenience, I'd say.' Denaos sipped his coffee. 'I mean, if you've got the pallor of a dead body, that's one less step before you're actually dead. I suppose the paint will let me know which corpse is yours when you wash up on shore.'

'If you live to see her die,' Lenk said.

Denaos stared at him blankly, disbelief straining to express itself in his eyes as a particularly venomous curse strained to break free from his lips. Lenk, for his part, merely smiled back.

'As the shict said, your God doesn't love you nearly as well as you'd hope.'

The rogue paused, opened his mouth as if to say something, but could find nothing more than a sigh to offer.

'I take it, then,' he said, 'that you've given some thought to the recovery of our precious tome.'

'I have.' Lenk nodded.

'Thusly, you've no doubt a plan.'

'I do.'

Denaos stared at him, purse-lipped, for a moment.

'And?'

The young man smiled gently. 'And you're not going to like it.'

Twenty-One

A SERMON FOR THE DAMNED

The frogmen, this one decided, still had needs.

It, for it was now far beyond a 'he', would have thought it slightly ironic, had this one still the capability to appreciate such a concept. This one had long ago grown past the desire for what it vaguely remembered as being needs. Comforts of family, of flesh and of company were no longer recalled; families died, flesh was weak, company had shunned him.

And yet, flashes of those necessities still clung frustratingly to this one, the claws of the weak and sorrowful creature this one had long ago sought to kill. While other frogmen had received Mother Deep's blessing and no longer felt the need for food or for air or for water beyond a body to immerse themselves in, this one still felt knots in its belly, could not remain underwater.

Nor, this one thought irately, could this one ignore the growing pain in its loins any longer.

Quietly, this one crept into an alcove, carved by the crumbling tower as walls fell and endless blue seeped in. This one glanced over its shoulder; if any of those ones had seen it, it knew, there would be shame, there would be pain, and Mother Deep's blessing would continually evade this one.

As it would continue to evade this one, it knew, after it

dropped its loincloth to spill its water in the shallow pool that had formed in the alcove's corner. To desecrate water blessed by the Shepherds, this one knew, was to displease Mother Deep. This one was not worried, however; Mother Deep was kind, Mother Deep was forgiving, Mother Deep had given this one the blessing of forgetting and a new life beneath the endless blue.

This one was not worried as it let itself leak out into the water with a great sigh.

This one was not worried as it felt the air grow a little colder.

It was only when this one noticed the rope descending from above that it felt the need to scream.

What emerged from its lips, however, was a strangled gargle as the thin, sharp rope bit into its neck and pulled. It felt itself slam against an unyielding surface, felt the rope knot behind its neck tighten. Its own voice fell silent as the yellow stream arced out in a terrified spray, its claws felt so feeble and weak as it raked at the rope.

'Shh,' something hissed behind it.

Its vision swam, eyes bulging from their sockets as though trying to escape. It kicked against leather, strained feebly to reach for the knife attached to the loincloth pooled around its ankles. Only as it felt its lungs tighten into pink fists inside it did this one remember the need to breathe.

A need this one never knew again.

Denaos caught the corpse as it slumped to the floor. Quietly, he laid it in the puddle of yellow filth and gave it a quick, distasteful shove. With barely a splash, it rolled over an outcropping and slipped into the black pool. No matter how shallow it might or might not have been, the frogman was well hidden from sight, and Denaos had no urge to see how deep such a pit went.

Instead, he rose and glanced out of the alcove, looking up and down the halls. The faintest traces of sunlight crept in through the faintest scratches in Irontide's hide, but even such a small source of light was not permitted to live long within the tower. It was consumed by the dark water, pulled below to die soundlessly in the brackish depths that drowned the hall.

The poetry, while not lost on Denaos, would have to wait. For the moment, he was thrilled to find no frogmen, no Abysmyths, nothing that stopped him from making a beckoning gesture. Footsteps, wince-inducingly loud, filled the hall as a pair of shadows slipped into the alcove from around a corner.

'Well done,' Lenk whispered as he hunkered into the crevasse. 'Clean and quiet.'

'Quiet, maybe,' Denaos mumbled. 'Clean, hardly.' He wrung out a lock of his hair, gagging at the drops of yellow that dropped to the floor. 'I suppose I deserve it. Silf wouldn't smile upon garrotting a man while he's draining the dragon.'

'What's …' Kataria grimaced. 'What's "draining the dragon"?'

'It's not important.' Lenk waved her down. 'Think, now. Where would they have the tome?'

'Somewhere they don't piss, I suppose.' Denaos sighed.

'Probably down there.' Kataria gestured further along the hall. 'Something's going on.'

'What's going on?'

The shict glanced at him, her ears twitching as though that would be enough. Blinking, she coughed.

'Oh, right, you're …' She shook her head. 'Never mind. It's hard to make out over all the water, but they seem to be ... chanting or something, I don't know.' She frowned. 'It's not a pleasant noise, I can tell you that.'

'Chanting is never good,' Lenk muttered. 'As if we needed any more reason to grab the tome and get out of here quickly.'

'Agreed.' Kataria nodded. She glanced between the two men. 'So, uh ... which one of you knows where it is?'

'You might be missing the point of this. If we knew where it was, we wouldn't be stumbling about in the dark waiting for our heads to be eaten.' Lenk glanced down the hall. 'I'll wager, however, that whatever there is to be found is probably going to be found with the chanting.'

'What we'll find is a bunch of bloodthirsty demons,' Denaos grumbled. 'And, given that we have the rare opportunity of knowing where they are, we should probably go in the other direction.'

'Do you have a better idea?' Lenk held up a hand before the rogue could reply. 'Do you have a better idea that *doesn't* involve running away or soiling ourselves?'

'Ah, well ... you've got me there.'

'Yeah,' Lenk grunted. He glanced out of the alcove, then back to Denaos. 'We'll continue as we have, with you on point and Kataria covering our ... or rather *my* rear.'

'And what will you be doing while I'm sniffing your farts?' the shict sneered. 'Put me in the lead.'

'Fat lot of good that piece of wood will do you in the lead.' Denaos pointed at her bow. 'It's too cramped in here to draw the damn thing, let alone hit anything.'

'And if *you* go in the lead, we'll be found out for sure.' She twitched her ears. 'I could hear that splash for ages after you dumped the body.'

'Well, I'm trusting our enemies *don't* have ears the size

of Saine.' He snorted. 'I seem to be doing a good job of it so far.'

'Any dim-witted *Kou'ru* can sneak around and strangle something,' Kataria hissed. '*True* stalking is a delicate practice, involving equal parts verbal and non-verbal.'

'Verbal … you *do* know the point is to stay silent, don't you?'

Whatever retort she had was cut off by the sound of legs splashing through the water, however. They tensed as one, waiting for the sound to pass. While it did so, they could still hear the heavy breathing of something just around the corner.

'Hello?' it gurgled. 'Is that one there?'

Before anyone could stop her, Kataria sprang out from the alcove and levelled her bow at the creature.

'No,' she replied.

Air split apart, there was a hollow sound, then the sound of something slumping quietly beneath the black waters. Kataria cast a glance over her shoulder at Denaos and grinned haughtily.

'Case in point.' She slung her bow over her shoulder. '*I'll* take lead.'

'For a fortress, there's not much to it, is there?' Lenk murmured as quietly as he could as they crept through the hallway.

Total silence had become unattainable; the water seeping into the fortress had drowned the halls in ever-rising tides. It was all they could do to restrain their fears of something reaching out and seizing them from below as they mucked through the knee-high deeps.

'I haven't seen any rooms,' he continued, 'no barracks, no kitchens, no mess …'

They hesitated where the hall forked into two black

paths. Kataria glanced up and down both, ears twitching, before gesturing for the two men to follow as she stalked further into Irontide. The sunlight, terrified even to peek a scant ray any further, completely disappeared, leaving them sloshing about in the dark.

'If rumours can be trusted,' Denaos replied softly, 'there used to be sleeping quarters down here.' He pointed towards the dripping ceiling. 'Business was conducted further up.'

'So what happened?' Kataria whispered.

'All I know is stories.'

'And what did they say?' the shict pressed.

She could feel his morbid grin twist into her back.

'Supposedly,' he muttered, 'when the Navy finally seized Irontide, they made their examples down here.' He rapped his knuckles against the stone. 'The smugglers barricaded themselves in here. The Navy responded by punching a hole through the wall with their catapults.'

'And?'

'And then … high tide.'

She paused at that, taking a moment to waste a sneer in the darkness.

'Dirty trick,' she muttered. 'But they're just stories.'

No reply from the back.

'Right?'

'They might be,' Lenk replied for the rogue. 'History's full of worse ways to die and the people who think them up.' He spared a stifled laugh. 'I suppose we should take a certain amount of pride in that we'll probably be experiencing some of the more awful ways first-hand.'

'You're a delight,' Denaos growled softly. 'Why have we stopped, anyway? At least with the sound of water, I don't have to listen to *you*.'

Kataria leaned forwards in the gloom, narrowing her eyes. The two men held their breath behind her, nearly springing backwards when they heard her morbid chuckle.

'There's light ahead,' she whispered, 'and voices, too. We're getting close.'

'What kind of voices?' Lenk asked.

'Frogmen.' She looked thoughtful as her ears twitched. 'Something else, too.'

'Abysmyths?' Lenk tightened his grip on his sword.

'No.' She shook her head and frowned. 'I thought I had heard something else, but I must have been mistaken.'

'You're never mistaken,' Lenk said, quickly correcting himself, 'when it comes to noise, anyway. What did you hear?'

'A female's voice.' Her frown grew so heavy that it threatened to fall off her face and splash into the murk. 'It almost … sounded like the siren.'

'Aha!' Denaos grimaced at his own cry. 'I could have told you. She's led us to our deaths.'

'Kat said it *sounded* like Greenhair,' Lenk replied harshly, 'we don't know if it's her or not.'

'How many things in this blessed world of ours sound like some fish-whore?' the rogue snarled. '*How many?*'

'I guess we'll find out, won't we?'

Lenk hefted his sword, gave Kataria a gentle push to urge her onwards. The shict responded by nocking an arrow, slinking forwards silently. Creeping into the gloom as they did, their steps heralded by the sounds of water sloshing, neither man nor shict glanced over a shoulder to see if the rogue followed.

Denaos had always thought of himself as a sensible man, a sensible man with very vocal instincts that currently shouted at him to turn around and let the others die on their own. It was suicide to follow; if, by some miracle of faith in fish-women, Greenhair hadn't betrayed them, there might be another siren within the forsaken hold.

He recalled Greenhair's song, her power to send men, even dragonmen, into slumber. The thought of snoring blissfully at some sea-witch's tune while an Abysmyth quietly munched his head down to the neck held no great appeal.

Even if they *did* survive long enough to lay a finger upon the tome, what then? How would they escape? Even if they survived and were paid in full, how long would it be before he was placed in another situation where head-eating was a very likely outcome?

The sensible thing, he told himself, *would be to turn back now, find a merchantman and hitch a ride back to decent folk.*

'Sensible,' he reaffirmed to himself, 'indeed.'

He knew that the tome lay with something that he did not seek to find. But he knew much more certainly that the things he didn't want to find were in the shadows that turned sensible men to cowards.

And, he reminded himself as he sighed and began to wade after them, he was a sensible man.

'I do not remember ever being loved by Gods.'

The frogman finished its sentence with a slam of its staff, driving it against the stones, letting the various bones attached to its head rattle against its ivory shaft. Dozens of pale faces looked up at the creature reverently, black eyes reflecting the torches that burnt with a pure emerald fire.

Dozens of faces, the frogman thought, free of scars, free of birthmarks, free of overbites, underbites, deformities, hair colours. Dozens of faces, all the same beaming pale-ness, all the same mouths twisted shut in reverence, all the same black eyes looking up at it, silently begging for the sermon to continue.

And the frogman indulged them.

'I do not remember a day without suffering,' it said, letting its voice echo off the vast chamber walls. 'And I do not remember a day when my suffering served any purpose but for the amusement of what I once thought of as beings perfect and pure.'

The faces tensed in reply. The frogman snarled, baring teeth.

'And I do not *want* to remember.'

At this, they bobbed their heads in unison, muttering quietly through their own jagged teeth.

'What I remember,' it hissed, 'is praying daily at the shores for a false mother to deliver food. What I remember is starvation. What I remember is those that I once called my family being swallowed up and the waves mocking me. I remember.' It levelled its staff at the congregation. 'And so do you.'

'Memory is our curse,' they replied in unison, bowing their heads. 'May Mother Deep forever free us.'

'I thought the sea to be harsh and cruel, then,' it continued, 'but that is when I heard Her song.' It tilted its head back, closing its eyes in memory. 'I remember Her calling to me, singing to me. I remember Her assuring me that my life was precious, valuable, but my body was weak. I remember Her leading me here, granting me Her gifts, to breathe the water, to dance beneath the waves,' its face stiffened, 'to forget …

'I do not remember Gods talking to me.' It craned to face the congregation once more. 'I do remember them asking me for my wealth and to deny others their wealth.' Its smile was broad and full of teeth. 'And so did Mother

459

Deep bid me to shatter their pretences by asking these ones to come, penniless and alone, fearful and betrayed, full of aching memory. She bade these ones to return and forget the lies they had been told. She gave these ones gifts and asked for but one thing in return.'

The faces brightened in response, reflecting the frog-man's smile.

'She asks,' they chanted, 'only that these ones aid the Shepherds as the Shepherds aid these ones.'

They spoke, and their voices reverberated through the water that had claimed the stones and the few stones the water had spared drowning. They spoke, and their voices caused the green flames to leap to life at their words as they burned in their sconces. They spoke, and a dozen as yet unheard voices, sealed behind sacs of flesh and skins of mucus, pulsated in response.

It would have thought them disgusting, it reflected, and chastised itself for the blasphemy. Something that it once was would have thought them disgusting, these glorious creations of Mother Deep that clung to the walls and pillars. Now, the frogman, the creature that it had become, knew them to be Her blessings made manifest.

They pulsated, beat like miniature hearts, bulbous and glistening, misshapen and glowing. Inside these great and vile creations of flesh and fluid, something stirred. Trapped within these skins, something sought to glow with the light of life. Beyond the glistening moisture that clung to them, something reflected only blackness.

'Disgusting,' Lenk muttered, sneering at the pulsating sacs. 'What *are* they?'

Neither rogue nor shict had a response for him beyond a reflection of his own repulsion. The vast and sprawling chamber, as though it had not yet been desecrated enough by the black water that drowned it and the green and red graffiti that caked its walls, was absolutely infected with the things. They clung to every corner, bobbed in the water, hung from every pillar. The largest of them was suspended directly above the circle of frogmen, twitching with a thunderous pulse, threatening to drop at any moment.

'I'm rather more concerned with what they're doing,' Denaos muttered with a grimace as the frogmen began to rhythmically sway. 'Any ceremony accompanied by ritualistic chanting tends to end with eviscerations, in my experience.'

'I *am* slightly tempted to enquire, but all the same.' Lenk nudged Kataria's shoulder. 'Any sign of Abysmyths?'

'Not that I can see.' Her eyes were narrowed, sweeping the chamber. 'Take that as you will, though. They're large, black things in a large, black room.'

'Well, we can hardly wait here for them to come and eat us,' the young man murmured. 'We'll have to move soon.'

'To where, exactly?'

Lenk glanced about the hall. Options, it seemed, were limited. The chamber had undoubtedly once been grand, though its vast ceiling had begun to sink, its marching pillars had crumbled and its floor was completely lost to the water, save for the sprawling stone island that the frogmen congregated upon.

He didn't even bother to note the torches crackling an unnatural green and the hanging sacs; there would be time enough to soil himself over those details later.

Though nearly unnoticeable through the gloom, he spied a crumbling archway at the chamber's furthest corner. Half-drowned, half-cloaked in shadow, what lay beyond it was veiled in forbidding void.

'There,' he pointed, 'that's the way.'

'How do you figure?' Kataria grunted.

'Because we seem to have a habit of going into places that would result in our deaths and I'd hate to ruin our rhythm.'

'Sound reasoning as any. However,' Denaos gestured to the prostrate frogmen, 'how do you intend to get past them?'

'Luck? Prayer?' The young man shrugged.

'Neither of which ever seem to work for *me*,' the rogue countered. 'Hence, before we decide to rush off all at once and possibly die together, let's do a bit of scouting.' He gestured to Kataria. 'Send the shict out first.'

The suggestion struck Lenk like an open-handed slap and he felt himself tense at it, fixing a scowl upon the rogue. In the back of his mind, he knew such an anger shouldn't have been stirred within him; after all, his companions had nothing in common save complete disregard for each other's well-being.

All the same, he couldn't help but tighten his grip on his sword irately.

'Yeah, that works.'

If Denaos had slapped him, Kataria's response all but knocked him into the water. He whirled on her suddenly with eyes wide.

'What?' he sputtered. 'Wait, why?'

'It makes sense, doesn't it? I'm the best stalker. I should go ahead and see if this even has a chance of working.'

She unstrung her bow and pulled a small leather pouch from her belt. Quietly coiling the string, she secured it tightly within the pouch before popping it into her mouth and swallowing it. Her unpleasant smile at the men's revulsion was accompanied by a wink.

462

'Wet bows don't shoot.'

'That's not what I'm worried about. You might get killed.'

She blinked at him.

'And?' Not waiting for an answer, she turned, crouching low into the water. 'Assuming you can see me when I reach the door, follow.'

'But ... Fine.'

Lenk found the words coming out of his mouth with more exasperation than they should have. He watched her slide into the water, her black-painted flesh melding seamlessly into the gloom. Only the tips of her ears, protruding from the surface like the dorsal fins of two fish, gave any indication of her presence.

It was only after she was almost totally out of sight that he whispered to her fading form.

'Be careful.'

'She'll be fine,' Denaos muttered.

'Of course, no great loss if she dies.' Lenk cast a cold, narrow scowl over his shoulder. 'Right?'

'Given the circumstances, I would think the opposite. I'd rather have a working bow than a corpse.'

'Don't act coy.'

'It's no act, I assure you.'

'Well, in case you hadn't noticed,' Lenk spat, 'I still hold a grudge over what you said on the beach.'

'You'll have to be more specific.'

'I mean—' The young man paused, scowling at his taller companion. 'You really are scum, you know that?'

'It has been suggested before.' The rogue shrugged. 'And yes, of course I know what you're talking about.'

'And?'

'And,' Denaos bit his lip contemplatively, 'I'm a tad hard pressed to care.'

Lenk had no retort for that, merely staring at the tall man with a blend of incredulousness and anger that vaguely resembled an uncomfortable bowel movement. Before he could even begin to think of something to say, however, Denaos held up a hand.

'And before you decide to see just how far up you can shove that sword, let me explain something to you.' He sighed a sort of sigh that a father reserves for uncomfortable discussions with a son aspiring to be a seamstress. 'Listen, you're still young, rather naive to the ways of the world, but I consider you enough of a friend to tell you that you're wasting your time.'

The rogue's words were lost on Lenk, so many unheard echoes in the void of his ears, fading quickly with every breath. And with every breath, another voice spoke more loudly in his head.

'*He is weak.*'

'You're a human,' Denaos continued, 'she's a shict. Don't get me wrong, I'm delighted you found a pointy-eared shrew to lavish undue affection upon, if only for the sake of loosening you up, but don't think for a breath that the feeling is shared.'

'*She is weak, as well.*'

'Whatever you may think of her, of everyone in the little social circle we've created, it's all completely pointless.'

'*They will both die here.*'

'In the end, you can't change what you are, and neither can she.'

'*We will live on, though.*'

'She's a shict. You're a human. Enemies.'

'*Our enemy lies within this forsaken church.*'

464

'Centuries upon centuries of open warfare won't lapse just for you, my friend.'

'*We will make our war upon the creature that leads these abominations.*'

'She'll shoot you in the back as soon as she feels the impulse.'

'*We will carve out the pestilence that festers here.*'

'So don't blame me for holding a view that the rest of the world knows to be true.'

'*We will cleanse this world.*'

'It's all moot, anyway. You clearly haven't heard a word I've said.'

'*And it begins ... now.*'

'Now ...' Lenk whispered.

'NOW!' another voice echoed.

They whirled about as one, suddenly aware that the rhythmic chanting had reached an abhorrent crescendo. The voices were incoherent, tainted by the sound of croaking and gurgling, punctuated by clawed hands raised, trembling, to the sunken ceiling. All knelt prostrate, all babbled wildly in mockery of a proper hymn.

All but one.

'Now is the time,' the frogman with the staff uttered, 'now is when these ones' suffering and hardships are rewarded.'

It raised its staff to the ceiling and the pulsating sac above responded. It ceased to beat like a heart and began to tremble furiously, shaking angrily against the thick strands of mucus that held it to the stones. Areas of it stretched, extended, indentations of thick fingers pressed against the viscous skin.

The frogmen responded, their voices rising and falling in ecstatic discord with every push from within the tumour-like womb. The staff-bearing creature seemed to rise higher, held aloft by their fervent chanting as it shook its staff at the ceiling.

'Come to these ones, Shepherd,' it crowed, 'and grant these ones the gifts that were promised.'

'Free these ones from the chains of memory and the sins of air,' the chorus chanted.

'The feasts that were promised,' the high frogman croaked, 'the gifts that were whispered, the song that is yearning to be heard ...'

'Sing to these ones,' the chorus spoke, 'and deliver the world—'

'TO ENDLESS BLUE!'

The frogman's invocation echoed through the hall.

It did not go unanswered.

There was the sound of flesh ripping as the sac split apart against the force of a long, black arm. It dangled, glistening like onyx, from the ceiling for but a moment before the ripping became a harsh groan.

Lenk's breath caught in his throat as the womb tore open violently, expelling a blur of blackness that collapsed onto the floor with a heavy, hollow sound. From the quivering strands of leathery flesh that dangled from the ruined womb, droplets of a thick, glimmering substance coagulated, shivered and fell. The frogmen rolled their heads back, expressions twisted into orgasmic mirrors of each other as the substance splattered across their faces.

There was no time for the young man to vomit, no breath left in him to even contemplate doing such a thing. Unable to turn away, he continued to stare as the blob of darkness began to stir in the circle of frogmen.

Without so much as a whisper, it rose to its knees. Even so prostrate, it towered over the row of hairless heads before it. Its body trembled, sending thick globs of the ooze peeling off its flesh. With a violent cough, expelling more of the foul stuff, its head rose: two vacant white eyes stared up, a jaw filled with white teeth lowered.

And, freshly born, the Abysmyth screamed.

'Sons of . . .'

The meagre breath that Denaos was able to conjure was still more than Lenk could manage. The young man's jaw hung slack, his sword limp at his side. He could not blink, for fear that when he opened his eyes again, the demon would still be there.

The creature took no notice of the men, however. It swayed upon its knees, oblivious to its surroundings as the frogmen crowded around it, scooping globs of the viscous ooze in both hands and devouring it messily, choking on their own moans as they shovelled, lapped and slurped the demonic afterbirth into their craws.

'*This is only the beginning*,' the voice murmured within Lenk's head, '*and we are the ending.*'

'Do we kill it?' Lenk asked quietly.

'Are you mad?' Denaos, incredulous, was unaware of the unseen speaker.

'*No. Too many tumours. We go deeper.*'

'At any rate,' the rogue whispered, 'we'd better get a move on. Kat's found the way.'

The mention of her name caused him to blink. The sight of a few bands of pale flesh at the furthest edge of the chamber caused him to smile. The shict, her eyes so wide as to be visible across the waters, seemed barely able to tear her attention away from the ghastly scene long enough to beckon them over.

'We go, then,' Lenk whispered.

He sheathed his sword and slid into the gloom, Denaos

467

close behind him. Quietly, they darted between the bobbing sacs, careful not to look too closely into any of them. Filling their ears were the sounds of things moving within and the choked moans of the frogmen's gluttony.

'Silf preserve me.' Denaos's grumble was mingled with the sound of water sloshing as he pulled himself up the steady slope and onto dry land. 'But in a fortress crawling with demons, breeches riding up on me should be the *last* of my problems.'

'Could be worse.' Kataria wrung her long braid free of the black water as she crawled out of the gloom. 'At least there *aren't* any frogmen here.'

'True.' Lenk was last to pull himself free. He paused, casting a glance down the twisting corridor they had just swum through; the chanting had begun again and now echoed listlessly. 'They're still far too close for my liking, however.'

'All the more reason to get moving.' Kataria held up a finger, then lurched. Her mouth opened, a vile gagging sound emerging from within. Her whole body shuddered, then the tiny leather pouch was in her hand. Pulling the string out, she began to reassemble her bow. 'Right, then. Where to?'

Lenk quietly surveyed their new surroundings, if only to avert his gaze from the shict's nauseating display. The hall was refreshingly large after the oppressively cramped passages of Irontide. The torches, while still burning an unnatural green, did so with as little malice as an unnaturally green fire could manage. All in all, he thought, the broad hall was rather pleasant.

That worried him.

The dilapidation that plagued the rest of the keep was strangely absent. The walls were of a smooth, polished stone that resembled emerald against the crackling torchlight. At the end of the hall, a tall, square doorway had been carved, the green light pouring from beyond like venom from a serpent's maw.

'I only see one way.' He sighed, gesturing with his chin. 'Denaos, take the lead.'

'Of course.' The rogue sighed dramatically. 'Why not? I've already been doused in some reeking foulness that's gone so far up my nose I can see the filth behind my eyes. Nothing else could be too much worse.'

'On second thought,' Lenk drew his sword, 'I'll take the lead.' Shoving the rogue aside, he strode cautiously towards the door. 'If there's something waiting up ahead to dismember us, I think I'd like to go first to spare me your whining.'

Despite weapons in hand and an irate growl from Denaos, their trek towards the doorway was less than cautious. *Why wouldn't it be?* Lenk thought. *It's not like anything can hide here.* For all the tension that coursed through them, the young man almost felt disappointed that their journey was so uneventful.

'Wait here,' he whispered.

'Be careful.'

He felt a hand on his shoulder and turned to face two hard emerald eyes. He cracked a grin that he hoped was reassuring and hefted his sword as he slipped through the massive stone frame. He could hear their held breaths with each step, their silence speaking the fear their voices could not.

'Think we're close?' Denaos whispered to the shict.

'Might be,' she grunted. 'I've never known Lenk to guide us wrong.' She smiled. 'He just takes us on unorthodox routes.'

'Unorthodox,' the rogue muttered, 'a much kinder word than I was going to use.'

Lenk paused beyond the doorway as he cast a scrutinising glance about this new chamber. Many moments passed before he turned around and shrugged, then returned to searching.

Kataria was about to take a step to join him when something struck her as amiss: she could hear her footsteps. The sound of silence was deafening in her ears.

'Do you …' she glanced at Denaos, 'hear anything?'

The rogue cast her a crooked scowl before the same realisation filled his eyes.

'Nothing,' he whispered, 'the chanting's stopped.'

Before Kataria could reply, she felt a sudden chill. Something cold and wet plopped upon her shoulder and trickled down her bare back. Swallowing hard, she reached behind and took a bit of it between her fingers. It was too thick for water, she realised, and carried a peculiar but familiar odour.

Sparing no words for surprise or disgust, she felt the chill grow colder, a long shadow descending over her.

'Oh,' she gasped, looking up, 'hell …'

She saw herself reflected in the Abysmyth's white eyes for a moment before a long, black claw seized her by the throat. Her scream was wordless and terrified as she was hoisted into the air.

Lenk whirled about at the cry, his sword up and feet moving before he even knew what had happened. He had barely taken a step, however, before the entire fortress trembled. A massive stone block fell with a thunderous crash, wedging itself firmly in the doorway and banishing Lenk behind a vast screen of grey.

Kataria barely had time to glimpse the sight of another

demon grabbing Denaos, the rogue going limp in its claws, before her captor whirled her about. Her bow effortlessly wrenched from her grasp, her quiver torn from her back and tossed to the earth, she was helpless as the demon presented her before dozens of pale faces, each one a perfect copy of the others, looking at her through malicious black eyes.

And at their fore was their staff-bearing leader, the only face to be twisted into a broad, needle-toothed grin as it croaked.

'Mother Deep ... has sent us much.'

Twenty-Two

THE COLOUR OF PAIN

Irontide was a thing oblivious to the sun.

As dark and foreboding in the bright afternoon as at dusk, it turned a stony and shadowed face to the shore, frowning with its many catapult-carved gashes, grinning with its corpse-laden spikes when the waters receded. A dispassionate monarch of the waves, Irontide was unmoved by the concerned stare that had bored into it since early morning, choosing to show the fate of those who defied it whenever disapproving eyes lingered too long.

The metaphor, Asper decided, was fitting. Irontide was a tyrant, complete with its own crown of parasites.

The Omens shimmered in the afternoon sun, ruffling feathers, heads twisting on stiff necks as they swept their bulbous eyes about the sea. The priestess was not afraid to stand openly upon the beach as she did; the little creatures showed no signs of moving. Rather, she found herself staring at them expectantly, holding her breath every time they chattered their teeth in a chorus, wondering if they would begin mimicking the sounds of her dying companions as they were torn into pieces by whatever lurked within the fortress.

The demons, to their credit, seemed to possess enough tact to spare her such a thing.

And yet, she thought resentfully, even a horrific echo

472

from their withered maws would give her at least *some* notion of what was going on inside. The Omens gave no indication that they had any more idea than she, and stood as they had for ages: organised in neat, white rows upon the battlements, wide eyes unblinking even as the light of an angry afternoon sun poured mercilessly into them.

A sun, Asper noted, that hung ominously high.

'Four hours.' She sighed.

While she hadn't expected any great outpouring of emotion from her companion, she felt compelled to scowl at Gariath as he stared off towards the jungle, snout upturned and nostrils flickering.

'Four hours since they went in,' she reiterated.

Gariath, apparently realising she wasn't going to be content with showing off her ability to tell time, flared his ear-frills aggressively and glared.

'And?'

'Shouldn't they be back by now?' she asked.

'Had I gone with them, they should,' he snorted. 'Since I'm here, however, their corpses might wash up in a day or two.'

'Are you being scornful,' Asper glared at him, 'or just insensitive?'

'I wasn't aware I had to choose between the two,' he replied, and turned his attention back to the jungle.

She would have suggested that they go in after their, supposedly, mutual companions, but wisdom held her tongue. Whyever Lenk had decided to go in with only Kataria and Denaos, perhaps two of the less reliable companions, to watch his back, she was certain he had reason.

It seemed to make sense to her, at any rate, since the remaining two members seemed to be less interested than she was. Dreadaeleon sat some distance down the beach,

473

babbling excitedly with Greenhair, who had yet to show even an ounce of concern, despite seeming the most knowledgeable regarding what might happen within the tower. Her apathy seemed to have infected the boy; he hadn't moved since luring the Omens away with his glamer long enough to allow Lenk and the others to slip in.

As for Gariath, she had to admit she was a tad surprised to see him so calm about being left behind. The dragonman, however, seemed even less concerned than the others. That was only surprising due to his eagerness to kill. Yet even that appeared restrained as he stared towards the jungle, inhaling deeply.

She had been content to allow him whatever eccentricities a two-legged reptile might be entitled to for the first three hours, but after so long without even a bat of his leathery eyelid, she took a step forwards.

'What *are* you doing, anyway?'

'I *was* ignoring you,' he replied calmly, 'but I suppose the spirits don't love me today, do they?'

'And these spirits allow you to remain so calm while our friends are possibly being eviscerated in there?' She gestured fervently to the tower. 'I must admit, I'm a bit intrigued.'

'First of all, they're not *all* friends to me,' he grunted. 'Secondly, the spirits have no use for weak and ugly creatures.' He rolled his shoulders. 'The spirits protect the strong. Lenk is strong. He will survive.'

'And the others?'

'Dead,' he replied. 'The pointy-eared one might die quicker than the rat, *if* the spirits are merciful.'

'I ... see. So, uh ...' She found herself eager to begin a new topic, if only to take her mind off which chunks of her friends might or might not be in the process of being torn

474

out at that moment. 'Is it ... the spirits you're smelling?'

'Don't be stupid,' he said, inhaling. 'I'm smelling a memory.'

'Oh ... well, I guess that makes sense.' She scratched her head. 'What are the spirits, anyway?'

'You wouldn't understand.'

'Oh, of course *I* wouldn't.' She rolled her eyes. 'Perhaps the only person of worldly faith amongst this whole Godless band of heathens, and *I*, of course, wouldn't understand the religion of a walking, bloodthirsty lizard.'

'No, you wouldn't.' The dragonman's tone was decidedly calm for the accusation. Or at least distracted, Asper thought; either way, she resisted the urge to take off running. He simply drew in a deep breath. 'It's not a religion.'

'Then what is it?'

'Live well, protect the family,' Gariath grunted. 'And the spirits are honoured enough to give you the strength to do it.'

'So ... it *is* a religion.' She chanced a step forwards. 'I mean, it's not so different amongst us ... er, amongst humans.'

'So I've noticed,' he replied without looking at her. 'Humans are rather fond of having so many different weak Gods from whom they claim to draw strength. And with that strength, they try to kill everyone who doesn't kneel before the right weak God.' He chuckled blackly. 'And somehow, no weak God gives their followers enough strength to *truly* bless the world and wipe each other out. There are always more humans.'

'Well, that's not *quite* how it works. I mean, Talanas is the Healer, He—'

'Gives you the strength to clean up after the other weak

Gods' messes,' Gariath interrupted. 'I suppose I have you to thank for knowing all this about humans and their useless faiths, since you never shut up about them.'

Asper self-consciously rubbed her left arm.

'It's ... not always about power.'

'Then what's the point?'

Asper found herself disarmed by the question. She had been mentally preparing her arsenal of responses, all sharply honed from years of debate with other scholars of faith. *Other human scholars*, she corrected herself; amongst her own people, her weaponry had always been enough. Her responses were accepted, her reasoning commonplace, her retorts cutting deeply against the shield of human rhetoric.

And yet, she stood still, too stunned even to be galled at the fact that she had been rendered speechless by a simple question. And yet, all the more galling, she had enough wits left about her to realise why it left her so paralysed.

She was, she realised, a custodian. She was a matron who had, thus far, kissed scratches and massaged bruises, whose limitations had been proven the day before. Kataria, breathless and still upon the sands, was still vivid and fresh in her mind. Now she saw the visions again, visions of things yet to pass: her companions bleeding out on the stones of Irontide, drowning in the clutches of demons, eviscerated on whatever infernal altars they had constructed in the tower's unhallowed depths.

And here she was ... left behind.

Now she knew why Lenk had chosen not to take her.

'Do the spirits make you a better fighter?'

Now it was the dragonman's turn to stand speechless. He cast her a glance that suggested he was unsure whether to ignore her or spill her innards upon the sand. She was

476

more than a tad surprised when he rolled his shoulders and answered.

'A spirit is only as strong as the body that honours it.' He raised an eyeridge. 'Why?'

'Can you teach me to fight?'

She held her breath as he looked her up and down, not with derision or scorn, but genuine appraisal. When he finally spoke, she was slightly less surprised that it was with swiftness and decisiveness.

'No.'

'Why not?'

'You're too weak, too stupid, too cowardly, too human,' he replied crassly.

'Humans have won many wars, you know.' She attempted to mime his tone. 'I mean, if you haven't noticed, we *are* the dominant race.'

'Humans only win wars against other humans,' he growled. 'You breed like cockroaches, fight like rats, die like mosquitoes and expect to receive any respect from a *Rhega*?' He waved a hand dismissively. 'Satisfy yourself with staying behind and cleaning up after real warriors.'

'You once told me that all dragonmen fight.' She furrowed her brow angrily. 'Doesn't that include the healers?'

'*Rhega* don't need healers. Our skin is strong and our bones mend as quick as yours don't.' He turned his back to her and flexed for emphasis, every crimson cord pronounced. 'I've got things to do now.'

'Things to smell, you mean?'

When he did not respond to her, she took a challenging step forwards, unaware of how softly her feet fell in comparison to his tremendous red soles. Perhaps it was the fact that he had turned his back on her that made her so bold, or perhaps she wished to prove to herself that she was made of sterner stuff than he suggested.

'If humans only win human wars,' she cried after him, 'why aren't there more *Rhega* around?'

What her motive might have been, even she did not know. As he turned and stalked towards her, with an air of calmness that suggested she wouldn't be able to run far if she tried, she steeled herself. She had issued the challenge, she told herself, and it was her time to stand by it.

'Hit me.' He spoke disturbingly softly.

'What?' She half-cringed, looking baffled.

'Here is where you learn to,' he replied calmly. 'Hit me as hard as you can.'

An unfamiliar sense of dread befell Asper, a stubborn battle between fear and pride raging inside her. It was never a good idea, in principle, to hit a creature bristling with horns and claws, even if he requested it. *No*, she scolded herself, *stand by the challenge.*

She simply had not realised when she had issued it how small she stood against his red mass. Nevertheless, with a clench of her teeth, she balled one hand into a fist and launched a swing against the dragonman's chest.

It struck with a hollow sound, which she, at that moment, swore reverberated like metal. She pulled back not a fist, but a throbbing, swollen red mass of skin and scraped knuckles.

It didn't even occur to her to moan in pain, nor even to wince, for the moment she glanced up, she spied a tremendous red claw hurtling towards her. The back of his hand connected fiercely with the side of her face and sent her sprawling to the ground, any sound she might have made gone silent against the crack of flesh against bone.

Pressing red hand to red cheek, she sat up slowly and

looked at the dragonman, her shock barely visible behind the massive bruise forming upon it.

'What ...' It hurt to speak, so she had to exchange the indignant fury broiling inside her mouth for something more achievable. '*Why?*'

'You hit me.'

'You told me to!'

'And what did you learn today?'

Every sound he made diminished her further. His footsteps echoed in her aching jaw, his tail lashing upon the ground made her hand throb all the worse. It was his back, however, turned callously towards her, that caused tears to well in her eyes, that caused her to rise.

Though her right hand had been the one to sting, it was her left arm that tensed so tightly it sent waves of pain rolling into her. That pain consumed all others, giving her the ability to trudge after the dragonman, her arm hanging low like a cudgel. And like a cudgel, spiked and merciless, she could see herself wielding it against him.

His neck looked so tempting then, blending in with her eyes as her vision reddened further with each breath. She could see herself through the crimson, reaching out to grab him, his neck a pulsing red vein that she need merely pinch shut and ...

'*No!*' She clasped her agonised hand to her left arm, the pain blossoming again like a garden. 'No ... no. Stop thinking that. It's not right. Stop it.' She struck her temple with her red hand. '*Stop it!*'

'Is that really intelligent?'

She resisted the urge to whirl about before she could wipe the tears from her eyes. Dreadaeleon appeared concerned as he saw her purpling cheek and reddening hand, though not quite as horrified as she thought he should.

'What happened to *you*?'

'Fight,' she grumbled, 'nothing much. Learned something ... I don't know. Gariath hit me.'

'Oh.'

In civilised countries, there would be a call to arms over a man striking a woman. In the quaint culture of adventurers, bludgeoning tended to be more on the unavoidable side of things.

'It ... hurts?' Greenhair was not far behind the boy, tilting her head curiously at the priestess, whose eyelid twitched momentarily.

'Oh, not at all,' Asper replied. 'Having my hand smashed and my jaw cracked seems to have evened out into a nice state of *being in searing pain. Of course it hurts, you imbecile!*' Wincing at her own snap, she held up a hand, wiggling red fingers. 'It doesn't seem to be broken ... I should be fine.'

'I could assist, if you so desired, Darkeyes.'

Asper had to force herself not to recoil at the suggestion.

She had felt the siren's song before, when the creature had offered her aid in treating the companions' injuries. The priestess thanked Talanas that hers were the least serious. The lyrics were more invasive than a scalpel, going far beyond her ears and sinking into her bones. Though she felt bruises soothed and cuts cease their sting, she was forced to fight the urge to tear herself open in a desperate bid to force the song out.

Bandages and salves were slower and sloppier, but they were natural and Talanas's gifts to His servants. *They're at least a sight more trustworthy than whatever some fish-woman-thing can spew out*, she thought resentfully. Instead of saying that, however, she merely forced a smile.

'I'll take care of it,' she replied with a sigh. 'It's not like

480

I've got anything better to do while the *real* warriors are off … warrioring.'

'Warring,' Dreadaeleon corrected.

'I knew that, you little …' She trailed off into incoherent mumbling as she began to trudge away. 'It just needs a splint, a bit of binding. It'll fix itself in a bit.'

'You didn't break it, did you?'

'First of all, I already said it wasn't broken.' She whirled on him with a snarl. 'And if anyone *did* break it, it would be Gariath.'

'He hit your hand?' The boy raised an eyebrow. 'That seems a tad indirect.'

'He *broke* it when I hit him in the mass of metal he calls a chest.'

'Well, no wonder he hit you.'

'He *told* me to hit him!' she roared. 'And what kind of logic is that, anyway? His fist is the size of my head! How is that at all justified?'

'Oh … um, are you being irrational?' The boy cringed. 'Denaos said this might happen while he was gone. And, I mean, you couldn't have been thinking too clearly to have actually thought hitting Gariath was a good idea.'

'I could clear your mind, Darkeyes,' Greenhair offered with a smile, 'if you so wished.'

She affixed a scowl to both of their heads, her only wish being that she could replace her eyes with a sturdy quarterstaff. Her rage only intensified as they turned, with infuriating symmetry, to look at Irontide, pausing to exchange an encouraging smile.

There was a time, she thought irately, when Dreadaeleon would have withered under her glare. Now, even the scrawniest creature posing as a man put up a defiant face

481

against her. And at that thought, her heart sank into a foetid pool of doubt.

Am I truly so weak, she asked herself, *that I can't even intimidate* him?

It would seem so. He stood tall upon the shore, taller than ever before. He stood uncrippled by his previous malady; *A malady that only I could cure. Up until now*, she added, scowling at Greenhair. Beside her, he stood erect, proud and completely oblivious to her best attempts to gnaw on his face with scornful eyes.

'Look at that.' He gestured to Irontide with insulting casualness. 'She ... it? Whatever hasn't stopped moving since dawn.'

Asper glanced up and frowned. It was difficult to maintain her anger at the sight of Irontide's crown; another more loathsome sensation crept over her.

The greater Omen skulked up and down the lines of its lesser parasitic kin like a general inspecting its troops. Of course, Asper admitted, there was no way to tell if the creature was even looking at the others; they were much too far away to make out even the barest detail of features besides the creature's size.

And yet, the revulsion it emanated was tangible even from the shore. Everything about it was horrible: its ungainly gait, its bobbing head, its messy, angular body. Asper admitted with momentary unabashedness that she would much prefer it to remain far away.

Of course, she thought with a frown, *Gariath wouldn't even hesitate to get up and tear its wings off ... Are those wings or hands?*

'Fascinating, isn't it?'

Her frown became a deep gash across her face; it

appeared that someone else wasn't at all bashful about the creature's presence, either.

'All those Omens,' Dreadaeleon gestured out to the tower, 'standing perfectly still.'

'It's not like they've got anything else to do,' Asper grunted.

'They are the vermin of hell, Lorekeeper,' Greenhair agreed. 'They bear not the gifts of thought and heart.'

'We know that much, certainly. But look, they aren't moping about.' He glanced at Asper. 'Recall that, whenever we've found them separated from an Abysmyth ... or should I say *their* Abysmyth, they've always looked addled, distraught.'

'We've only seen that happen once,' Asper replied.

'Twice – Gariath said they were acting in such a way when he was disposing of them.' He paused, licked his lips. 'I guess I wouldn't know for certain, though, since apparently no one noticed he had left me for dead at that point.'

'Perhaps you should thank him.' She forced acid through her grumble. 'After all, you found fine company in a sea-trollop.'

'Trollop?' Greenhair tilted her head. 'That is ... what you call a shellfish, yes?'

'It's some manner of fish, all right,' Asper seethed.

'*As I was saying,*' Dreadaeleon interrupted with a snarl far too fierce for his frame, 'these particular Omens don't seem at all bothered by the fact that there isn't an Abysmyth in sight.'

'I can appreciate that feeling.'

'As can we all.' Dreadaeleon nodded. 'But consider the events of this morning when I lured them away with my glamer.'

Asper nodded grimly, remembering the situation all too vividly.

The larger parasite had reacted swiftly, hurling itself off the tower with a piercing wail. Echoed by its lesser kin, the shriek tainted sky and sea as they descended in a stream of white feathers and bulbous eyes upon the illusory blood-stain Dreadaeleon had cast upon the sea.

She winced, recalling the even louder scream when they discovered it was false. Far too late to even notice Lenk and the others slipping in, they had simply returned to the battlements, where they now roosted.

'They followed the big one,' Asper muttered, 'like duck-lings following their mother.'

'I was going to compare them to lemmings, but your analogy might be better.' Dreadaeleon grinned. 'At any rate, the greater Omen seems to act as a substitute for the Abysmyths, if you will, giving orders in place of them.' He tapped his cheek thoughtfully. 'Though they don't seem that much brighter than the small ones, do they?'

'Not especially, no.' She glanced at him. 'I suspect you have a reason for thinking about this?'

'While knowledge is its own reward, I do. If the big one gives the orders, then it stands to reason that we can effectively render all those little ones a moot issue.' He extended a single finger out towards the tower, aiming it at the greater Omen, and grinned. 'Zap.'

'That's … actually not bad.' Asper felt slightly frustrated at having to compliment the boy, but nodded apprecia-tively regardless. 'Cut off the head and the body falls. If it was that simple, the way for Lenk and the others would be clear.'

'Right.' Dreadaeleon nodded. 'If they come out.'

'*When* they come out,' she snapped. Turning back to the

484

tower, she bit her lower lip. 'The trick, then, would be to kill the big one before it could reach them.' She glanced him over appraisingly. 'Could you hit it from here?'

'If I could, I would have done so.' He shook his head. 'No, I'm assuming that Lenk is a quick enough swimmer that he could draw it close enough for me to plant a lightning bolt in its face.'

'Lightning—'

'It's the only thing accurate enough to hit from such a distance.'

'Of course … you realise that lightning and water aren't precisely the best of friends.'

'Well … I mean, yeah.' He straightened up. 'Of course I know that. If I can figure out how to throw lightning out of my damn hands, I can figure out *that*.' He cleared his throat, attempting to maintain his composure. 'Naturally, there might be some collateral damage, but—'

'There is no good way for you to end that thought.'

'Listen, the overall objective is to get the tome, isn't it?' He glanced to Greenhair, who offered a weak nod. 'Right, so, even if something *does* go wrong, so long as we can remove the greater Omen as a threat, we can fish the tome out of the water at our leisure.' He turned a nervous glance to Asper. 'Or rather, you could.'

'What?' Her tone was teetering between incredulous and furious.

'It's only fair. I'm the one who has to kill the thing.'

'That wasn't …' Her pain and words alike were lost in a sudden flood of anger driven by a storm of righteous indignation. 'You're talking about our friends, our companions, *dying*.'

'I …' His words failed him as he shook, turning a grimace

towards Greenhair, who offered nothing but a concerned glance. 'I mean, I thought we always did that.'

'We don't talk about murdering *each other*,' she roared. 'These are our friends, *your* friends, dying by *your* hands.'

'First of all,' he mustered a new semblance of confidence in a growl, 'I said there *might* be collateral damage.' He offered a weak smile, a crack in his facade. 'And, I mean, that would be totally inadvertent, so, it's really more like dying by my finger.'

Whatever rage might have boiled inside her was not shown on her face. Rather, as though water had been poured over her, she hardened and grew cold, regarding him through an even, unquivering scowl.

'You make jokes … about murdering them.'

'Why are you getting upset at me for being pragmatic?' He shifted, unsure as to whether he should puff up or back down. 'You never get this upset at any of the others.'

'They can't be helped! You—' She moved forwards, both fists clenched and ready to strike him in spite of the pain in her right hand. Her face clenched harder, finding it very difficult to summon a reason not to. 'You …' With a sigh, she reached out and gave him a shove. 'Damn it, Dread. You're supposed to be the good one.'

He collapsed onto his rear.

Whether it was because he had been rendered stunned by her words or because she had seen him shoved over by toddlers before, she didn't stop to think. And when he stared at her through an unblinking mask of flattery and confusion, she did not smile.

'I … thought it … uh …' He blanched. 'What?'

She opened her mouth to say something when she suddenly became aware of Greenhair. Or rather, became aware of Greenhair's lack of awareness towards them both.

486

'And you've nothing to say about this?' Asper growled to the siren's back.

Apparently not, for the siren merely stared out over the sea, fin erect, gills fluttering. Asper stalked towards her, perhaps intent on forcing her to participate in the fight, perhaps on forcing her to suggest some way to help.

She did neither, however, for as soon as she came up beside the siren, her gaze, too, was locked on the sea and the black ship that stained it.

Creeping across the waves with ebon oars, like the limbs of some great spider, the ship made only the slightest of ripples in the water, cutting through the surf with a jagged, black bow. With singular speed and purpose, it eased itself inevitably towards the shore.

'What is it?' Asper glanced over her shoulder at Dreadaeleon, who was also staring at the vessel, unblinking. 'More pirates?'

'Not like any I've seen.' The boy shook his head.

'I have … made a grave sin.'

They turned towards Greenhair, who now backed away, eyes wide with fear.

'It was my error to seek help so promiscuously,' she uttered, wading into the waves.

'What are you talking about?' Dreadaeleon asked.

'Forgive me, lorekeeper,' she replied, frowning. 'Forgive me for what I was forced to do and for what may yet happen. Permit me to attempt to atone with a final wisdom.' She grimaced, her face going rock hard. 'Hide.'

Before either of them could form an objection, opinion or question, the siren sprang to her feet and tore into the surf. With a graceful leap, she dived beneath the lapping waves and vanished under a blanket of sand and spray, her form sliding further up the coast.

'Well.' Asper coughed. 'That's … ominous.'

'Greenhair!' Dreadaeleon called, tearing off down the beach. 'Wait! Come back!'

'Dread, you fool!' Asper hissed after him, but she could spare no more time for him.

Her attention was seized by the ship; in the moments she had been looking away, it had crept closer. So close, in fact, that she could now make out its crew.

Eyes the colour of milk. The sound of metal clanking against metal. Alien voices uttering foul indecipherables.

Skin the colour of a fresh bruise.

'Preserve me, Talanas,' Asper, alone, whispered, 'purple-skinned longfaces.'

Twenty-Three

THE PROPER MINDSET

Restraint, Denaos thought, was a vastly unappreciated trait.

All tense situations relied on it, he knew from an experience that had been long and not fatal, which was more than most in his profession could claim. Restraint was the idea of being the centre of calm in a raging storm, so that while all around would be rent asunder by torrid winds and gales, the centre would remain unnoticed, unscathed.

It had served him well in every situation in which he had hoped to never find himself, from negotiations with watchmen clamping irons about his wrists to talking down a particularly passionate young lady with a sharp knife and an overzealous love of fruits.

Of course, he thought as he felt moist talons dig into his neck, *those were all mostly reasonable people.* As he glanced out of the corner of his eye at the Abysmyth regarding him dispassionately, he could think of more ideal situations.

And, he added with a sidelong glance at his fellow captive, *more ideal companions.*

Kataria, it seemed, had no talent or appreciation for restraint. Within the demon's grasp, she writhed, snarled, spat and gnashed her teeth. While undoubtedly she thought of herself as some ferocious lioness, in the creature's grasp she more closely resembled a particularly fussy kitten.

The frogman standing before them appeared to share Denaos's thoughts. Leaning heavily on a staff carved of bone, it ignored the rogue to regard the shict with what looked a lot like haughty mirth. Denaos arched an eyebrow at that; this frogman's face was twisted in a grin, distinctive from the legions of identical faces past shoulders bereft of their collective stoop.

'Does it not hurt?' he asked, and Denaos noted a distinct lack of needle-like teeth in his mouth. 'Is the futility not agonising? Do you not despair to look upon the rising tide and know that you are so much froth in an endless sea?'

The rogue tightened his lips, regarding the creature suspiciously. He did not recall the frogmen having either a speech pattern unslurred or a penchant for obvious metaphors.

'The tide cannot be stopped.' The frogman shook his head. 'But yours is not a plight without power.' He leaned closer, his grin becoming more abhorrent than the needle-toothed smiles of the creatures behind him. 'Surrender to the tide, flow with it as it flows over the world, and become a part of the endless blue.'

'Drown in it,' Kataria spat back, with as much force as her position allowed. 'When you wash up, I'll kick the crabs out of your carcass.'

'Sun and sky have blinded you. Wind and dirt have rendered you deaf.' He made a sweeping gesture and Denaos noted that all five of his fingers spread themselves into thin, pale digits, free of any webbing. 'Open your ears to the song of Mother Deep. When the earth is drowned and the sky kneels before the sea, it will be far too late to repent.'

Her ears folded flat against her head as she bared her teeth at him and snarled. The frogman, undeterred, reached out with a trembling hand to cup her by the chin. It was with that gesture, that familiar quiver in the fingers which suggested needs far beyond those that could be satisfied by the company of demons, that the realisation finally dawned upon the rogue.

'You're human,' he whispered breathlessly, as though it was some damning discovery.

The unblinking, symmetrical expressions of the Abysmyths and the frogmen beyond him indicated, however, that it was not. The creature himself did not so much as cringe at the accusation, instead turning his leering grin upon the rogue.

'You are cruel to notice,' he replied. 'But Mother Deep needs many mouths, and I am the one selected to remain cursed with the sins of flesh and earth so that others may be guided to Her waiting heaven.' The frogman twisted a bald head to regard the masses behind him. 'And am I not rewarded with the adoration of the devoted?'

'The pain is fleeting,' the frogmen echoed in unified chorus, 'the blue is endless.'

'So says the great Ulbecetonth.'

'May She reign over a world without the agony demanded by false Gods.' The frogmen raised their webbed hands and extended them towards the black water. 'May these ones see Her restored to a throne built over heaven.'

'It is not too late.' The leader turned his attention back to Kataria and a sudden light filled his eyes. A desperation, Denaos saw, that he had seen in every man who hungered for the same thing. 'Forsake your false Gods, as they have forsaken you. Abandon the sins of memory and sky. Feed the Mouth of Mother Deep.'

His lower lip trembled in time with his hand as it and his eyes, now wide and unblinking, lowered themselves to Kataria's taut, pale form.

491

'And he shall speak well in your name.'

The shict's answer was less eloquent.

Heralded by the sound of ripping flesh and an all-too-mortal squeal, her head shot down like an asp's to seize the frogman's hand in her teeth. After a quick, canine jerk, he pulled back a bloody hand and the pain that lit up his eyes seemed even more foreign in the wake of his inhuman congregation. He stared at her, shocked, as she flashed a smile that was morbid and red, chewing on the pink for a moment.

'Not the mouth you were expecting to be fed,' she said before spitting it at him, 'was it?'

The frogmen congregation recoiled in collective horror. They turned to their leader with a terror reserved for those who had seen idols desecrated and loosed a chorus of disharmonious agitation at the pain that flashed across his features and the blood that dripped to the floor. For his part, the Mouth seemed far less confused.

'Swear unto Her,' he seethed through clenched teeth. He twisted the head from his bone-carved staff to reveal a jagged blade. 'Feed Her flock.' He lunged forwards, seizing her by the throat as he raised the blade, quivering and whetted with his own blood. 'It matters little to Her.'

Kataria met the threat with teeth bared and a snarl choked in her throat, defiant even as the jagged edge of the blade grinned green against the unnatural torchlight. Denaos, though he was certain some God somewhere hated him even for the effort, had to fight his own grin back down into his throat.

Silf help him, though, it was hard not to be pleased when opportunity bloomed into so sweet a flower.

Quietly, his eye slid up towards the bulbous ivory sphere that stared out blankly over the impending bloodshed. The

Abysmyth's expression hadn't changed since first laying eyes and webbed hands upon his throat. If not for the shallow breaths that shuddered through its emaciated abdomen, it would be hard to declare the creature alive at all.

It was impassive. It was inattentive. It was uncaring. Enough, he reasoned, that it wouldn't notice the dagger until Denaos had jammed it deep into that vast, unblinking stare. Immune to mortal weapons or no, the rogue imagined that two fingers of steel rammed into gooey flesh would at least give the demon an itch.

An itch it would have to scratch.

That, of course, left the frogmen to deal with. The congregation stood, enraptured by their leader's quivering, bleeding hand. They were intent on the human, blank, sheep-like eyes upon their shepherd. So intent, he reasoned, that they had been sent into utter confusion at the little nip Kataria had given him.

A well-placed slice to the jugular, he imagined, would shock them enough that they'd hardly miss him.

So, one knife in the eye, he told himself, feeling the familiar weight of the weapon tucked neatly in his belt, *one in the neck*, feeling his heart beat against the cold steel strapped to the inside of his vest, *and a spare for whoever else isn't shocked*, clenching his buttocks tightly.

All that was needed was an opportunity. An opportunity, he noted with some dismay, that was particularly slow in coming.

Of course, the loss of Kataria would be lamentable. She wasn't entirely unpleasant company, as women went, nor entirely unpleasant to look at. However, she was still just a shict. He knew it, and his companions would understand. Dreadaeleon would have a few forced words of grief,

493

Gariath some callous commentary and Asper all manner of harsh words for him not being able to save her.

Lenk, of course, would likely have reacted far worse, if he was still alive. Failing that, however, Denaos thought the young man would have been pleased if he and the shict had both died in the same place, separated only by a mere stone block.

Kataria's death was regrettable, but necessary, he reasoned with a restrained nod.

Or it will be, if it ever happens …

The quiver with which the frogman held the dagger was familiar to him; he had seen it in hungry men who had been consumed with desires that the company of other men, or demons, could not satisfy. The broad eyes, angry and hungry at once, suggested that the frogman was caught between the desire to spill blood in retribution and the very grim knowledge that this was likely to be the last female he, all too human, would see in quite some time.

Of course, the rogue might have been more sympathetic to the Mouth's quandary if not for the webbed fingers wrapped about his throat.

As it was, he made a quick note to feel guilty twice when he made his escape. Once for having to bite back his sigh of finality when the frogman at last overcame his indecision and drew the blade back, and twice for forcing himself to resist the urge to shout in exasperation when the creature staggered backwards suddenly.

Such a temptation passed quickly, overcome by a far more pressing urge to cover his ears. A cacophony of whispers filled the room, a high-pitched whine seeping through the stones, a guttural murmur rising between the ripples in the waters. And yet, it wasn't within his ears that the rogue was assaulted. The sound permeated every part of him, vocal talons clawing past every pore to sink into his body and reverberate inside his sinew.

His were not the only sensibilities to be so flagrantly violated. Kataria writhed about in her captor's grasp, snarling with such ferocity as suggested she was straining to block out the noise with one of her own. The Mouth, too, reacted in such a way, drawing concerned looks from his congregation and impassive stares from the Abysmyths.

'Yes, yes,' he whispered to no one, 'I hear you.' With a sudden growl, he clapped hands over his ears. 'I SAID, I HEAR YOU!'

The dagger dropped from his fingers, forgotten along with his imminent sacrifice as he trudged past Kataria with a sudden weariness, ignoring her spitting and snarling. Denaos tolerated the noise long enough to note the intensity with which the Mouth gazed upon the stone slab at the end of the hall behind which Lenk had disappeared.

'What is it?' the Mouth muttered, then shrieked. '*WHAT IS IT?* I can't ... it's hard to ...' He bit his lower lip, narrowed his eyes upon the stone. 'Fine. I just ... what? They're coming? How close?'

Denaos felt the creature behind him shift and dared to look up enough to see the Abysmyth's gaze also locked upon the rock. The impassiveness in the demon's eyes had also shifted, as much as an expressionless fish face would allow. It stared without the hysteric intensity of the Mouth, but rather with the attentive silence of an eager pupil.

What lessons it sought to learn in the agonising noise, Denaos did not dare guess.

'They can wait,' the Mouth replied, his voice suddenly a whine. 'I've business to ... what? No, it's not as though—' He paused, hissing angrily at the stone as he gestured wildly at Kataria over his shoulder. 'She insulted me! She insulted *you*! Now you wish to—'

The sound intensified. Denaos could no longer resist, forcing his hands to his ears as the murmurs became thunderous bellows, the whining a chorus of angry shrieks. The congregation cowered at the unseen speaker and even the Abysmyths shifted uncomfortably.

It was Kataria who drew Denaos's attention, however. The shict's writhing became a frenzy, kicking, frothing, emitting howls that went silent beneath the onslaught of sound. Her arms firmly locked behind her, her ears twitched and bent wildly, trying to fold over themselves and block out the sound.

The rogue grimaced. Despite his earlier plot, it was difficult not to share his companion's pain. Besides, he reasoned with as little resentment as he could muster, if she decided to simply collapse without blood or fanfare, there'd be no escape for him. That thought fled him the moment she looked up to meet his gaze, however.

Her eyes were wide and terrified, like a beast's. *No*, he thought, *not an animal … she looks like … just like …* He blinked. When he opened his eyes again, she was someone else, another woman, another life ending with blood seeping out of her throat. She mouthed something, his ears were deaf to it, but his mind was not.

'*Help me, tall man.*'

He shut his eyes again. When he opened them, the shict hung limp in the Abysmyth's grasp, her breathing shallow, buds of red beginning to blossom inside her ears.

'No! No more! *No more!*'

His attentions were drawn back to the Mouth, collapsed before the stone as though it were an altar of adoration.

'I do your bidding! I serve the Prophet!' He crushed his

head to the floor in submissive fervour. '*I will serve!*'

The silence that followed seemed deafening in the wake of such a hellish chorus. Even though it had dissipated, Denaos couldn't shake the reverberation, the sensation of ripples sent through his blood. It wasn't with anything but irritation that he recalled where he had first felt such a sound, such a violation of flesh by song.

'Greenhair,' he whispered.

'What?' The Mouth rose on shaky feet, not turning about. 'What is it?'

'Of course, it was a set-up.' His callous laughter, he hoped, disguised fury and fear he dared not show before his captors. 'You've been working with the siren the whole time.'

'Blasphemy,' the Mouth replied. 'There are no blind servants to false Gods in this place.' He turned, and the hunger that had once filled his eyes was replaced with a madness yet unseen in the empty stares of the Abysmyths and symmetrical glowers of the frogmen. 'This ... this is a holy place.'

'Defilers have arrived,' the Abysmyth holding Kataria gurgled. 'Offenders to Mother Deep ... slayers of the Shepherds.'

'So it is noted,' the Mouth grunted, stalking back to the dagger.

'The longfaces return,' Denaos's own captor added. 'The Prophet demands vengeance.'

'There is yet time.' He leaned down to pluck the weapon up. 'I am yet the Mouth of Mother Deep. I demand vengeance of my own.'

'The Prophet is the Voice.' The Abysmyth regarded Kataria, limp and motionless in its grasp. 'This vessel is empty. There is no further need.'

'What have you done with her, you sons of fish-whores?' Denaos demanded, scolding himself immediately afterwards. *So much for restraint …*

'I know not from whence this wretch came,' the Abysmyth replied, 'but it is a blessed one to have heard the voice of the Prophet with such clarity.'

'A Prophet,' Denaos muttered, eyeing the door. 'You worship a block of stone.'

Mock them, he told himself, *brilliant.*

'I suppose that makes as much sense as anything else related to a bunch of walking chum and their hairless androgynous toadies.'

They're going to kill you, no matter what. Go out with some class.

'You also reek.'

Well done.

'You dare to blaspheme—' the Mouth snarled, stalking towards him.

'The words of the faithless are nothing to the graced ear.' The Abysmyth's grasp grew tighter around Denaos' throat. 'The Prophet shall cleanse what mortal filth taints these hallowed halls. As we shall march in Mother's name to cleanse the impending blasphemers.'

'Is that easier or harder to do with only one eye?'

Before the Abysmyth could so much as grunt, the blade was out and flashing in Denaos's hand. He twisted in the beast's grasp, arcing the dagger up and sinking it into a gaze that remained blank even as the hilt kissed its pupil.

With a triumphant cackle, he kicked at the creature's ribcage, leaping away from it and tearing towards the water. His heart raced with elation as the frogmen reacted just as he had hoped, recoiling and parting with collective horror at the desecration that had occurred before them.

He glanced over his shoulder as he sped towards shadowed freedom, grimacing at Kataria's limp form. Sparing a moment to mutter a prayer that the shrieking had killed her before the demons could have the pleasure, his attention was suddenly seized by the Mouth.

Odd, he thought, that a man so thoroughly defiled would be smiling.

Then he felt webbed fingers seize him. The Abysmyth's long arm jerked him off his feet, staring at him through the wedge of steel lodged in its skull. The hilt shifted with an unnerving squishing noise as the creature's eyeball rolled about in its socket.

'Blessed is he who stands to face his judgement,' the creature gurgled. 'Blessed is he who perishes in the name of Mother Deep.'

Its arm snapped forwards with surprising speed, sending Denaos hurtling towards the wall. He struck it with a crack, bouncing from the stones to land in a puddle of salt water. Through hazy vision, he was barely able to make out Kataria's pale body flying over him as she was likewise discarded.

'So, then, are all blessed in Her eyes and heart.'

With that, the creatures turned and stalked through the congregation, followed by a begrudging Mouth. So, too, did the congregation turn to vanish down the hallways, following the Abysmyth's empty voice.

'Defilers approach. All are needed. We go to water, to weapons, to war.'

Left alone in the silence of the hall, accompanied only by the crackle of green fire and the lonely drip of water, Denaos could hear the sound of his heart slowing, the sound of red seeping into the puddle that was his grave.

It was the groan behind him that caught his attention, however, the voice that rose faintly.

'Lenk,' Kataria whispered, her voice wet, '... I'm coming.'

No matter; he reminded himself to appreciate the irony when he reached the afterlife.

She's alive, he thought, unable to summon the breath to chuckle.

Twenty-Four

THE OPPORTUNE MOMENT

It was with great clarity that Asper recalled the very first time she wondered whether Talanas truly loved her.

One year ago, following a short, wiry young man with silver hair, as his barbarous shict followed him, her doubt had been a brief, niggling gnat she could easily swat away. A disciple of the Healer's pilgrimage, after all, required many opportunities to witness and learn from injury as well as to see what good could be wrought from those situations.

While most joined their local militias or armies, Asper was handed the bad luck to be born in an era where no one was particularly eager to slaughter each other on a mass scale. Adventurers, at the very least, provided ample opportunity to observe injury and all manner of wounds and diseases.

Her doubt had grown with each member added to their band: the murderous brigand, the heathen wizard and the savage monster. When they had finally met Miron Evenhands and agreed to aid his mission to commune with the heavens, it had dissipated.

But now, as she squatted in the underbrush of Ktamgi's forest, watching the prow of the black vessel carve through the water, her doubt returned. And like a rash left untreated, it blossomed with a triumphant festering.

The ship, carved long and sleek from a wood so dark

as to devour the sun, slid along the shoreline. With every push of the thick oars, every grunt of effort from those who pushed them, the crew became distinct, each one an ugly purple bruise upon the ship's low-set deck.

At first, she wondered if she might be hallucinating, wondered if some native pollen had seeped into her nostrils and twisted her sight into some miasma of ebon and violet. She certainly had never seen such creatures as dotted the benches on the vessel.

Their purple flesh, generously exposed by the hammered sheets of iron they wore over their chests, was pulled hard and taut over muscles that flexed and shimmered in sweat-laden harmony. Their black hair resembled a row of hedges, each one trimmed with similarly violent style and cut close to their powerful jawlines.

It was their eyes that caught Asper's attention, however: rows of narrowed, white diamonds without pupil or iris, each one set deep into the sockets of a long, narrow face.

Asper felt herself cringe inwardly. These, then, were the source of the carnage upon the blackened beach. She found it easy enough to believe; as the ship pulled closer, she could make out the thick iron blades strapped to their belts, two to each man, dark and ominous against their muscular purple thighs.

And yet, for all their menace and jagged edges, they appeared to be nothing more than ordinary blades. Not even well-made ones at that, she thought, each one resembling little more than a long spike. What, then, enabled these men to slaughter the demons as they had done?

That question suddenly became far less relevant to her as another one forcefully entered her mind through her widening eyes.

Are ... are they ... slowing down?

'*NYUNG!*'

She winced at the sound: a harsh, alien bark that was difficult to distinguish between an actual spoken language and a bodily function. Whichever, the men seemed to understand it well enough. With an equally unintelligible roar in reply, they dug their oars into the sands of the shoals, bringing the ship to a sudden halt, bobbing ominously in the surf.

Though she was shocked to admit it, her first thought was not for herself, but rather for her companions. Gariath and Dreadaeleon were still vanished, chasing whatever it was that made each of them respectively useless at that moment. What would happen, she wondered, fearful, if they should stumble upon the purple creatures disembarked and eager to dismember?

Then again, she reasoned, perhaps their disappearance upset her for the sole reason that magic and claws would be much better for a potential fight than a hefty stick and harsh language.

Whenever her companions planned on returning, however, they'd have to deal with whatever metal bits would be inevitably jammed into their orifices themselves. She had no intention of moving from her cover in the first place, and the sudden sound that arose from the ship's deck did nothing to persuade her.

There was a sharp groan, followed by a heavy slamming sound, as though someone thought it a good idea to drag a bag of particularly old door hinges in a particularly thin sack across the deck. With each passing breath, the sound grew to resemble the distinct pound of footsteps. And with each heavy fall of the heel, the realisation grew in Asper's heart with a chill.

Talanas help me ... they're coming ashore.

From the rear of the ship rose a great white plume, stalking between oarsmen who, at its presence, lowered their heads. It strode to the prow of the ship and Asper could see it was a stiff topknot stretched tightly above a particularly long face. The man, noticeably taller and more muscular than his dark-haired companions, stood at the vessel's bow and swept a white-eyed glare across the shore.

Asper had to clap her hand over her mouth at the sound of shattered surf as he placed a gauntleted hand upon the railing and hoisted himself over. Trudging through the waves with a contemptuous stride, he emerged onto the shore, purple flesh and black armour glistening.

Despite his proximity, close enough for her to see the hard sneer etched into his long, hairless face, Asper couldn't help but lean closer to study the man. There was something off about him, she noted, for as tall and powerful as he was, there were too many decidedly unmasculine qualities to him.

The skirt-like garment that hung from his belt exposed legs that should have been covered in greasy, grimy hair; even Dreadaeleon had that. But his legs were smooth, as was the rest of his purple flesh. His armour, a haphazard collection of blackened chain and plate, was sparse, exposing a muscular abdomen that was also hairless. It was the particular curvature of his breastplate that caught her eye, though: the metal was curved, seemingly needlessly, as though it had been wrought to fit ...

The realisation knocked her to her rear.

'Sweet suffering Sun God, it's a woman.'

Why wouldn't they be? she asked herself. Females more massive than men would certainly fit with the absolute nothingness she knew of these alien things.

The rest of them, she realised, were also female. Their

curves became more apparent, though hard and unyielding. Their chins bore a feminine angle, but only vaguely. Their faces resembled first the same hard iron they wore, but secondly women.

Women, she realised, but only barely so; the one standing upon the beach even less.

Taller than a man, lean and hard as a spear, she surveyed the shore through a long, narrow face. Her eyes were hard and white, not the colour of milk but of angry quartzites, sharp enough to draw blood with a mere gaze. Even her hair was menacing, topknot rising like a white spire from the crown of her head, the rest of it pulled tightly against her skull.

For as much ferocity as she oozed, however, it was nothing compared to the weapon clenched in her hand. Resembling nothing so much as a broad, flattened sheet of iron with a hilt jutting from it, the sword looked to be easily the size of a small man, yet this longface, this woman, clenched it with familiar, five-fingered ease.

No, wait, Asper noted, *four fingers.* The gauntlet covering her hand had only three digits and one thumb, the middle being decidedly larger than the others. She blinked, took a moment to consider.

Four-fingered, purple-skinned, white-haired, longfaced women who carry giant slabs of metal, she paused to swallow, *and kill demons.*

Quietly, she looked up to the sun, beaming proudly upon this towering woman and asked.

'Why?'

'*SCREAMER!*'

Asper staggered back twice; once for the sudden snarl from the woman's mouth and twice for the fact that she was apparently speaking the human tongue. She froze, fearing that the sound of her rump scraping across the dirt might have attracted attention. For the strange woman's part, however, she seemed much more concerned with the state of the beach than anything else.

And the beach seemed to annoy her immensely. With another growl, she hefted her huge weapon and brought it down in an explosion of sand. Sand, Asper noted, that was suddenly green as it landed in sizzling blobs upon the shore.

She squinted and, upon eyeing the sickly emerald shimmer to the weapon's edge, the reason for the Abysmyth's death at the longfaces' hands became apparent.

'*Semnein Xhai!*'

Another voice, far less hurried and harsh, lilted from the ship as another figure stepped to the prow.

In shocking contrast to the others, this woman was a head and a half shorter than the rest, clad in silken fineries as opposed to heavy black plate. Her face was more rounded, as though better nourished. The billowing velvet of her black and gold robe could not obscure her figure, either. Where the others were lean and hard, this one was frail and slender, where the others bore the modest swell of breasts …

'Oh, you can't be serious …' Asper muttered to no one in particular.

The male looked wildly out of place amongst the metal and muscle. Where the females sat attentively, grips shifting between oars and weapons, he reclined lazily upon the prow, daintily covering a yawn with a slender hand.

He looked almost approachable, Asper thought, at least compared to the others. The images of the frogmen, frozen upon the earth, and the Abysmyth, shrieking out its last breath, were fresh in her mind. That, and the imposing white-haired female between them, kept her still and silent.

For that reason, though, a thought occurred to her. Fierce as they were, these longfaces *had* slain an Abysmyth, an impossible task done to an impossible foe. Whatever their motives, they had removed one more piece of filth that stood between herself and the tome.

After all, she reasoned, it wasn't as though she travelled with the most gentle-looking people herself. Perhaps these longfaces could be trusted, perhaps these longfaces could be her key to delivering Lenk and the others from Irontide.

Of course, perhaps they'd simply carve her open and wear her intestines as laurels and call it a day.

At the very least, it would have helped to have known what they were saying.

The male at the prow called to the white-haired warrior with a lazy lilt, the language not quite so foul from his lips. In response, she whirled about, howling what were undoubtedly curses in her twisted tongue. The male repeated himself with a smirk, holding up a single digit, one of five, Asper noted, and wiggled it.

The female bristled, hard body trembling with restrained fury.

Though she looked like she would have, and could have, hurled her giant cleaver at the male, she settled for stalking back to the ship. Her angry snarl commanded the sound of two sets of boots rumbling up the deck and, within moments, two more of the females had disembarked and stood before her with hard-faced attention.

She barked orders, accompanied alternately by wild gestures and ironclad slaps across the chin. Barely fazed, the females grunted in response, smashing gauntleted fists together in a gesture that appeared half-salute, half-challenge and uttering a unified roar in response.

'*QAI ZHOTH!*'

The white-haired female gave them a long, hard stare, as though appraising them. Apparently satisfied, she snarled at them and hefted her weapon over her shoulder. Asper noted grimly the ease with which she hoisted both herself and the weight of metal upon her back into the ship. Tense as she was, though, she couldn't help but spare a relieved breath as the females' grunting rose with their oars, pushing the ship away from the shoreline.

The longfaces were departing, leaving her with two heavily armed, possibly deranged purple women.

The thought momentarily crossed her mind to make her move now: as powerful and fierce-looking as these two were, they still resembled dainty purple milkmaids in the shadow of the white-haired one. Perhaps the opportunity to discover what they were about and whether they might be of use was now.

She quickly retracted that thought as they slid short, stabbing spikes of iron from their belts. Exchanging a momentary scowl with motives unreadable, they turned and began to stalk off towards opposite ends of the beach. Like narrow-faced hounds, they swept the shore with hard stares, searching.

But for what?

Horror's icy fingers suddenly seized her by the throat, her breath dying with the sudden realisation: it didn't matter what they were searching for, so much as what they would find. And, if their eyes were for more than just looking menacing, they would undoubtedly find tracks.

Her tracks.

If they didn't think to search the forest after that, she would have been shocked. However, an old adage involuntarily came to her mind: the Gods frequently offered gifts in threes. Given that she had already been handed giant purple men-women in addition to giant black fish-things, it would seem a shame if they *both* didn't try to kill her.

Her options were so slim as to be an emaciated wretch begging for food.

Running was clearly futile; deserted islands tended to leave very little room for evasion. Fighting them was similarly discarded; neither longface's unyielding muscle seemed to suggest that a staff's blow would have any greater result than a stern talking-to.

Clearly, then, she reasoned, someone else would have to do the fighting.

She glanced up and down the beach and frowned; each one of the longfaces had departed in the same directions her companions had. If she didn't find them first, the females undoubtedly would. Then she might never find out if they were friend or foe before the others decided to eviscerate or burn them alive.

That was, of course, if they didn't simply gut her companions first.

Then again, she thought, rubbing her jaw where Gariath had struck her, *maybe that's not so bad.* She growled, giving herself a light thump to the head. *No, no, no. Stop thinking like that. Don't end up like them.*

She would stick to the forest, she imagined, skirt the trees to keep out of their sight until she could find Dreadaeleon or Gariath. Even if the longfaces *were* allies to be won, negotiations would go much easier accompanied by four hundred pounds of red muscle or one hundred pounds of fire and lightning.

The sole question remaining, then, was why there was so much activity atop Irontide's battlements.

She wouldn't have noticed it had it not been so prominent.

509

The crown of white was now alive, the Omens writhing and hopping about, emitting all manner of chattering jabber that carried over the waves. The sight of them, their countless bulbous eyes shining like ugly, unpolished jewels, made Asper's stomach roil; they had been bad enough when they stood still.

And yet, it wasn't until she noticed a distinct empty space that she truly began to worry as another question crept intrusively into her mind and onto her lips.

'Where'd the big one go?'

Her question was answered in the chattering of teeth that filled the air behind her, carried on a cloud of acrid fish reek. She felt the hair on the back of her neck stand up, kissed by a wisp of salt-laden, hot breath. The fear came over her in a cold blanket, freezing muscles that begged her to run, paralysing a neck that shrieked at her to turn around.

Heat returned to her as she heard something behind her speak in a guttural mimic of her own voice.

'Where'd the big one go?'

She whirled, eyes going as wide as the eyes staring into hers. Two bulbous blue orbs stared at her, unblinking, from an old crone's face. Asper's lips pursed for a moment, unable to find the words to form a prayer holy enough to ward against what she saw.

The creature's eyes stared at her from where the chin ought to have been, the hooked nose curving sharply above them like a long, fleshy horn. Breathlessly, the priestess stammered, trying to form a curse, and her words were echoed back to her from a pair of jaws creaking open upon the creature's forehead.

Trembling hand clenching her pendant, she muttered a word.

'Run,' she gasped to herself, 'run.'

'Run,' her own voice replied from the creature's jaws.

Legs refusing to obey, she all but collapsed backwards out of the foliage and onto the beach, arms swiftly dragging her away from the creature. The Omen was not deterred, and leapt from the underbrush in a great flap of white wings to land before her.

In the daylight, the thing was even more horrific. From its upside-down face ran a long neck, leading to a body that resembled an underfed stork. The creature crawled forwards on bony hands blue with swollen veins that jutted from its wing-joints. Its face was blank and expressionless, teeth chattering as its eyes locked on to Asper, who sat frigid and unable to move before it.

The Omen rose up on webbed, yellow feet and spread its wings, exposing a pair of withered breasts that trembled as the creature drew in a deep breath and dropped its massive, inverted jaws.

Whatever sound it might have made, whether a curse or the shrill mockery of Asper's own terror, was lost in a whining shriek and a hollow slamming sound. Something silver whirled violently through the air. Asper blinked and, when she opened her eyes, a leather-bound hilt jutted from the creature's neck. With its face still unchanged, the Omen gurgled slightly, lowered its arms and keeled over.

The Omen lay leaking dark red upon the sand. Asper could not find the breath to scream, nor to do anything but stare open-eyed and open-mouthed at the twitching corpse before turning to gawk at the sound of heavy boots crunching across the sand.

The longface's stride was casual and unhurried as she stalked towards the Omen, her face appearing more perturbed than anything. Completely heedless of the priestess sitting paralysed beside it, she merely leaned down and pulled the long blade, its edge jagged and thick with life, from the creature, her only expression being the hint of a smile that emerged alongside the choked squawk from the parasite as she ripped the weapon free.

When Asper finally spoke, the words came as a shock to her.

'Th-thank you,' she gasped.

The longface turned and lifted a black brow, as though she hadn't noticed the woman until just now. Despite the not-entirely-friendly expression, Asper shakily rose to her feet and dusted her robe off, offering the woman a weak smile.

'If you hadn't come along just now ...' She cleared her throat. 'Can you understand me?'

The longface cocked her head at that and Asper sighed. *Of course*, she muttered in her head, *that was* much *better*.

'All right,' she said resignedly. 'You can't understand me. We'll work around that. But you did help me and you *did* kill what I'm supposed to be killing. So, for now,' she extended a hand and a broad smile to her purple rescuer, 'we can satisfy ourselves with that, can't we?'

The longface regarded Asper's hand with apparent concern, eyeing it for a moment as if unsure what to do with it. For a moment, the priestess felt her heart stop as the longface shoved her bloodied blade back into her belt without cleaning it. While the sensation she felt as the purple female seized her hand in a red, sticky gauntlet was not what she thought she could call 'good' in all conscience, it was with no small relief that she saw the longface smile back, exposing rows of jagged teeth.

The feeling was decidedly ruined when the longface

pulled her forwards violently and drove a purple knee into her belly.

She staggered backwards, clutching at her stomach. Her left arm throbbed angrily, pulsing with a life all its own, a foreign, fiery blood coursing through it. Swiftly, she seized it with her weak right hand, clutching it as though it were a feral dog.

No, no, no! NO! Not now! She grimaced at her arm, and it seemed to scowl back at her, as if to ask, *Then when?*

She found no ready answer as the longface stalked forwards, eyes glimmering cruelly in their sockets. Feebly, the priestess held up her right hand, half in futile warding, half in unpitied plea.

'No! *No!*' she hacked. 'That's … not … I didn't want to …' She staggered to her feet, knees threatening to give out beneath her as she backpedalled awkwardly. 'Listen. *Listen!*'

She stumbled backwards, saved from falling only as the red gauntlet reached out to seize her by her collar. With a harsh jerk, she was brought face to longface, a jagged, white smile added to the ivory stare. And the longface spoke with a voice as harsh and grating as the iron spike sliding from her belt.

'I heard you, pinky.'

'You,' Asper gasped, 'speak my language?'

'I do.' The longface's smile seemed too wide for her narrow visage as she levelled the spike at Asper's. 'That's what your weak breed calls "irony", isn't it?'

'It's not irony, it's coincidence!'

'Arguing languages while you're about to be skewered?' The longface shook her head. 'Your death will be a boon to your race.'

Before she knew what was happening, Asper's left arm,

burning under her sleeve, snapped up to seize the woman by her throat. The voice shrieking inside her mind, begging for control, fell quiet against a violent crackle inside her. The fire in her veins slid through her fingers, up her shoulder and scorched a bare-toothed snarl upon her face.

'I'm not going to die, *heathen*.'

The longface's smile only grew broader, a predator feeling its prey squirm inside its jaws. Without a thought for the unnatural tension in Asper's hand, she raised her spike and aimed the point directly at the priestess's face.

'*VERMIN!*'

The bellow degenerated into a wordless howl that rent the air. Eyes, white and pupilled alike, turned upwards to regard the massive wall of crimson muscle standing upon the shore.

Gariath's own dark orbs were fixed upon the longface, apparently heedless of the captive she held, as he unfurled his wings, dropped upon all fours and charged, leaving sundered earth in his wake.

'Not yet, anyway,' the longface muttered, dropping the priestess and turning her weapon to face the new threat.

She did not have to wait long.

With a roar, Gariath sprang from the sand, wings flapping, claws outstretched and aiming for a tense purple throat. What he received instead was a vicious handful of iron as she raised her spike to strike at him. He seized it and twisted it away. She was driven backwards by the force of his lunge but did not stagger, her heels digging deeply into the sand.

His free hand came up, claws glistening, and was caught in her grasp. His muscles tensed, eyes widened, if only in momentary appreciation for a hand large and strong enough to hold his killing grasp at bay. *A good fight*, his toothy smile said without words, *a good opponent*. And, as he reared his head back, his horns finished the thought.

Not good enough.

His skull crashed against her nose, snapping her head backwards. When he drew away a face glistening with a moisture not his own, his eyes spoke of a deeper surprise. The longface's grip held firm, her hands unshaking, as she turned upon the dragonman a scowl burning white through the crimson dripping down her face.

She snarled, a noise as vicious and fierce as Asper had ever heard Gariath utter, and returned the gesture, slamming her face against his snout. He reeled and Asper's breath caught in her throat; Gariath had never reeled before.

He made a long, slow effort of drawing his face back up. And it was with longer, slower and far more unpleasant effort that he drew his tongue across his lips, tasting the red that dripped upon it.

'Oh,' he said through his smile, 'I *like* you.'

His nostrils flared, snorting a cloud of crimson into her eyes. Her flinch left her unprepared for the head that followed. His skull smashed against hers; she quivered. His horns crushed her forehead; she released him and staggered backwards.

As if infuriated by the sudden lapse in her strength, Gariath drove his head forwards a third time, sending the longface to her knees. His rage-laden howl became the song of a violent choir as he brought his fists down upon her back. She withstood two hammering blows before buckling, collapsing to the earth.

Not nearly satisfied, Gariath fell on her, continuing to rain fists upon her until the sound of meat slapping meat became the sound of thick branches snapping.

It wasn't until the sound of a particularly moist sponge

being wrung reached her ears that Asper finally spoke up.

'Enough, Gariath.'

'You're right.' The dragonman rose, flicking thick droplets from his hands. 'This one's almost finished.' At an errant twitch from the purple body, he brought his foot up and then down, smiling at the sound of undercooked porridge being spilled. 'Tough one, though.'

'There are more of them.'

His eyes lit up with a glimmer that Asper often found charming in children being handed presents.

'Where?'

'Later. We need to find Dread and—'

'*Where?*'

He stood before her, the stink from his body, and parts of the longface's body, roiling into her nostrils. She did not turn away, despite the pleas of her senses; his twitching arms suggested that there was only one acceptable gesture to make. And, with a sigh, she pointed out over the sea to the black vessel.

He shoved her aside, scowling across the waters. The ship cut through the froth like a black spear, propelled by its harmony of oars. Purple bruises lined the low deck, and in each pulse of purple muscle, Gariath saw something that made his smile threaten to split his face in two.

'They're not so fast,' he grunted, stalking towards the water. 'I can still catch them.'

'Catch them?' Asper turned an incredulous glare on him. '*Catch them?* There are over thirty of them on that ship!'

'A ship heading for the tower,' Gariath pointed out. 'A tower filled with Lenk and two other weaklings.'

'Don't insult my intelligence by pretending you care about them.'

'Fine, but only because I can insult you in so many

other ways. Like this.' His hands went limp at the wrists as he began dancing from foot to foot on his toes, whining through his teeth. 'Oh! Oh! A bunch of scary purple women! Whatever shall we do?' He gasped, reached out and slapped her face hard. 'How about we *kill* them?'

'Just because that's the only answer you know doesn't mean it's the right one,' she snarled, rubbing her face. 'They're dangerous. That last one almost killed me.'

'Such a phenomenon ceased being interesting the last four hundred and twenty-six times it happened.'

'With Dread, we can—'

'*You* can. With the skinny little runt, *I* can sit around listening to *two* spineless imbeciles and waste time that could be better spent killing.' He waved her off, stalking into the surf. 'See you in the afterlife, if you ever make it.'

'You expect to die,' she called after him, 'and you're still going?'

'It should have ceased to be shocking after the four hundred and twenty-seventh time.'

The curse she flung at his tail was lost, as was the tail, behind a screen of froth. She watched him become a red blur, his wings, arms and legs pumping to propel him beneath the waves and towards his target. She snarled, stamped her foot and found herself caught between cursing and envying him.

He, at least, would be doing something to help the others.

Gariath's words were true, she knew; should their companions run into the longfaces, there would likely be nothing left to drift ashore. She admitted to herself with less shame than she expected that the dragonman had voiced concern for their companions before she had.

Now he was off, with at least a shallow facade of

compassion behind him, to at least attempt to help Lenk and the others. And she stood on shore, helpless, left arm burning with impotent fury.

'Where's he going?'

She glanced up at Dreadaeleon's approach, immediately noting the smoky tendrils he flicked from his fingers.

'What happened to you?' she asked.

'Found something purple further up the beach,' he replied, 'fried it.'

'It's not important. Look, there's—' She paused, blinked at him. 'Wait, what? Fried her? Just like that?'

'Her?'

'It was a woman.'

'Oh … wait, really?' He flapped a hand. 'It … she had a sword, she was waving it at me. I was busy searching for Greenhair, I didn't have time *not* to fry her.' He stared out over the sea. 'But where's Gariath going?' His eyes went wide at the sight of the black ship. 'Furthermore, what's *that*?'

'A ship,' she replied curtly. 'Isn't that obvious? It's also full of more purple women, all armed, all irate, *all* heading for Lenk and the others.'

'As well as the demons,' Dreadaeleon pointed out.

'Right. There are demons in there, too.' She began to wade into the surf. 'Gariath's heading out to help and we have to, as well.'

It wasn't until the water was up to her thighs that she realised both that she was not dragonman enough to swim out to Irontide and that Dreadaeleon was still standing on the shore, staring at her in befuddlement. She whirled, turning a scowl upon him.

'What are you waiting for?' She gestured wildly at the

water. 'Make an ice bridge … or an ice boat, some kind of ice … whale. *Do something.*'

'Like what?' He held his hands out to his sides. 'It doesn't seem like anything needs to be done. The longfaces hate the demons. We hate the demons and the longfaces. Let one kill the other and we can clean up afterwards.'

'If Lenk and the others get caught between the demons and the longfaces, there won't be enough left of them to clean up with a dirty rag,' she snarled. 'If you won't help, sit here and wallow in a pool of your own cowardice, but at least call Greenhair to see if she can help me.'

'*Call* her? She's not a dog.' He snorted. 'Besides, I couldn't find her. She vanished beneath the water.'

'All the more reason for you to help me,' she replied hotly. 'What do you suppose will happen to her when whoever's the victor of this little clash comes out?'

'What do I suppose will happen to a siren capable of hiding anywhere in the limitless blue sea?' He tapped his chin, her scowl deepening with each strike of his finger. 'Goodness, maybe she'll come out and ask for a hug?'

Her face grew red with the scathing fury building up behind lips twisting into a grimace fierce enough to spew it. Her left hand trembled at her side, burning angrily, demanding to be wrapped about the boy's throat. If he noticed such a thing, however, he paid it only as much care as was required to wave a hand as though batting away a particularly irate gnat.

'It may seem callous,' he continued, turning to walk away, 'but my solution is both logical and fair. They'd abandon us in a heartbeat and you know it.'

'Being an adventurer isn't about being *fair*,' she snarled, tearing through the water towards him, 'it's about suffering every miserable person the Gods deem fit to throw into your company.' She raised a fist angrily, his head a greasy black pimple waiting to be popped. 'And dealing with it the best you can at the mo—'

The burning in her arm dissipated with such force as to be painful. Quietly, she lowered it, stared at it with wide eyes. It felt strange in its socket: no longer so heavy, no longer so hot. It felt exactly like her right arm, it felt ... normal.

That, she thought, *has never happened before.*

But it paled in comparison to the sensation that followed.

A feeling straddling pain and ecstasy swept over her. Her flesh grew gooseskin beneath her robe, a chill crept down her back, wrapping about her spine like a centipede with icy, frigid legs. She felt her voice catch in her throat, unsure how to respond to the feeling. Then, with a suddenness that made her knees buckle, the chill twisted inside her body, becoming violently hot.

The sun seemed incredibly oppressive at that moment, as though it reached down with a golden hand to glide past cloth, flesh, muscle and bone. It seized her essence in a scalding, fiery grip and shook vigorously. She could feel it pushing down upon her, a great pressure forcing her skin in upon itself.

She would never have noticed Dreadaeleon's hand clenching about her arm had she not spied his scrawny fingers. He seized her with a strength belied by his frailty, he stared at her with an intensity she'd never seen in him. Behind the dark orbs of his eyes, crimson light danced like a flock of agitated fireflies.

'What ...' Her voice came reluctantly to her lips. 'What are you—'

'You feel it.' He spoke with a firmness not his own.

'Feel … what?'

'*It.* Cold. Hot.'

With surprising strength, he tightened his grip on her left arm. She felt her heart leap into her throat. *He knows,* she screamed in her own mind, *he knows, he knows, he knows. Of course he knows. He knows everything. He knows what it is.* She tensed her fingers, the burning returning. *It's hot enough to torch him. He knows.*

If he intended to act on that knowledge, however, he did not. At least, not the way she expected. Instead, he pressed his palm against hers. It felt freezing, then hot enough to rival even her own heat.

'You can sense it,' he whispered, 'can't you?'

'Sense what?' she asked, hysteric as she tore her hand away from his. 'I don't know what you're—'

'Venarie. Magic.'

The fireflies behind his eyes, the ever-present, if faint, mark of wizardry in his stare, went alight. His gaze became a pair of pyres, crimson energy seeping out in great flashes. He turned his scowl out to sea, the pyres becoming thin red gashes.

'There is … a wizard out there.'

Her gaze followed his, towards the only thing present upon the sea.

The black ship drew into Irontide's ominous shadow, blending into the darkness. But Asper could still see it, clear as a fire on fresh-fallen snow. Though she knew she stared into darkness, she felt the ship, sensed it as she might an itch between the shoulder blades. She felt it throb, felt it twitch.

And then she felt it stand up and stride to the prow of the ship.

Something stirred atop the tower's battlements. A

521

chorus of chattering teeth and throaty gibbers cut through the sky. The great crown of white shifted as a hundred bulbous blue eyes spotted the ship.

Like a wound bleeding white, the Omens toppled from the tower, pouring over the side with flapping wings and gnashing teeth. In twisting, chattering harmony, they reared, their mimicked voices of the long dead clashing off one another in a hideous howl as they rose, then descended upon the purple invaders.

'*NYUNG!*' The command went up from the longfaces, audible even over the cacophony.

The vessel came to a sudden halt, bobbing upon the water like a floating coffin. Purple figures rose, drawing back bows made of the same black wood as the ship, arrows aimed at the descending gibber.

The male stood before them, his white hair whipping about his face, his robes billowing about his frail body as he turned a defiant stare towards the winged frenzy.

'Here it comes.'

Asper was numb to Dreadaeleon's voice, numb to everything save the freezing sensation coursing through her body and the sudden weight in her left arm.

The Omens swooped upon the ship in a twisting column, shadow and sky painted writhing white as they tucked their wings against their plump bodies and turned their hooked noses and yellow teeth to the longfaces.

With an eerie casualness to his movements, the male raised his hands. His purple, bony fingers knotted together in agonised symmetry as they bent in ways they were not meant to. He shouted a chorus of words not in his own tongue, nor the tongue of humans. They were familiar, if incomprehensible to Asper, and her eyes widened as she realised she had heard them from Dreadaeleon's mouth before.

'Magic,' she gasped.

His voice boomed, granted an unnatural echo. An unpresent wind swept his hair back, revealing a frigid blue glow engulfing his eyes. He continued to speak the words and the azure energy bathed his fingertips, sweeping up his arms.

The spectacle was not lost on the Omens.

Those in front reared in mid-descent, colliding with the ones still swooping, and the column became a messy cloud. The flying parasites beat each other with their wings, bit each other with their needles, struggling to get free of the mob of feathers and flesh. Their crazed gibberish became a unified howl of terror as the blue glow rose from below.

'This,' Dreadaeleon gasped, 'will be big.'

He was not mistaken. The longface's words of power ended with an echo that stretched into eternity as his mouth opened wide. In the wake of his voice, a howl rose.

The ship shuddered as an angry gale tore itself from the longface's mouth. The air became blue, shimmering blades tinged with razor shards of frost. From the slight, wispy creature, a maw of frigid azure and ivory swept up to crunch rime-laden teeth about the Omens.

The gale grew high, kissing the battlements and devouring the creatures' wailing. The Omens were swept inside it, caroming off one another in bursts of black blood and broken bones. They thrashed, bit, rent each other as they struggled to escape. Many died immediately, limp bodies twisting silently in the wind. More lived, thrashing even as their feathers hardened upon their flesh.

The maw glowed with a horrific blue. The Omens lost their colour in it, frozen bodies becoming so many flakes inside it. Still and silent, the statues clashed against each other, frozen anatomies snapping to become lost in the wind. Hooked noses, lipless mouths, bulging eyes: one by one, they snapped off, crashed against wings, feet and heads before twisting off to crash into torsos, tails and scalps.

Only after there was nothing left to crash did the longface close his mouth.

His trembling fingers undid themselves, his eyes returned to their heavy-lidded whiteness and the wind that had whipped his hair vanished. Folding his hands inside his sleeves, he turned and took a seat at the end of the ship.

As though nothing had happened, the females took up their oars in resignation to duty. The chant resumed, the rowers worked. The ship glided across the sea, towards Irontide, through an artificial snowfall of powdered blood and pulverised flesh.

Asper could but stare. In an instant, the harbingers of hell, the precursors of horror, the Omens had been reduced to nothing. Reduced to nothing, she added to herself, by a display of magic she had not even dreamed possible. And now the ship continued forwards, the male's expression as casual as the hand that brushed red flakes from his shoulder.

Asper could but stare as they continued towards Irontide. Asper could but stare as such a force continued towards her friends.

Dreadaeleon seemed much less indecisive.

'Come,' he said, brushing past her with a forcefulness that she might have gone agog at, were she not already dumbstruck. 'We have to go.'

'What?' she gasped, breath returning to her. 'Now?'

'That longface is a heretic.'

'You don't even know what religion he is.'

'*Not* a heretic of whatever made-up god you choose to serve,' the boy snarled at her. He gestured towards the ship. 'Look at him! He's not even breathing hard!'

Asper frowned; she could sense his calm well enough, as she had sensed his power before. Without seeing the longface, she knew Dreadaeleon was right. Dreadaeleon, of course, wasn't waiting for her approval. He waded out from the shore, inhaled deeply and blew a cloud of frost over the ocean. In the few gasping breaths that followed, a small ice floe had formed, bobbing upon the surface.

'It violates all laws of magic, all laws of the Venarium.' The boy climbed upon the white sheet, surprisingly sure-footed. 'That, at least, is worth getting involved over.'

'But not your friends?' Asper asked, raising a brow.

'Friends die. Magic is for ever.' He glanced down at her, extended a hand that seemed far too big for him. 'Are you coming, or would you rather sit and savour the irony for a bit?'

She glanced out over the sea at a sudden stirring. The male was up and at the prow again, she sensed, his hands outstretched. She felt with her arm the explosive power boiling between his palms. She saw with her eyes the prow aimed at Irontide's great, rock-scarred wall.

Waiting to see what he was about to do seemed decidedly unwise. With a grunt, she waded into the surf and took the boy's hand.

'It's not ironic ...'

Twenty-Five

THE PROPHET

The explosion came to Lenk as a muted thump, shaking the stones in the ceiling and sending gouts of dust to lie upon the black water. He rose to his feet, scrambled to the wall.

'Kat?'

The wall gave no answer.

'*Kataria?*'

The stone offered no reply.

'*Kat! Denaos!*'

His fist against the rock slab was half-hearted, all his energy drained from previous pummellings with nothing to show but throbbing fingers and a stone that seemed to smile at the futile effort. He did not expect it to miraculously crumble under his desperation, but the dull rumble spurred him to action.

If his pitiful attempts could be called such, he thought.

He had heard only faint noises since the slab had fallen behind him: the gurgling sounds of the Abysmyths, a shrill whining and the collective croak of the frogmen. Of his companions, he had heard nothing; nothing to suggest they had heard his furtive cries, nothing to suggest they were still alive.

What, he wondered, had made him not listen to Denaos? What had made creeping into a demon-infested, dying fortress seem the logical choice? Greed? Some bizarre, misplaced desire to do the proper thing? *No*, he told himself, *that doesn't work for adventurers.*

A lust for some breed of unpleasant death, then?

That seems more likely.

Whatever the reason, the stone did not answer. With no more hope to drive him to beat answers out of it, he sought to bring it down with his head. Sighing, he rested a hot brow against cold rock, giving up on it as he had given up trying to find a way out of the forsaken chamber.

He had wondered, when panic had dissipated and calm prevailed, if there was a mechanism of some kind to make the slab rise. After all, he had thought, something must have made it fall. That hope was foetid and rotting now as calm gave way to futility. He swept his gaze about the large, circular room; if such a device existed, he'd never find it.

What floor there was extended ten paces before him into a stubborn outcropping of rock. The rest had long disappeared, swallowed up by a pool of black water that writhed like a living thing. Torches burning emerald lined walls that rose high to form a domed ceiling, glistening with a macabre shimmer of green and ebon.

Whatever had operated the slab before was long-decayed or long-drowned.

The meek thought of searching the waters had been banished long ago. Black enough to eat even the emerald light, there would be no way of finding anything in its depths. The thought of something lurking in there, like the somethings he had seen lurking in brighter waters, was just one more reason to stay on land, however meagre.

Logic and sense abandoned to futility, he turned and, with nothing else productive to do, screamed.

'KATARIA!'

He froze. His echo was joined.

A melodic giggle reverberated through the chamber, bouncing off walls like a chorus of tinkling bells. The harmony was tainted, however, as though those bells were scratched and cracked. He felt it, rather than heard it, slithering across the water, over the stone, through the leather of his boots and into his skin.

He whirled, eyes narrowed, hand on sword. Nothing but stale air and flame shared the room. Or rather, he corrected, shared the part of the room he could see. With the laughter ringing in his bones, he felt his gaze going ever wider, pulled to the water.

'No,' he muttered, 'not a chance.'

The giggle emerged once more, twisting in the air and becoming a stinging cackle. It rang familiar in his ears; his face twisted into a scowl.

'Greenhair.'

At the accusation, the laughter became a horrid, shrieking mirth, loud enough to urge his hands to his ears. Resisting, he instead slid his sword from its sheath and snarled at the water.

'And what's so damn funny?'

'If you knew, it wouldn't be quite so.'

The voice was alien and convoluted, as though it couldn't decide what it wanted to convey. It was deep and bass, but tinkled like glass, and carried with it a shrill, mirthful malice.

'Tell us,' it spoke, 'what drives the landborne to try the same thing over and over and expect different results?'

Lenk arched a brow. Wherever the speaker was, it seemed to see this.

'You have been pounding at the stone for some time.'

It sighed. 'Have you not yet realised it moves by will? *Our* will?' It giggled and spoke at the same time. 'All moves at our will, at Her will, earth and water alike.'

'You haven't moved me.' He spat into the water.

'Haven't we? You drew your horrid metal at the sound of our song.'

'Conceded,' Lenk muttered, 'but it's no great accomplishment that the sound of your voice makes me want to jam something sharp into you.' He raised the weapon in emphasis. 'Show yourself so we can get this over with.'

'Curious. What is it that drives you to fight? To think that we wish to fight you?'

'I've been doing this sort of thing long enough to know that if someone's referring to themselves as "we", they're typically the kind of lunatic I'll have to kill.'

'Astute.'

'Time is too short for that sort of thing, you understand.'

'One would think all you have is time, unless we decide to move the stone.'

Lenk ignored the echoing laughter that followed, searching the waters for any sign of the speaker.

The stirring began faintly, a churn in the water slightly more pronounced than the others. He saw a dim shape in the gloom, the inky outline of something moving beneath the surface. Soon, he saw it rise, circling at the very lip of the rock.

It was when he saw it, so dark as to render the void pale, that it dawned on him.

'Deepshriek ...'

'The servants of uncaring Gods and the blind alike have spoken that name,' the creature replied, its voice bubbling up from the gloom. 'To others, we are Voice and Prophet to Her Will. The landborne forgot all those names long ago, however.' Its voice was quizzical. 'Tell us, what green-haired maidens have you been consorting with?'

'Hardly the point.'

'The point? *The point?*' It became wrathful, a great churning roar that boiled to the surface. 'What heathen consorts with blasphemy with such casualness? Such callousness?'

'Yeah, I hear that a lot.'

'Speak to us.' The black shape twisted towards his outcropping. 'What did she promise you in exchange for vengeance? Treasures of the deep, perhaps, the laden gold of the drowned? Or were you overcome with sympathy for her plight? Perhaps she appealed to your love of false, uncaring deities.' Its voice became a slithering tendril, spitefully sliding up from the deep. 'Or are you the breed of two-legged thing that lusts to lie with fish-women?'

'I've come for the tome.'

The shape froze where it floated. The voice fell silent, its pervasive echo sliding back into the deep.

'You cannot have it.' It spoke with restrained fury. 'Landborne … you all covet things you have no desire to learn from, you seek to steal them from their proper authority.' Its echo returned with a tangible, cutting edge that seeped into flesh and squeezed between sinew. 'Do you even know what holy rites this book contains?'

'I don't care,' he snarled through gritted teeth. 'I gave my word I'd return it.'

'Your word is an iron weight in deep water. What is your true purpose to come with such heresy in your heart?'

'One thousand pieces of gold,' he answered without hesitation.

'Meagre riches!' the Deepshriek roared. 'Fleeting! Trifling!

They give you pleasures you will forget and in exchange forsake your purity and chastity. You would trade power, *the* power to return the Kraken Queen to her proper seat for shiny metal? There are infinite worlds of golden garbage in the deeps, forever clenched in the drowned hands of those who would die with it. You are no different.'

'I haven't been paid yet. If I die, I won't even have gold to drown with.' The irony was lost on him in a sudden fury. 'I've seen what comes out of the deeps. I've seen it die, too.'

'So it was you,' the Deepshriek seethed from below. 'I heard the cries of the Shepherd as you callously cut it down. And so did Mother Deep hear the wails of Her children.'

'I didn't kill it,' he replied, 'but I put a sword in it. That's one thing I can do to demons.'

'Demon?' It loosed an infuriated wail. '*Demon?* A word birthed by the weak and covetous to rail impotently against the righteous. You display your ignorance with such callousness.'

'I don't care.'

'*You* are blinded and deafened by hymn and terror for your false Gods. You would deny your place in the endless blue. You were not there, as we were, in ages past when Great Ulbecetonth reigned with mercy and glory for Her children.'

'If you really are so old as that, you're well past due for a sword in your face.'

'This book has the power to return Her,' the Deepshriek ignored him, 'to return Her from worlds of fire and shadow to which She was so cruelly cast.' Its voice became shrill, whining, pleading. 'Join us, landborne. It is not too late to forsake this quest and aid our glorious mission. You, too, have a place in the endless blue ... for the moment.'

'I've heard stories that a demon's promise is the bait to hook the mortal soul.' Lenk eyed the shape, growing larger and darker beneath the surface as it slid towards his ledge. He held his sword tightly, planted his feet upon the stone. 'I'd sooner believe that shicts bottled my farts than believe … whatever in Khetashe's name *you* are.'

The black shape rose wordlessly to the surface. Straining his eyes, Lenk thought he could make out the edges of stubby, jagged fins, like those of a maimed fish, and a long, thrashing tail that spanned an impressive distance from the creature's already impressive mass.

Shark, he recalled, was the name of such a thing.

'We tried, Mother Deep, how we tried.' The Deepshriek muttered, whined and snarled all at once. 'Let this waste of promise not enrage You.'

The surface rippled, parted. Lenk hopped backwards, levelling his sword before him. A pair of glittering, golden eyes peered up at him and he stared back, baffled. A woman's face blossomed from the gloom in a bouquet of golden hair wafting in the water behind her.

Somehow, he had expected the Deepshriek to be more menacing.

Slowly, her visage rose from the gloom entirely and Lenk found himself staring at a pair of enchanting eyes set within a soft, cherubic face the colour of milk. She smiled; he found himself tempted to return the expression.

And she continued to rise. There were no shapely hips or swelling breasts to complement the beautiful face. From her jawline down, she rose from the darkness on a long, grey stalk of throbbing flesh. Her smile was broad, delighting in Lenk's visible repulsion as he recoiled, sword lowered.

But he could not turn away, could not stop staring. He spied another feminine face, another pair of golden eyes framed by hair of the blackest night. Another bobbed up beside it with a mane of burned copper. They shared their golden-locked companion's smile, revealing sharp fangs as they rose on writhing stalks.

In hypnotic unison, they swayed above Lenk, their sharp teeth bared, golden eyes alight against the green fire. They glided gracefully through the water to the outcropping's flank, visibly delighted as Lenk hesitated to follow their movement.

'What,' he finally managed to gasp, 'in the name of all Gods *are* you?'

'We,' they replied in ghastly symphony, 'are your mercy.'

The golden-haired head snaked forwards suddenly, its lips a hair's width from Lenk's face.

'And no God will hear you down here.'

The demon threw back all its heads and let out a hideous, screeching laughter that echoed through stone and skin alike. Lenk resisted the urge to clutch his ears, finding solace in the grip of his sword. He eyed the stalks the heads were mounted upon; they looked flimsy at a glance, like boiled corn.

Corn cuts easy. He took his weapon in both hands, narrowed his eyes and prepared to strike.

The golden-haired head snapped forwards once more, eyes unnaturally wide, mouth agape to an extent that should not have been possible. Lenk stared, horrified, as the very air trembled at the beast.

A great bulge rose up through the fleshy stalk. The demon's mouth stretched even wider. The remaining two heads smiled broadly as, in one great exhale, the Deepshriek screamed.

The air was robbed from him, turned into a fist that

struck him squarely in the chest. His ears threatening to burst in tiny blossoms of blood, he was hurled from the outcropping to slam against the chamber's rough-cut wall.

His sword fell from his hand, disappearing beneath the waters. He didn't feel it, didn't feel his heart slowly stopping, didn't feel his body peeling off the wall to slide slowly into the waters, so numb it was.

Fear was forgotten, fury fled. The creature's wail had robbed him of all sense and emotion; he had not the feeling left within him to know to scream before his head slipped beneath the blackness.

Through the gloom of the water, he saw it. The fish hurtled towards him like a grey arrow, skin the colour of rock, save for its bone-white underbelly and spattered maw. Three fleshy stalks crowned its forehead, snaking about in the water. Somewhere far above, he heard three laughing voices.

As he saw the fish's white, gaping jaws and the rows of jagged teeth, he wondered absently if he would feel it when they ate his head.

Twenty-Six

A BEAUTIFUL DEATH

It wasn't until after Gariath pulled himself up out of the water and into Irontide's gaping wound that he felt his breath stop. Ear-frills spread, eyes wide open, he was terrified to blink for fear that he might miss a single moment of what unfurled before him.

He had begun to think he'd never see it. He had begun to think he was doomed to die a miserable, peaceful death, slipping away in his sleep or being laid low by a particularly noisome cough. He had begun to think that he would never see what all *Rhega* yearned to see before they left this world for the spirits.

Beautiful.

It occurred to him that others might think him morbid for describing the carnage blossoming before him in such a way. But then again, he reasoned, that was why they were stupid and dead and he was *Rhega*, soon to die.

Carnage, a symphony of metal and screaming, permeated the vast hall, pain and glory bled out of the gaping hole in Irontide's hide on saltwater tides.

That he had missed the beginning of it all bothered him little. The fight was still unfolding when he arrived, a humble child well on its way to becoming a furious adult of slaughter. And Gariath could see that it grew amidst the

535

great mass of purple and white in the centre of the vast and sprawling chamber.

That the longfaces held the advantage was obvious enough. They moved in tight, concentrated packs, bristling with their iron spikes and circular shields. Frogmen descended upon them with wailing fervour, undeterred as one after another were impaled and tossed into growing piles of humanoid litter.

But the creatures did not falter, compensating for their lack of skill and weapons with their sheer press of flesh. The passages and archways of the hall were choked with rivers of them, pouring out in ever-greater numbers to fight the violet invaders.

One of the muscular women went down, skewered by a press of five bone-tipped spears. *Magnificent*, Gariath thought.

A jagged throwing blade was hurled, bouncing off the stone floor to catch a charging frogman in the groin. *Incredible.*

A white-haired female at the centre cut down throngs like great hedges, shearing through bone with a massive blade. *Beautiful.*

And all through it, the shrieks of battle filled the air, striving to be heard over the din of agony.

'*Ulbecetonth!*' the frogmen screamed, rattling spears. '*These ones shall be rewarded!*'

'*Qai zhoth!*' the females roared in their guttural language, banging iron to iron. '*Akh zekh lakh!*'

'*Let all defilers know Her mercy!*' the pale creatures shrieked.

'*Chew them alive, netherlings!*' the white-haired female howled, the human tongue delightfully harsh on her tongue. '*Akh zekh lakh!*' Her roar sent the tiny pale creatures scurrying into the water, sent her purple fellows shrieking with collective fury. '*EVISCERATE! DECAPITATE! ANNIHILATE!*'

At that moment, Gariath decided he liked her best. She would be the last, he told himself, the one to give him his beautiful death.

It was only out of a fleeting sense of fading loyalty that he scanned the melee for any signs of pink flesh. Amongst the fluids and metals exchanged, the humans were nowhere to be seen. Perhaps they had fled, or perhaps they were already dead.

Perhaps, he told himself, *is a good enough reason for vengeance.*

The thrum of bowstrings was an insult to the glory of personal combat, and its sound annoyed Gariath. Quickly spying its source, a trio of the longfaces loosing jagged-headed arrows into the throng, he narrowed his eyes.

Cowards would serve as decent preludes.

They did not deserve to be made aware of his presence, he knew, but for this death to be true, they would have to. His chest expanded, his roar was a flash of thunder, coursing over the melee and lost in the sound of battle. The rearmost archer turned to regard him curiously, no trace of fear in her white eyes.

He smiled at that; he had forgotten what such a thing looked like.

Honour was satisfied. His presence was announced. Whether the females realised it or not, the time for fighting had come.

He lowered his head and rushed towards them, salt kicking up behind him, eyes alight with fury. His intent was unmistakable; a cry of warning went up, a clumsy arrow flew over his head. He fell to all fours, another pair of arrows shrieked towards him, one sinking into his shoulder.

He did not feel it. He did not hear their threats. There would be time for pain later. There was time for fear never. His horns went low, glittering menacingly. More arrows flew, nicking his flesh, kissing the stones.

By the time they were throwing their bows down to draw swords, he was already laughing.

The archer at the fore was met in a violent burst of crimson. His horns found a hard, purple belly and dug in. His laughter grew to be heard over her howling as his head jerked upwards, his horns grating against her ribcage. He rose to his full height, the female kicking and shrieking like some macabre living hat.

With a great snap backwards, he sent her flying, then skidding, leaving a smear of red upon the stones.

His remaining foes were painted red in his eyes. Their horror was momentary, replaced by expressions that seemed to vaguely resemble jagged smiles. With eager glee, they kicked their bows aside and drew hard iron.

Gariath had to fight the urge to shed joyful tears.

The more eager of the pair rushed him; no shriek determined to intimidate him, no scowl to mask her fear. There was nothing on her face but a hard smile to match her iron. There was no sound from her but the thunder of her boots and two words tearing themselves from her lips.

'QAI ZHOTH!'

He caught her chop in his hand, feeling the metal bite into his palm. His grasp had tasted blades before; he did not flinch. Snarling, he tore it away from her as a stern parent takes a toy from a petulant child. Tossing it aside, he snapped both hands out to wrap around her throat.

It was almost disappointing to feel the weakness with

which this one fought back: not quite as firmly as the one on the beach, but equally as fierce. There was no confusion in her milk-white eyes as he had seen in the eyes of humans, no unspoken plea, no desperate murmur to a God suspected to be merciful. Instead, she spat into his eyes as he hoisted her from her feet. Her hatred was unabashed, her fury pure, her fate sealed.

Refreshing.

With another snap of his arms, he brought her crashing down to the stones. Bones shattered, salt water sprayed, and the longface still twitched. He did not laugh as he seized her by the hair and forced her to kiss the rock once more; he owed her that much. And in return, she did not scream, did not beg, did not put up a pathetic struggle.

When he rose, he did not see a wretched corpse, a dead coward. He had taken that from her, leaving only a good death.

A beautiful death.

Even if she wasn't quite as strong as the one on the beach, hers would be a death better than most. The same could not be said of her companion. He glared over his surroundings; nothing but the clash of battle and the sound of carnage. Wherever the third one had gone, she apparently had found a better way to die than at his hands.

'Coward,' he snorted. Just as well, her death would have given no satisfaction.

His ear-frills pricked up. The sound of whirling metal was faint, but distinctive enough to be recognised between the sound of someone grunting behind him and something sinking into his back.

He jerked forwards, his own growl more angry than painful. Something gnawed at his flesh, worming its way in deeper on jagged metal legs with every twitch of his body.

Far too concerned with who had thrown it, he ignored the sensation of warm liquid trailing down to his tail and turned with anger flashing in his eyes.

This one's smile was not eager, but haughty. It was the breed of grin reserved for a weakling who believed themselves to have struck a decisive blow through cowardice. *A human grin.*

Gariath could not help but grin back; he had always enjoyed the mess of teeth and gum such grins inevitability became. If the longface saw her fate in his teeth, however, she did not show it. Instead, she slammed her spike against her breastplate in a challenge.

'You pinks should pay more attention,' she spat through her teeth. 'Bites hard, doesn't it?'

Gariath had no reply that could be voiced with words. He merely stalked forwards, his grin broadening as she took a cautious step backwards. In two quick strides, his claws were outstretched and he opened his jaws wide to offer his answer.

There was little about Gariath that surprised Asper any more. That hardly made him any less pleasant to be around, but while she might never grow used to his style of solving problems, she wasn't prone to go running and screaming from him any more.

Though, she had to admit, when she pulled herself into Irontide to find him standing over a trio of corpses, a leather-bound handle jutting from his back, chewing what vaguely resembled a piece of jerked meat well, *well* past its intended consumption date, the urge was hard to resist.

In light of that, the concerned pair of words she uttered was a reasonable response, she thought.

'You're hurt.'

'Good eyes, stupid.' He spat something red and glistening onto the floor, licked his chops. 'Better hope they don't get cut out, otherwise your only use will be as food.'

Asper looked past him, to the thundering melee. Her first thought was not for the chaos raging in the hall, the bodies falling, the metal flashing, but rather for the pulsating sacs that hung from the pillars, the ceiling, that bobbed in the swiftly draining water. Amidst the bloodshed, they seemed disturbingly placid, like fleshy, throbbing flowers in a red-stained garden.

Occasionally, a longface broke free from the melee to dig a sharp implement into one of them. The frogmen shrieked in response, turning attentions away from other opponents to descend upon the assailant in a hail of spears and daggers.

The longfaces fought with equal vigour, welcoming the attacks with an upraised shield and a cruel smile, warding off their web-footed foes as their fellow females hacked into backs with spikes and jagged blades. The fight seemed scarcely even to Asper, with only five longface corpses on the ground and many more standing, against the quickly piling heaps and shrinking throngs of frogmen.

It was just as she had turned her attention back to Gariath and his new, metallic growth that the stones shook.

Heralded by a great, choked roar, they came pouring out of the fortress's orifices: great, white serpents of salt and spray, churning the waters ivory in their wake and kicking up bubbling clouds as they swept towards the battle.

As titanic dead trees, their bodies glistening onyx, their eyes vacant and expressionless even in fury, the Abysmyths exploded from the water. With gangly, ungainly grace, they swept towards the throng, heedless of the cheering fervour from their smaller, paler companions. Claws lashed as they waded into the purple, rending flesh under talons, snapping bones in great webbed hands, tossing bodies aside with contemptuous disinterest.

The longfaces scurried backwards, closing against each other. In the span of a few screams, the three demons had diverted the tide, crushing and scarring without the slightest thought for the iron sinking into their hides.

Asper fought the urge to look away as an abominable claw seized a longface by her throat. Her struggling, snarling and kicking were nothing to the creature. Her companions, like so many gnats, were swept away by its free claw. In one blink of her white eye, the creature's hand brimmed with glistening mucus.

In another breath, she hung like a limp, lamentable trophy in its grasp.

A silver blur cut the air. With an angry popping sound, the demon's emaciated arm twitched, then fell from its shoulder. It looked to the stump with momentary confusion for the pulsing green ichor that gnawed at its flesh. It could scarcely form a surprised gurgle before metal flashed once more and a great, single-edged blade burst through its ribcage.

The sound of the creature's agony was not a pleasant one. Asper threw hands to ears at the wail that burst from its jaws, winced as it collapsed to knees. In a spray of emerald, the blade was out and painting a silver moon at the thing's neck. When she blinked, the fish-like head sank into the water with a plop.

'*QAI ZHOTH!*' the longfaces howled.

'*ULBECETONTH!*' the frogmen shrieked.

The Abysmyths remained silent, looking up from their slaughter as a hard, purple figure rose atop the fallen fiend's corpse.

Asper immediately recognised the stark-white hair of the leader, her heavy iron wedge slick with green and black as she held it aloft and loosed a cry to her underlings. The shout was taken up, the throng was pushed forwards, and the killing began anew.

'Ha,' Gariath chuckled blackly. 'Now it's a fight.'

Asper was hard pressed to disagree as the female leapt from the demon's body and hacked a swathe through frogmen, wading deeper into the battle. With purpose, the priestess realised, noting the shadowy archway at the farthest corner towards which she was cleaving.

Gariath, apparently, noted it too, taking a step forwards before she cleared her throat.

'You're aware there's a knife jutting from your back, aren't you?' She took a step towards him, reaching for the handle. 'Here, just hold on for a moment and I'll—'

'*NO!*'

He whirled on her with eyes flashing and the back of his hand colliding with her jaw. She collapsed to the floor, more shocked than pained. The dragonman loomed over her, blood pooling in the furrows of his scowling face, and levelled a single accusatory claw at her.

'*You will* not *ruin this for me.*'

'Ruin ...' There was not nearly enough room on Asper's face to express her incredulousness. 'Are you demented?'

'This is a beautiful fight,' he said, sweeping a trembling arm over the melee. 'You don't belong here.'

That wasn't entirely untrue, she realised as she clambered shakily to her feet. There was no reason to be here, trying to convince a murderous reptile to let her pull a chunk of metal out of his back. There was no reason to be here, in the midst of a battle between two breeds of creatures that should not be. There was no reason to be here, chasing friends who would kill each other in a heartbeat and undoubtedly deserved to die on their own merits.

Then why am I here? she wondered as she rubbed at her left arm. It still burned, seared her from the inside. She grimaced; the pain was coming in sharper now. It wasn't supposed to come so soon, she thought, not after what had happened on the *Riptide*. But it still throbbed, still seared, still was angry.

Perhaps that was why she was here. For as she looked out over the melee, filled with people who wanted to kill her, to kill her companions, she knew of only one way to make it stop hurting.

No, no, no. She shook her head. *Bite through it. You know you can. You don't have to—*

'GNAW! BITE! GNASH!'

The war cry shattered her thoughts. She looked up as Gariath whirled about, both spying simultaneously the frenzied longface charging with shield and spike held high. Shrieking, the female lunged into the air, her weapon slick and whetted, her eyes crazed and bulging.

There was little time to appreciate the howl, however, for the echoing word of power that resounded behind her drowned out all other noise. There was the crack of thunder as a jagged bolt of electricity split the air to pierce the longface, reaching through her breastplate, through her breast, and leaping out of her back.

She landed, a smoking hole in her chest, muscles twitching with involuntarily convulsions, teeth forever locked in a sudden rigor. They both turned to regard the scrawny boy lurching forwards, Asper with shock, Gariath with ire. Dreadaeleon seemed rather unconcerned with either them or the woman he had just struck from the sky.

'That one,' the dragonman growled, 'was *mine.*'

'If I had thought you were capable of killing her in a timely manner, I would gladly have let you trade blows until one of you wet yourselves.' The boy blew on his smoking fingertip. 'I didn't think I had time for that, though.'

Asper noted the tremble in the boy, the limp that was swiftly developing in one of his legs. He made no effort to hide it, nor his heavy breathing or the sudden bags that hung like purple fruits under his eyes.

'You should probably sit back for a while,' she suggested. 'You ... don't look so good.'

'How about that,' Dreadaeleon muttered, 'I wasn't actually *lying* when I said magic drains me. Thus, forming a raft made out of ice using only my *brain* actually *might* leave me looking not so good.'

'There's no need to get all smarmy about it.'

'He gets smarmy over everything. The little runt could pull a gerbil out of his pants and he'd somehow manage to end up in a coma *and* complain about it.' Gariath snorted, prodding the boy in the chest. 'I've got a *knife* in my back, but I don't go crying about it. You don't get hugs for doing things right.'

'What do I get for killing that last longface?'

'Punched in your ugly face.'

'The fact that you're decidedly unbothered about a knife in your back and the troubling questions it raises does not concern me now.' The wizard swept a glare about the carnage. 'Where is the heretic?'

'The what?'

'The renegade,' Dreadaeleon hissed. 'The defiler of law. The male. Where is he?'

Answer came in the form of a sudden pyre that cast the room into a glowing orange hell. A vast circle formed within the battle, charred black figures collapsing around its centre. The male longface, however, seemed to pay these no mind as he turned the plume of flame that leapt from his palm upon the pulsating sacs infesting the hall.

With methodical patience, he reduced them to ash. With contemptuous casualness, he flitted a hand at any frogman that rushed towards him, sending them spiralling against the stones.

'Ah,' the dragonman replied, 'there he is.'

'Incredible.'

The male, having torched one cluster of the fleshy sacs, strode across the water upon stepping stones of ice, smirking slightly as he drew back curtains of frogmen to make a path for himself towards the next.

'Simply incredible,' the boy repeated, narrowing his eyes.

'How so?' Asper asked. 'You can do the same thing, can't you?'

'Not like that,' the boy muttered. 'I made a boat out of ice and almost lost consciousness.' He pointed a trembling finger. '*He's* channelling three schools of magic at once *after* doing what he did to the Omens and he's not even sweating.'

'So … he's better than you.'

'It's simply not possible!' His protest came as a wheeze. 'Spells can't just be hurled about without regard! There are laws! There must be pause, there must be rest, there—' He stiffened suddenly, turning the expression of a scolded puppy upon Asper. 'Wait, you think he's better than me?'

'Well … I mean, *you* said he was.'

'I said he did something different. That doesn't make him better than me.'

'I'm sure you're very talented in other respects, but …' She scowled suddenly. 'Does it really matter now?'

'No,' Dreadaeleon muttered. He studied the male through a scrutinising squint, his lip crawling further up his face with every spell cast. 'If his magic were just stronger, I'd sense it. I'd *know* it.' With cognitive suddenness, he slammed a fist into a palm. 'He's *cheating*.'

'Cheating.' Asper raised a brow.

'Well, he is!' Dreadaeleon stamped a foot. 'Even in the most skilled hands, magic is a controlled burn. It strains the body, but not *his*. He's not even breathing hard. He's … I don't know … *using* something.'

'Search him when he's dead,' Gariath growled.

With a low snarl, he reached behind him. His body jerked, spasmed, then relaxed at the sound of particularly thick paper being torn. Asper cringed as dark rivers poured down his back, then fought violently against the rising bile as he thoughtfully flicked a glistening fragment of red from one of the blade's sharp prongs.

'For now,' the dragonman grunted, 'there's plenty to kill. If you're smart, you'll sit back and wait for a real warrior to finish it.' He looked over the pair contemptuously. 'Being that you're human, though—'

'Naturally.' Dreadaeleon's fingers tensed, beads of crimson glowing at their tips. 'I don't care who kills him. The laws of the Venarium must be upheld.'

With grim nods exchanged, the dragonman and not-yet man turned and stalked grimly towards the melee, ready to rend, to freeze, to bite and to burn. The battle raged with a yet-unseen fury, tides of pink and purple flesh colliding as the Abysmyths waded through to leisurely pluck opponents up and dismember them with disinterest.

Beautiful, Gariath thought.

The dragonman snorted. The wound felt good in his back. He would not be walking away from this fight, he

547

knew. All that remained was to make certain that he got there before nothing was left to kill.

'Wait!'

His eyelid twitched at the shrill protest. He scowled at Asper over his shoulder, meeting her objecting befuddlement with abject annoyance.

'What about the others? Lenk, Kataria, Denaos—'

'Dead, dead, dead quickly,' he replied. 'Honour them. Give them company in the afterlife.'

'But I …' she whimpered, 'I can't fight.'

'So die.'

'I left my staff behind.' Her excuse was as meek and sheepish as her smile. 'I'm not much use. I … could remain here and tend to you, though. You are bleeding quite badly and I—'

'*Moron!*' he roared, turning on her. 'There will be *nothing* for you to tend to here. Nothing will survive if I can help it.' He stomped towards her, scowling through his mask of gore. 'You cried about wanting to fight.' He thrust the jagged blade into her hands, staining her robes red. 'Now prove if you're worthy of life.'

'I … no, it's not that.' She tried to return the blade, her grasp trembling. 'I don't want to … I mean, I can't. My arm, you see, it—'

'I don't care,' he snarled in reply. 'No one will ever care what you did while you're still alive.' He snorted, spraying a cloud of red into her face. 'Your life will be nowhere near as great as your death, if you manage to do it right.'

Her eyes were those of an animal: frightened, weak, quivering. But she held on to the blade, he thought, and more importantly, she stopped talking. For the moment, that was enough for him; if she managed to do something worthwhile in the time she still breathed, it would be a pleasant surprise.

She disappeared from his thoughts and his sight as he turned his back to her, stalking towards the throng. He ignored her cries of protest, ignored the boy who had already disappeared into the battle, ignored the thought of the other dead humans. He would mourn for Lenk later, laugh at the rest of them with his last breath.

The wound in his back felt good, the chill that filled him refreshing. The sound of his life spattering onto the ground was a macabre reassurance that he would not be walking away from this fight, that he would be seeing his ancestors before the day was done.

And he would not be going alone, he resolved.

When the first of the longfaces looked up at him, pulling her spike out of a pale corpse and loosing a war cry, it was not death that he smelled, nor sea, nor salt, nor fear. There was only the scent of rivers as she charged him.

Rivers and rocks.

Twenty-Seven

TO SEE WITH EARS

'*Kat?*'
That was her name, wasn't it? No shict had ever
called her that, of course; shicts had full, proud names that
all meant something. Kat meant nothing, Kat was not a
name, Kat was not a word.

'*Kat!*'

Kat was her name, she remembered. Not her true name,
not her shict name. Kat was a name that some silver-haired
little girl had called her. No, she remembered, he had been
a man. A human.

'*Kataria!*'

She remembered him now. Skinny fellow, not at all
impressive to look at; but she looked at him often, didn't
she? She followed him out of a forest, a year ago. Where
was he now?

His voice was hard to hear. Her ears twitched against her
head. They felt disembodied, hanging from her head and
heavy with lead. Too deaf to hear her own breath, much
less some weak little human girl ... man.

But she heard him, still crying out her name, still shrieking, still screaming as if in pain. He had a lot of pain, she
remembered.

What was his name again?

'Lenk.' Her lips remembered. 'Don't be dead.' The

words came unbidden. They were not shict words. 'I'm coming.'

'Well, that's just delightful. I'm sure if he wasn't already dead, he'd be thrilled to hear it.'

Another voice: grating, simpering, unpleasant. She frowned immediately, her eyelids flittering open. The face she recognised: angular and narrow, like a rat's, except more obnoxious. His wasn't entirely concerned, his frown not particularly sympathetic.

'Denaos,' she hissed. Her voice was a croak on dry lips.

'Oh, good. You remember my name. Everything else upstairs working?' He tapped her temple with a finger. 'Nothing feel loose? Leaking?' He waved a hand in front of her. 'How many fingers am I holding up?'

'However many as will fit up your nose if you don't get away from me,' she snarled, slapping at his appendage. She rose from the stones beneath her, head pounding with the blood that rushed to it. 'What happened?'

'So, you *are* whole in the mind, right? That question was just your natural stupidity?' He sneered and gestured down a dark, drowned hall. 'Just listen, nit.'

She didn't have to strain her ears; even weakened as they were, the distant furore sounded violently close. There was the sound of weapons clattering to the floor, harsh and croaking war cries mingling. Mostly, there was the screaming: loud and sporadic, flowing into a continuous river of agony that flooded into her ears and filled her mind like a bubbling pot.

She winced, folded her ears over themselves. They ached terribly; why did they hurt so bad? With a pained expression, she reached up and rubbed them gently. Her horror only grew at the flecks of dried crimson that crumbled out into her palms.

'Ah, yes,' she muttered, remembering. 'Screaming.'

'Plenty of it,' Denaos confirmed. 'So, if you wouldn't mind, I'd like to do this nice and quietly.'

'Do … what?'

Denaos rubbed the bridge of his nose. 'I'd *like* to get out of here without having anything stuffed inside me that I didn't put there.' He eyed her warily. 'Are you sure you're all right? Because I'm starting to think this might be easier if you were dead.'

'Get out of here?'

Kataria looked over her shoulder. The great stone slab loomed at the end of the hall, the cracks in its grey face made haughty, shadowy grins against the emerald torch-light. It was mocking her, she realised, as she recalled what had happened. As she recalled who lay beyond it.

'We aren't going anywhere,' she muttered, rising to her feet. Her bones groaned in protest. She ignored them, as she did the throbbing of her ears, the agony of her body. 'Not without Lenk.'

'I'm sure he appreciates the sentiment.' Denaos crossed his arms and rolled his eyes. 'However, given the fact that he's behind Silf knows how much solid stone and we're out here and … you know, *alive*, he probably wouldn't hold it against us.'

She ignored him, collected her bow and quiver from puddles of salt and slung them over her shoulder. With equal contempt for the limp she walked with, she trudged to the stone and ran her fingers down it.

'It's rather large, if you hadn't noticed,' Denaos muttered. 'And thick. I checked.'

She looked over her shoulder at him with an even stare.

'Admittedly, with not much care.' He sighed. 'There was the issue of the half-dead shict to attend to.' He clapped his hands together. 'But you're up. You're moving about. Whatever else is down here is distracted, thus leaving us a fairly good opportunity to do that activity I enjoy so much where I don't get my head chewed off.'

'You could have run already,' she replied, turning back to the stone.

'I stand a better chance with you watching my back.'

'And we'll stand an even better chance with Lenk watching both our backs. Help me look for it.'

'For what?'

'A switch ... a lever ... something that moves this thing, I don't know. You're supposed to be good with these things, aren't you?'

'With hopeless situations?' He shook his head. 'Only by virtue of experience. If there was anything that could move that thing, I'd have found it. The only chance you have at this point is to bash it down with your ugly face.' He sneered. 'Granted, while it seems tempting ...'

His voice faded into another babbling tangent, easily ignored as she pressed her ear against the rock. The noises were faint: scuffling, splashing, something loud and violent. Through it, though, there was a familiar, if fleeting, sound.

He's alive.

At least, he sounded alive to her. It was difficult to tell; what she heard was but a fragment of his voice. It was a weak and dying noise, there and gone in an instant. Perhaps, she wondered, she imagined it?

A trick of her mind or her bloodied ears? Or maybe, in her heart if not her mind, she knew he was already dead and heard the last traces of his breath escaping this world before he followed it. Either way, it was a flimsy, weak excuse to linger in a forsaken fortress filled with demons.

Still, she thought as she cracked her knuckles, *I've gone off less before.*

'Hurry it up,' she growled as she leaned down to inspect the bottom of the slab. 'He's not well.'

'Compared to you?' She heard Denaos's long sigh. 'Good luck.'

She turned at the sounds of boots scraping across the stones. Denaos, with no particular rush or hesitation, stalked down the hall towards the drowned section. She quirked a brow.

'Where are you going?'

'Let's not belabour this, please. We all knew there was going to have to be a parting of ways, eventually.' He threw his hands up in resignation. 'I did what I could. Let Silf bear witness.'

'You did *nothing*!' she spat at his back, as though her words were arrows. 'I know your petty round-ear God rewards cowardice, but I don't. Now get back here and help.'

He could feel her eyes boring into him, that emerald stare that he had seen even Lenk flinch at. But he was not Lenk. He was not Gariath. He was not Kataria. He was a reasonable man. He was a cautious man. He was a man who knew when to run.

Keep telling yourself that, he thought. *Eventually, you'll believe it.* He stooped, making certain that the shict wouldn't see his bitter frown, hear his sigh. *Don't turn around*, he reminded himself, *don't turn around. She doesn't deserve a second look from you. None of them do. You told them. You warned them. They didn't listen and this is what happened.*

It's not your fault.

He paused at the edge of the water, blanched at its blackness and noted that it wasn't nearly black enough to hide the frowning face that looked back up at him.

No … still don't believe it.

His thoughts were interrupted by the sound of a bow-string drawn. He couldn't say that the sight of her eyes, narrowed to venomous slits over a glistening arrowhead, was particularly unexpected.

'No clansman is left behind,' she snarled, 'ever.'

Steady now, he told himself, holding his hands up for peace. *She's clearly lost what little mind she had.*

'Must we do this *now*?' he half-whined.

Brilliant.

'It should have been done long ago,' she hissed, pulling the fletching to her cheek. 'I've been lingering amongst your diseased race for too long. I wanted to believe the stories my father told me weren't true.' He caught the briefest sliver of a tear murmuring at the corner of her eye. 'I *wanted* to believe that.'

Sweet Silf, she's completely mad. Mad, he realised, and perceptive. His hands twitched, fingers eyeing the dagger at his belt. She responded, string drawing taut, teeth clenched.

'But every time I try, every legend proves true, every story about your cowardice and sickness …' Her eyes went wide, like a crazed beast's. 'All of it was true.'

Grief-ridden, perhaps, he suspected. *Gods know Lenk was a decent man, but this seems a bit extreme.* He noted the trail of blood that had dried upon her temple. *Maybe that last blow did it …* His attentions were drawn back to the arrow. *Either way …*

'If I can't do anything for Lenk …' She growled, her fingers twitched anxiously. 'I have to do *something*.'

'He's not a shict.'

Her fingers twitched, bowstring eased just a scant hair.

Good enough, he thought as his hand slid a little closer to his belt.

'W-what?' Her expression seemed to suggest she hadn't contemplated that fact in some time.

'He's human, you know,' the rogue continued, pressing a thumb to his chest. 'Like me, not you.' He raised one hand in appeal, all the better to draw attention from the other. 'You call him "clansman", like that means anything to him ... to *us*. But it only bears any weight on long, notched ears.'

There might still be a way out of this, he told himself, *you don't have to kill her.* Yet, as his fingers brushed the weapon's hilt, it seemed to add: *But just in case ...*

'Lenk's ... not like you,' she muttered without much conviction.

'Fair enough. What would he suggest you do, then?' The rogue shrugged. 'Sit here? Wait for whatever's happening out there to find its way in here?' He shook his head. 'No, Lenk might not be like me. He's reasonable. He's cautious.' He levelled an even stare at her. 'He would run ... but he would want you with him.'

I can't really afford to make that kind of choice right now, he added mentally. *I'm sorry, Kat.* The dagger slipped into his palm. *This isn't my fault.*

He didn't believe it then, either.

Something heavy slammed against the stone, water erupted behind him.

He whirled about, springing backwards at the sight of the great, white-eyed shadow barrelling out of the darkness. The Abysmyth clawed its way into the corridor, dripping water and black ichor from a number of festering emerald wounds that criss-crossed its body.

Denaos held the dagger high, ready to throw as the beast

stretched out a claw. Yet, as vacant as the creature's stare was, there was no mistaking its direction. The Abysmyth looked past Denaos, past Kataria, to the great, stone slab. Its mouth dropped open.

'Prophet ...' it gurgled, 'why ... won't you help—'

Its question ended in a violent sputter and a blossom of iron. Faster than Denaos could even gasp, a great wedge of metal burst out from between the thing's jaws. It spasmed as green-tinged froth spilled out of its maw to splatter on the floor, twitched as something pulled on the metal and ripped the weapon free from the back of the demon's skull. It toppled forwards and Denaos immediately forgot how close he had been to killing his companion.

The appearance of the newcomer demanded far more attention.

The woman, or what appeared to be a woman, swung her massive weapon over her shoulder, heedless of the black liquid dribbling down its length. With equally callous casualness, she stepped atop the creature, iron boots crunching upon spine and ribs.

Kataria met her gaze. It occurred to her that the stare, milky white, was not unlike the slain Abysmyth's. Where the demon's was vacant and unfeeling, however, this ... woman's stare leaked hunger and scorn as though they were tears.

Her purple flesh was as lean and hard as her black armour. Even her face was long and thin like a spear. The fact that her metal was still slick with the Abysmyth's essence did not encourage the shict to lower her weapon. She had cut down a demon with such cruel callousness and now regarded the rogue and shict with an angry ivory scowl. Any idiot could tell she was no ally.

And, as if on cue, Denaos rushed up to meet her.

'Well done!' He slid about the female, seeming to place her between himself and Kataria. 'Quite a fine blow there.'

You can't be serious, Kataria thought. Was the woman's malice not apparent to him? Did she strike him as another lusty tramp eager for his seduction? She would have put an arrow through the woman in that breath, but white eyes held her in check, daring her and warning her at the same time.

'Any lady that is a foe to any Abysmyth is a friend of ours,' he said, smiling broadly to compensate for the cold scowl she shot him.

'Abys ... myth?' Her voice was a knife, raspy and cold. 'Is that what they are called? Master Sheraptus refers to them as "underscum".'

'A fine term.' Denaos's laugh was a bit strained. 'What does he call us humans?'

'Overscum.'

'Clever. And what do we call you?'

The woman regarded him cautiously for a moment, then turned her gaze back to Kataria. Her eyes narrowed, she forced the word into a sharpened blade aimed at the shict's head.

'Xhai.' She swept that scornful gaze about the corridor. 'Semnein Xhai.' She waved a hand. 'Unimportant. Where is the leader of this weak gathering? Where is the Deepshriek?'

'We're not entirely certain,' Denaos replied. 'Our friend slipped into that room there, see, and—'

'Useless.'

His jaw became a gong of bone and blood, her gauntlet the hammer that sent it ringing through the hall. His whimper was somewhat less impressive as he crumpled to the floor in a whisper. She spared a derisive glob of saliva for his body before turning to the shict.

There was no time for Kataria to wonder whether her companion still drew breath. Her bow was up and levelled. All that stayed her arrow was the odious malice that oozed from every inch of the female's skin.

'Your males,' the purple woman muttered, 'have a great love of hearing themselves speak.'

'Stay back, longface,' Kataria hissed in reply.

'Longface?' The female arched a white brow. 'We've been called that before.'

'It's slightly less of a mouthful than "white-haired, narrow-jawed, purple-skinned man-woman".'

'We are netherling, overscum,' the woman snarled. '*You* would do well to shove the proper respect in your mouth when addressing the First of Arkklan Kaharn's Carnassials.'

'Whatever you like to be called, you're not needed here.'

'We go where we please.' The netherling tapped her sword against her shoulder. 'I have come for …' Her long face twisted in thought. 'A book, is it called?'

'The … tome?'

'Ah. That does sound more impressive.'

'That isn't yours to take.'

'Ours is the right to take.' Xhai levelled a metal finger at the shict. 'Your fortune is to stay out of our way when we choose to allow you to. Now … embrace your luck and get out of my way. I have much killing to do.'

'So have I.' Kataria drew back the arrow to her lips. 'And I was here first. Get out.'

'Or?'

Her bow sang a melancholy tune and, as Kataria

witnessed wide-eyed the woman stagger back only half a step as the arrow sank into her ribcage, she couldn't help but wonder if her weapon sang her own dirge. The Carnassial glanced down at the shaft quivering in her flesh and grinned broadly.

'Weak.'

Stone groaned, metal shrieked, the netherling was rushing. Her long blade dragged behind her, spewing emerald-tinted sparks. Kataria fired again, hastily, clumsily, and the arrow lodged itself in the netherling's biceps. Her grin broadened as she hefted the blade in both hands.

Stop, Kataria told herself. *Breathe.* The arrow slid into her fingers eagerly. *Focus.* She drew back the missile. *Steady.* She narrowed her eyes as the netherling raised the weapon above her head and shrieked.

Shoot.

The arrow howled, found its mark in a splitting squeal and bit deeply into a purple armpit. Iron clattered, the Carnassial shrieked and pressed a hand against the red blossoming under her arm.

Kataria smiled. All humans, purple or pink, never saw that one coming. The victory was as brief as the Xhai's pause, and Kataria's smile died and withered into a terrified gape.

She's not stopping.

Another arrow flew, ricocheted off an armoured shoulder that collided with her chest. The shict felt something shift inside her violently. Her bow was torn from her grasp as she was torn from the floor, sent skidding across the salt and stone.

She could barely clamber to her knees, barely muster the energy to cough and send a thick liquid spattering onto the floor. *Not good*, she realised, *not good, not good*. Sounds were distant, sights varying shades of grey.

'That's it, is it?'

The netherling's voice echoed against her skull. She looked up just in time to see a pair of milky orbs, a broad, jagged smile to match the shimmering sword held high above her head.

Move.

It was more of a lurch than a roll, but the sudden movement served well enough to place Kataria out of the way of the crashing blade. It devoured the stone in a shower of fragments, embedding itself hungrily in the floor. Xhai snarled, tugging violently at the weapon's handle. She didn't even bother to look up at the sound of boots crashing on the stone.

'*Surprise!*' Kataria roared.

She leapt, took the woman about the waist and sent them both tumbling to the ground. Xhai tossed her off as though she were an overenthused puppy, leaping atop her opponent.

But Kataria's instincts were swift as her legs. Boots were up and planted into the Carnassial's belly with a ferocity the shict was not even aware of. Even less aware of the roar tearing itself from her lips, she drove her feet against her foe's stomach again. The netherling was hoisted up and over her to sprawl upon the floor in a crash of iron.

She should have run then. Some part of Kataria knew that was a good idea. But that part was far away now, bleating impotently against the howling within her.

Kataria could feel the roar, rather than hear it. Something forced undiluted rage from her heart, through her veins and out of her mouth. Something bit her muscles with sharp, angry teeth. She went taut, hard, her blood straining to feed her fury as her ears folded against her head in a feral display.

And through her bared teeth, her flashing canines, she could only say one thing.

'No clansman is left behind,' she snarled. '*EVER!*'

Xhai didn't seem to notice, far more concerned with the foot that crashed down upon her face as she tried to rise. Kataria swept upon her, straddling her waist and seizing her by the jaw.

The sound of bone cracking upon the stone did not cause her to relent, could not drown out the roar. What dwelt within her screamed long and loud, sent its victorious, unpleasant laughter rushing into her ears and past her teeth. She brought her fist up and down, pumping with feral rhythm against the Carnassial's bony cheek.

So loud and proud did it call, so fierce and feral did it roar, that she never even noticed that her foe was growling instead of flinching. She did not see that the netherling barely bled from her wounds. She did not see the metal-clad fist rising.

'*ENOUGH*,' Xhai shrieked.

The iron was a blur, crashing against Kataria's jaw and sending her reeling to the floor. Her foot was a spear, kicking the shict hard against the ribs and sending her curling, her howl abandoning her in an agonised cacophony.

Where is it, she asked herself, *where is the howling? I can't hear it any more ... I can't ...*

There were many things that she could not.

She could not feel a heavy weight straddling her back, cold iron wrapping about her wrist and twisting her hand behind her back. She could not even roar in pain any more. When her arm was wrenched up so that her wrist pressed against her shoulder blades, it was a weak, meagre whimper that came out of her lips.

'Stop.' A second hand seized her by her braid and pressed her face forwards against the stone. 'Do not taint the fight with weakness.' She could feel Xhai's smile bore into the back of her head. 'I knew somewhere in this stupid horde of weakness, someone could fight. Naturally, I found it in a female.'

How, Kataria asked herself, *how am I supposed to kill her? What was I supposed to do?* The howling within her was silent, offering no answers. *WHAT?*

'Don't misunderstand, of course,' Xhai continued, 'I'm still going to kill you, but I'll ... regret it. That is the word for it, yes? But not yet. I need you to speak.' She rubbed the shict's face in the salt water. 'Your brains have yet to leak out onto the floor, so use them. Tell me what I want to know or I'll wrench your arm off.'

'Then do it.' Kataria's voice, weak and foreign to her own ears, did nothing to convince herself, let alone her captor.

The Carnassial's derisive snicker confirmed as much. 'Obey and I leave you whole. I understand whatever weak deities you overscum worship frown on followers in pieces.' She pulled her prisoner's face up that she might better hear the snickering spike being driven into her ear. 'That's all up to you, though.' She pressed the shict's face back to the stone. 'Where is the book?'

'I ... we don't know.'

'There are more of you, are there?' The Carnassial snorted. 'Odd that so many weaklings would congregate in one place. Were you all drawn here by some stink?' The woman snarled, twisting the shict's arm further. 'Or were you sent?'

563

Kataria could hear her own bones creaking, feel her own fingers grazing the nape of her neck.

'G-Greenhair,' she half-growled, half-whined, a wounded beast. 'S-siren—'

'The screamer?'

Xhai's recognition should have alarmed Kataria, would have alarmed Kataria if not for the fact that there was no room for panic or fear left in her. Nor was there any room left in the netherling for mercy, for as Kataria pounded the stones for mercy with her free hand, her captor merely let out a contemplative hum.

'She is too loose with her allies,' the white-haired woman muttered.

Whether out of mercy or out of boredom, she released Kataria's arm and rose up and off her. Kataria gasped, biting back the scream in her throat. Her arm felt weak and useless, freedom a sudden unbearable agony. Straining to keep from shrieking, straining to keep her breath, she struggled to rise. Even her free arm ached, groped about with blind fingers.

It was by pure chance that she felt a handle amidst the salt water. It was with pure fury that she wrapped trembling fingers about it. It hurt to grin, but she couldn't help it. *Apparently*, she thought as she looked into the blade of Denaos's fallen dagger, *he's good for something*.

'After all, she chose you two weaklings rather poorly.' The woman's voice was only slightly harsher than the sound of her blade being jerked free from the stone. 'I must admit, I was surprised.' Kataria heard the whisper of air as the blade was raised. 'Still, for a female, you are weak. Are all your kind?'

'No.'

Xhai whirled, the great wedge of metal slicing off the

scantest of hairs atop Kataria's head as she drove the knife forwards. It found flesh and drove deep into the netherling's hip. Kataria's cry of joy was as short as her foe's cry of anger.

Run.

She did, but the effort was hindered by a desperate limp. Still, she reasoned, if her pain was only a little less than that of having a dagger driven through a hip, she should be able to get away.

Unfortunately, she realised as a gauntleted hand clasped upon her shoulder, things rarely went as they should.

Stone struck her back, air was struck from her lungs as Xhai shoved her against the wall. With scarcely any breath left to scream, much less to marvel at the ease with which the netherling hefted the great chunk of metal, Kataria gritted her teeth, folded her ears against her head and hissed as she raked the woman's metal-clad wrist.

She wasn't quite sure what she hoped to accomplish. The unstable twitch that consumed the woman's eyelid suggested she was as far beyond intimidation as she was beyond mercy.

'Clever, clever little runt,' the netherling snarled. 'Cleverness never prevails against the strong. The netherlings are strong.' She slammed Kataria against the wall again. 'Semnein Xhai is strong.'

There was no room left for fear or pain within Kataria. She had done her part, she told herself, fought as best she could. The knife and arrows jutting from the woman testified to that. The netherling would remember her, long after she killed her. She tried to take comfort in that, but found it difficult. As difficult as she found it to keep a defiant face directed at the Carnassial. Her neck jerked involuntarily, drawing her attention back to the stone slab that loomed with granite smugness at the end of the hall.

'Lenk,' she whispered, though she could no longer hear her own voice, 'I'm sorry.'

She expected the blow to come then: a quick, sudden sever that she would never feel, perhaps swift enough to allow her to stare up at her own neck as the rest of her rolled across the floor. The blow did not come, though. Reluctantly, perhaps afraid that the netherling was simply waiting for her to watch it come, Kataria turned back to face the woman.

What she saw was a black hilt jutting from the Carnassial's collarbone, her face contorted in a sudden agony, iron rattling in her trembling arm. A sudden splitting of flesh drew Kataria's eyes down to the gloved hand wedging a second blade into her flank. The woman staggered backwards as a pink face marred by a black eye and split with an unpleasant grin rose over her shoulder.

'What was that about cleverness?' Denaos hissed, twisting the knife further.

The female shrieked, whirling about to bring her sword up in a frenzied circle. The rogue was already out of reach, retreating nimbly as another dagger leapt to his fingers.

Xhai roared, hefting her sword as she stepped towards her new foe. Like a sparrow, the dagger danced off his fingers, tumbling lazily through the air to impale itself in the netherling's knee. Her foot collapsed under her, she fell to one knee.

She seemed shattered in that moment, swaying precariously as a hand pressed against her as though straining to keep pieces of her from falling apart. Her wounds seemed to bloom all at once, life coagulating in the contours of her muscles. The mask of fury slipped off her face, exposing a slack-jawed, incredulous mockery of a warrior.

'What … I'm …' She touched her knee, eyes widening at the sight of red smearing her fingers. 'I … you can't …' She tried to rise, her voice caught in her throat as she winced. 'It hurts.' As though this were something alien to her, she looked to Denaos. 'You *hurt* me.'

'It's what I do,' he replied casually.

'Impossible. I am … unscarred.' She rose to shaky feet. 'I could kill you … both of you!' She jerked a dagger free from her side, hurling it to the floor. 'I *will* kill you! *All of you!*'

Xhai hefted the sword and buckled under its weight, choked by an agonised whimper. The Carnassial, so strong and relentless, became a weak and meagre thing, Kataria thought. The fact that she still held a massive wedge of iron, however, kept the shict from savouring her pain. Instead, she retreated cautiously, eyeing her bow.

'Stay back!' Xhai roared, holding up a hand as she trembled to her feet again. 'Stay away from me!' Her eyes darted between them, crazed, before settling upon Denaos. 'I will … *kill* you.'

Her voice hanging in the air, her blood pooling beneath iron soles, she spat a curse in a harsh, hissing language. Her sword groaned as she dragged it behind her, Denaos's dagger still lodged in her collarbone. She limped over the fallen Abysmyth into the watery passage and vanished into the gloom.

The air left Kataria in a sudden sigh as she collapsed to her rear. She could hear nothing but the pounding of her own heart and the lonely drip of salt water falling from the ceiling to dilute the sticky red smears on the floor. She felt the sweat of her body cold upon the stone, she felt her breath come in short, ragged bursts.

'Sons of the Shadow,' Denaos gasped, crumpling against the wall. 'I thought she'd never leave.' He glanced down to his belt, ominously empty. 'Pity ... she took my best knife with her.'

'If you'd like, I'm sure she can come back.' Kataria resisted the urge to laugh, pressing a hand to her sore ribs. 'How do you feel?'

'About the same as any man who's been beaten by demons and purple harlots in the same day. How do I look?'

'About the same.'

'Yeah? You should take a look at yourself before you decide to sling stones.'

Kataria didn't doubt his claim. She didn't need eyes to know the extent of her injuries. She could feel the purple bruise welling up on her midsection, the blood dripping from her nose, the lungs that threatened to collapse at any moment. She smiled, hoping the gesture was as unpleasant as his grimace would suggest.

'I'll be even less of a prize when we're done.'

'We are done,' Denaos replied. He rose from the stones, knuckled the small of his back. 'There's nothing more we can do here, Kat.' He gestured to the great stone slab. 'We couldn't lift that even if we *weren't* both half-dead.'

The realisation hurt worse than any of her wounds. He was right, of course. Staying behind was lunacy, a short period of contemplation and repentance before a demon or another netherling stumbled upon her. And, as she heard her next words, she knew there would be much to repent for.

'I'm staying.'

He looked at her, frowned.

'He's not a—'

'I know.'

Quietly, he nodded. He plucked up her bow and quiver from the floor, giving a quick count before tossing it to her.

'Thirteen arrows left,' he said. 'Unlucky number for round-ears.'

'Shicts, too.'

'Mm.' He lingered there, watching her readjust her weaponry. 'It seems a shame to leave you after you threatened to kill me for leaving earlier.'

'You'll get over it.' She gestured down the hall. 'Go. Don't choose now to pretend we've got camaraderie.'

He nodded, turned. 'I'll bring back the others.'

'No, you won't.'

'I might.'

She made no reply, merely staring at her arrows. He paused at the edge of the water, looking over his shoulder at her.

'What are you going to do, anyway?' he asked.

'Something.'

He slipped into the water without a sound, vanishing. The sound of carnage was quieting now, nothing more than whispers of pain on a stale breeze. A pity, she thought, there might be no one left to come and kill her.

That might be less painful, she reasoned, than living to see the shame of waiting for a human she had dared to call her own.

Twenty-Eight
TASTING THE SCREAM

S o ... that's *why it's called the Deepshriek.*
The musing flitted through Lenk's brain, swimming
on a ringing cacophony and disjointed panic. He could feel
laughter echoing in the water, crawling over his lobes on
skittering, shrieking legs. Even through such a wretched
fury, however, the voice was clear and cold.

'*Air,*' it commanded, '*we need air!*'

Eyes snapped open, aching reverie was banished. The
water was thick and oppressive around him, clung to him
with a lonely desperation and smothered him with black
liquid quilts.

Not nearly black enough, he noted, to obscure the horror
barrelling towards him.

The Deepshriek's six golden eyes, alight with wicked
glee, were a stark contrast to the shark's glimmering
onyxes, just as the fiend's great white teeth were a terrifying comparison to its dead stare.

'*AIR!*' the voice shrieked.

Fear fuelled his legs, tearing his body from the foggy
trance. He struggled, kicked, thrashed as though he were
on fire. He pulled himself up to the shimmering green light
above him. The water moaned frothily as he shattered the
surface, begging him to return, groping with lonely liquid
claws.

It shuddered beneath him at the passing of the shark. That was a fleeting terror; for now, he sought to fill his lungs with every stale breath he could. It was only after the danger of drowning had passed that he felt the first pangs of cold fear.

The liquid trembled in sympathy. Six golden eyes peered out of the blackness, three fanged grins pierced the gloom. A great, axe-like fin broke the surface of the water, drifting with a casual menace before vanishing again.

'*Toying with us . . .*' The voice, its need for breath satiated, was a fiercer cold than any fear. '*Take us to land.*'

'Right,' he muttered in reply.

He spied the decaying stone ledge hanging over the water, reaching with fumbling hands. Breath burned in his lungs as he flailed, struggling against the fierce water. His heart thundered in his chest, sending ripples upon ripples. Undoubtedly, he thought as he felt something pass him, it did not go unnoticed.

The outcropping grew closer.

He yearned for a sword, leather, something solid to wrap his hands around. A man with a sword was a man with a chance, however thin either might be. A man with a sword had a satisfying death to look forward to, a shrug of the shoulders and a knowledge that he had done all he could. A man without a sword was nothing more than . . .

'*Bait,*' the voice suggested in response to his thoughts.

He ignored it. The outcropping was within arm's reach.

His hand shot out desperately as a chorus of twisted laughter filled the air. He snapped his head about, regarding the three feminine faces snaking high above the water, staring back at him with broad grins and wide, excited eyes. More distressing than that was the great grey fin jutting between their stalks, looming over Lenk's head.

'Oh, damn,' he whispered.

He saw the crimson first, the thick red upon the darkness, before he felt the teeth sink into his thigh. His scream was short and stifled. The shark, unsympathetic, continued to swim, deaf to his agony as it dragged him through the murk. Lenk threw back his head, opened his mouth to scream again.

'*Bad idea*,' the voice snarled.

The shark dived. Darkness filled Lenk's mouth as the green firelight waxed and grew fainter above him. He was pulled deep, to the bottom of the foetid pool, leaving a crimson cloud behind. He flailed, pounded the shark's head, raked at its rock-hard flesh with painfully human hands. The sheer futility did not occur to him. He was well past the point for logic to be of any use.

The shark's teeth dug further into his flesh in response. He screamed, his voice lost on bubbles and blackness, and through thoughts clouded by pain he wondered why the demon simply hadn't sheared through his leg.

The beast twisted, turned sharply upwards to bring him to the surface. He was spared a choked gasp, a triumvirate of giggles, before the shark angled sharply and pulled him under.

It's ... he realised, *it's tasting me.*

And it did so with macabre discerning. It chewed on him thoughtfully, fondled his thigh with a thick tongue, saliva cold even in the brackish depths. The three heads shifted, licking their own lips, sharing their grey host's experience with water-choked enthusiasm.

And Lenk continued to strike it, still. The liquid slowed his fists, pulled at him, defending the demon even as impotent as his assault was. And yet, such a futile fury was all that kept him alive. When he ceased struggling, when

panic faded, the abomination would be

Hunger, if the thing did indeed ea
behind.

But his body was running out of fear
His lungs tightened, vision darkened. A
though the water seeped into his very
panic, consuming fear and replacing it
tion.

This is how it ends. The thought was
bubbles, a slowing of his fist. *Eaten by*
heads. His strike was an infant's agains
make a good story, at least.

His thoughts were faint against the
All sounds were fading, drowned by the
his ears. Even the sound of his heart
burst in a sloppy eruption, was but a dis

It wouldn't be long. And, as the water
his mind with liquid tendrils, that didn'
thing.

'*Fight.*'

The voice, colder than all the water
through him, muttered from a distant co

'*Kill,*' it uttered, faint, like someone
behind a great wall of ice, but growing st
'*Kill!*'

As water reached from without, someth
within. A hand with fingers of frigid mist
his body, expelled the invading liquid. His
stopped beating. The fear that such a react
was gone, the need for air less desperate.
leg was gone, the limb felt numb even u
teeth.

'*Kill!*'

573

ıe numbness spread to his entire body, a coldness that
ed the demands of his flesh, silenced the shrieking
ıter. He could not feel his arms moving, but saw his
ırs guided by something not himself. They slid down
focused precision to the shark's side, sank into some-
ʒ soft and fleshy. He did not know the beast's weak-
ɛs, but whatever moved his limbs did, and it seized
ı, merciless.

'ILL!'

ɛnk felt his hands dig into the ridges of the gill slits.
felt an impassive, uncaring strength course into his
. He felt flesh tear.

gout of red wept in the gloom. The shark's groan was
ʒ and echoed through the blackness. The heads above
t into a snaking, writhing agony, sputtering through
cloud of blood that drifted into their faces. The jaws
ıquished him to the water and he watched the thing
t sharply, retreating into the darkness.

Ie remembered air, the taste of it in his lungs. He saw
green light shimmering above him. But the strength
t coursed through him, the rivers of ice that replaced
blood, would not let him go to it.

nstead, his legs became as lead, pulling him to the bot-
ı. He did not resist, did not feel fear at such a thing, did
hear the cry of his body for breath. All thoughts were
ıe, retreated from the voice that muttered in his brain,
ʒden in some forgotten corner of his mind.

Iis eyes were jerked, forced upon a glimpse of metal
the darkness. He swam to it, heedless of his bleeding,
ɛdless of his need for air. He felt the massive demon
ɔop over him, heard it scream, but ignored it. Only
ɛr existed.

His fingers groped the rocky bottom of the pool, the

glint of silver vanishing as his shadow fell over it. He caught something in the darkness, a strap of some kind. Unthinking, he took it in one hand and reached again. His hand felt a familiar hilt, a leather-bound grip in his own.

Lenk remembered his sword.

'*And now, we are strong.*' The voice spoke to him with what sounded like an attempt at soothing reassurance. It would have caused Lenk to cringe, if not for the smile he felt creep across his face. '*Kill*,' it commanded.

And, in the death of sound that existed between the blade sliding from the rocky floor and the tightening of his hand around its hilt, Lenk answered.

Yes.

The presence fled him in an instant. He was once more aware of the blood pumping in his arms, out of his leg. He felt his heart pound in his chest. He remembered the need for air.

Twisting, thrashing, he pulled himself skywards. Out of the corner of an eye wide with returned fear, he spied the Deepshriek spearing towards him. Its jaws gaped, six golden eyes narrowed furiously. He thrashed harder, straining, lusting for the surface.

The water stirred under him, the sound of bone cracking filled the dark as teeth clamped shut over emptiness. It sped beneath him. He felt three pairs of fangs gnash at him, grazing the leather of his boot and growling in frustration.

Lenk sundered the surface with a gasp and tore towards the outcropping. He grunted, grabbed and hoisted himself upon the rocky ledge. The stale air felt as sweet to his lungs as the hard, unyielding granite felt welcome to his body. He lifted his sword above him, smiling at the thick steel as he would an old friend.

575

And in his reflection, his old friend smiled back.

It wasn't until he rose that he felt the weight in his other hand, the leather strap wrapped around his fingers. A satchel, he realised, water dripping off its black, slick leather. Its mouth hung loosely open, exposing a glimpse of its contents. Yellowed parchment, he recognised with widening eyes, bound between planks of dark leather that reflected no light.

As he stared down at it, the book stared back up at him with papery eyes and smiled.

'It can't be—'

'*VILE LANDBORNE FILTH!*'

He looked up, simultaneously tossing the satchel behind him as he took up his sword in both hands. Three heads snaked before him, ominous golden scowls narrowed upon him as they spoke in a unified trio of spite.

'What disease of your feeble grey brain afflicts you so to persist in this stupidity?' they snarled. 'You know nothing, less than a fraction of what lingers within those pages, and you come, suffer *our* wrath, even as your fellow mortal pests are butchered beyond this chamber.'

'What?'

Lenk knew he shouldn't have said it, shouldn't have let the fear show even for a moment on his face. He should have ignored the demon, drowned its words, but they echoed in his ears.

'This … shocks you?' The three heads bared fangs in unpleasant smiles. 'We see all that occurs in this tomb of rock and froth. We see mortals dying, blood being spilled, agony, fear, panic—'

'*It lies*,' the voice came rushing back into his brain. '*Kill it now.*'

'They are broken, mortal.' Their mouths twisted, caught

between joyous grins and hateful grimaces. 'They have suffered much. They begged for salvation from uncaring Gods.'

'*Ignore it.*'

Lenk could not hide the despair flashing on his face, despite the voice's command. Did it truly lie? The demon had powers, powers he could not contemplate. Could it know? Could it speak the truth?

'And when none came,' the heads spoke, 'they begged for death.'

'*Kill it now!*'

Lenk's sword drooped in his hands and he stared out into nothingness. He didn't notice the golden-haired head rising above its swaying kin on a neck gone rigid.

'Fret not, poor creature,' the red- and raven-coloured heads purred. 'Your fates are tied. Their mercy was cruel, but swift.'

'*LOOK, FOOL!*'

Lenk spied the bulge rising up the centre stalk. The golden-haired head's mouth stretched impossibly wide.

'*YOURS*,' the other two heads shrieked, '*WILL BE MUCH MESSIER!*'

The air shattered, the stones trembled. Lenk's vision rippled as the shrieking thunder split the world before him. He flung himself to the side, narrowly avoiding the vocal onslaught as it bit into the stone slab, digging a crater in a spray of granite shards.

Snarling, he pulled himself away from the edge. His ears rang, but he heard nothing, not the lapping of water or stones sinking into the gloom or the curses of the Deepshriek.

He heard but one cold, angry voice that swiftly became his own as he tightened his grip on the sword.

'DIE!'

Three great bulges rose up the stalks, three mouths gaped wide.

Silent, ignoring the voices of reason and instinct, he charged. Silent, ignoring the quake of his heart and the scream of his leg, he leapt. Silent, heeding only the voice in his head and in his hand, he struck.

He landed, straddling the shark's slippery back. He teetered, narrowly avoiding toppling back to eager jaws by reaching out to grasp the central stalk. The golden-haired head let out choked protest, jerked down as he struggled to keep atop the beast.

The air split with the other heads' shrieks, their fury launched at nothing. His grip tightened as he pulled himself to his feet. The other heads snaked about, snapped at him, nicking multiple cuts on his arms. He ignored them, focusing only on the central head's bulging eyes and the sickly shade of blue it turned as the bulge of air was choked beneath his grasp.

His sword came up and down in a silver blur, sundering the thick flesh of the stalk. His grip slipped as golden locks tumbled into the air and disappeared beneath the water with a satisfying plop.

Time stopped suddenly. The shark came to a halt, the four remaining eyes went wide, and even the blood from his wounds seemed to stop seeping.

Then, chaos.

Their screams filled the chamber, their heads flailed with such fury as to seem ready to rip off from their stalks. The air within the now-headless central stalk came bursting out, heralded by a torrent of black, sticky blood. Lenk released it, seizing the shark's fin as the stalk went wild, spewing black ichor.

The remaining heads shrieked in unison, barely audible through their agony. 'What have you done, mortal? What wicked blade do you possess?'

Odd, he thought as he reached for the red-haired head, until that moment, he had never wondered if demons felt fear. Nor did he care as he raised the sword, ready to add another head to his tally.

His arm was jarred as the entire chamber shook. The shark rammed its snout into the rocky wall, causing Lenk's swing to go wide. He snarled, swept his blade up to carve a gaping gash into the beast's hide. It groaned, thrashed suddenly and sent him flying to crash against the wall.

He peeled himself from the stone, winded, but still with his wits about him as he hit the water. His sword was up, its silver bright in the water's gloom as he prepared to finish the demon off.

Through the water, though, Lenk spied the Deepshriek, thrashing madly, its heads screeching. He watched it, squirming about like a wounded animal before it turned to the bottom. He watched it as it passed through the floor, staring in curiosity as its tail vanished into a gaping, black hole, its screaming echoing off the water as it disappeared.

He stared at the hole, waiting for it to return. When moments had passed, he surfaced. His breath was heavy as he hoisted himself onto the outcropping once again. Heavy, but clean.

He stared at the waters for ages, sword clenched tightly as he waited for the demon to return. The surface would yield no signs from its blackness, though, and, with a great sigh, he allowed his sword to fall and himself to collapse onto his back.

His head felt like lead, but through his hair he could feel

something resting under his skull. He remembered then: leather, unadorned and black, in the satchel. What he had come all this way for ...

'The tome,' he whispered, smiling.

And under his head, it smiled back.

Twenty-Nine

BURN

A blade was a peculiar thing to feel, Asper thought. She had never held one before, only stared at them with envy as they danced to a tune played by more capable hands. Now that she did feel one, it was heavy in her grip, like an iron burden wrought with jagged teeth.

Dripping with blood, she added mentally, *Gariath's blood*. The thought of holding such a thing had occasionally crossed her mind, in her darkest anger against the dragonman.

But now that she held it . . .

'I can't do this,' she gasped, 'I can't do this, can't do this, can't . . .'

Reassuring denial was lost in an errant roar from the distant hall.

The battle, as Denaos might say in his cruder moments, had long since spent its best affections and now slid into sluggish, sleepy, blood-glutted cuddling.

The precise strikes from the longfaces' iron spikes had become vicious, slovenly chops as their purple kindred lay beside their feet. The endless stream of frogmen had choked to narrow trickles, the pale creatures glancing around with dark eyes to seek out their emaciated Shepherds. The demons themselves had either fled or lay in smoking husks that still sighed white plumes of steam as they sank into the salt.

And even the water seemed disgusted, sliding out of the great wound in Irontide's hide in an effort to escape the battle. Water shunned the place, she thought, and begged her to go with it. Neither of them belonged here.

They were healers. She was a healer. She served the Healer. What place did she have in this slaughter?

She did not desire an answer, but received one, anyway, at the end of her left arm. It twitched now, throbbing angrily. It did not doubt, it snarled. It did not beg, it demanded. And with each moment, it grew harder to ignore.

'Not now,' she whispered to her appendage. '*Not now.* I can fight this. I can resist this.' Only remotely aware of how much of a squealing whisper her voice was, she felt the tears slide down her cheek to land upon her sleeve. '*Not ... now.*'

'Then when?'

Asper's head snapped towards the longface standing over her. For a woman bludgeoned and cut, she looked remarkably calm, regarding the priestess from behind a circular iron shield. The unpleasant grin that split her face, however, left no motive unclear.

'You look lost, pinky,' the longface said. She raised her iron spike, slammed it against her shield. 'Need some help?'

'S-stay back.' Asper retreated a step, raising her left hand, then forcing it down against her side and holding up the blade. 'I've got a weapon.'

'One of our own gnawblades.' The longface tilted her head to note the gore dripping down its handle. 'But you don't look like you could have done *that* with it.'

'I ... I did.'

'I haven't seen you in the fight. Hiding is reserved for males.' The longface smiled, took a step forwards. 'Females fight.'

'Stay away from me!'

'Do your breed proud and stand,' the woman hissed. 'If I have to stick you in the back, I'm going to be unhappy.'

Asper took a step backwards and the longface's grin grew broader. *Unhappy, indeed.* Calling the woman a liar would seem a bit futile, though. Instead, she tensed, ready to turn, ready to flee.

'*QAI ZHOTH!*' A grating roar split the air. '*DIE, OVERSCUM! AKH ZEKH LA—*'

The war cry was cut short with the sound of paper splitting. Both longface and Asper looked up, seeing a great red fist thrust into the mouth from which it had poured. Gariath offered no war cry in retort, no insult or unpleasant cackle. His blow was vicious, but his fist hung in the air long after his victim collapsed. When he finally lowered it, he gasped with such exhaustion that the rest of him threatened to follow his hand to the floor.

Still, it was enough to send three other longfaces leaping backwards, shields raised. And in the parting of purple flesh, Asper could see the red pools at his feet, the tears dripping from his flesh, the waning hatred in his eyes. His knuckles were purple, wings flaccid on his back, but his smile was large and unpleasant.

'Lucky, lucky.'

Her attention was brought back to the longface before her, who snorted, spat and hefted her shield.

'Looks like the darker you pinkies get, the more trouble you are.' She flashed a grin at the priestess. 'I don't need you any more. I don't want you any more.'

'What?' Asper could not help but look incredulous as the longface stalked away. 'That's it?'

'I'll be back later.'

'But … you were going to … I mean, I've … I've got a gnawblade!'

'There are always more weapons.'

'You can't just—'

Stop that. Her thoughts echoed in the sound of iron soles. *This is your chance. Run. You don't belong here.* Her eyes narrowed upon Gariath, swinging wide against an encroaching longface. *He doesn't want you here. He wants to die.* She swept the rest of the battle. *No sign of Dreadaeleon, either. He's dead … you can't bring people back from the dead. No one can.*

There's nothing you can do here.

The longface swung her iron spike, testing its weight. Her left arm twitched.

You shouldn't even be with these people.

Gariath buckled to one knee under a sudden blow from behind. Her left arm throbbed.

What, she asked herself, *could you even do?*

She clenched her jaw, tightened her grip upon the weapon. And, in the faint flash of crimson that ran down her arm in time with the beating of her heart and the burning of her skin, she knew her answer.

The longface's ears twitched at the sound of whistling iron. She whirled, just in time to see the blade go spinning past the side of her head. The blow was slight, a faint tug on her shoulder that she might have ignored if not for the trail of red that followed the tumbling weapon.

Lips drawn tightly, the woman regarded the empty, trembling pink hand extended at her.

'Fine, then.' The longface rolled her shoulder, even as her wound wept. 'There's plenty of time left in the day.'

'Stay away from my friends,' the human female warned.

The longface smirked at the sudden hardness in the

human's voice. 'Stay away from you, stay away from your friends.' She hoisted her weapon and advanced in slow, clanging strides. 'Make up your mind.'

One quick swing, the longface thought, and it would be over. Pink flesh was soft, weak and tore like paper saturated in fat. If the female turned and ran, it would take only a little longer. Even though the longface's own gnawblade was quivering in a motionless body somewhere, the chase would be a pleasant distraction before returning to the business of slaughtering underscum and whatever the winged red thing was.

The human did not turn and run, however. Her advance came in bold, decisive steps. 'Bold', the longface had learned, was the overscum word for 'stupid, but admirable'. That made sense, the purple woman decided, since this one approached her without fear. Without weapon, without armour, but without fear, the human extended her left arm like a fleshy, flimsy shield.

'Master Sheraptus would like you,' she said.

The woman showed no reaction, no wide-eyed honour that such a proclamation should entail. The longface narrowed her eyes. This one's death suddenly became more necessary.

They closed without haste, the longface swung without urgency. One quick swing, she thought in one moment and cursed in the next. The woman side-stepped the blow; clumsy, the purple creature scolded herself, but nothing urgent. The next one would do it.

The woman's left arm shot out, clamped around her throat, and the longface couldn't help but smile at the weak and sweat-laden grip.

'This is it?' she chuckled. 'You won't be a great loss to any—'

In a twitch of muscle, the pink arm became something else, something stronger. The fingers tensed, skin tightening around the bony joints as they dug into hard, purple flesh. The longface's voice was strangled as she felt her own blood mingle with the cold sweat. Impressive, she thought, but netherlings were hard, netherlings were strong.

That thought abandoned her, a sudden panic seizing her as the human female's hand began to glow. Her eyes went wide, alternately blinded and captivated by the pulsating light that drifted between bright crimson and darkest black.

'*Nethra*,' she tried to sputter through the choking grasp.

No more time wasted, she resolved. No more humouring the little pink weakling. One quick swing and it would be over. She kept that thought as she raised her iron spike to the sky.

'No,' the human whispered.

There was a sudden red flash. The longface became a trembling symphony, her shriek accompanied by the sudden snapping of bone, the snapping of bone accompanied by her sword falling to the stones. She looked to her arm, the folded, bunching mass that used to be her appendage as it twisted of its own sudden, violent accord, cracking and bending backwards like a wet branch.

She had felt bones broken before, blood spilled, iron in her flesh. This pain that raked through her was nothing like that, no cause, no physical presence. It was simply a blink of the eye, a twitch of muscle, a snap, and then her arm folded over itself violently again, her elbow touching her shoulder.

'What ...' she screamed through the sound, 'what is this? *WHAT IS THIS?*'

'I'm sorry,' someone sobbed.

She turned to the human female, saw the tears in her eyes, flooding down her cheeks with unrestrained swiftness. She saw the sleeve of the pink creature's robe rip and burst apart into blue ribbons, exposing an expanse of glowing red beneath. The light that engulfed the woman's arm pulsed, and with every heartbeat, blackened bones, joints and knuckles flashed through the crimson.

'I'm so sorry,' the woman whispered again.

'Then stop! Stop it! *STOP*—'

Another snap. The netherling collapsed to her right knee, her left leg a knotted mass of folded bone and sinew, her heel touching her knee, her iron-clad toes brushing against her rear. The woman collapsed with her, her entire body shaking, save for the arm that dug its skeletal claws deeper into the purple throat.

'I can't,' the human whimpered, 'I can't … I can't stop.'

The sensation of tears was alien to the netherling. She had never cried before. Netherlings were hard. Netherlings were strong. Netherlings did not cry. Netherlings did not beg.

'Please,' she shrieked, 'please! It hurts! It hurts so—'

Snap.

She felt her teeth touch the back of her tongue, her jaw folding once, twice over itself. Salty tears pooled in her mouth, leaking out over her shattered jaw. She felt her spine bend, groaning like an old and feeble tree before breaking.

Snap; her other arm.

'It's not my fault,' the human whispered.

Snap; her other leg.

'What could I do?' the human whimpered.

Snap; her neck.

587

'Forgive me,' the human pleaded.

Asper would have thanked Talanas for her tears, thanked the Healer that she could not see the abomination she had created through the liquid veil. She would have praised Him for the fact that she could not hear the screams emanating from what used to be a mouth over the shrieking inside her mind. But she could not bring herself to utter any thanks, to remember that she had lips with which to praise.

The pain, the searing red and black that engulfed her, would not allow it. The arm could not let her stop.

Her body was limp behind it, so much useless flesh leaking tears that hung from the rigid, glowing appendage. She could not pull her arm from the longface's throat, could not form a prayer for salvation. She could do nothing but close her eyes.

She tried to ignore the loud cracking sound that followed. She tried to ignore the feeling of her palm closing in on itself. She tried to ignore the bright flash of red behind her eyelids.

She tried, failed, and whispered, 'Forgive me ...'

She had prayed before that she would never see what she did when she opened her eyes again.

There was nothing left of the longface. There was no iron, no black hair or even a trace of purple flesh. Nothing to even suggest that anyone had ever stood there, knelt there, died there.

Nothing, except Asper, upon the floor, and the black, sooty stains that surrounded her. Her arm was a testament, a whole, pink thing that now lay in her lap, satiated. It was whole again, free of burning, free of glowing. It felt normal, good.

Why, she asked her thoughts, *does it feel good?*

Whoever heard her had no answer.

Three times now, she thought next. Once for the frogman in the *Riptide*'s cargo hold. Twice for the longface. Three times—

That was an accident, she interrupted herself, *no ... that was ...*

'Interesting ...'

She didn't bother to look up at the sound of the masculine voice. It was far away now, the shadow cast by his slight form nothing but a wisp of blackness to join the smears upon the floor.

'What do you call that?' he asked.

'A curse,' she whispered in reply, 'that the Gods won't take away.'

'There are no such things as Gods.'

She had no answer.

'Power, however, is absolute. And you, little creature, have such a thing.'

Asper craned her neck up, feeling its stiffness, to regard the man. The male longface, clad in robes that looked untainted despite the water, blood and ash that seeped through the great hall, looked almost friendly compared to the woman. His face, narrow as it was, had a smile that was not unpleasant and his eyes flashed with an intrigue, rather than malice.

Or perhaps she was just too numb to see it.

'I ... I killed her,' was all Asper could choke out through her tears.

'She is ... was just a female. There are more.'

'I ... but ... I didn't just kill her. I ... made her go away.' She stared down at her arm again. 'There's nothing left of her.'

'*Truly* impressive.' His bony hands applauded. 'Imagine

589

my shock. I had no idea females could even use *nethra*, much less to such ... ends.'

'It's a curse,' she repeated, more to herself than to him.

'Whatever you choose to call it, it's worthy of the attention of Sheraptus.' She felt his eyes wander over her, felt his grin grow broader. 'Other appreciable qualities considered.' He thrust his hand towards her like a weapon. 'So, if you would please rise – our business here is concluded and we must be off.'

He was right, she thought as she looked up. The hall was largely abandoned now, the battle concluded in the moments when she had held her eyes tight and asked questions no one would answer.

Who had emerged victorious, she could not say.

The defeated lay dead in the dozens, stacked in heaps, strewn across the floor, floating listlessly in the pools of salt water. Flakes of ash drifted lazily on the breeze as the pulsating, fleshy sacs still burned like grotesque pyres. There were grunts called out in harsh tongues, iron scraping on stone as the longfaces hurried back to their vessel, leaving the bodies of their comrades where they lay.

Of her own companions, there was no sign.

Not such a bad thing, she reasoned; they wouldn't have seen what she had just done. They wouldn't have known she had the power ... the curse to unmake people, to reduce them to nothing. Dreadaeleon's magic still left ash behind, Gariath left bodies in his wake. Of her foe, there was nothing left: no skin, no bone.

No soul.

She had not the strength to explain it any more, to justify it to them, to whoever Sheraptus was, or to herself. She could not bear to look upon the arm masquerading behind its pink softness, concealing the crimson and gloom. Three times had it emerged, two times it had left nothing, a thousand times had she looked up to the sky and asked why.

And a thousand times, no one had answered.

The male looked up at the sound of a wailing, warbling horn and frowned. 'The time has come to depart, I'm afraid.' He scrutinised her through his white eyes. 'It has been a long day. Frankly, I am not sure you are worth the trouble it would take to bring you along.' He snapped his fingers, sending a blue electric glow crackling at the tips. 'Your arm will have to suffice. You can keep the other parts.'

Asper looked up as he levelled the finger at her, watching the sphere of lightning grow. It was not with apathy that she stared, but weariness, relief that came with the grim knowledge that there was only one way to ensure there would never be a fourth time.

The male muttered a word of power. The electricity burst forth with a loud cracking sound. Asper stared at it through eyes with no more tears to shed. The male's own stare went alight with energy. One more word, she knew, and it would all be over.

That, too, was not such a bad thing.

'BURN, HERETIC!'

A wall of flame erupted between the two of them. The electric blue faded as the male recoiled, snarling angrily. He turned, more annoyed than anything else, to regard the boy standing at the end of the hissing fire.

Dreadaeleon looked ready to keel over at any moment. His coat hung loosely, tattered in some places, bloodied in others, from a body that appeared shrunken and withered. The veins creeping up from his jawline and the violent quaking that seized his body suggested that whatever

591

damage had been done to him was by his own hand, his magic having eaten at him deeper than any blade.

Asper could muster no excitement at his appearance, nor concern for his frailty. She felt a twinge of scorn, diluted by pity. All this meant was that someone else had to die before her curse could finally be lifted.

'Ah.' The male longface smiled at the newcomer with the familiarity of two old friends meeting. 'I was wondering who that was.' He glanced at the wall of flame and, with a word and a wave, reduced it to a sizzling black line upon the floor. 'Decent enough work, really. I was beginning to wonder if any of your breed could use *nethra* at all.'

Dreadaeleon tilted his head to the side. The male grinned and held up a hand.

'Apologies. "Magic" is your word for it, I believe.'

'We have laws for it, too,' the boy said sharply. 'There are rules to practice by.'

'Law ... rule ...' The longface shrugged. 'I have not learned those words yet. They sound like weakness to me, though.' He smiled. 'I suppose I should not be too surprised, though, since all your language seems to convey varying degrees of that. From my home, we—'

'Clever,' Dreadaeleon interrupted, taking a step forwards. 'I'm less interested in where you came from and more in how you're still standing.'

'Ah, after this, you mean?' He gestured over the burning sacs, the seas of ash. 'Duty, I suppose someone of your breed might call it. The underscum are in our way. Sheraptus desires them dead and ... well, look. The price one pays for *nethra* would be a further detriment. Thusly ...' He snapped his fingers, smiled. 'We removed it.'

'Impossible.'

'We do not know that word, either.'

592

'How many of you are there?' the boy demanded. 'How many heretics remain?'

'Perhaps you refer to males, the only ones capable of *nethra*.' The longface shrugged. 'Not so many, but if power were not a rare quality, any thick-of-skull female could do it.' He glanced sidelong at Asper. 'Speaking of which, I have business with this one. If you had claims on her arm, you must live with that disappointment.'

'Arm?'

In any other moment, Asper's pulse would have risen, mind gone racing for excuses. Now, what did it matter what Dreadaeleon knew? He would be dead. She would follow. Nothing remained to be spoken, nothing remained to resist as the longface took a step forwards.

'As well as whatever else I can salvage,' he said, chuckling. 'An arm is not such an important thing to one who carries no weapons, is it?' His eyes ran up and down her body hungrily. 'Particularly when the rest of her can be put to a much more proper use.'

His purple hand extended with the vaguest hint of an excited tremble coursing down his digits. His tongue flicked out, a tiny line of pink sliding across long, white teeth.

'*GET AWAY FROM HER!*' Dreadaeleon's roar was followed by a racking cough, a shudder in his stance. The longface, if his quirked brow was any indication, seemed less than impressed.

'This belongs to you? I am sorry in a terrible way, but I must damage your property. I need the arm.' He waved dismissively. 'You can have the rest when I am finished.'

'I said,' the boy uttered against the hiss of flames, 'stay away from her.'

At that, Asper's eyes did go slightly wider. The flames that danced on Dreadaeleon's outstretched palm were barely stronger than that of a candle, but every moment they burned caused his body to shudder, to tremble. *Why*, she asked him silently, *why don't you do it? Burn your heretic. Save your laws.*

She then saw the longface's hand, also outstretched, a single finger pointed directly at her. She glanced back to Dreadaeleon. *No*, she wanted to cry out to him, but had no voice in her raw throat, *don't do it. Not for me, Dread. I want this to happen ... I want—*

Dreadaeleon shuddered suddenly. The longface's grin broadened as the boy shifted slightly, trying to conceal the dark stain that appeared on his lap.

'Pushed yourself too far, it is apparent.' The purple man laughed. 'Is it really worth the shame, pinkling? I am no bloodthirsty female. Step aside, let me do my business, and you may clean yourself in peace. I have no wish to harm a fellow user.'

'I'm not your fellow.'

'Whatever laws separate us are as trivial and fleeting as the gods your breed claims to love.'

'It's not about laws.'

'Oh ...' The longface's mouth twisted into a frown. 'All this over a *female*, then? You do not have many where you come from?'

'Stop talking about her,' the boy spat. The sphere of flame growing in his palm bloomed into an orchid of fire. 'I'm the only one standing in your way. Face *me*.'

The only one ... Asper let that thought drift into nothingness as the male longface raised his hand, levelled it at Dreadaeleon.

'Point,' he said simply, 'goodbye.'

The longface thrust his hand forwards with a grunt. The air rippled as an invisible force struck Dreadaeleon, his fire extinguished and his frail body sent flying to crash against a pillar. He staggered to his feet, swayed precariously with only a moment to cast a desperate stare in her direction before crashing upon the floor, unmoving, unbreathing.

'Dread.' Asper could do no more than whisper, could find no strength. That was going to happen, she knew, he would die before she did, as the only one who had stood in the longface's way. That was logical.

Why, then, did she want to cry out so much louder?

'Annoying,' the male muttered, turning back to her. 'Perhaps it is worth taking whatever consists of your thoughts to find out what makes you do things like that.' He flicked his fingers and spoke a word that called flames to his palms. 'Small steps, I suppose. Arm first. Brain later.'

'Dread ...' she whispered again, watching the boy lying motionless in a puddle of salt water.

He could have stayed behind, she knew, he could have crept up on the longface and struck him from behind. If she had died, his laws would have been upheld, his faithlessness upheld. *Maybe even proven*, she thought.

Instead, he had stood against the longface, weakened as he was. He had died, his pants soiled, face-down upon unsympathetic stones. *For what?* That he might preserve her? Though he might not have known it, all he had preserved was a curse. And not knowing that, all he had done was give her the few breaths it took for the longface to approach her.

Where was the reason? Where was the logic?

By the time the longface stood over her, all teeth and fire, she had no answer and Dreadaeleon was still dead.

'Do not think this to be unkind, little pinkling.' He extended his hand, the fire engulfing it from tip to wrist. 'It is the way of things, you find, as all others shall. We are netherling. We are Arkklan Kaharn.' He narrowed his eyes, glowing red. 'Ours is the right to take.'

There was no cry from her, no protest as he eyed her arm hungrily. She barely had eyes for him and his wicked fire. Her gaze was upon Dreadaeleon, her lips quivering as they sought the words to offer his limp body.

You shouldn't have bothered, she thought. *It's better this way … you didn't have to die, Dread. I did. You shouldn't have become involved.*

'Forgive me,' was all she whispered.

All that she heard, however, was the throaty, ragged breath from above. Longface and priestess looked up as one, seeing the massive, red chest that rose and fell with each red-flecked burst of air. They looked up further, past the massive, winged shoulders and into the narrowed, black eyes that stared down contemptuously upon them.

'Oh … my …' The longface swallowed hard at the sight of rows of white, glistening teeth bared at him.

Gariath's jaws flashed open, his roar sending the male's white hair whipping across his purple face. The netherling responded swiftly, hands up like torches against the night, mouth straining not to fumble in fear as he uttered the words that caused the flames to leap from his palms and into the gaping maw of this new aggressor.

The dragonman vanished behind the curtain of fire for but a moment before emerging, flesh smeared black, blood boiling in the crevasses of his scowl, eyes painted a ferocious orange by the flame. His hands rose, pressing against the fire, containing it within his claws until he reached down to seize the netherling's own digits with an extinguishing hiss and a sputter of smoke.

The longface's shriek was louder than the sound of his fingers snapping, the tears streaming from his eyes thicker than the blood coating his foe's face. He staggered backwards as Gariath released him, his appendages hanging limply at his sides, oozing liquid that sizzled as it spattered upon the ground.

'You … you *dare*!' the longface tried to roar, but could only whimper as he fought to scowl through his sobs. 'It is futile, beast! Your whole fleeting life is nothing but a sigh on the wind before Sheraptus finds you! Both of you! *ALL OF YOU!*'

Gariath ignored him, stalking towards the netherling with claws flexing.

'We are netherling!' the longface continued to shriek. 'We come from nothing! We return to nothing! And *nothing* you do can change—'

'Stop.'

Gariath interrupted the longface, sliding the tips of his claws between delicate teeth. He hooked another two digits under his prey's upper jaw. The skin of the netherling's mouth gave one groan of protest, choked on the man's terrified sob.

'*Talking.*'

Asper was jolted by the sound. The sudden rip, the shudder of the longface's body as it twitched, then hung in Gariath's grasp for a moment. When the body hit the floor, when Gariath stood, breathing heavily, streaked with blood and black, something purple, white and glistening clenched in his hand, she realised.

I'm still alive.

For all the death that surrounded her, all the ash pervading the air, all the blood on the stones, the only person who should have died was still alive. Her, she realised, and Gariath.

But Dread …

'Dread,' she said suddenly, clambering to her feet. She looked to Gariath with desperation. 'He's—'

'Still alive,' the dragonman grunted, tossing the glistening object of purple and white over his shoulder to clatter and bounce across the floor.

'He ... is?'

He is. She could see it, the faint stir of his body as he pulled himself out of the salt water, only to collapse again.

'He is! He's still alive.'

'*I* am still alive.'

Asper looked up, took a step back as Gariath staggered forwards. The murder in his eyes had not dissipated, the red did not coat his hands entirely. His teeth were bared at her, his body shuddering with every haggard step he took towards her.

'Still alive,' he repeated, '*because of you.*'

'Because of ...' She glanced over his body, saw the gaping wounds, the chunks of missing flesh, the countless bruises. 'Gariath, you need help.'

'You already helped me,' he snarled, taking another step forwards. 'You fought that one longface, left me with three others.' His wings twitched and his lip curled. 'Does it look like *three* could kill me?'

At that moment, it looked like a half-blind, incontinent kitten could kill him, but she chose to say something more sympathetic.

'I can tend to you, Gariath. I can—'

'What can you do?' he roared and his body trembled with the effort. 'You cannot kill. You cannot let me be killed. You can't do *anything*!' She recoiled, not at his bared teeth, but at the tears that glistened in his eyes. 'I should be dead!

I should be with my ancestors! I should be with my *family*!'
He levelled a finger at her. 'And all I have now … is *you*.'

'I … didn't—'

'And you won't.' He drew his arm back. 'Ever again.'

The blow came fiercely, but slowly. Asper instinctively darted away from it, but it did not stop. His great red fist became a falling comet, dragging the rest of him to the floor where he struck with a crash. She remained tense, even as he dragged himself towards her, extended a quivering hand and uttered two words.

'Hate … you …'

And he fell. Still breathing, she noted, but not moving, like Dreadaeleon, like the rest of Irontide. Whatever it had been before, before it was taken by pirates, before it was taken by demons, it was truly forsaken now.

Bodies lay everywhere, the salt choked with blood, the stones littered with flesh, the air tainted by ash. Whatever netherlings had escaped were gone now, their snarling cries absent in the silence as smoke and water poured out of Irontide's jagged hole. Death drew a merry ring about the hall, haphazard bodies scattered artistically in a ritual circle at the centre of which stood Asper, still alive, still breathing.

Still cursed.

'Why,' she asked as she collapsed to her knees, 'why am I still alive?'

'Good question.'

Denaos did not look entirely out of place, standing nearby, hands on hips as he surveyed the carnage. Clad in black, his flesh purple in places from bruising, he looked the very spectre of Gevrauch, come to reap a bloody harvest from the white and purple fields. The rogue merely scratched his chin, then looked to her and smiled.

'Still alive, I see.' His eyes drifted to Gariath and Dreadaeleon. 'And them?'

'Yes,' she replied.

'Not by much, it looks like,' he said, wincing. Quietly, he stepped forwards. 'Netherlings gone?'

'Yes.'

'Demons dead?'

'Yes.'

She felt his shadow, cool against the heat of the flames. She felt his hand on her shoulder, strong against the softness of her aching body. She felt his eyes on hers, hard and real, full of questions and answers.

'Asper,' he asked, 'are you all right?'

She bit her lower lip, wishing more than anything that she had tears left to weep with. Instead, she collapsed forwards, pressing her face against his shoulder as she whispered.

'Yes.'

Thirty

MORE PERSONABLE COMPANY

L enk held his hand before his face, turning it over.
'That's odd,' he muttered.

'*Hm?*' someone within replied.

'My skin ... I don't remember it being grey.'

'*An issue worthy of concern.*'

'And my head ... it feels heavy.'

'*Moderately distressing.*'

'Only moderately?'

'*In comparison to the fact that we're still alive, I should have added. Apologies.*'

'It's fine.' He blinked, lowered his hand to feel the cold rock beneath him. 'I am still alive, aren't I?'

'*We are, yes.*'

'Apologies. I forgot you were there.'

'*Think nothing of it.*'

'I thank you ...' Lenk furrowed his brow. 'You know, I don't ever recall you being quite so chatty. Usually, it's all "kill, kill" with you.'

'*You haven't really cared to hear what I have to say,*' the voice replied. '*When one speaks to closed ears, one places a priority on available words.*'

'Point taken.' He let the silence hang inside his head for a moment. 'Who are you?'

'*Pardon?*'

'We've never been properly introduced.'

'*Is that really necessary at this point?*'

'I suppose not ... but I feel I should know who you are if you're going to do what you did back in the water.'

'*Excuse that intervention. Things were looking quite grim.*'

'I suppose they were. But there are no worries now.' He smiled at the familiarity of the satchel beneath his head, the tome safe and supportive within. 'We have the book. The Deepshriek is gone. It's over.'

'*It is not.*'

The voice was painfully clear and crisp now, as though it was hissing in his ear. He could almost feel its icy breath upon his water-slick skin. And yet, he did not so much as shiver. The chill felt almost natural, as did the presence that settled all around him, within him. It felt familiar, comforting.

And cold.

'I ... beg to differ,' he replied. 'We're alive. We've got a tome and a sword. What else do you need?'

'*Duty. Purpose. Death.*'

'There you go with the "death" thing again—'

'*You think it wise to leave the Deepshriek alive?*'

'No, but I—'

'*You chopped off a head. It has three.*'

'That usually suffices with most people.'

'*That thing is not people.*'

'Point taken.'

'*What of the others? They are weak ... purposeless. Let us lie here if you wish them all to die.*'

'The Deepshriek said—'

'*Three mouths to lie with ... apologies, two now. We should have killed it when we had the chance.*'

'It ran.'

'We could have pursued.'

'Through water?'

'Through anything. It fears us. It fears our blade.'

'Our blade?'

'The hand that wields it is nothing without the duty to guide it.'

'I'm … not quite up for philosophy at this point. How do we get to the others?'

'Others?'

'Kataria … the others—'

'Ah. That remains a problem.'

Lenk looked upwards. The stone slab loomed, impassable as ever despite the deep gash that had been rent in its face. A tiny fragment of grey broke off, tumbling down the depression to bounce off the ledge and strike Lenk's forehead.

'It's mocking me,' he growled.

'It's stone.'

'Have you any idea how to get out?'

'I do.'

Lenk waited a moment.

'Well?'

The voice made no reply.

Water lapped against water, against stone. Fire that had shifted from unnatural emerald to vibrant, hissing orange sputtered and growled in the wall sconces. The waves made lonely mutters against the stone wall. Something heavy bumped against the outcropping.

Wait …

He rolled over and stared into the water, into the golden eyes staring back up at him. He froze momentarily before realising the eyes did not blink, the mouth lay pursed, the golden hair wafted in the waters as the head bobbed up and down with the rhythm of the churning gloom.

Lenk grimaced. He was a moment from turning his gaze away when a hint of movement caught his eye. He leaned over, staring intently at the severed head. The eyes twitched, he felt his heart stop.

Is ... he thought to himself, *is that thing ... still alive?*

Fingers trembling, he reached down and poked it. It bobbed beneath the waves, then rose again, still staring. Swallowing his fear and his vomit, he seized it by its hair and pulled it out of the water. The eyes twitched, glanced every which way, as if seeking the shark it had been attached to. Its lips quivered, mouthing wordless threats to empty air.

'Disgusting,' he said, blanching. He caught an errant glance of himself in the void-like waters, then raised a brow. 'That's ... unusual. I don't really ever recall having—'

'*Time is limited,*' the voice interrupted. '*We must focus on this newfound gift the Deepshriek left us.*'

'I beg to differ.'

He was prepared to throw it back into the gloom, regardless of the answer, when he heard it. A faint, barely audible sound, as though someone whistled from miles away. Against all wisdom, he drew it closer to his ear.

Wordlessly, an almost-silent breath hissed between its teeth. He turned it over, glancing where its stalk-like neck had been attached. A blackened, bloodied hole stretched from hair to jaw beneath. Air murmured through it, emerging from the creature's fanged mouth.

'Sweet Khetashe,' he fought bile to speak, 'it *is* alive.'

'*It has a new duty now,*' the voice replied.

Lenk turned to the stone slab, watching another shard crumble and slide down like a drop of stone sweat. He smiled, rose to his feet, sheathed his sword and slung the tome's satchel about his shoulder.

'*We have but to give it that duty,*' the voice said, and – how, he had not the faintest idea – Lenk knew what it meant.

He walked before the slab, dangled the decapitated head by its golden tresses and whispered a word.

'Scream.'

Even over the explosion, the stone shattering and the hail of rock chips, Kataria could hear the shrieking. In fragments of sound, it had been painful, uncomfortable, but tolerable. Bared to its full vocal fury, it was agonising. And in response, she became a creature of folds: folding her ears over themselves, folding her hands over her ears and folding her body over itself.

Shards of grey bit at her bare back, the earth settled ominously under her feet, dust poured into her nostrils. None of that mattered, none of that pain needed to be felt. All she thought of was the hideous wail that defiled the air, and keeping it from turning her ears into flayed pieces of glistening bacon hanging from her head.

How long it lasted, Kataria did not know, and she did not care. When it finally ceased, it still echoed in the hall, reverberating off stones and ripples and breaths she took. After an eternity of darting eyes and nervous twitching, she took her hands away from her ears, breathed a word of thanks mingled with a curse, and turned around.

And then, the screaming suddenly didn't seem so bad.

Two thin pinpricks of light, cold and blue, stared at her from behind a cloud of dust that, mercifully, showed no signs of dissipating. She swallowed hard, clenched her teeth.

'Lenk,' she said, rather than asked. There was no mistaking him or his stare.

The two tiny spheres flickered, a shadow moved behind the dust cloud. It shifted against the curtains of pulverised grey, as though agitated or confused.

'I think ...' a voice, faint and freezing, spoke, 'she's talking to you.'

The voice was familiar to her. She remembered it as well as she remembered Lenk's own. And now they spoke in unison, each one with a crisp clarity that settled upon her skin like rime.

She could feel her heart sink. Whatever dwelt on the other side of the dust cloud was not completely Lenk. *Perhaps*, she thought, *maybe not even Lenk at all.*

'What?' When he spoke next, it was with his own voice, but it was frightened, shrill, like a small child's. 'No, I didn't mean ... stop. Don't yell at me!'

This was it, she knew, the sign she had been waiting for. He was a disease within a disease now, completely lost to whatever plagued him. These were the moments she should be running instead of staring at his shadow through the veil of dust. These were the moments she should turn, leave this human – *all* humans – behind her and thank Riffid for giving her the clarity to be free of her shame.

'Stop it ...' he whimpered, his voice rising into a roar. 'I said *stop*!'

He would never hear her footsteps as she walked away. She kept that in mind as she turned to the water, reassuring herself. He would think it all a dream in his fevered mind, he would think she was dead. He would never suspect that she had left him behind.

And still, she cursed herself. She should be braver, she should be able to stand before the human disease, the great sickness that plagued the world, and spit on him through a shictish curse. Her father would have wanted that. Her people would have wanted that.

For her part, Kataria merely wanted to fight back the urge to turn around.

'Kat ...'

Damn it, she muttered in her mind as she halted, *damn it, damn it, damn it*.

She turned, only to be greeted by another sign. The curtains of smoke parted, layer by layer, exposing the shadow behind in greater detail. Her blood froze at the sight, the distorted shape of the young man, the jaggedness of his outline and the bright, ominous blue with which his eyes shone.

He extended a hand to her, trembling, far too big to be his own and whispered.

'Please ...'

This was the final sign, Riffid's last mercy to her. She should turn, walk away, run away, leave this human and whatever he had become in the shadows behind her. Her ancestry demanded it. Her pride as a shict demanded it. Her own instincts demanded it.

Kataria listened carefully. And, in response, she drew in a sharp breath and walked into the cloud of dust.

'I'm here,' she said as she might speak to an injured puppy, her hands groping about blindly. 'I'm here, Lenk.'

She found him in a sudden shock as her hands clasped around flesh that froze like a fish's. She swallowed hard, ignoring this sign as she had done the last, hearing in the faintest whispers Riffid cursing her for her stupidity.

Another hand reached out to clasp about hers and she froze. Through the leather of his glove, through the leather of hers, she could feel it, a sensation that caused her to go breathless as he squeezed her fingers in his.

Warmth.

'You're alive,' he spoke.

He spoke, she told herself, unable to fight back the smile creeping onto her face. *Lenk spoke. No one else.*

'Come on,' she urged, pulling at him.

They staggered out into the stagnant air and the dying light of the torches. She drew in a sharp breath before looking at him, afraid to find grey flesh or pupilless spheres staring back at her.

Instead, she saw a man barely alive. His shirt was tattered and clung to a body that was stained red in areas. His leg, rent with a jagged cut, barely seemed capable of supporting the rest of his wiry frame. Deep circles lined his eyes and his smile was weary and accompanied by a sharp wince.

He looks so weak, she thought, *like a sick dog or something.* Why she should find that endearing, she did not know. The faint smile that crept to her face quickly vanished by the time her gaze drifted to the black-stained blade and the severed, golden-haired head in his grasp, however.

She cleared her throat. 'Busy in there?'

'A bit,' he replied as he tucked the head's glimmering locks into his belt.

He paused at the centre of the corridor, noting grimly the Abysmyth corpse striped by sizzling green lacerations. Quietly, he looked her over, frowning at the bruise upon her flank, the cuts criss-crossing her pale skin, the dried trail of blood under her nose.

'How was your day?' he asked.

She sniffed a little. 'Pleasant.'

'So long as you kept yourself occupied.' He took a step forwards, then winced to a halt. Smiling sheepishly, he extended his arm to her. 'Help me?'

'Help *you*?' She gestured to her own wreck of a body. 'I fought a hulking, purple-skinned white-haired man-woman!'

He patted the severed head at his belt. 'I took the skull off a three-headed shark-lady.'

'She kicked me,' Kataria said, gesturing to the long bruise running down her flank, 'might've broken my ribs, too. This was all *after* I stabbed her.'

'Yeah? Well, she ...' Lenk looked at the head disparagingly. 'She yelled at me.'

Kataria stared at him blankly. He coughed.

'*Really* loudly.'

She pursed her lips. He sighed and offered his shoulder to her.

'Fine, get on.'

'No.' She took his arm instead, draping it over her shoulder. 'You'd probably soil yourself with the effort, anyway.' She grunted, bolstering him. 'You owe me, though.'

'I'd offer my blood, if I hadn't left it behind.' He chuckled, then winced. 'It hurts to laugh.'

'Then stop telling terrible jokes.' She guided him down the corridor. 'Denaos lived.'

'Pity,' he replied. 'And the others?'

'Possibly.'

'Possibly what?'

'Either.'

He squeezed her hand and she froze. His grip was still warm.

'You're alive,' he whispered, the faintest edge of hysteria in his voice.

'I am,' she replied in a voice just as soft.

'And you're still here.'

She hesitated, looked down at the ground and frowned.

'Yeah … I know.'

'I didn't think—'

'Don't ruin it by starting now.'

And so they hobbled in silence until they reached the water's edge. There they stopped, there they stared at themselves in the gloom.

The liquid seemed slightly less oppressive now, the air a bit cleaner, if tinged by a distant stench of burning. Kataria glimpsed Lenk's reflection in the water as it twisted and writhed. Odd, she thought, but as distorted as it was, she could still pick out his features, his silver hair and his blue eyes.

What comfort she took in that was lost the moment she spied her own reflection, however. The creature of pale skin and green eyes stared back up at her, twisting, contorting and fading. She frowned, for even as her reflection re-formed, she still didn't recognise the shict looking back at her.

'Kataria,' Lenk began, sensing her tense under him, 'I—'

'Later,' she grunted, adjusting herself and him as they slid into the water.

If there was a later, she would handle it then. Whatever excuses needed to be made, whatever apologies had to be voiced to herself, to her Goddess, to her kin, could be made later. For now, they were both alive.

And Kataria couldn't help but think it would be easier if one of them weren't.

Thirty-One

THAT WHICH FADES

Denaos had never believed the idea that one of his particular talents should prefer the darkness. The sun was far more pleasant; it illuminated, it warmed, and didn't mind at all if one happened to admire it nude, unlike certain people with primitive notions of modesty and boundaries.

'We could learn a bit from you, my golden friend,' he whispered to the great yellow sphere, reaching down to scratch a particularly errant itch.

After the eternity it had taken to leave Irontide, the sun was a particularly welcome sight. It was two long days in a dank, decrepit stone hall stinking of ash and blood before they were rested enough to make the long swim back to Ktamgi. The effort was made all the harder by the grievous injuries sustained during their excursion to the crumbling fortress. Even Asper had tended to them with a degree more listlessness than usual; many of his companions still lingered in uncertain fates.

But, he thought, *they aren't here now.*

And so Denaos lay upon a beach blissfully free of demons, netherlings or hulking she-beasts while at least three of his companions were threatened with the imminent possibility of a slow, agonising death.

It was a good day.

611

Naturally, the thought occurred with a twitch of an eyelid as he heard the sound of footsteps on sand, *someone has to come and ruin it*.

'Hey.'

Lenk's voice, he thought, was a dull and unenthusiastic brick hurled through a pleasant stained-glass window depicting a rather tasteful scene of curvaceous nude women and apple trees. Knowing that such a thing would be lost on the young man, he chose to say something different.

'Naked here. Go away.'

'We've got work to do,' Lenk replied with an unsympathetic tone. 'The boat needs to be repaired. There's wood to chop and nails to hammer.'

'Why in the name of all good and virile Gods did you think that coming to a naked man with messages of chopping wood and hammering nails would persuade him?' Denaos snorted. 'Get someone else to do it.'

'Everyone else is gone.'

'Gone where?'

'I don't know, just ... *gone*. I can't find any of them.'

'Well, why don't you scurry off and see if they left any scat to track them by?' He snorted and folded his hands behind his head. 'Or, for a better idea, why don't you just go and rest yourself? Your leg can't be feeling too well.' He coughed. 'Not here, of course. Go find your own stretch of beach.'

'I feel fine.'

Denaos arched his neck, regarding his companion who stood, he thought, far too close. Still, the young man looked to be standing firm, favouring his uninjured leg, to be sure, but largely unaffected. It struck the rogue as odd that someone who had been bitten by a demon shark should be standing only two days later, but that was a concern for another time.

'I'm incredibly comfortable right now, I'll have you know,' the rogue muttered. 'I'm not sure if you're aware of this, but it takes a considerable amount of effort to achieve the precarious position in which sand does *not* reach up into my rear end with eager, grainy claws and I'll not have you ruin it.'

A period of silence, punctuated by the idle banter of the surf, followed before Lenk spoke again in a voice decidedly meeker than his own.

'Please?'

'Whatever for?'

'I need to talk to someone.'

'About what?'

'Things … you know.'

'So talk,' the rogue replied. 'I'm not going anywhere.'

'I can't … I mean, not here.'

'Why not?'

'Well, back in Steadbrook, whenever we needed to talk about something, we'd do it over work.' Lenk rubbed the back of his neck. 'And it's not like we can get off the island until someone finishes the vessel, anyway.'

'I think I see,' Denaos said, humming thoughtfully. 'You'd like to talk to me, but instead of doing it like a human being free of mental illnesses, you'd like me to indulge you in this quaint little ritual devoted to furthering your already stunted social skills and rewarding you for not acting like a normal person.'

'Basically.'

Denaos yawned, then pulled himself to his feet. 'Fine.'

'I mean, it's nothing all that important,' Lenk said to the

rogue's back as the taller man began walking towards the pile of nearby tools. 'I'm just a little … confused.'

Denaos froze for a moment, then sighed. He waved a dejected hand as he turned around and began walking to his discarded clothing.

'Hold that thought. This sounds like the kind of conversation I'll need pants for.'

It dangled like an ugly fold of aging flesh, Dreadaeleon thought as he stared at his reflection in the shore's tidepools. The filthy grey streak of hair that hung over his brow continued to mock him, continued to chide him for his stupidity.

He had suspected this might happen, which was why he made a point of staying far away from his companions. They wouldn't understand; how could they? None of them had the Gift, none of them had the mental capacity to comprehend a fraction of magic's laws and extents, let alone its prices.

The Venarium's records were full of cautionary tales of those who had overextended themselves: flesh melting from bones, bodies exploding into flames after misspeaking a word, young ladies giving birth to two-headed calves after being a bit too close to a wizard when he sneezed during an incantation.

Rapid, concentrated aging was the most common – and the most lenient – of the punishments. He supposed he should be grateful that he would only suffer from one marred lock.

Regardless, he lifted his shirt, checking his torso for any sign of liver spots, wrinkles, prominent veins. Nothing, he noted with relief, as there had been nothing when he checked twenty breaths ago.

The grey lock was warning enough, though, and he absently considered keeping it as a reminder of his failure. His companions wouldn't understand, of course, but why should they? They weren't the same as he was. They were lesser, stupid, still clinging to the belief that gods and spirits would protect them.

Ridiculous, he thought, the notion of beings in the sky that could reshape mountains and raise the dead without a thought. Power had a price, any logical mind knew. Nothing could be created without being taken from somewhere else, whether it was fire from the heat of a palm or ice from the moisture of a single breath. That was the law, the law of magic, the law of the Venarium.

Or, he thought as he reached inside his coat pocket, *that* used to be *the law*.

He pulled the red jewel out, observing it as it dangled on the black chain before him. Perfectly spherical, save for a noticeable chip on its face, the jewel ate the light of the sun, rather than reflected it. That, he told himself, was the sign that this was it, the tool that the longface male had used to cheat the laws of magic.

I mean, he told himself, *what else could it have been?* He had searched the corpse thoroughly, inside and out after performing a bit of impromptu dissection. Nothing differentiated the longface from himself, save for his purple skin and this ... this tiny jewel.

That particular heretic was dead, it was true, but how many more were there? Where did these 'netherlings' come from and what did they hope to gain by fighting demons? Who was this 'Sheraptus'?

And what, he asked himself with a sudden surge of fury, *made them look at Asper the way that one did?*

The memory of the long face, and its broad grin and

hungry eyes, still burned in his mind with an anger far greater than any heresy the black-clad wizard might have committed. The memory of a purple hand extending to touch her, *her*, *his* companion, sizzled within his skull. The stink of his own soil filled his nostrils at the thought of it.

Dreadaeleon sighed, pressing his face into his hands. The strain had been too much to bear, he knew, and undoubtedly she would, too. Still, even after that, after drawing upon so much that even his bladder could not hold, he hadn't even been able to save her. Gariath had to do that, leaving him as nothing more than an afterthought with wet pants and a breathing problem.

Somehow, he had imagined the scenario working out far more gallantly.

He should have pushed himself further, he knew, he should have had the strength to fend off that netherling and a hundred more. He should have flung them aside on waves of fire and roars of lightning, creating a ring of destruction to shelter her from the carnage.

He was a wizard! He *was* the absolute power!

Power, he thought ruefully, *so limited* …

But instead of all that, he had soiled himself and crumpled up in a heap, leaving her to whatever malice the netherling had planned for her. And once again, it had been Gariath, superstitious, brutish, barbaric Gariath, who had done what he could not. And if it hadn't been Gariath, he told himself, it would have been Denaos with a dagger in the back or Lenk with a killing blow of his sword.

Or even Kataria, standing triumphant over an arrow-laden corpse as Asper swooned at the shict's feet.

While not an entirely unpleasant image, the fact of the matter remained that it would not have been him who saved her. It would never be a scrawny boy in a dirty coat. He would never have that kind of power.

At least, he thought as he wrapped his hand about the crimson jewel, *not on my own*.

'You are well, Lorekeeper?'

Dreadaeleon found himself incapable of starting at the voice. It was far too melodic, far too soothing to cause anything but a smile. He looked up, wearing that smile, to regard an angular, pale face framed by flowing locks of kelp-coloured hair and a pair of feathery gills.

'I am, thank you,' he replied.

'Your hair …' Greenhair noted, frowning at the lock of grey.

'Yeah, well … prices and the like,' Dreadaeleon muttered as he climbed to his feet. 'You know how it is.'

'I do not,' she replied flatly.

'Oh.' He paused, cleared his throat. 'Well … it's, ah … difficult.' Forcing a larger, far more awkward smile onto his face, he continued, 'Where did you scamper off to, anyway? We missed you.'

'Oh,' she said, blinking. 'Did you throw something at me?'

'No, I mean …' He held up a hand, drew in a deep breath. 'Where did you go?'

'I went …' A pained expression crossed her face, though Dreadaeleon found it hard to decipher that from her features. 'Away.'

'Where?'

'Somewhere else, Lorekeeper. It is not important.'

'Why, then?'

'That is even less important.' She eyed the boy curiously for a moment, something dancing behind her alien eyes. 'You … were victorious in Irontide?'

'Roughly,' he replied. 'It was difficult. There were demons, some kind of … sacs, I don't know.'

'Even fiends have mothers, Lorekeeper, and they are all birthed from the wretched womb of Ulbecetonth.'

'Those things,' Dreadaeleon said, cringing, 'were *eggs*?'

'They were nothing meant for this world. What is important is that they are destroyed.' She leaned in to him, regarding him through a wary expression. 'You *did* destroy them?'

'Not personally, no. There was a longface there. He burned them with fire.' The boy scratched his chin. 'Fire that wouldn't go out …' He scratched a little harder. 'He was defying the laws, he cheated.' His teeth clenched unconsciously as he scratched harder at his hairless chin. 'He … he almost …'

'Lorekeeper …'

He felt his blood on his hands the moment she spoke. Muttering a curse, he wiped his chin off on the lapel of his coat, hiding it from the siren's curious gaze. A futile gesture, for her eyes seemed to focus on something past the dirty fabric, past his skin and bone.

'You are … not well,' she observed.

'I'm fine,' he replied coldly. 'It's just …' He sighed, looking at his hands, so scrawny, so feeble. 'I should have been the one.'

'To kill the Abysmyths?'

'To kill the Abysmyths, the frogmen, the longfaces, to find the tome, to kill the Deepshriek, to …' *To save Asper*, he added mentally, *but all I did was piss myself and fall down, like an old man, with barely any blood on my hands.*

'So long as they are dead, what does it matter?'

Because what's the point of having the power if I can't use it? Because why is it fair that I can be beaten by brute force and

618

superstitious myth? Because why can't I be the one to turn the tide, to get the treasure and win the woman?

'Because,' he whispered, 'there are laws.'

He continued to stare at his hands as the pale, webbed fingers slid around his own, closing tightly over them. Quietly, his stare was drawn up and into her fathomless eyes, her gentle, thin-lipped smile.

'Laws are not important,' Greenhair whispered, her voice but a ripple on the water.

He could feel his breath catch in his throat as he stared into her eyes, his hands go so weak and malleable under hers as she pushed them aside. He could feel his legs cross awkwardly over each other in a vain attempt at concealing as she drew herself closer to him, feeling the chill of her body through the garment wrapping her.

Oh Gods, he muttered inside his own mind, *quick, say something clever.*

'So ... what is important?' he squeaked.

Moron!

'What is here. What is now,' she replied, low and breathless. 'What has occurred is but one wave, come and gone. What is now is you.'

She raised a hand to her shoulder and, with digits working slowly, let her silk-like garment fall from her body.

'And me.'

His eyes went wide, wide enough to leap out of his skull, yet nowhere near wide enough to take all of her in. He could only steal glimpses: gentle curves like the bend of a river, skin that shimmered between pristine ivory and pale azure as the light glimmered off her body, and rivers of hair that flowed down her body.

'Uh ... should I ...'

Dreadaeleon was silenced with a sudden chill as she

619

pressed her mouth to his. His eyes threatened to melt as hers closed. Thoughts slid through his mind as easily as her tongue slid past his lips.

Oh Gods, oh Gods, oh Gods, he babbled inwardly, *if there were Gods, that is. This is it! This is it! This is what it feels like! This is what it tastes like.* He blinked, his tongue shyly brushing against hers. *Salt? That makes sense, I guess. She's a siren. Does the rest of her taste like—*

Something stiffened beneath him and he swallowed hard.

Keep it together, old man, he chided himself mentally. *Here and now, like she said, focus on the here and now. One moment ... what does that even* mean? *Am I ... am I supposed to lick something? I think I'm supposed to lick something. I should lick something ... but what? Oh Gods ...*

Her tongue seized his forcibly, wrapping around to caress softly. He felt her breath upon his face, the gentle whisk of sea spray that tingled in his nostrils. He felt her slide a hand up and behind his head, pulling him further into her.

I think I'm supposed to do that ... aren't I? Denaos always says that the male is supposed to be aggressive. But ... but what does that mean? Do I ... do I pin her down or something? Is that romantic or rape? His hands absently brushed against her arms. *Nevermind it, she feels pretty tough. Gods, why do I always have to meet muscular women? Well, I can't just sit here and let her do everything ... do something, you fool!*

But what?

I ... uh ... grab something! His hand lashed out and clasped, quivering upon her round buttock. *Not there, you fool! She'll think you a pervert! Wait, no, you fool! She's already naked, how much harm could you possibly do? Okay ... okay ... everything's okay. It's just—*

'What does it matter,' she whispered on a wisp of breath as she pulled slightly away, 'that you were not the one to slay the demons?'

Wait, what? That hardly seems like a nice thing to ... steady. Steady! You're losing it!

'It is what you *will* do that matters most,' she continued.

Oh Gods, is that a joke? Can she feel it getting soft? Steady! Denaos always says this sort of thing happens ... but only with lots of whiskey.

'You have the tome.' She drew herself closer, one ivory thigh easily brushing his leg aside and sliding up and down.

Well, yes, we have it, but Lenk took it ... no! No! Think positively! It's not about Lenk! It's about you, you ... you throbbing stallion, you rapturous lord of the sheets, you amorous bullfrog. Wait ... wait ... ignore that last part.

'And you will bring it to me ...'

What?

'What?' He said as much.

'Is it not wise?' She pulled him closer, smiling as she felt him go rigid against her. 'The tome is an item of such knowledge.' She leaned in, her whisper carried on the tongue that flicked against his ear. 'Such *power*.'

'Power ...' He could feel himself lost on her whisper, set adrift on the sea that was her voice.

'Your companions would not understand it.'

'How could they?' he muttered. 'They know nothing but gold.'

'They would hate me for it.'

'I ... I'd protect you.'

'You would save me?'

Her gasp caused him to shudder as something within

him yearned to be free, yearned to burst out and seize her, to force her upon the sands and savage her in ways he had only heard about second-hand. It pushed at him, demanding he forget the idea of betrayal, demanding he take her in his arms and deliver to her what she demanded herself.

He reached up, seizing her by her naked shoulders and pulling her close, feeling her breasts press against his chest, feeling the breath on his cheek as her lips parted in a faint gasp, feeling her webbed fingers slide down to his belt.

'I would save you ...' he whispered.

'On waves of fire,' she replied, 'and roars of lightning?'

'Yes ...'

Wait ...

With her words sliding like veils over his ears, he felt it. Something twitched in the back of his head, as though a cockroach had skittered upon his brain while she spoke and stood stock still, desperate not to be noticed. But with those last words, he could feel it, the brief twitch of antennae.

Dreadaeleon pushed himself away from her, his eyes narrowing. Greenhair recoiled. Though it was difficult to tell, Dreadaeleon could make out upon her angular features not shock, but the sudden fear of being discovered.

'You're in my head,' he whispered, his voice seething.

'It is ... it is not what you think, Lorekeeper,' she protested.

'How is it *not* exactly what it seems?' he snarled, advancing menacingly. 'You never told me you could read thoughts ... then again, if this is what you were planning, I suppose that makes sense.'

'The tome is dangerous, Lorekeeper! There are powers at work here that you do not understand! The Sea Mother—'

'Is false! Like all Gods!' Dreadaeleon blinked, his eyes opening with a burst of crimson power. 'Like *you*!' He levelled a finger at her. 'You wanted to *use* me! All to get some stupid book!'

'It is no mere book, Lorekeeper,' she said, fumbling for her garment. 'It has knowledge, it has darkness, it has—'

'Power,' he finished for her. 'And so do I.' He spoke an echoing word and his finger burst with electricity. 'Get out of here.'

'It is also to save you,' she protested, backing away. 'The darkness will come after *you* now that you have the tome! I can protect it! I can protect *you*, Lorekeeper.'

He roared another word that thundered off the sky, punctuated by a sudden crack of lightning leaping from his digit. She shrieked and collapsed. Only when the echo of thunder passed did she look up at him, his finger angled high and smoking.

'My name,' he said, 'is Dreadaeleon.'

The boy could not recall in what order it happened: his threats, her wailed excuses and pleas, his collapsing, her fleeing into the water to vanish into the sea. He could only sit and stare out over the waves as a tear trickled down his cheek and into his mouth, leaving him with the fading taste of salt.

Thirty-Two

AN UNCARING WING

Denaos poised the hatchet over the wooden block, closed one eye and swung. It split smoothly down the centre, each half flying off to join the two piles of similar semicircular shapes. He smiled at his work momentarily, admiring the even cleave, before sinking the tool into the tree stump that served as a chopping block.

'Your turn,' he said.

Lenk looked up through a sweat-stained face, incredulous.

'What?' He looked down at the piles, his piles, with Denaos's addition lying smugly on top like fruits on a dessert. 'You only chopped one?'

'I chopped one *exquisitely*,' the rogue corrected. 'If I wanted to beat you in a contest, I could hack circles around you, throwing off so many lacklustre splinters like you did.' He plucked up his product and one of Lenk's, holding his up. 'Look at this: a nice, delicate blow, revealing every tender secret of the wood. Now look at yours. *Where's the heart?*'

Lenk mopped his brow, looked down at the piles, then looked back up at his companion.

'It's wood.'

'A true artist never makes excuses.' The rogue added an insulting sashay to his walk as he turned away from Lenk.

'Anyway, you're the one who wanted work ethic and talk. It's only fair that I get laziness and listening.' He pulled himself up onto a low-hanging tree branch and lay down. 'So, go ahead.'

'Fine,' the young man said, grunting as he hefted the hatchet and placed a fresh block of wood onto the stump. 'I'm having some trouble with—'

'Oh, wait, we're going to talk about *you*?'

'Well … yeah.'

'Why can't we ever talk about *me* for once?' the rogue muttered, settling himself further into his boughy sling. 'Everyone comes to *me* with their problems. Why can't I ever get the same treatment?'

'Because all I know about *you* is that you're a coward, a lech, a lush, a brigand, a bigot and a piece of offal masquerading as a man,' Lenk snarled, bringing the hatchet down in a vicious chop. 'Did I miss anything?'

'Yes,' the rogue replied, 'I also play the lute.'

'Fine, then. We'll talk about you.' Lenk set a new piece of wood up, glancing at his companion. 'You never told me what you did before becoming an adventurer. Are you married?'

Denaos sat up at that, lips pursing, regarding Lenk through narrowed eyes.

'Any children?' Lenk asked.

'You know, I think I am in the mood to talk about you.' With noticeable stiffness, the rogue settled back into his tree branch. 'So, do go on.'

'Um … all right, then.' Lenk brought the axe down again. 'I'm having some difficulty understanding women.'

'Ah, yes.' Denaos scratched his chin. 'The eternal question on two legs that only gets more annoying with every passing thought.' His hand drifted lower, scratched something else. 'Fortunately for you, I'm something of an expert on the subject.'

'Yeah?'

'No doubt,' the rogue replied. 'What do you want to know?'

'I suppose …' Lenk's hum hovered in the air as he leaned on the hatchet's handle, staring contemplatively out at the forest's greenery. 'Why?'

'The best place to start,' Denaos said, nodding. 'Well, to understand women, you must first understand their place in the world. And to that end, you must first know how they came to occupy this world alongside us.'

'How?'

'The theories vary from faith to faith, but here's how it was explained to me.' He cleared his throat, sitting upright as though he were some scholar. 'The Gods first created man and gave to him their gifts. From Daeon and Galataur, we received the art of war. From Silf, we received the talent of deception. And from Khetashe, as you know, we received the urge to explore.'

'Go on.'

'But there was a difficulty. Mankind lacked purpose. There was no reason to go to war, no reason to lie, no reason to wander far and wide.'

'And?'

Denaos shrugged and lay back. 'And then the Gods created women and suddenly everything made sense.'

'Oh …' Lenk scratched his head. 'Well, how does that help me?'

'If you haven't reached that conclusion from that particular story, there's really nothing I can do to help you.' The rogue waved a hand dismissively. 'What do you even care? When we return the tome, you'll have enough money

626

to buy several whores, make one of them your wife and die a slow, lingering death at the bottom of a tankard like any decent man.'

'What if I don't want any of that?'

'Then give me your share.'

'I mean,' Lenk said, setting down another log, 'well … let me ask you this. Have you ever wanted something desperately, but you knew it just wasn't meant to be?'

The rogue fell silent, absently scratching his chest. The wind shifted overhead, parting branches that sent shadows dancing over his face, chased by eager fingers of sunlight upon the giggles of a playful breeze. Quietly, he reached up, fingers outstretched as though he sought to grab them.

'Yeah,' he replied, 'I've wanted that.'

'So, what do you do?'

Lenk brought the hatchet down, splitting the log and sending its halves flying off. The echo of the chop lasted an eternity throughout the forest, silencing the laughter of the wind.

'I suppose,' Denaos whispered, 'you ask "why"?'

Taire was her name.

Asper remembered that about her, remembered it the first day she had heard it.

'Like … *a paper tear?*' she had asked the girl, scrunching up her nose. '*What kind of name is that?*'

'*What kind of name is Asper?*' she had replied with a smile, sticking her tongue out. '*The name of a slow-witted tree or a snake with a lisp?*'

Her tongue was long and pink, never coated. Her eyes were big and blue, not cold like Lenk's, but vast like the sky. Her hair was long and golden, not dirty like Kataria's, but glistening like the precious metal.

She was always smiling.

Temple life was hard. Asper had been told that before she ever felt called to join. She learned it in the days that followed, during the dissections of the dead to discover what they had died from, ferrying salves and medicines from the apothecary to the common floor where the elder priests tended to the sick and the dying, forced to look upon men, women and children as they coughed out their last breath so that she might know why she served the Healer.

Taire was never shy, never afraid, life never seemed hard for her. She was always the first to peer curiously into the open corpse, the fastest to get the medicine to the common floor while greeting every patient that walked in, the only one who would hold someone's hand as they left the world on Talanas's wings.

Taire had taken Asper's hand and placed it on the dying. Taire had helped her fumble with the medicine. Taire had stayed up reading the tomes on the human body, late into the night, with Asper. Taire was not the reason Asper had entered the temple. Taire was the reason she served the Healer.

Taire had begged.

Her disappearance was officially marked down as 'lamentable', never pursued with any particular interest. Children fled from the temple all the time, even the brightest and most enthusiastic students occasionally finding it too stressful to continue with the training. The gravedigger had looked half-heartedly about the temple grounds. The high priest sighed, gave a prayer and made a note in the doomsday book. Taire's belongings were folded into a bundle and put into storage in the bin marked 'unclaimed'.

There was no corpse, no suicide note, nothing to indicate

she had ever existed besides the sooty mark on the floor of the dormitories.

And Asper.

No one had asked the shy little brown-haired girl who was always rubbing her left arm where Taire had gone. No one had paid attention to the shy little brown-haired girl who cried in the night until long after Taire was forgotten by all.

All except the one who knew that she had begged, like the longface, like the frogman.

She hadn't forgotten any of them. She hadn't forgotten the pain she felt, that they shared, as her arm robbed them of all. She could still feel it, would feel it long after whoever kept track of such things forgot that the longface in Irontide had ever existed. She would hear them scream, hear their bones snap, hear their bodies pop, hear them beg.

Her arm was one part of the curse. That Asper would never forget was another.

And she hadn't forgotten that, for as many times as she looked up to the sun and asked, 'why?' no one had answered her.

'It happened again,' she whispered, choked through tears brimming behind her eyes.

Asper turned. The pendant did not look particularly interested in what she was saying as it lay upon the rock. The forest danced, shifted overhead, casting a shadow over the silver-wrought phoenix. Its carved eyes turned downcast, its gaping beak resembled something of a yawn, as though it wondered how long her weeping confession would last.

'It happened again,' she repeated, taking a step closer. 'It happened again, it happened again, it happened again.' She took another step with every fevered repetition until she collapsed upon her knees before the rock, an impromptu altar, and let her tears slide down to strike upon the pendant. 'It happened again.

'Why?'

The pendant did not answer her.

'Why?' she said, louder.

'Why, why, why, why?' Her knuckles bled as she hammered the symbol, straining to beat an answer out of it. 'Why does this keep happening to me? Why did you do this to me?'

She raised her hand to strike it again. The phoenix looked out from behind the red staining its silver, uninterested in her threat. Like a parent waiting for a child to burn itself out on its tantrum, it waited, stared. Her hand quivered in the air, impotent in its fury, before she crumpled beside the rock.

'What did I do to deserve this?'

Asper had asked that question before, of the same God, on her first night in the temple. She had knelt before his image, carved in stone instead of silver, far from the loving embrace of her father and mother, far from the place she had once called home. She had knelt, alone, and asked the God she was supposed to worship.

'*Why?*'

And Talanas had sent Taire.

'*Because,*' the young girl who was always smiling had spoken from the back of the chapel, '*someone has to.*'

And Taire had knelt beside her, before the God that seemed, in that instant, better than any parent. Talanas was loving, cared for all things, sacrificed Himself so that humans might know what death was, what sickness was, and how to avert them. Talanas cared for His priests as much as He did His followers, and in the instant Taire had smiled at her, Asper knew that Talanas cared for them both, as well.

'*Has to what?*' she had asked the girl then.

'*Has to do it,*' Taire had replied.

'*Do what?*'

'*That's why we're here,*' the girl had replied, reaching out to tap the brown-haired girl on the nose before they both broke down into laughter.

'I don't deserve this,' Asper whispered, broken upon the forest floor. 'I didn't do anything to deserve this.' She raised her left arm, stared at it as it grinned beneath its pinkness, knowing it would be unleashed again. '*You* gave this to me.'

She rose to her knees, thrust her left hand at the pendant as though it were proof.

'*You* did. It isn't what I wanted. I … I wanted to help people.' She felt her tears sink into her mouth as she clenched her teeth. 'I want to *help* people.'

'*To serve mankind,*' Taire had said as they flipped through the pages of the book. '*To mend the bones, to heal the wound, to cure the illness.*'

'*What for?*' Asper had asked.

'*You're weird, you know that?*' Taire had stuck out her tongue. '*Who else is going to do it?*'

'*Talanas?*'

'*You don't pay attention during hymn, do you? Humanity was given a choice: free will or bliss. We chose free will and so it's up to us to take care of ourselves. Or rather, it's up to us, His faithful, to take care of everyone else.*'

'*Why would anyone not choose bliss?*'

'*Huh?*'

'*I would forsake free will in a heartbeat if it meant I didn't have to feel pain any more, if I didn't have to cry any more.*'

'Well, stupid, you'd be a slave, then.'

'What's wrong with that?'

'What's wrong …' Taire had sputtered, looking incredulous. *'What would be the point of life if you never knew pain? How would you even know you were alive?'*

Asper had felt pain. Asper had felt Taire's pain, that night in the dormitories. Asper had felt it as her friend begged and she could do nothing about it. Asper had felt it for the years after, as she had grown up, told herself it was an accident, told herself that she needed to atone for it by following Talanas.

'Well, I have followed you,' she whispered to the pendant. 'And you've led me to nothing. I … I always wondered if I was doing good, being amongst these heathens. Never once did I suspect I was doing wrong.' Her tears washed away the blood on the silver. *'Never*, you hear me?

'But what am I supposed to do with this?' She grabbed her arm, its sleeve long since destroyed. 'What good can come from this? From leaving nothing to bury? From robbing someone of *everything*? *What good?'*

The pendant said nothing.

'Answer me,' she whispered.

The wind shifted. The pendant shrugged.

'Answer me!'

She turned her arm, levelled its fingers at her throat.

'If you're there, if you're listening, you'll tell me why I shouldn't just turn this on myself and end it all.' She shook her arm. 'I'll do it. I'll do the one good thing I can with this arm.'

A tear of salt leaked past its beak. The pendant yawned. She looked around furtively, found a hefty brown stone. She pulled it up, raised it above her head, fingers trembling as she aimed it over the pendant.

'This,' she said, shaking the rock. 'This is real. This rock is real. Are you?' she snarled at the pendant. '*Are you?* If you are, you'll tell me why I shouldn't just destroy you. If you aren't, you end with this pendant. All you are is silver ... just a chunk of metal.' She growled. 'A chunk of metal with three breaths. One.'

The pendant did not do anything.

'Two.'

The pendant stared at her through hollow eyes.

'Three!'

The rock fell, rolled along the earth to bump against the trunk of a tree that loomed over a brown-haired girl, crumpled before a mossy altar, clenching her left arm with tears streaming down her face as a chunk of metal looked upon her with pity.

Thirty-Three

MEEK EXPECTATIONS

'So,' Denaos spoke loudly to be heard over the sound of hammering, 'why the sudden interest in the fairer sex?'

Lenk paused and looked up from his duty of nailing wood over their wrecked boat's wound, casting his companion a curious stare.

'Sudden?' he asked.

'Oh, apologies.' The rogue laughed, holding up a hand. 'I didn't mean to suggest you liked raisins in your curry, if you catch my meaning.'

'I ... really don't.'

'Well, I just meant you happened to be all duty and grimness and agonising about bloodshed up until this point.' Denaos took a swig from a waterskin as he leaned on the vessel's railing. 'You know, like Gariath.'

'Does ... Gariath like raisins in his curry?'

'I have no idea if he even eats curry.' Denaos scratched his chin thoughtfully. 'I suppose he'd probably like it hot, though.'

'Yeah, probably.' Lenk furrowed his brow. 'Wait, what does that mean?'

'Let's forget it. Anyway, I'm thrilled to advise you on the subject, but why choose now, in the prime of your imminent death, to start worrying about women?'

'Not "women", exactly, but "woman".'

'A noble endeavour,' Denaos replied, taking another swig.

'Kataria.'

There was a choked sputter as Denaos dropped the skin and put his hands on his knees, hacking out the droplets of water. Lenk frowned, picking up another half-log and placing it upon the companion vessel's hole.

'Is it that shocking?' the young man asked, plucking up a nail.

'Shocking? It's *immoral*, man.' The rogue gestured wildly off to some direction in which the aforementioned female might be. 'She's a *shict*! A bloodthirsty, leather-clad savage! She views humanity,' he paused to nudge Lenk, 'of which *you* are a part, I should add, as a disease! You know she threatened to kill me back in Irontide?'

'Yeah, she told me.' Lenk began to pound the nail.

'And?'

'And what?' He glanced up and shrugged. 'She didn't actually kill you, so what's the harm?'

'Point taken,' the rogue said, nodding glumly. 'Still, *that's* the sort of thing you're lusting after here, my friend. Say the Gods get riotously drunk and favour your union, say you're wed. What happens when you leave the jam out overnight or don't wear the pants she's laid out for you? Do you really want to risk her making a necklace out of your sack and stones every time she's in a mood?'

'Kat doesn't seem like the type to lay out pants,' Lenk said, looking thoughtful. 'I think that might be why I ...' He scratched his chin. 'Approve of her.'

'Well, listen to you and your ballads, you romantic devil.' The rogue sighed, resting his head on folded arms. 'Still, I might have known this would happen.'

'How's that?'

'Well, you've both got so much common,' he continued. 'You, a grim-faced runt with hair the colour of a man thrice your age. And her …' Denaos shuddered. 'Her, a woman with a lack of bosom so severe it should be considered a crime, a woman who thinks it's perfectly fine to smear herself with various fluids and break wind wherever she pleases.' His shudder became an unrestrained, horrified cringe. 'And that *laugh* of hers—'

'She has her good points,' Lenk replied. 'She's independent, she's stubborn when she needs to be, doesn't bother me too much … I'll concede the laugh, though.'

'You just described a mule,' Denaos pointed out. 'Though you grew up on a farm, didn't you? I suppose that explains a lot. Still, perhaps this particular match was meant to be.'

'What do you mean by that?'

'I mean you're both vile, bloodthirsty, completely uncivilised and callous people and you both have the physiques of prepubescent thirteen-year-old boys.' The rogue shrugged. 'The sole difference between you is that you choose to expel your reeking foulness from your mouth and she from the other end.'

'Glad to have your blessing, then,' Lenk muttered, hefting up another log. 'So, what do you think I should do?'

'Well, a shict is barely a step above a beast, so you might as well just rut her and get it over with before she tries to assert her dominance over you.'

'Uh … all right.' Lenk looked up, frowning. 'How do I do that?'

'How'd you do it the first time you did it?'

'What, with Kat?'

'No, with whatever milkmaid or dung-shovelstress you

happened to roll with when you first discovered you were a man, imbecile.'

Lenk turned back to the boat, blinking. He stared at the half-patched wound for a moment, though his eyes were vacant and distant.

'I ... can't remember.'

'Ah, one of *those* encounters, eh?' Denaos laughed, plucking up the waterskin from the sand. 'No worries, then. You might as well be starting fresh, aye?' He brushed the dirt from its lip and took a swig. 'Really, there's not much to it. Just choose a manoeuvre and go through with it.'

'What, there's manoeuvres?'

'Granted, the technique might be lost on her ... and you, but if you've any hope of pleasing a woman, you'll have to learn a few of the famous arts.' A lewd grin crossed his face. 'Like the Six-Fingered Suldana.'

'And ...' Lenk's expression seemed to suggest a severe moral dilemma in continuing. 'How does that go?'

'It's not too hard.' The rogue set down the waterskin, then folded the third finger of each hand under it, knotting the two appendages over themselves. 'First, you take your fingers like this. Then, you drop a gold piece on the ground and ask the woman if she wants to see a magic trick, then you—' He paused, regarding Lenk's horrified expression, and smiled. 'Oh, almost got me to say it, didn't you? No, no ... that one's a secret, and for good reason. If you tried it, you'd probably rupture something.'

'Maybe all this is for nothing,' the young man said, turning back to the boat. 'I mean, it's not usual to ... do this sort of thing right after confessing your feelings, is it?'

'Love has nothing to do with *feelings*, you twit. Or at least, lovemaking doesn't. It's an art, created to establish prowess and technique.'

'I'm … I'm really not sure I want to do that, then.'

'Fine.' The rogue sighed dramatically. 'I was trying to spare you some embarrassment, since I severely doubt your capabilities of conveying anything remotely eloquent to her. Then again, she is a barbarian, so perhaps just grunting and snorting will do.'

'I was planning on something like that,' Lenk said, grinning. 'But, out of curiosity, if Khetashe *does* smile upon me … what manoeuvre *do* I use?'

'Something simple,' Denaos said, shrugging. 'Like the Sleeping Toad.'

'The Sleeping Toad?'

'A beginner's technique, but no less efficient. You simply request that your lady wait until you're asleep, then have her do her business with such delicate sensual eroticism that you barely even stir.'

'Huh … have you ever tried it?'

'Once,' the rogue said, nodding.

'Did it work?'

Denaos looked out over the sea thoughtfully, took a long sip from the waterskin. 'You know, I really have no Gods-damned idea.'

The coconut was a hairy thing, a small sphere of bristly brown hair. Kataria scrutinised it, looked it over with an appraising stare as she took out her hunting knife. With delicate precision, she jabbed two small holes into two of the nut's deeper indentations. Quietly, she scooped a chunk of moist sand out of the forest floor and smeared it atop the coconut.

It looked at least *vaguely* silver in the shimmer of the sunlight, she thought, but there was still something missing. After a thoughtful hum, she brought her knife up and gouged a pair of scowling lines over the nut's makeshift eyes, finishing the product with a long, jagged frown underneath.

'There,' she whispered, smiling as the hairy face scowled at her, 'looks just like him.'

She traipsed over to a nearby stump sitting solemnly before a larger tree and set the face down upon it. Then, backing away as though she feared it might flee if she turned around, she reached for her quiver and bow. In a breath, the arrow was in her hand and drawn to her cheek, the bowstring quivering tautly.

The coconut continued to frown, not an ounce of fear on its grim, hairy visage. *Just like him*, she thought, *perfect*.

The bow hummed, the arrow shrieked for less than a breath before it was silenced by the sound of wood splitting and viscous liquid leaking onto the sand. The face hung by its right eye, the arrow having penetrated it perfectly and pinned the nut to the tree trunk behind it. Its expression did not change as thick milk dripped out of the back of its head and its muddy hair dribbled onto the earth.

The shict herself wore a broad, unpleasant smile as she stalked back to her impaled victim and leaned forwards, surveying her work. She observed the even split in the nut's eye and nodded to herself, pleased.

'I could still kill him,' she assured herself. 'I could do it.'

He was the tricky part, she knew, the only one she would have trouble killing. The rest were just obstacles: shifty hares in a thicket. He was the wolf, the dangerous prey. But that was hardly a matter. She could kill him now, she knew, and the rest would be dead soon after.

With that, Kataria jerked the arrow out of the face's eye and watched it fall to the earth. Wiping the head off on her breeches, she slid the missile back into her quiver and turned to walk away. She had gone less than three paces when she felt a shiver run up her back.

The nut was still staring at her, she knew, still frowning. It demanded an explanation.

'All right, look.' She sighed as she turned around. 'It's nothing personal. I mean, I don't *hate* you or anything.'

The coconut frowned, unconvinced.

'You had to know this was going to happen, didn't you?' She scratched the back of her head, casting eyes down to the ground. 'How else could it end, Lenk? I mean, we're … I'm a shict. You're a human.' She growled, turning a scowl up. 'No, you're a strain. You're part of the human disease! It's up to *us* to kill *you* before you become unsatisfied with the parts of the world you've already contaminated and infect the whole thing!'

The coconut did not appear to share the same sentiments. As she fell to her rear, Kataria realised she didn't either.

'We had fun, didn't we?' she asked the nut. 'I mean, I had fun at least. After a year around you, I'm not infected.' She sighed, rubbing her eyes. 'That's not true. I am infected. That's why I had to do what I did … sorry, why I *have* to do what I'm going to do.'

She didn't bother explaining the rest to the coconut. How could he understand? she asked herself. Humans didn't understand the Howling, couldn't hear it, couldn't comprehend what it was like to hear it again after a year of silence.

But Kataria did.

She had heard it, in fleeting echoes, during her battle with Xhai. And in those few moments, she had felt it, everything that it meant to be a shict. She could hear all the voices of her people, her ancestors, her tribesmen.

'My father,' she whispered.

Quietly, she reached up and ran her finger down the notches in her long earlobes, counting them off. One, two, three, she switched her hand to the other ear, four, five, six. The sixth tribe. *Sil'is Ish*. The Wolves. The Tribe that Hears.

And what good was it to be a part of the sixth tribe if she was deaf to the Howling? What would her people say if they knew such a thing? To know that she only used her ears to be a glorified hunting hound for a pack of inept, reeking, diseased monkeys?

What would her father say?

A brown shape caught her eye and she spied another coconut, this one apparently having landed on a rock when descending from its leafy home. Its face looked sunken, frowning, disapproving.

Much like him.

'*Naturally, I'm disappointed,*' she imagined the coconut saying, '*you are a shict, after all.*'

'What does that even mean, though?' she asked.

'*If you've forgotten already, then the answer as to what you should do is quite clear.*'

'But I don't want to do it,' she replied.

'*If we could all do what we wanted to, what would that make us?*'

'Human.' She sighed, rubbing her eyes.

'*Or?*'

'Tulwar,' she recited with rehearsed precision, 'or Vulgore, or Couthi, or any number of monkeys that claim to be a people.' She looked to the coconut with a pleading expression. 'But it's not like we have to kill them all.'

'*Just the ones that make us forget what it is to be a shict.*'

'It's not like that—'

'*Was it not you who just said such a thing?*'

'It's complicated.'

'*It is not.*'

'*He's* complicated.'

'*He's human.*'

'I have no reason to kill him. I don't hate him.'

'*It's not a matter of hate.*' She could hear the deep, resonant tone of a voice used to speaking to a people, for a people. '*Any monkey can hate, no matter what race he claims to be. Shicts are as beyond hate as the human disease is beyond redemption. We do not hate the disease, we cure it. We do not kill, we purify. This is simply what must be done and no other race has the conviction to do it. After all ... we were here first.*'

'Right ...'

Her father had always been hard to deny, for both herself and her tribe. He had shed little blood himself in years past, but had kept their home free of filth and degenerates. It was his leadership that turned back three individual human armies seeking to cross their domain. It was his confidence that led the three tribes to unite under him.

It was his plans, the houses that burned, the wells that were poisoned, the lack of mercy for anything with a round ear, regardless of age or sex, that kept humans far away from their borders.

No one could say what might happen if a human did contaminate a shict. Her father had made certain there would never be an opportunity. Now that Kataria herself felt it, felt the distance, felt the need to ask what it meant to be a shict, his speeches and sermons made much more sense than they ever had when she was small.

And yet, she wasn't quite ready to pick up arrows and start firing.

It could have been something else that infected her,

something else that made her forget the Howling. She had been around many humans, after all, and other races as well. Any number of them could have been the cause.

But then, she told herself, *you wouldn't have been exposed to any of them if not for him.*

Kataria lay back upon the sand. Her head throbbed, ached with the weight that had been put upon it. Her father was right, she knew; humans had done too much damage to be considered anything but a threat. She was proof enough. But if he was right, why hadn't she done what needed to be done in the first place?

Opinions contradicting her father's were few, but there was one that could be counted on always.

At that, she folded her arms behind her head and stared up at the sky, wondering what her mother would have said.

'*Well, it's not like it's some great loss for a human to die,*' the crisp, sharp voice came cutting on the wind, '*but when is it really necessary?*'

'You killed humans at *K'tsche Kando*,' Kataria retorted, 'many.'

'*Hundreds.*' There was a morbid laughter on the wind. '*But that was different.*'

'Forgive me for not seeing how.'

'*A human encroaching on our land is no different from any other race encroaching on our land. If they stay on their own side, they can do whatever they want. It's when they start pretending they belong somewhere else that they need to be culled.*'

'Not quite the message I'd hoped to receive.'

'*Well, you're forgetting a very important aspect.*'

'What's that?'

'*I didn't go to* K'tsche Kando *for any shict. I went there for you.*'

'I don't understand.'

'*If you did, you wouldn't be hallucinating now, would you?*'

'I thought this was the Howling,' Kataria said, frowning. 'Am … am I actually going mad?'

'*If you choose to. After all, no matter what your father says, it's all down to choice. He didn't want me to go, but I chose to, because if the humans set one foot upon our sister tribe's land unchallenged, they'd come to our land, too, bolder and more virulent than ever.*'

A brief silence hung over them. Kataria absently sighed up to the sky, hoping that whatever was looking down upon her did so with a frown that matched her own.

'Did you choose to die there?' she asked.

'*Can you choose that? I chose to kill there. What do you choose?*'

'I'm … not sure.'

'*Then what do you want?*'

Kataria sat up, staring at her hands as they lay in her lap, calloused and well used to the shape of the bow, feeling the breeze kick the feathers in her hair against her notched ears, hearing the distant howl upon the wind.

'I …' she said reluctantly, 'I want to feel like a shict again.'

'*Then,*' the sky and coconut answered as one, '*you already know the answer.*'

The hunting knife seemed much heavier when she picked it up. Her body felt like lead as she pulled herself up to her feet. The realisation that they were right was so thick as to choke her when she took in a deep breath.

The coconut with its eye put out now looked cold, stale. In the moments before the last of its milk had sloshed onto the sand, its face had changed. No longer did it demand explanation or look at her with disapproval. It merely seemed to stare blankly, as if to ask what it had done wrong to deserve such treatment.

She had no answer for it, no answer for herself as she tucked the knife into her belt and turned to join her companion for the last time. All she had left was a question that she asked herself with every footstep.

How else could it end?

Thirty-Four
WHAT IS LEFT

Irontide no longer loomed against the orange setting of the sun. Irontide was no longer capable of looming. Instead, the massive fortress sagged, leaned drunkenly with a long, granite sigh as though it strained to clutch at the gaping hole in its side and lamented its lack of arms. Instead of looking fearsome, instead of looking forsaken, it looked at peace, a great, grey old man ready to go with a stony smile and an undignified stumble into the water.

Salt still wept from its wound, though in small, murmuring trickles. The tide had settled over its spike-encrusted base. Soon, the whole structure would crumble and vanish beneath the waves. The weapons and bodies entombed within would be forgotten. The sea, ever rising, had already forgotten Irontide.

Lenk, however, had not.

He wondered if he could still swim to the fortress, how long it would take him with his injured leg. How long would it take him to revisit the chamber with the black water and the rocky outcropping? How long would it take him to sink to the bottom once more and leave behind what had come out of the chamber with him?

'I hear it more often now,' he whispered, perhaps to whatever God might be listening. 'It's so loud, so clear.' Absently, he rubbed his leg. 'So cold.'

And with the voice had come the memories, the images that he remembered forgetting before. He saw them in flashes, in the moments when he blinked, and heard them in the moments when he held his breath. He could remember a strange weight upon his head, as though his skull had been coated in lead. He could remember the distinct lack of warmth and not being bothered by such a thing.

He could remember seeing his hands before him, covered in grey skin.

Now they lay before him, pink. But he remembered what they had done, whose head they had taken.

'Demons can't be harmed by mortal weapons,' he muttered to himself. 'Demons can't die by mortal hands. That doesn't happen.'

But it did, didn't it?

'Did it?' he asked himself. 'Maybe the whole thing was ... was imaginary, a hallucination. It could have been a trick of the mind.'

You did take several blows to the head.

'Yes, several blows,' he agreed.

Not as grievous as those the Deepshriek took, of course.

'Exactly, I—'

Lenk paused and looked up, eyes wide as he felt his blood go cold. Somewhere inside him, a chuckle slipped through his brain and slid down his spine on freezing legs.

'Not so chatty now, are you?'

'What?'

'I said, not so talkative any more? No more questions?'

Lenk turned about, regarding the rogue standing behind him. Denaos flashed a grin as he stalked towards the young man, taking a seat beside him on the beach.

'Any other inane enquiries about the female question? Perhaps you'd like to know where babies come from?'

Lenk regarded the taller man through eyes that suddenly felt heavy, as though he had just been deprived of a year's worth of sleep in a breath. He pulled his knees up to his chest and stared out over the ocean.

'No. I don't want to talk any more.'

'Oh? Did we run out of work to do?' Denaos glanced down the beach where their vessel lay, its hole patched with conspicuous timber. 'Not the best job, I admit, but hardly a reason to stop conversing. I was rather enjoying myself towards the end.'

'I don't want to talk—'

'Then maybe you ought to listen.' The rogue scratched his chin. 'Frankly, I think I might have misjudged your chances with Kataria.' At the young man's worried look, he grinned. 'There, I thought you might find that interesting.'

'I don't understand.'

'Shocking.' Denaos rolled his eyes. 'Anyway, it strikes me that, if plays are any indicator, a great deal of romance tends to end in death. Suicide, frequently, or murder ... and if the script's any good, sometimes both.' The rogue shrugged. 'Given your mutual professions, I think your chances for either are rather good. Violence, it seems, makes a fertile garden for love to blossom.'

'Love ...' Lenk repeated to himself, staring at his hands.

And who could love someone who ... did what you did? Someone who is what you are?

'*Who even requires love?*' the voice asked.

'Shut up,' Lenk hissed.

'No, no, hear me out,' Denaos insisted. 'Given that she's a shict, I think the chances of her killing *you* are excellent. And that's almost exactly how *The Heresy of Vulton Husk* ends, if you've ever read it.' He made a soft applause. 'A great tragedy of our time. Truly inspired.'

'You've …' Lenk began, glancing at the rogue, 'been in love?'

'I've been married.'

'Same thing.'

'Oh, Gods no.' The rogue shook his head vigorously. 'Marriage, you see, is an invention of man. It's a trick in which you deceive someone into cleaning up after you when you're too old to care whether you're wearing pants when you piss. If it's love … true love, one of you dies before the other realises they hate you.'

'*And she will die long before us,*' the voice whispered threateningly, '*they all will die, you know. They're obstacles. They're hindrances.*'

'Stop,' Lenk muttered.

'Yes, I suppose it's a little late for such quandaries, isn't it?' The rogue clapped the young man on the back as he clambered to his feet. 'But I'm glad we had this talk. If nothing else, you can always buy your answers with your reward when we hand over the book.'

Denaos's feet crunched upon the sand, leaving Lenk staring at his hands, straining not to blink, not to breathe. When the taller man's footsteps were barely audible, the young man looked up and spoke to no one.

'Who are you?' he whispered. 'What do you want?'

'*It is not a matter of want. It is a matter of what must be done.*'

'I'm not the man to do it. Not if it means that she—'

'*We are the one to do it. All obstacles fade or are torn down, even her.*'

'How do I get rid of you? How?'

'*There is no such thing.*'

'What do you do,' he muttered, 'when you want to be with someone … but you want to kill yourself?'

'Ah,' the rogue called, distantly, 'that's most definitely love.'

There was nothing left.

The stench of blood and cowardice, the reek of smoke and salt, the foul aromas of humanity and weakness were all vanished. Even the air hung still, carrying no scent of moisture rising from the earth or breath hissing from the trees. The world was as it was intended to be, free from all imperfect stenches.

All that remained was Gariath and the scent of rivers and rocks.

His legs felt weak underneath him as he pushed his way delicately through the jungle, following the memory's trail. His wounds had since begun to heal, the burned flesh peeling off and the cuts scabbing over. It was something else that made him hesitant, made him wary of continuing, a sensation he hadn't been able to smell through the stench of his own anger and the sheets of blood that he covered himself with.

His knees were soft as they had been when he first learned to hunt alongside his father. His bowels quivered with excitement as they had when he tasted the meat of his first prey. His chest trembled and felt as shallow as it had when he first mated. His arms felt weighted and weak as they had when he first held two wailing pups in his grasp, when he first learned he was a father.

That, all of it, was gone now. Only Gariath was left, of his family, of the *Rhega*. When he realised that, when he realised why he had followed a weak, scrawny human away from what had once been his home, where his family had once lived, where his children had cried and his father had bled, he realised what the sensation was.

Fear.

It was a foul emotion, Gariath thought, anger was much better. Within anger there was certainty, there was predictability, and he always knew how everything would end. Within fear, there was nothing. There was nothing to expect and nothing to keep hope from spawning inside him.

Hope died. Anger lived.

But it was with hope that he walked, following the scent as it wound its way through the jungle paths and into the heart of the forest where no one but he was meant to go. The spirits let him pass, drawing back their fronds and branches, leaving their rocks and roots out of his path, chasing the noisy beasts and birds from their crowns that he might hear.

Hear and smell.

The scent became overwhelming as he placed a claw upon the thick, leafy branch. The last branch, he realised, before he faced what lay upon the other side. It would be better to go back now, he knew, to go back to the certainty of anger and the predictability of bloodshed. It would be better to go back, safe in the knowledge that there were no more *Rhega*, that his father and his mate and his children were all gone.

It would be better to forget that he might have ever hoped.

But, still, he pushed past the branch.

The glade greeted him with the murmur of a stream and the gentle hum of sunlight peering through the branches. The earth was moist, but hard and green under his feet. It pressed against his soles affectionately, as if it were welcoming him back after a journey so long only the earth could remember him.

It knew his feet.

The water greeted him eagerly, lapping up to his waist as he waded through the shallow stream towards the verdant chunk of earth in the centre of it. It giggled, laughed and jumped up to grab at him, trying to invite him to swim as he had once before, before he had known what anger was.

The water knew him.

He reached down, leaving a hand in the stream as if to assure it that he would be back before too long. He ignored the splashing moans of disappointment as he climbed onto the chunk of green. The great stone loomed over it, tall, grey and jagged. An elder, he realised as he brushed a hand over it, who had seen the stream born, the forest born, and so much more.

He knew the stone.

He breathed deeply, inhaling the memories. The elder was free with his tales, let the scents escape his soil and fill Gariath's nostrils. They came quickly, almost overwhelmingly.

Taoharga was born here, he knew, *and she was the swiftest runner in the land. The earth scorned her feet and the beasts feared her approach.*

He inhaled again. *Gathar stood here and sheltered his children beneath his wings when the storms came and did not relent for three days.*

The sound of breath. *Argha and Hartaga were born here. They stood, they fought, they hunted and they bled together.*

They came one after the other, his breaths short and ragged. *Gratha laughed while she mated here. Harathag roared to the sky here as his children died before he did. Iagrah watched her son catch a fish and wrestle with it here.*

652

'There …' Gariath whispered, his voice afraid to confirm what he knew, 'there were *Rhega* here.' His eyelids twitched. His hand pressed hard against the stone. 'They were … *we* were here.'

Were.

It was not the name of his people or his family that echoed in his mind. It was that ugly, muttering qualifier that caused his brain to ache and his lips to quiver. *Rhega were here. They are not any more.*

That should have been the end of it, he knew, one more reason why hope was stupid, one more reason to go running back in tears to the comfort of hatred and the warmth of anger. He should have gone back, back to fighting, back to bloodshed. But he could not bring himself to walk away, not yet, not before he looked to the elder and asked.

'Where did they all go?'

Gariath's ear-frills twitched as he heard the sound of leaves rustling. He cast a glower out over the surrounding underbrush. Had one of the weakling humans followed him to this place where they weren't meant to go?

Just as well, he thought as he flexed his claws. There was no more reason to continue this imaginary game of pretending they didn't deserve to die. There was no more reason to keep them alive. They were the answer to his question, *they* were where the *Rhega* went.

No more questions. No more excuses. This time they all died.

'Come out and die with a bit of dignity,' he growled, 'or start running so I can chase you.'

His unseen spy answered, bursting from the foliage in a flash of red. It moved quickly, tearing so swiftly across the green and through the stream that he did not even lay eyes upon it until it was upon him.

There was a sudden pressure upon his ankle, warm and almost affectionate. Slowly, he glanced down, his claws untensing, wings furling themselves as he stared at the tiny red muzzle trying to wrap itself around his foot.

The pup, apparently, did not sense his smile and the young creature renewed his vigour, clawing at Gariath's leg with short limbs, trying to coil a stubby tail about the taller *Rhega*'s leg to bring him to the ground.

Gariath reached down and tried to dislodge the pup with a gentle tug. The young *Rhega* only held on faster, emitting what was undoubtedly intended to be a warning growl. His body trembling with contained mirth, Gariath hooked his hands under the pup's armpits and pulled him up to stare into his face.

From behind a short, blunted muzzle, the pup stared at his elder. His ear-frills were extended, not yet developed enough to be able to fold them. His wings were tiny flaps of skin hanging on his back, the bones not strong enough to lift them yet. His stubby little red tail wagged happily as he stared at Gariath through bright eyes.

That's right, Gariath remembered with a smile, *our eyes are supposed to be bright, not dark.*

'I almost got you,' the pup growled. He bit at Gariath's nose, the taller *Rhega*'s nostrils flickering.

'I don't know,' Gariath replied with a thoughtful hum. 'You're a pup.'

'I'm a *Rhega*.'

'You're small.'

'I'm *big*.'

'Big enough to be held like a pup, maybe.'

At that, the pup emitted a shrill snarl and bit Gariath's finger. The sensation of tiny teeth grazing his tough hide was familiar. He remembered a pair of jaws nipping at him in such a way, two equally small voices insisting how big they were.

The smile he offered in response, however, did not feel so familiar.

'Fine, you're huge.' Gariath laughed, dropping the pup.

The smaller *Rhega* landed with a growl and a scrabble of short limbs as he scrambled to his feet. Gariath, in response, fell to his own rear, taking a seat opposite the pup. He could not help but stare at the small creature; he had forgotten how small he had started as. The pup was tiny, but not weak, unharmed from the fall, back up and on all fours as he growled playfully at the older *Rhega*.

Did I ever growl like that? Gariath asked himself. *Were my eyes ever so bright?*

'I might not be so big now,' the pup said, making a feinted lunge at the older *Rhega*, 'but my mother says I will be someday.'

And at the pup's words, Gariath felt his smile drop, fade back into a frown.

He doesn't know, he realised.

And how could the pup know? He couldn't see himself, couldn't look at the way the sunlight occasionally passed through his body. He could not see the distance in his own eyes, suggesting just how long he had been so small. He could not see that the earth did not depress beneath him when he rolled and jumped.

He couldn't possibly know he wasn't alive any more.

'What's wrong?' the pup asked, tilting his head to the side.

'Nothing is wrong,' Gariath replied, forcing the smile back onto his face. 'It's … just been a long time since I've seen one of you … one of us.'

'Me, too,' the pup said, plopping onto his rear end.

'There used to be lots of us.' He looked around the glade and frowned. 'I wonder when they're coming back.'

Tell him, Gariath told himself, *he deserves to know. Tell him they're not coming back.*

'I'm sure they will soon,' Gariath replied instead.

Coward.

'I hope so … they left a long time ago.'

'Where did they go?'

The pup opened his mouth to speak, then frowned. He looked down at the earth dejectedly.

'I … I don't know.'

'Then why are you still here? Didn't your father take you with him when he left?'

'My mother was supposed to,' the pup replied. 'My father left … long ago, long before she did.'

'He died?'

'I … think so. It's hard to remember.'

The pup placed two stubby clawed hands on the tiny bone nubs that would someday be two broad horns. *Would have been*, Gariath corrected himself.

'My head hurts thinking about it,' the pup whined. 'You're not going anywhere, are you?'

'Of course not,' Gariath said, smiling. 'What's your name?'

'Grahta,' the pup said. 'It means—'

'*Strongest*,' the older *Rhega* finished. He flashed a coy smile. 'Are you sure it's accurate?' He prodded the pup, sending him tumbling over. 'You don't look very strong.'

'I will be someday!' Grahta scrabbled to his feet and lunged at Gariath's hand as he pulled it away. 'It's a much better name than whatever yours is, anyway.'

'My name,' the older *Rhega* said, drawing himself up proudly, 'is Gariath.'

'*Wisest?*' Grahta laughed. 'That can't be right.'

'What makes you say that?' Gariath asked, frowning. 'I'm plenty wise.'

'You're plenty beat up, is what you are.' Grahta poked his stubby finger against the cuts crossing Gariath's flesh, the traces of black where his skin had been burned. 'What happened to you?'

Gariath stared down at that finger, prodding so curiously, taking everything in through a tiny digit. *They had fingers so tiny*, he recalled.

'I ...' he whispered with a sigh, 'I hurt myself.'

Tried to kill myself, he added mentally, *tried to join you, Grahta, and your mother and father and my—*

'That wasn't too smart,' Grahta said, frowning. 'Aren't you supposed to be the smart one?'

'What do you mean?'

'I've heard you talk to the other creatures you walk with. You yell at them, call them names, try to hurt them.' The pup's frown deepened, his eyes turning towards the earth. 'My father used to talk like that.'

'I'm sorry. I didn't know you were listening.'

'You didn't sound very happy.'

Gariath followed the pup's gaze. 'I'm not.'

'Why? Don't you have enough to eat?'

'I have enough to eat,' Gariath replied. 'I just ... I don't have anyone to talk to.'

'What about those creatures?'

'The humans?'

'Is that what they're called? They smell bad.' The pup tilted his head to one side. 'Is that why you're not happy? Because they smell bad? Maybe you could ask them to wash.'

'Humans are ...' Gariath sighed. 'They smell bad no

matter how much they wash. And they only smell worse the more of them that are around.'

'Are there a lot of them?'

'Many.'

'More than the *Rhega*?'

Many more. Thousands more. There are no more Rhega. *Tell him. He deserves to know.*

'You don't have to worry about humans,' Gariath said, 'so let's not talk about it.'

'All right,' Grahta said. 'How come there's only one of you?'

Gariath winced.

'I mean,' the pup continued, 'don't you have a family?'

'I did ... I do,' the older *Rhega* said, nodding. 'I have two sons.'

'What are their names?'

Gariath paused at that, staring intently at the pup. 'Their names are Tangahr and Grahta.'

'Like me!' The pup ran in a quick circle, barking excitedly. 'Is your son the strongest, too?'

'He was ... very strong,' Gariath whispered, his voice choked suddenly. 'His brother was, too. Much stronger than their father.'

'I'm sure you'll be strong too, someday,' the pup said, nodding vigorously. 'You just need to eat more meat.'

'I'm ... sure I will be.'

'Not as strong as me, though.'

'Of course not.'

'I'm very strong, you know. Once, I even killed a boar on my own. It was back when—'

The stream whispered quietly around them, no other sound to distract Gariath from hearing the pup. Every word echoed in his mind, every word felt like a claw dug into his chest that he couldn't dislodge. He could hear himself in the pup's voice, he could hear his own shrill bark, his own boasts, his own proclamations that he had made to his father when he was so young.

The proclamations his sons had made to him.

They were so boastful, he thought, smiling at the pup, *they talked so much ... they never stopped talking until ...*

'Grahta,' he interrupted softly, 'why aren't you with your family?'

'I ... I'm not sure,' Grahta replied, scratching his head. 'I think ... I think Grandfather asked me to wait. He asked me to stay awake.'

'For what?'

'For you,' Grahta said, looking up at the older *Rhega* intently.

'I'm here now.'

'And you're not going anywhere, right?'

'Right.'

'Okay, good.' The pup scratched his head. 'Grandfather ... Grandfather said ... uh, he wanted me to tell you something.'

'What?'

'He told me to tell you ... not to follow me.'

Gariath felt his heart stop, his eyes go wide. 'Wh-what?'

'He said you can't come where he went, where I'm supposed to go, not yet.'

Something welled inside Gariath's throat, lodging itself there. 'But ... why not?'

'I don't know,' Grahta replied, shrugging. 'But why would you want to go? I'm right here. We can play!'

No, Gariath told himself, *we can't play. You have to go,*

Grahta. You can go, now. You can fall asleep. I've heard the message. You can go.

Gariath looked at the pup, eyes wide, teeth so small in his smile. *Tangahr smiled like that. Grahta's eyes were so bright.*

No ... NO! he roared inside his own head. *Tell him. Tell him he can go! Tell him he can sleep! He's been awake for so long!*

Grahta fell to all fours, tail upright as he barked a challenge at the older *Rhega. Tangahr always barked like that. Grahta didn't like to fight ... Tangahr teased him. What ... what* Rhega *doesn't like to fight?*

Tell him ... TELL HIM! YOU CAN'T DO THIS TO HIM!

'Grahta,' Gariath whispered, 'how long have you been awake?'

'A ... a long time, I guess,' the pup replied, sitting back down. He yawned, a shrill, whining sound accompanied by exposed rows of stubby white teeth. 'I'm very tired now, since you said it.'

Good, Gariath told himself, inhaling sharply, *he can rest. He deserves to rest. He deserves to ...*

Gariath watched the pup walk in a circle, then curl up, folding his tail towards his snout. His eyes went wide.

Tangahr ... Grahta ... used to sleep like that.

'Grahta,' he whispered. Upon hearing no reply, he said loudly. 'Grahta!'

'What?' the pup asked, opening one bright eye.

'Don't fall asleep yet!'

'But I'm so ...' the pup paused to yawn, 'so tired. I've been up for so long.'

'I know, but stay up a little longer.' There was no reply from the younger *Rhega. 'Please.'*

'I'll be back, Gariath. I just want to sleep a little.'

'No, Grahta, don't fall asleep. Please don't fall asleep.' Gariath was up on his knees now, standing over the pup. 'Don't leave me alone, Grahta. I ... I've been alone for a long time now. Please, Grahta ... *please*.'

'Maybe you should ... should go and see Grandfather,' Grahta suggested, yawning. 'He said you should go and see him.'

'Where? Where did he say he would be, Grahta?'

'Somewhere ... north? I don't know what that means.'

'Then how am I supposed to find him?'

'You're ... you're Wisest, aren't you?'

'I'm not very smart, Grahta. I need you to stay up and give me directions. Please, Grahta, stay up a little longer. Stay awake, Grahta.'

'I ... I'm sorry,' the pup said, almost snoring. 'I just ... I'm so tired.'

'Not yet, Grahta. Talk to me for a little longer. Tell me ... tell me about your mother.'

'Oh, my mother ...' The pup smiled wistfully, even as his red eyelids drooped. 'My mother ... her name was Toaghari ... it means ...' He opened his mouth wide in a yawn. 'It means ... *Greatest*. I ... I hope she comes back ...' He settled down upon the earth, pressing his face against his tail. 'Soon.'

The sound of the pup snoring carried over the sound of the brook whispering, but it faded with every passing breath. More sounds returned to the world: air from the trees, breezes blowing over the sand, moisture rising from the earth. Grahta's sound of slumber was a distant part in the world's great chorus.

As was the sound of Gariath's own voice.

'Don't blink,' he told himself, gripping the earth in two trembling hands. 'Don't blink. He'll go if you blink.'

661

He tried to hold the image of the little red bundle, his side rising and falling with each breath, in eyes that were quickly streaming over with tears.

'Don't blink.'

He tried to hold the image of wings too small to flex, a tail too small to do anything but wag, eyes that were bright as his once had been.

'Don't blink.'

He tried to hold the image of two similar bundles, rolling over each other at his feet, barking and nipping, wagging and whining, their voices fresh in his frills as they boasted, proclaimed, roared, growled, snarled and snored.

'Don't—'

When he opened his eyes again, Grahta was gone. The earth was not depressed where he had been, the sunlight continued to pour despite his absence. The sound of his sleeping was lost on the wind.

'No,' he whimpered, pawing at the ground. 'No, no, no, no, *NO!*' His roar killed the sounds in the air as he threw back his head. '*Hit something,*' he told himself, sweeping his gaze about the glade. 'Hit! Kill! Make it bleed! Make it die! Kill something! *KILL!*'

The only thing that shared the glade, that could possibly satiate the urge, was the impassive elder stone looming over him. Snarling, he levelled an accusatory finger.

'*YOU!*'

He struck the stone, felt his hand crack, and fell to the earth with a cry. There was nothing to hit. Nothing to kill. No anger, no hatred. He was left alone with hope. Quietly, he laid his head against the rock, his body trembling as tears slid down his snout to trickle across the rim of his nostrils and fall to the unmoved earth.

Grahta was gone. The *Rhega* were gone. Gariath was alone.

With the scent of nothing but salt and wind as the world continued around him.

Thirty-Five

NOTHING REMAINS

There was very little in the supply crate to suggest that Argaol ever really expected them to return alive, Denaos thought as he rummaged blindly through the various sundries and goods within. The moon was not much help in illuminating his search.

'Blankets ... fishing line ... but no hooks,' the rogue muttered, rolling his eyes. 'Rope ... who needs *rope* on an island? Waterskins, empty ... bacon ... dried meat ... salted meat ... *dried salted meat.*'

His hands clenched something long and firm. Eyes widening, he pulled something stout and rounded free. Scrutinising it in the darkness, he frowned.

'A ... lute.' He blinked at the stringed instrument. 'What ... did he just throw whatever he could spare into this thing?' Quietly, he noted the inscription on the wooden neck. 'Not a bad year, though.'

'Could you possibly hurry it up?' someone called from behind. 'I'm sort of ... you know, trying to keep someone's leg from becoming gangrenous and falling off.'

'If the Gods had mercy, such a fate should befall my ears,' the rogue muttered.

Sighing, he sifted through everything else the captain had deemed worthy for chasing demons. His persistence, however, eventually rewarded him with the knowledge that the old Silfish prayer had yet to be proven false.

'Gods are fickle, men are cruel,' he recited as he wrapped his hand around something smooth and cold. He pulled the bottle from the crate and watched his own triumphant smile reflected back to him in its sloshing amber liquor. 'Trust only in yourself and what lies in your cup.'

That smile persisted as he walked back to the fire, back to his doubtlessly grateful companions. Who else would have had the foresight to smuggle out a bit of liquid love, after all? *Granted*, he reasoned, *it's stolen love. But what is love if it doesn't leave someone else unhappy?*

He couldn't honestly say the thought of Argaol's furious face, screwed up so tight his jaws would fold inwards and begin to devour his own bowels, caused him any great despair. *After all, the man gave us a* lute.

Besides, he reasoned, whatever price Argaol demanded could be paid out of his earnings. *One thousand gold*, he told himself, *divided amongst six … one hundred sixty five pieces, roughly. My share, plus Asper's, equates to three hundred and thirty. This bottle*, he paused to survey the golden-stained glass, *can't be more than thirty. Expensive, but still enough to buy many more and a new bowel for Argaol.*

The good captain's sacrifice would not be in vain. Silf demanded sacrifice for His role in their victory, the recovery of the book. Fortunately, the Patron was, if His own scriptures were to be believed, satisfied with whatever revelry that might occur being done in His name.

And what was not to revel about? The book was in their possession, patiently waiting to be exchanged for hard, shiny coin. The demons were fled for a glorious three nights, the longfaces gone, as well. And, as an added answer to an oft-muttered prayer, both Gariath and Dreadaeleon had been strangely absent for the past day and night, leaving

665

Denaos alone with two lovely women who would no doubt be at least tolerable when the bottle was drained.

And Lenk, too, he thought disdainfully, *but let's not dwell on the negative. Tonight is a night of revelry! Silf demands it! He demands empty bottles, drunken dreams and remorseful lamentations in the morning! He demands satisfied women, wrinkled skirts and trousers that can't be found in the morning! He demands riot, revel and, at the absolute minimum,* three *violations of scripture by* two *women with a strong desire to explore their own mystique.*

What greeted him when he arrived, however, was not revelry or riot. There was hardly a smile shared around the fire, much less two women committing blasphemies on the sand. Their faces were sombre, their eyes hard and their mouths stretched into frowns so tight they might as well have come off a torturer's rack.

'Frankly,' he said aloud, placing hands on hips, 'I'm wondering if I might not find a livelier bunch in Irontide.'

'Amongst the maggots and corpseflies, perhaps,' Asper muttered, looking up from Lenk's leg. She eyed the bottle with scrutiny. 'What's that?'

'Huss's Gold Cork,' the rogue replied, holding up the bottle triumphantly. 'The finest whiskey ever to be wrought past the last Karnerian Crusade. Only one hundred barrels of this made it out of the empire before liquor was outlawed there.'

'Where'd you get it?' the priestess asked, lofting a brow.

'Argaol so generously donated it to our cause.'

'Uh-huh. And why don't I believe you?'

'Likely because you have two working eyes and at least a tenuous grasp on the concept of behavioural patterns.' The rogue batted his eyelashes sweetly. 'Or maybe Talanas just loves you.'

'Sure, fine.' She held out a hand. 'Give it here.'

'A zealous little one, are you?' He slipped the bottle to her. 'By all means, begin your indulgences first. The tightest buttocks require the most lubrication, after all.'

Asper ignored his remark, seemed to ignore the bottle as she studied Lenk's leg. The young man's trouser leg had been sheared off above the knee, pulled back to expose the jagged wound in his thigh. It had since been treated, the dead flesh removed, the salve applied, the skin pulled together and stitched tight with black gut thread. All the same, Asper scrutinised it with the same sort of frown she might an oozing, infected, scabrous thing.

She uncorked the bottle and held a white cloth to the mouth. Quietly, she tipped it and stained it amber, wiping it upon the young man's leg.

The scream of agony came not from Lenk.

'What are you doing, heathen?' Denaos shrieked as he shoved her over and wrenched the bottle from her hand, cradling it to his chest as he might an infant. 'This is none of your wretched Talanite swill! This … is … *liquor.*'

'It's alcohol,' she replied, scowling as she righted herself. 'It'll fight infection.'

'If you were any kind of decent healer, you'd have fought it with another weapon already.'

'I wanted to make sure.' She shrugged. 'What else am I supposed to clean it with?'

Denaos glanced from the bottle, to the priestess, to the young man's leg. He snorted, a wet, rumbling sound coursing through his nose, and spat a glistening glob upon the stitched wound.

'Walk it off,' he snarled.

'Yeah, sure,' Lenk muttered. 'You've been trying to

indirectly kill me for as long as I've known you. I suppose you had to escalate at some point.'

'You didn't cry out.'

Lenk turned a hard stare upon Kataria. It was with a frown that Denaos noted the shict had affixed such a stare to the young man ever since they had settled around the crackling fire. He would have hoped that her gaze would have turned to him by now, or at least to Asper.

Then again, he thought, noting the particular hardness and narrowness of her gaze, *perhaps it's all for the best*.

'What?' Lenk asked.

'You didn't cry out,' she repeated, gesturing to the bottle. 'Didn't that hurt?'

'It might have.'

'But you don't know.' Her ears twitched with a sort of predatory observation. 'Humans are supposed to cry out when they get hurt.'

'And what do you think that means.' It was not a question that came out of Lenk's mouth, and the cold hostility with which it was delivered indicated no particular concern for whatever Kataria might have to answer.

For her part, the shict said nothing. It was with some concern that Denaos noted the hunting knife securely strapped to her belt. He hadn't ever noticed her wearing it when not hunting, but that was far from his largest concern.

'Oh, let's not do this now, shall we?' Denaos took his place around the roaring orange. 'We've a victory to celebrate, after all, and it's two days overdue.'

'Victory?' Lenk asked, raising a brow. 'We barely escaped alive.'

'Barely counts.'

'We're wounded and tired,' Asper pointed out.

'But alive.'

'For now,' Kataria muttered.

'And now, we *need* to celebrate. We *need* to get drunk, roll around in our own vomit and lick whatever amphibious wildlife we can catch in our stupor.' The rogue paused, blinked and cleared his throat. '*Granted*, in practice, it's a lot more amusing, which is all the more reason to start drinking.'

'I don't feel the need to,' Lenk replied harshly.

'But the *need* feels you ... to—'

'That doesn't make sense.'

'It doesn't have to! We're celebrating!'

'Celebrating what?' The young man rose, his injured leg shaking beneath him. 'What did you do that's worthy of celebration?'

'Well, I—'

'Did *you* fight the Deepshriek?'

'No, but—'

'Did *you* get wounded?'

'I was fairly well—'

'When you close your eyes, what is it that *you* see, Denaos?' Lenk snarled.

The rogue glowered, his lips twitching as if ready to deliver some scathing retort to that. After a moment. his face twisted, cracked around the edges, and he quickly looked down at the earth.

'I'd rather not say,' he whispered. 'But I do know that liquor often helps it.'

'Then you keep it,' Lenk muttered, turning around. 'Thank whatever kind of God Silf is that your problems can be fixed like that.'

Denaos did not try to stop him as he stalked away from the fire and vanished into the night air. Silf hated melodrama, after all.

'Well, fine.' The rogue snorted and spat upon the earth. 'That's just glorious. He can go and sulk and wait for someone to come and rub his back and tell him that everyone loves him and *we* shall have a good time all our own.' He took a brief swig from the bottle. 'So, why don't we enjoy ourselves? Kataria, you take off your tunic and I'll show you both a magic trick.'

'She's gone,' Asper said.

Denaos's frown only grew deeper as he stared at the indentation where she had been sitting. At what point she had decided to go, he could not know, nor did he particularly care. *All the better, all the better*, he told himself with a bit of hysteria edging his inner voice, *that just leaves me and …*

Asper, he finished with a sigh. Zealous, purist, morally irreproachable Asper. Asper, who had never done anything wrong in her life. Asper, who complained every time he stuck a knife into anything. Asper, who tried to use Huss's Gold Cork as a disinfectant.

Maybe I should just save myself the trouble and go to sleep now.

He was about to rise when he heard the sand shift, sensed someone come up beside him. He felt soft brown hair laid down upon his shoulder as she pressed her body against his, resting her head upon him as she stared into the fire. So stunned was he that he didn't even try to resist as she took the bottle from his hands and pulled a long swig from its neck.

'Well,' he said softly, eyeing the eager pulse of her throat. 'Dare I ask what drives you to such extremes?'

'You dare not,' she replied coldly.

'Dare I hope where this might lead?'

'You dare not.'

'Well, then what's the bloody point?' he muttered, snatching the bottle back from her.

'I need you,' she said, simply and without anything behind it.

'I've heard that from a few women in my time,' he said bitterly, taking a swig. 'In my experience, it never quite works out in a way that's beneficial for me.'

'Well, I don't need *you*, specifically.' She wrapped her arm around his, clutching it with a tightness he found uncomfortable. 'I need a rock.'

'A rock.'

'I need something real. I need something that talks back to me.'

He smiled at that. It was only with the night time, the starlight that made her skin glow, the scent of smoke that contrasted with her own delicate aroma, that he noticed her. It was only now, as he felt her body rise and fall with each breath, pressing against his, that he noticed how her body curved in a way that could not be hidden by robes.

She reminded him of ...

He blinked. The images flashed before his eyes. Blood. A dead stare locked upon the ceiling. Laughter.

Someone else.

Asper was not someone else, though. It was only at that moment that she was no longer a priestess, he no longer a rogue. She no longer pious, he no longer vile. Between the darkness and the bottle, they were but woman and rock.

That thought brought a smile to his face as he upended the bottle into his mouth.

'Rocks don't drink,' she pointed out.

'Rocks also don't finger your asshole while you sleep.' He exhaled, then took another swig. 'Looks like you're in for several disappointments tonight.'

'That's funny,' Asper said. 'I'm not laughing … but it's funny.' She eyed the bottle thoughtfully. 'We should make a toast, shouldn't we?'

'We should. The Gods would demand it.' He raised the bottle, observed the amber sloshing inside. 'To the Gods, then?'

'Not the Gods,' she said coldly, snatching the bottle back.

Denaos felt her breath catch in her body, linger uncertainly there for a moment. He could feel her press more firmly against him, her grip tighten on his arm. He could feel her fingers slide up his arm, searching for something.

Smiling, he reached out, letting her hand find his, letting hers grip his tight.

'To rocks, then,' he whispered.

'To rocks.' She threw back her head and the bottle at once.

Lenk did not remember when the sun had shone so brightly. The golden orb cast a warm, loving caress upon the fields below, setting the golden wheat to a shimmering blaze against the blue sky. Below the ridge, Steadbrook continued its quiet existence as if it had always existed.

He could see the people as distant, vague shapes. They dropped sheaves of wheat, wiped their brows. They rolled up their sleeves and tended to swollen udders. They watched dogs rut, drank stale beer and muttered about taxes in the village's dusty lanes.

It was a quiet life, the most notable occasion being a farm changing hands or an infant from the womb of woman or cow being born. It had never seen plague, famine or weather in enough ferocity to warrant worry over such things. It was a quiet life, far from the grimy despair of cities and away from the greedy hands of priests and lords.

It was a good life.

'*Had been, anyway.*'

He suddenly became aware of the figure sitting cross-legged at the ridge's edge beside him. He stared at the man, observing his silver hair, dull even in the sunlight, his wiry body tensed and flexed despite his casual position. The sword lay naked in his lap, its long blade dull and sheenless, catching the light upon its face and refusing to let it go.

'I can't really be blamed for being nostalgic,' Lenk replied, looking back down over Steadbrook. 'There are times when I wish it still stood.'

'*That would imply there are times when you prefer things as they are.*'

'For certain reasons.'

'*Such as?*'

'None that you would approve of.'

'*Doubtless.*'

'If things hadn't happened as they had,' Lenk muttered, resting his chin in his hand, 'I wouldn't have met any of my companions.'

The man beside him drew in a deep breath. No sigh came, nor any indication that the man would ever exhale. Lenk raised a brow at him.

'What?'

'*You believe all the good that came of what happened to this village was that you met a few other people?*'

'Well ... one of them, at least.'

'*Ah, yes. Her.*'

Lenk frowned. 'You don't like her.'

'*We don't need her,*' the man replied. '*But I digress. You owe much to this village, you know.*'

'Obviously, I was born here, raised here.'

'*Apologies, that was not my intended meaning. It would have been more proper to say that we owe much to this village's destruction.*'

'You're treading on dangerous ground,' Lenk growled, scowling at the man.

'*Am I?*'

The man's sword rose with him, so effortless and easy in his grasp. He turned to face Lenk and the young man blanched. The man's face was cold and stony, a mountainside carved by eternal sleet. His eyes were a bright and glowing blue, glistening with a malevolence unmarred by pupils.

'*Look at me,*' the man demanded.

'I am.'

'*You're not. You look through me. You look around me. You don't hear me when I try to speak to you and you refuse to do what must be done.*'

Lenk rose to his feet. Despite standing the same height as his counterpart, he couldn't help but feel as though he was being looked down upon.

'You don't say anything I don't already know,' he retorted.

'*You know nothing.*'

'I know how to kill.'

'*And I have taught you.*'

'I taught myself.'

'*You're not listening to me.*'

'I am.'

'*Are you aware of what we are?*' the man asked. '*Are you aware of what we do? What we have done? What we were created to do?*' The man's eyes narrowed to angry sapphires. '*Do you see our opponents tremble? Do you hear them scream and beg? Do you remember what we did to the demon?*'

'Only vaguely,' Lenk replied.

'*Understandable,*' the man said, '*it was mostly my doing.*'

'I drove the blade into the Abysmyth,' Lenk replied. 'I killed it. That's not supposed to be possible.'

'*Then why will you not say such to your companions? Why will you not answer her?*'

'I don't want her to worry.'

'*You don't want to look at her, either. You don't want to listen to her. If you did, you would know she means to kill us.*'

Lenk did not start at the accusation, not raising so much as an eyebrow at the man. Instead, he drew in a sharp breath and looked back over the ridge. Steadbrook continued under the sun, unmoved and unmotivated by the presence of demons or the whisper of swords. He, too, was once so unmoved.

'Maybe,' he whispered, 'that's not such a bad thing.'

'*What?*'

'Demons can't be killed by mortal hands.'

'*We are more than mortal.*'

'Exactly my point,' Lenk replied, looking up sharply. 'That's not supposed to happen. *She* can never know.'

'*Why should she not?*'

'Why *should* she?'

'*They all should know,*' the man said coldly. '*They already know we are superior to them.*'

'No, we're not. I'm just a man.'

'*You? You are weak. We are far more than a man. Why did they follow us? Why do they continue to follow us? Why do we suppress their greed, their hate, their violence and make them do as we say? Even the lowliest of beasts recognise their master.*'

675

'I don't want to be anyone's master,' Lenk snarled suddenly. He stabbed a finger at the man, accusing. 'I … I want *you* to go.'

'*Go?*'

'I want you to get out of my head. I want to stop hearing voices. I want to stop feeling cold all the time. I … I …' He clutched at his head, wincing. 'I want to be *me*, not us.'

The man's face did not move at the outpour of emotion, did not flinch in sympathy nor blink in scorn. He merely stared, observed his counterpart through cold, blue eyes, his hair unmoved by wind and heedless of sun, just as Steadbrook was heedless of them upon the ridge.

'*Look.*'

Lenk blinked and felt cold.

The sun sputtered out like a dying torch, consumed behind a black veil of darkness. The golden fields below were bronzed by the fires engulfing Steadbrook, moving in waves of bristling, crackling sheen. The livestock lowed, their cries desperate to be heard over the roar of fire, their owners and tenders motionless in the red-stained dirt. Shadows moved amongst them and where their black hands caressed, people fell.

Lenk felt his heart go cold, despite the fires licking the ridge. He had seen this happen before, had watched them die before, his mother, his father, his grandfather. He could not recall their names, but he could remember their faces as they fell, nearly peaceful, herded to the darkness upon the whispers of shadows.

'This …' he gasped, 'this is—'

'*How we were created,*' the man finished for him. '*What we were created to stop.*'

He caught sight of figures in the distance, out of place against the common folk lying in the streets. These figures fought, resisted the shadows. One by one, they looked up, and he saw the faces of his companions turn pleading gazes to him.

'*Look*,' the man commanded, and it was so. '*They are lesser than us.*'

Gariath howled, swinging his arms wildly before the shadows fell upon him, consumed in swathes of blackness. Lenk winced, eyes unable to shut themselves against the stinging smoke.

'I don't want to ...' he whimpered.

'You *do not have a choice*,' the man uttered. '*We have our duty.*'

Asper shrieked, fervently babbling indecipherable prayers as the shadows dragged her into the gloom. Lenk felt tears brimming upon his lids.

'Please—'

'*And our duty*,' the man continued, unheeding, '*is to cleanse. As we cleansed the Deepshriek, as we cleansed the Abysmyth, so we shall continue. We shall do as we must, for no one else can.*'

Dreadaeleon collapsed, the fire in his eyes sputtering out to be replaced by blackness.

'No, it can't—'

'*It will. You cannot recall what suffering was necessary to create us. If more suffering is needed to remind you of our duty ...*'

Denaos twitched, convulsed, tore apart as the shadowy tendrils raked and whispered at his body.

'I want—'

'*Your wants are meaningless. Our duty is all. They are hindrances.*'

Kataria's body was pale against the gloom as they lifted her up to the black sky, as if in offering. The fingers shivered and trembled against her skin, flowing over her stomach,

677

wrapping about her neck, snaking over her legs as she was cocooned in the gloom. Her head rolled, limp, to expose her eyes, bright and green, locked on to his. She stared at him as she vanished into the darkness.

And smiled.

'*NO!*' Lenk roared, collapsing to his knees. 'No, no, no ...'

When he opened his eyes again, he was in a vast field of darkness, no flames, no death. All that remained were him, and the two great blue eyes focused upon him, pitiless and cold.

'*The gift shall not be wasted,*' the voice whispered. '*The duty is all encompassing. Do what must be done.*'

Lenk opened his mouth to scream, his voice silenced as the darkness flooded past his lips and filled him completely.

He awoke not with a start, but with a snap of eyes. Not with fear, but with a cold certainty. Not with thunder in his heart, but a single drop of sweat that slid down his brow and murmured as it dripped past his ear.

Do what must be done, it uttered, voice mingling with the murmur of the surf, *if more suffering is needed ...*

And his hand was slow and steady, balling up into a determined fist as he understood what the voice told him.

But he did not rise, suddenly aware of the weight upon his chest. He didn't even see her until she peered down at him through a pair of hard, green eyes, glittering in the darkness. Her knees were on his chest, hands on his shoulders, the knife dark and grey against the moonlight.

'Hey,' Kataria muttered.

'Hey,' Lenk replied, blinking at her. 'What are you doing?'

'What I have to.'

She means to kill us, he heard within his own mind, but paid the warning no heed. *Maybe that's not such a bad thing.* He eyed the blade in her hand, its edge a line of silver in the darkness. *No*, he told himself, *no, you can't ask her to do that.*

'Can it wait?' he asked.

The shict's face twisted violently, her eyes softening as her mouth fell open, as if she hadn't expected that one answer of all of them. 'Wha-what?'

'I need to do something,' he said, placing a hand on her naked midriff. Her body shuddered under his touch, like a nervous beast. 'Get off, please.'

She complied, falling off him as though she was pushed. On shaking legs, his arms barely strong enough to draw him, he got to his feet. He suddenly felt very weak, his body pleading with him to lie back down, to return to sleep and think upon this in the light of day. He could not afford to listen to it, could not afford to listen to his instincts or his mind.

They, too, were tainted, speaking with a voice not their own.

No, he told himself while he could still hear his own voice inside him, before it was drowned out completely, *this is what it has to be.* He staggered forwards, nearly pitching to the earth. He maintained his footing, his shaking hand rising and reaching for the sword lying upon the sand. *This is how it has to end. There's no other way to get rid of it …*

'Hey,' he heard a voice call from behind him.

Do what must be done.

'Hey!'

This is how it must be.

'*HEY!*'

'*WHAT?*' he roared, turning upon her. She stood before him, ears bristling, teeth bared. 'What do you want?'

'I could have killed you there!' she snapped, pointing to the knife. 'I ... I could have—'

'You didn't,' he said simply. 'You had every chance in the world, but you didn't.'

So I have to, he finished mentally, turning back to the sword.

'No,' she whispered, eyeing the weapon. 'You can't do that.' *I have to*, she finished mentally, reaching out.

This is how it has to be, he told himself.

How else could it end? she asked herself.

One blow. He reached out for the weapon.

Clean and quick. She reached out for him.

Her hand fell upon his shoulder.

This is what has to be done.

They both froze, each one suddenly aware of the other as they connected, hearing each other's breath upon the night wind, feeling each other's heart beat through each other's skin. They felt so weak, all of a sudden, his legs barely able to keep him up as he turned to regard her, her arm barely able to hold up the knife above her head.

Her eyes glittered in the darkness, so soft suddenly, quivering like emeralds melting. His shimmered in the gloom, so warm, ice under sunlight. Her arm shook, the knife trembling in her hand as he stared at her, not with challenge, not with threat, but with a pleading he wasn't even aware of. Her teeth clenched behind her lips, body shaking.

The blade fell to the earth, crunching into the sand, as his body fell into hers. She caught him in her arms, wrapped them about his waist and drew him in closer, tighter. Against each other, they found a strength too weak to keep them up, enough to keep their arms about each other, but not enough to keep them from falling to their knees, the earth's pull suddenly so strong.

'I could have killed you,' she whispered, running a hand down his hair.

'Yeah,' he said, feeling her heartbeat through his hands. 'You could have.'

'I didn't,' she said.

'Thanks,' he whispered.

The surf yawned against their legs, as if disappointed that it ended in such a way. The moon waned with a staggering breath of relief and the stars allowed themselves to blink. They rested there, upon their knees, barely aware of the world moving again beneath them.

Thirty-Six

TRAGIC

The Aeons' Gate
The Island of Ktamgi
Summer, late ... date unknown ... who cares?

No one picks up a sword because they want to.

It's a matter of need. People are called to wrap their hands about the hilt, even if they can't hear what calls them. The noblest of us do it out of what they call duty, the desire to serve their country, their lord if they have one, or their God. The pragmatic amongst us do it out of a need for work, for coin, for respect.

And the lowest, meanest of trades picks up a sword because that's all we know how to do. Violence is all we know, all we will ever know, everything else having long been burned away and fled to the shadows. The irony of it is that the mercenary, the soldier, the knight must all carve their own way through life, but there's always enough violence and hatred in the world that it will make room for the adventurer.

I remember now, if only in fleeting glimpses, when the rest of it was burned away for me.

Not shadows, but men, who swept into Steadbrook with candles, not torches, and set the dry hay ablaze. They killed while the flames still whispered, vanished when the fire started to roar. That was enough time for them. Mother, Father, Grandfather ... all dead ... me, still alive. I don't know why.

Maybe that's how adventurers are made, maybe an act of suf-
fering and violence is necessary as the forge that shapes the metal
or the knife that shapes the wood. To that end, I don't suppose
anyone can blame us for doing what we do, even if they don't
like it. I don't suppose I can blame anyone for thinking what they
think of us, even if I don't like it.

At the moment, I have larger problems than other people's
opinions.

The tome is ours, but so many questions are unanswered. Will
we even be able to get to Teji? If we do, will Argaol have kept
up his end of the deal? Does Miron have that sort of sway over
him? Does Miron even care?

And what of the demons? Do so many of them just let their
precious book escape without a fight? If not their book, will one
of them come back for their head? I'm not stupid. I know they
haven't just rolled their shoulders, given up and gone back to hell
for tea and toast. But will they at least stay in the shadows until
we can reach dry land?

On a deeper level, should I even give this tome to Miron?
Does any one man have the right to carry such a thing?

I don't have the answers. Really, I don't care. Someone else
can worry about them on their time. My time is worth exactly
one thousand pieces of gold. Past that, I don't really mind what
the demons, longfaces or beasts of the world do. The world will
continue without the actions of adventurers, long after the pro-
fession has died out.

My companions are solemn as we set out for Teji, untalkative,
not even mustering the will to fight with each other, for once.
At the moment, our humble little vessel resembles something of
a flower with half its petals missing. Each of us stares over the
edge into the water, watching ourselves, not even aware of the
people next to us.

I should be pleased, I know. After so long spent in prayer, the Gods have answered me and finally taken their tongues. But now ... I want them to talk. I want to hear a distraction, another noise, if only to divert me from the other ones.

The voice ... is not gone. I know because it murmurs to me, still, in the time between my breaths. But it is quieted, put down slightly. I don't know why and, again, I don't care, so long as it's quiet again.

Another few days until we reach Teji. A haven, supposedly, friendly to us, our kind. Is that true? I'm not too sure, really. Argaol doesn't really seem the type to make himself useful to us, in any way possible. But I can deal with that when I come to it.

Kataria just looked up at me. She seems to be doing that a lot tonight. I try to smile at her ... no, I want to smile at her, but she doesn't make it easy. But it's not because of all those questions, oh no. The demons, longfaces, Argaols, Mirons, Deepshrieks, Xhais and tomes of the world can all go burn.

I've got bigger problems.

Epilogue
TEARS IN SHADOW

The silhouettes moved viciously against the cavern wall. There was no grace in them, nor gentleness as they twisted against each other. Between the snarls and cries emerging from the back of the cavern, the shadows found individual shapes. A man, tall and lean with long flowing hair. A woman, her curves indistinct as they quivered against the man's movement.

Greenhair could not see the smile on the man's face, nor the tears on the woman's cheeks. But she heard his teeth grinding, her liquid pooling upon the floor in quiet splashes. It was the only noise she allowed herself.

And the siren cringed, the only one to hear them.

'Cahulus is dead,' one of them said at the fore of the cavern. 'Over *twelve* of the warriors were lost in the battle. That's nearly half of the force we sent.'

'Nearly is not all. Nearly is not even half,' a second, snider voice retorted. 'We still emerged victorious, with the underscum cleared out.' A thin body settled into a large chair. 'Besides, Cahulus was an idiot.'

There was a terse silence before the other voice spoke. 'He was your brother.'

Greenhair looked to the pair of longfaces seated before her. Clad in flowing robes of violet and red, respectively, they narrowed white eyes at each other from their black wooden thrones. A great, ebon mass separated them, obscured by shadows cast from torchlight.

This was once a sacred place, Greenhair remembered, a place of devotion to the Sea Mother. The holy writ upon the walls had been seared away by fire. The relics and offerings lay shattered upon the floor. The worshippers ...

A scream burst from the cavern's mouth, cut short by the crack of a whip and a snarling command. She was the only one to hear it echo on the stone.

'*Our* brother,' the longface on the right continued, heedless. This one was short and thin, his head swivelling back and forth with a rehearsed sense of ease, like a wispy plant. He smoothed the crimson robes over his purple body as he spoke. 'And that does not change the fact that he was weak. The youngest is always the least talented.'

'Talent or no, he shouldn't have been able to die at all.' The longface on the left, harder and broader than his brother, stroked a white goatee. 'Our tools should have ensured that this did not happen. What good are the red stones if they fail?'

'Netherlings can still die, if not stones, Yldus,' the other pointed out. 'Cahulus was cursed with weakness *and* stupidity. He was overconfident.' He waved a hand and sighed. 'But was it not the duty of Semnein Xhai to protect him?'

'True enough, Vashnear.' The one called Yldus looked up and over Greenhair's head. 'And, I ask again, Semnein Xhai, what is your explanation?'

Greenhair looked over her shoulder and saw that no explanation was forthcoming. The female longface did not so much as adjust her gaze to even acknowledge the two males. She stared instead at the shadows, grinding and jerking upon the wall. Her ears were pricked up, sensing every sound that emerged from the lit space behind the thrones.

686

And with every sound of ecstasy or agony, her white gaze grew more hateful.

'She will not answer you.' Vashnear sighed. 'And why should we ask? It is clear by her wounds that she was as unprepared as Cahulus.'

The reference to the bandages wrapped about the female's ribcage, hip and neck got her attention. Xhai's stare jerked to the longface, her lip curling upwards in a snarl.

'Cahulus *was* weak,' she growled, 'and he died sobbing. If it hadn't happened this time, it would have happened in the next raid. Nothing I could have done would have cured his weakness.' She folded her arms over her chest, drummed three fingers upon her biceps. 'Be thankful he didn't piss himself before he died.'

'And yet, for all that sacrifice, you *still* don't have the tome,' Yldus said, steepling his fingers. 'Nor did you even *encounter* the Deepshriek, much less kill it.'

'An issue I will take up with Master Sheraptus,' Xhai replied coldly, returning her attention to the shadows.

The red-clad netherling looked over his shoulder at the cavern wall and giggled. 'He might be a while.'

Xhai's mouth dropped open, her three fingers balling up into a fist. 'You wretched little—'

'And what of you, screamer?' Greenhair felt Yldus's hard gaze upon her. 'We make no inconsiderable compromise to our worth by admitting you in here. What do you have to say for yourself?'

'I ...' The siren hesitated, wincing. 'What I speak is reserved for the greatest longface.'

'His *name* is Sheraptus,' Xhai growled, giving the siren a harsh shove. '*You* will call him Master.'

'A-apologies,' she said, feeling the blow ache between

her shoulders. 'But the information is great, it must be—'

'Reserved for the greatest.'

All eyes looked up at the new voice. This one lacked the harshness of the others', bearing no snideness, no hatred, no concern. It was slow and easy, like languid falls over smooth rocks, like …

Mine, Greenhair thought.

And this new longface looked nothing like the others. He was tall, but not menacing, lean, but not hungry-looking. His eyes sparkled instead of scowled and his smile was pleasant, not cruel. His robe hung open around a body developed to the point of attractiveness, not grotesqueness.

Greenhair pursed her lips. If she hadn't heard his smile, hadn't heard the tears he caused, she might think him a good man on sight alone.

'A sound policy,' the new longface said, closing his robes and stepping out from the darkness.

He made a beckoning gesture and there was the sound of bare feet scraping against the stone. The human female who followed him did not bother to close her robe, nor even look up. She shuffled forwards as though her legs strained to die beneath her. Her eyes were wide and vacant, hands limp at her sides, hair hanging over her face like a veil to hide her shame.

Not nearly long enough to hide the tear streaks, Greenhair thought.

'Now then,' he said, taking a seat upon the black mass and gesturing for his consort to kneel beside him. 'What is it that makes everyone so talkative during my private time?'

'You could always order us out,' Yldus muttered, pointedly looking away.

'I like an audience,' the longface said, smiling, 'a respectful one, though. I can only assume it was pressing business that made you all so chatty.' He steepled his long fingers and stared at Greenhair over them. 'So ... chat.'

'Longface—' she whispered, cut short by the blow to the back of her head.

'*Sheraptus*,' Xhai snarled. '*Master* Sheraptus.' She delivered a booted kick to Greenhair's legs, forcing her to the earth. 'And you will kneel before your betters.'

'Do calm down, Xhai,' Sheraptus said, sighing. He directed a sympathetic smile to the siren. 'Apologies. She and her fellow warriors are all so excitable. They learn a new word and they're just *dying* to use it. I'm sure you've heard them with their chants: "eviscerate, decapitate" and so forth.' He laughed, waving a hand. 'Females, hm? You know how it goes ... well, of course you know.'

'Sh-Sheraptus,' Greenhair whimpered from the earth.

'*Master* Sheraptus,' the tall longface replied. 'Xhai is enthusiastic, but not mistaken in this case.' He laughed again, a gentle, resonant sound. 'But we can discuss titles later. Let me hear you.'

'Scream the way you do,' Xhai warned in a low snarl from behind, 'and I carve you open.'

'I ...' Greenhair tried to speak with the threat lingering in her ears. 'I know where the tome is, Master Sheraptus.'

'And you waited until *now* to tell us?' Yldus leaned forwards in his throne, scowling. 'We could have had a ship brimming with warriors and ready to take it ages ago.'

'I am sure she had a good reason,' Vashnear suggested.

'I do!' The siren rose slightly, resting upon her haunches. 'I ... was conflicted. The demons, too, seek the tome. It would have been folly of me to put my faith in those who could not defeat them.'

'You dare to insinuate—' Xhai began to snarl, silenced by Sheraptus's raised hand.

The tall longface merely smiled, raised a finger to the sky, and spoke a word. Fire erupted from the purple tip in a great blaze, illuminating his black seat. Greenhair's voice caught in her throat.

It was still recognisable as an Abysmyth, but barely. Its arms had been twisted, crushed to resemble armrests. Its ribcage had been turned into a headboard and its skull decorated the top of the throne, eyes glassy and vacant in death as its toothy jaw hung slack over Sheraptus's head. Then the longface spoke another word, doused the flame and rested his hand in his lap.

'I trust that will prove sufficient evidence for your faith.'

'It … it does!' Greenhair stammered. 'But I have seen your power displayed on the blackened sands of Ktamgi, Master Sheraptus. I do not doubt your strength.'

'Oh.' Sheraptus's eyes went wide, then narrow. 'Well, then why do we even *have* this gaudy thing?' He thumped a hand-turned-armrest. 'I despise it.'

'She betrayed us once already, Master Sheraptus,' Xhai growled. 'She was not there when we struck against the demons, as she said she would be. We did not know about the … complications because she was not there.'

'Complications?' Sheraptus raised a brow.

'Overscum,' Vashnear answered. 'Five of them, all told. Two of them lived, three of them died, likely.' He cast a smug smile toward Xhai. 'One of them gave the First Carnassial her lovely little scratches.'

'There are six of them,' Greenhair spoke before Xhai could, 'and none of them are dead. They have the tome … and weapons.'

'Six weapons are nothing against two hundred,' Vashnear replied, sighing.

'One of them uses magic,' the siren said.

'*Nethra?*' Yldus blanched. 'Are they even capable of that?'

'Not nearly to our mastery, I am sure.' Vashnear smiled, tapping the shining red sphere about his neck. 'Whatever little users they have will be ash when we find them.'

'Which begs the question,' Yldus muttered, leaning forwards, 'why tell us this? Do you overscum loathe each other so much?'

'I think only of duty. The humans … they are incapable.' Greenhair's face felt heavy, pulled to the ground. 'They cannot protect the tome and I cannot see it fall to the Deepshriek again.' She forced her gaze up to the tall longface, her expression pained. 'But you are—'

'I am,' Sheraptus said, his nod slow and deliberate. 'And you are most perceptive.' His eyes lit up with hunger. 'As well as …'

Shcraptus tapped a finger to his cheek thoughtfully, his gaze lingering on Greenhair with what appeared to be only a partial concern for what she had to say. His gaze drifted over her, observing her curves, sliding over her body. She swallowed hard and eyed the female kneeling beside him, her eyes wide and dead, her breath shallow.

For a moment, she saw herself there, her eyes so dead, her voice so silent. Quickly, she coughed.

'Six of them,' she reiterated, 'four men, two women.'

Sheraptus's brow raised. Xhai's face twisted into a snarl as Yldus sighed.

'Intriguing,' the tall longface said. 'And you can find them for us?'

'If you swear to take the tome from them.' Greenhair nodded. 'If you swear to protect it.'

'Let us go for the tome, yes,' Yldus said. 'But you don't need more women, Sheraptus. You had two and you already lost one of them.'

'As well as the boat she escaped in,' Vashnear muttered, glowering at Xhai. 'Another of the First Carnassial's triumphs.'

'That was an internal issue due to our unpreparedness when we first arrived on this world,' Sheraptus retorted before Xhai could. 'Our security is much improved now.'

'Still,' Yldus said, 'it's hardly necessary—'

'I don't *need*,' Sheraptus growled, 'I *want*. I am *saharkk* of Arkklan Kaharn, Yldus. *Mine* is the right to take.' He cast a glance down to the female kneeling beside him, stroked her hair thoughtfully. 'Besides ...'

He muttered a word. Blue electricity danced along her head, coursed through her body. It shuddered once, then went still, collapsing to the side as smoke hissed from her mouth and ears. Her stare did not change, even as she lay dead.

'This one is broken.' He smiled, languid and easy, as he leaned forwards in his throne of flesh and rested his chin on his hands. 'And you can guarantee that the tome will be ours once the overscum are dead?'

'There's no need to kill them,' Greenhair replied quickly. 'Display your force, show them your might, and they will flee. It is their nature.'

'Indeed ...'

Sheraptus regarded the collapsed woman, her eyes reaching out into the darkness as the last light faded from them. His smile was as long as his face.

'The nature ... of a human ...'

Acknowledgements

This book was made with no small help from people with more scrutinizing eyes than myself. Danny Baror, my extremely canny agent, was able to get the book to Lou Aronica, an exceedingly savvy editor who helped shape and skin this story to a point where Danny could get it to Simon Spanton, my other editor, for even further and finer hammering. It's because of these fine fellows that the book is what you're reading right now.

Along the way, though, my gurus of quality, psychology and evisceration helped in no small part: Matthew 'Danger King' Hayduke, John 'Duke of Branle' Henes and Carl Emmanuel 'Mighty Thesaurus' Cohen all contributed their diverese and violent qualities to help fine-tune the story.

None of this would be possible without the help of many people, and one in particular. Hopefully, they will all burble with as much pride as I do over the finished story.